The Telegraph

BONKER, BOUNDER, BEGGARMAN, THIEF

The Telegraph

BONKER, BOUNDER, BEGGARMAN, THIEF

A COMPENDIUM OF ROGUES, VILLAINS AND SCANDALS

Aurum
Press

Quarto is the authority on a wide range of topics.

Quarto educates, entertains and enriches the lives of our readers—enthusiasts and lovers of hands-on living.

www.QuartoKnows.com

First published 2016 by Aurum Press Ltd
74–77 White Lion Street
London N1 9PF

A catalogue record for this book is available from the British Library.

ISBN 978 1 78131 544 6
eISBN 978 1 78131 548 4

10 9 8 7 6 5 4 3 2 1
2020 2019 2018 2017 2016

Typeset in Electra LH by SX Composing DTP, Rayleigh, Essex

Printed and bound in Great Britain by CPI Group (UK) Ltd, Croydon, CR0 4YY

FSC
www.fsc.org
MIX
Paper from
responsible sources
FSC® C020471

Contents

Introduction

'I love scandals about other people, but scandals about myself do not interest me. They have not got the charm of novelty.'

Oscar Wilde, *A Picture of Dorian Gray*

You might think that by 2016 a kind of tedium should attend stories about scandal, whoever they concern. Just as there are a mere seven endlessly deployed plots available to writers of fiction, so, in theory, there is only a limited number of ways to make sure the general public choke on their cornflakes as they read the newspaper over breakfast. There is much to be said for this argument, but ultimately it doesn't quite satisfy. The human weaknesses for sex or drugs or money (or a combination of all three) are eternal verities, but so is the insatiable desire to read about them. Suetonius' *Lives of the Caesars*, Procopius' *The Secret History* and Edward Gibbons' *The History of the Decline and Fall of the Roman Empire* – to pick a handful of classics at random – might all be insightful, elegant and psychologically acute historical and literary documents, but they are also packed to the gills with deviancy and moral squalor.

And the corpulence of these books is in turn another clue to the enduring appeal scandal holds for us: its inexhaustible variety. There may only be a finite quantity of themes, but it appears there's an infinite number of ways to interpret them. This book has the Reverend Paul Flowers creating his own unholy trinity of rent boys, hard drugs and financial malpractice; Silvio Berlusconi using his position to arrange parties his imperial Roman forebears could only have dreamed of attending; and the Duchess of Argyll proving that a co-respondent in a divorce case can still have an impact, even if they're only (un)identifiable from the waist down. Though previous generations may have wished to gain access to the private communications of Lady Hamilton or Nell Gywnn, there was very little they could do, short of intercepting their letters: one imagines that any future editions of a *Telegraph* book of scandal will place a far greater emphasis on the way technology is able to facilitate indiscretion, as well as to create an indelible record of any given individual's bad behaviour.

Scandal is perhaps an underrated metric for measuring social change, and the pages collected here are an eloquent testimony to the evolution of public and private morals in the century and a half since the *Daily Telegraph* was first printed. In 1855 homosexuality was illegal, but the ingestion of cocaine was not. Women could not vote (though, in truth the franchise was so limited that many men could not either) but they could be raped, as long as the man forcing intercourse upon them was their husband. Had he been born even fifty years later, Oscar Wilde's life would not have been disfigured by scandal – or, at least, not the same kind of scandal.

It might be said that in some ways, what was *not* printed in the past is as eloquent as what was. For a long time the press were so deferential towards politicians that leading public figures were able to conduct lengthy affairs, confident that they would not suffer the shame of exposure (of course it might be suggested that this discretion was simply a more restrained and mature judgement as to what truly constituted the 'public interest'). Herbert Asquith wiled away dull Cabinet meetings writing love letters to his mistress Venetia Stanley, and during the twenties a compromising photograph featuring a nude Oswald Mosley and another man's wife did the rounds of the House of Commons – none of this reached the front pages of the newspapers. And even such details as did slip into print were innocuous in the extreme. It is said that on one occasion when Roy Jenkins was spotted by a newspaper's diary editor having an intimate lunch with a woman who was most certainly not his wife, the only item that made it into the journalist's column the following day was that the noted bon vivant Jenkins had committed the cardinal sin of drinking red wine with the fish course. I cannot imagine that the obituaries of MPs Bob Boothby or Tom Driberg – neither of whom ever bothered concealing their proclivities whilst they were still alive – would be quite so coy about their subjects' sexual preferences if they were to be written tomorrow.

At the same time, there is much pleasure to be had in tracing the strong veins of similarity that connect events many decades apart. The financial shenanigans that distinguished swindlers like Horatio Bottomley or Charles Ponzi would not be unfamiliar to anyone who witnessed the collapse of Enron, or to the thousands of victims of Bernie Madoff's cynical frauds. The fraudulent 'deaths' of the Johns Darwin and Stonehouse have much in common, not least the vast distances they were each able to travel (Australia and Panama respectively) when they were supposed to have been resting in peace.

For a number of the subjects of this book, scandal was for them what water is to the fish: a necessary and enveloping constant in their lives. For instance, Oliver Reed gave a very good impression of a man for whom his career – acting – was of only secondary importance to his passion – raising hell. Indeed, it might be said that for the Soho provocateur Sebastian Horsley, scandal *was* his career. By contrast there are others, such as John Profumo, who dived briefly into scandalous behaviour (and it should be said in Profumo's case, quite deeply also) only to emerge soon after and devote their existence to good works. Or, more tragically, Dr David Kelly, a perilously shy scientist who discovered that public exposure could be merciless and, ultimately, unendurable.

This volume does not pretend to be a comprehensive collection, but I hope the reader will feel that it is representative – and, more importantly, entertaining. Some candidates (Nixon and his involvement with Watergate springs to mind here) have been omitted for reasons of space and others from prudence: lawyers are attracted to scandal, and many of those who have been stung once by notoriety are quick to litigate if it means they can avoid another spell in the limelight. Occasionally absences have been dictated by the fact that a portion of the historical reporting is too unwieldy, detailed, or, to modern eyes, dull, to be included here. Similarly, one is left wishing that the revolution in the *Telegraph*'s obituaries pages – which transformed the simple fact of marking a notable figure's death into something approaching an art form – had occurred earlier than 1986: what fun they could have had with people like Tallulah Bankhead or Lord Haw-Haw. But I have tried to include as broad a sweep of characters as possible, which is why a cold-blooded killer like the sinister Dr Crippen sits beside the genial madam Cynthia Payne (could there be a more quintessentially suburban and English way of paying for sex than luncheon vouchers?). And how many other books would give equal billing to both Kate Moss and Colonel Gadaffi?

One final note. Watching another person's fall from grace, their public humiliation, can easily lead to feelings of schadenfreude or moral superiority, but there is perhaps a more appropriate and reflective response to displays of human fallibility: There but for the grace of God go I.

The Editor
London, 2016

Jonathan Aitken

"Libel is not a game."

Until 1995 Jonathan Aitken (grand-nephew of notorious press baron Lord Beaverbrook) had largely managed to avoid the infamy that settled upon many of his fellow Conservative MPs. This might in part be because he had spent much of his career as a backbencher (allegedly because he'd offended Margaret Thatcher by breaking up with her daughter, Carol). In 1992, John Major made him Minister of State for Defence Procurement (the previous incumbent had been perennial scandal-magnet Alan Clark), and two years later he entered the Cabinet as Chief Secretary to the Treasury. Not long after, though, the *Guardian* printed a series of allegations about his conduct at the MoD, allegations that Aitken denied forcefully. The allegations were serious enough that he resigned, but also launched a libel case against the paper. In 1997 matters deteriorated further for Aitken. In short order he lost his seat in Parliament, and then a month later his case collapsed after the *Guardian* was able to produce definitive evidence to back up its claims. By the time of his trial for perjury and perverting the course of justice, he had acquired a new daughter (via DNA testing), but had lost a wife and many of the friends who had supported him previously.

11 April 1995
Aitken attacks Press "cancer"
Minister sues over report of girls for Saudi prince
By George Jones

Mr Jonathan Aitken launched a high-risk crusade last night against the tide of "sleaze" claims threatening to overwhelm the Government. The Treasury Chief Secretary declared that he would fight against the "cancer of bent and twisted journalism".

Mr Aitken had earlier denounced newspaper claims that he tried to arrange girls for a Saudi prince and his entourage at a Berkshire health farm of which he was a director.

He stunned Westminster by calling a press conference at Conservative Party headquarters to announce that he was launching a libel action against the *Guardian* for publishing "wicked lies" about his business activities.

Mr Aitken also warned Granada TV's *World in Action* that he would sue if it repeated the allegations last night. Granada went ahead with the 30-minute programme, which described him as "Jonathan of Arabia" and claimed he had repeatedly hidden the extent of his business dealings with the Saudi royal family.

However, it was updated to include sections of Mr Aitken's statement denying the main allegations. A spokesman said Mr Aitken was now considering whether to sue *World in Action*.

The spokesman added that "loud laughter" had been heard coming from Mr Aitken's room at the Treasury as he watched the programme. The Chief Secretary was said to have been amused by the programme's "amateur theatricals" – the use of actors to portray his alleged business dealings with leading Arabs.

Mr Aitken's decision to sue is a high-risk strategy and could lead to him being cross-examined in court over the allegations. However, political colleagues said the charges against him were so serious that he had no alternative but to take action if he wanted to remain a frontline politician. He has the party's backing in his fight.

His move came 24 hours after Mr Richard Spring, MP for Bury St Edmunds, resigned as parliamentary private secretary in the wake of a newspaper report of a "three in a bed" sexual liaison.

Mr Aitken made clear he was launching a crusade to halt what many Tory MPs and ministers believe is a media witchhunt which has resulted in 15 Tories having to resign office since September 1992 because of newspaper allegations about their private lives.

Mr Aitken said he was taking legal action not simply to clear his name but for wider public interest issues. He will pay his own legal costs.

"If it falls to me to start a fight to cut out the cancer of bent and twisted journalism in our country with the simple sword of truth and the trusty shield of British fair play, so be it."

Mr Aitken said he was "shocked and disgusted" by the very serious allegations made against him. He had no hesitation in stating categorically they were "wicked lies" and he had therefore issued a writ for defamation against the *Guardian*, its editor-in-chief, Mr Peter Preston, and the journalist who wrote the article.

He said the main allegation that he tried to arrange girls for Prince Mohammad bin Fahd, son of King Fahd of Saudi Arabia, and his entourage during a stay at Inglewood Health Hydro, Berkshire, was "an outrageous falsehood". He said Prince Mohammad had only made one short visit to Inglewood for lunch 13 years ago and no girls were present.

The allegation was made by a former matron. Mr Aitken claimed that a matron was dismissed "for dishonesty following a police investigation".

But Mr Robin Kirk, a former principal of Inglewood, said on *World in Action* that Mr Aitken had himself called in the police after a dispute with staff over a demand for £15,000 commission, which was refused. He did not say what the money was for.

The investigation was abandoned some months later, with no charges being pressed, but had been called purely to "destroy our credibility", Mr Kirk claimed.

Mr Aitken also denounced as an "outrageous falsehood" an allegation by the *Guardian* that while Minister for Defence Procurement in 1992–94 he had improper commercial relationships with two British citizens of Lebanese origin.

"The total picture for the *Guardian's* report is therefore one of deliberate misrepresentations, falsehoods and lies and is clearly part of the paper's long campaign of sustained attempts to discredit me," he said.

Last autumn, Mr Aitken was involved in a furious dispute over a payment of his bill at the Ritz Hotel, Paris. It was revealed that the *Guardian* used a forged fax to obtain details of the bill.

More recently the *Independent* had accused Mr Aitken of being involved with a company – before he joined the Government – that breached an arms embargo on Iran. Ten days ago he accused the BBC of political "bias" and has now decided to make a stand on behalf of his colleagues against "media harassment".

9 June 1999
Aitken's ruin ends in prison:
Daughters weep as father is jailed for 18 months
Ex-minister "wove a web of deceit", says judge
By Colin Randall

Jonathan Aitken was jailed yesterday for 18 months for perjury and perverting the course of justice, completing what was described at the Old Bailey as his self-inspired professional, political and personal ruin.

Mr Justice Scott Baker told the 56-year-old former Chief Secretary to the Treasury that it was his duty to send out a message "loud and clear" that such crimes were likely to lead to condign punishment.

Seated alongside the dock, Aitken's 18-year-old twin daughters Victoria and Alexandra burst into tears as he was sentenced. They had arrived at court hand in hand with Petrina Khashoggi, their father's illegitimate daughter by Soraya Khashoggi.

The young women joined his mother, Lady Aitken, in waving and blowing kisses as Aitken was led down to the cells.

Aitken will be held for some weeks at Belmarsh high security prison in south-east London before an assessment is made of where he should serve his sentence. He will be released after nine months, the remaining half of the sentence then to be suspended until the full 18 months have elapsed.

Aitken admitted that he lied when he told a High Court libel case in 1995 that his wife, Lolicia, paid the bill of about £1,000 for a weekend stay at the Ritz Hotel in Paris. In fact, it was paid by an old friend and business contact, Said Ayas, an adviser to Prince Mohammed, son of King Fahd of Saudi Arabia.

Yesterday Aitken stood to attention but betrayed little sign of emotion as the judge told him: "For nearly four years you wove a web of deceit in which you entangled yourself and from which there was no way out unless you were prepared to come clean and tell the truth. Unfortunately you were not.

"You hoped that by committing perjury and perverting the course of justice the truth of who paid the bill for that weekend at the Ritz would never see the light of day."

The judge condemned Aitken on two "particularly serious aspects" of the offences. "First, this was no passing error of judgment," he said. "It was calculated perjury pursued over a period of time. Second, you swept others, including members of your family, into it and most particularly one of your daughters who was only 16 at the time."

This was, the judge said, a "gross and inexcusable breach of trust".

The court had heard earlier of Aitken's deep sense of remorse, especially about his actions in drafting a statement for Victoria to sign in support of his account.

The former Tory MP was said to have involved his daughter in a desperate attempt to salvage his libel action against the *Guardian* newspaper and Granada Television, maker of a *World in Action* programme about his affairs. Although during the 1995 trial the paper and television station had withdrawn some of the more serious allegations against Aitken, suggesting sleaze and corruption, evidence had emerged to challenge his story about the Ritz.

In a statement admitting to his lies, Aitken had said he would bear the burden for the rest of his life of having "misled and manipulated" some of those close to him to lie on his behalf. The judge accepted that the offences were committed in the context of Aitken's belief that a number of serious allegations against him were false.

He also accepted that his "paramount" objective in bringing the libel action had been to protect his reputation and not to earn money.

He added: "But the fact remains that you knew perfectly well when you brought them that who paid for that weekend was a central plank in your case and that you could only succeed on that issue by committing perjury."

No one, whatever his position or status, was entitled "dishonestly to manipulate the evidence to his advantage". Perjury and perverting the course of justice were serious offences because they struck at justice itself.

Mr Justice Scott Baker gave Aitken credit for pleading guilty at the earliest opportunity. He had already suffered other penalties arising from his actions: bankruptcy, impaired health and the loss of his career, reputation and marriage.

He had also been a successful government minister who contributed very significantly to the interests of the country and a highly regarded constituency MP.

Sir John Nutting, QC, defending, said Aitken had brought about his own destruction and suffered "absolute" public humiliation.

It was to Aitken's profound relief that the Crown Prosecution Service had decided not to prosecute Victoria, and later to offer no evidence against Mr Ayas, who had also been charged in connection with the affair.

"He has always wanted to shoulder the blame alone," Sir John said. "It is the greatest consolation to him that he, the sole author of his misfortune and that of others, is to be punished alone."

Aitken left the Old Bailey cells for Belmarsh Prison in a custody van which he shared with six men facing murder charges, five accused of armed robbery and two on rape allegations.

The *Guardian* editor Alan Rusbridger said in a statement last night: "This case was about more than Jonathan Aitken. It was about the dishonest misuse of our libel laws to close down legitimate scrutiny of the people we elect to govern us.

"If Mr Aitken had won, he would have dishonestly taken up to £2m from the Guardian by way of costs and aggravated damages.

"The case should serve as a warning to future litigants who may be set on stifling scrutiny. Libel is not a game: it is too often used by the rich, the powerful and the crooked to suppress proper reporting and fair comment.

"No one using the law against others can complain if the law is, in turn, used against them."

Lolicia Aitken announced the couple's separation immediately after the libel case and is suing for divorce.

She now lives abroad because she fears that she might be arrested on returning to Britain for her part in her husband's attempt to deceive the High Court.

Maria Aitken, Mr Aitken's sister, is to become the children's guardian. A trust fund has been set up for the twins and their brother William, 16, who is at Eton. Petrina Khashoggi is also a beneficiary.

9 June 1999
The self-destruction of Jonathan Aitken
By Colin Randall

Jonathan Aitken will live forever with the shame of having involved his teenaged daughter Victoria in an attempt to deceive the High Court, the Old Bailey was told yesterday.

The former Cabinet minister's remorse about the effect of his actions on those close to him came in a statement of confession which he made when it became clear he faced criminal charges.

Aitken had claimed when giving evidence in his 1995 libel case against the *Guardian* and Granada Television that his wife Lolicia had paid the bill for a weekend stay at the Ritz Hotel in Paris in September 1993.

In fact the bill was paid by a long-standing friend and business associate, Said Ayas, an adviser to the Saudi royal family.

When evidence emerged during the libel trial to cast doubt on Aitken's claims, he drafted a statement which his daughter Victoria, then 16, agreed to sign in support of his story. The case collapsed when it was shown that Mrs Aitken and Victoria had never been in Paris on the weekend in question.

David Waters, QC, prosecuting at the Old Bailey where Aitken appeared for sentencing yesterday, said Aitken ended his statement with expressions of regret to the "large number of people" he had misled with his lies about who had met the cost of a weekend he spend at the Ritz.

It went on: "I am especially full of remorse for the actions I took to mislead or manipulate Victoria, Lolicia, Nadia Azucki [his mother-in-law], and Said Ayas into signing witness statements which contained lies.

"This is a burden I will have to bear for the rest of my life. I am sorry and ashamed."

In a lengthy speech of mitigation, Sir John Nutting, QC, for Aitken, said: "In a real and fundamental sense this defendant had brought about his own destruction.

"Not since the days of Oscar Wilde has a public figure who told lies in a libel case suffered such humiliation, media vilification and personal vindictiveness from his enemies as this defendant.

"The fall from grace has been complete. His marriage has broken down, he has lost his home, he is one of only three people this century who felt compelled to resign from the Privy Council, he has been declared bankrupt and his health has suffered.

"His public humiliation has been absolute. For someone in his position, these are real punishments in themselves."

Earlier, outlining the case against Aitken, Mr Waters had said the libel case ended when documents obtained from British Airways showed that the former minister's family was not in Paris but flew straight to Switzerland, where Victoria, then 13, was starting at a new school.

Aitken had claimed the visit to Paris was social. After being delayed by another engagement, he spent a quiet weekend, working on his biography of Richard Nixon and meeting friends.

He said his wife returned from Geneva to the Ritz on Sunday to meet him after dropping off his daughter at the school, Mr Waters said, and that she had paid his bill in cash.

When Mr Waters referred to Victoria's statement, Mr Justice Scott Baker interrupted to ask how old she was at time. Told it was about the time of her 17th birthday, the judge said that Aitken's involvement of her was a "very grave" feature of the case.

Sir Malcolm Rifkind, who volunteered to give character testimony on Aitken's behalf, said he had visited his Westminster home on several occasions for meetings of the Conservative Philosophy Group.

"I thought of him as a very able, intelligent and articulate MP, someone who had very considerable experience and who was always thought to be of potential ministerial calibre," he said.

When Sir Malcolm became Defence Secretary, John Major appointed Aitken as a junior defence minister, and it was clear that he was in a unique position because of his close contacts with influential Middle East royal families with whom Britain wanted to do business. Sir Malcolm described his former colleague as the most able junior minister he had come across during his years in government.

He had access to top levels of government in Saudi Arabia and other countries which were usually exclusive to the Prime Minister or senior Cabinet members.

On separate occasions, Aitken used his influence to help persuade Kuwait and Saudi Arabia not to cancel lucrative contracts with Britain, safeguarding thousands of British jobs.

The Saudi intervention required him to set up a meeting between King Fahd of Saudi Arabia and Mr Major, which prevented a £4bn contract going to the United States.

He had no reason to believe that Mr Aitken had ever benefited personally from his contacts. "I felt he was carrying out his work in a very responsible way," said Sir Malcolm.

The court was told that Aitken's false denial, in a response to a letter from Peter Preston, then editor of the *Guardian*, that Mr Ayas had paid his Ritz bill, effectively trapped him into perjury once the lie became part of the libel case.

Sir John said the downfall of Aitken was a devastating example of how a "lie with small beginnings", told by the defendant because he hoped it would put the newspaper off a scent he believed to be wholly false, could snowball. He was horrified when the *Guardian* published allegations that he was financially dependent on Prince Mohammed, son of the Saudi king, had concealed his links with Arab businessmen, had procured prostitutes for Saudi contacts and had arranged arms deals to regimes to which the sale of weapons was forbidden.

Aitken was by then in the Cabinet as First Secretary to the Treasury. "It is difficult to imagine more serious allegations against a minister or ones more certain to question his fitness for office or more likely to undermine his role as an MP," Sir John said.

He felt he had no option but to sue. "He was faced with a very genuine dilemma whether to say nothing and allow very serious allegations, the falsity of which he believed he could prove, to go unchallenged or to sue, knowing that in relation to the Ritz hotel he would have to tell a lie."

It was important to recall the atmosphere of 1995, when the Government was beset by allegations of sleaze, Sir John said.

He pointed out that the *Guardian* and Granada had been forced to withdraw some of the allegations against Aitken during the libel trial.

But Aitken had committed himself to his lies about the Ritz bill and repeated the lies in conversations with the Prime Minister and Cabinet Secretary, Sir Robin Butler.

It was inconceivable that he would have done so had he realised at the outset that it would lead him to give untrue evidence in witness statements and on oath. The prosecution and defence counsel referred in disapproving terms to the method used by the *Guardian* – a fax on House of Commons notepaper purporting to come from Aitken's private secretary – to obtain details of how the Ritz bill was settled.

Mr Waters said the newspaper had described its tactic as a "modest subterfuge", but others would be less restrained.

Sir John said it was a forgery. It was arguable in any case whether he was in breach of rules governing ministerial acceptance of gifts or services. There was no question of payment for his hotel stay placing him under any obligation to Mr Ayas or Prince Mohammed, with whom he had been friends for several years, and frequently exchanged hospitality.

Aitken had been an admired journalist, a successful merchant banker, a respected biographer of Richard Nixon and a "remarkable" MP and an effective minister, Sir John said.

"But for what of this will he be remembered? How will he be remembered? There can be only one answer. He will be forever remembered for the odium of being the MP who lied to try to pervert justice."

John Amery

"They called you traitor, and you heard them."

Today John Amery is, at best, remembered as only a slightly unsavoury historical footnote. But during the 1930s and 1940s he enjoyed two bouts of notoriety. He was the son of Leo Amery, a leading Conservative figure; and his brother, Julian, served his country with distinction during both the Second World War and as a minister in Ted Heath's early 1970s government. John, however, was delinquent, deviant and destructive, often at the same time. Having shocked his way out of Harrow (during his time there he apparently acquired syphilis while working as a male prostitute) he set up a series of film production companies, which invariably collapsed in a morass of recklessness, extravagance and deceit. His first brush with infamy came when he was arrested in Paris for diamond fraud. The press revelled in the story of how he and his new bride, Una Wing, who called herself an actress but whom everyone knew was a streetwalker, had eloped to Greece and converted to Orthodoxy because his parents wouldn't give them permission to marry. He disappeared from the public eye – busy gun-running for Franco's rebel forces in the Spanish Civil War – until later in 1942, when he delivered a series of propaganda broadcasts on behalf of the Nazis. By the time he was arrested in Italy (by Alan Whicker!) more lurid allegations still were brought against him.

31 July 1945
John Amery for trial on treason charges
Asserts aim was to create anti-Bolshevik front

After a six-hour hearing at Bow-street police court yesterday John Amery, 33, was committed for trial at the Old Bailey on charges of treason.

It was stated during the hearing that Amery had gone to prison camps where British civilians were held and had attempted to form a "Legion of St. George" to fight against "the menace of Bolshevism".

The charge alleged that between 22 June 1941 and 25 April 1945, being a person owing allegiance to his Majesty, he adhered to the King's enemies elsewhere than in the King's realm: to wit, in the German and Italian realms and in those parts of the continent of Europe occupied or controlled by the King's enemies, contrary to the Treason Act, 1351.

A second treason charge was that he had made propaganda speeches for the enemy in several European countries. A third charge referred to his alleged regular broadcasts for the enemy.

Mr L. A. Byrne stated the case for the prosecution. He said that on two occasions, the last on 31 July 1942. Amery had applied for a passport and stated that he was a British subject by birth.

Mr Byrne said: "It is alleged that the prisoner on behalf of the enemy urged British subjects, both soldiers and civilians, who were interned in France to join a military force called the 'Legion of St. George'.

"In his attempt to obtain recruits he visited an internment camp at St. Denis where British subjects were interned. He made speeches to them in which he urged them to join the Legion of St. George and he told them that if they joined they would be used to fight against the Russian army and not against their own countrymen."

A printed proclamation was issued to British prisoners stating that 150,000 of their fellow-countrymen were in prison in their home country because they had declared themselves against a fratricidal war.

It said that American troops had occupied Ulster and were arriving in increasing numbers and that British naval bases were to be handed over to the Roosevelt administration.

The proclamation, signed by Amery, went on: "I appeal to all Britons to answer this call to arms in the defence of our homes and children and of all civilisation against Asiatic and Jewish bestiality."

All ranks in the "Legion of St. George" were guaranteed permanent and well-placed jobs in the British administration and all priority in any other employment after the signing of peace with the possibility of forming the elite of the British Army.

It was signed "John Amery, 20 April 1943".

Amery's own explanation of his actions was contained, Mr Byrne said, in a statement he made when he was an internee in Italy and in another, a copy of a memorandum to the German Foreign Office, which came into the possession of the British military authorities.

On 22 May this year; Amery was seen by two British intelligence officers, Maj. Burt and Capt. Fish. Amery typed out a long statement, which Mr Bryne read to the court.

In this statement Amery explained that he was in the South of France winding up some business affairs when the French Army collapsed.

The armistice was signed," he wrote, "and I found myself virtually trapped in the free zone of France where by the terms of the armistice visas outgoing were not granted to British subjects of military age.

"In June, 1941 the war with the Soviets broke out. It was my considered opinion and that also of my friends, and notably Doriot and Deat, that Europe was in the greatest peril of a Communist invasion; that this invasion would sweep the whole Continent and that nothing could stop it unless the different countries of Europe pushed through a social revolution which would spike the guns of the Communists."

"It was also our view that the Jewish race was mixed up and working hand-in-glove with Moscow. In consequence of this it came as a very great shock to me when I heard that England and Soviet Russia had become Allies; so much so that I thought that the people responsible in London were acting in a manner that no longer coincided with British Imperial interests.

"I went, therefore, to Vichy to see what was going on, determined to do what I could to create a situation whereby a united front of all nations might be organised against Russia. I found that Vichy was an ultra-reactionary Government, of priests, the worst type, in my opinion, of French industrialists and militarists.

"In November 1941, on a frivolous pretext, they threw me into gaol at Vals Les Bains, where I found myself with Paul Reynaud and Mandel, of all people. The united efforts of my friends, Jeanine Amery-Barde and Doriot, extracted me from there after 18 days."

He then tried to get in touch with Grandi, the former Italian Ambassador in London, but failed.

"Now it became my turn to be visited by a certain Graf Ceschi, German Armistice Chief for Savoy, whom I had known slightly in Vienna. The suggestion was made that I should go to Germany and discuss my point of view with them.

"After a few days in Paris and travelling under the names of Mr and Mrs Browne I arrived in Berlin early in October 1942, where I began to discuss those problems with a certain Dr. Hesse. He had a kind of autonomous situation with Minister Schmidt (Hitler's interpreter).

"As is well known there were numerous other Englishmen in Berlin, notably William Joyce and his friends, and Baillie Stewart and his.

These people had come to Germany on or before the declaration of war. Also they had adopted German nationality and considered themselves Germans. In consequence their views and outlook widely differed from mine.

"It was in my view quite insane to carry on as they did calling the British 'the enemy' and so forth as was their custom.

"I told Dr. Hesse perfectly frankly that I was not interested in a German victory as such, that what interested me was a just peace, where we could all get together against the real enemies of civilisation, and that the British Empire as it was intact must be a part of this and not independent of such a regroupment; that I considered, if, as an Englishman, with the collaboration of others we could speak uncensored and uninterfered with in a special British hour on the radio and they would give precise guarantees, at least to us, concerning British imperial territory, and consider their policy as remaining based on the proposals of the German Chancellor to the British Government of July 1940, then we could attempt something.

"He asked me how much I wanted for myself. When I told him that far from wanting anything I was not disposed to accept anything, other than that he considered me as a guest having no resources of my own available, he seemed quite taken aback.

"When I next saw him he told me that I could consider myself a guest of the Reich, that I could go where I pleased, and that he suggested I should make on the radio a series of weekly speeches which would be officially dissociated from the German senders and entirely uncensored."

In January 1943, he went to Paris. The news from Russia was "pretty bad" and that in France worse.

"Doriot's view," he wrote, "was that it was better to go to the front, in Russia and to make things abundantly clear, and when I come back with the Iron Cross I will send this bloody Embassy to hell."

I tackled Hesse again. He was a man who had never got over the criminal folly of the bombardment of England in 1940–41 and he listened patiently to us.

"I told him that in my view we must also create a British anti-Bolshevik Legion, however small, and that perhaps on the things going on in other countries of Europe would it be possible for me to attempt to help some sort of improvement of the situation based on the following principle: If England saw that Europe was uniting against Bolshevism she would come in as well.

"On 7–8 April my beloved friend and brave political revolutionary, Jeanine Barde, died. I buried her in her native Bergerac, went to see her child, and stayed in France from 15 April to June 1943.

"I paused at St. Denis (civilian internee camp) to test whether there might or might not be volunteers for the British Legion. Considering the general difficulties I was impressed by the fact that out of some 30 or 40 people there were four or five volunteers, but I was too distraught to pay any great attention at the time.

"At the end of September I received an invitation from the Italian Government telling me that Mussolini wished to see me. I set out in the middle of October and saw him on the Lake of Garda at the end of that month.

His view was that he had made a great mistake in 1922 in not carrying through what he was now attempting, i.e., to create a social republic.

"In Italy I spoke in Italian to the Italians over the Republican network, uncensored, and made some speeches in Geneva, Turin, Biella, Remona and Milan.

"Mussolini had by mid-April moved definitely to Milan, where I saw him on 23 April. The military situation had so degenerated by this time that his view was that there remained only to betake ourselves to the mountains, where a great stock of food, munitions, radio apparatus &c., was to be laid in.

"In accordance with this suggestion he offered me a commission in the 'Brigade Nera.' I told him that I could not accept that because such an acceptance might involve me in firing on my fellow-countrymen, and this I was unwilling to do, but that I would certainly go with him and address myself in a manner that my opinions should be unmistakable.

"I decided to go over to Como to see what was happening there. I left Milan on the night of the 25th, and two-thirds of the way along the autostrade to Como I was surrounded by partisans and made prisoner.

"On my insistence they finally consented to hand me over to the British authorities. The rest is known."

Amery's statement ended: "I particularly want to draw attention to the fact that I defy anyone to find in my speeches, radio or otherwise, my conversations in private and of what I have written, one single solitary word against my country – on the contrary.

"Considering (unless time proves all these anti-Communists to have been insane) that Russia and her Communist satellites will prove a great danger to the civilised world and to the British Empire in particular before very many months have gone by . . . may I be permitted to suggest to the political and intelligence departments of his Majesty's Government that in some form or other I can still carry on my life's political work and render very considerable services to my country?"

Mr Byrne held up a large red-bordered poster written in Italian with a photograph of Amery in the centre, which said: "Who ordered the indiscriminate bombing of women and children? Churchill and his gang did not hesitate to drag the flag and the fair name of England in the mud."

Mr Byrne added: "Those are the documents, which indicate quite plainly the prisoner's personal activities which, in the submission of the prosecution, are nothing more nor less than a confession of treason."

Pte. David Watson Philp, of the Black Watch, stated that he was a prisoner at St. Denis. Amery asked him to join the "Anti-Bolshevik League," telling him that he would be taken to a camp near Berlin where he could receive all his letters and parcels from home and "no one would be any the wiser".

"He said we would be promoted to officers," Philp added, "and would become the élite of the British Army when England had fallen to Germany. I lost my temper and attempted to strike him."

He was then taken to another camp and kept in the cells for three weeks. For four days he had only bread and water.

Royston Francis Wood, of Rue de l'University, Paris, who was interned at St. Denis, declared that Amery visited the camp on 21 April 1943, spoke of the Legion of St. George, and promised them their freedom if they joined it. The internees booed Amery as he left.

Percy Glyn Davies Pugh, of Rue Joseph Bara, Paris, who was the camp secretary during his internment at St. Denis from July 1940, to August 1944, stated: "When John Amery left, the attitude of the internees was exceedingly hostile. They demonstrated in the only way they could – by hooting and booing.

Jacques Girard, a Paris police inspector, told of a speech given by Amery in the

Gaumont Palace in Paris on 7 May 1944, to about 2,000 people. Amery spoke in French, saying: "Don't expect an Englishman to speak badly of his country. I love my country very much. If I am among you to-day it is because I detest the people who have thrown my country into war."

He was antagonistic to the Churchill Government and said that there were about 150,000 English people who were in internment camps in England.

When Amery was committed for trial, Mr E. P. Lickford, defending, said that Amery pleaded not guilty and reserved his defence, and added, "he desires through me to take the opportunity of stating that he has a complete answer to this charge. He wishes to take the opportunity of stating that none of his actions has been directed against the British Empire, but that he is now and always has been pro-British."

29 November 1945
John Amery's guilty plea in eight-min trial
Death sentence
By a *Daily Telegraph* reporter

John Amery, 33, described as a politician, was yesterday sentenced to death at the Old Bailey after pleading guilty to eight counts of high treason. The case lasted just eight minutes.

Amery heard the sentence with composure. When it was over he bowed gravely to the judge, Mr Justice Humphreys, turned and walked quickly to the back of the dock and disappeared down the stairs to the cells.

While the court was waiting for the case to open, a dramatic scene was being enacted in Amery's cell below No. 1 Court. The case was due to come on at 10.30 a.m., but it was 11.30 a.m. before his name was called.

In the meantime his counsel, Mr G. O. Slade K.C., and Mr John Foster, were trying to persuade him to adhere to his original plea of "Not guilty". It was an unexpected development when he decided to change it to one of "Guilty".

Counsel pointed out that his decision would inevitably mean the death sentence.

After the Clerk had read the indictment, Amery said: "I plead guilty to all counts."

Mr Justice Humphreys: "I never accept a plea of guilty on a capital charge without assuring myself that the accused thoroughly understands what he is doing, what the immediate result must be, and that he is in accord with his legal advisers in the course he is taking. Can you give me that assurance in this case?"

Mr Slade: "I can. I have explained the position fully to my client, and I am satisfied he understands."

The Judge: "Let the plea be recorded."

Before passing sentence, Mr Justice Humphreys addressed Amery with these words: "John Amery, you have forfeited your right to live. You now stand a self-confessed traitor to your King and country.

"I am satisfied that what you did you did intentionally and deliberately, after you had received warnings from more than one of your fellow-countrymen that the course you were pursuing amounted to high treason.

"They called you traitor, and you heard them. In spite of that you continued in that course."

Amery stood perfectly still. The ghost of a smile spread across his face as the black cap was placed on the judge's head and sentence of death pronounced.

The second indictment alleging treachery was not read. At the preliminary hearing at Bow-street a statement, alleged to have been made by Amery, was read. In it he said that he went to Berlin in 1942 and made speeches and broadcasts of an anti-Bolshevik character.

After the trial Amery was driven to Wandsworth Prison, where Joyce is held awaiting his appeal to the House of Lords.

20 December 1945
John Amery executed

In a drizzle of rain a warder yesterday morning stepped outside Wandsworth Prison and on the great main doors, fixed formal notices stating that John Amery, self-confessed traitor, was dead.

The execution took place while the bells of a distant church were chiming 9 o'clock. It was carried out by Albert Pierrepoint, who had recently returned from the Belsen executions.

The posting of the notices was watched by a small group of soldiers from a nearby stores depot and a few passing workmen. Amery was visited in prison by all his family the evening before he was executed.

About three hours after the execution Mr Hervey Wyatt, the coroner, held an inquest in the prison. The jury returned a verdict of judicial hanging. Dr. Cedric Simpson the pathologist, said the post-mortem examination revealed no disease of any kind.

Jeffrey Archer

"I have never denied what I was; I was a prostitute.
But I wasn't a liar. He is."

In November 1986 the *News of the World* ran a story claiming that Jeffrey Archer, the novelist and deputy chairman of the Conservative Party had met 35-year-old prostitute Monica Coghlan, and then paid her £2,000 to buy her silence. A week later the *Star* repeated the allegations and also suggested that they had had "kinky sex". Outraged, Archer swiftly brought a libel action against both papers. His suit against the *Star* appeared in court first, and as more details spilled out, he accomplished the unlikely feat of ensuring that the plot of his own life appeared subject to the same kind of lurid melodrama that had made his books bestsellers. The case, described by the judge as "as big a libel as has ever been tried this century" was eventually decided in Archer's favour, and he was awarded record damages of £500,000. Fourteen years later, substantial evidence emerged that immolated the credibility of Archer's alibi; gratifyingly, for those fond of dramatic justice, it was his own ambition and carelessness that led to his ultimate downfall.

8 July 1987
Archer "pleaded with editor to save political career"
"Outside chance of Tory chairmanship if this dies down"
By Robert Reid

Hours before the story that led Jeffrey Archer to resign as Tory party deputy chairman reached the streets in a Sunday newspaper, he pleaded again and again with its editor for his political future, a libel jury heard yesterday.

He even confided to Mr David Montgomery, *News of the World* editor: "I believe I have an outside chance of being chairman of the party if this dies down and doing some work in my life I can be proud of."

But unknown to Mr Archer the story alleging he had paid £2,000 to prostitute Monica Coghlan to buy her silence was already in print and waiting only to be despatched to newsagents round the country.

Minutes later when 47-year-old Mr Archer learned that the story would not be "killed", he berated Mr Montgomery over the telephone.

"I have rarely seen a bigger set-up," he told him in a call punctuated throughout by each calling the other by his first name.

"If you are in the game of taping phone calls and following people around, David, you are not the man I thought you were when I first met you.

"I hope you live with this for the rest of your life. When my resignation is announced, I hope you smile. You have broken my career."

Tapes of this and other conversations were played at the High Court yesterday in the second day of a libel suit brought by Mr Archer not against the *News of the World*, but against the *Star* newspaper and its editor, Mr Lloyd Turner.

The *Star* carried a story a week later on 1 November last year, after Mr Archer had denied the Sunday paper allegations, repeating its claims and suggesting Mr Archer had paid for intercourse with the "kinky sex" girl in the case.

Another action being brought by Mr Archer against the *News of the World* is still pending and not expected to be heard before 1989.

So packed was Court 13 for yesterday's hearing that the judge, Mr Justice Caulfield, delayed the start for nearly half an hour to allow adjustments to be made to public seating arrangements. A balcony was opened to take the overspill.

Mr Archer, watched from the front of the court by his wife, Mary, 41, resumed his evidence interrupted by Monday's adjournment. It is thought he could spend much of the week in the witness box.

He briefly went over earlier evidence of five telephone calls made to him by Miss Coghlan and taped by *News of the World* reporters in which she claimed that another client – solicitor Aziz Kurtha – had recognised him (Archer) as the man who had sex with her at the Albion Hotel, Victoria, last September.

Mr Archer repeatedly denied even being there and advised her time and again to go to the police.

He admitted later arranging for her to be paid £2,000 to take her and her 10-year-old son on holiday, but claimed that was because he believed her story that she was being harassed by Kurtha and the press and that her home in the north of England was virtually under siege.

In court, Mr Archer admitted he was "frightened" of a false story of this kind appearing in the papers. With a General Election in the offing, he said, it was the last thing he wanted.

During the Conservative conference at Bournemouth around this time last year, Mr Archer said he twice had lunch with Mr Montgomery. There was no talk then of any story being "peddled" around Fleet Street about him and the girl.

When he finally obtained Mr Kurtha's address from the girl, Mr Archer contacted his solicitor who wrote to Mr Kurtha warning of legal action if he continued spreading or trying to sell his story.

"I was not deterred by the realisation that such a step would make the story public," said Mr Archer. "It was not true."

"It was going on for weeks and I was becoming absolutely sick of it. The only way to deal with it was to ask my solicitor to handle it in the appropriate manner."

He first learned of the *News of the World* story at about 4 p.m. on the Saturday it was being printed.

"I rang David Montgomery because I just did not believe it was possible," he said. Mr Archer asked: "Do you accept that this is a story on which I could resign?"

"I am not in your shoes, Jeffrey," came the reply.

Mr Archer: "I want to tell you there is no truth in it and my wife is here in tears."

Mr Archer then talked with *News of the World* reporter John Lisner and denied everything that was subsequently to appear in the paper.

"I have to say to you, and will say to your editor, that this is not true and I will issue a writ immediately.

"I shall sue and I shall win. You will ruin my career. It will take three years to get to the courts and by then my career will be wrecked."

The reporter then apologised, but reprimanded Mr Archer for having been "very indiscreet".

Mr Archer later pleaded: "I would like you and your editor to sit down before you print this and say out loud: 'We are going to ruin this man's career.'"

Mr Lisner's response was that it would not be the newspaper's doing.

At this point the judge warned the jury to ignore any facial expressions they had seen being made in the public gallery and he advised members of the public to be still during evidence.

Mr Archer said it was only when he had seen the content of the story in print that he realised the *News of the World* had recorded all five calls between himself and Miss Coghlan. He accused the paper of printing parts of only the last conversation "knowing very well they were going to ruin my career".

He added: "They didn't use the first four conversations, only the fifth. They behaved quite dishonestly."

In a final plea to Mr Montgomery, Mr Archer said: "If that article goes in, I am going to tell the Prime Minister I am resigning and I am going to sue you."

He admitted he had been "very foolish indeed" and added: "I beg you not to put it in."

The editor responded: "I am very sorry, I can't kill this story. I have to go the way my conscience dictates and I believe it to be true. I can offer you a platform to reply."

Within 60 seconds, Mr Archer learned from the editor of the *News of the World's* sister paper, the *Sunday Times*, that the story was already in print.

Mr Archer said: "The way the story was written, anyone reading it, even of a fair mind, would be bound to believe that there was only one phone call and, on the basis of that one call, I had sent money to a prostitute to get her out of the country."

He made the decision then to inform Mr Tebbit immediately of events but not to speak to the Prime Minister.

But after consulting with his solicitor, Mr Archer decided to resign to avoid any harm to the party.

Mr Archer said that after the story was published "I think it became clear among decent-minded journalists, this was a set up. The Press reacted accordingly with generous tributes in almost every national newspaper.

"I think my wife and I, towards the end of the week, were feeling that we were out of the worst of it. Although I had made a fool of myself, no one actually believed I had met the girl.

"So when I learned on the Saturday of the *Star's* article suggesting I had not only met her but had sexual relations with her, both my wife and I were very distressed indeed."

Asked if he believed up to that point that he could salvage his political career, Mr Archer replied: "It is very hard to judge whether those who offer high political office would have considered that it would need a long period of time to be accepted in the party again."

The hearing was adjourned.

9 July 1987
Archer denies telling newsmen he met "sex" girl
By Robert Reid

Jeffrey Archer, fighting to clear his name of newspaper allegations that he had "kinky sex" with a prostitute then tried to buy her silence with a £2,000 "pay-off", vigorously denied in court yesterday that he had told two other papers he had "met the girl, but not slept with her".

It was the former Tory party deputy chairman's third day in the witness box at the High Court libel hearing.

He is suing the *Star* and Mr Lloyd Turner, its editor, for libel over front page claims last November.

He has maintained since the hearing opened on Monday that he had never met 35-year-old Monica Coghlan, the woman at the centre of the scandal that led to his resignation as Mr Tebbit's Number Two and "wrecked" his political career.

In continuing cross-examination by Mr Michael Hill, QC, yesterday, it was suggested that on the Saturday night the story first appeared in the News of the World, Mr Archer himself had told reporters from *Sunday Today* and the *Observer* that he HAD met her.

"That is absolute bunkum," said an angry Mr Archer, "and I can prove it."

Extracts from the papers were read to the court. In *Sunday Today*, Mr Rupert Norris, a reporter, wrote: "Mr Archer was telling friends last night his career is finished.

"He told me last night: 'I am consulting my lawyer. That is all I can say.' But he has told friends that he had met the woman once, but denied sleeping with her."

In the *Observer*, Mr Adam Raphael, political editor – who was, Mr Archer conceded, a "respected journalist" – wrote: "Archer is claimed by friends to have met Monica Coghlan only once, and very casually, six months ago."

Again Mr Archer cut in. "Absolute bunkum," he said.

He was asked repeatedly if he had in fact used those words to the journalists concerned on an "off the record" basis, and whether they had used the device of "friends" as a means of quoting him without attribution to him.

"Certainly not," he replied. He had never met the woman, he insisted, and had never told any reporters otherwise.

He said he had received 50–60 telephone calls at his home the night the story broke. He could not recall the details of all of them, or who had rung. But he had never said to any of them that he had met the prostitute.

Mr Archer, 47, told the court that newspapers "do get things wrong", and quoted from a report of this case earlier this week in the *London Daily News*, where a completely wrong and "damaging" interpretation had been put on his past financial difficulties.

Mr Hill quoted from Mr Archer's statement after he quit as party deputy chairman. "I have never, I repeat never, met Monica Coghlan, nor have I ever had any association of any kind with a prostitute," he said.

Mr Hill asked: "Not even for book research?" The millionaire author admitted: "Some years ago – four of five, I think – I approached a man called Ian Scarlette, who is an expert on prostitution, and he advised me on a set-up I wanted to use.

"I believe on one occasion he did bring with him a girl who claimed to be a prostitute."

He was then asked: "Is there no possibility you were involved in a research way with Monica Coghlan?" "Absolutely not, Sir," he answered.

Two more newspapers entered the picture when cross-examination was turned to examining Mr Archer's diaries, and what the author himself has called his "alibi" that he was dining with friends and associates the night he was said to have spent with Miss Coghlan.

Mr Nicholas Constable, a reporter, wrote in *Today* that Mr Archer said he had been "at a meeting with 50 other people" that night.

Mr Tony Dawe, a reporter on the *Daily Express*, had been told, Mr Hill claimed, that Mr Archer had been at a function with 40 other people. Mr Archer had told the *Express* he had been discussing an impending Cabinet reshuffle with Mr John Wakeham, Government Chief Whip, and had driven a colleague home from Conservative Central Office.

"I suggest you were putting forward a very different account then than you are giving here now," accused Mr Hill.

Again Mr Archer argued that newspapers sometimes get their facts wrong. "The relevant thing is that I was in a room with 50 other people, nine of whom will come forward and confirm it, he said.

Earlier, Mr Archer had clashed angrily with Mr Hill over the QC's suggestion that he was "trying to wriggle off the hook".

Denying the claim, Mr Archer snapped back that counsel was being "aggravating". "You are repeating exactly the same things today that you did yesterday," he said, "then telling the jury when I repeat the same answers that I am making speeches."

During heated exchanges in the packed courtroom yesterday with Mr Hill, Mr Archer accused the *News of the World* of being "a bunch of liars who had set me up".

The case was adjourned until today.

11 May 1987
Archer had sex with me, says prostitute
High Court hears of "midnight approach in a Mayfair alleyway"
By Wendy Holden

The prostitute at the centre of the Jeffrey Archer High Court libel case yesterday identified the former Deputy Chairman of the Tory party as the man who had sexual intercourse with her in a London hotel.

Petite mousey-haired Miss Monica Coghlan, 36, from Rochdale, Lancashire, was appearing as a witness on the fifth day of the action brought by Mr Archer against the *Star* newspaper, which published allegations last November that he had "kinky sex" with her and then paid her £2,000 "hush money".

Mr Archer resigned his party post as a result of the allegations, but has maintained since the case began on Monday that he had never met Miss Coghlan, and that the £2,000 he paid her was for "holiday expenses", after she had told him she was being hounded by the press.

Her voice quivering with nerves, Miss Coghlan avoided the glare of Mr Archer's wife, Mary, sitting a few feet from her in the front of the court. She told the court she had a two-year-old son, lived in a bungalow in Rochdale, and had taken up prostitution two years after leaving school at 16.

She commuted to London for three or four days a week, staying at the Albion Hotel in Victoria, before going home to spend the next week to 10 days with her son, she said.

On the night of 8 September last year, when Mr Archer has claimed he was with friends at a London restaurant until 1 a.m., Miss Coghlan said a man approached her from an alleyway in Shepherd Market, Mayfair, at about midnight.

"I was wearing black fishnet stockings, black patent shoes, a black handbag, black PVC wet-look skirt, with a black leotard underneath, and a white chunky-knit wool jumper on," she said.

She had already been with two clients that evening, who had paid her £120, when the man walked up an alleyway opposite the one she was standing in.

"He walked right past all the other girls, and came straight towards me. He was familiar and I put it down that he could have been an ex-client of mine, but when he came up to me, I realised that he wasn't a client, but he was still familiar," she told the packed courtroom.

"He said 'Hello, are you free?' and I answered 'Yes.' I said that it was £50 and he said that was fine. When he agreed I suggested that we walked down into Curzon Street and got a black taxi back to the Albion Hotel, but he said he had a car on the corner," she said.

The man said he would prefer it if he went to get his car alone, while she waited, and so she did. But, when, after a few minutes he had not returned, and another client approached her, she decided to go off with him in his Mercedes to the hotel.

Her "business", as she described it, with that client only took about 20 minutes, and when she came out of the hotel with him, she saw a Jaguar car on he other side of road, flashing its headlights. As she walked towards the car, the man she had seen in the alleyway got out the Jaguar.

"Which man?" counsel for the *Star*, Mr Michael Hill, QC, asked.

Miss Coghlan raised her right arm and pointed her finger at Mr Archer, sitting at the front of the court next to his wife.

"That gentleman there. The gentleman with the red tie on," she replied. Mr Archer looked at her, then down at his tie, and then directly back at her again.

Her previous client called her over to him, she said, as she and the Jaguar driver walked towards the hotel.

She said: "He said to me: You have hit the jackpot this time. Do you know who that is? It is Jeffrey Archer, the well-known author, and then he said something about being an MP. I just shrugged my shoulders – the name meant nothing to me."

She took her client up to the second floor to her room, Room 6A, where he gave her a £50 note.

"I told him that if he took his time and I took my time and made it last a bit longer, it would be another £20, and he gave me a £20 note. Then we undressed," she said.

"And, then?" inquired Mr Hill. "He commented on how lovely I was. He was quite surprised by my nipples."

"What did he get for his money."

"Sex."

"How long were you in that room?"

"Not very long. It was over very quickly, about ten minutes, what with getting undressed and the actual sex."

"And after the sex what happened?"

"Because it was over so quickly I suggested that he relax for a while and he could try again. I took the Durex off first and washed him and cleaned him up with tissues and dried him. I lit a cigarette and I laid down on the bed with him.

"Go on."

"Well, to sort of break the ice and probably because of what my previous client had said I was a bit intrigued and I asked him what he did for a living. He said 'I sell cars,' and he had no sooner said that when he jumped of the bed and said he should go and move his car.

Her client then got dressed and left the room, she said. She watched him go to his car, from the window, and then she did her hair and reapplied her make-up, and when he had not returned after ten minutes she decided to return to Shepherd Market in a taxi. By then, she said, it was between 1.20 a.m. and 1.30 a.m.

The following Saturday, she said the client in the Mercedes, who she now knew as Mr Aziz Kurtha, a solicitor, contacted her and they arranged to meet. He paid her £60 and they had sexual intercourse at the Albion Hotel, and then he talked to her about the previous weekend.

"He asked me to go and see two journalists or reporters from *Private Eye* magazine to describe what happened to me that night, the night of 8 September," she said.

The sum of between £700 and £800 was mentioned as a payment to her, she added, and the suggestion that she should she agree to the proposition, she said, "terrified" her.

"Mr Kurtha mentioned that the gentleman they were talking about had quite possibly recognised him also. He said he had been on television, in the *Eastern Eye* programme, and that they moved in the same circles. He said he was a solicitor and he also told me he was very rich, a millionaire, she added.

She said she told him that she was not interested, and he left but not long after a man had phoned her earlier and made an arrangement to meet her "for business", arrived. He paid her £70, but they did not have sexual intercourse, she said. She met him again after that.

Mr Hill asked her: "Did you eventually learn his occupation?"

"Yes, he was a freelance journalist," she replied.

Mr Hill had opened the *Star's* defence case by telling the jury that they would have to decide whether his case proved, to the necessary standard, that Mr Archer did have sexual connection with Monica Coghlan on 8/9 September.

"There is a strain on the British character which requires of those who are in position of power, or prominence in the public eye, that they should behave themselves according to the highest standards," he said.

"And when they do not and are discovered not to have done so, their falling from those highest standards damages their reputation and standing."

He added that the period following discovery would be agonising and desperate for the person concerned, although society was compassionate.

"What society regards as least acceptable is somebody caught out in that position who does not confess, and lies."

Earlier a defiant Mrs Archer spoke out in anger for the first time, a day after she broke down in tears and was led weeping from the witness box.

Mrs Archer, 42, a former Cambridge don, appeared calm, arrogant and defiant as she answered questions for over an hour from Mr Hill.

Asked what impact the *Star's* coverage of the hearing had on her this week, she commented that she knew it was "perfectly proper" for Mr Hill to put the *Star's* case, and even to suggest that her husband had told a "pack of lies".

But when asked what she thought of the paper's front page headline, "You Lied and Lied and Lied", earlier this week, she replied:

"It is perfectly proper for Mr Hill to say that my husband lied and lied and lied but we all heard my husband say with equal conviction that he had not."

Then, leaning forward and directing her comments to Mr Lloyd Turner, the paper's editor, sitting ten feet away, she almost spat out the words:

"Mr Turner, your paper cannot keep a consistent line from week to week."

And when Mr Hill jumped to his feet to object and said: "Madam I cannot keep silent," Mrs Archer turned on him and retorted: "I have been long silent."

Mrs Archer, who has been married to the novelist for 21 years, and is the mother of his two teenage sons, continued to answer cross-examination in a defiant tone.

At one point in the questioning, her husband's counsel, Mr Robert Alexander,

QC, jumped up to object, but the judge, Mr Justice Caulfield, told him: "You may think that the jury may think that Mrs Archer is looking after herself very well."

Later, she recalled how she was "dumbfounded" when she heard her husband tell a reporter on the telephone: "If I did meet her [the prostitute] I don't know about it. If there is a photo of me with her then I don't know about it."

Mrs Archer said: "I asked him what on earth made him say that, and he said it had occurred to him that the *News of the World* could have contrived some meeting, at some kind of public function, when very many people do come up to Jeffrey, shake his hand, sometimes even throw their arms around his neck and kiss him."

She said later that she thought that the reason she was not told by her husband about the prostitute ringing him up several times about the matter was "very simple".

"It is simply that Jeffrey didn't take it seriously for a very long time."

The High Court then heard from Mr Richard Cohen, a publishing director who had dinner with Mr Archer at the Caprice Restaurant in Arlington Street, Westminster, on the night of 8 September last year.

Mr Terence Baker, a film and literary agent, said that he met Mr Archer in the restaurant at about 11.15 p.m., and that Mr Archer stayed in the restaurant, until driving Mr Baker home to Camberwell some time after 1 a.m. The hearing was adjourned until Monday.

12 July 1987
Archer lives the part
A celebrity trial staged in a heatwave
By Megan Tresidder

They were packing the aisles last week in the liveliest court drama of the year: Archer versus the *Star*. And who can blame them, those members of the public who adopted notebooks as camouflage to pour into Court 13, leaving the gentlemen of the press to take their shorthand standing?

Here was, as the plaintiff would himself blurt out, "an evil little story" about a vice girl and a millionaire worthy of the fluent pen of the author, Archer, himself, yet allegedly entirely produced by others, namely the *News of the World* and the *Star*.

And yet, as Archer, again would several times admit, it was a story into which he had managed to write himself, in a pretty big way. The two poles of fact and fiction were melting before our eyes. At times, they appeared to run together.

Phrases that came from witnesses seemed to have jumped out of Archer's novels, or from the script he has already prepared for a courtroom drama.

Was he speaking as a thrilling writer or as a plain man when he told the court "I realised I had what I think is called an alibi"? What book or play had Michael Hill, QC, the *Star*'s Counsel, been reading when, quizzing Archer about his dinner at Le Caprice on 8 September, he asked, "House wine or cellar wine?"

The jury did not look as if it were composed of wine buffs but then there did not seem to be any legal point resting on the distinction between house or cellar wine.

What the question did do, when answered by Archer with "Oh, cellar wine, probably", was restore the image of a millionaire.

That high-living image had been cruelly punctured earlier in the discussion about the dinner at Le Caprice, where the bill had only been £51.75, plus a £6 tip – for three! When a man has been described in court as a millionaire whose life is "a big dipper ride", you expect him to tip with his cufflinks, at least.

Small wonder then, as the court case turned into a play within a play, that the judge showed so much concern for the jury of eight men and four women, asking if they could bear "ten minutes' injury time."

Mr Justice Caulfield quickly established himself as a character to watch: with a dry humour that belied his face of livid fury beneath a tattered, grey wig. "Can we get the clicks over before we start?" he asked the jurors as they fiddled with the ring-binders.

The judge's wit could not crack the ice that formed round the *Star*'s QC, better known for his work in the criminal courts. For four days he cross-examined Archer whilst hardly ever looking at him. His technique was harsh and wearing: "Mr Archer, do you really mean that?" or "Mr Archer, would you like to reconsider your answer?" or "Are you sure, Mr Archer?"

Mr Archer met Mr Hill's attack with a cold courtesy that only cracked occasionally, at the end of the long days. With "no sir," "absolutely not, sir" and "I fear I cannot, sir," he deferred to Mr Hill so often that the judge finally told him to stop being so polite.

Mary Archer needed no such urging on Day Five. In an astonishing contrast not just with her brief and tearful scene in the witness box on the previous afternoon but also with her nervous and intent appearance all week, she tore through all the unrealities and surrealism in court 13.

But Jeffrey Archer's wife betrayed nothing when Monica Coghlan was brought in that last afternoon.

Act Two of the courtroom saga commences tomorrow morning at 10.30 am. There won't be a seat left in house.

24 July 1987
Archer: what the judge told the jury
The Jeffrey Archer libel case jury is now considering its verdict. Here we publish an edited version of the summing-up given to the jury by the judge, Mr Justice Caulfield. He began on Wednesday afternoon

"Just harken to me, please. Harkening means more than listening, and not in haste we are going to review the issues and the evidence in this very grave and serious trial.

Jeffrey Archer, who sits before you, has by his own brain pulled himself from great debt to possibly considerable wealth in a few years. In material terms he can be described as rich. At this moment in reputation you may think he is a pauper, and if your verdict goes against him, you may think he is destined to endure the rest of his life as a social leper in a social workhouse for hypocrites. You can see how grave this trial is.

"Assuming he is defeated today and you conclude that the *Star* has proved its case, you can imagine, can you not, a graveyard for lost reputations. You can imagine, can you not, the memorial that would be raised for the lost reputation of a man with the distinction and the abilities of Jeffrey Archer.

"That gravestone could possibly have just two words quoted from the banner headline of the *Star* newspaper for 1 November, 'Poor Jeffrey' and underneath you might find on that imagined monument: 'This monument has been donated, erected and inscribed by the proprietors of The Star and its editor, who wish to acknowledge the co-operation of those who helped to erect it. We acknowledge,' it could read, 'the co-operation of Monica Man Coghlan, a well-known trader in Shepherd Market, and the co-operation of Aziz Kurtha, one of the many thousands of customers, satisfied customers, of Monica.

"'A lawyer, a gambler and a writer of articles part-time. There are others, too, who have helped in this monument. Eddie Jones, Jo Fletcher. Gerry Brown and John Lisners, the protectors of Monica. Signed Lloyd Turner, editor, the Feast of All Saints 1986.' That was the day of publication.

"Put in that imaginary form, you as jurymen should be able to visualise the gravity of this case, and you should be able to recognise the burden which is upon you, and upon you only to give a true verdict according to the evidence.

"You will find when I come to make my comments that there will not be many sugared almonds and there will be quite a few acid drops, but make up your mind when you hear them.

"The *Star* in this libel action says: 'You, Jeffrey Archer are a liar when you said that you had never, repeat never, met Monica Coghlan. Secondly,' says the *Star*, 'you did consort and enjoy the body' – if enjoyment is the word – 'of Monica Coghlan some time round about twenty minutes to one or thereabouts in room 6A of the Albion Hotel on 9 September last year.'

"The *Star* has the burden of proving to your satisfaction that those allegations are probably true.

"In this trial, you have seen loads of copies of newspapers. You could almost become a newsagent with the newspapers that have been put before you. You might have thought before this trial that what you read in the newspaper is fact, namely, that it is true. Well, goodness, if you had such a thought, it must have disappeared from your minds long, long ago in this trial.

"You might rely on the sporting columns to see the horses running at Haydock Park, and they are generally right about that. But as regards matters of fact connected with this case, do not work on the basis that any matter of fact asserted in a newspaper is evidence of truth.

"The evidence in this case is concerned with identification. The person who does the identification in the first place is Aziz Kurtha.

"Have you ever said to a friend, perhaps a relation: 'I saw you at Chelsea last Saturday'? 'Don't be stupid,' he said, 'I went to Lowestoft with my wife.' 'Did you?' 'Yes.' 'Well, I could have sworn it was you.'

"That is a mistake made in identification by somebody who is not looking for money, not looking for gain, but has plainly, as an honest person, made a mistake. It does happen. Of course it happens where the person is asserting that he has seen somebody when the person he has seen is not known to him. Mistakes can grow, and if the identification is in the dark when the circumstances are difficult, there is more error."

The judge then adjourned the hearing until yesterday morning.

"I come to look generally at this situation of Jeffrey and Mary Archer. Who are they? How do they live? What do they look like? What are their attributes? What are their interests? What is their family life like?

"I do that because you are entitled to look at all the possibilities. You are entitled to consider the whole situation of the Archers at the Old Vicarage in Grantchester, and at the life – perhaps an extremely busy life – of a deputy chairman of a leading political party – it matters not which party.

"Remember Mary Archer in the witness box. Your vision of her probably will never disappear. Has she elegance? Has she fragrance? Would she have, without the strain of this trial, radiance? What is she like in physical features, in presentation, in appearance? How would she appeal? Has she had a happy married life? Has she been able to enjoy rather than endure her husband Jeffrey? Is she right when she says to you, you may think with delicacy, 'Jeffrey and I lead a full life.'

"They were married, if my memory is right, twenty-one years before the first Saturday of this trial, which was their anniversary. They are blessed, no doubt they would say, with two sons, who are possibly at their most attractive ages and interesting periods of 13 and 15.

"Though her husband is obviously busy and leads a careering political life throughout the country, he comes home at the weekends. A couple of days a week, Mary, who has great distinction in her own right, is in London, perhaps two or three days a week. So is there any abstinence from marital joys for Jeffrey Archer?

"Look at him. What is his history? His history, you might think, is worthy and healthy and sporting – which is ordinary. A great attribute of the British is their almost adoration, besides enjoyment, of good lawful sports like cricket and athletics.

Jeffrey Archer, himself, was president of the Oxford University Athletic Club. He ran for his country. You may think he is fit looking, and you may think he is still interested in an athletic life.

"Is he in need of cold, unloving, rubber-insulated sex in a seedy hotel round about quarter to one on a Tuesday morning, after an evening at the Caprice with his agent or editor?

"There is no accounting for the tastes of even happily married men . . . It is possible even for the most happy, successful and respected married man to seek adventure in physical contact with persons who will not tell. But reflect, would you, upon the position.

"If Jeffrey Archer was in need of physical adventure with a prostitute, his need must have been very demanding; his sexual urge must have been very sustaining and may not have been very discerning.

"Because, on the version put forward by the newspaper he had the briefest of encounters with 'Debbie' [Monica Coghlan] in Shepherd Market, leaving her, after the briefest of conversations, to collect his car.

"His sexual urge driving him, as well as being driven in his powerful Daimler no doubt, he follows the prostitute, who is now accompanied by Kurtha. He follows them down Curzon Street, along to Park Lane. They turn left on to the nearside carriageway. They pass the Grosvenor, down to Hyde Park Corner, where even the most skilful drivers have to be tremendously alert. He trails that car with his prostitute in it and Kurtha to a part of London to which no tourist ever goes for the fun of seeing it.

"A seedy street called Gillingham Street. A seedy hotel, if that is the title for it, called the Albion. He must have arrived in time to see the entry of that couple up the grey steps of the Albion. Still his urges and his senses are such that he is willing to wait and say, with imagination – this is not evidence – 'After you, Aziz.'

"You have to bear in mind the attributes, past attributes of Jeffrey Archer, to consider whether his taste is such that he can take his place in virtually a queue – it is only a queue of two – for the services that 'Debbie' had to offer.

"I am now going to give detailed evidence of Aziz Kurtha . . . because you may think Aziz Kurtha is the foundation of the case against Archer. His name is not Peter, it is Aziz. But is it a case, or is it not, of 'Thou art. Aziz, and upon thy rock will I build this stone', if it is a rock?"

The judge then recalled that Kurtha, having had sex with "Debbie" in the Albion, spotted her next customer outside and told her it was Archer.

The judge referred to Kurtha's inability, because of his colour blindness, to be sure of the colour of the car Archer allegedly was driving.

The judge went on: "Aziz Kurtha has been, he said, a TV presenter. Not being able to recognise red, green or brown, he is hardly likely, is he, to be the presenter of Pot Black or a commentator at the Crucible Theatre in Coventry?

"And if he did play snooker (if he could), you would not mind having a game with him, would you?

"And if you had a side bet, would you not lay guineas to gooseberries you would win? Green, brown, and red. And if he ever had the good luck to get a ticket at Cardiff Arms Park when Wales in their red were playing Ireland in their green, perhaps it is too cynical to say he would have to wait for the singing, the beautiful singing of 'Bread of Heaven' to get the result.

"And if he ever went to the races, he would need all the help he could get from Peter O'Sullevan and, to level it up. Lord Oaksey. Those are cynical comments, of course they are. Everybody will recognise them as cynical comments, but you are dealing with identification evidence, with a big car outside the Albion Hotel.

"There are many situations when the perception and appreciation of colour is important, when you would wish to enjoy the blushing fresh green of spring and the rosy-red roses in your garden, when you would enjoy the parade at the Grand National and when you would enjoy Ian Rush in his all-red strip in the six-yard box at Anfield.

"And those powers you may appreciate are important if you are called as a witness in order to convince a jury that what you saw on a particular night in a well-lit street are true.

"I have made some cynical comments about Kurtha. But remember, would you, in his favour that he is a professional man, that he seems to have good business contacts, that he is successful, that he must know as a solicitor the nature of his oath, and he is asking you to believe him, and he reiterates and emphasises that he is telling the truth on the main issue.

"On the fifth day of the trial we saw as the first witness for the defence the woman Monica Mary Coghlan. Whatever money she has made since she became a prostitute in the well-known Moss Side area of Manchester, graduating to the more elite Shepherds Market, she obviously has had a miserable life.

"There will be, no doubt, on the part of everybody, a great deal of pity for her. Of course when you are trying an action such as this, you do not decide it according to pity. When she was in the witness box under very strong, but legitimate, cross-examination from Mr Alexander [Archer's counsel] she wept and she wept and she wept.

"She hurled accusations at the man who denied that he had been with her, namely. Archer. She screamed at him and she screamed at Mr Alexander. Again do not condemn a person because she breaks, that her tension compels her to break out as a violent witness in court.

"But you may have to consider eventually whether this girl or woman is sincere, or whether she is in the clutches of the News of the World and remains in their clutches, and whether she has continued with this allegation against Archer at the behest of people whom you have never seen.

"If they have persuaded this young woman to proceed with this allegation against Archer on flimsy grounds, they are the people who, you may think, are responsible for the tears.

"You do know that in the taped conversations with Archer, of which you well know, she showed guile and cunning, you may think quite clever cunning. Archer is probably not a man who is not resilient, but she seems to have worked on him with tremendous success. But was it Monica Coghlan who was doing the work or was it those people who were so-called protecting her, who were feeding her from time to time with £500 in cash, according to her, to the extent of £6,000?

"You will consider – I will mention it when I come to review her evidence – how she came to go and have her photographs taken. The photographs were the tantalising, titillating photographs which we see every day on Page Three of a bust, and for which she got, she says, I think £5,500.

"So there are features of Monica Coghlan to consider, many features, besides the breakdown in the box and besides her tears and besides her accusations made in this court. Those who do not (and perhaps those who do) consort with prostitutes have some sympathy for all of them, that they have to make their living in that way.

"You do not know, some of them may want to do so, some of them may be attracted by the money, some of you might think that £350 a night for little outlay is a fair reward. So that £1,750 minus expenses, including fines, taxis and clothes and heavy rents, is an attraction to somebody who is not particular about what she does.

"But there is no doubt, she is a common prostitute and has been since the age of 18. I think on the evidence. She was a common prostitute long before her son [Robin] was born.

"Of course Robin, who was born three years ago, was born at a time when she had already been in business as a prostitute for about 12 or 13 years When she says that she really is a prostitute, follows this horrible trade because she loves her child and it was the child that caused it, you may have to ponder upon that assertion, and I do not pour any cold water upon it, make up your own mind.

"But Monica is an important witness in the case. She is important because she says she lay on top of Archer for 10 minutes. She is important because she is the person who was making the telephone calls and ultimately, in her green leatherette, received the wad of £50 notes.

"She is a Lancashire girl who left school at the age of 16. She lived in Manchester as a prostitute for five years between 1968–73. Her son was born on 9 August 1984. After about seven or eight months, that is after the birth, she came to London. She has lived in flats, she has lived in Islington with her common-law husband, who at one time she thought was a millionaire. He died five years ago.

"When she is at work her pattern is fairly regular. She leaves her abode, whether it is a flat or a hotel, at about half past eight, going for a meal in a good restaurant in Curzon Street, the title of which was not given, but was an Italian restaurant. Once she has had her meal and she is fortified for her night's activities, she begins them at ten o'clock or thereabouts in the evening.

"She has casuals, many casuals, but she also has regular customers. Her trade is such that she even takes cheques, provided they are backed by a banker's card, which might surprise you.

"So let me come to Monday, 8 September 1986. When she came out of the Albion hotel she was told by Kurtha – whether she knew his name or not then, we know not – that somebody was flashing. 'Somebody is flashing you, Debbie,' he said.

"'When I looked to my right on the opposite side of the road there was a dark Jaguar car and it was flashing its headlamps. I said goodnight to Kurtha and he walked towards his car and I went to walk across the road. Before I had actually crossed the road, this man opened the door, stepped out of the car and I noticed straightaway it was the gentleman who had been talking to me in the Shepherd Market a little time before.

"'I walked in front of the car and before I even reached him he said: "I hope you don't mind me following you."'

"We would expect Mr Jeffrey Archer, would we not, not necessarily, of course, not to breach the rules of grammar, but still that is what the girl said. 'I hope you don't mind me following you.' 'I said: "No, that's fine, it's better for me." With that, he locked his car. I went the way I was and we met each other on the other side, the other side of the road outside the Albion.

"'Then from my right Kurtha came back and said: "Excuse me, Debbie," or something like that. I walked up to Kurtha and he said: "You've hit the jackpot tonight, Debbie. Do you know who that is?" I said: "No." Kurtha said: "It's Jeffrey Archer, the well-known author."'

"Whether it hurts Jeffrey Archer or not. Debbie said: 'The name Jeffrey Archer meant nothing to me.'

"Now let us go to this article of the *Star* newspaper. And Debbie went through it. What did she tell you? 'Save for the mention of what I told my sister, and save for the reference to my affection for Robin, that article is sheer fantasy.'

"You may think that rather astonishing: you may not.

"So here we are in as big a libel as has ever been tried this century and the girl at the centre of the article is saying. 'This article is sheer fantasy, save for the exceptions that I gave you.'"

The judge then described Archer's career at Oxford, in politics and as an author. Finally he referred to Archer's attitude to his wife.

"He said she was the most remarkable woman when he met her and the most remarkable one now, and he asserted that he had had a very happy married life, and is having a very happy married life."

20 July 2001
The end: Archer goes to jail
Peer gets four years for lying
By Sue Clough

The roller-coaster career of Jeffrey Archer, politician, failed businessman and millionaire novelist, came to a dramatic halt yesterday when he was jailed for four years for lies he told in his libel action 14 years ago.

After four days of deliberation, an Old Bailey jury convicted him unanimously of two charges of perjury and two of perverting the course of justice.

The judge, Mr Justice Potts, said the case was "the most serious offence of perjury I have experienced" and that Archer must serve at least two years. The 61-year-old peer will start his sentence at high-security Belmarsh prison, south-east London.

In the libel trial, Archer won a record £500,000 from the *Daily Star* over allegations that he slept with Monica Coghlan, a prostitute "willing to engage in perverted sexual practices".

Yesterday the judge told him that if the libel jury had seen the evidence he had seen, "it is unlikely in the extreme you would have succeeded".

The paper is demanding its money back, with damages and interest, totalling £2.2m. The *News of the World*, which settled a separate libel action, is seeking repayment of £500,000. These demands, with Archer's own legal costs, could bring his total bill to more than £4m.

The judge appeared to question the evidence of Lady Archer, who accompanied her husband to court, as she had done throughout.

As Nicholas Purnell, QC, pleading for Archer's freedom, he said that his client had not compounded any lies told 14 years ago by evidence in the trial, the judge said: "What about the evidence of Lady Archer?"

Police said later that they were considering whether to investigate Lady Archer's evidence.

When the four guilty verdicts were given by the jury of six men and five women at 12.20 p.m., there were cries of "yes" from the public gallery. Archer and his wife remained motionless.

He was cleared of a further charge of perverting the course of justice. His co-defendant, Ted Francis, a film producer, was acquitted of the one charge he faced: of perverting the course of justice by providing a false alibi for Archer for the night it was at one point said he had a £70 sex session with Miss Coghlan in a London hotel room.

The judge said that Archer had been convicted on clear evidence.

"Sentencing you, Lord Archer, gives me no pleasure at all, I can assure you. It has been an extremely distasteful case. The fact is that in January 1987 you set out dishonestly to manipulate the proceedings that you had chosen to institute against the *Star*."

It was Archer's ambition to be the first mayor of London that led to his conviction. Francis, an old friend with whom he had fallen out, went to the *News of the World* after the former Conservative Deputy Chairman had been selected as the party's candidate in the mayoral election. He told the paper that he had constructed a false alibi for him for the night in September 1986 that it was at first suggested he had been with Coghlan. He had originally agreed to this because he thought he was covering up a dinner date that Archer was keeping with his then mistress, Andrina Colquhoun. He realised only much later that the alibi was for the libel trial.

Archer promised in return a £20,000 loan to help pay for a film Francis was hoping to make. The relationship between the two men cooled when, at one of Archer's vaunted Krug and shepherd's pie parties at his penthouse on the Embankment, he told another guest in Francis's hearing: "You want to watch this fellow. I lent him £20,000 and I'm still waiting for it to come back."

At the libel trial, Francis's alibi was not needed in the end because of a mix-up over the dates of the sexual encounter. Instead, Terence Baker, Archer's agent, who has since died, said he had met the peer by chance on the crucial night and they had talked until well after the time the *Star* claimed that he had picked up Miss Coghlan in Shepherd Market.

The criminal case revolved around a diary kept by Angela Peppiatt, Archer's personal assistant. Because Mrs Peppiatt's genuine diary of appointments listed a meeting with Mr Baker for the next night, Archer ordered her to make new entries in a blank diary. It was this diary which was used in the libel case. It has since disappeared.

Worried about the dishonesty her employer had involved her in, Mrs Peppiatt kept her genuine diary as "an insurance" and handed it to police in 1999.

During seven days in the witness box, Mrs Peppiatt was accused by Mr Purnell of faking the diary to cover up that she was fiddling her expenses. This she angrily denied.

It was Lady Archer's evidence about the diary that was questioned by the judge. She said she remembered the main office diary for 1986 being of A4 size, whereas Mrs Peppiatt and another witness said it was smaller.

Archer's involvement of Mrs Peppiatt drew particular criticism from the judge. He had drawn her in knowing that she had suffered a broken marriage and had children to support, he said.

He ordered Archer, who will be able to retake his seat in the Lords when he is freed, to pay £175,000 towards prosecution costs with an extra year's jail in default.

Lady Archer left the Old Bailey with her sons William, 29, and James, 27, without comment. But Tony Morton-Hooper, her husband's solicitor, said: "Lord Archer and his family are shocked and disappointed. We shall be lodging an appeal."

Miss Coghlan, who was killed shortly before the trial when a robber crashed into her car, always maintained that the sex session Archer denied had taken place.

She said: "I want him to suffer like I have suffered; I want him to squirm. But most of all I want him to tell the truth. I have never denied what I was; I was a prostitute. But I wasn't a liar. He is."

Also 20 July 2001
He lied, paid and sued his way to the top. Yesterday his world collapsed
Ultimately, the best-selling novelist became the author of his own downfall
By Caroline Davies

In 1998 Jeffrey Archer published a novel, *The Eleventh Commandment – Thou Shalt Not Be Caught*. Within a year he had broken his own fictional commandment.

But fact and fiction are inextricable when attempting to understand the rise and fall, and rise and fall, of Baron Archer of Weston-super-Mare of Mark in the County of Somerset.

Reputation is everything to Archer. He has lied for it on oath. He has sued for it. He has repaid, often in cash, those who helped him maintain it. He has clung to it desperately throughout his adult life.

It was in seeking to hold on to the standing in society he had sought since early manhood, and which he eventually achieved through his own extraordinary efforts, that he made the "silly mistake" that finally brought him down 14 years later.

He still has his millions in the bank, his properties and his art collection. But the thing he valued most was annihilated in Court 8 at the Old Bailey. He was, said the prosecuting barrister David Waters, "entirely the author of his own misfortune".

Jeffrey Howard Archer was born on 15 April 1940, the son of a convicted conman and former bankrupt and a devoted mother, Lola, who wrote a column *Over the Teacups* in her local newspaper in Weston-super-Mare.

Readers were entertained with anecdotes about the cherished son she nicknamed "Tuppence". He was destined to fill many thousands more column inches, much of it less flattering.

Archer was an unremarkable pupil at Wellington School near Exmoor, not to be confused as occasionally happened later with the better known Wellington College, in Berkshire.

He acquired three O-levels, English Literature, Art and History, and, according to his unofficial biographer and bête noire, Michael Crick, the reputation of being "as near to illiterate as you can get". But, even then, fellow pupils saw in him an utter self-belief and absolute determination to progress; qualities witnessed by many more as he propelled himself ever upward.

For example, he detested being nicknamed "the pune", and so embarked on rigorous weight training and gymnastics, soon building up his slight physique.

His political ambition was not immediately apparent. On leaving school he seemed at a loss over which career to follow. A brief spell as an Army recruit did not go smoothly. One fellow recruit said he was regarded as a young man who was "hugely insensitive and amazingly pleased with himself".

What followed is something of a mystery, but he appears to have attended a short course in physical education in America. This would appear on subsequent job and college application forms as a full degree.

By 1960 he was on the beat in Brixton, south London, as PC 149055. His flirtation with the Metropolitan Police force lasted only five months, but he excelled at its athletics championships.

Next, he took up the position as physical education instructor at Vicar's Hill, a small private boarding school near the New Forest. But it was his move to Dover College, a minor public school, that set in train the metamorphosis of Jeffrey Archer, the games master, to Lord Archer, the politician and multi-millionaire novelist.

The new games master became J. H. Archer FIFPC BSc, and posed for school photographs in a graduate gown of indeterminate origin and unrecognisable colours. He was now, students were proudly told, a Fellow of the International Federation of

Physical Culture, which, although no one had heard of it, was assumed to be an American institution.

Archer's assault on Oxford University was equally impressive. Backed by Dover College, his application as a mature student for a one-year Diploma of Education at Brasenose was accepted.

By now, according to his letter of recommendation, his academic achievements encompassed six O-levels, three A-levels, a two-year anatomy course at the University of California, as well as being an "FIFPC".

It was 30 years later, when Crick was researching his biography of Archer, that he discovered that the FIFPC was a body-building club, advertised through newspapers and which you paid to join to help develop muscles through home exercise.

Getting to Oxford, albeit by a back-door route, would transform Archer's life. He prolonged his one-year course to three with "extra research". He became president of the Oxford University Athletics Club and gained national newspaper prominence as the confident extrovert who persuaded The Beatles to endorse a £500,000 fund-raising campaign for Oxfam.

He left Oxford with an athletics Blue, and with friends who would become MPs, ministers, newspaper editors and City financiers.

He also left with the hand of Mary Weeden, an intelligent, attractive chemistry student at St Anne's with a formidable list of would-be suitors. They were introduced by Nick Lloyd, future editor of the Daily Express, who worked with Archer on The Beatles campaign.

Archer later said of Mary: "She was stunningly beautiful. It was love at first sight for me, but I don't think it was for her." He pursued her relentlessly, telling her he was "going to get an Olympic silver medal in the 200 metres, become a millionaire, and possibly become Prime Minister", one friend said later.

First stop on this heady journey was the Greater London council, where he is chiefly remembered as "Mr 10 per cent" for helping councillors fill out their expenses for a cut of the proceeds.

Next he became an MP. After two attempts, he was on the verge of being confirmed as Tory candidate for Louth in Lincolnshire, a safe Tory seat. Win it and he would be set for a life in politics.

But, as so often in Archer's life, the past came back to haunt him. He had been working as a fund-raiser for charities and one, the United Nations Association, hit on some alleged discrepancies in his expenses claims for expensive meals, such as in the Rib Room at the Carlton Tower Hotel.

Rumours of this reached Fleet Street, and just before his selection was due to be confirmed, John Clare, now education editor of the Daily Telegraph but then a young reporter on The Times, was sent to investigate. He caught up with Archer on the train from Louth to King's Cross.

According to Clare, Archer "burst into tears" and begged him not to write the story because it would hurt his wife. It appeared, says Mr Clare, in truncated, unrecognisable form because, he was told, his editor felt sorry for the would-be MP.

Next, he threatened legal action, and issued a writ for libel against Humphry Berkeley, chairman of the UNA, who had by now confided to senior Tory party officials his concerns over Archer's suitability as an MP.

The writ stymied further debate before his selection was confirmed. Louth Tories decided the claims were rubbish and selected Archer. He romped home.

His libel action against Mr Berkeley dragged on for three years and was settled out of court in a deal brokered by the man who would one day be a Cabinet minister and later a convicted perjurer, Jonathan Aitken. Terms remain undisclosed, but Mr Berkeley did not retract and Archer paid both sides' costs.

Now, as an MP before the age of 30, Archer could concentrate on his political ambitions and getting rich. He and Mary set up home in a £100,000 house in the exclusive Boltons in Kensington. He became a member of Lloyd's. They had the trappings of wealth, with a Coutts bank account and personalised number plate ANY 1, and had started a family.

Then came Aquablast, Archer's first unfortunate experience with stocks and shares, and it blasted his career and his fortune away. Acting on information from acquaintances, he was persuaded that shares in the Canadian industrial cleaning system would go through the roof because of a gadget the company had invented to cut carbon monoxide emissions. It was a scam and led to a high-profile prosecution in Canada.

Archer was one of the biggest victims. Without his wife's knowledge he had taken out a second mortgage on their house to invest and, convinced this was an ideal "get rich quick" scheme, borrowed £172,000 from Anthony Bamford, of the JCB family. He bought 101,500 shares at 345p each, for about £350,000. When the shares plummeted, Archer lost everything. Mary, seven months pregnant with their second son, James, was at home organising a second birthday party for their first son, William, when he walked in and told her.

She said later: "I felt weak at the knees. But there was nothing else to do except carry on with the party."

Bamford had no option but to begin proceedings to declare Archer bankrupt. But this was one avenue Archer, unlike his father, would not take. With the help of his long-standing friend and confidant, Victor (now Lord) Mishcon, he drew up a repayment schedule.

Though his immediate political career was over and he was forced to quit his parliamentary seat, he showed again his indomitable self-belief, his constant determination to rise from whatever pit he might find himself in. Almost immediately, he began writing Not a Penny More, Not a Penny Less. Jeffrey Archer the best-selling novelist was born.

There was another little hiccup when, whilst in Canada giving evidence to the Aquablast inquiry, he was stopped in a department store with three suits he had inadvertently forgotten to pay for. He explained the problem away and no charges were brought. He probably forgot about the incident until it too came back to haunt him 20 years later in 1998 while he was campaigning to be London mayor.

Then, when questioned, he relied on an explanation put forward in Crick's book that he may have inadvertently walked over an internal footbridge linking two stores, without realising he had left one and was entering another. The only problem was that the footbridge, although there now, had not been built at the time of the incident. No other explanations have been offered.

For the moment, though, he was once more in the ascendancy. He bought his Thames-side penthouse and the Old Vicarage at Grantchester, Cambs, the former home of the poet Rupert Brooke. His shepherd's pie and Krug parties for the great and good became legendary. Guests at these lavish functions who asked the way to the lavatory were told "straight down the passage, just past the Picasso".

But, while his apartment overlooked the Houses of Parliament, he was on the political outside, and desperate to get back in.

Margaret Thatcher offered just the opportunity. Describing Archer as the "extrovert's extrovert", she sought to exploit his gift as an entertaining public speaker to energise the party grassroots by making him the unpaid Deputy Party Chairman.

He bounced around the country, happy again to be a player. He must have thought the chairmanship within his grasp.

Monica Coghlan put paid to that a year later. In October 1986 the News of the World splashed "Tory boss Archer pays vice-girl" on its front page, with a picture of Coghlan, aka street girl "Debbie", at Victoria station being offered an envelope crammed with £50 notes, an estimated total of £2,000, by Archer's friend Michael Stacpoole. The story said Archer had told Coghlan to go abroad. The paper did not state that Archer had slept with her, but the implication was clear.

The Daily Star followed it up, but went further, alleging that Archer had sex with her. Archer resigned as Tory Deputy Chairman then sued for libel. The celebrated libel action in July 1987 was at the heart of this case and, 14 years later, finally brought about his downfall. Not for the last time Archer found himself in court, listening to conversations secretly taped by the News of the World.

In the tapes of six conversations, Archer denied meeting Coghlan, but he eventually offered her money to go abroad to escape the media she said were hounding her. His gesture, the jury was told, was not that of a man guilty of sleeping with a prostitute, but an act of philanthropy to a distressed woman.

Critical to his case was his alibi on the night of Monday, 8 September 1986, when, the Daily Star alleged, he was with Miss Coghlan. Friends gave evidence that he left Le Caprice restaurant at about midnight, and then gave Terence Baker, one of his film agents, a lift back to Camberwell.

Also crucial was the presence of the "fragrant" Mary, who so bewitched the judge Mr Justice Caulfield. She told the jury the thought of her husband with a prostitute was preposterous as "anyone who knows him well, knows that far from Jeffrey accosting a prostitute, if one accosted him he would run several miles in the opposite direction, very fast".

In an affirmation she would be forced to repeat 14 years later in a different courtroom, she told the jury that she and her husband had a "happy marriage" and enjoyed "a full life".

Archer won £500,000 damages, a new British record. But for the matter of a second alibi and an office diary, no more would have been heard of it.

Once more he had salvaged his reputation. His wealth increased further through television and film deals. Apart from the libel damages handed over by the jury, his fortune was an estimated £50m, and he enjoyed an art collection worth £20m including works by Picasso, Lowry, Sisley, Miro, Vuillard and Monet.

His wife's career was also flourishing. As well as her academic career she was undertaking television work and the year of Archer's libel success she was invited on to the board of Anglia TV as a director.

It was during the Anglia takeover talks in 1994 that Archer bought two large batches of shares in Anglia, although this time not for himself, but for a Kurdish friend, Broosk Saib. But the purchase led to a DTI investigation and claims that Archer had used information to which his wife was privy, to predict a rise in share price – insider dealing.

The investigation cleared him, but it dealt another blow to his political ambition at a time when the Tory party was fighting accusations of sleaze.

In August that year Archer conceded that he had made a mistake, but this time he had dragged his wife into it.

He had made "a grave error", said a statement issued on his behalf. "His deepest regret is the embarrassment needlessly caused to Lady Archer." Despite his exoneration, she resigned from Anglia four months later.

Chastened, but undeterred, Archer then set his sights on being mayor of London. It was "arguably the second most exciting job in England", he said.

William Hague, Conservative Party leader, endorsed his bid. "This candidate is a candidate of probity and integrity," he said. But others were underwhelmed by the prospect.

With the Archer election machine in full flow, a nervous Ted Francis picked up the telephone and called the *News of the World*.

The ensuing story opened the floodgates. Once more Archer was forced to resign.

Five months later, in April last year, Lord Archer was formally charged with perjury and perverting the course of public justice. "What a silly mistake I made," he told journalists.

Clearly, as yesterday's verdict showed, this was much much more than yet another "silly" Archer misjudgment.

Also 20 July 2001
A Tory disaster waiting to happen
By Andy McSmith

For 20 years it was understood in the highest Tory circles that Jeffrey Archer was a useful fellow to have about because of his bubbly personality and immense wealth, but not someone to be wholly trusted.

Lady Thatcher explained in her memoirs why she decided to appoint Jeffrey Archer in 1985 to the unpaid post of Deputy Chairman of the Conservative Party.

He was "the extrovert's extrovert, he had prodigious energy, he was and remains the most popular speaker the party has ever had".

"Unfortunately, as it turned out," she added, "Jeffrey's political judgment did not always match his enormous energy and fund-raising ability."

That is the only mention of Archer in Lady Thatcher's 860-page account of her premiership.

She continued to be on good terms for many years, but she never gave him another job.

John Major, similarly, described Archer glowingly as a friend, and awarded him a life peerage, but never took the risk of offering him a responsible post.

By contrast, Mr Major was prepared to offer a Cabinet seat to Jonathan Aitken, another Tory whom Lady Thatcher did not trust, who was to be found guilty of lying in court, dragging his family into the deceit.

Mr Aitken, however, had a long record as a serious parliamentary debater and the books he had written, in contrast to Archer's, were considered to be serious academic works.

Archer was apparently condemned to be forever regarded as a political lightweight.

But in 1999 William Hague – the one Tory leader whom the wayward peer had never cultivated socially – made the catastrophic mistake of allowing him to take centre stage as the authorised voice of the Conservative Party in London.

He compounded this error by accepting Archer's offer of free use of a private gym where Mr Hague and his chief of staff, Seb Coe, the double Olympic 1,500m gold medallist, could practise martial arts.

It was not that Mr Hague had been badly advised. Every official in Conservative Central Office who voiced an opinion at the time seemed to have seen Archer as a disaster waiting to happen.

One former Central Office worker said: "Everybody said, 'No, no, no, you should not do it.' Everybody said to William, 'You shouldn't go to his summer party, you shouldn't use his gym.' Archer had a highly controversial past, but he was still a popular figure. He was good old Jeffrey Archer, a good old rogue.

"Who was to know that there was really serious stuff waiting to come out about him?"

Knowing that members of the London Conservative Party would vote for Archer in preference to almost any other potential candidate, they wanted Mr Hague to intervene before it reached the membership ballot.

One idea was that Mr Major would be asked to persuade Archer to pull out. But Mr Hague refused.

Ceri Evans, who joined the Conservative machine as Director of Presentation early in 1999 said that he encountered a "deafening silence" on how the Conservatives would handle the impending mayoral election.

"I don't believe you would have to be a genius to know somewhere along the way that Archer would self-combust," Mr Evans said.

"But you must understand the depth of the party's financial problems at that time, and Lord Archer is a very rich man.

"To have a candidate who was prepared to pay the bill for his own campaign was a dream come true. It was a contest they didn't want, an issue they hadn't thought about.

"They never thought they could win the mayoralty because London is a Labour city.

"In that deafening silence, all you could hear was the clamour of Lord Archer's campaign."

He added: "Is it any wonder that they were happy for Lord Archer to be the candidate?"

It was a misjudgment which Mr Hague would bitterly regret.

After he had announced his resignation last month, Mr Hague confided to *The Sunday Telegraph* that the discovery of how badly misled he had been by Archer had contributed to his decision to resign immediately.

Having failed for years to play a truly significant role in the Conservative Party, Archer at last had one dubious distinction: he helped bring down William Hague.

Also 20 July 2001
A roving eye for debs, strippers and call-girls
By Caroline Davies

Jeffrey Archer's extra-marital affair with Andrina Colquhoun, his former personal assistant, was to feature prominently in the trial, alongside allegations that she was not the only girlfriend at the time.

Or, indeed, after.

Even as lawyers were preparing their case against the novelist, he was enjoying a South African holiday with Nikki Kingdon, the 51-year-old former wife of a plastic surgeon.

Archer was photographed walking hand in hand with Mrs Kingdon.

On examining the grainy pictures, many assumed the long-haired blonde to be Sally Farmiloe, an actress and Tory fund-raiser who claimed a three-year affair with Archer, beginning in 1996.

Miss Farmiloe, 53, who starred in the 1980s television series *Howard's Way*, was, like his long-term lover Miss Colquhoun, a former debutante. The daughter of Sir Thomas Farmiloe, a Hampshire farmer and yacht broker, she was an active Conservative Party member.

Disclosing their affair shortly after the alibi story broke, she said she had met Archer at a Valentine's Day ball in 1996, had fallen deeply in love with him and hoped for marriage.

During their affair, they made love at his London flat, in a suite at the Café Royal and even in Archer's Mini in an NCP car park.

"I really love him and he loves me," she said at the time. "Well, he told me he did many times. And he was still telling me up to last week.

"It was a love job. It wasn't the cheap affair it has being made out to be. Everybody is feeling so sorry for bloody Mary Archer but she doesn't need feeling sorry for. I cannot believe Jeffrey has abandoned me. I refuse to believe it.

"He carried on with his secretary after their relationship was supposed to stop and I don't see why we can't carry on where we left off. But I suppose the Fragrant One won't allow it."

Aside from the affairs, Archer has been dogged by allegations that he used prostitutes, always denied. Monica Coghlan, the prostitute at the centre of the 1987 libel action, went to her grave claiming he had paid her £70 for sex after picking her up.

She was killed a few weeks before this trial when her car was hit by a getaway driver.

During the libel action, the *Daily Star*'s lawyers were contacted by Dorrett Douglas, another prostitute who claimed that Archer had picked her up in Mayfair.

Dorrett, then 21, claimed that Archer, whom she did not recognise, took her back to his flat where he paid her £50 for sex.

They had sex, she said, on a white leather seat in an open plan part of the flat. "He came across as a true gentleman. He looked good, smelled good and he was polite, even when we were having sex. I think that was what I really liked about him.

"So I stretched it out for him so he would really enjoy himself. He thanked me afterwards. I was there about four hours. He seemed lonely and was very grateful. He just wanted some company and some pleasure."

Michael Stacpoole alleges that, during his friendship with Archer, they regularly went out to strip clubs and sleazy bars. He particularly remembered one on Gower Street, near Tottenham Court Road, to which Archer said he had once been taken.

"This was basically a drinking and strip club. It was a very dingy, dirty, small bar and there was a dance floor where the girls would strip."

He looked at one black girl, said Stacpoole, and said: "I fancy that one."

"I said, 'I'll bring her over'."

He said Archer took her to his flat. "The next day I rang him up and asked if he had had a good time. He replied, 'Yes, thanks very much'."

21 July 2001
Archer in jail hospital with train robber Biggs
By Caroline Davies

There must be few places in Britain where Lord Archer can pass unrecognised after his trial for perjury. And Belmarsh top security prison, where he spent the first night of his four-year sentence, is not one of them.

The peer needed no introduction when he walked up to a fellow prisoner with hand outstretched and said: "Hello, I'm Jeffrey Archer."

The inmate, named Clint, replied: "Yes, I know."

Details of Archer's first night in the category A jail in Woolwich, south east London, were told by a 21-year-old inmate called Del, who was released yesterday.

The 61-year-old novelist, who is undergoing routine assessment in the hospital wing, was also introduced to Ronnie Biggs, the Great Train Robber, receiving treatment on the same wing.

Fiona Gavriel, a solicitor visiting a client at the jail, said: "Lord Archer was introduced to Biggs in the exercise yard. He just shook hands with him and chatted to him very briefly."

Archer spent his first night in the prison's health care unit undergoing routine assessment.

Describing the induction process for new inmates, Del, who has just completed a one-month sentence for deception, said: "You go to reception and are held in a little steel cage with glass sides. You're there for a couple of hours and then you move on to induction to learn about the regime before going to the cells.

"When you first go into reception, you're strip-searched, which is humiliating, and then you spend three days on induction in the hospital wing, which is called Beirut as you go in there with nothing and it is like a war zone."

One prison officer, who saw Archer during the night shift, said: "He looked very low. When he first came in, he smiled a bit and exchanged a couple of jokey comments with officers.

"But when I saw him later in the evening he was very quiet and very sad. He hardly said a word to anyone all night. There is obvious concern about how he will cope with his sentence. But there is also the added strain of his mother's death."

Mr Justice Potts, the trial judge, has made a recommendation that Archer be allowed temporary release to attend the funeral of his 87-year-old mother Lola Hayne, who died as the trial was nearing its conclusion.

The private funeral is expected to take place today at Cambridge Crematorium at Madingley, followed by a service at St Andrew's and St Mary's Church in the village of Grantchester, where the Archers have a family home.

While in Belmarsh, Archer can choose to wear his own clothes or blue jeans and a blue and white shirt, or a burgundy tracksuit.

Lady Archer will be allowed to send him six books, a pack of playing cards, a board game and, ironically, a diary. During her visits, she will have to be searched, her coat X-rayed and have an ultra-violet stamp put on her hand.

Police sources said it was unlikely that there would be a criminal inquiry into possible perjury by Lady Archer in her evidence in her husband's defence case.

A senior Tory MP joined the clamour to strip peers of their titles and right to sit in the Lords on conviction for serious criminal offences.

Sir Teddy Taylor, MP for Southend East and Rochford, said: "If the House of Lords is going to retain its respectability, I think people found guilty of crimes should be quietly excluded from it."

Duchess of Argyll

"What I can only describe as disgusting sexual activities to gratify a basic sexual appetite."

28 July 1993
Margaret Duchess of Argyll

Margaret Duchess of Argyll, who has died aged 80, was one of the most photographed and publicised beauties of the 20th century and a seemingly indomitable social figure.

But between 1959 and 1963 she was involved in a sensational and sordid divorce case, when her second husband, the 11th Duke of Argyll, Chief of the Clan Campbell and Hereditary Master of the Royal Household in Scotland, sued her for divorce on grounds of adultery.

The court case lasted 11 days, and its piquant details included the theft of a racy diary, in which the Duchess listed the accoutrements of a number of lovers as though she was running them at Newmarket. The 50,000-word judgment, in which the Duke was granted a decree, was one of the longest in the history of the Edinburgh court.

The Duchess was found to have committed adultery with three men named in her husband's petition and with a fourth, unidentified figure. A pair of photographs was produced in court showing the Duchess, naked save for three strings of pearls, engaged in a sexual act with a man whose face was not shown and who passed into folklore as "the Headless Man".

Lord Wheatley, who tried the case, described the Duchess as "a completely promiscuous woman . . . Her attitude towards marriage was what moderns would call enlightened, but which in plain language was wholly immoral".

Nor were the Duke's morals found to be above rebuke. The judge found his fondness for pornographic postcards especially deplorable.

A host of other legal actions delighted the press before and after the actual divorce hearing. Accusations about trust funds, libel and conspiracy to defraud were played out, at an estimated cost to the Duchess of more than £200,000.

One particularly juicy action concerned the Duchess's outrageous suggestion that her recently widowed stepmother was having an affair with her estranged husband.

Margaret Argyll continued to be a favourite subject of gossip columnists long after the furore about her divorce had died down. Her feuds with her family, her landlords, her bankers and her biographers were all lovingly documented, usually with her own connivance.

As recently as 1989 she was involved in a highly public prosecution of her Moroccan maid, who had run up a telephone bill of thousands of pounds. The maid said that the Duchess had given her permission to call her family in North Africa but was unable to remember having done so because of her inordinate consumption of whisky.

The maid's stories were dismissed and she was given a suspended sentence, but the case sparked off a debate about the servant problem. The Duchess was herself an old hand with recalcitrant maids, suffering a series of unhappy arrangements after she dispensed with the services of the redoubtable Edith Springett, who looked after her for more than a decade.

Springett fell out with the Duchess after being found unconscious on the floor of Her Grace's bedroom, with an empty bottle of her whisky lying close by. The Duchess dispatched solicitor's letters instructing Springett to desist from calling her a "Mayfair whore" and a "silly old bitch" in front of guests.

In her later years the Duchess fell on hard times, although she still retained the shadow of her remarkable beauty – melting green eyes and pale magnolia skin.

At one point her debts were gallantly paid off by her first husband, the American golfer Charles Sweeny. The Duchess later recalled of that marriage that she had felt "like a bird in a not-so-gilded cage".

She reserved her virulence for her second husband. "Ian Argyll," she would announce at regular intervals, "was a fiend and a sadist."

Ultimately Margaret Argyll became a figure of pathos, the harder to help for lingering vestiges of arrogance.

The daughter of George Whigham, a self-made businessman from Glasgow who founded the British and Canadian Celanese Corporations, she was born on 1 December 1912 and christened Ethel Margaret.

She was educated at Miss Hewitt's Classes in New York, at Miss Wolff's in London, at Heathfield and with Mlle Ozanne in Paris. Miss Whigham was launched as a debutante in London with an extravagant coming-out ball in 1931.

Her striking looks and perfectly formed figure immediately made her the toast of numberless hopeful swains.

In later years she would look back on this period of her life with rage in her heart, claiming to have grown up in a world where innocence marched hand in hand with ignorance, in which money and a title were the only goal for wayward Cinderellas.

She was briefly betrothed to the 7th Earl of Warwick, but shied away from matrimony after the invitations for the wedding had been sent out, on the grounds that she "did not love him sufficiently".

Instead she married, in 1933, Charles Sweeny, a tall, dashing American.

Their wedding at Brompton Oratory drew a crowd of 3,000 onlookers.

A son and a daughter followed in quick succession, and Margaret Sweeny appeared to carry all before her.

Cole Porter immortalised her in his hit song "You're the Top" from the musical *Anything Goes*: "You're the nimble tread of the feet of Fred Astaire You're Mussolini You're Mrs Sweeny You're Camembert . . ."

But the Sweenys were divorced in 1947, and four years later she became the third and penultimate wife of the 11th Duke of Argyll.

Margaret Argyll continued to throw lavish parties at her Grosvenor House apartment throughout the 1970s and 1980s, although as time went on it was less easy to detect any particular merit in her guests. She favoured Americans for their natural courtesy and their dollars.

Although she was not a witty woman – "She don't make many jokes" was the pithy conclusion of one peer who sat next to her at dinner – Margaret Argyll was the mistress of boring banter, delivered with a drink in one hand and cigarette-holder in the other.

Her memoirs, *Forget Not* (1975), were generally judged a disappointment. No clues were offered as to the identity of the "Headless Man", and no mention made of her much-publicised estrangement from her daughter, the Duchess of Rutland.

Reviewing the book, Alastair Forbes observed: "Her father may have been able to give her some fine ear-rings but nothing to put between them."

The Duchess was interviewed about the book on a literary programme on television, and was asked why she had not employed a ghost. She seemed flummoxed by the question, since she had obviously not written a word of the book, and directed her melting green eyes with memorable ferocity towards her interlocutor.

In 1979 she was given a gossip column in *Tatler* magazine ("Stepping Out with Margaret Argyll"), but was defeated by the difficulties of spelling names correctly. By 1981 her soporific social jottings had been reduced from two pages to a small corner of one, and the connection was severed entirely the following year.

Although Margaret Argyll may not have been accepted in the "Establishment", she enjoyed star status in the world of showbusiness and money.

She presided over a lavish party for Paul Getty's 80th birthday at the Dorchester, attended by King Umberto of Italy and Tricia Nixon, daughter of the American President.

Nor was her life devoid of good deeds. She adopted two boys, Jamie and Richard Gardner, whom she put through school, and also espoused a campaign to save the Argyll and Sutherland Highlanders from disbandment, energetically assisted by Lt-Col Colin "Mad Mitch" Mitchell.

The Duchess also delighted in dogs. She kept a series of miniature French poodles – 14 altogether, most of them black. She was an inveterate campaigner for animal rights and served for many years as president of the Bleakholt Animal Sanctuary in Lancashire.

In 1990 Margaret Argyll was evicted from her suite at Grosvenor House over unpaid rent; she later took up residence in a nursing home in Pimlico.

"I do not forget," she concluded. "Neither the good years, in which I laughed and danced and lived upon a cloud of happiness; nor the bad years of near despair, when I learned what life and people and friendship really were . . .

"Unfortunately I am only too aware that I am still the same gullible, impulsive, over-optimistic 'Dumb Bunny', and I have given up hopes of any improvement."

9 May 1963
Duchess a promiscuous woman says judge
Photos showed her nude near undressed man

The Duchess of Argyll, 49, was described by Lord Wheatley in the Court of Session in Edinburgh yesterday as "a completely promiscuous woman whose sexual appetite could only be satisfied with a number of men".

He granted a decree of divorce to the Duke of Argyll, 59, of Inveraray Castle, on the grounds of the Duchess's adultery. The judge found that the Duchess had committed adultery with three men named by the Duke in his petition, and with an unknown man who was shown in a batch of photographs.

These pictures showed the Duchess in the nude "in close proximity to a nude male".

The three men named are: Baron Sigismund Von Braun, brother of Dr. Wernher von Braun, the former German and now naturalised American rocket expert; John Cohane, a wealthy American business man, now living in Eire; and Harvey Christian Rupert Peter Combe, 37, a former Press officer at the Savoy Hotel, London, who lives at Strathconon, Muir of Ord, Ross-shire.

Only Mr Combe denied the Duke's allegation. The Duchess did not attend the court. The Duke sat with his legal advisers a few feet from Mr Combe.

The Judge said that the Duke, by continuing to co-habit with his wife, had condoned her adultery with Baron von Braun and the unknown man in the photograph.

"I shall spare her the indignities of what those photographs depict. In them, the persons were indulging themselves in a gross form of sexual relationship.

"They showed that the Duchess was a highly-sexed woman who had ceased to be satisfied with normal sexual relations and had started to indulge in what could only be described as disgusting sexual activities."

The Duke claimed that a "cryptic symbol" in the Duchess's personal diaries, denoted she had had intercourse when it appeared. The significance the Duke attached to this had not been established.

Love letters which the Duke took from the Duchess's flat in Upper Grosvenor Street, were a "library of mementoes of her affairs".

Mr Cohane was a "self-confessed wolf". He held that he and the Duchess had committed adultery at 10 o'clock in the morning in a New York hotel.

He quoted from one of Mr Cohane's letters to the Duchess,

" . . . I have thought of a number of highly intriguing things we might do, or that I might do to you . . . " These words were sufficient to confirm an adulterous association.

Evidence had been given that the Duke was "not averse" to carrying pornographic pictures, which he had shown to a mixed crowd at a party in New York. "I can only deplore his taste and standards of value," said Lord Wheatley.

The 50,000-word judgment, which took 3 hours 10 minutes to read, was the longest delivered in Scottish divorce action.

The tiny court room was crowded, with people standing at the back as Lord Wheatley read out 160 pages of typed judgment at the rate of about 250 words per minute. He paused for a few brief moments to sip from a glass of water.

Lord Wheatley began his judgment by saying that the allegations of adultery related to the Duchess's association with three men. Only one had entered an appearance as party minuter to resist the accusation of adultery made against him.

A further allegation of adultery was based on an inference sought to be drawn from photographs said to have been found in the Duchess's depository. Two depicted her in the nude in close proximity to a nude male and in positions which clearly indicated intimate sexual relationship. The Duchess resisted that allegation.

In both photographs the head of the male figure was excluded. The Duke alleged that these indicated adultery. He said that he was not the male but the Duchess said he was.

Lord Wheatley said the Duke had been married twice before. The second wife divorced him in 1951, when the ground of the divorce was adultery with the present defender.

The Duchess was married once before. That marriage was dissolved in 1947.

The Duke and the Duchess lived mostly at Inveraray Castle and at Upper Grosvenor Street, London, which was the Duchess's residence. The relationship was said to be unhappy. The Duke attributed their unhappiness to the Duchess's insatiable desire to participate in social life. He preferred a quiet existence.

The Duchess said his drinking habits and his dislike of social engagements left her dependent on the company of others. What seemed clear was that by the beginning of 1959 relations between, the parties were strained.

About that time the Duke and the Duchess went on a World cruise. The Duke said he taxed the Duchess with misconduct which she admitted. The Duchess denied this admission.

The Duke returned from this trip some days before the Duchess and went to the house in Upper Grosvenor Street with the avowed intention of obtaining, if possible, evidence of her adultery. He employed a locksmith to open a cupboard, in which he found letters and photographs.

An unusual position arose about the possession of the material. The fact that the Duke required the services of a locksmith suggested that this was a private depositary to which he was not supposed to have access.

The Duke, on the other hand, maintained that this was a cupboard to which they had joint access. It was most improbable that the Duchess would leave incriminating letters and photographs in a cupboard used by both of them.

Letters from Baron von Braun and Mr Cohane formed the basis of the Duke's case for adultery with these men. The photographs formed the case for adultery with the unnamed man or men.

The Duke had said he found in the cupboard what he considered to be the most important document of all. This was said to be a "mock-up" of fragmented documents, pasted on to a piece of notepaper from an hotel.

This appeared to be a letter written and signed by the Duke's second wife. The contents of this were highly derogatory to the Duke and the children of the second wife.

The Duke was suspicious that the Duchess was the author of a campaign and stated that the finding of this document confirmed his suspicions. Several blank pieces of notepaper from the hotel were also found.

The Duke had said that he extracted from an unlocked drawer in a desk in the drawing room a number of articles, including two diaries. One was dated 1948–1951 and the other related to the years 1952–1955.

There was a list of men's names in the Duchess's handwriting which, for some reason, had not been produced. The Duchess maintained that these were kept in a locked drawer. But once again he preferred the Duke's account.

Lord Wheatley said that in April 1959, the couple had a violent quarrel and had had no marital relations since, except on one night in June of that year. The Duke said that he had a bolt put on to his bedroom door to prevent the Duchess getting into his room and into his bed with him.

The couple had met in Paris and had dinner together on the night of 2 June 1959. The Duchess maintained that the main purpose of the meeting was to try to effect a reconciliation and save a marriage which she was anxious to preserve.

The Duke took her back to her hotel in the early hours of the morning. He stayed in her bedroom.

The Duke said that they spent the time arguing about an injunction. No intercourse took place, he added.

The parties later left the castle and went to London, travelling on different dates. The Duke went to his rooms in St. James's Street and the Duchess to the house in Upper Grosvenor Street. Apart from that night in Paris, it was clear that they had no marital relations since.

In September 1959, the Duke accompanied by his daughter, let himself into the house in Upper Grosvenor Street. He went to the Duchess's bedroom and grabbed a diary which she kept either on her bedside table or in the bedside table drawer.

Lord Wheatley dealt at length with this diary and with two others which the Duke had taken from an unlocked drawer in the house when he and the Duchess were living together. It had been her practice to write up the diaries late at night. Each covered a four-year period.

These diaries did not record her "innermost thoughts". The general pattern was a record of places she had stayed at. Although in the last diary there was an occasional cryptic symbol "B" which, the Duke held, meant that she had had intercourse with von Braun on that date.

In support of this, he pointed out that his own initial appeared in her diary for 4 April 1950, when he first had intercourse with the Duchess, at that time being married to his second wife.

This seemed "somewhat double-edged". There was no "J" on the date on which the Duke alleged that the Duchess misconducted herself with John Cohane.

He was led, however, to the conclusion, that on the standard of proof required, it would be wrong to attach such evidential significance to a symbol that it was an admission of intercourse. The diaries' only evidential value was to establish where the Duchess was in 1948 and 1950.

Lord Wheatley said the Duchess had claimed confidentiality for the diaries but two covered periods during which she was living with the Duke. They were left in an unlocked drawer where he could see them.

So far as the third diary was concerned, the "plain unvarnished fact is that the Duke deliberately went to her house to obtain that diary. His foray into her bedroom at six a.m. was obviously to catch her unawares."

After quoting from several cases which dealt with similar circumstances, Lord Wheatley said he had concluded that the diaries were admissible. It would be contrary to the interests of justice to prevent a husband discovering evidence of that nature, from using that evidence against his wife for what it was worth.

Of the last diary he said: "There was a deliberate raid on her house during the time they were living apart to recover that diary. The pursuer thought it would be useful to him as evidence of her infidelity.

"I have reached the conclusion that this diary should be admitted to evidence as it reinforces my conclusion about the use to which it was put in evidence, as an *aide memoire* to the Duchess as to dates and occasions."

Dealing with the allegations of adultery during 1956, Lord Wheatley said that two were based on letters to the Duchess from Baron von Braun and Mr Cohane. The third was based on the photographs.

The Judge continued: "The photographs are said to be indicating an association between the Duchess and an unknown man or men. Two of the photographs are proved to be the photographs of the Duchess taken during the marriage.

"They not only establish that she was carrying on an adulterous association with those other men or man but revealed that she was a highly-sexed woman who had ceased to be satisfied with normal relations and had started to indulge in what I can only describe as disgusting sexual activities to gratify a basic sexual appetite."

The photographs showed the body of a nude male but did not show the head. He had no doubt that the woman in the photographs was the Duchess. The real question was whether the Duke had proved he was not the man.

Lord Wheatley said he would spare the Duchess the indignity of describing the photographs. The only inference that could be drawn from them was that the persons in them were indulging in a gross form of sexual relationship.

An expert had made an examination of the Duke and a comparison of the photographs and had concluded that the man in the photographs was the same in each case and was not the Duke. He accepted that opinion.

The camera used was of a Polaroid type which took the photographs and printed the films, which was an advantage to people who wished to take that type of pornographic photograph.

The Duke denied taking the photographs and said that neither he nor the Duchess possessed such a camera. The Duchess said the Duke had borrowed one for the occasion.

He held that two of the photographs depleted the Duchess in a position which demonstrated she was engaging in a sexual association with the male in the photographs and that the male was not the Duke. The photographs were taken during the marriage, probably in 1956.

The Duke said he found the photographs together in a cupboard in the bookcase enclosed in a piece of paper which contained writing in printed capitals. This he accepted was not the Duke's writing.

The Duchess denied keeping the photographs. She suggested they were part of a catalogue of pornographic photographs kept by the Duke.

The Duke had admitted showing the photographs to a mixed party in New York and seemed to think it was a joke. "I do not commend his standard of tastes and habits."

The photographs seemed from the contents to be more the type of photograph carried by a woman with a sex perversion than by a man by a sex perversion. He accepted the Duke's evidence that he found the photographs among papers kept by the Duchess.

While it seemed strange that a married woman should keep such incriminating photographs in a place to which her husband had access, it was no more strange than keeping them in the same place as love letters from other men.

"It seems to be not inconsistent with the attitude of men and women whose life was characterised by promiscuous sexual relationship, the satisfactions of which was not confined to normal sexual relationship."

During a visit to New York the Duchess went to a party on 10 January 1956. Mr Cohane tried to make an appointment with her but succeeded only in getting an invitation to cocktails two days later in her hotel suite.

He took her to the airport when she returned to England on 13 January and wrote letters to her afterwards. Allegations of adultery said to have taken place on 13 January in the Duchess's suite were based on an entry in her diary "Jackie 9–10."

He had seen the Duchess in the witness box but not Mr Cohane, whose evidence was taken on commission. His evidence was more unreliable.

Mr Cohane thought there were 200 at the party at which they met. The Duchess thought there were 50.

Mr Cohane said the Duchess was not introduced to him as the Duchess but was introduced to him by her former name. "This I doubt. I doubt if a New York hostess would miss the opportunity of introducing a Duchess to her guests."

He was voluble and some of his explanations became more incredible as a result of his verbosity. "Even she, with all her quickness of mind, could not square some parts of his evidence with her own."

Despite the lack of response to his advances, Mr Cohane stated that he was anxious to pursue his assault on the chastity of the woman. He tried to "date" her for lunch or dinner engagements.

Mr Cohane was "a self-confessed wolf" who admitted he was immediately attracted physically to the Duchess. He wanted to set in train the machinery culminating in sexual relations.

The Duchess was concerned only about getting back to her husband. Mr Cohane learned that she was the wife of someone who wanted to make a success of her second marriage.

Dealing with an entry in her diary "Jackie 9–10," Lord Wheatley said it would not be surprising if he had advanced to "Jackie" in her mind if the relationship had also advanced.

Mr Cohane had been anxious to establish that he was not in her hotel suite on the day she went to the airport and he denied going up to the suite to collect her, thereby contradicting the Duchess.

The Duke said that on her return the Duchess told him that Mr Cohane had entered her suite on the morning of departure.

Lord Wheatley referred to letters exchanged between Mr Cohane and the Duchess. It could be assumed from various expressions in them, such as "Dearest Margaret" and "Darling Margaret", that a close personal relationship existed between the two.

The Duchess had explained one letter by stating that Mr Cohane had approached her to see if there was any chance of her returning to New York. She had told him that there was not.

It did not appear to be a letter from a man whose advances had been rebuffed. It seemed to seek a continuation of a relationship. It appeared that some suggestion had been made by the Duchess that they might meet in Paris.

He could not regard this as consistent with the situation in which Mr Cohane's advances had been repulsed by a married woman who wanted to have nothing to do with him.

Mr Cohane's phrase, "you are an incredibly exciting woman", was further proof of the nonsense of the explanation that there was nothing in their relationship. Although no letters from the Duchess to Mr Cohane had been produced, the whole tenor of the correspondence suggested that they had been mutually canvassing ways of getting together again.

The Judge read a passage from one letter which said: "I am completely frustrated as to how we can get together. I would like to be with you in Paris – what a titillating idea – but I just can't get away."

The Judge read another phrase: "I really would love to be with you even for a few days, and my not having written does not mean that you are not inflaming my imagination."

The date of the letter was unknown, but Mr Cohane said that he would be engaged from June until September when he should have some freedom. He went on: "I have thought of a number of new, highly intriguing things that we might do, or I might do to you."

The clear implication was that they had already engaged in a number of "highly intriguing things". It was conclusive of a previous adulterous association.

The final sentence of the letter informed her that he had to leave. "Darling, I have to leave. I miss you enormously and I never knew that such a short acquaintance could keep a hot flame burning so high for so long. Much love, Jack."

Lord Wheatley referred to another letter, which said: "Tell me where you will be, and somehow I will get to you."

The contents of the letter bore no other construction than that they were part of a correspondence between a man and a woman who were having an adulterous intercourse. He rejected the contention that this was a unilateral correspondence, conducted only by Mr Cohane.

He did not believe the Duchess, when she said that the man who was alone with her in her hotel on the morning of 13 January 1956, was not Mr Cohane. From the letter and the draft replies he was satisfied that they were sexually attracted to each other and, that this attraction was consummated.

There was the opportunity that morning and he found that there was sufficient evidence to establish facts, circumstances and qualifications to infer that the Duchess committed adultery with Mr Cohane then.

Turning to the allegations of adultery with Baron von Braun, Lord Wheatley said he would spare the Duchess further embarrassment of quoting in detail from the letters. The Duchess admitted that they were written when she was having a sexual relationship with von Braun. She asserted that this was between 1946 and 1947, and in 1950, before her marriage to the Duke.

In some letters the top of the first page had been torn off. The Duchess suggested that this had been done by the Duke after he recovered the letters. But he did not accept this suggestion, "which was typical of many suggestions advanced by the Duchess".

There was an arrangement between the Duchess and Baron von Braun that they exchanged self-addressed envelopes. The Duchess had advanced what could only be described as "a fantastic story" to explain this exchange.

In a cable there was a reference to "ghosts all around me". The Duchess stated that this cable was from the Duke.

"I don't believe her. There is a reference to ghosts in the correspondence and I find that this would seem to be an expression used between von Braun and the Duchess.

"The Duchess admitted this but asserted that this was an expression also used between herself and the Duke. I don't believe her."

The correspondence between Baron von Braun and the Duchess related to 1956 and "spelled out in large capitals that they were having an adulterous association". The evidence, facts, circumstances and qualifications inferring the Duchess's adultery with Baron von Braun.

Lord Wheatley turned to the plea that there might be special circumstances for condonation constituting a general forgiveness of adultery with men unknown to her husband, such as in the case of a wife who had embarked on a life of prostitution.

In April 1959, the Duke discovered letters from Mr Cohane and Baron von Braun and the photographs, when he had more than a suspicion of the Duchess's infidelity. He was then looking for evidence.

In May 1959, he lived with the Duchess again. His explanation of this was that he was "so shattered at finding the letters that everything else was excluded from his mind".

He did not believe the Duke when he said that this preoccupation did not give him time to examine the letters and photographs and draw the conclusion that she had been unfaithful. The photographs must have struck him straight away.

He said he could not know when these photographs were taken. As one showed that it was taken in the bathroom at the Upper Grosvenor Street house, this explanation was highly improbable.

He was satisfied that at that early stage the Duke was satisfied that his wife had committed adultery. It might seem strange that they resumed marital relations after such a discovery.

There were two possible explanations. They were that he was unable to resist her physical attractions and that his main anxiety at the time was to get her to submit to the injunction.

He found that the adultery was committed by the Duchess and the man or men in the photographs.

The Duke had said it was only in September 1959, that he was able to make a detailed examination of the letters and satisfy himself that he had sufficient evidence of her adultery with Baron von Braun and Mr Cohane.

Of the period during which the Duke and the Duchess lived together after the discovery by the Duke of the letters and photographs. "I am quite prepared to believe that in this period his anxiety was to get her to submit to an injunction. That, however, does not mean that he had no reasonable grounds for believing she had committed adultery with Baron von Braun."

It was not without significance that immediately after the Duchess submitted to the injunction the Duke instructed a solicitor to "begin divorce proceedings".

In these circumstances what took place after 9 May 1959, was important. There was a great deal of evidence that when the parties were at Inveraray, marital relations took place on several occasions.

When they met in Paris the explanation probably was that he had been a great deal in her company. He went back to the hotel, succumbed to her physical charms and spent the night in her bedroom in circumstances which inferred that relations took place.

Such condonation did not operate as a general forgiveness of all adultery with men unknown to him at the time.

In the case of the letters from Baron van Braun, they were signed in some cases "Sigis", an unusual name in this country. There seemed sufficient to establish that the Duke had reason to believe that his wife had committed misconduct with Baron von Braun.

The position regarding Mr Cohane was different. The letters were signed "Jack" with no date and address. Presumably the link with him was established only after the diary was found.

He found that the Duchess's adultery with Mr Cohane had not been condoned.

The Duke's evidence on condonation was unconvincing and the Duchess did not impress him at all.

"Her explanations of many incriminating documents were unconvincing and he thought she was lying on various points." She did not shrink from casting aspersions on anyone who seemed to be giving evidence contrary to her interests. She seemed to be a malicious woman.

"When a woman's chastity and character are being impugned, it is not surprising that she is hostile to those whose evidence seems to support the attack. But the general effect on her evidence, particularly on the questions touching her adultery, were most unfavourable."

The Judge considered the Duke's allegation of the Duchess's adultery with Mr Combe. There was sufficient to establish that she was a sexually promiscuous woman. On her own admission she committed adultery with the Duke before her marriage and with Baron von Braun between 1947 and 1950.

"She seemed to think association with a married man, or indeed adultery with a married man, was not a serious breach of the moral code if the man was not happy with his wife.

"There is enough in her own admissions to establish that by 1960 she was a completely promiscuous woman whose sexual appetite could be satisfied only by a number of men. Her attitude to the sanctity of marriage was what moderns would call enlightened, but in plain language could only be described as wholly immoral."

These might seem harsh words to use about a woman, but she had qualified for them by her own actions.

The Duke said that in 1960 the Duchess was associating with Mr Combe, It transpired that the association lasted longer than that.

On a number of occasions it was said that Mr Combe had been acting as an escort for the Duchess, who was then without the partnership of her husband, who had left her. Sometimes they were in the company of other people and sometimes on their own.

There was evidence of familiarity between them. The Duke's case rested on this association over an extended period.

The Duke had referred to two occasions, on the early morning of 14 July 1960, in Upper Grosvenor Street, and on 23–25 September 1960, when they were in Spain. The Duchess and Mr Combe denied that adultery ever took place.

Inquiry agents watched the Duchess's house on the night of 13 July. At about 9.10 p.m. Mr Combe arrived in an old Ford car. He went into the house and when he came out he took three dogs back in with him.

The Duchess and Mr Combe went to a night club and remained until 1.25 a.m., when they drove back to Upper Grosvenor Street. At 3 a.m. Mr Combe came out and walked with the dogs to the car.

The Duchess's explanation for Mr Combe's staying so long was that the dogs had "made a terrible mess and that he had spent the time cleaning up the mess and having a goodnight drink".

If the period spent in the house was one and a half hours, some explanation was called for if the old-fashioned, if realistic, inference was not to be drawn.

Their evidence was far from convincing. He found it difficult to believe that the dogs were given the free run of the house and not placed under the supervision of a member of the staff.

The stories of the witnesses differed in regard to the damage to furniture and the mess they made.

It was difficult to believe that a Duchess with a substantial staff should engage in such an unpleasant "chore" even when the damage and the mess were caused by the dogs of her escort.

He had reached the conclusion that they were not aware of the presence of inquiry agents outside and the evidence that they knew they were being watched was fabricated.

The Duchess made no reference to Mr Combe staying for a drink. When the point was put to her she said she had no recollection of it.

Later she said he did stay for a drink, but made no reference to the playing of gramophone records, which had been elsewhere in the house.

He thought the impression that the story about the dogs having done damage was invented or exaggerated to explain Mr Combe's long stay in the home that morning.

The Duchess and Mr Combe were seeing each other in July 1960. Most of their meetings were of a social nature. Both denied adultery.

During a trip abroad by the Duchess and Mr Combe, it was admitted that he was in her bedroom shortly after arrival, drinking champagne. That established that he had access to her bedroom.

The reason for their trip abroad had been given as an interest in the acquisition of land. Her real interest was another matter.

Mr Combe was uncertain about a number of important details such as where the land was to be acquired, what was to be done with it and how much money would be needed.

"The fact that no land has been acquired is not a surprising sequel to the whole affair."

The Duchess appeared vague about where the land was to be acquired, whether for development, for resale or capital gain. She was of the opinion that Mr Combe wanted her to invest about £1,500 although he had no idea how much money was required.

He reached the conclusion that the so-called business trip was an excuse to enable her to spend a few days with Mr Combe, with whom she had a close association.

Even taking into account the kind of social life led by people in the social set in which they moved, the number of outings together went far beyond the limits of normal friendship.

He was a man 12 years younger than herself and he could well imagine that the Duchess "just had to indulge herself by going out to theatres and night clubs and just had to have an escort on such occasions".

It might be that there would be an opportunity to be something more than just friends. Such a woman might be prepared to satisfy her sexual urges and take risks that a normal woman would not have taken.

In his opinion, the role which Mr Combe played "in this sordid, sinister projection was much closer and intimate than either is prepared to admit".

During the trip to Spain their "primary purpose was to spend some days together under the cover of a nebulous business deal. Of a woman of her propensities I am entitled to infer that she committed adultery with Mr Combe during their stay there.

Referring to the evidence of a man called Peach, a former valet of the Duke, who later entered the service of Mr Combe, Lord Wheatley said: "My impression of him was that he was a liar and a person in whom no trust could be placed."

Lord Wheatley granted the Duke a decree on the ground of the Duchess's misconduct with Mr Combe.

On the Duchess's answer, he found that the Duke had condoned her adultery with Baron von Braun and with the unknown man in the photographs. He found that her adultery with Mr Cohane had not been condoned.

After giving judgement, Lord Wheatley listened for about 15 minutes to the submissions of counsel for the parties in payment of the expenses of the action. He said he would take the question of expenses to deferred judgment.

Under Scottish law a husband is normally liable for all the costs, even if he wins a matrimonial action. But when the wife is known to have sufficient means in her own right she may be ordered to pay all or part of the costs.

The divorce action brought by the Duke began in November 1959, and a cross-petition by the Duchess in which she alleged the Duke's adultery with her stepmother, Mrs Jane Whigham, 47, of Cookham Dean, was withdrawn. Litigation between the two parties continued for the next three years.

The Duke's first marriage to Miss Janet Aitken, daughter of Lord Beaverbrook, was dissolved in 1934 after she obtained a divorce. The next year he married Louise Vanneck, daughter of the late Henry Clews, of the Chateau la Napoule, Alpes Maritimes, formerly the wife of the Hon. Andrew Nicholas Armstrong Vanneck. She obtained a divorce in 1951, on the grounds of the Duke's adultery with the present Duchess.

The Duchess's first marriage to Mr Charles Sweeny, the American golfer and financier, was dissolved in 1947.

A decree of divorce under Scottish law is immediate, but like all other Scottish law decrees, it is subject to appeal within 21 days. If a party awarded a decree was to remarry within that time and an appeal was lodged and upheld, the marriage would be declared null and void.

Lance Armstrong

"I am not the most believable guy in the world now."

For years, the brash but hugely charismatic Texan Lance Armstrong towered over the sport of cycling. His seven consecutive victories in the Tour de France between 1999 and 2005 displayed just how complete was his physical and mental domination over his rivals. What made his achievements seem even more impressive was that earlier in his career he had recovered from potentially fatal metastatic testicular cancer and through his Lance Armstrong Foundation he raised millions of dollars for charity. He was an inspirational figure, but also one who attracted controversy. After years of persistent rumours that he had been using performance-enhancing drugs, in 2012 a United States Anti-Doping Agency investigation concluded that Armstrong had used doping during his career. More than that, in a phrase that was redolent of Mafia kingpins, they named him as the ringleader of "the most sophisticated, professionalised and successful doping programme that sport has ever seen". Armstrong continued to deny the allegations until, finally, he staged a televised confession.

19 January 2013
In weasel words, Armstrong writes his own epitaph
Chilling in what it revealed and disturbing in what it did not,
interview confirms central character's flaws
By Paul Hayward

Lance Armstrong's "confession" should have taken place in front of "a man with a badge and a gun", to use his phrase from the Oprah Winfrey show, rather than a hotel room in Texas where he could keep his world of lies intact.

"This story was so perfect for so long," he told the world as Livestrong gave way to Live TV. "It was a mythic, perfect story – and it wasn't true."

Like a movie director contemplating his owned ruined narrative, Armstrong invited us to believe the holy light of truth had broken in. But that was not what this toe-curler was all about. The deceit goes on, the evasions multiply.

In the early hours of this morning, night owls in the UK will have seen Armstrong talk about the "$75m day" when his sponsors ran for the hills, the disastrous effect on his cancer charity, Livestrong, his 13-year-old son defending his father against innuendo (Armstrong cried about that) and the distress inflicted on his mother.

Before we could reach that point, we heard final confirmation of cycling's dirty secret. Armstrong said: "There will be people that say, 'OK, there are 200 guys on the Tour, I can tell you five guys that didn't [dope], and those are the five heroes', and they're right."

That statement sticks and festers in the brain and re–raises the unavoidable question: how clean is cycling now, and have other drugs come along to replace the chemicals Armstrong and many others imbibed so greedily? To Winfrey's interviewee, EPO, testosterone and human growth hormone were "like saying we have to have air in our tyres or we have to have water in our bottles. That was, in my view, part of the job".

Today's cyclists, with their biological passports and zero-tolerance contracts, are bound to squirm at Armstrong's depiction of a "level playing field" of cheating. Sir Bradley Wiggins, the recently knighted reigning Tour de France champion, is now the standard bearer in a sport where drug use was as much part of winning as pedalling, and where refuseniks were coerced or thrown off teams.

For sure this has been a great global moment of exposure to compare with other historic unmaskings. The "mafia" the United States Anti-Doping Agency report talked about has been busted.

The gulf between the confected celebrity life (the cancer, the yellow jerseys, the philanthropy) and the debased reality has never been so vast in sport.

Ben Johnson was a doper in a culture of cheating individuals. Juiced athletes were assisted by chemists and coaches. But not on the scale of professional cycling, where helicopters were on hand to fly riders to Spain for blood transfusions, and used syringes were stuffed in coke cans in motorhomes while fans mingled outside.

Armstrong is probably right to assert that the East German state doping programme of the 1970s and 1980s was bigger, but this one is more disturbing, for its flagrancy, its systematic intimidation and what it says about cycling in general and the Tour de France in particular. Never mind drugs helping a cyclist ride up hills for almost a month.

Armstrong's testimony says it was not possible to win the race in those years without a Hunter S. Thompson bag of pharmaceutical boosts.

A self-confessed "bully" of infinite calculation, Armstrong told the world he knew he was in big trouble when the feds began a Department of Justice investigation into his industrialised performance-enhancing drug use, but then he relaxed again when the case was dropped. "I thought I was out of the woods. And those were some serious wolves." he told Winfrey. The fall of the world's 'greatest' cyclist is surely one for the cops and prosecutors, not the stuff of light entertainment.

His partial mea culpa was compelling for reasons he did not intend. It showed him sticking to the lie that he raced clean in 2009 and 2010 in his comeback phase.

"The evidence from Usada is that Armstrong's blood tests show variations in his blood that show with absolute certainty he was doping after 2005," John Fahey head of the World Anti-Doping Agency, responded. "Believe Usada or believe Armstrong? I know who to believe."

Fahey's belief is that Armstrong was trying to avoid saying anything that "might be picked up under the US criminal code". He accused him of giving "weasel answers" in a "controlled PR exercise". His control-freakery survives. A "flaw" of his nature," he confessed, was an obsessive need "to control outcomes". But what was his appearance on Oprah, if not an urge to micro-manage his own downfall and our emotions? Fahey said: "The Usada invited him to come clean and advised he would have to give evidence under oath and provide substantial assistance and, if he indicated the nature of the evidence – and he would have to name times, dates, people – there may be a consideration of reducing his life sentence to a term of years. But he never came back, he went to Oprah instead and that indicates how sincere he really was. He wanted to control the way his story was told."

The most damning aspect is Armstrong's insistence that he stopped cheating eight years ago when Usada shows otherwise. "The last time I crossed that line was 2005," he told Winfrey. "Does that include blood transfusions? No doping or blood transfusions in 2009, 2010?" Winfrey asked. "Absolutely not," Armstrong replied.

For these answers to be given first from a TV studio rather than in front of federal agents, lawyers and police is, of course, a grotesque affirmation that law and order has limited jurisdiction in the fight against doping, despite there being clear evidence of fraud: obtaining money by deception. In part two, Armstrong remembers losing $75m (£47m) in sponsorship in one day. "Nike – they're out," he says.

With careful choreography, and a reduction in his lifetime ban, Armstrong will probably replenish his bank accounts. The future is less clear for those he impugned, vilified and sued for libel and slander. Among Winfrey's best questions was: "Suing people and you know they're telling the truth. What is that?" Significantly, a psychologist might say, Armstrong started to smile or giggle in parts of the inquisition but then stopped himself. Contrite Lance was trying to stay in the saddle. It was not hard to detect a deeply sadistic streak, a nature that has detached itself from reality. Had he not sued Emma O'Reilly, the whistleblower masseuse? Armstrong's answer: "To be honest, Oprah, we sued so many people I don't even [know]. I'm sure we did."

There were many, like O'Reilly, who were "run over and bullied", as Armstrong accepted, including Betsy Andreu, wife of Frankie, who went on CNN yesterday to express outrage at her tormentor's refusal to apologise to her on air. Andreu also alleged: "He had the UCI [cycling's governing body] in his back pocket." The UCI denies that accusation and was doubtless relieved to hear Armstrong deny any connection between his $100,000 (£63,000) donation to the organisation and its repeated failure to catch him out: "That story isn't true. There was no positive test. No paying off of the lab. I'm no fan of the UCI."

Armstrong also stuck by Michele Ferrari, the team doctor now serving a lifetime ban. He told Winfrey: "There are people in this story, they are good people, we've all made mistakes, they are not toxic and evil.

I viewed Dr Michele Ferrari as a good man and I still do."

There is a measure of fear in that statement. Ferrari may know more about

Armstrong's doping than anyone so his reluctance to provoke his old mentor is understandable.

With the choreography of remorse comes an offer to help. The burglar goes back into the house to clean up. The person who defiled the sport poses as its saviour. The reward: a reduced sentence. So Armstrong said: "I love cycling and I say that knowing that people see me as someone who disrespected the sport. If there was a truth and reconciliation commission and I'm invited, I'll be first man through the door."

Thus "one big lie" has become one big self-preservation exercise. But there is no getting away from his podium speech in Paris after his seventh Tour win: "To the cynics and the sceptics – I feel sorry for you that you can't dream big – and I'm sorry you can't believe in miracles."

Calling those who challenged him "crazy" or a "whore" or "a bitch" was his modus operandi. And there was no better insight into his psyche than what he said of Betsy Andreu: "I did not call her fat."

Armstrong treated us to the following exchange with Winfrey, ice cold in tone.

Winfrey: "Was it a big deal to you, did it feel wrong?"

Armstrong: "No. Scary."

Winfrey: "It did not even feel wrong?"

Armstrong: "No. Even scarier."

Winfrey: "Did you feel bad about it?"

Armstrong: "No. The scariest."

Perhaps his most valuable contribution to this whole burlesque was to write his own epitaph.

"I am not the most believable guy in the world now."

Richard Bacon

"Blue Peter presenters have to be squeaky clean – he knows that."

19 October 1998
Sack for *Blue Peter* drug man
By A. J. McIlroy

Richard Bacon, one of the presenters of BBC Television's *Blue Peter*, has been sacked after he admitted taking cocaine.

His contract was terminated to protect the wholesome image of the children's programme, which celebrated its 40th anniversary last week, a BBC spokesman said last night. He is its first presenter to have had his contract ended prematurely.

Lorraine Heggessey, head of BBC children's programmes, said the decision had been taken after allegations that Bacon, 22, of Chiswick, west London, snorted cocaine during a 12-hour drugs and alcohol session.

"It is sad that such a talented presenter as Richard Bacon has not only let himself and his colleagues down but, most important of all, he has let down the millions of children who watch *Blue Peter*," she said.

"For 40 years, *Blue Peter* has been a force for good, providing positive role models for children to follow and helping them to become responsible and caring adults. It is vital that nothing tarnishes that reputation."

She said it had not been decided how to tell viewers when today's pre-recorded show, which does not include Bacon, is broadcast.

Bacon, who joined the programme in February 1997, said in a statement: "I fully accept and agree with the decision that has been taken. I regret what I did but it was in my personal time and I therefore hope that it does not reflect on the show.

"I am very grateful to *Blue Peter* for the opportunity it has given me and am very sorry that I have let everybody down."

He had impressed BBC bosses with a likeable, easy-going manner during his audition, which included making a Christmas card, bouncing on a trampoline and handling a snake.

At the time, he said: "I remember seeing Caron Keating filming *Blue Peter* when I was with my family. I was about 10, but I had dreams that it would be me one day. I couldn't believe it when I heard I had got the job."

Born in Mansfield, Notts, he started his career at BBC Radio Nottingham before joining *Blue Peter*.

The show's presenters have not been entirely free of scandal. In 1980, it was revealed that Peter Duncan had once featured in a porn film.

In 1985, video footage of Michael Sundin emerged showing him dancing in his underpants with a male stripper in a nightclub.

The revelations came three months after he had left the show but led to revelations about his gay lifestyle. He died in 1989 at the age of 27.

In 1987, controversy surrounded the news that another presenter, Janet Ellis, was an unmarried mother.

20 October 1998
Sacked *Blue Peter* presenter's parents tell of drugs shame
Our foolish son has let everyone down
By Maurice Weaver

The parents of Richard Bacon, the Blue Peter presenter sacked by BBC Television for taking cocaine, spoke of their family's shame yesterday.

As the BBC apologised on air to viewers who had been "let down badly" by the presenter's behaviour, his father Paul, a solicitor, said at his home in Mansfield, Notts, that the news had left them "totally demoralised".

He added: "We cannot defend it in any way. It is the worst day of our lives."

He and his wife, Christine, said they were standing by their 22-year-old son, whose premature departure from the cast of the children's programme was announced to viewers early yesterday evening.

Mrs Bacon said her son had been a fool but added: "I love Richard and will support him."

Bacon is the first *Blue Peter* presenter to have his contract terminated prematurely. He has a flat in Chiswick, London, and has yet to return home to face his parents since his fall from grace. The couple said they had not heard if and when he planned to do so.

Chosen to present the programme because of his wholesome, clean-cut image, he was sacked after he admitted snorting cocaine and drinking vodka during 12 hours of partying a few days before hosting *Blue Peter*'s 40th anniversary party.

His father said that since news of their son's disgrace broke at the weekend his two sisters, Helena, 20, and Juliet, 19, had returned home from university to be with their family while they coped with the distress.

"I agree with the decision to sack him, as does he," he said. "If any message can be sent out as a result of this it is that drug-taking is wrong and should be punished.

"It is a dreadful situation to be in and we are totally demoralised and disappointed. It has all been a bit much to take in and we will need a bit of time before any of us start planning.

"Richard very much regrets what has happened and I think he is just trying to be as stoic as possible.

"The family is sticking by him. He did have the courage to admit that he'd done wrong.

"He has no plans for the immediate future and is obviously considering his position."

Mrs Bacon said: "My son is very disappointed with himself. He knew when the story got out that the consequences would be that he would lose his job.

"*Blue Peter* presenters have to be squeaky clean – he knows that. But he has been a fool, he realises that, and he is really sorry.

"I think he has been easily led but he shouldn't have done it. I'm sure he wishes he hadn't. He's sorry but hopefully he will bounce back."

But the presenter's humiliation intensified with the disclosure last night that an anti-drugs group in which both he and his family have been involved is considering recalling publicity literature featuring his name and picture.

DARE, an acronym of Drug Abuse Resistance Education, was set up in Mansfield four years ago, backed by Nottinghamshire Police. The presenter's father donated £1,000 to help it to get started.

The scheme had proved successful, with other forces adopting it and building on the *Blue Peter* link to persuade youngsters of the perils of drug-taking.

James Sprey, DARE's administrator, said: "Clearly, Mr Bacon's actions do not represent the sort of message we want to put across."

He said he would like the link with *Blue Peter* to continue.

Norman Baillie Stewart

"There is nothing we can say. The whole thing is damnable."

Norman Baillie Stewart's trial for passing secrets (via his lover) to the Germans helped briefly entertain a British population sunk in the middle of the Great Depression. Twelve years later, Baillie Stewart was arrested in his lederhosen halfway up an Austrian mountain. Having moved to Germany before the war, and taken

German nationality, after the conflict broke out he broadcast for a while alongside the more notorious William Joyce. They were both, for a while, identified as Lord Haw-Haw, before Joyce took definitive possession of the soubriquet. In 1946 he was sentenced to five years' imprisonment for aiding the enemy by broadcasting from Germany. Summing up, the judge, Mr Justice Oliver said to him: "You are, I suppose, one of the worst citizens any country has ever produced."

21 March 1933
"Country sold for £50 or more"
Charges against tower officer
By our special representative

Lt. N. Baillie-Stewart, of the Seaforth Highlanders – the officer whose detention in the Tower since early in February has aroused intense public interest – was charged yesterday before a general court-martial on ten counts.

They were summed up by Major H. Shapcott, the prosecutor, in one phrase:

"The prosecution contend that Lt. Baillie-Stewart sold his country for £50 or more."

The charges relate to an alleged betrayal of military secrets, concerning tanks, rifles, formations and organisation, to a German agent known as Otto Waldemar Obst. An astonishing story of secret visits to Holland, payments of £50 and £40 in English banknotes to the lieutenant, and alleged veiled communications signed with code names was unfolded by Major H. Shapcott, of the Judge Advocate-General's office, in his presentation of the case for the prosecution.

The trial is expected to last for three or four days. Parts of it are to be heard in camera.

A bare, bleak setting of green distempered walls, a few tables covered with dark-blue cloth, and rows of unpainted garden seats.

Seven officers in khaki, and the Judge-Advocate in wig and gown seated behind a table on a dais, the red tabs and decorations on their uniforms providing the only flash of bright colour – these are the elements of the strange drama which is taking place in a drill hall at the Duke of York's headquarters in Chelsea.

It was a brisk, business-like opening. A sharp word of command from the curtained entrance by the dais, and the President, Major-Gen. W. J. Dugan, entered, followed by the tribunal. The Judge-Advocate, Mr P. N. Sutherland Graeme, took his place at the President's right hand. There was a pause, and the President's voice came quietly and clearly, "Bring in the accused."

Lt. Baillie-Stewart, with his escort, an officer of the Grenadiers, strode in through the curtains, sprang to attention, and saluted the President. He was swordless, and without his Sam Browne belt.

He took his place at a small table to the right of the court, next to the table where his counsel, Mr Norman Parkes, was already busy with his papers. The members of the court were ten sworn.

There was tension of anticipation as the Judge Advocate prepared to read the first charge. It was broken, unexpectedly, from the back of the hall.

A middle-aged clergyman was on his feet holding aloft a Bible. "Mr President," he shouted. "In the name of Jehovah I protest against this officer being sent to the Tower."

The interrupter was escorted from the court by military police and the charges were read.

Then came the strange anti-climax which so frequently haunts the court of law. Scarcely had the full significance of the ten counts become divested of their shroud of legal language in the minds of the listeners when Mr Parkes had lodged a legal objection to four of them.

For twenty minutes the quiddities of interpretation were discussed – whether in a clause in the Official Secrets Act of 1920 the word "and" should or should not be considered to mean "or". Finally, the court retired for a few minutes and the objection was overruled.

The prisoner pleaded "Not Guilty" in clear, firm tones to all the ten counts. On each and all of them, Major Shapcott indicated later, a person was liable to a maximum of 14 years' imprisonment.

It was a strange, vivid story which Major Shapcott unfolded. It began with the reading of a letter alleged to have been received by Lt. Baillie-Stewart about 14 November, signed "Marie Louise." The writer thanked him for a loan he had made to her to help her continue her studies, part of which she was repaying. The letter contained ten £5 notes.

"You will have Lt. Baillie-Steward's banking account in front of you," said Major Shapcott. "You will see that at no time during this material time did he have £50 in it to lend to anybody."

Another letter, addressed to Otto Waldemar Obst in Berlin, acknowledging receipt of money, and signed Alphonse Poiret, is read. "Alphonse Poiret is Lt. Baillie-Stewart," said Major Shapcott.

A further letter with £40 from Marie Louise is read, and the Court is suddenly brought to the moment when the lieutenant is questioned by an officer on 20 January.

The explanation he is alleged to have given then is that Marie Louise is a woman who has paid him "for services rendered". He had made love to her. He knows her by no other name than Marie Louise, and he describes her as 22 and fair. He said that he had nothing but his word to prove his story.

24 March 1933
Tower officer's own story
New Description of "Marie Louise"
By our special representative

The trial by court-martial of Lt. N. Baillie-Stewart, who is charged with communicating military secrets to a man believed to be a foreign agent, reached a dramatic stage yesterday.

For more than two hours the young officer gave evidence under examination and cross-examination. He answered all questions in a clear, resonant voice, and the nonchalant demeanour which he has maintained throughout the trial remained unchanged.

He gave in his own words an account of his first introduction to "Marie Louise" by Obst in a Berlin cafe, and of his subsequent relations with her.

His visit to Holland, in August, which he said was not a secret one, he declared to have been for the purpose of meeting her again, and getting money from her. He admitted receiving money from her on this and subsequent occasions, in addition to the £50 and £40 which she is alleged to have sent him in a letter.

Cross-examined by Major Shapcott, the prosecutor, Lt. Baillie-Stewart described Marie Louise as "five and a half feet high, with blue eyes and a good figure". He had been unable to find out her surname, her occupation, or her address. He met her by appointment on a number of days, and "dropped" her at the end of a street at the end of the evening.

They made several excursions to the Wansee (a lake outside Berlin), where she either owned or had the use of a canoe, and intimacy took place, on several occasions, always on the shores of the lake.

At one point in the cross-examination the President of the Court, Major-General W. J. Dugan, interpolated the question: "Did she not strike you as rather a mystery woman?"

"Well, sir, all foreigners are mysterious, in a way," replied Lt. Baillie-Stewart.

Asked by Major Shapcott why he had not attempted to find out more about Marie Louise, he said, "I saw no reason why I should look a gift horse in the mouth."

Marie Louise had sympathised with him when he told her he had sold his car, and hinted at "a pleasant surprise" for him later. He was to try to get over in the spring to see her.

At the end of his visit to Berlin he suggested meeting her in Holland, where she was going to stay with friends. He had not meant it seriously, but she sent for time-tables, and he made the note of train times which was afterwards found in his rooms.

Lt. Baillie-Stewart denied that he had any idea that either Marie Louise or Obst was a Secret Service agent. "We never discussed military subjects," he said.

Mr Norman Parkes, in opening for the defence, said he would call a witness, a man of eminent respectability, who had met Marie Louise in Berlin. Having read an account of the trial in the Press, this witness had communicated with the War Office, had been "passed on by telephone from department to department" without finding the right authority to whom to tell his story, and had then got in touch with the defence.

Referring to the accused's relations with Marie Louise, Mr Parkes said he had "a peculiar attraction for women and a peculiar attitude towards them – rather a lack of chivalry". The reason for the subterfuge of fictitious names and communications through the man Obst was that they were in a situation which was discreditable to both of them.

Before the Court rose for the day the President put several questions to Lt. Baillie-Stewart concerning the nature of his confinement in the Tower, saying that many people imagined it to mean being "locked in a dungeon". (Laughter.)

Lt. Baillie-Stewart agreed that his quarters were the same as those available for officers stationed at the Tower.

28 March 1933
Court-martial to end to-day
Counsel's plea for accused

The trial by court-martial of Lt. Norman Baillie-Stewart, Seaforth Highlanders, on charges alleging offences under the Official Secrets Act, will conclude to-day at Chelsea.

Mr Norman Parkes addressed the Court for an hour and a half yesterday on accused's behalf, and was followed by Major H. Shapcott, the prosecutor.

When the Court re-opens this morning the Judge-Advocate, Mr P. N. Sutherland Graeme, barrister of law, will sum up. The Court will then consider its verdict in private.

The procedure behind closed doors is a little peculiar in that, the evidence having been discussed, the President first calls on the junior member of the Court to give his opinion as to the proper verdict to be returned. The President expresses his opinion last.

The verdict having been decided upon, the accused is marched into court, with the witnesses.

If the verdict is not guilty it is announced forthwith. If, however, the accused is found guilty, the sentence is not disclosed, as it has to be confirmed.

In this case the proceedings are transmitted by the Judge Advocate-General direct to the convening authority, and the latter forwards them with his recommendations and remarks to the Judge Advocate-General. If the sentence is one that requires to be confirmed by the King, the Judge Advocate-General transmits the proceedings to the Secretary of State for War for this purpose.

Only after confirmation is the sentence promulgated.

A breeze
Counsel and decoded telegram
From our special representative

Challenge and counter-assertion in an afternoon devoted to the concluding speeches of Mr Norman Parkes, for the defence, and Major H. Shapcott, the prosecutor, marked the trial yesterday.

The speeches were listened to intently by a quietly dressed, sad-voiced middle-aged woman and a young lieutenant who sat by her side. They were the prisoner's other and elder brother, both of whom had given evidence in the morning.

There was less smoothness in the proceedings than previously. An atmosphere of tension and suspense mounted steadily through the afternoon in the crowded drill hall as the two explanations of the lieutenant's conduct were laid before the Court. At the outset there was a sharp passage of arms between Mr Parkes and Major Shapcott when the latter, just before the speech for the defence, announced that he had received a decoded telegram which "might be of assistance". He handed a sheet of paper to Mr Parkes, and the President asked if the Court was to see it.

Major Shapcott appeared to indicate that he had no objection. Mr Parkes at once interjected:

"My friend knows quite well that the court can only see evidence which is produced in a proper manner. This is an effort—"

Major Shapcott sharply retorted "It is not." Mr Parkes: "Very well. But I do not know why my friend wished to announce in open court his intention of handing it to me. He has, however, done so, and I will return it."

The Major received back the telegram with a smile.

Mr Parkes, in his speech for the defence, referred to two roads which might alternatively be taken by the court. That suggested by the prosecution led to a conclusion so unbelievable, so dreadful that the court would hesitate a long time before taking it.

"Nothing but surmise and suspicion" had been offered to induce the court to take that road. Mr Parkes enumerated points of evidence at which a red lamp warned that the direction indicated by the prosecution would "lead to a most dreadful disaster".

"In this case," said Mr Parkes, "this officer's life is ruined whatever the result of it may be, and he knows it. His career in the Army, of necessity, is ended.

"Any possible life he may continue outside the Army will be a life which is wholly worthless, whatever the result of this case may be."

His explanation was a discreditable one, but it could not be excluded as impossible. It was not so surprising and unbelievable as that offered by the prosecution. Mr Parkes spoke for one hour and fifty minutes.

Major Shapcott declared in his reply that the prosecution's case was in exactly the same state as it had been a week ago. The explanation offered by the defence was "the most remarkable story certainly that has ever been put before any court-martial; probably the most remarkable story which has ever been put in any court of law".

Major Shapcott quoted a previous case to show that direct evidence of communication was not essential. It might be inferred from the payment of a reward.

The morning's evidence given by Mrs Wright, the mother of the accused, had concerned her occasional gifts of £3 or £4 at a time to her son. Lt. Eric Wright, elder brother of the accused, described how he and his brother spent their holiday together at Southsea. He had seen a blank sheet of Berlin paper – that on which notes of military matters were now written – in his brother's possession. He had discovered the character of Lt. Baillie-Stewart's relations with Marie Louise at Christmas, and had "jumped pretty heavily" on him for it.

29 March 1933
Officer goes back to the tower
Not guilty on three charges
By our special representative

The trial of Lt. N. Baillie-Stewart is ended.

He returned last evening under escort to the Tower, there to await the promulgation of the Court's decision upon seven of the ten charges which are laid against him. Upon three charges he was found "Not Guilty", at the direction of Mr Sutherland Graeme, the Judge Advocate,

In the remaining charges the lieutenant accused of obtaining, collecting and communicating to Otto Waldemar Obst, of Berlin, information which might be useful to an enemy, and of performing acts preparatory to the committing of these offences.

The finding of the Court was announced after over two and a half hours of deliberation in private. The prisoner heard it unmoved, standing at attention. He gave no sign of emotion when he saluted the President, and left the Court for the last time.

In the caressing spring sunshine of the afternoon the sightseers waited in the grounds of the Duke of York's Headquarters. The summing-up – a masterpiece of weighed judicial oratory – had ended shortly after the luncheon adjournment, and now all eyes were turned towards the great stone portico, where a little group of officers and court officials were chatting. Lt. Baillie-Stewart, with the escort and his brother, strolled up and down by the grass edge smoking cigarette after cigarette.

Minutes became hours, and still the seven officers deliberated. Any sign of movement among the officers beneath the portico was the signal for a stampede of the watchers towards their seats in the court room. But it was not until 5 o'clock that the court reassembled in the drill hall.

Again the sharp word of command as the members entered. But now the hall had become strangely, incredibly silent. The routine phrase, "Bring in the accused", was spoken by the president almost in an undertone.

Again the familiar thud of footsteps behind the blue curtain, and Lt. Baillie-Stewart entered, saluted, and took his seat, removing his Glengarry.

For the first time it seemed, one noticed that the strain of the trial had left its mark upon him – his mouth seemed a little drawn, and there were dark marks under his eyes. But there was no sign of fatigue in his bearing. His brother sat behind the counsel for the defence. He rubbed his hands together nervously.

The President motioned the prisoner to rise. He stood at attention, bare-headed, his shoulders squared.

From a paper before him the President began to read.

"The accused, Lt. Norman Baillie-Stewart, Seaforth Highlanders, on probation, Royal Army Service Corps, and attached to the Second Battn. Coldstream Guards for safe custody, is not guilty of the third, fifth and tenth alternative charges."

To very few members of the public present can the full significance of the pronouncement have been conveyed. But with scarcely a pause the President, speaking so softly that his words were scarcely audible, called for evidence of the prisoner's character. Major Shapcott was ready and the Adjutant of the Coldstream Guards was sworn. Once again the cold formality of official evidence, cut as short as possible, at the President's own request.

Lt. Baillie-Stewart, seated once more back in the shadow, listened. Then came Major-Gen. Dugan's signal: "The accused may go."

He sprang to his feet, looking neither to right nor left, stepped forward three brisk paces, faced the President at attention, saluted, turned on his heel and strode firmly from the court.

15 April 1933
Tower officer in Wandsworth Prison
Sentence received calmly

Found guilty of seven of the ten charges preferred against him at the court-martial at Chelsea last month, Lt. Norman Baillie-Stewart, the Seaforth Highlanders, the "officer in the Tower", has been sentenced to be cashiered, and to suffer penal servitude for the term of five years. There is no right of appeal.

"Cashiering" is more severe than mere dismissal from the service, inasmuch as it disqualifies from entering the public service in any capacity, which dismissal does not.

The sentence will be served at Maidstone Prison. It is assumed that the prisoner, like other convicts, will be able to earn a remission sentence, amounting to three months a year, for good conduct.

The War Office, announcing the sentence, states: "The King, on the advice of the Secretary of State for War, has confirmed the findings of the Court on the 2nd, 4th and 9th charges laid under Section 41 of the Army Act of obtaining, collecting and communicating information which might be useful to an enemy for a purpose prejudicial to the interests of the State, contrary to the provisions of the Official Secrets Acts, 1911 and 1920.

"Confirmation has been withheld by his Majesty from the findings of the Court on the 1st, 6th, 7th and 8th charges, which only relate to subsidiary incidents of the same transactions as form the subject of the 2nd, 4th and 9th charges.

"His Majesty has confirmed the sentence of the Court and has directed that it be carried into effect."

The three counts on which the Court found accused "not guilty" were alternative charges.

When the sentence was read to him at the Tower, where he had been detained since the close of the court-martial, Lt, Baillie-Stewart maintained the calm he showed throughout the seven days of the trial.

Soon after four o'clock on Thursday afternoon – when few people were about – the saloon car which had been used to take Lt. Baillie-Stewart to and from the court-martial was driven through the gates of the Tower. In it, dressed in civilian clothes and with an escort of an officer and a regimental sergeant-major in uniform, was the prisoner.

He was being conveyed to Wandsworth Prison. Here he will serve the first part of his sentence before being removed to Maidstone convict prison.

On reaching the prison the prisoner was formally handed over to the custody of the governor by his escort.

His own clothing was taken from him, and after he had bathed he was provided with a complete kit of prison uniform, underwear, socks and boots.

The prisoner will receive the same treatment as is accorded to any civilian sentenced to penal servitude. He will remain at Wandsworth for a few weeks, and will then be transferred to Maidstone prison, where convicts of the "star" class, serve their terms of penal servitude.

"Star" class convicts are those men who have not been previously convicted of grave crime, and are not likely, in the opinion of the authorities, to lead a life of crime after being released.

Like other convicts, he will be questioned regarding his abilities, and a suitable task will be allotted to him.

Lt.-Col. C. H. Baillie-Wright, accused's father, said when news of the sentence was communicated to him at his Southsea home:

"It is ghastly. The sentence is awful.

"I am not satisfied with the trial. I consider there was not evidence sufficient for conviction. There may have been for assumption, but not for conviction. In a civil court, in my opinion, the accused would have got the benefit of the doubt."

Col. Baillie-Wright expressed the opinion that the constitution and methods of courts-martial ought to be altered, as at present there was chance of a grave miscarriage of justice. He looked upon the position of Deputy Judge Advocate, for instance, as being tantamount to that of a second prosecutor, although he made no reflections on the Deputy Judge Advocate in this case.

Mrs Baillie-Wright bore traces of the great shock she had received. "There is nothing we can say," she said. "The whole thing is damnable."

The findings of the Court, which have been confirmed by the King, state that Lt. Baillie-Stewart collected information at or near Aldershot concerning modern formations, war establishment the handling of tank battalions, automatic rifles and other technical matters, and communicated it to Otto Waldemar Obst, of Berlin, who is believed to be a foreign agent.

Evidence was given that he had received £90 in banknotes from a person known as "Marie Louise".

In his defence the lieutenant declared that the money had been given him by a German girl of that name, with whom he had contracted a liaison while he was on holiday in Berlin.

Peter Baker

"One can hardly imagine a worse type of commercial fraud."

If his life had worked out differently, Peter Baker might have been remembered as a war hero, a leading politician or a successful businessman. Unfortunately, the dashing former officer who was elected to Parliament at the age of just 28 had a streak of dishonesty – perhaps if he'd spent less time with *Mirror* crook Robert Maxwell and traitor Kim Philby he would have been able to steer a more honest course – in addition to his undoubted gifts, and he will instead be remembered as the last MP to be expelled from the House of Commons to date.

1 December 1954
Capt. Baker M.P. sent to prison for seven years
Forgeries involved £88,000 loss to finance houses
By a *Daily Telegraph* reporter

Sentence of seven years' imprisonment was passed on Capt. Peter Arthur David Baker, 33, Conservative M.P. for South Norfolk, by Mr Justice Lynskey at the Old Bailey yesterday.

Baker pleaded guilty to six charges of uttering false documents which involved losses to finance houses amounting to £88,000. He pleaded not guilty to one charge of uttering a forged document, a form of guarantee purporting to be signed by Sir Bernard Docker, on 29 October 1953.

The Judge said: This case is extremely serious. You have deliberately forged the names of people who apparently helped you by guaranteeing your liabilities, or the liabilities of your companies on other occasions.

"When forged documents are put forward in the course of financing companies one can hardly imagine a worse type of commercial fraud. I take into account your excellent record and the great service you have given to your country.

"I am not satisfied that you did not know what you were doing and I am not satisfied you did not intend to do what you were doing." Baker stood stiffly to attention and after the sentence bowed deeply from the waist, leaving the dock without, showing any signs of emotion.

Mr Christmas Humphreys, for the Crown, who accepted the pleas, said that the frauds were all concerned with guarantees given by Baker to finance houses, mostly banks. The guarantees were for money he wanted for overdrafts both for himself and for companies.

In every case the person concerned was a director of one of the many companies run by Baker, or who had previously either guaranteed some overdraft or guaranteed money for one of the companies.

The frauds took place in a very short space of time. In Just over five months £103,000 was involved and the downfall of seven or eight of the companies. Eight of the 17 companies were then in liquidation, to a deficit of at least £652,000.

On 7 October Baker handed the Edgware Trust 12 bills of exchange dated 6 October. They were purported to have been accepted by Sir (Edward) John Mann and endorsed by himself, payable monthly from 6 December.

On 9 June, six of the bills having already been paid before they could reach maturity, the seventh bill was presented for payment. Someone noticed the signature differed, the bill was dishonoured and the Edgware Trust lost £6,600.

On 23 November 1953. Baker went to Barclays Bank for a loan of £49,000 which he wanted for Peregrine Press Ltd. He said it would be secured with guarantees from Sir Bernard Docker. Mr N. R. Reynolds and Sir John Mann.

When the £49,000 guarantee was presented to him last May, Baker said: "I feel pretty sure in a state of alcohol and general breakdown I put in Docker's and Mann's signatures myself."

Chief Det.-Supt. Robert Stevens, of New Scotland Yard, said Baker was married, with two young children. His character had been exemplary, in 1945 he was awarded the M.C. for "penetrating into enemy territory, obtaining information and effecting rescue of men".

He helped to get 137 men back to British lines. After the battle of Arnhem he volunteered to establish an escape line by getting in touch with the Dutch Resistance. As a result many Arnhem survivors were rescued.

Mr R. C. Levy Q.C., defending: Do you know that his father provided a great deal of money for the companies and has completely ruined himself through their activities to the tune of tens of thousands of pounds.

Dr. G. Garmany, of Harley Street, consulting psychiatrist at Westminster Hospital, said that he had examined Baker 11 times, once at a nursing home. Baker then "presented an extraordinary appearance, lying on the bed in his dressing gown, unshaven, with papers littered all over the place and a Dictaphone by his side.

"He interrupted me constantly to use the telephone. His language to me was perfectly friendly, but it was facetious and frequently obscene. His deportment was quite out of touch with the man's background."

Baker was suffering from hypomania, a state of over-excitement and over-activity produced by alcoholism. It was a state in which judgment was much impaired.

Baker started his career as a publisher with less than £1,000 and founded the Falcon Press. Within seven years he had built his interests into a group with assets valued at more than £1m.

His failure was due mainly to his desire to be known as a captain of industry, whatever the cost. He had big ideas but lacked the ability to carry them through. His lavish spending on unnecessary things such as office equipment, entertainment and the purchase of political manuscripts with a limited appeal, lost a lot of money.

Although he was getting deeper and deeper into financial difficulties he tried to maintain his pose of success. He cared little about his clothes or looks but people who knew him saw only in his unkempt appearance another affectation.

Baker had an outstanding wartime career marked by rapid promotion. It led him to believe that he could be successful at anything and neither lack of business training nor experience deterred him.

Educated at Eastbourne College, he was waiting to enter Trinity College, Cambridge, when the war started. He enlisted in the Royal Artillery and served eight months in the ranks before being commissioned.

After distinguished service in N. Africa and Italy he was captured by the Germans in Holland at the headquarters of an underground resistance group behind the German lines. Brutal treatment by the Gestapo affected his health. During six months in prison camps he made two attempts to escape. He also wrote two books.

Two years after starting his publishing career at the end of the war Baker was adopted prospective Conservative candidate for Norfolk South. He won the seat in 1950.

A number of prominent men and politicians at one time belonged to his companies. Among them were his father, Major R. Baker, President of the British Film Producers' Association; Viscount Astor; Mr Hugh Fraser, Conservative M.P. for Stafford and Stone; and Major H. Legge-Bourke. Conservative M.P. for the Isle of Ely.

The group of companies included publishers, printers, consulting engineers, whisky blenders and an organisation for packing books for export. From the Falcon Press, Baker developed other publishing companies and the Dunstead Trust, an investment company which became the "parent" of several of the Baker enterprises.

The first public indication that the Baker empire was crumbling came early this year when the Peregrine Press, formed in February 1947, began to fail. Within a few months winding-up orders were made against it, the Falcon Press and a subsidiary and finally against the Dunstead Trust.

The winding up order against the Dunstead Trust, of which Baker was chairman and principal shareholder, was on a petition by his father, supported by Lord Astor. It had a capital of £35,620 in £1 shares.

Baker frequently used the precincts of the House of Commons to meet people he wanted in his companies. He arranged many parties there for his "contact work".

When he got into financial difficulties he finally had to resort, when the funds of one company were drained, to borrowing from another to pay printing bills and royalties.

Baker also founded and became chairman of an organisation called the Association of Commonwealth Venturers. It was formed to spend £1m on Commonwealth development.

The collapse of the Baker group has affected a large number of people and caused heavy losses to some of the smaller printing firms. One of them is owed £5,000.

It was Baker's practice to farm out his printing, paper-making and binding to small firms all over the country. When his companies began to fail in 1950 the larger firms would not accept his work without full pre-payment. There are substantial stocks of books in sheet form, uncut and unbound, in the smaller printing houses. The liquidators are trying to trace them.

17 December 1954
Capt. Baker writes from prison
By our own representative

A letter from Wormwood Scrubs prison from Capt. Peter Baker, former Conservative M.P. for South Norfolk, was read to-day to a crowded House of Commons by the Speaker (Mr W. S. Morrison).

Capt. Baker was sentenced at the Old Bailey on 30 November to seven years' imprisonment for uttering forged documents. His letter read:

Dear Mr Speaker,

By the kind dispensation of the Governor, I am at last able to write you this short letter to offer my most humble apologies to you, and through you to the Prime Minister and the House of Commons, for the trouble I have caused you and any discredit I have, inadvertently, brought upon the House over the past months.

As you know, proceedings commenced while I was recovering from my illness and I discovered to my dismay that I was unable to vacate my seat in any way while the matter was sub judice. I hastened the proceedings as far as was possible and refused to appeal so that you can now dispossess me of my seat without delay

I must end as I began by begging the House of Commons to accept my most sincere apologies. I can only assure you that my regret, remorse and repentance during the past three months were doubled by the knowledge that in addition to my friends and colleagues elsewhere I had also embarrassed my friends and colleagues in the House of Commons.

I can only ask you, and through you, them, to accept this expression of these regrets.

I cannot ask you for your forgiveness. I dare to hope for your pity and your prayers. I hope, too, that you will receive with compassion and some measure of understanding this letter to testify to my sorrow that I should have involved in my own personal misfortunes the House of Commons of which I was so proud and honoured to be a member.

I am your humble and obedient servant,

Peter Baker

Mr Crookshank, Leader of the House, said the House would share his feelings that the moving of the motion to expel Mr Baker was "a most melancholy task". Speaking quietly in a silent Chamber, he added:

"Cases of this sort are fortunately very rare. I believe I think aright when I say that I hope the House will not desire to go further in this matter."

Members, with almost inaudible consent, signified their approval and the motion "that Mr Peter Arthur David Baker be expelled this House" was carried.

Colonel Valentine Baker

"I am sorry I did it, I do not know what possessed me,
I being a married man."

On the afternoon of 17 June 1875, a railway porter encountered a panic-stricken girl on the Portsmouth to London train.

"She was on the step, and I helped the guard and the engine-driver to get her down."
"In what condition was she?"
"She was very distressed, in great alarm, but very self-controlled at the same time."
"Did you see where the defendant was?"
"I saw his face in the carriage."
"What did Miss Dickinson say to you?"
"'I will not ride any longer with that man.'"

"That man" was the 49-year-old Colonel Valentine Baker, an intimate of the Prince of Wales, and an officer in the 10th Hussars considered to be an expert in military tactics. He was, a witness claimed, "one of the army's greatest ornaments".

The subsequent trial, in which Baker was accused of indecent assault and intent to ravish – he had allegedly tried to force his hands into Miss Dickinson's underwear – was a sensation. It was conducted in front of packed crowds, which included a number of Baker's most blue-blooded friends. It was their presence, and his proximity to royalty, that suggested to most people he would be dealt with leniently. Suspicions confirmed by the judge in his summing-up, who suggested that Baker's chief concern was to save Miss Dickinson from falling off the train's running board, and that he had no "intent to ravish". His casuistry impressed the jury whose decisions led to the judge giving a relatively generous sentence of a year in jail and a fine of £500. The public was not impressed. After serving his sentence, the disgraced Baker moved with his wife and children to Istanbul, where he served the Ottoman army with some distinction. He subsequently took a police post in Egypt, where he died in 1887 of typhoid. Queen Victoria, who had previously been unbending in her condemnation of his behaviour, cabled that he should be buried with full military honours.

3 August 1875
Colonel Baker's trial
Evidence, cross-examination, verdict and sentence

How great was the interest which the public took in the trial of Colonel Baker on the charge of assaulting Miss Kate Dickinson, in a carriage on the South-Western Railway, was evidenced by the fact that fully two hours before the time appointed for the commencement of the legal proceedings the Town Hall in the High-street of Croydon was besieged by an excited and anxious crowd of men and women, many of whom had come down specially from the metropolis by the early trains. The authorities had not apparently anticipated such a large gathering of people, and the small police force in attendance was soon found to be inadequate to maintain order and decorum. It was with difficulty that those who had business at the court, or who had obtained from the Sheriff tickets of admission, succeeded in effecting an entrance to the small and inconvenient hall which, long before Mr Justice Brett took his seat, was crowded to the utmost. The learned gentlemen engaged in the case were able to reach their places only by passing through the criminals' dock, while some ladies, whose eagerness to listen to the trial overcame any weak feminine scruples, permitted themselves to be lifted over the heads of the crowd, and through a window into the courthouse, amid the jeers and shouts of the throng outside. Throughout the morning the disappointed public, who had wasted great part of the Bank Holiday in the vain pursuit of the privilege of being present at a sensational trial, remained massed together, surging to and fro in front of the Town Hall, and occasionally making desperate but unsuccessful attempts to effect an entrance. Vehicular traffic in the High-street was for a time perforce suspended, and the noisy demonstrations of the outsiders almost drowned Mr Serjeant Parry's eloquence, until the police, stimulated by a peremptory order from the Judge, succeeded in securing comparative quiet. The scene in court presented a subdued reflection of the excitement outside. Every nook of the building was occupied, and it is needless to say the audience comprised many officers of the Army and other friends or acquaintances of the prisoner. County magistrates were there in unusually large numbers, occupying privileged seats; and the Bar, of course, was strongly represented. Prominent among those in court were General Sir Thomas Steele (commanding at Aldershot), the Earl of Lucan, and Sir W. Fraser, M.P. The defendant entered the dock shortly after ten o'clock, and formally surrendered, when called upon by the Clerk of Arraigns to do so. Colonel Baker was then standing at the bar with his hat in one hand, but some time afterwards was accommodated with a seat, where he had to submit to an inconvenient amount of scrutiny and curiosity on the part of the spectators, among whom were a number of ladies of all ages. It must have been some relief to the prisoner when the prosecutrix, accompanied by her mother and brother, entered the court, and thus partially diverted from him the eyes of the curious. As soon as the jury had been sworn and the defendant had pleaded, Mr Serjeant Parry – who had sufficiently recovered from a serious fall he sustained in alighting from a train at Croydon Station on Sunday evening to fulfil this important engagement – opened the case in a brief and temperate speech, after which the witnesses were called, and the trial, all the details of which were fully reported below, went on to its conclusion.

Serjeant Parry said: I regret, gentlemen, the position in which the defendant stands. He is a colonel in the Queen's Army; he holds or held a staff appointment at the camp at Aldershot; he is a married man; he is about 50 years of age; and he stands before you this morning charged with a cowardly and unmanly outrage upon a young lady whom he met for the first time in his life in a railway carriage on the 17th June last.

The prosecutrix was then called into the box, but some few minutes elapsed before she was able to make her way through the crowd from the entrance set apart for the legal profession. Miss Dickinson is a young lady of prepossessing appearance. She did not betray the slightest emotion on entering the court, but had evidently nerved herself for the very trying and unpleasant ordeal through which she had to pass. Accompanied by her mother, a widowed lady, and her brother, Dr. Dickinson, she stepped into the box, and her modesty of demeanour at once won the sympathy of all present. Her dress was of black silk, trimmed with lace and bugles, and she wore a black hat and feather, with lavender gloves; and without the slightest hesitation she gave the following evidence in support of the charge:

Mr Poland: Your name is Rebecca Kate Dickinson? – It is.

In June last were you living at Durnford, near Midhurst? – Yes.

With your mother and two unmarried sisters? – Yes.

Had you been living there since September of last year? – Yes, I had.

Had you previously all your life lived at New Park, near Lymington? – Yes.

From the time you were a child? – Yes, since I was six weeks old.

Now you are 22 years of age? – Yes, on the 10th of this month.

On Wednesday, the 16th June, had you arranged to go to Switzerland with your married sister. – Yes.

Was she the wife of Dr. Bagshaw, a physician practising at St. Leonards? – Yes.

Had you received a telegram on Wednesday with reference to your making arrangements for your journey? – Yes, on Wednesday afternoon.

Were you to join your brother-in-law, Dr. Bagshaw, in Wimpole-street on the following day (Thursday)? – Yes.

I believe your sister was to go from Hastings straight to Dover and wait there for you? – Yes.

On the Thursday afternoon did you start for your residence and go to the Midhurst Station? – Yes.

Did your sisters accompany you in your carriage? – Yes; my two sisters.

Did they see you into the train? – Yes.

With your luggage? – Yes, with my luggage.

Did you proceed from Midhurst to Petersfield to join the Portsmouth train? – Yes.

Had you at Petersfield to change carriages? – Yes.

And at that station did you get into a first-class compartment of the Portsmouth train? – Yes, with my luggage.

That was the three o'clock train from Portsmouth? – It was.

In the same compartment was there any one else? – No; it was an empty compartment.

Was your luggage put in with you? – Yes, it was.

That consisted of a portmanteau and three packages? – Yes; a bag and two other packages.

Had your portmanteau any address on it? – It was labelled "Dr. Bagshaw, Dover."

Where did you sit in the carriage? – In the corner, with my face to the engine.

On which side of the carriage? – The platform side.

Did you travel on in that way till you got to Liphook? Yes, I did.

The next station was Liss, and then Liphook? – Yes.

At Liphook did the defendant get into the carriage? – Yes.

Did you know him at all before? – No.

Whereabouts did he sit? – Right opposite, on the middle of the seat.

With his back to the engine? – Yes.

When you left the station at Liphook, was the window open? – Yes.

Were you facing the wind? – Yes.

After you had started did the defendant say anything to you? – He asked me if I felt the draught.

Just use the same language as far as you can. – He said "Don't you feel the draught?"

Did you make any reply? – Yes; I said, "No, thank you, I rather like it."

Did he say anything further? – Not then.

After some time, however, did he say anything more? – At Haslemere, the next station, he remarked upon the general prettiness of the line, and especially with reference to the station.

Did you make any reply? – I said it was very pretty – that it was the prettiest part of the branch from Petersfield to Midhurst.

Did any further conversation pass between you? – He said that Midhurst Station was a very convenient place for Goodwood time.

Had anything previously been said about Midhurst? – No.

What did you say about Midhurst? – I said we lived near the place.

Besides this was there anything said about Aldershot? – Yes.

What was that? – He said, "Have you ever been to Aldershot?"

And what did you say? – I said, "Yes; we had a brother in the Engineers stationed there, and only a short time ago we went to the steeplechase ball."

When you said that, what did he say? – I said my brother was away camping out from Aldershot, and he replied, "Pontooning?" and I remarked, "Yes, something of that sort."

What else did you say? – I said to him, "What is your regiment?" and he replied, "I don't belong to any regiment; I am on the staff at Aldershot."

What further? – I said, "At the South Camp?" and he remarked, "No, North Camp."

Can you tell when you had this conversation about Aldershot? – It was on the Liphook side of Guildford. I do not remember more than that.

Besides that, did you have any other conversation with him on that part of the journey? – Yes.

Did you talk about the Academy? – Yes.

And about the theatres? – Yes.

You have mentioned that your portmanteau was labelled "Dr. Bagshaw, Dover?" – Yes.

Was anything said about that? – Yes; he said, "I see your luggage is labelled Dover. Are you going there to-night?"

What did you say? – I replied, "Yes, and we cross to-morrow morning."

Was there anything more said about Dover and your crossing? – Yes; he asked me if I was going down alone.

What did you say? – I said, "No; I am to meet my brother-in-law in town."

Anything further? – He said, "You will have two hours to wait."

Yes; what else? – "You ought to stay a few days in town."

Anything further? – I said, "We have previously been to town at my brother's."

Was anything said as to how long you were going to be away? – Yes. He said, "How long will you be abroad?" and I replied, "A month." "Exactly a month?" he observed; and I said, " No, perhaps three weeks."

Did you continue conversing until you arrived at Woking? – Yes.

After leaving Liphook did you travel on to Haslemere, Witley, Godalming, and Guildford, to Woking? – Yes; we journeyed from Liphook to Woking.

That occupied about fifty minutes? – Yes; about that time.

When the train stopped at those stations did any one else get into your compartment? – No.

At Woking did anybody get in? – No.

Without changing your carriage, did you continue, taking your luggage with you? – Yes.

Up to Woking was there anything in the conversation or demeanour of the defendant to alarm you? – No, nothing.

And you still occupied the same seat? – Yes.

Where was the defendant sitting on leaving Woking? – He was sitting in the opposite corner to me.

Now, when you left Woking did you know where the train would next stop? – Yes.

What station? – Vauxhall.

What made you think that? – He had said so on the way.

After leaving Woking what did he say? – He said the train stopped at nearly every little station until we got to Woking, and then it went right through.

After leaving Woking what first occurred – what was said or done? – He said, "I suppose you don't often travel alone?"

What did you say? – "Never." He said, would I fix a time to be on the line again.

What did you say? – "No."

What did he say? – "You won't?"

What did you say? – I said nothing.

What next? – He said, "Will you give me your name?"

What did you say? – "I shan't."

What next? – "You will give me your name, that I may know when I hear."

What did you say? – I said "I shan't."

What next? – "Why not?" "Because I don't choose." I did not see any reason why I should.

What then? – He got up and shut the window. Anything more said about your name? – "Will you give me your Christian name?"

What did you say to that? – He sat beside me then, and I said nothing. He came to sit beside me after he shut the window.

Was there any division in the seat, or was it that kind of carriage where two can sit? – There were no arms.

One arm, and then room for two to sit? – Yes, I think it was one of those.

What did he do or say when he sat beside you? – He took hold of my hand, and said, "Will you give me your name?"

What did you say? – I said, "Get away; I won't have you so near," and pushed him off.

What did he say? – He said, "You're cross. Don't be cross."

Anything more? – He put his arm round my waist.

The Judge: Which arm? – The left arm, and held me in front with the other and kissed me.

Mr Poland: Where did he kiss you? – On my cheek.

More than once? – No; once only.

What did he say? – He said, "You must kiss me, darling."

The other arm was where? – He held me in front.

What did you do when he held you so and kissed you? – I pushed him off.

The Judge: He held you in front? – Yes.

The Judge: Round your waist, do you mean? – Yes.

The Judge: Where was he sitting then? – He was sitting beside me.

Mr Poland: What did you do then? – I got up and tried to ring the bell and call the guard.

Was the bell in the centre compartment? – Yes.

You tried to give the alarm by that? – Yes.

You found it would not act? – No; the glass was broken away.

Did he say anything? – He said, "Don't ring; don't ring; don't call the guard."

What happened next? – When he found it would not act, he forced me back in the same corner where I had been sitting, against the cushions.

Was he standing? – Standing. He kissed me on the lips many times. I was quite powerless. I could not move at all.

Did you do anything? – No; nothing.

What took place? – As soon as I could speak I said, "If I tell you my name will you get off?" He said nothing.

Did he prevent your speaking before? – He was kissing me.

What did he do then? – He sank down close in front of me.

What then? – I felt his hand underneath my dress.

Whereabouts? – Above my boot.

The Judge: He had not got you round the waist then? – No; I was quite free.

Mr Poland: Did you see what he was doing with the other hand? – I had an impression, nothing more.

Mr Poland: What was your impression?

The Judge: No, you must not ask that. You may ask her if she saw what he was doing with the other hand.

Witness: I had an impression; I cannot say I saw.

Mr Poland: What did you do? – I got up suddenly, and pushed the window with my elbow to see if I could break the glass.

Could you break it? – No, I couldn't.

What did you do then? – Got the window down, and put my head out and screamed.

Did you scream at all before you put your head out? – No, I think not.

What next? – I forced myself out with my elbows.

Outside? – Yes.

What did the defendant do? – He pulled me back, and I felt quite strangled.

The Judge: Did he put his arm around you? – I cannot tell what he did.

Mr Poland: Did he pull you back? – No, I screamed once more, fearing it was all I should be able to do.

What then? – I was twisting round the handle of the door at the same time.

Then? – I got out backwards.

What did you step out on to? – The footboard.

How did you hold on? – With my left hand I held on to the outside handle of the carriage. The door opened towards the engine.

The Judge: Was that the handle of the door? – No; it was the handle of the carriage.

The Judge: Was your arm through the window? – No; I was outside.

The Judge (surprised): Outside! Where was your other arm? – With my right hand I had hold of his arm.

The Judge: Did you take hold of him? – I think he caught hold of my hand. He held firmly to me by my arm while I was outside.

The Judge: How was he – standing or sitting? – I don't know.

The Judge: You can't recollect? – No.

The Judge: Did he say anything? – He said, "Get in, dear; get in, dear. You get in, and I will get out at the other door."

Mr Poland: What did you say? – I said, "If you leave go I shall fall." I had seen the other door locked at Guildford.

Was anything more said? – No; nothing more was said.

Did you travel on in this way outside the carriage for some distance? – Yes; I spoke to some gentlemen in the next compartment. I asked them, "How long is it before the train stops?" The wind was so strong that I could not hear what they said. I thought one of them said, "I don't know," but I was not sure about it.

Did the train travel on in this way until it was stopped at Esher? – Yes.

Did your hat blow off? – Yes, as soon as I got out.

Now, when the train was stopped, did any one come to your assistance? – Yes.

Did the defendant say anything? – He said, "Don't you say anything – you don't know the trouble you will get me into."

Anything more? – Yes. "Say you were frightened. I will give you my name or anything."

Did you say anything about it? – Nothing.

In what state were you at this time? – I was nearly exhausted.

Did you know how many minutes you had been outside the carriage? – No, I did not.

Then persons came to your assistance, and you were lifted off the carriage? – Yes.

Where was the defendant. Did he get out of the carriage? – Yes, so soon as it stopped.

Did they say anything in his presence when you got down? – They said, "What is the matter?"

And what did you say? – I replied, "That man will not leave me alone."

Did the defendant say anything to that? – No.

He was put into another compartment? – Yes.

Did you go back into the same compartment of the carriage in which you had been assaulted? – Yes, when they said "We have removed him; get in again."

What did you say? – I said, "I cannot go alone."

Did the Rev. Mr Brown get in? – Yes.

Into the same carriage with you? – Yes.

Then you travelled from Esher to Waterloo Station? – Yes.

And then you went into the inspector's office? – Yes, at the station.

Was the defendant brought there? – Yes.

Did you give your name and address? – Yes; I had previously given them to the guard.

I believe you said you would consult your brothers? – The defendant said, "I know your brother very well indeed."

Was that said at the station? – No, as we were going along.

Anything further? – Yes, "Give me his name and address, and I will write to him."

What reply did you make? – "You may do what you choose."

Did you give him your address? – No.

I believe you left the station with the Rev. Mr Brown? – Yes.

Where did you go? – To my brother's house, in Chesterfield-street, Mayfair.

On the following day did you go with your brother to Guildford? – Yes, on the following morning. We started at half-past nine o'clock.

And there your brother obtained a warrant for the arrest of the defendant? – Yes.

Did some of the railway people go to Guildford with you? – Yes; a porter.

The Judge then proceeded to sum up, as follows: Gentlemen of the jury, if I did not knew how thoughtless people are who are not responsible for giving decisions, I should have been more annoyed than I have been at the interruptions that have taken place in this court to-day. You will remember that you are no longer a part of the public audience, but are people who have a grave responsibility cast upon you, and that is, nor to follow your own inclinations, not to give way to your sympathies, but to decide according to the law. It was well, therefore, for those who are not responsible to applaud when it was said that an attempt to seduce a young and inno-cent girl was as bad a criminal assault upon her; but even if you shared those sentiments – which if you inquired carefully you would not – you would have no right now to act on them. You have only to answer the questions I shall put to you as you really believe they ought to be answered; and even though you should not that is answering them a result will be arrived at which your own feelings will sympathise with, still you must only answer the questions truly, because you are now become a part of the tribunal which is to administer the criminal law of this country. That tri-bunal consists not of you only, but of me also, and we each have our part of the responsibility. I have now to tell you the questions you must answer me, and I will tell you that if you answer them in one way you are bound to convict the prisoner, and if you answer them the other way you will acquit him. You have simply to obey what I tell you is the law, and I have nothing to do with the answers you give to the questions that I put to you. You are alone responsible for the answers you may give, but you are to answer the questions, not according to your wishes, but as you conscientiously believe the truth requires. Forget, therefore, all you have heard of expressions of opinions from the people who are not responsible, and think of your own responsibility, which is that you should give a most calm, dispassionate, and careful consideration to the evidence in this case, and give the answers which you honestly consider ought to be given. The defendant at the bar is first charged with an assault upon this young lady, and if, with a very strong feeling in his mind, he even laid his hand on her without her consent, that is an assault; but he is farther charged under a statute with an indecent assault. The statute says it shall be a crime or an offence to commit an indecent assault. I have to define that particular law, and the definition I give you is this: if any man assaults a female, and does it in such a way that men of ordinary right mind and feeling would say that it is an indecent way, then you should find that it is an indecent assault. I cannot lay down to you as law what is or is not indecent. I say that that is indecent which all ordinary men of right and wholesome feeling would say is indecent. I will endeavour to explain that in language which you cannot mistake. It is said that the defendant here took this young lady round the waist, that he kissed her on the mouth, and took other liberties, all that being against her will. Therefore if you are satisfied that he did that, you can have no further doubt about his having been guilty of an indecent offence. I say to you, as I said to the grand jury, that even though you should suppose he only kissed her, you would have to consider what is the nature of the kiss which he gives. It is for you to decide. I believe all men will say that the kiss of a father to his daughter is not an indecent thing: it is the most holy endearment that can pass. If boys at any time of festivity were with some violence to kiss a girl, as at Christmas-time, if they did it without her consent, it would be an assault, but do you think that any person of right feeling would say it was indecent? They would say it is violent, but not indecent. But if a man kiss a young female against her will, with some further intent, do you or do you not say that people of right minds and feeling would come to the opinion that that is an indecent thing? If you believe that that is an indecent thing to do, and that all people of right mind and feeling would so regard it, then I tell you that such a kiss is indecent: if you believe otherwise, then it is not. You must say, first, whether he has been guilty of an assault; and, secondly, whether that assault was an indecent assault. You have heard the powerful counsel who has addressed you, who has hardly combated what he believes will be your decision on that – that he is guilty of an indecent assault. Then comes another accusation which is of the highest importance in this matter. The defendant is charged under a section of the statute with an assault with intent to commit a felony. Under that statute it is an offence to assault a person with intent to rob, or to assault a female with intent to violate her. The defendant is indicted for assaulting the prosecutrix with intent to violate her. I wish you most carefully to attend to what I am about to say. In my opinion it is not correct to say that the question is whether he had determined to stop if he found her resistance to go beyond a certain point. The question is whether he intended to violate her, and he cannot be found guilty of that offence unless you are of opinion, not that he would have had it in his mind afterwards, but that he had it in his mind sometime before she saved herself, notwithstanding all the resistance she made or might make. How are you to find out what was in his mind? How are you to tell any man's mind? Only by a careful consideration of what he did and of what he said, or of both, inasmuch as he never said he did intend to force her to the last extremity, notwithstanding all her resistance, he has said the contrary, you are left to infer what was in his mind mainly from what he did, and I shall point out to you the facts which will tell against him and those which tell for him. I must tell you first what is the regard to your mode of interpreting facts. Here it is not for you to do as you like, but to act according to the law, and the law is that the jury, in regard to any doubtful fact, shall give to it the most merciful interpretation as concerning the prisoner. If you have no doubt about the meaning of the attack, act on that conviction; but if you have any doubt as to the meaning of any particular evidence, it is your duty to give the most indulgent inter-pretation of it in favour of the prisoner. If you have no doubt you must give effect to your conviction, even though it be to the destruction of the prisoner. I have called attention to your duty because no one can fail to see that there must be a strong sym-pathy in favour of the young lady who was before you, and that it requires the greatest care on the part of every one of us to act calmly and dispassionately, and not allow ourselves to be led away. This young lady entered a compartment of a railway car-riage and travelled for a time alone. Eventually the defendant got into a compartment with her and was alone with her. You have seen them both. She is on the point of being twenty-two years of age. The age of the defendant has been stated to be some-where towards fifty. You can judge for yourselves, and certainly he is a far older person than she is. The defendant got in at Liphook, and began a conversation with her. She did not refuse to converse with him, but, on the contrary, conversed with him in a manner, of which you will have to say whether there was any incitement in it, anything wrong in it, anything which the most innocent and virtuous girl might not carry on with a man who appeared respectable, and whose demeanour towards her was respectful, That conversation was carried on from Liphook to Woking, nearly an hour, on different subjects, and she says that until they arrived at Woking there had been nothing wrong, nothing that she could complain of. That upon which your opinion is to be founded happened between Woking and the time when she was outside the carriage. I cannot think that anything done after she was outside can help you at all. Whatever intention he had had, that act of hers put an end to it. What he did afterwards was to prevent the terrible result of his former misconduct, and he was attempting honestly to save her. That is her own view. It would be a mon-strous thing to conceive that after what he had done he would not do all he could to save the life of an innocent woman. Up to the time of reaching Woking he was sit-ting opposite to her: but soon after leaving Woking, when near the Dramatic College, he said something to her in which there was no offence, and now you come to this scene. He pulled up the window, and you will have to consider what was the mean-ing of that. On the one side it is said that he had made up his mind she would resist him and scream, and that he shut it to prevent her being heard. Another suggestion is that if he did not think she would scream he thought he ought not to have the win-dow open while such a transaction was going on as he contemplated. That is a fact against him, and you must put the true construction upon it. The prosecutrix tells us,

"He asked if I could fix a time to be on the line again?" How does that strike you? Is it an endeavour to induce her to enter into such familiar relations with him that if he could not persuade her to submit on this occasion he might at some future time? She says, "He then asked me to give him my name, and I said 'I shan't'." At that time he was holding her hand, having moved so as to sit next her. You must ask yourselves whether that was not an endeavour to her into such relations with him that if she should not consent between Woking and London she might consent at some future time. That would be the beginning of a seduction. He continued to converse with her, and used terms of endearment, saying, "You must kiss me, darling. Ask yourselves when a man uses back an expression as that to a girl against her will, whether an indecent assault is not already committed. He pulled her towards him with his left arm, and his right arm was round her. She then pushed him off. Do you think he had made up his mind to use irresistible force, notwithstanding all she might do to the contrary? If he had, how do you think she was able to get away from him? or do you think that, wicked and abominable as his conduct was, he was hesitating then, and that, considering their relative strength – the inference is that he was a wicked man and an indecent man, but that he was a hesitating man and that he had not made up his mind to that extremity of violence which is necessary to constitute an intention to violate. When she got up to reach the bell he leaned towards the bell and said, "Don't ring." He would be rather behind her, but on her right side, and he must have thrown her back in her place or pulled her back from behind. She was then in a slanting position, and she explains that the defendant was leaning over her so as to have the weight of his chest or body upon her. She cannot tell what he did next, only she knows that she was powerless. One would suppose that his arm was over her in some way so that his weight would of itself render her powerless, but that is not quite what her words represent. Looking to the graver charge, if he had intended to force her, you must consider what was his advantage then. He had her down on the seat, and was over her, and you must consider whether he might not have got more over her. At that moment the prosecutrix appears to have thought she could persuade him to desist, and she said "If I satisfy you by giving you my name will you desist? Perhaps intending to mislead him by the idea that he might have some other opportunity. She says he then sank upon his knees, and she felt his hand upon her stocking. Do you think she can be mistaken in this? If not, it must be obvious that that was an indecent assault, and that would show to a great extent what he must then have desired and hoped – if not more – that he could induce her, or force her, or half induce and half force her, to yield herself to his will. You must ask yourselves whether he did not intend to use all the force of which he was master, and brutal violence, to effect his purpose, notwithstanding all the resistance she could make. If he had intended that, would he not have been putting his hand on her mouth, or holding her down with both hands instead of one? Do you think he could have left her entirely free? At that moment, by an almost miraculous act of courage and presence of mind, she jumps up.

Her position is such that she can jump up. You must ask yourselves what is the fair and just conclusion from that. Do you think, looking to the circumstances, that at that moment he had made up his mind to go to every length? Do you think the prosecutrix could have so far escaped as to stand up and open the window if he had not been, although wicked, yet hesitating? She describes how she got out, and says he attempted to pull her back. Did he do so with any intent except to prevent her screaming, and so exposing what he had done? She says she felt strangled, he must have pulled her by her dress, which, if it caught about the throat, would make her feel as if nearly strangled. That looks more like the act of a man preventing her going further than if at that time he intended to proceed with his worst intentions. When he said, "If you leave go I shall fall," what he said in reply shows that he had given up the intention of ill-using her. He said, "Come in, and I will get out at the other door." I think it very unlikely that she should have been calm enough at that moment to remember that the other door had been locked at Guildford; she has probably remembered that since, but there is no indication that the defendant knew it was locked. As to the defendant's dress having been disarranged, I should have advised you not to act upon the evidence of the guard alone, because he was entirely wrong as to the defendant standing on the gravel, and he is a man without such habits of accuracy as to be sure of conveying the exact truth; but other gentlemen testify to the same fact, and if you believe that his dress was disarranged then you must conclude that his intention was not to seduce at some future time, but then and there. You must bear in mind the relative strength of the two parties, and the fact that she twice escaped from him. If he had made up his mind to overcome any resistance, however brutal the force that might be necessary, then he was guilty of an assault with intent. If you believe his idea was to induce her, however reluctantly, to yield, that does not amount to an assault with intent, and you ought not to find him guilty on the first count.

You must now bring your intelligence to bear upon the evidence without any feeling of passion, and ask yourselves are you satisfied that he had the worst intent? If you are you, must find him guilty; if you think that, although a wicked and hesitating man you have some doubts about the intent, you ought to say he is guilty of the crime, and that he is guilty of an indecent assault, of which you can have little doubt. Finally, there is one thing more important than that a prisoner should be convicted or acquitted, and that is that a jury constituting a great part of the criminal administration of this country should be absolutely honest. Do not think therefore of what the punishment may be in one case or the other. With that you have nothing to do. Exercise your minds and intellect, and not your passions and your feeling, and say what are the right answers to the questions I have put.

The jury, at twenty-five minutes past five, returned into court, when their names were called over and the defendant stood forward to receive their verdict.

Mr Avory: Have you all agreed upon your verdict? – Yes, sir.

Do you find the prisoner, Valentine Baker, guilty or not guilty of criminally assaulting Rebecca Kate Dickinson?

The Foreman: Not guilty. (Applause.)

Mr Avory: Do you find him guilty or not guilty of an indecent assault?

The Foreman: We find him guilty of that.

Mr Serjeant Ballantine: I wish to call your lordship's attention to the position of the defendant and to call witnesses on his behalf I desire also to show what the consequences of this decision will be.

The Judge: Very well; call your witnesses.

Sir Richard Airey, Adjutant-General to the Forces, examined by Mr Serjeant Ballantine: How long have you known Colonel Baker? – Upwards of twenty years now; first in the Crimea, where he commanded the escort of the Commander-in-Chief. I know him intimately well, and have seen him every day. I have watched his career with great interest and very great admiration. He has devoted all his energies to his profession of a soldier, by which means he has risen to high rank and the highest reputation as a cavalry officer; indeed, he is one of the army's greatest ornaments.

I believe he served during the Caffre war, also in India, and elsewhere, and that he marched his troops from the East to join the army in the Crimea? – I believe so. I have known him in my position as Adjutant-General. Every officer comes more or less under my observation, and of Colonel Baker I may say I have never known anything in his conduct that was discreditable or against his honour.

Sir Thomas Steele, called and examined by Mr Serjeant Ballantine: What is your rank in the army? – I am a Lieutenant-General, and command the forces at Aldershot.

Are you well acquainted with Colonel Baker? – Yes.

Throughout the whole of his public career? – Yes.

You have heard the account given of him by Sir Richard Airey? – No ; I was not able to hear what Sir Richard said.

What is your opinion of Colonel Baker? – I consider him one of the most valuable cavalry officers that we have. He is a man of the greatest energy, and possesses all the qualifications of an officer in every point of view. He is, indeed, as good a soldier as any that her Majesty has.

Has he always been a man who, with reference to his character, has been honourable with his brother officers. Has his conduct always been irreproachable? – Oh yes, quite, as far as I know.

The Judge then proceeded to pass the sentence of the law.

His Lordship, in a loud and clear tone, said: Prisoner at the bar – When this story was first published, a thrill as of dishonour went throughout the country when it was told that a young and innocent girl travelling by the ordinary conveyance of this country had been obliged to risk her life in order to save herself from a gross outrage. Every part of society, every householder in this kingdom felt as if they had themselves received a personal injury; and when they heard that her assailant was a gentleman, a soldier, and an officer – an officer high in command – a thrill of horror, if not of disgust, went through them. Notwithstanding you have had, what everybody must admit to be a calm and dispassionate trial, the jury, about whom some fear was expressed, have known how to discriminate between the charges made against you, and have most honestly, most fearlessly, and most properly absolved you from the heaviest part of the charge, but have found you guilty of that which no man who has heard this case can doubt. Now, with regard to this young lady, I have heard it said that she ought not to have remained in a railway carriage alone for such a time with a man. It seems to me that such a suggestion about the state of society in this country does not exist in any part of it. It seems to suggest that a defenceless woman in a public conveyance in this country, if she is alone with a man, may expect to suffer outrage from him. Such, I believe, does not exist in truth in any part of society, from the highest to the lowest. It may be there are people who now and then give way to vile passion, but this is not a characteristic of this country, and I wholly deny there is anything wrong in a woman, however young, travelling alone in a railway carriage with a man who appears to be respectable. If it were otherwise, I say that the law would with outstretched arm put an end to everything of the kind, and that women generally, however unprotected, are safe. It has been further suggested that this young lady was wrong in entering into a prolonged conversation with you, who, up to that time,, were a stranger to her. I cannot agree to that. It seems to me that it suggests rather a prurient fear than it does that feeling of self-respect and safety which every innocent woman in this country has in her heart. It may be suggested that the libertine outrage which you committed upon her has defiled her. I say again distinctly it has not. She walks and goes from this court as pure, as innocent, as undefiled as ever she was – (applause) – nay, more, the courage she has displayed has added a ray of glory to her youth, her innocence, and her beauty. When I say what I have already pointed out, that you were not only of the rank of a gentlemen of position, but that you were an officer – an officer high in command – it seems to me that, of all the people in the train on that day, you were the last who ought to have been expected to do anything but absolutely to protect a defenceless woman – I say advisedly, in the presence of all here, that even if a girl so young had behaved herself with imprudence or indiscretion, it was nothing but your duty – the manly duty of a person in your position and of your age – to have protected her, even against herself; but there is nothing from the beginning to the end in your conduct which can palliate or excuse, in the slightest degree, that most dishonourable conduct towards the prosecutrix in the crime you committed; therefore, as I say, I can see no palliation whatever. It is, when I think of her, when I think of you, and of the circumstance itself, a crime as bad as it can be, but there are circumstances of which the law always takes notice, and of which I am bound to take notice in the discharge of my duty. It seems to me, considering the character you have received – it seems to me that this was a sudden outrage of wickedness on your part. I have heard from the highest military authorities – from two of the first officers in the army – not only of what your position is as a soldier, but I have heard that up to this fatal day they believed you to be a honourable man. Yours is not the case of a person born to a high position – you have attained the high rank you hold and the high estimation in which you are held as an officer by your own individual exertions. I ought not to forget either that you have by brilliant services made your country, so far as you have been a soldier, indebted to you. I therefore have to treat this as a wicked outrage – nay, more, believe me when I say it was a dishonourable, a cowardly outrage; nay, trust me if I think that you, in your future life, will pass that judgment upon yourself. Notwithstanding that I have to consider it was a sudden outrage, and it was a sudden outrage on the part of a man who up to this time has held an honourable character by his own exertions, yet if the jury had found you guilty of the greater charge I should have thought It my duty to pass upon you the fall sentence of the law in all its severity. I should most certainly have imprisoned you, and kept you to hard labour for two years, which is the heaviest punishment the law allows; but the jury have rightly and truly found you had not made up your mind to the degree of wickedness. You were, as I have said, a hesitating man, although you acted wickedly towards the young lady. It seems to me that if I were to pass upon you a sentence carrying with it all the personal degradation, all the physical degradation, which follows from the ordinary sentences, I should be submitting you to a punishment which in your case would be far greater than it would be to other persons who might be guilty of the same offence. I cannot but think that if I submit you to what I call the physical degradation of a jail it would be an absolute torture to you from day to day – it would prevent you, even by long repentance and even by any amount of future service, from any way doing away or re-instating yourself in the eyes of your country.

I therefore purpose not to submit you to those physical indignities which to you would be so terrible, hoping that by long repentance on your part, and in some distant day, you may again, although I cannot answer for it, not knowing what the rules of your service are, but in hopes that, by long repentance and at some distant day you may be allowed by some brilliant service – of which you are undoubtedly capable – to wipe out the injury which you have done to your country. (Applause.) The sentence which I shall pass upon you will be a severe one; but I hope that it will save you from that absolute destruction which another sentence would impose. The sentence I pass is that you be imprisoned in the common gaol of this county, in such a way as shall not subject you to the physical degradations of which I speak, for twelve calendar months; that you be fined £500, or be further imprisoned until you pay that fine; and that you pay the costs of the prosecution, and be imprisoned for a further time not exceeding three months until you have paid those costs.

The prisoner then shook hands with several of his friends who stood beside him in the dock, and proceeded to the cells below, and the court rapidly cleared.

Jabez Balfour

"When in difficulty start a new company."

Jabez Balfour has the unsavoury distinction of being probably the biggest fraudster in British history. He grew up a sober, high-minded household and, on the face of it, the Liberator Building Society, which by the age of forty had made him one of the richest men in the country, was a faithful reflection of his family's radical, dissenting background. It presented itself as an institution that allowed honest hard-working families to buy their own homes, and thus escape the tyranny of unscrupulous landlords and shoddy rented accommodation. Unfortunately, it evolved into a vehicle to ensure that Jabez could continue to live in the manner to which he had become accustomed. He may have paid lip service to non-conformist values, such as temperance, but this did not stop him from, for instance, filling his cellars with the best French champagne money could buy.

This dissonance was eventually resolved once an economic downturn, and a subsequent dip in profits, prompted an unprecedented curiosity as to how Balfour's business was actually run. Those possessed by this desire to know more were soon horrified by what they found. The company was buoyed only by a mixture of greed, bluster and gross dishonesty, all of which emanated from Balfour's person. At a stroke, many hundreds of people were left near destitute, a nasty foretaste of the impact of some of the financial scandals that have so disfigured lives in recent years.

25 February 1916
Jabez Spencer Balfour
Story of the "Liberator"

The report of the death of Jabez Spencer Balfour, announced in our later editions yesterday, recalls memories of the cruellest financial disaster of this generation. The name of the "Liberator" is still an abomination in thousands of homes. The interest excited by the news of Balfour's death is a tribute to one of the most grandiose of swindlers such as he himself would have loved. To tell the story of his career adequately would require Defoe's genius for detail and for the nuances of rascality. But the plainest version is exciting.

Jabez Spencer Balfour was born in 1842, and brought up in the odour of sanctity and total abstinence. His father had been a marine store dealer, and subsequently was a messenger of the House of Commons. But he was also employed on evangelical work and total abstinence propaganda, in which his wife was actively associated. Mrs Clara Lucas Balfour used to write fiction and verse for the "Temperance Weekly Journal", edited by the Rev. Jabez Burns. From that gentleman Balfour the younger derived his first name. The son of the Rev. Jabez, the Rev. Dawson Burns, married Jabez Balfour's sister. The connection is of importance, as throughout his career Jabez made great play with appeals to those interested in religious and total abstinence societies. He was a master in the exploitation of philanthropic finance and financial philanthropy.

Such were the moral influences of Jabez Balfour's youth. His business training was acquired in the office of a Parliamentary agent. But, like other great men, he matured early. He was only 25 when the Liberator Building Society was introduced to an admiring world. We must go back a little. A more cautious man than Jabez Balfour might have thought the moment bad for such a scheme. Only the year before a number of similar societies known as the Alliance Group, with which his brother-in-law and future colleague, the Rev Dawson Burns, was associated, and which made a special appeal to the small investor who was also a total abstainer, had gone to hopeless ruin. There was a touch of greatness in Jabez Balfour's decision that the very same class could be brought to support another and more pretentions scheme of the same kind. Hence the Liberator.

The very name was a piece of cunning typical of the ways of philanthropic finance. Its ostensible explanation is to be found in the motto of the society, "Libera sedes liberum facit", a free home makes a free man. But there is no doubt that the name was chosen to catch the support of ardent Nonconformists by suggesting a connection which did not exist with the Liberation Society. An appeal was made to Nonconformist ministers and those associated with total abstinence propaganda to promote the interests of the Liberator. In its first year they received 1 per cent. commission on the shares and deposits, and subsequently ½ per cent., and in the end a round sum of £141,000 was paid in this way.

A good many swindlers have known how to draw their profit from the religious and moral instincts of mankind. But none was ever more successful than Balfour. When the Liberator began to feel itself established, and moved into new offices, his board passed this resolution:

That on the occasion of taking possession this day of our new premises, the directors desire to record their own sense of thankfulness for the prosperity with which, as they believe, God has hitherto blessed their efforts in the establishment of this business.

He was careful in maintaining an air of devotion. He was the most regular of worshippers at chapel. The appeals of religion always found his purse open. To the militant Nonconformist's mind he had also the supreme virtue – bitter hostility to the Established Church. On the very eve of his downfall he was a valued speaker at anti-Church meetings. Here is a glimpse of him at the 1892 assembly of the Liberation Society.

The next speaker was Mr J, Spencer Balfour, who, if I am not mistaken, is the son of Clara Lucas Balfour, once a popular writer of stories. He is florid, portly, more than middle-aged; and it looked at first as if he was to miss fire. His speech was an indictment of the Church of England clergy for their neglect of country parishes, and he went over the rates of wages and the prospects of agricultural labourers till he was brought to book by "Question" shouted from the gallery. Mr Balfour had good cause to bless the interrupter, for he warmed up immediately, and in a most telling way compared the questions with which parsons were actually concerned, and those about which they had never troubled themselves. I am not sure but that this was the most effective of all the speeches. It roused the meeting to a high pitch of enthusiasm.

Politics also had his attention, and from the last days of Disraeli to the last days of Gladstone he was one of the most effective platform speakers of the Radicals. It is indeed understood that he expected high office in the Gladstone Government of '92. The post to which he aspired was that of Postmaster-General, and when he found that Mr Gladstone had other views he declared that "the Liberal party would never see the colour of his money again". It is fair to add that after the smash every penny of his subscriptions to the party, £700 in all, was returned to the Liberator Relief Fund. He entered Parliament as member for Tamworth in 1880, and sat till 1885. After some defeats he was returned for Burnley in 1889, and held the seat by a large majority in 1892, just before his ruin. He was also the first Mayor of Croydon, where he had a large house, and for some time his portrait adorned the Croydon Council Chamber.

The original appeal of the Liberator Building Society was based upon the claim that, above all things, it was safe. To the very eve of the disaster the directors pretended that its operations were of the ordinary building society character. But less than ten years after the foundation of the Liberator allied companies began to come into existence, the operations of which were far more ambitious. It may be said that the hard-earned savings of the Liberator members were used to support grandiose speculative schemes of land development and building over which no one exercised control, and which at the best were reckless, and at the worst fraudulent.

The secret of the finance of Jabez Balfour was, "When in difficulty start a new company." Dependent upon the Liberator there sprang up a series of companies of which nobody but Balfour himself seemed to have any control. The other directors, the officials, the shareholders, the depositors bowed to Balfour's will. A certain builder became, under his ægis, involved in colossal enterprises, including the erection of the huge blocks which are now the Hotel Cecil and Whitehall Court. When he failed his schemes had involved the Liberator to the extent of £2,000,000. This is not the place for a complete account of the Liberator schemes, but it may be said that while disaster followed disaster the directors throve. From the seven leading companies of the group Balfour and his colleagues received as remuneration £178,534. The final collapse involved some £7,000,000 of capital.

Rarely has a financial failure spread such misery. The shareholders and depositors of the Liberator were almost entirely of the lower middle and middle classes, and had trusted their whole resources to Balfour's grip. Thousands were absolutely penniless and had to seek relief from charitable sources.

He was cunning to the last. When the crash came and his tools, dupes, or confederates, had to face exposure, Jabez Balfour was safe out of the country. There was then no extradition treaty between England and the Argentine Republic, and to the Argentine Jabez fled. He was for some time lost to sight, and the official description issued in hope of his apprehension has interest now:

Jabez Spencer Balfour, late Member of Parliament, absconded, charged with fraud as director of a public company, and obtaining money by false pretences. Sums charged in warrants, £20.000. Balfour believed to be residing in Buenos Ayres. Age, 50, looks 55: height. 5ft 6in: broad shoulders: very corpulent: hair dark, turning grey, parted centre, thin top of head: eyebrows dark, nose short: face full: complexion florid; straggling beard: dark, slight whiskers, turning grey: dark, slight moustache: appearance of having weak legs: usually dressed in dark jacket; gentlemanly appearance.

After some time London learnt that a gentleman just returned from Argentina "recognised some weeks ago Jabez Spencer Balfour while riding in the public Gallera. Balfour was then living in semi-Sultanic luxury in a fine hacienda at Flores. According to report he is engaged in various enterprises, and is credited with having considerably added to his banker's balance during his stay in Argentina."

The diplomacy of Lord Rosebery persuaded the authorities of the Argentine to surrender the much-wanted man, and on 15 January 1894, Jabez Spencer Balfour was arrested at Salta, in the province of Sujury, where he had purchased a brewery. On 28 November, after a trial of twenty-four days, Mr Justice Bruce sentenced him to fourteen years' penal servitude. So he vanished. He was released in 1906, and has since lived in obscurity, his last place of residence having been in Ladbroke-grove, W., where he and his wife occupied apartments.

Silvio Berlusconi

"They were cheerful, elegant dinners."

Any one of the numerous financial and sexual scandals in which Silvio Berlusconi, the cruise-ship crooner turned media magnate and politician, became embroiled would have been sufficient to destroy another figure. But the perma-tanned Berlusconi always seemed to emerge, if not stronger, then at least unbowed. He was "the Jesus Christ of politics", he claimed, "I am a patient victim, I put up with everyone, I sacrifice myself for everyone." It was a charge of tax fraud that finally put paid to one of the most colourful careers in world politics, but his infamous 2011 Bunga Bunga parties are what will forever define him in the eyes of the British public. He was still prime minister at the time that the "cheerful, elegant dinners" took place, and despite the crass and often lascivious buffoonery for which he had become famous – as well as the fact that two years previously his ex-wife had written an open letter telling the world that she could not "remain with a man who consorts with minors" and who "is not well" – it was still a shock. He is currently facing several court cases, and previous convictions mean that he is, for the moment at least, banned from holding public office.

16 March 2011
Berlusconi and "Ruby" shared 13 sex acts, say Italian prosecutors
By our foreign staff

Silvio Berlusconi allegedly had 13 "sexual acts" with under-age prostitute Karima El Mahroug at his villa near Milan last year.

In a report by prosecutors, who ended their investigation yesterday, it is alleged that Mr Berlusconi's parties began with dinner and ended with the prime minister selecting a sex partner, or partners. The Italian prime minister, 74, is accused of having sex with Miss El Mahroug, a Moroccan belly-dancer known as Ruby the Heart Stealer, when she was aged 17. He will face trial on 6 April. The report also recommended that three friends of Mr Berlusconi face trial for procuring prostitutes on his behalf.

Nicole Minetti, a regional councillor in Lombardy; Emilio Fede, a television executive and Lele Mora, a talent scout, are all accused of procuring the sexual services of Miss El Mahroug and 32 other women. All three have denied the allegations.

The prosecutors allege that the aides acted together in a criminal scheme to induce Miss El Mahroug into prostitution.

In an eight-page document the prosecutors indicate the alleged offence of exploiting an under-age prostitute took place between September 2009, when Ruby was aged just 16, and May 2010. The timing implies that the prosecutors believe Miss El Mahroug was being groomed from the moment she was first noticed at a beauty contest in Sicily, long before she attended what investigators believe was her first dinner in Mr Berlusconi's Arcore mansion on 14 February last year.

The document says that Miss El Mahroug "committed sexual acts with Silvio Berlusconi, for payment in cash and other compensation, at his residence" on 13 occasions from 14 February to 2 May 2010. According to the document, the evenings proceeded in three phases. Dinner was followed by erotic dancing, dubbed "bunga, bunga". During this phase, the women were either masked, did a striptease or erotic dance.

The evening ended when Mr Berlusconi chose "one or more girls with whom to spend a night of intimate relations, people who were paid sums of cash, or other compensation beyond what was given to the other participants".

The document alleges that Miss Minetti arranged payments to the women, while Mr Mora and Mr Fede "identified young women disposed to prostitute themselves in the Arcore residence of Silvio Berlusconi".

Both Mr Berlusconi and Miss El Mahroug deny that they had a sexual relationship.

17 March 2011

Berlusconi: even a rascal like me does not have the stamina for 33 women

By Nick Squires in Rome

Silvio Berlusconi has ridiculed claims by Italian prosecutors that he paid 33 women for sexual favours in a matter of months, saying he would need the stamina of a man four decades younger to maintain such a vigorous private life.

The Italian prime minister, who will stand trial on 6 April on charges of having intercourse with an underage prostitute and abuse of office, offered an angry defence against the accusations, contained in court documents released on Tuesday.

"I'm 74 years old and even though I may be a bit of a rascal . . . 33 girls in two months seems to me too much even for a 30-year-old."

He condemned investigators for citing the women in their dossier because "for the rest of their lives they will be branded with an indelible label: prostitute".

He claimed to have a long-standing "girlfriend" who, he said, would never have allowed him to behave in such a way. He did not name the woman. "If I'd done everything they say I've done, she'd have gouged my eyes out. And I can tell you, she has very long finger nails." He said he had paid for dentistry bills, university tuition fees and medical treatment on behalf of his female friends, but that he did so out of personal generosity, seeking nothing in return. "I'm a walking charity," he said. "I'm happy to be able to do it."

He made the remarks to *La Repubblica*, a left-leaning national newspaper that has repeatedly called for his resignation over the scandal. Prosecutors have accused the 33 women of prostituting themselves for money, jewellery and other gifts with the billionaire tycoon, who denies all the allegations.

Of the 33 women, about a dozen have not been publicly linked to Mr Berlusconi before. They include Ludovica Leoni, 23, a showgirl and reality TV contestant; Ambra Battilana, 18, who is of mixed Italian-Philippine heritage and was last year crowned Miss Piedmont; and Raffaella Fico, 22, a men's magazine model and former contestant on Italy's version of *Big Brother*, who two years ago auctioned her virginity for €1m (£870,000).

She was also linked to Cristiano Ronaldo, the footballer in 2009.

Prosecutors say the women took part in "bunga bunga" orgies at Mr Berlusconi's imposing residence at Arcore, near Milan, involving "masks, stripteases and erotic dances".

The prime minister denied paying the women for sexual intercourse, saying they simply attended private dinners held at his mansion.

"They were cheerful, elegant dinners. The women went for a little dance in the disco – on their own because I've never liked dancing. Nothing more than that. I will go on television to explain everything, to defend myself and these women."

He promised to turn up for every hearing in the four trials in which he is now involved. The three others involve allegations of corruption, bribery and tax fraud relating to companies in his media empire.

Conrad Black

"Humility is a good quality, though it can be overdone."

14 July 2007
Black, the fraudster
Tycoon faces 15 years' jail, financial ruin and threat to peerage

Conrad Black, the former media tycoon, last night faced years in jail after an American jury found him guilty of criminal fraud and obstructing justice.

The Canadian-born peer, once the head of the world's third largest newspaper group, which included the *Daily Telegraph*, was cleared of nine other charges, including racketeering. His lawyers said he would appeal.

Prosecutors said he could expect to go to jail for at least 15 years, though the potential sentence is more than twice that.

He could also be forced to pay back millions of dollars in fines and forfeitures to reimburse shareholders in the company he once controlled. Hollinger International, now called the Sun-Times Media Group, is suing him for $540m over alleged negligence, breach of contract and "unjust enrichment".

His conviction prompted the Conservatives to disown him by removing the whip in the House of Lords and last night MPs called for him to be stripped of his peerage. Black's elevation to the Lords in 2001 was the high point of a glittering financial career. When he took his seat, he was introduced by Margaret Thatcher.

But his spectacular fall from grace was complete at the end of a four-month trial in which he was compared to a bank robber who "lied and stole and betrayed the trust of thousands of shareholders".

Prosecutors said he and three others stole millions in a scheme that involved falsifying documents and lying to shareholders to cover it up.

The jury in Chicago, which took almost a fortnight to consider its verdicts, heard a tale of greed, lavish living and corporate intrigue during a trial likened to a circus, a soap opera and a re-run of *Citizen Kane*.

Throughout, Black maintained a lofty disdain for the proceedings, which he once called a "toilet seat" hanging around prosecutors' necks. His defence team did not put him on the stand to give evidence on his own behalf.

His composure deserted him towards the end of the hearing when he gesticulated angrily at reporters.

His wife, Barbara Amiel, herself a journalist, called her colleagues covering the trial "vermin".

Black left court holding the hands of his wife and his daughter, Alana, 25. He made no comment.

His lawyer, Edward Greenspan, said: "He came here to face 13 counts. Conrad Black was acquitted of all the central charges. We intend to appeal. We disagree with the government's position on sentencing. We believe, based on the convictions, the sentences are far less."

Black, 62, was charged after an investigation into his activities at Hollinger International in 2004 concluded that he and other executives oversaw a "corporate kleptocracy."

He was also accused of using the company as a "piggy bank" to fund his billionaire lifestyle.

Accommodation, personal staff, food, opera tickets, holidays, club membership fees, restaurant bills, jogging attire and even charity donations were charged to the company.

But his undoing was not the use of a private jet to travel on holiday to Bora Bora or the houses in London, New York and Palm Beach – he was acquitted of improperly using company money to subsidise his lifestyle.

He was brought down by a device known as a "non-compete fee", under which he paid himself and his co-defendants for agreeing not to compete with themselves. They received the money from a subsidiary of their own company that owned only one paper and was in the process of selling it. Black and his cohorts kept the money without passing it on to his company shareholders.

Of the total £3.2m that was stolen from the company, Black personally received £1.7m, although his lawyer claimed the figure was £1.4m.

One of those who benefited was David Radler, Black's right-hand man for most of his meteoric rise up the corporate ladder. But Radler turned against him and gave evidence for the prosecution in a deal under which he pleaded guilty in exchange for up to 29 months in jail.

Three other Hollinger executives, Jack Boultbee, 64, former chief financial officer, Peter Atkinson, 60, former vice-president and Mark Kipnis, 59, a lawyer, were all found guilty of the same fraud charges as Black. They each face up to 15 years in prison.

Black was additionally found guilty of obstructing justice by removing files from his office in Toronto to stop them falling into the hands of the authorities. A CCTV camera filmed him doing so.

When the first guilty verdict was read out, Black bowed his head and looked pale. He quickly regained his composure and sat impassively as the rest of the verdicts were read out. His wife and daughter, sitting in the first row of the public gallery behind him, remained stony-faced.

Eric Sussman, the prosecutor, wanted Black remanded in custody, claiming there was a risk he would flee to Canada. "He has had his day in court – my concern is whether he will return for his day of sentencing," Mr Sussman said.

Edward Greenspan, Black's lawyer, said his client wanted to return to his home in Toronto until he was sentenced but said he had no intention of fleeing.

However, Black was instructed to hand over his passport and remain in Chicago until the court ruled next Thursday whether he should be placed in custody. He was released on his conditional $21m bail.

Although there were calls for Black to be stripped of his peerage, there is no provision for this. The Government once proposed such a law after Jeffrey Archer was jailed for perjury but it was never introduced.

David Heath, the Liberal Democrat justice spokesman, said a way should be found as part of the reform of the Lords planned by Gordon Brown.

Also 14 July 2007
A ruthless tycoon brought down by greed and arrogance
The life of the media mogul who yesterday lost the biggest
battle of his audacious career
By David Litterick

Every day of his fraud trial, Conrad Black sauntered into the courtroom in Chicago with the disdainful air of a man who had seen it all before. The attacks on his character, the carping at his business dealings and the outrage – tinged with envy – at his lavish lifestyle; Lord Black has made a career of taking on his critics and winning.

While many men would have buckled under the relentless storm of disapproval, Black carried on, fortified by his trademark characteristic – the supreme self-confidence that brooks no dissent.

"Humility is a good quality, though it can be overdone," he once told the *Wall Street Journal*, in a line that many critics and admirers would think a suitable epitaph.

Even his Canadian lawyer, Edward Greenspan, admitted in interviews before the trial that Black could appear to display "tremendous arrogance".

But arrogance can only carry you so far, and it was this, coupled with extreme intelligence, that brought Black to his position as one of the most powerful media moguls on the planet, as well as one of the most controversial.

Certainly Black has never been one to bow to convention.

Born into a wealthy family in Montreal in 1944, his upbringing was unorthodox from the start. He was expelled from two schools – once for selling exam papers to fellow students – before graduating with a BA in history from Carleton University in Ottawa. Said to be neither athletic nor sporty as a youth, he would throw himself into his study of history, later writing a number of erudite and well-received biographies.

In every life there are particular events on which the future turns and Black arrived at his first in 1969, when he met David Radler, the man who would become his business partner for more than 40 years. With a mutual acquaintance, Peter White, the men bought the Sherbrooke Record – one of only a handful of English-language local newspapers in Quebec.

It was the beginning of a fruitful business partnership, but if the two men could ever be described as friends, it was a friendship based on respect and mutual gain rather than genuine warmth.

As the court in his fraud case heard, they spent one single holiday together – a weekend trip to New Orleans early in their partnership. It was, as Black's defence sarcastically noted, a trip so successful it was never repeated.

Black and Radler were different beasts with wildly different attitudes to life. As Paul Healy, a former vice-president at Hollinger, recently told *Vanity Fair*: "Black spent every dime he ever had, and Radler still has his first nickel." Despite their contrasting personalities, the partnership worked well. The court heard how Radler held the purse strings, while Black contributed articles and oversaw the editorial of the small paper. Between them, they made the venture a success. The court heard how Black and Radler worked day and night to turn the loss-making paper into a venture turning healthy profits within a few months. Buoyed by their achievements at the Record, they sought other papers for sale offering the same potential. Before long, they were running a good-sized chain of local newspapers and profiting handsomely from it.

But Black had a vision that demanded more. Before the venture reached the heights of the third largest newspaper publisher in the world however, Black suffered a personal setback with the death of his parents in 1976 within two weeks of each other.

His father, George Montegu Black, had run Canadian Breweries and was a successful businessman in his own right until disputes with his board of directors led to him being fired. Black senior is said to have deteriorated into bouts of depression and melancholy following the incident – something that moved his son greatly.

Crucially, the elder Black also owned a huge stake in Argus Corporation, Canada's largest holding company with interests that crossed every industry and every province of the country. It owned some of Canada's corporate jewels, among them a mining group, a large grocery chain and the Massey Ferguson tractor business.

Bequeathing the shares to Conrad – then in his early 30s – he set his son on the road to his fortune.

Even then, he was displaying the chutzpah that came to define his business dealings. In 1978 Bud McDougald, then regarded as an almost legendary businessman in Canada, died, leaving a power vacuum at the top of Argus. Two months later, Black convinced the dead magnate's wife and sister-in-law to sign documents that gave him effective control of the empire. Rivals wondered how he had managed it. Even the two women later expressed a wish, in hindsight, that they had acted differently.

Black swiftly antagonised many in the Canadian business world. There were disputes over employee pensions and arguments over money transfers between companies in a presage of events that came to haunt him at Hollinger.

At about that time, his first biographer, Peter Newman, embarked on a series of interviews with him. He recently recalled one particular conversation that he said chilled him. "Greed", Black confessed, "has been severely underestimated and denigrated, unfairly so, in my opinion . . . It is a motive that has not failed to move me from time to time."

As Newman wrote afterwards, "There exists a mile-wide streak of righteousness in the man, a glut of self-confidence that transcends run-of-the-mill arrogance."

Yet it brought with it no small measure of success. With the takeover of Argus, Black had turned the £3.5m inheritance from his father into a conglomerate worth £2bn.

Some believed that the company could have become the General Electric of Canada, but Black had other ideas. By 1985, he had sold most of the company's assets and folded what remained into a newly formed company, Hollinger Inc, which effectively returned Black to his roots as a newspaper operator.

Shortly afterwards, he struck gold by buying a stake in the *Daily Telegraph* – in a transaction described by the late Robert Maxwell as "landing history's largest fish with history's smallest hook".

Black eventually bought the rest of the Telegraph, along with hundreds of other newspapers, and later floated a Hollinger subsidiary, called Hollinger International, on the New York Stock Exchange.

Crucially, that gave Hollinger international investors for the first time and brought the company under US corporate governance rules.

By then his first marriage to Joanna Hishon – with whom he had two sons, Jonathan and James, and a daughter, Alana – had ended. In 1992, when his divorce was finalised, he married the conservative columnist Barbara Amiel. Together, while Hollinger International was at its height, the pair lived a gilded life, enjoying homes in Toronto, New York, London and Florida and a staff of butlers, drivers, gardeners and chefs.

They moved in exalted circles, enjoying the company of the super-rich as well as ambassadors, politicians, entertainers and opinion formers. The jurors in his fraud case heard plenty of evidence as to the extent of Black's lavish life.

The apartment in New York was decked out with *objets d'art* costing tens of thousands of dollars. There were marble elephants, oriental rugs, figurines, even a wooden cabinet containing the porcelain bottle Napoleon had used during his 1812 invasion of Russia.

The court also heard about the £30,000 birthday party thrown for Lady Black in the exclusive Manhattan restaurant La Grenouille – part of which was paid with company money. Even jogging kit for Lady Black was said to have been bought by Hollinger.

Then there was the trip to Bora Bora – a resort in French Polynesia – that the couple took on Hollinger International's jet. Despite the cost, it was not a success.

Black wrote to a friend afterwards: "We just got back yesterday from a shambles of a trip to the South Pacific, where I came down with bronchitis and almost died snorkelling as a result. We felt like geriatric freaks among a sea of honeymooners – loutish young men and their perky wives."

There were rumblings about the cost of the flight, putting Black on the defensive in the bombastic style that was his trademark.

"There has not been an occasion for many months that I got on our plane without wondering whether it was really affordable," he said in a revealing 2002 email that formed part of the prosecution case but was never presented to the jury. "But I'm not prepared to re-enact the French revolutionary renunciation of the rights of the nobility."

Similar views would be repeated in numerous emails shown to the court. "We have a certain style that shareholders were aware of when they came in," he wrote, "We should fine-tune that style, not revolutionise it with a Damascene conversion to vows of poverty."

By the latter years of the 20th century, just as Black was fighting Canadian politicians over his right to take up a seat in the House of Lords, his acumen led him to presume – rightly, as it turned out – that the valuations of newspapers had reached their peak.

The growth of the internet led many readers to get their news elsewhere, and that, coupled with the debt with which Hollinger had saddled itself, persuaded Black to begin a root and branch sale of the local newspapers that had served the company so well. At some point during these deals – at least according to Radler – occurred the brainwave that led to Black standing trial. When companies sell newspapers, the deals often include non-competition agreements which include payments to the sellers to prevent them using their local knowledge to set up a rival newspaper to the one they have just sold. Such agreements were common in the deals Hollinger struck when selling its newspapers. But payments to individuals, rather than the companies they represented, were not.

However Radler testified that when the disposals were under way in 2000, he had a key conversation with Black. "He suggested that we insert ourselves into the non-compete process and I agreed," Radler said in evidence.

In subsequent deals, Black, Radler – who pleaded guilty to one count of fraud – and other executives all received hefty payments. Whether these payments were justified or were approved by directors was the subject the jurors spent the past four months contemplating. A letter from one investor in 2003 complaining about the way the company was run prompted other shareholders, regulators and ultimately US prosecutors to take a closer look at Hollinger International's dealings, and the company subsequently unravelled fast.

As his empire collapsed around him, Black never entertained the thought that he would be found guilty. In an emailed message to a documentary maker in 2004, he suggested: "It will startle an entire burgeoning industry of pundits, eulogists and curio-vendors, but I'm far from dead. When everyone is finished dancing on my grave, they may be disconcerted to find I am not in it."

Cherie Blair

"Sometimes I feel I would like to crawl away and hide but I will not."

Cherie Blair, a notably gifted QC, has at times displayed a talent for misjudgement in exact proportion to her considerable intelligence. One manifestation of this was her close relationship with Carole Caplin, who nominally advised her on fashion and fitness, but appeared to have exerted a far greater influence. The scandal was initially limited to the revelation that Cherie Blair had used Caplin's boyfriend, Peter Foster, a convicted fraudster, to help arrange the purchase of two flats in Bristol. It later emerged that papers on his legal battle against extradition had been faxed to her private study in Downing Street. The furore around the affair – arguably the first major scandal of Blair's reign – eventually died down. Though the Blairs' perceived cupidity, and curious blindspots regarding people with whom they do business (in particular a string of despotic leaders) has become increasingly apparent in the years since Tony left front-line British politics, it's worth noting that in this instance Cherie displayed commendable loyalty to a friend who had dragged her into an awkward situation in which she was guilty of nothing more than an error of judgement.

5 December 2002
No 10 "lied" over role of conman in helping
Cherie Blair buy flats
By Toby Helm

Downing Street was accused last night of lying over claims that a convicted fraudster acted as a financial adviser to Cherie Blair during the purchase of two flats in Bristol.

Under a front page headline, "Cherie, a Crook and the Proof that Number Ten Lied", the *Daily Mail* claimed to have evidence from a string of emails that No 10 had covered up the facts.

The paper, which devoted nine pages to the story, alleged that Peter Foster, a convicted fraudster, had exchanged numerous emails with Mrs Blair that showed an "extraordinary degree of familiarity". In the emails, Mr Foster discusses the price of the flats and the potential profit the Blairs might hope to make on them.

Downing Street, which over the past four days has denied that Mr Foster acted as a financial adviser to the Blairs, refused to comment on the alleged new details.

Mr Foster, who is said to have boasted to friends about helping the Blairs to buy the flats, is in a relationship with Mrs Blair's "lifestyle guru", Carole Caplin. Miss Caplin advises Mrs Blair on fashion and fitness. Mrs Blair is understood to have met Mr Foster at least once.

One of the flats is believed to have been bought for the Blairs' eldest son, Euan, who is at university in Bristol. The other is thought to have been acquired as an investment.

According to the *Mail*, the alleged emails show that Mr Foster saved Mrs Blair £69,000 on the purchase of the two flats by negotiating personally with the vendor.

The paper also claims that he offered her the services of his own accountant and offered to pay the accountant's fees himself.

In an email said to have been written by Mrs Blair, she apparently described Mr Foster as "a star" and someone with whom she was on "the same wave-length".

Mr Foster, a former boyfriend of the model Samantha Fox, became involved in buying the flats after viewing properties with Miss Caplin.

To begin with, the *Mail* says, the flats were on the market at £297,000 each. Mr Foster managed to beat the price down to £265,000 and later to £260,000 for one of the flats.

In the correspondence he allegedly had with Mrs Blair, Mr Foster raises the possibility of trying to get the price below £250,000 so that it would be below a threshold for higher stamp duty. He advises against trying to achieve the lower price.

"As for the stamp duty issue, the tax man recently sent out a circular to all accountants advising them that they are keeping an eye on all property sales just under the 250K mark for that very purpose, so to try and do something could be risky and unadvisable."

Since last weekend No 10 has refused to answer detailed questions about the story.

The Prime Minister's official spokesman said on Tuesday that any negotiations that may have taken place would have done so between Mrs Blair and her lawyers.

Mr Foster, 39, who has served a jail term for fraud, was named last month by the Australian competition and consumer commission as the "mastermind" in a scheme to market a slimming product, Trimit, through Chaste Corporation Pty Ltd, which is in liquidation.

The company was accused of "engaged in misleading and deceptive conduct".

11 December 2002
"I have made mistakes but I was only trying to protect my family"

Tearful Cherie says sorry for fiasco over fraudster

By George Jones

Cherie Blair delivered an unprecedented and highly emotional public apology last night for embarrassing her husband, her family and the Labour Government by her relationship with the convicted fraudster Peter Foster.

The Prime Minister's wife was in tears as she admitted that she had made mistakes in an attempt to protect her family's privacy.

But she raised fresh questions about the extent of her involvement in Foster's battle against deportation when she disclosed that she had checked the court lists for the name of the judge involved.

She indicated that her decision to break her silence on her role by making the televised statement followed reports that some newspapers were about to allege that "I tried to influence a judge".

Any suggestion that she sought to influence the judicial process would be highly damaging for Mrs Blair, who is a QC and part-time judge.

She denied that she had acted improperly, but did not explain why she had checked the name of the judge.

Her personal statement came after Downing Street accused sections of the media of a deliberate campaign of false accusations and "character assassination".

She was clearly concerned that what she described as "frenzied and inaccurate" allegations would become so damaging that they could threaten her legal career as well as causing further embarrassment to Tony Blair.

Her surprise statement was a high-risk gamble to try to extricate the Blairs from the biggest crisis to engulf the family since they entered Downing Street five years ago.

In an appeal to the public to give her the benefit of the doubt and forgive her mistakes she revealed the pressures she had been under.

She said she was "not Superwoman" and that in juggling her roles as a wife, mother, prime ministerial consort at home and abroad, barrister and charity worker, "some balls get dropped". But she delivered a defiant defence of her friendship with Carole Caplin, her fashion and fitness adviser, whose boyfriend Foster was.

She said Miss Caplin had been a trusted friend and "a great help" to her when she suddenly found herself the wife of the Labour leader and future Prime Minister.

Mrs Blair said she did not know the full details of Foster's background "until a couple of weeks ago when the police alerted us that a newspaper was trying to set me up in a meeting with him".

But it was not her business "to choose my friends' friends".

Despite Mrs Blair's insistence that she did not know "the full story" about Foster until a couple of weeks ago, friends of Miss Caplin insisted yesterday that the Prime Minister's wife was told about his past in the summer.

They said that like many close girlfriends Mrs Blair and Miss Caplin did not keep secrets from each other, particularly on something as central as a new boyfriend.

Mrs Blair's statement was part of a choreographed counter-attack by Downing Street, which included the publication by the Home Office of a detailed chronology of the proceedings to remove Foster from Britain.

It came as the Tories stepped up the pressure on the Prime Minister for an independent inquiry into events surrounding the purchase of two flats in Bristol and the actions of ministers and officials in moves to speed up Foster's deportation.

Her decision to break her silence was a recognition that the drip drip of disclosures about her relationship following her initial denials had called into question her judgment and integrity.

It had caused a major breach with the media and severely strained relations between the Blairs and their senior advisers in No 10, including Alastair Campbell, the Prime Minister's director of communications.

The Blairs have also been left with flats which have cost them £500,000 but which they will not be able to use because of security concerns. They may have to sell them, possibly at a loss.

Throughout the day it became evident that Downing Street had failed to draw a line under the affair and that Mr Blair could face embarrassing questions from Tory MPs at question time in the Commons this afternoon.

Mrs Blair used a scheduled appearance at an awards ceremony for childcare projects at a restaurant close to Parliament to deliver her statement.

She referred to her husband, Miss Caplin and her son Euan by their first names – but spoke of Mr Foster, and did not refer to him as Peter.

It was an indication of her anger and dismay at the way she had become the latest victim of such an accomplished conman, who had stolen her reputation and made her an object of ridicule.

Although the statement raised more questions about Mrs Blair's role in the controversy, its emotional delivery showed the strain she has been under since news of her links with Foster broke 10 days ago.

"I now realise I made two mistakes," she said. "My immediate instinct when faced with the questions from the *Mail on Sunday* 10 days ago was to protect my family's privacy and particularly my son in his first term at university living away from home."

She sobbed as she added: "This instinct, which I think any mother would have, and my desire not to open myself up to any and every question which the press should choose to ask me led to this misunderstanding in the press office and I think they know I did not in any way set out to mislead them.

"The second mistake I made was to allow someone I barely knew and had not then met to get involved in my family's affairs."

Mrs Blair said she had "only wanted to protect my family and to help my friend Carole. I am sorry if I have embarrassed anyone but the people who know me well know that I would never want to harm anyone – least of all Tony or the children or the Labour Government or misuse my position in any way."

She added: "Sometimes I feel I would like to crawl away and hide but I will not."

Mrs Blair defended her conduct in telephoning Foster's solicitors with Miss Caplin to ask about his deportation proceedings. She said Miss Caplin was unclear about the legal process concerning Mr Foster's right to remain in the country.

"I phoned Mr Foster's solicitor simply to put her mind at rest that the normal process was being followed. I emphatically did not try to influence this one way or another, I was simply trying to help my friend Carole find out the facts. It is now being suggested that beyond this I also spoke twice to Mr Foster himself, I did not."

Mrs Blair also rejected allegations that she or people in Downing Street had phoned the Home Office and the Immigration Department to take up Mr Foster's case "or depending on which allegation you listen to, to kick Mr Foster out of the country".

Officials said she checked the judge's name as part of a "reassurance" exercise for Miss Caplin, who was worried that it was a different judge from the tribunal which first heard Foster's case.

12 December 2002
Blairs pay back conman over flats mortgage
Prime Minister praises his wife: It's been a horrible time for
Cherie – I'm very proud of her
By George Jones

Tony Blair and his wife Cherie severed their final link with the Australian fraudster Peter Foster last night by reimbursing him for the cost of arranging a mortgage on two flats he helped them to buy in Bristol.

Mr Blair paid an emotional tribute to his wife's "courage" in admitting mistakes in dealing with Foster, the boyfriend of her lifestyle guru, Carole Caplin.

As No 10 disclosed that the Blairs were no longer under a financial obligation to him, the Prime Minister said he was proud of his wife for making her televised apology.

Cabinet ministers rallied round, accusing her critics in the press of waging a vendetta to drive the Prime Minister and his wife out of public life.

After days of stonewalling on Foster's claim that he had paid £4,000 in fees for arranging the mortgage, Downing Street said that the bill had been settled – although officials said it was for a smaller sum.

In an email to Mrs Blair in October, Foster had said that the mortgage would be handled by his accountant, Andrew Axelsen, who it later emerged was awaiting trial at the Old Bailey on charges relating to suspected money laundering.

Foster wrote: "He will not charge you for his services as I will pay him for his time and efforts through my company."

He later said he had paid £4,000 and had not asked Mrs Blair for reimbursement. He told friends: "I would have been embarrassed to ask."

Since the allegations surfaced, Downing Street has refused to answer questions about the payment or whether Mr Blair intended to declare it as a benefit in the MPs' register of interests.

However, given the embarrassing publicity that Foster's fraudulent past and prison sentences have attracted, it would have been impossible for the Blairs to remain financially beholden to him.

Mr Blair's official spokesman said that any fees involved in the mortgage would be paid by the Blairs and had probably already been settled. He described Foster's £4,000 figure as a "total fabrication" but refused to say what the Blairs had paid.

Mr Blair used a visit to a domestic violence refuge in London to express his support for his wife after her friendship with Foster had plunged the family into its biggest crisis since he became Prime Minister. He said it had been a "horrible time" for Mrs Blair. He was proud of her televised apology because it had been very difficult for her to do.

"She has integrity and decency," he said, "and some of the things that have been written bear absolutely no resemblance to the person who is my wife."

Around the country, people supporting Mrs Blair were in the minority. Sixty-two per cent of those taking part in an online poll conducted by a Manchester newspaper said they had found her unconvincing.

On a Capital FM phone-in in London, 86 per cent of listeners said she was like an Oscar-winning actress.

Cabinet ministers toured the broadcasting studios to try to turn the spotlight away from questions about Mrs Blair's involvement in Foster's legal battle against deportation and on to the media treatment of the family.

Margaret Beckett, the Environment Secretary, protested at the "vicious" way Mrs Blair was being "hounded".

She said: "There are clearly quite a large number of people who loathe Cherie Blair, loathe Tony Blair even more and would love to drive him out of public life – through his family if that is the only way they can get at him."

Jack Straw, the Foreign Secretary, spoke of his admiration for Mrs Blair – "someone I know as a friend, a wife, a mother and a human being".

Downing Street made clear its desire to end the controversy. Officials refused to clear up questions about how the Blairs had used money in their blind trust to finance the purchase, or Mrs Blair's disclosure that she had checked the court lists for the name of the judge hearing Foster's deportation case.

Mr Blair authorised the release of a letter from Sir Andrew Turnbull, the Cabinet Secretary, saying that he had not broken the ministerial code of conduct by using the blind trust to buy the property.

Iain Duncan Smith, the Tory leader, accused Mr Blair of "extraordinary complacency". He said that, after days of "half truths and evasions", questions remained over the changing of deportation orders for Foster and the integrity of the No 10 press office.

Mr Blair said there was nothing that warranted an independent inquiry.

13 December 2002
Conman fax sent to Cherie's flat
No 10 accuses Foster as PM's wife faces new claims

Cherie Blair was last night fighting against a fresh wave of allegations about her links with the fraudster Peter Foster after it emerged that papers on his legal battle against extradition were faxed to her private study in Downing Street.

Tony Blair rounded on his wife's critics after the controversy pursued him to a summit of European leaders in Copenhagen. He challenged her accusers to put any evidence of "criminal, illegal or improper" behaviour to the proper authorities.

Otherwise, he said, "I think everyone's had their pound of flesh and now it's time to move on."

Iain Duncan Smith, the Conservative leader, who was also in Copenhagen, called for an independent inquiry to establish the truth. He said that No 10 was "drowning in very murky water".

Downing Street pointed the finger of blame at Foster as fresh allegations about his contacts with Mrs Blair were made.

Carole Caplin, Mrs Blair's lifestyle and fashion adviser, reignited the controversy by admitting that she had asked Foster, her boyfriend, to fax papers relating to his deportation to her while she was in Mrs Blair's flat.

The *Scotsman* newspaper alleged that the Prime Minister's wife was more intimately involved in the extradition case than she had so far admitted. It claimed that she reviewed the court papers prepared by Foster's lawyers and the official Treasury solicitor's papers demanding extradition.

The newspaper also said that Mrs Blair had commented on the judge likely to hear the case and advised Foster to make a "human rights issue" of the fact that Miss Caplin was pregnant.

A Downing Street spokesman, highly embarrassed, admitted that it was the first No 10 had heard that additional legal documents had been faxed on Mrs Blair's private telephone line.

At a tense and heated briefing in Whitehall, Godric Smith claimed that "basic inaccuracies" were being presented as fact. He suggested that Foster was behind the latest allegations.

"We are not going to dance to the tune of Mr Peter Foster, a convicted conman," he said.

On Tuesday another of the Prime Minister's official spokesmen, Tom Kelly, told journalists that Mrs Blair had neither asked for nor read the papers; nor did she know their content. He also made clear that the papers had not been sent to Mrs Blair on an unsolicited basis.

Yesterday Mr Smith insisted that Downing Street had not been evasive on the issue.

"These papers were not sent to Mrs Blair," he said.

Even if No 10 had known about the fax, the answer would have been the same – "Different papers, same response," he said.

Miss Caplin said she had arrived at Downing Street on 22 November "pregnant and very worried". She confirmed that she brought with her some of the papers relating to the extradition case and, while there, asked for more to be sent over.

She insisted that she and not Mrs Blair had asked to see the legal papers. She claimed that Mrs Blair had refused to read them – even though an hour earlier Mrs Blair had taken part in a conference call with Foster's lawyers about the extradition case.

"Cherie told me it would not be right for her to read them, as it was not her case," Miss Caplin said. "So I folded them up, put them in my bag and took them home, basically."

Mr Blair's spokesman did not explain why Miss Caplin had used Mrs Blair's personal fax or needed the additional papers to be sent over while the two were closeted in Mrs Blair's Downing Street study.

David Janes, of Foster's London solicitors, Janes, denied "knowingly" faxing papers on the extradition case to Mrs Blair. He rejected any suggestion that his company had sought or was offered any advice or influence by the Prime Minister's wife.

In another twist, tape-recorded conversations with Foster were published in which he talked of selling his story for £100,000. According to transcripts of the tapes in the *Sun*, Foster claimed that he could destroy Mrs Blair's professional and personal image.

The newspaper did not disclose where it obtained the tapes. In them Foster said: "I might as well get something out of this." The tapes give some weight to Downing Street's claim that Foster is deliberately targeting Mrs Blair and may be behind the latest series of allegations about her role in the controversy.

However, they are a further indication of how No 10 has lost control of events, with the Blairs' reputation increasingly at the mercy of an accomplished conman who managed to get close to the Prime Minister's wife.

Foster challenged Mrs Blair's denial that she looked at the legal papers about his extradition. In a conversation with his mother, he discussed yesterday's disclosure that papers relating to the case were faxed to Miss Caplin in Mrs Blair's study.

His mother asked if it was true, as No 10 and Miss Caplin claimed that "Cherie never read the papers".

He replied: "No, of course not. She read them." He added: "I think Carole was stupid. She was trying to protect a friend and it was a knee-jerk reaction."

Downing Street was clearly exasperated by the story's continuing prominence despite Mrs Blair's televised statement on Tuesday admitting mistakes.

Mr Smith denied that she had expressed opinions on the judge who would be dealing with Foster's case – because she did not know him.

Downing Street threatened to stop answering further questions about the affair, even though many issues are unresolved.

Inquiries by the *Daily Telegraph* indicate that Mrs Blair may have been told some of the detail of Foster's criminal past as early as July, three months before he became involved in buying two flats for the Blairs in Bristol.

Miss Caplin had wanted to invite Foster, whom she met in June this year, to her 40th birthday party, which was hosted by the Blairs at Chequers in July.

She told friends at the party that Foster could not attend because he had failed a police vetting process. Security around Mrs Blair has been stepped up since the 11 September attacks and more checks are now being made on people entering her circle.

The heightened vetting is believed to have led to the discovery last month of a tabloid newspaper's attempts to set up a meeting between Mrs Blair and Foster.

A Downing Street spokesman said: "Peter Foster has never been on the guest list for any event at Chequers and has never been to Chequers."

Foster told an Australian newspaper that the scandal could end his relationship with Miss Caplin. "I am feeling very homesick," he said. "I would like to come home and lick my wounds."

Labour MPs sent flowers to No 10 in support of Mrs Blair, while Robin Cook, the Leader of the Commons, said that after two weeks of allegations nothing illegal or improper had been shown.

Gordon Brown's allies were at pains to quell suggestions that the Chancellor was not doing enough to support the Blairs.

17 December 2002
Charlatan remains convinced of his own lies
Peter Foster tells the world he is a flawed man
By Sean O'Neill

After Cherie Blair's confessional moment, it was time for the conman to come clean. Last week the ball-juggling Prime Minister's wife, QC and part-time judge admitted: "I know I am not Superwoman."

Yesterday the serial fraudster who landed Mrs Blair in the biggest mess of her life conceded: "I know I am a flawed man."

There were times when one wondered if the two statements might not have been written by the same hand – moments of high emotion combined with bursts of indignation and pleas for understanding.

Underlying the statements of Mrs Blair and Foster was the view that although they were not perfect, they had not done much wrong. The whole affair had been drummed up by a hostile press.

Foster, a man with a 20-year record of deception and dishonesty, claimed that he was the subject "of the most extraordinary character assassination" by the media.

The Australian – who is facing deportation from Britain because of his criminal past – made his televised statement at the studios of ITN in central London.

Foster did his best to look sincere as he read from his script. The Australian accent faltered a little as he described his first "chance" meeting with Carole Caplin – Mrs Blair's fashion and fitness adviser – in July this year.

"I was smitten . . . the reasons any man would become attracted to Carole are obvious," said the man, who previously fell for and conned Samantha Fox, almost conned Tara Palmer-Tomkinson and tried to con Pamela Anderson.

Later he added: "I will always love her."

Although his recollection differed markedly from that of Mrs Blair, there was no hint of malice in his voice as he delivered his account of the discounted-flats-for-legal-advice scandal.

Yes, he had secured a £69,000 reduction for Mrs Blair on the price of two flats in Bristol. But no, he was not "working an angle", it was all down to "the art of negotiation". Foster added: "I did not seek anything in return, although I remain appreciative of the later, innocent advice given to me, by Cherie. At no time did she seek to interfere with the legal processes, nor did I ask her to.

"Cherie simply passed on to me a professional view of where I stood on the case. The notion I was attempting some elaborate sting on the Blairs is laughable. As everybody around me knows I had many opportunities and invitations to meet Tony and Cherie. I consistently turned them down, aware my background could cause embarrassment."

Foster pleaded that he had "made mistakes and paid the price for that". Despite that the press had described him as a liar and a fantasist and told endless untruths about him – including the allegation that he had been trying to sell his story.

"I had no chance to challenge these lies," said Foster – although at no stage in the past two weeks has he returned calls from this newspaper in which he could have given his account. "Could it be that I had to be discredited by the establishment?" asked the man who is not a fantasist.

Perhaps most astonishing was Foster's claim that despite his string of convictions and a long list of unhappy investors he had never defrauded anyone. He said: "No one has ever lost money through my enterprises." Yet he is currently being sought by the Australian consumer authorities in connection with a slimming pill scheme in which 70 investors claim to have lost £1.4m to a company run by Foster.

Finally Foster asked for "peace and quiet" to complete the autobiography he says he has been writing for the past year – a clear appeal to any publisher to come forward and offer an advance.

Esther Rantzen, whose *That's Life* programme first exposed Foster's fraudulent business schemes, watched his statement with a sense of amazement. "He says no one has ever lost money through his enterprises," said Miss Rantzen. "The reason we exposed Peter Foster over and over again in about 30 different programmes, was because of the scams he used.

"I assume that having heard that, thousands of people will be queuing up to say 'in that case can I have my money back'. I thought it was interesting when he said he was not a fantasist, then created a fantasy that he had been discredited by the establishment, when he was discredited by hard working police and trading standards officers in three different continents."

Euan Blair

"I guess most of us at the age of 16 have done
something we might later regret."

7 July 2000
A good kid really, says Blair after drunk son is held
Euan found lying in Leicester Square
By Caroline Davies, George Jones and Andy McSmith

Tony Blair was close to tears last night as he spoke of the difficulties of bringing up children while being Prime Minister after his 16-year-old son, Euan, was found drunk and incapable in Leicester Square in London.

Choking with emotion, he said on BBC TV *Question Time*: "It has not been the greatest of days – let's put it like that. But my son is basically a good kid really. He will get through this.

"We are a strong family and we will see him right and we will get to the other side."

Referring to the fact that Euan lied to police about his identity and age, he said that he had been trying to save his family embarrassment.

Mr Blair was challenged to justify his suggestion of on-the-spot fines on young people for disorderly behaviour – an initiative dropped after police chiefs dismissed it as unworkable – and asked whether such a law would have deterred his son.

He said: "We should take action against violent, aggressive and disorderly conduct and I'm afraid that applies to my son as well as anybody else's.

"I don't ask for any special preference for my kid. I guess most of us at the age of 16 have done something we might later regret. Not everybody has to see it in the newspapers, but that is the life we have to lead. I hope he would be deterred from behaving wrongly."

Earlier in the day, in an unscripted address to black church leaders in Brighton, Mr Blair became emotional as he spoke of faith, strife and the perils of parenthood.

Euan was held at Charing Cross police station after being found lying on the pavement outside the Odeon cinema shortly before 11pm. He gave a false name to police, a former address and suggested that he was 18. His identity was discovered only after he was searched. Special Branch officers were immediately sent from Downing Street, where his father, who had returned from a Labour fund-raising dinner, had become worried that his eldest son had not come home. Euan was released from custody shortly before 1am.

His mother, Cherie, was not at home. She was on a break in Portugal with her mother and baby Leo, but flew back early to London last night.

The two other children, Kathryn and Nicholas, were looked after by a nanny while Mr Blair was at the dinner.

A Downing Street statement said: "Euan was out last night with friends to mark the end of his GCSEs. The police late last night saw him lying on the ground in Leicester Square.

"He was clearly ill and had been vomiting. An ambulance was called, but ambulance personnel decided he didn't need hospital treatment and he was then taken by the police to Charing Cross. He was, in the view of the police, drunk and incapable.

"He gave his name during the interview as Euan John. He gave an old address and a date of birth which suggested he was 18. The police searched him and established his correct identity.

"They immediately called the Special Branch, who went to Charing Cross and identified him. He was then processed, released and taken home.

"Euan is very sorry for the inconvenience he caused to the police, the state he was in and for the false statement that he made.

"He is in no doubt of the seriousness of it and the view that his parents take of it. They will of course fully co-operate with any further action the police propose to take.

"In the near future he will have to return to Charing Cross with his parents to hear what, if any, action is going to be taken. The Prime Minister and Mrs Blair appreciate that as this is a case of under-age drinking requiring the involvement of the police, the press will report this.

"But they will continue to do all they can to protect their children's privacy and ensure as normal an upbringing as possible."

Although there was no attempt by opposition politicians to make political capital out of Mr Blair's family difficulties, Euan's arrest was highly embarrassing for the Prime Minister in view of his recent attacks on drunken yobs.

The incident will add to the pressures on Mr Blair, who is going through his roughest patch as Prime Minister.

In the Commons on Wednesday he received a mauling from William Hague. Colleagues believe that Mr Blair has been showing signs of strain since the birth of

Leo seven weeks ago and that he is finding it increasingly difficult to balance family and political commitments.

After being up until the early hours dealing with Euan, he faced a hectic round of political and public engagements yesterday.

In the morning he chaired the weekly meeting of the Cabinet. Then he travelled to Brighton to address the church leaders before his *Question Time* appearance.

Downing Street acknowledged the public interest in the arrest and provided a full briefing on what had happened.

Alastair Campbell, the Prime Minister's spokesman, stressed that the Blairs, who were "strict disciplinarians", would be fully involved in any follow-up action, including going back to the police station with Euan.

Asked if Mr Blair felt guilty about putting his son in a position in which he was exposed to publicity, Mr Campbell said that Mr and Mrs Blair "believed in the job", but were aware that it exposed the family to "extra pressures".

Lord Wakeham, the chairman of the Press Complaints Commission, urged newspaper editors to take into account the Blairs' "clear commitment to do all they can to protect the privacy of their children".

As pubs in Leicester Square denied knowledge of Euan's drinking at their premises, there was sympathy for Mr Blair and his son. Mr Campbell said: "Euan will not be the only teenager out last night celebrating his exams; he won't be the only one who got worse for wear, but he will be the only one splashed all over the papers and the television."

John Prescott, the Deputy Prime Minister, said: "It is about growing up, isn't it, and we will all have a little smile at the same time, won't we?"

Mo Mowlam, the Cabinet Office Minister, said: "I have teenage stepchildren, so it's a problem that can arise."

Had Euan been an adult, he would probably have been released with "no further action". But youth justice procedures are different. He will have to return to the police station, where he may receive a verbal reprimand, a recorded warning or a charge, although that is extremely unlikely.

Sir Anthony Blunt

"It is the first time I have got near the truth."

Scholar (his monograph on Poussin was considered definitive), aesthete, administrator, establishment linchpin (he had been Surveyor of the Queen's Pictures) and almost painstakingly discreet homosexual, Sir Anthony Blunt was a public figure who guarded his privacy closely; so to the British public his exposure as a Soviet spy came as a terrible shock. The same cannot be said of MI5 (nor the Queen) who had known his secret for over a decade: on being identified as the fourth member of the Cambridge Spy Ring – it later emerged that his own KGB handler described him as an "ideological shit" – Blunt was given immunity in exchange for a full confession. If Kim Philby remains the most famous member of the group of traitors, it's arguable that Blunt's actions were most damaging. During the war he had passed the Russians detailed information about the highly secret Ultra programme as well as German spy rings operating in the Soviet Union. Almost allergic to the glare of publicity that shined on him, Blunt withdrew from society and died of a heart attack four years later.

16 November 1979
Spy to lose knighthood
Queen's art adviser was defectors' "fourth man"
By Guy Rais

Sir Anthony Blunt, 72, the Queen's former art adviser, was named by the Prime Minister in the Commons yesterday as a spy for the Russians – the "fourth man" who helped Burgess and Maclean to flee Britain in 1951.

As this sensational disclosure was made, a Buckingham Palace announcement said that Sir Anthony was being stripped of the honour – Knight Commander of the Royal Victorian Order – awarded to him by the Queen in 1956. The decision was made personally by the Queen and will take effect today.

Sir Anthony confessed to having passed information to the Russians in April 1964 – seven months after Guy Burgess died in Moscow – and was given immunity from prosecution in return for helping the security service's investigations into the defections of Burgess, Maclean and Kim Philby.

Last night, hard on the heels of Mrs Thatcher's Commons statement, came a further revelation by Mr Andrew Boyle, whose book *The Climate of Treason*, led to the Government's disclosures. Mr Boyle claimed that 25 people were involved in the Philby-Burgess-Maclean spy network, of whom "one or two are in influential positions."

Sir Anthony Blunt disappeared from his sixth-floor flat off the Edgware Road, London, early on Wednesday.

A porter at the block of flats said he had "gone for a holiday in Italy", but Mr Christopher Price, Labour MP for Lewisham – one of two MPs who had put down a question concerning Sir Anthony's activities – suggested in the Commons that he had been "tipped-off" about the Prime Minister's statement.

The announcement from the Palace that Sir Anthony was being stripped of his title said that he had been informed of the Queen's decision, but it did not disclose how this had been done.

It was most likely that the Queen would have consulted the Prime Minister about the action Mrs Thatcher was taking – probably at their regular meeting on Tuesday – and that it was then decided that the Palace announcement would be made at the same time as the Prime Minister's statement in the Commons.

Mrs Thatcher's written statement was in reply to the Labour MP, Mr Ted Leadbitter, who had asked for a statement "on recent evidence concerning the actions of an individual, whose name had been supplied to her in relation to the security of the United Kingdom".

Mrs Thatcher's statement began: "The name which the hon. gentleman has given me is that of Sir Anthony Blunt.

"In April 1964, Sir Anthony Blunt admitted to the security authorities that he had been recruited by, and had acted as a talent-spotter for Russian Intelligence before the war, when he was a don at Cambridge, and had passed information regularly to the Russians while he was a member of the Security Service between 1940 and 1945.

"He made this admission after being given an undertaking that he would not be prosecuted if he confessed."

Mrs Thatcher said inquiries were "of course" made before Blunt joined the Security Service in 1940, and he was judged a "fit person".

He was known to have held Marxist views at Cambridge, "but the security authorities had no reason either in 1940, or at any time during his service, to doubt his loyalty to his country".

She revealed that Blunt first came under suspicion following the defection of Burgess and Maclean in 1951, but that during 11 interviews he "persisted in his denial, and no evidence against him was obtained". Inquiries which preceded the exposure and defection of Philby in January 1963, produced nothing which implicated him, although in 1964 new information was received "which directly implicated him."

It did not, however, "provide a basis on which charges could be brought.

Mrs Thatcher said that in April 1964, the then Attorney-General (the late Sir John Hobson in the Conservative Government), authorised immunity from prosecution to Blunt if he confessed.

"Blunt then admitted that like his friends, Burgess, Maclean and Philby, he had become an agent for Russian intelligence, had talent-spotted for them at Cambridge during the 1930s and that he regularly passed information to the Russians while he was a member of the Security Service, and that, although after 1945 he was no longer in a position to supply the Russians with classified information, he used his old contact with Russian intelligence to assist in arrangements for the defection of Burgess and Maclean."

Mrs Thatcher, in a reference to Blunt as a double-agent, added that both at the time of his confession and subsequently "Blunt provided useful information about Russian intelligence activities and about his association with Burgess, Maclean and Philby."

She further revealed that the Queen's Private Secretary in April 1964 (Sir Michael, now Lord Adeane), had been informed of Blunt's confession and his immunity from prosecution. Sir Anthony was not required to resign his appointment in the Royal household as Surveyor of the Queen's Pictures – a post he held until his retirement in 1972, when he became picture adviser to the Queen.

Explaining why Blunt had not been asked to resign, Mrs Thatcher said his unpaid appointment "carried no access to classified information and no risk to security".

A Buckingham Palace spokesman confirmed last night that at the time Blunt was made KCVO "nothing was known."

Sir Anthony, a bachelor, who today will revert to plain Mr Blunt following the promulgation of his loss of a knighthood in the *London Gazette*, is one of the art world's most distinguished figures.

An art historian, he served as director of the Courtauld Institute of Art for 27 years and was considered brilliant while at Cambridge.

It was at Cambridge that he recruited Philby, Burgess and Maclean before the war, and continued to feed Moscow with information until 1945.

The present deputy director of the Courtauld Institute, Prof. Alan Bowness, said: "Those who knew Sir Anthony well also knew that he been mixed up with Guy Burgess from university days.

Sir John Hobson, the Attorney-General in 1964 who took the decision not to prosecute Blunt, died in 1967, aged 55.

At the time he made the decision, there was no Director of Public Prosecutions because Sir Theobald Mathew had died and Sir Norman Skelhorn was not appointed to that office until May 1964.

It was known that Sir John had consulted an Assistant Director of Public Prosecutions before taking his decision.

Last night the DPP's office was not prepared to name the Assistant DPP, whose advice had been sought.

Mr Andrew Boyle, the author of *The Climate of Treason – Five who spied for Russia* was at one time an executive editor for the BBC's *World at One*.

It was his book which sparked off speculation about the identities of the unnamed fourth and fifth men in the spy drama which resulted in Mrs Thatcher's statement yesterday.

Mr Boyle did not name the fourth and fifth men who were involved in the Philby-Burgess-Maclean affair, but his book refers to "Maurice" and "Basil," the code names he said were given to them.

It was "Maurice" [now known to be Sir Anthony Blunt], "who worked so hard for the Communist Party in Cambridge in the 1930s, who tipped off Maclean about his imminent arrest, and who subsequently made a confession of his lies and misdeeds to the Security Service," Mr Boyle says in his book.

Last night Mr Boyle, 59, said that Philby, Burgess and Maclean had "up to 25 accomplices".

Emphasising that he did not want "to start taking part in a numbers game," Mr Boyle added, "but I could name a few of them."

"Some have died, and quite a few – half a dozen – are walking free. One or two are still in influential positions, but I think they have long ago been neutralised."

Mr Boyle, said he "had nothing but a feeling of satisfaction" after yesterday's disclosures by Mrs Thatcher.

He expressed the view that Blunt had been granted immunity because of his knowledge of the other side of the Iron Curtain – confirming Mrs Thatcher's remarks that he was a double agent.

Two Labour MPs – Mr Christopher Price and Mr Dennis Skinner (Bolsover), had tabled questions due to have been answered next Monday by the Attorney-General, Sir Michael Havers.

Under the rules of Parliament, questions once tabled have privilege from legal proceedings.

It was left to Mr Leadbitter, MP for Hartlepool, to put down a direct question to the Prime Minister, and faced with growing Parliamentary demands for information on Blunt's involvement in the affair, Mrs Thatcher decided the facts should be revealed, As head of Britain's security services, she alone made the decision to be as frank as possible in a situation involving national security.

Mrs Thatcher was obliged to answer the Parliamentary question put down by Mr Leadbitter, which had a priority classification, but it was her decision to decide how much substantive information was to be given.

Lord Home, Prime Minister at the time of Blunt's confession, was last right at his Castlemain, Douglas, Lanarkshire, home, but was "not available" for comment

Lord Butler, Foreign Secretary in Lord Home's Government in 1964, said last night that he had heard nothing about Blunt while he was in office and knew nothing further until he had heard of what had been revealed in the House.

Blunt's brother, Mr Christopher Blunt, 75, a retired banker, described the news as "a very great shock. I had absolutely no knowledge.

"It is the first time I have got near the truth."

Mr Blunt, who lives at Marlborough, Wilts, said he had no idea what his brother would do now. But he said his attitude to him would not change. "After all he is my brother."

Blunt's wife, Elizabeth, said the family was in a state of "severe shook" and had no idea of Sir Anthony's whereabouts

Another brother, Mr Wilfred Blunt, 78, curator of the Watts Gallery in Compton, near Guildford, said he was "amazed at what I have read in the newspapers. I can give no information on the whereabouts of my brother."

Mr Tony Marlow, Tory MP for Northampton North, last night tabled a Commons question asking the Home Secretary how Sir Anthony Blunt got out of the country and whether he intended to involve Interpol.

Mr Marlow said: "If the man is a traitor I resent the fact that he has been given immunity and if it is humanly possible he should be pursued and prosecuted."

Bob Boothby

"His faults were as well known to his friends as his qualities."

The almost pathologically discreet tone of this obituary means that the roguish drift of Booth's life might be inferred, but none of the details revealed. This was partly because the press, though aware of the more colourful elements of his discreetly conducted private life, declined to publish them. Perhaps this was a measure of the affection with which he was held: the Queen Mother described him as a "bounder but not a cad". In addition to his affairs with women such as Dorothy Macmillan, wife of the Conservative prime minister, he was openly bisexual at a time when male homosexual activity remained illegal. It was this proclivity that brought him into the Kray's inner circle – allegedly, in exchange for supplying young men, Boothby performed personal favours for Ronnie in return. Though he was too rebellious to ever achieve high office, he was a radical and often very prescient voice in British politics throughout his career – and he deserves to be remembered for his contribution to public life more than he does his enjoyment of his private one.

17 July 1986
Boothby: charmer with brilliant touch

British public life has lost one of its few really colourful characters by the death, aged 86, of Lord Boothby. His talents and his charm in his later years won him an immense following among the television viewers.

They were both so great that his friends viewed his failure ever to attain high offices as an almost sinful waste of good material. There was a time when he was regarded by many as a future Prime Minister.

His critics, many of whom could not resist affection for the object of their criticism, declared him to have too strong a strain of the playboy in his composition. It is probably true that in character, though not in views, he belonged more to the 18th than the 20th century.

At his best he was the most stimulating and intelligent of companions. At his bellicose worst he could be unreasonable and offensive. He had much in common with Randolph Churchill.

Robert John Graham Boothby was born just too late for service in the 1914–18 war. Indeed he used to tell his friends that he was the only person who wept on Armistice Day, 1918, because he had been robbed of the chance of serving his country in the field.

His zest for the dramatic side of life found an outlet in politics. He was elected as a Conservative for East Aberdeenshire in 1924, and this constituency stuck to him through thick and thin for 34 years.

He had a magnificent grounding by serving for three years as the Chancellor of the Exchequer's Parliamentary Private Secretary. The Chancellor was Winston Churchill.

The experience gave Boothby a life-long taste for speaking on economic matters and an equally ineradicable tendency to disagree with the "Treasury view".

He was a (slightly unpredictable) prophet of Keynesianism and reserved his finest diatribes for conventional finance and failure to export herrings.

In the later 1930s an extensive knowledge of Central Europe – he was incidentally, from first to last a fervent European – added another topic to his repertoire. He was furiously opposed to appeasement and found his spiritual home among the small band of anti-Munich Churchillians.

May 1940, brought him his first taste of administrative office as Parliamentary Secretary to the Ministry of Food. But alas, a previous error of judgment caught up with him.

He had been a protagonist in pressing, after Hitler's rape of Czechoslovakia, for the payment of compensation to Czech refugees, with one of whom he was on terms of friendship, out of the frozen assets of the Czech Government in this country.

It was alleged that he had an interest in such payments and, though he declared that he had never himself received a penny, he had clearly failed, although a Minister of the Crown, to disclose his connection with the affair when it came up for scrutiny. The House of Commons was indignant.

A Select Committee found against him and Lord Simon, the Lord Chancellor, went so far as to consider impeachment.

Churchill, who had more important matters on his mind, stamped on that suggestion but Boothby's political prospects were irrevocably destroyed and suspicion of his integrity was never finally dispelled.

He resigned office to become adjutant of a bomber squadron, but even in that capacity he was soon in official trouble for making indiscreet revelations at a dinner party.

He did not resign his seat which he hoped to use as his launching pad for a new post-war career.

As has happened before, his constituents took an officially proclaimed sinner only more to their hearts, and increased his majority in 1945 when many of his judges were ejected by the Labour landslide.

His new career proved to be a startling success in broadcasting and television. Never has a rounder peg dropped into a round hole. He had everything – a splendid voice, a quick wit, an appearance like an American senator, and an eye at once slumberous and twinkling.

In 1953 Churchill helped to take the sting out of memories of the Czech assets affair by recommending him for a KBE. This was indeed balm, not because of the honour itself, but because his father, whom he regarded with deep love and affection had held the same distinction. Then, five years later Harold Macmillan, whom he had wronged in other ways, was so magnanimous as to be recommend him for a life peerage.

His faults were as well known to his friends as his qualities, for he never concealed either. Behind and beneath the attractive mould of Eton and Magdalen there was the core of a lovable human being and the world is the poorer for the loss of any man of whom that can be said.

Unfortunately, he had an uncontrollable passion for adventure, which combined with a genuine interest in people, of whatever origin, sometimes led him into trouble. When he was photographed in company with the Kray brothers, even the friendliest of eyebrows were raised.

In August 1964, the International Publishing Corporation owners of the *Sunday Mirror* and the *Daily Mirror*, made an unqualified apology to Lord Boothby and announced they had paid him £40,000 compensation and paid his costs. This followed publication of an article in the *Sunday Mirror* about his association with the Krays and his homosexuality.

From the compensation Lord Boothby gave money to charity, including £5,000 to King Edward VII Hospital for Officers.

He had as he grew older more than his share of illness.

"I drink a great deal of alcohol," he said with cheerful frankness in 1962. "I have had cardiac trouble and very nearly thrombosis, I have had bronchitis every year for four years. I am overweight. I fear the doctor because I know exactly what he is going to tell me and that it is true."

Ill-health did not interrupt a steady flow of comments, mostly critical, which derived increasingly from a Radical standpoint. He developed a passionate if posthumous admiration for Lloyd George and somewhat ungratefully, was highly critical of Churchill.

All the radicals were disfranchised, he lamented in a letter to the *Daily Telegraph* towards the end of 1963: "This is a pity because they comprise the cream of the country, including yours faithfully, Boothby."

He was Rector of the University of St Andrews from 1958 to 1961, chairman of the Royal Philharmonic Orchestra from 1961 to 1963, a founder member of the of Royal Philharmonic Association and president of the Anglo-Israel Association. In 1950 he was appointed an Officer of the Legion of Honour.

He gave a party in November 1969, to celebrate 45 years of unbroken service in both Houses of Parliament.

In 1935, Lord Boothby married Diana Cavendish, daughter of Lord Richard Cavendish. She divorced him in 1937. He married in 1967 Miss Wanda Sanna, a Sardinian, then aged 34, whom he had met in Monte Carlo.

Horatio Bottomley

"Success turned his head."

Bottomley was one of the most noted patriots of the First World War, and the founder of the demagogic *John Bull* magazine. He was unfortunately equally famous for his financial disasters (he had to resign from Parliament on being declared bankrupt), which people were inclined to view with a degree of indulgence, at least until the full extent of his fraudulent behaviour became known. He died penniless in 1933, perhaps relieved to be spared the humiliation of continuing a precarious existence as a music hall novelty, the only avenue left to him after he had exhausted all others.

30 May 1922
Penal servitude for Horatio Bottomley
"Heartless frauds"

Sentence of seven years' penal servitude was passed on Horatio Bottomley, M.P., at the Old Bailey yesterday, when he was found guilty of fraudulently converting to his own use large sums of money entrusted to him for investment in the Victory Bond Club and other similar schemes. Mr Justice Salter referred to the case as of great importance from the point of view of public rectitude and commercial morality. He referred to defendant's long series of heartless frauds, and said he could see no mitigation whatever. The crime was aggravated by defendant's high position, by the number and poverty of his victims, by the magnitude of his frauds, and by the callous effrontery with which they were committed and sought to be defended. Defendant intimated that it was his intention to appeal.

Counsel for the Crown were: Mr Travers Humphreys, Mr H. D. Roome, and Mr Vernon Gattie. Defendant conducted his own case, assisted by a representative of Messrs. Lloyd, Richardson, and Co. Mr G. W. H. Jones held a watching brief.

Mr Travers Humphreys, continuing his address at the close of the defence, said he agreed with Mr Micawber's historic dictum, "Your financial position does not depend on your income but on your expenditure." "One man may have £40,000 a year and yet hardly have a shilling to bless himself" said counsel, "while another man may have only £250 a year and yet be a happy, free, and a comparatively wealthy man, because he owed no man anything, and even had £5 to spare." It was fortunate in the present case they had the best possible evidence of defendant's real financial position in May and June 1920. There was an old judgment debt against defendant, who was anxious to annul his bankruptcy, and on 4 May 1920, he swore an. affidavit in which he stated that his total income was £11,000 a year, of which for that year only £3,000 was free income. That was the position when he was drawing these colossal sums from moneys which did not belong to him. He said now that his income was £25,000 a year, at the end of 1919, and that by the middle of 1920 it had grown to £40,000. The jury could choose between the evidence of Mr Bottomley on oath in 1920, when he made the affidavit, and his evidence on oath in 1922, as to his income. Counsel asked the jury to accept the statement of Mr Bottomley in 1920, when at that time he was a poor man surrounded with difficulties and had to borrow a large sum of money in order to get his bankruptcy annulled, and, to use his own expression, he was struggling to get himself out of his liabilities.

Mr Bottomley, at the close of counsel's speech, rose from his seat at the solicitors' table, and, addressing his lordship, said, "I will now go, my lord, to the place where accused persons usually go." He then entered the dock and faced the court.

His lordship then commenced his summing up. The case, he said, had been well conducted on both sides; by counsel for the prosecution with great care and conspicuous fairness, and by the accused with great vigour and ability. By the jury the case had been followed with unflagging attention. They had been told by both sides that this was a simple case, and when they thrashed the matter out thought they would agree with that opinion, although it had occupied eight days. Questions regarding the history, management, and the financial position of the clubs had been responsible for a good deal of the time that had been occupied, but these only incidentally related to the charge against the defendant. The charge was not that he mismanaged the clubs, but that he fraudulently converted to his own use moneys entrusted to him, and that he did that on twenty-three different occasions. On each one of these the jury must determine, because these were twenty-three separate charges, and they must find him guilty, or not guilty on each. It was not necessary, in considering the case, that defendant should have been a trustee of the moneys in a technical sense. As a matter of fact, there was no doubt he was a trustee, but the things that must be proved by the prosecution in order to establish the guilt of the accused were three – the first was that he received the moneys for and on behalf of others; next, that he in fact converted the sum in question in each case to his own use; and, thirdly, that when he did that he did it dishonestly and fraudulently, knowing at the time that he was doing a dishonest thing. He might well have hoped to repay the money; no errand boy who stole a shilling out of the till but hoped to be able to repay it. The hope of replacing it was neither here nor there. The question was, was there conscious dishonesty at the time the money was appropriated? The onus of proof of those three things was upon the prosecution. If in any one of those cases the prosecution failed to satisfy them, it was the duty of the jury to acquit the defendant. Certain things had been talked about during the hearing or the case which the jury must put out of their mind in coming to a decision. One of those was the public and political position of the defendant; another had reference to patriotic service, and payment for lectures. All these things the jury must dismiss from their minds.

If it was not proved that defendant had not fraudulently appropriated this money he was entitled to an acquittal whether he was paid for his patriotic work or not, or whether he was a big or a little man. On the other hand, if the charges were proved their verdict must be one of "guilty". The case was in no way an exceptional one or different from any other precaution of alleged fraudulent appropriation, except in the amount of the alleged defalcations, which certainly were very large. They had a sequence of events in three periods. The period of 1918 was the first period – that of the War Stock Combination, the time when the moneys were paid into the Northern Territories Syndicate (No. 3) account. The second period was the last five months or so of 1919 – that was the period of the Victory Bond Club. The last period was the first five months of 1920 – that was the period when the Thrift Prize Fund had been formed. The moneys were in the Victory Bond Club account at the time, and that account contained the sums deposited in all three clubs. During the first period the defendant was charged with having fraudulently appropriated money in two cases amounting altogether to £17,500. In the second period he was charged with fraudulently appropriating in eight cases sums amounting to £90,000; and in the third period he was charged with fraudulently appropriating in thirteen more cases a little over £61,000. During the ten months defendant was dealing with the Victory Bond Club account he was charged with misappropriating sums amounting to £150,000, the total alleged defalcations being £170,000.

The clubs, his lordship went on to say, came to disaster, and in the end the Receivers appointed by the Court of Chancery took possession of what was left of the assets. There was not much left – only about £23,000. The jury were not concerned with the merits or demerits of Premium Bonds. This was not a question between the defendant and the depositors; it was a question between the defendant and the law. His lordship said he supposed it was plain enough that the outlook was not hopeful for those people who had not yet got their money, but the jury must on no account convict the defendant because they were sorry for the position of the unpaid depositors; they were on no account to convict merely because there was a deficit and some people would go unsatisfied. If the jury were convinced that the defendant put the money into his own pocket knowing he was doing a dishonest thing, then it was their duty to convict; and it was no use or excuse for the defendant to say, "I will make restitution." Dealing with the way in which the accounts had been handled, his lordship said there was such a thing as a stupid muddle, but there was also such a thing as a clever muddle – an intentional confusion. He pointed out that no trustees were appointed and no auditor; "But even if auditors had been appointed I don't know what there was for them to audit," he remarked, and added that the jury must also take into consideration what the defendant had said with regard to the fees asked for by auditors. One firm asked him as much as 7,000gns. "But I am not sure," his lordship went on, "when a man is dealing with other people's money to the extent of not far short of £900,000, that even 7,000gns might not be very wisely expended in seeing that everything was in order and above board." No record was kept of money received, and it was for the jury to judge whether a man who was taking other people's money as a trustee would not desire first, and above all things, to make a record of the amount for which he was answerable. A very valuable record might have been kept merely by using counterfoil certificates, and had the counterfoils been preserved, there would have been a complete record of the number of certificates that went out. He pointed to the discrepancy of the evidence of defendant and another witness on this question: but if the evidence of the witness was correct that counterfoil books were used, where were the counterfoils? This was not a case of some uneducated person who had a few entrusted to him and got into a muddle; it was a case of a very able and experienced business man, who received very important sums of money from people who trusted him – a man who appreciated as well as any business man in the City of London the importance of correct accounts when dealing with other people's money. Any honest account, however kept, would have rendered it impossible for the defendant to have appropriated, honestly or dishonestly, these great sums without immediate detection. His lordship went on to deal separately with each of the twenty-three counts in the indictment, reminding the jury that there had been twenty-four, but one (the seventh) had now gone. The Victory Bond Club account, he pointed out, was not only a trust account but a trust fund, and, in fact, contained only the money of those who had trusted the defendant On certain of the counts the defence was that the depositors owed defendant the money, that he had paid on their behalf more than he withdrew: "But," said the judge, "if I have got a man's money in my hands as a trustee – say, £100 – and he becomes indebted to me for £100, that does not make his property mine." Dealing with the count involving the largest sum, £37,000, which was realised on the sale of an allotment letter for £100,000 worth of bonds, his lordship asked what could be the defence. Up to that time, on defendant's own showing, the clubs were owing him nothing. There was the money taken and there was no existing debt. In all defendant had converted to his own use £150,000. The jury had to decide whether that was a fraudulent thing to do, and whether defendant must have known that at the time.

His lordship, resuming his address to the jury after lunch, mentioned that during the interval he had received a communication from the defendant with regard to the comments which he made during the morning concerning the £57,000 paid for newspapers. "The last thing in the world that I would desire is that anything he wishes should be placed before you which might assist him, should not reach you," said his lordship. Mr Bottomley had said he had in his bed-room in St. James's-street a chest containing £60,000 in small change, and some of the payments – so Mr Bottomley said – had been made out of that chest. His lordship did not think that in any way affected the point, but it was his duty to put it before the jury. He still contended there was no indebtedness to the defendant at the time the £57,000 was withdrawn. His lordship went on to deal with the defence that these great conversions of £150,000 of trust money were not fraudulently made because an equal amount had been paid by the defendant out of his own pocket. Were the jury going to believe he did pay these great sums/of money out of his own. private means for the benefit of the depositors? They know what sums were drawn out by him during ten months. In the 1919 period he drew out about £64,000, and it was charged against him that £33,000 of that was fraudulent conversion. That left between £30,000 and £31,000 drawn out by defendant during five months to which no objection was taken. In the first five months of 1920 the amounts drawn out were rather more than £124,000, and out of that it was alleged, that £64,000 was fraudulent conversion. That left a balance of £65,000 to which no objection was taken. Altogether, therefore, something over £90,000 had been properly taken out during ten months, and properly expended. There would also seem to have been available for expenses and repayments the £50,000 bonds of the War Stock Combination, so that altogether there would be available something like £140,000. In addition to that great sum they were asked to believe that defendant paid out of his own pocket and advanced to the clubs a further £150,000, making altogether not far short of £300,000. His lordship did not suppose anyone would doubt that defendant expended large sums in paying people off. The point was whether he paid them out of his own pocket.

Naturally, said the judge, there was evidence of large repayments. The money had all gone except £23,000, which the Receivers took over, and no one could doubt the bulk of the money had properly gone in repaying people. Defendant had these large sums of trust money out of which to pay off. The question was did he pay off any of it out of his own pocket. Where was the evidence except his own statement that he ever put his hands in his pocket to pay out a single person? The jury must consider the defendant's financial position at the time. Was he a man not merely rich, but so rich as to be able to produce these great sums of ready cash at the rate of £15,000 a month, or was he, on the contrary, at that time, embarrassed, pressed with liabilities and money troubles, so that he might be tempted to lay his hands upon trust funds in the hope that he might be able to restore it later? If these great sums of money came from the sources referred to by defendant, where were the documents, where were the receipts, and where were the bills? Defendant had known for some two or three months the case that was being made against him. If this £150,000 had really been paid by him would he not have come with a mass of documentary evidence, proving beyond doubt the payment by him out of this own resources of large sums for the benefit of these clubs? So far as his lordship was aware, they had not seen documentary evidence of the payment of a pound or a shilling. "If this trustee can defend himself in that way," said his lordship, "so, I suppose, can any other trustee. Considerable public responsibility rests upon you members of the jury to whom it has fallen by chance to decide this case, which is undoubtedly of importance from the point of view of public rectitude and commercial morality. I say to you frankly that if the mere assertion on oath of the defendant is to be accepted as sufficient in a case of this kind by a jury in the City of London, it is difficult to see how any trust fund can ever be protected and safe for those for whom it belongs."

Mr Justice Salter had spoken for an hour and a half, and when the jury retired to consider their verdict, the defendant went below from the dock.

After an absence of twenty-five minutes the jury returned with a verdict of guilty on twenty-three counts. On the direction of the judge a verdict of not guilty was returned on the seventh count, which related to a sum of £5,000, which had been withdrawn from the trust funds and afterwards repaid.

Mr Justice Salter asked Mr Travers Humphreys if there was anything further that he ought to know before passing sentence.

Mr Humphreys: I think not, my lord.

Mr Justice Salter then turned towards the defendant, who stood in the dock closely guarded by a couple of warders, and said: "Horatio Bottomley, you have been rightly convicted by the jury of this long series of heartless frauds. These poor people trusted you, and you robbed them of £150,000. The crime is aggravated by your high position, by the number and poverty of your victims, by the trust which they reposed in you, and which you abused. It is aggravated by the magnitude of your frauds, and by the callous effrontery with which they were committed and sought to be defended. I can see no mitigation. The sentence of the Court upon you is that you be kept in penal servitude for seven years."

Defendant, who appeared to be far less concerned than most of the spectators in the crowded court, asked if he could have an opportunity of consulting his solicitor with a view to an immediate notice of appeal.

Mr Justice Salter: Yes.

Defendant: And I take it that at this stage the question of bail does not arise?

Mr Justice Salter: "The question of bail does not arise at all. You may see your solicitor, but whether it will be allowed you to see him here or somewhere else will rest with the prison authorities. Subject always to the prison rules, you can have an interview with him."

Defendant, still leaning his arms on the rail in front of the dock, said: "I was under the impression that the question was sometimes put to accused persons whether they have anything to say before sentence is passed."

Mr Justice Salter: It is not customary in such cases of misdemeanour.

Defendant: I am glad it is not, because I should have said something rather offensive to the summing up.

Defendant was then taken below by the warden.

His lordship exempted the jury from further service in that court for five years.

Also 30 May 1922
The Bottomley sentence

The jury at the Central Criminal Court have decided that the charges of fraud and theft made against Mr Bottomley were proved. So ends the last, hardest struggle of an adventurous and melodramatic career. The verdict was not unexpected. No one who has read the evidence with care can doubt that many thousands of pounds of other people's money did stick to Mr Bottomley's fingers. The prisoner in his elaborate orations thought it best to leave the facts of the case alone. But till the moment that the verdict was given, judicious and experienced minds thought it something more than possible that the appeal of the Bottomley eloquence might lure the jury to an acquittal or to disagreement. He failed. His defence consisted of rhetoric and histrionics, protestations of patriotic and religious emotion, and a display of tears. It was well that he should fail. It is not in the public interest that such schemes as his should escape punishment, or that such advocacy as his should influence or bemuse a jury. But while we must approve the conviction, it is not irrational sentiment which persuades us to express regret that the career of a man of such powers should have ended in such merited disaster. This case was a monstrous example of fraud upon the public and abuse of public confidence. By a skilful mixture of appeals to patriotic feeling, to thrift, and to the appetite for speculation, Bottomley induced great numbers of small investors to entrust him with their money. They were promised, for example, a "unique chance to help our French Allies, and, at the same time, win a fortune". Of the funds which came into his power large sums were used to finance dubious enterprises and to provide for his private extravagance. When the man against whom these things were proved protests as his defence that to convict him would be "a shock to every man who fought for his country", he does not inspire sympathy. For the first time in his life, perhaps, he made the worst of a bad case against himself. There was only one verdict possible to jurors who kept their heads. It is not to be denied that the sentence of seven years' penal servitude was justly due. Yet those to whom the theatrical emotions of the speeches for the defence are most repugnant may not refuse to admit some pity for the man in his downfall.

A criminal who is past sixty and has before him such a sentence is at the end of his life. Bottomley's story, if we met it in the pages of Balzac, would seem to us rather a masterpiece of grandiose fancy than persuasively real. For he was not only such a chief among gamblers and cheats as Balzac loved to imagine; he had a singular power of demagogy, he was a *chevalier d'industrie* and a tribune of the people in one, and in both parts supreme. He began life as an office boy in a City warehouse. He learnt something of law in an attorney's office, which also taught him at an early age that the Tichborne claimant's belief in the division of mankind into rogues and fools was not unfounded. His legal education was extended by service as a shorthand writer in the law courts. His turn for popular oratory and popular writing was developed by an association with Charles Bradlaugh. There followed experiments in journalism which were not fruitful, and the adventurer sought a more profitable profession in the flotation of companies. The echoes of the great crash of the Hansard Union sound faintly on our ears, but the exploit of Bottomley in defending himself against all the resources of the Law Officers of the Crown and winning in the process the regard of a Judge who did not incline to sentimentality, Lord Brampton, is not likely to be forgotten by lawyers or laymen. The Hansard Company was not the only one of his promotions which went awry. His self-defence before Lord Brampton was the beginning of a series of cases. But fifteen years ago Bottomley was only thought of as a speculative financier, with a peculiar ability for legal procedure. Only in the last quarter of his life were his most remarkable powers discovered. He entered the House of Commons, and he set up a weekly journal of his own. His career in Parliament was interrupted by financial disasters, but there were good judges who thought it possible that he might have had there great success. There was no doubt about the success of his paper. He hit off with extraordinary skill the taste of the mass of uneducated people. Their feelings, their thoughts, were expressed for them with a flamboyant vigour such as they found nowhere else. He had no high aims. He simply sought to say to-day what the crowd were saying yesterday, or would probably say to-morrow. And he found that it gave him wealth and what, to do him justice, he valued as much as wealth, importance. It is idle to deny or minimise his appeal to great audiences, whether as speaker or Journalist. He gave them the rhetoric which moved them, and the emotions by which they desired to be moved. And a fair critic would admit that at times the rhetoric and the emotions were sound enough.

Success turned his head. There is little doubt that he came to believe himself not merely a rhetorician who put into words what crowds wanted to hear, but a leader whom crowds would follow. He did not, to be sure, know where to lead them. His policies were mere words. But he sought to set himself up as a dictator of opinion. He would found a party in the State. He would speak through many newspapers. And he found that he had misjudged the people whom he boasted himself to know through and through. He had taken Horatio Bottomley seriously, and that was beyond their understanding. While he spoke as the knowing Cockney gamin, his first and most sincere pose, they applauded and laughed with him as well as at him. When he professed an ardour of violent patriotism they became critical. When he tried to give the fervour of his rhetoric a religious spirit they were puzzled or disgusted. The general public who had watched, not without goodwill, his adventures, his desperate escapes, and his infinite ingenuity, had no sympathy for the mingling of financial schemes and scatter-brained politics with calling upon the name of God and protestations of loyalty to the men who fell in France. They could be indulgent to the escapades of a gallant gambler, but they were not inclined to be merciful to hypocrisy. Yet it is possible that a wise judge of human nature would pronounce Bottomley no less sincere in his virtuous rhetoric than in his earlier jovial cynicism as the average sensual man. At the moment they were uttered he may well have believed in both professions of faith. He was even capable of believing both at once. His success depended upon his skill in catching the tone of the hour. He had no principles to interfere with his denunciation of Serbia on the eve of war. He could become at a moment's notice more warlike than the most determined friend of France. No sceptical mockery from his past disturbed him when he found that religion was a living reality to the masses whose spokesman he was determined to be. His convictions could always be changed. As he never thought anything out, it is probable that he was sincere in his most unpleasant mingling of arguments to cupidity and to loyalty to the dead. There was to him nothing nauseous in the desire to make the best of both worlds. It seemed to him – the fact is written large in his success and his failure – the governing emotion of the natural man. For the right analysis of his character would find in him a compound of the gambler and the emotional rhetorician. He had the daring and the cunning, the fantastic hopes, and the cold cynicism of the man for whom the excitement of gambling is the greatest joy in life. He had the gambler's generosity and the gambler's heartlessness. But no less potent in him was the temperament of the rhetorician. He could believe anything while he was saying it or writing it. If he was in the vein he could make the great mass of the uncritical believe it too. But his greatest power was found in persuading them that they were wise and noble creatures to think what they were thinking, and believe what they had come to believe. It is an ability which, in our modern world, will carry a man far. The disaster which ends Bottomley's career may serve to point the old warning that men and women are not so foolish as the cynics and the sentimentalists fancy, that the demagogue and the charlatan are not the natural rulers of mankind, and that in the end of the day common-sense and reason assert their power and deliver us from the sway of those who trade upon the passion of the hour.

Boulton and Park

"It was an outrage upon public decency which every
right-minded person would say should not be tolerated."

In 1871 Thomas Ernest Boulton and Frederick William Park were charged "with conspiring and inciting persons to commit an unnatural offence". They were cross-dressers who liked to be known as Fanny and Stella. The case centred on an attempt to prove they engaged in anal sex and the evidence featured an incredibly intrusive examination designed to establish this beyond doubt. This it was unable to do. Nor were they able to persuade the jury that wearing women's clothes was in any sense a crime, so Thomas and Frederick (or Fanny and Stella) walked free.

16 May 1871
The Boulton and Park prosecution
The hearing of this case was resumed yesterday,
at the sitting of the Court of Queen's Bench

The Crown and the defendants were represented as on the former days.

Proceedings were commenced by the examination of Eliza Clark, the witness whose absence had been much remarked upon in earlier stages of the trial, and whose attendance had been secured by the earnest exertions of Mr Lewis, the attorney for the defendants Boulton and Park.

Eliza Clark was called, and examined by Mr Digby Seymour. She said: In May 1868, I was in the service of Mrs Peck, in Southampton-street, and left in April 1869. I was there during the time Lord Arthur Clinton and Mr Boulton lodged there. I was housemaid. Maria Duffin was there a part of the time, She was there one month. Mr Boulton dressed as a man. I only saw him dressed as a woman once. Mr Park was dressed as a woman on that occasion. They were going to private theatricals. Lord Arthur Clinton and Mr Boulton always occupied separate rooms. Mr Boulton's father and mother called once or twice to see him. It was my duty to make up the rooms and take in the breakfast. Lord Arthur Clinton and Mr Boulton always conducted themselves as gentlemen. I have heard Mr Boulton sing, and used to accuse him of being a female. He passed it as a joke, and laughed. I remember Lord Arthur Clinton being ill. A young lady called to see him. I let her in and let her out. She gave the name of Lady Albert Clinton. She did not send in a card.

Cross-examined by the Attorney-General: I came back to Mrs Peck, and was in her service when I was examined at the police-court. Maria Duffin sometimes helped me to make up the beds. I was examined at the Treasury. What I stated was correct. I was examined before the magistrate.

Did you say at the Treasury, "We all thought for the first month that Boulton was a woman dressed in man's clothes?" – I said I believed he was a woman until his father and mother came.

But did you say what I have read to you, that for a month you all thought they were women? – I might have said so.

Did you say that Mrs Peck said he must be a man, as his father and mother came to see him, for that they would not come if he were a woman dressed in man's clothes? – Yes.

Did you go on to say, "I and my fellow-servant still believed that he was a woman?" – Yes.

And was that true? – Yes.

Did you believe he was a woman all the time he was there? – I did.

Cross-examination continued: I said that Park used to come for two or three days, and then go away for about the same time; and that was true. I do not know which room he occupied. Lord Arthur Clinton, Boulton, and Park had each a latch-key. Cummings and Thomas used to visit Lord Arthur Clinton while Boulton and Park were there. Lord Arthur Clinton, Boulton, and Park used to go out to dine in the evening, and seldom returned till after we were in bed. I cannot say whether Boulton and Park powdered their faces.

Did you not say before the magistrate, "Boulton and Park used powder to their faces. I thought Park was a woman as well as Boulton?" – I cannot remember saying it.

Did they use powder to their faces? – I cannot remember.

Did you say you thought Park was a lady as well as Boulton? – I think I said that.

Did you say that a hairdresser came every day to curl their hair? – No, sir.

What did you say about a hairdresser? – That he came once or twice a week.

What for? – To curl their hair.

Whose hair? – Boulton and Park's.

And Lord Arthur Clinton's? – No, sir.

Re-examined by Mr Digby Seymour: Did you tell at the Treasury the name and address of the hairdresser? – Yes.

Did Boulton and Park go out to dine dressed as gentlemen? – They did.

You heard Boulton sing? – Yes, sir. He sang like a woman.

Was it from his voice you judged he was a woman? – From his voice and appearance.

The Lord Chief Justice: You say that Maria Duffin was there only a month? – Yes.

How do you know that? – Because she said to me at the end of a fortnight the work was too hard for her, and that she was going to be married.

Did you hear her speaking to the defendant Boulton about his being a woman? – I did.

What did she say? – Just the same as I said myself.

What was that? – "I believe you are a woman."

What was his reply? – I do not recollect.

How was he dressed then? – To the best of my recollection as a man – at least I know he was.

The Attorney-General then replied on the part of the Crown, He said he should have been most happy could he have refrained from addressing the jury; but, if he did, he should be guilty of a dereliction of his public duty. They had heard no fewer than eight speeches from his learned friends, who had used on behalf of the defendants all the eloquence and ability and practiced dexterity of which they were capable. The jury had before them the accused, and it was almost impossible not to sympathise with men – whether they were innocent or guilty – who were undergoing a grievous ordeal. But there was another great party to the case – the public – a mere abstraction, with whom it was difficult to sympathise, but whose interest in the case – great as was that of the accused – was paramount. He had little to complain of in the speeches of his learned friends. They had spoken of him on the whole with a good deal of kindness and courtesy. Sir John Karslake had imputed to him a good deal of blame, but in a kind and considerate, he might almost say a condescending manner; and at last he acquitted him of everything hut negligence. He was deeply obliged to his learned friend, but had to say that, whatever might be his sins – and he dare say they were numerous – negligence was not one of them. Whether he had acted rightly or wrongly was matter of opinion; but the course he had taken had been anxiously considered by himself, his colleague, the Solicitor-General, and by the experienced and permanent advisers of the Crown; and his opinion of the course they had adopted was not affected by the disapprobation of Sir John Karslake. His learned friend was of opinion that there ought to have been two trials – one in London, and one in Scotland; and he ventured to say that if ever there was a case in which there should be one trial, and one only, it was this. He admitted that, in considering the case, the evidence ought to be regarded as it bore upon the differ-ent defendants; and he had been careful to distinguish between them in dealing with the case. His learned friends, who were great rhetoricians, had – as had been stated during the course of the evidence – created giants for the purpose of slaying them. With the utmost gallantry they had stormed and waved the flag of victory over positions which nobody occupied but themselves. He would not say they had mis-represented, but they certainly had misunderstood, some of the propositions he had advanced. He had never said that the theatricals in which the defendants indulged were other than innocent. On the contrary, in his opening address he had distinctly pointed out that, in that respect, the proceeding of the defendants was perfectly legitimate. But while evidence was given of their acting at the Egyptian Hall, at Scarborough, and elsewhere, all the evidence pointed to a time anterior to the taking of the lodgings in Wakefield-street, and it had not been shown that those lodgings had ever been used for the purpose of dressing for theatricals. His learned friends had promised to identify the dresses produced in court with parts which the defend-ant had sustained on the stage.

Mr Serjeant Parry said that several of the dresses had been identified.

The Lord Chief Justice said that the evidence fairly pointed to the dresses hav-ing been originally obtained for theatrical purposes. It did not follow, however, that, although they were obtained for a lawful, they had not been afterwards used for an unlawful purpose.

The Attorney-General went on to say that the proceedings of the defendants Boulton and Park had been defended on the ground that they were larks and frol-ics. If they were, the larks and frolics were long continued. Was it a mere frolic to walk about the streets of London at night in women's clothes, and that constantly, in Regent-street, the Burlington Arcade, and the casinos? Was it a frolic to go to the Alhambra dressed as men, but in such a manner as to lead every one who saw them to believe that they were women, and so behaving that they were several times turned out? The learned Attorney-General commented at great length upon the evi-dence, which, he submitted, pointed to the guilt of the accused. On behalf of the

Crown he was not interested to obtain a verdict of guilty if the defendants were innocent. On the contrary, it would be his duty, if he thought them innocent, to withdraw the charge against them. His only interest was to secure, as far as in him lay, that justice should be done. His learned friend Serjeant Parry had called on them for the sake of the character of the country to acquit the prisoners. The character of the country would not be affected by their conviction, but it would be if crime detected were allowed to escape unpunished.

The Lord Chief Justice then proceeded to sum up the case to the jury. He said, advocacy had fulfilled its task and discharged its duty. It was now for them, with such assistance as he could give them, to bring their minds calmly and dispassionately to the consideration of the entire case. And the case was assuredly one which required the utmost discrimination and care at their hands, not only on account of the interests of public justice, but the parties now standing accused, and not the less from the form in which the case was presented. They were trying the defendants for conspiring to commit an offence, and to prove that it was necessary also to prove the perpetration of the offence. Now, that was not a course which appeared to him to commend itself to their approbation. He was strongly of opinion that whether the proof intended to be submitted to the jury was proof of the fact, it was not a proper course to charge the parties with conspiring to commit it. His reason for saying this was that it manifestly operated unjustly, unfairly, and oppressively against the parties. The prosecution was enabled to combine in one indictment a variety of offences to the prejudice of particular defendants, who were deprived of the invaluable advantages of being able to call as witnesses the parties who were indicted with them. He did not say this merely on his own authority. He had the authority of one of the ablest judges of our time – the late Lord Cranworth – for the view which he then propounded – who said, in reference to a case then before him, that although the course to which he objected could be legally pursued, it never was satisfactory. He (the Lord Chief Justice) must say that it would have been far better if those persons who were indicted for the offences of a separate character had been put on their trial separately in respect to those things for which they were personally liable. However, the case was before them, and they must deal with it. There was this further difficulty, however, in the way. There were two indictments, only one of which was then for trial. On the second indictment, which was not before them, the defendants were charged with conspiring to outrage public decency, and upon that indictment the defendants could be hereafter tried. But in this case the whole evidence was given – evidence which must necessarily operate most materially to prejudice the defendants, if they did not carefully bear in mind that they were trying the defendants not for an outrage upon public decency, or for conspiring to commit such outrage, but for conspiracy to commit the felony charged in the present indictment. Unless they were satisfied of that, no amount of misconduct, however repulsive or offensive, would justify them in giving a verdict against the defendants. With these observations he would endeavour to lay before their minds the material facts of the case. It divided itself into two branches – one relating to the public conduct, and the other to the private relations, of the defendants. There could be no doubt that for some time before their apprehension two of the defendants, Boulton and Park, had been in the habit of conducting themselves in public in a most odious, offensive, and reprehensible manner. It had been distinctly proved that, sometimes in the dress of females, with tawdry finery, sometimes dressed as men, but so powdered and painted as to appear to be women, these two defendants were in the habit of appearing at the Alhambra, the theatres, and other public places. On four occasions they were compelled to leave the Alhambra through the confusion which their appearance caused. They were also ordered out of the Burlington Arcade, although very likely, if they had bribed that austere guardian of the public morals, Mr Smith – (laughter) – they would have been allowed to remain. From their lodgings in Wakefield-street they were in the habit of going to different places dressed as women, stating that they were about to appear in private theatricals, but he thought the jury would agree with him that that was a mere pretext. They were seen at the Holborn Casino – a place of resort of a certain description – and also, late at night, in Brunswick-square, walking like women of the streets. They were also seen at theatres. The evidence on that subject began with that of Mr Mundell. His lordship then read Mr Mundell's evidence, and also that in reference to the visit to the Lyceum Theatre in female attire, and that which he termed the revolting incident of Boulton going into the ladies' room. When arrested they endeavoured to get off by bribing the officer. The fact should not be lost sight of, but ought not to be strained against the defendants. It did not follow that they were conscious of the charge now preferred against them, and they knew that exposure of a painful nature was certain, and that, in all probability, punishment would follow for the offence of appearing in women's clothes. It was impossible to speak in terms too strong of the conduct of the two defendants, Boulton and Park. No one could doubt that it was a gross outrage upon public morals and public decency – one which deserved not only reprehension, but actual and severe punishment. It was an outrage upon public decency which every right-minded person would say should not be tolerated; but in his opinion, even if it were done for frolic and amusement, it ought to be the subject of summary and severe punishment. He could not help thinking that it was an offence to which the provisions of a most useful Act which dealt with offences against public propriety, and made them subject to summary punishment, ought to be extended. If the law as it stood could not reach it, he could not help saying it ought to be the subject of legislation, made punishable by three or four months' imprisonment; and, if that had not the desired effect, a little exercise on the treadmill and a little wholesome corporal discipline, not only in this, but in all cases of outrages against public decency, would be a useful and salutary mode of teaching people to behave with propriety. But it was not that offence for which the defendants were being tried. They should not allow their feelings, in reference to those proceedings, to warp their judgment in trying the far more serious accusation against the defendants. It was said that no inference but one could be drawn from the fact of their putting on tawdry finery and imitating the manners of what were called "gay women", but what they would call prostitutes. In considering that question, they should not allow themselves to be carried away by their natural indignation at the conduct of the defendants, lest they should do injustice to those who had so painfully misconducted themselves. The defendants say, "You accuse us of having been wearing female dresses. Well, we can account for having them," and the evidence no doubt fairly accounted for their having had the dresses for a legitimate purpose. He said legitimate purpose, because, although they might think it a custom more honoured in the breach than the observance for a man to appear on the stage in female characters, it was not an offence against law or public morals, however it might be a matter of bad taste. They sought to account for their appearance in places of public resort by saying that it was a matter of vitiated taste. Mrs Boulton, who gave her evidence in a manner which commanded their respect, spoke of the aptitude of her son from an early age for personating female characters, of his taste for music, and of his feminine appearance and grace. That taste was not – as it would be well if it had been – checked. It was, on the contrary, encouraged – and it gave rise to that vanity which would not probably be objected to in a female, but which in a man was contemptible and repulsive. All that, it was said, suggested to the two defendants in question the idea of going about dressed as females. It was for the jury to say whether it sufficiently accounted for conduct as extraordinary as had ever been heard of. He was bound to say that, after carefully sifting the entire evidence, it seemed to be wanting in proof of the purpose alleged in the indictment being carried out – and that, notwithstanding the fact that the police had their eye upon the defendants for a long time, and they were seen in all the public places which had been spoken of. They should also remember that on the occasion of which Mr Mundell spoke the defendants did not by word or gesture offend against propriety. He should now refer to the private relations subsisting between the parties. His lordship then read and commented on the evidence in reference to Lord Arthur Clinton and the defendant Boulton lodging in Southampton-street, and the letters written by Boulton and Park to Lord Arthur Clinton. The letters, he said, were remarkable, and were certainly capable of the construction put on them by the Attorney-General. But was there no solution consistent with innocence? One had crossed his mind; he did not say that it was satisfactory: and it was this: Those parties were mixed up in theatrical performances, and Lord Arthur Clinton and the defendant Boulton had taken the parts of man and woman on the stage, and it was said that Boulton, in consequence of his success, assumed the name of "Stella". It might be that off the stage they spoke to and of each other as they did on the stage, and, that the practice became a habit. That might account for the extravagant and unnatural language which they found in the letters. He now approached the case in reference to the defendants Hurt and Fiske, and he did so with pain. In his opinion – and he said so emphatically – Hurt and Fiske ought never to have been included in the indictment. It was a grievous injustice to them to have mixed them up with proceedings which were peculiar to the other defendants, with which they had nothing in common, and which were calculated secretly to prejudice them. The administration of justice was seriously affected by the course which had been adopted. They must be satisfied that there was a conspiracy in this country. Over what might have happened in Scotland they had no jurisdiction; and if there was a conspiracy in Scotland it ought to have been investigated there. It was an oppression for a man to be taken from the country in which he lived and could readily have called witnesses to another country in which he could only do so at great expense, and to mix him up in indictment with the proceedings of others with which he had nothing to do, and against which, indeed, Mr Hurt had remonstrated, as in his letters he stated his disapprobation of Boulton going about in woman's clothes. It was hard upon a man to be subjected to prejudice which attached to others. How it came about was manifest. The police took the case into their own hands, and the case illustrated the necessity of some one being appointed who should control such proceedings. The police arrested the defendants Boulton and Park for an offence against public decency, for appearing in woman's clothes. One of the police went to Edinburgh, where, without any authority whatever, he took possession of the letters found in the houses of the defendants Fiske and Hurt. The police knew that Hurt was in London; they took him into custody, and then they handed the case over quietly to the Treasury, and, to his utter astonishment, the Treasury and the public prosecutor adopted the whole proceedings, and treated these two defendants as though the offence were committed in this country. It had been done, however, and the jury should deal with the case. They should not think he had made those observations to deter them from a stern – the sternest – discharge of their duty. He made them with a view to influence the course to be taken in future cases; as, being engaged in the administration of justice, he confessed he regarded as not only impolitic but improper, the course that had been adopted. His lordship then read and commented upon the letters written by the defendants Fiske and Hurt, and stated that the defendants were charged with conspiracy, and that conspiracy was the common action of at least two minds. Before, therefore, convicting the Scotch defendants of conspiracy, they should be satisfied as to reciprocity of sentiment existing on the part of the defendant Boulton. The medical evidence was next reviewed, and his lordship said that Mr Paul had acted most unwarrantably in having examined the defendants without any authority whatever. He hoped that gentleman would know better in future, and he could not help thinking that if he had had to deal not with effeminate, but with strong men, he might have met with summary punishment. Nothing tended so strongly to prejudice the public mind as to the guilt of the accused as that evidence of Mr Paul – evidence which was opposed to the testimony of the eminent surgeons who had been examined. Having concluded his review of the evidence, his lordship said he had now gone through the whole of that most painful case, and it was for them now to form an impartial and dispassionate conclusion with reference to it. It was one, no doubt, of great public concern. He concurred with the Attorney-General that where crime was detected it was the duty of a jury to discharge their duty sternly. Justice should, however, be tempered with just consideration of the interests of those who were accused. If they thought the case had not been made out – even if they thought that it was doubtful whether it had been made out – they should give their verdict for the defendants. There was but one point in the speech of Serjeant Parry – that speech distinguished by its manly energy, its simple beauty, and real genuine oratory – to which he took exception, and it was that in which he asked the jury to allow their view to be influenced by considerations for the moral character of the nation. It would be fatal to the character of the country if guilt, when detected, was allowed to go unpunished. The first and greatest attribute of a great nation was the moral character of its people: the second, almost of as deep importance, was the pure administration of justice. If they were satisfied of the guilt of the accused, then they should not be afraid of the consequences of saying so. Their sole duty was to consider the evidence, and to decide upon it. In that sacred temple of justice no considerations save those of truth and justice should be entertained; no passion, no prejudice should be allowed to enter that sanctuary.

They had to take care, on the one hand, that guilt proved should find no means of escape, and. on the other hand, that innocence, or even doubtful guilt, should receive that protection to which, according to the sacred principles of be law, it was entitled.

The Jury retired at four o'clock to consider their verdict.

A few minutes before five o'clock they returned into court, and handed in a verdict of acquittal of the four defendants on all the counts in the indictment.

The announcement of the verdict was followed by loud applause in court.

The defendant Boulton, on hearing the verdict, fainted. Some water was procured, and he shortly afterwards revived.

The Lord Chief Justice, addressing the Attorney-General, said: I Suppose, Mr Attorney, you will not proceed with the other indictments at this late hour. This is the last day of the sitting, and there would be no time to try the case. It had better stand over until next term.

The Attorney-General said that would be the better course.

The defendants shortly afterwards left the court with their friends.

John Bryan and Sarah Ferguson

"Just good friends."

Sarah Ferguson had long been a tabloid favourite, even before the pictures of her dalliance with John Bryan emerged. With Prince Andrew frequently away on Navy business, she was considered to spend too much time in the company of other men. The more unkind quarters of the press responded to this perceived *lèse majesté* by dubbing her the "Duchess of Pork". In retrospect the incident is as notable for the debates it prompted about media ethics – obsessed by their circulation figures, the British red tops were sent into an unseemly feeding frenzy – and the invasion of privacy. Fergie and Andrew separated within the year and divorced in 1996.

21 August 1992
Snatched photos spark Fleet Street battle
Legal threat as the *Mirror* keeps grip on a cut-price coup
By Maurice Weaver

The *Daily Mirror* printed an extra 80,000 copies yesterday to satisfy the curiosity of readers about the controversial and much-vaunted pictures of the Duchess of York romping beside a holiday swimming pool with her wealthy Texan friend, Mr John Bryan.

But the paper's satisfaction at its coup was tempered by the appearance of identical pictures in the rival *Sun* and *Today* tabloids, and executives were gearing up for a legal wrangle over breach of copyright.

Some of the 22 colour photographs, surreptitiously snatched using a telephoto lens by Daniel Angeli, an Italian photographer, show the 32-year-old Duchess wearing only a bikini bottom.

The *Mirror* is believed to have paid about £50,000 for exclusive UK rights. If correct, this would be regarded as cheap, considering their explosive nature.

Because they depict the wife of the Queen's second son in a series of apparently compromising positions with Mr Bryan, they have become one of the hottest photographic properties for years and the focus of intense interest by British tabloids.

They were also published widely in Europe and America. The pictures were taken at Le Mas de Pignerolle, a St Tropez villa where the Duchess was on holiday with her two children, Beatrice, four, and Eugenie, two.

Mr Bryan, 37, a businessman who has described himself as "a friend and financial adviser", was also there.

In 12 of the shots the Duchess and Mr Bryan are seen on sunbeds. One of these shows him kissing her foot while in another, carried prominently on the *Mirror*'s front page under the headline "Fergie's stolen kisses", the couple are entwined.

Among a variety of other scenes is one showing the pair standing up kissing while Eugenie looks on, and a series of happy shots of the Duchess, Mr Bryan and the children cavorting in the water.

Although the Duchess is topless her breasts are covered in all the pictures by her arms or the angle from which the photograph was taken. However, the *Mirror* promises "more sensational pictures" this morning and these are thought to be considerably more revealing.

Angeli, who is one of Europe's most successful paparazzi, is well known to the picture editors of tabloid newspapers and magazines for his pictures of Princess Caroline of Monaco and pop stars like Mick Jagger.

He has sold his work to the *Daily Mirror* in the past and has many personal contacts on the paper. He approached it last Thursday afternoon offering a portfolio of 50 spy-camera pictures of the Duchess and friend on holiday.

A senior *Mirror* executive travelled to Paris to see the pictures before agreeing a deal. Angeli was simultaneously placing his work in other countries. The takers included ¡Hola!, the Spanish sister publication of Britain's *Hello!* magazine, the Swiss journal *Blick*, *Oggi* of Italy, *Das Neues* in Germany and the American supermarket tabloid the *Star*.

Paris Match was also reported to be interested, but its editors fell foul of French press laws when Mr Bryan sought a last-minute injunction. At a confused hearing in Paris the magazine's lawyers denied that the magazine possessed such pictures.

They were given until 11.30 a.m. today to produce a clear response.

The failure of a similar move by Mr Bryan in the British High Court left the *Daily Mirror* and its sister paper, the *Scottish Daily Record*, free to publish. Copies of the *Mirror* were not circulated in France yesterday because of confusion there over the legal situation.

The *Mirror* normally sells 2.8 million copies at this time of year, but printed 3.5 million on Wednesday night. A spokesman said newsagents had reported that these had sold out by 9 a.m. yesterday, depriving regulars of their copies – so a further 80,000 were run off.

He added: "These figures show there is enormous public interest in the subject."

The *Daily Record* also increased its normal run of about 750,000. The *Mirror* issued a warning that the pictures were its copyright and BBC1's *Breakfast Time* programme, which normally shows the day's front pages, displayed the *Mirror* with the Duchess's picture blacked out.

¡*Hola!* published its pictures yesterday as did the American paper. So far Angeli is believed to have earned about £250,000 from his undercover work in St Tropez and this could well double as the pictures are sold throughout the world.

Several other magazines are known to be interested, though the legal delicacy has made them touchy.

Staff at Germany's Bauer publishing house, which produces the downmarket *Neue Blatt* magazine, said that a management gag on the subject had been applied.

One editor said: "I cannot deny we have the Fergie pictures. Nor can I can confirm it.

"An order to remain silent on the subject has been circulated by management."

The *Daily Mirror's* tabloid rivals, meanwhile, faced the prospect of being left out in the cold – an alarming prospect for their editors, given the saucy nature of the pictures and the fact that they feature the Duchess, a figure they have long loved to pillory.

In a 'damage control' exercise Stuart Higgins, deputy editor of the *Sun*, who is editing this week, and Martin Dunn, editor of *Today* – both News International newspapers – decided to use the ploy of reproducing some of the pictures that appeared in yesterday's edition of the Madrid-based ¡*Hola!* magazine.

Both chose the same picture for their front pages, showing Mr Bryan kissing the Duchess's foot, and each carried the masthead of the Spanish magazine.

The *Sun's* splash headline spoke of "Toe-Job Fergie", while *Today's* simply said "Scandal".

The catch-up must have demanded rapid movement by staff of the two papers on Wednesday night. Their first editions went without the pictures from ¡*Hola!*, whose copies were not running off the Madrid presses until late that night.

It is thought that the *Sun* and *Today* had someone in Madrid grab magazine copies hot off the press and transmit the pages by wire to London. The ruse incensed Richard Stott, editor of the *Mirror*, who had bought UK rights to the originals. Mr Charles Collier-Wright, the *Daily Mirror's* legal manager, said yesterday: "We believe the *Sun* and *Today* are in breach of our rights and are considering such steps as are appropriate."

These could be an action for damages or an injunction to stop the papers repeating the exercise with other pictures. Although "fair dealing" clauses of the Copyright, Designs and Patents Act, 1988, does allow newspapers to reproduce the work of others "for the purpose of reporting current events" this applies to words and not to photographs.

It also seemed that the editorial management of ¡*Hola!* was not approached by the two London editors for permission to lift their material. The magazine's staff said they had no knowledge of what was going on.

If the *Sun* and *Today* had assumed that crediting the magazine by carrying its title with the pictures would placate the editors of ¡*Hola!* they seem to have been mistaken. A spokesman for the magazine said: "We are indignant."

There was a further mystery. The ¡*Hola!* masthead superimposed over the picture on the *Sun's* front page showed the issue number as 2,505 and the specific date in

August had been deleted. The actual issue of ¡Hola! published yesterday and carry-ing the Duchess pictures was 2,507 and carried the publication date 27 August.

This led some *Mirror* journalists to claim that the *Sun* had copied its pictures from their first editions and superimposed an old ¡Hola! masthead to disguise it.

Asked to comment on the allegation, the *Sun* was only able to field Mr Bill Newman, its managing editor, who said: "I wasn't involved so I don't know anything about it."

Also 21 August 1992
The embarrassment of two "just good friends"
By Dan Conaghan

Yesterday did not begin too well for 37-year-old American businessman John Bryan.

There was, of course, the matter of the morning newspapers sporting pictures of him in intimate commune with the Duchess of York.

But then his red Vauxhall Astra hire car, standing illegally on yellow lines outside his flat in Cheney Place, Chelsea, was wheel-clamped. "It doesn't matter who he is," said PC Nigel Legg, doing his duty. "He's going to have to pay. It will cost him £98 in fines and to have his vehicle freed."

At 1.30 p.m., wearing a blue pinstripe suit, the balding Mr Bryan emerged into a scrum of reporters.

"I'm sorry, I have no further comment to make in addition to the comments and statement I made last night," he told them.

Then he sped off in the back of a white chauffeur-driven Mercedes Benz to lunch at Santinis restaurant in Ebury Street with two business associates.

He returned smiling just before 3 p.m. in a different car and went into the flat without talking to reporters.

Such uncommunicativeness is unusual in the genial man who, following the Duchess of York's separation from her husband, swiftly assumed several roles.

He became "financial adviser" to the Duchess, her "unofficial press spokesman" and "honest broker" helping to patch up her broken six-year marriage. It was he who escorted her on a Far Eastern holiday in April to recover from her parting with the Duke of York.

When the holiday was over, it was he who returned to Sunninghill Park to brief the Duke – for five hours – on how things stood.

Revelling in the role of unofficial private secretary, he became her compan-ion-around-town, arranging meetings with bankers and shepherding her to parties.

He grinned relentlessly, but was always careful not to be photographed too close to her. He and the Duchess were, he maintained, "just good friends".

In June the Duchess and Mr Bryan was seen shopping for men's boxer shorts in New York. They flew to the United States, booking separate rooms at a four-star hotel. As speculation grew over the extent of their friendship, Bryan said: "There is absolutely no question of any romance between us at all. Nor will there ever be."

He dismissed as "lies" a claim that he had moved into Romenda Lodge, the Duchess's £4,000-a-month rented home in Wentworth, Surrey.

But his smooth confidence has been shaken in the past 48 hours: what began as a friendly professional relationship has been disclosed as an embarrassingly intimate one.

The pair seem suited to one other and have much in common. Bryan lacks the Hooray bumptiousness of the Duchess's other male friends.

He is equally at home skiing, riding to hounds in Gloucestershire with the Berkeley or pumping iron at the Bath and Racquets Club, in Mayfair. He also has expensive tastes.

Both he and the Duchess frequent Annabel's, the Berkeley Square nightclub.

One acquaintance, Taki, the wealthy Greek social columnist, upbraided Bryan for not paying debts back quickly enough.

Taki lost $50,000 he invested with the telecommunications company EnCom, which Bryan set up in 1985 and which foundered four years later.

Recently Taki told the *New York Observer*: "After the company failed, he went doggo for a while and then turned up again with Fergie. Let's face it, he's a flake (eccentric). But he's great at handling the press."

The Duchess and Bryan come from broadly similar backgrounds and both are at ease in the company of affluent American and English friends.

Armed with a respectable, if routine, education, Bryan became a businessman.

He has inherited his father Tony's entrepreneurial style and the pair now use London as their base and share a modest Chelsea flat. Though Bryan is often described as a millionaire, it was probably a "paper" one – and some years ago. His business dealings do not always run smoothly.

The Bryans' last venture, a marine electronics and construction company called Oceanics Group, recorded share losses of £7.5m in 1990 and they were forced to sell up. Bryan is now an "executive" with a German health care company.

While he has had varied business success, socially he has been accomplished to the point where travelling and partying now seem to fill most of his time.

He moves in a crowd of the youngish rich, including the Texan Steve Wyatt, whose presence in holiday snaps with the Duchess has been partly blamed for her marriage break-up.

His former girlfriends include Flora Fraser, daughter of Lady Antonia, and Geraldine Ogilvy, daughter of Viscount Rothermere. His name has also been linked with the banking heiress Natasha Grenfell and Lady Liza Campbell.

22 August 1992
Royal Family present united front over more photos of Duchess
By Caroline Davies and Tim Witcher

The Royal Family stuck to their traditional Balmoral holiday schedule yesterday, after further revealing pictures of the Duchess of York and wealthy Texan Mr John Bryan, secretly photographed in intimate poses on holiday, were plastered over the British tabloids.

The Queen and her family presented a united front of complete normality.

But there was increasing media speculation that the Duchess would not remain long at Balmoral and would fly from Aberdeen to Heathrow and then abroad, possibly to Argentina to her mother, Mrs Susan Barrantes. There was no sign of the Duchess as she kept a low public profile while the other members of the Royal Family continued their holiday pursuits.

It is thought it would be difficult to give a public show of family unity at the traditional church service tomorrow following the damaging photographs.

Legal moves by Mr Bryan to prevent the French magazine *Paris Match* from using the photographs failed yesterday.

Other legal moves to seize the negatives from the Paris-based photographer Daniel Angeli, said to have taken the pictures, are still under way.

Buckingham Palace was adamant there was to be no comment from the Queen yesterday, following Thursday's statement expressing "disapproval" of publication of the photographs.

Mr Bryan, 37, the man described as the Duchess's "financial adviser" and whose kisses and caresses at the St Tropez villa were captured on film, spent the morning at his apartment, in Cheyne Place, off London's Chelsea Embankment, apparently in a business meeting.

The Press Complaints Commission is unlikely to launch an inquiry into publication of the photographs unless it receives a request from the Duchess or Mr Bryan. Director Mr Mark Bolland said yesterday that neither the Duchess or Mr Bryan had contacted them but five letters of complaint had been received.

The Commission also received up to 50 calls from the public, most condemning the newspapers involved, but some praising the publication of the photographs, one of which shows a side view of the Duchess with one of her breasts clearly exposed.

In Paris, where Mr Bryan hoped to stop publication in *Paris Match*, Judge Jean Favard said the photos were undoubtedly an intrusion but added that as they had already been published in Britain "the damage has already been done".

He added: "You cannot help but see the photos. I saw a copy of the *Daily Mirror* at Gare de Lyon station this morning and whichever television station you turn on seems to be talking about it."

Around the world, the story of the Duchess and the pictures have dominated the popular press.

In Italy, the Turin daily, *La Stampa*, said the affair amounts to "monarchy in the mud. This explosion deepens the cracks in a monarchy which a number of Britons have for some time regarded with a mixture of indifference and contempt," the newspaper said.

Switzerland's French-language tabloid *Le Matin*, said the pictures had "provoked the most serious royal crisis since the 1936 abdication of Edward VIII".

In America, the *New York Post* gave the story a large display under the headline "Brits in a snit over Fergie's topless romp". The *New York Daily News* called the Duchess "The Duchess of Vulgarity".

Germany's mass circulation *Bild* splashed the story under the headline: "Fergie naked during love play. Her child looked on".

France's *Le Parisien* tabloid declared: "Fergie takes top off, crown trembles". The Conservative French paper, *Le Figaro*, said the pictures had had the effect of a "bomb at Balmoral".

The Belgian daily *La Lanterne* says the photographs sent a shiver through the Royal Family.

The latest issue of Spain's mass circulation magazine, ¡Hola!, carries 23 photographs of the Duchess, her children and Mr Bryan.

Dutch newspapers also devote many column inches to the "compromising" photographs. The Amsterdam national *Het Parool* headlines "Queen angry with the *Mirror*" and says the Royal Family is furious at photographs depicting the Duchess "as good as naked". The *Telegraaf* says they have caused consternation in Britain.

10 December 1992
Duchess wins £90,500 over pool photos
By Tim Witcher in Paris and Jonathan Petre

The Duchess of York and her Texan friend, Mr John Bryan, won their French lawsuit yesterday over publication of intimate photographs of their Riviera holiday and were awarded damages equalling the French record.

A court ordered *Paris Match* magazine and papparazo photographer Daniel Angeli to pay the Duchess and Mr Bryan a total of 740,000 francs (£90,500) in damages and costs for breach of France's privacy laws.

After legal fees are deducted, the money will go to charity.

Lawyers for the couple demanded 22 million francs (£2.6m) when the case was launched in October and expressed disappointment at yesterday's award.

Mr Henry Page, of the Paris office of the English law firm Withers, representing the Duchess, said during the hearing her reputation had been "left in tatters".

He added: "From being an admired public figure, she is now a figure of ridicule."

The court also heard the damage to the reputation of Mr Bryan, 37, had been equally grave. He had been "treated as a liar and hypocrite" and his business had suffered as a result.

Though not high by British standards, the sum equals maximum amounts won in recent years by French personalities in privacy cases.

The Duchess could get more from another civil action to get the negatives returned.

In a written decision, Judge Germain Foyer de Costil said the glossy magazine had "blatantly and with intention to harm" published the photographs, some showing the Duchess topless at the poolside of her rented holiday villa near St Tropez.

In one, the Duchess was shown smoothing suntan lotion over Bryan. In another, they were embracing. The Duchess's two daughters were with them.

But Judge Foyer de Costil, president of the tribunal sitting at Nanterre, near Paris, ruled they were a clear infringement of France's privacy laws.

"It is exploitation of a topic for purely money-grabbing reasons that flagrantly infringed the intimacy of the Duchess of York and Mr John Bryan," he added.

Paris Match and Angeli must each pay the Duchess 250,000 francs (£30,500) and Mr Bryan 100,000 francs (£12,500), with the remainder covering legal costs. A claim against the French NMPP press distribution company was thrown out.

Angeli, a Paris-based magazine photographer of international repute, still denies he or his staff took the pictures.

Bienvenida Buck and Sir Peter Harding

"My ex-wife is a very temperamental lady."

By 1994, after a succession of scandals, Prime Minster John Major could be forgiven for wincing every time he opened a copy of the *News of the World*. At least in the case of Sir Peter Harding it was a member of the defence establishment rather than one of his own MPs causing the scandal, but it remained yet another embarrassment for an administration struggling to cope with a succession of damaging revelations.

14 March 1994
Defence chief resigns over affair
Pictures and intimate letters betray
liaison with Spanish wife of former Navy minister
By George Jones and Peter Almond

The Chief of the Defence Staff, Sir Peter Harding, resigned last night after the publication of allegations of an affair with the Spanish wife of a former Navy minister. The resignation of the top military officer in the country is a further blow to Government efforts to re-establish the integrity of those in public life after a series of sexual scandals.

Sir Peter stepped down from his £112,083 a year post within hours of details of his relationship with Miss Bienvenida Perez-Blanco – former wife of Sir Antony Buck – becoming public. The speed of his resignation was an indication of the new tougher attitude ordered by Mr Major towards those whose indiscretions could compromise the Government.

The Ministry of Defence said: "Marshal of the Royal Air Force Sir Peter Harding, Chief of the Defence Staff, has tendered his resignation with immediate effect. This has been accepted by Malcolm Rifkind, Secretary of State for Defence."

Details of the affair between Sir Peter, 60, and the former Lady Buck, 37, were published in yesterday's *News of the World*. Sir Peter is married with four children.

The newspaper said the relationship began early in 1991 and ended several months ago. However, the two met at the Dorchester Hotel in London last week, where they were photographed together by the newspaper. It claimed that over lunch with Miss Perez-Blanco Sir Peter was dismissive of the Prime Minister – whom he advises on issues such as the deployment of more British troops to Bosnia – describing him as "a nice enough man, but just not strong enough".

Initially Mr Rifkind said he had "total confidence" in Sir Peter's professional abilities. But once it was known that the newspaper had videos, tape recordings and intimate letters, Sir Peter had no option but to quit.

In his letter of resignation to Mr Rifkind, he wrote: "You will have seen the news reports concerning me and Lady Buck. The content of these reports is not entirely right and there are some errors in them, but it is counter-productive to relate them in detail. The point is that I have not acted in a manner that befits the holder of the post of Chief of the Defence Staff.

"I therefore believe that the only honourable thing for me to do is to resign my post with immediate effect, and I ask you to accept this.

"I deeply regret the embarrassment that this has caused for you, the Government, my colleagues and the Services; and I am grateful for your support over the last 15 months, which has been considerable."

Mr Rifkind replied: "I am very saddened that recent circumstances have led you to reach this decision; but I understand and respect your wishes.

"May I pay tribute to the many years of dedicated service that you have given to the Royal Air Force and the Armed Forces. In your earlier career, as Chief of the Air Staff, and again as Chief of the Defence Staff, you have exhibited professionalism, energy and skill of a very high order.

"I very much regret that we will no longer have the benefit of your advice and judgment. I know that you feel that your resignation is in the best interests of the Royal Air Force and the Armed Forces and that is, if I may say so, characteristic of the loyalty and commitment you have always given to your colleagues."

Labour called for an inquiry to ensure that Sir Peter's affair had not given rise to any security breaches. Mr David Clark, Labour's defence spokesman, said: "This man knew all our military secrets and one must be absolutely certain that there have been no lapses."

The disclosure of the affair was deeply embarrassing for the Defence Ministry because the Army had recently reissued its Code of Conduct for officers and men. It said that married or single officers who enter into an adulterous affair outside the military community jeopardised their status should it become public. The code also referred to a steady decline in society and said that the services had to be different.

The RAF does not have a similar code of conduct, but as Chief of the Defence Staff Sir Peter was head of all three services.

Sir Antony, 64, who stood down as Tory MP for Colchester North at the last election, was a junior defence minister in the Heath government in the 1970s.

He married Miss Perez-Blanco, nearly 30 years his junior, in 1990, after divorcing his previous wife. Their colourful marriage broke up last September in a highly publicised fashion.

He confirmed the contents of letters written to Miss Perez-Blanco by Sir Peter, but said that the relationship did not directly lead to the break-up of his marriage.

"Judging by what he wrote, he and my wife were on intimate terms," he said. "It is not for me to use the word 'lovers', but it certainly looked that way to me. Despite everything, I would have wished that this affair remain a private matter. But my ex-wife is a very temperamental lady."

Sir Antony expressed regret over Sir Peter's resignation. "I think it is absolutely tragic because he is a brilliant officer. But, given the background, you cannot expect me to be overwhelmed with grief. I am sad and for Sheila, his wife. It is a miserable time for us all."

The news of Sir Peter's resignation shocked MPs and defence chiefs, and is the first time that the Chief of the Defence Staff has had to resign in such circumstances.

Sir Peter, tall, debonair and highly articulate, had worked his way studiously to the top of the RAF, taking a number of key appointments, including one at Nato's military headquarters. Senior RAF officers were upset by his resignation. One wing commander said: "Some of the other chiefs were too quiet or just got walked over by the politicians. Sir Peter gave as good as he got."

Sir Peter's vice chief, Admiral Sir Jock Slater, is likely to succeed him, although the Army's Chief of Staff, Gen Sir Peter Inge, is also in a strong position. The job has gone twice to the Army and twice to the Air Force in recent years.

Guy Burgess and Donald Maclean

"There appear to be no political implications in the matter."

Donald Maclean, at the time the outwardly highly respectable head of the American department at the Foreign Office, had long been suspected of being a spy, and finally in 1951 he was persuaded to defect. No such suspicions were attached to the flamboyant, if grubby, Guy Burgess, who, after a promising start to his career had started a drunken drift from one embarrassment to another; but he accompanied Maclean on their flit to Russia all the same. The exact route the two Cambridge Spies took across the Iron Curtain remains a mystery to this day, and it took five years for Khruschev to even acknowledge that they had indeed defected. Burgess would lead a lonely and booze-soaked existence in the Soviet Union. Maclean embraced life in Russia with much greater enthusiasm and success, though his marriage – his wife Melinda joined him in the USSR – did not survive his own heavy drinking and promiscuity. Both men died in Moscow.

8 June 1951
All-Europe hunt for two Britons
Foreign Office men away without leave
By a *Daily Telegraph* reporter

Police in Britain, France, Germany and Austria were last night searching for two Foreign Office officials who disappeared from London on 25 May. The men, absent without leave, are: Mr Donald Duart Maclean, 38, who since November last has been head of the American Department of the Foreign Office. He held the rank of counsellor. Mr Guy Francis De Moncy Burgess, 40. His appointment to the Embassy in Washington as an executive officer with the rank of second secretary had ended and he was in this country awaiting re-posting.

Mr Maclean's wife and Mr Burgess's mother yesterday received telegrams purporting to come from the missing officials from Paris stating that they were all right.

The telegrams bore the Paris postmark. The Foreign Office is trying to trace the originals to ensure that they are genuine and were in fact sent off by Mr Maclean and Mr Burgess.

The counter-espionage section of the French Ministry of the Interior stated that they had been asked to help to find the men, who were known to have gone to France. Strict check was made on the border between the British and Soviet zones in Austria.

In Germany watch was kept at airports, ports and road check-points. Britain, it is believed, has also asked the Swedish, Danish, Norwegian and Finnish Governments whether they have any trace of the officials.

The Foreign Office issued this statement yesterday:

Two members of the Foreign Service have been missing from their homes since 25 May. One is Mr D. D. Maclean and the other Mr G. F. de M. Burgess. All possible inquiries are being made.

It is known that they went to France a few days ago. Mr Maclean had a breakdown a year ago owing to overstrain, but was believed to have fully recovered.

Owing to their being absent without leave both have been suspended with effect from 1 June.

In answer to questions a Foreign Office spokesman said that there was no reason to believe that the two men had taken official papers with them. The Foreign Office had no information of their whereabouts since they left this country.

Asked about suggestions that Mr Maclean and Mr Burgess may have gone to Russia, the spokesman again pointed out that there was no information about the men's present whereabouts.

In semi-official circles and among friends of the two men there was no support for the theory that they may have gone to an Iron Curtain country. A general view was this: "There appear to be no political implications in the matter."

Two Scotland Yard men who are helping in the search in Paris are detectives who are permanently stationed in the French capital. The inquiries are being directed by the Yard Special Branch.

Mr Maclean and Mr Burgess have been friends since they were undergraduates at Cambridge. Both were members of the Gargoyle Club, Dean-street. Soho, which they visited fairly frequently.

Friends of the men in England and America said last night that both were the last people one would associate with Communist views. They thought the two "will turn up from some remote place where they have gone to get away from the rush of civilisation".

Both men, it was learned, left one of the Channel ports by ship for France on 25 May.

Mr Burgess, a bachelor, was a member of the Reform Club, Pall Mall. He last visited the club on 24 May, collected letters and made a telephone call to Sonning, Berks.

At Falcon House, Sonning, Mr Goronwy Rees, to whom the call was reported to have been made, said that Mr Burgess had been a friend for some years. He refused to make any statement on the disappearance.

Mr Burgess was granted a certificate for Branch B of the Foreign Service on 1 October 1947. He was appointed to be an officer Grade IV, with effect from 1 January 1947, and was transferred to Washington as second secretary in 1950.

During the war he was a member of the Foreign Office news department. For a while he was private secretary to Mr McNeil, Secretary for Scotland, when Mr McNeil was Minister of State.

Mr MacLean is the son of Lady Maclean and the late Sir Donald Maclean, the Liberal leader. He entered the Foreign Service in 1935. In 1938 he went to Paris, and in 1940, just before he left there, he married Miss Melinda Marling, an American. They have two sons.

In 1944 Mr Maclean was transferred to Washington and became acting first secretary. In 1948 he was appointed counsellor at Cairo. It was last November that he came back to London as head of the Foreign Office American Department.

Lady Maclean yesterday declined to see callers at her Kensington flat, to which she moved a few weeks ago. One of the staff said: "Lady Maclean is very distressed, and is resting under doctor's orders."

12 June 1951
Missing men: security aspects investigated
M.P.s ask Mr Morrison about Russia and private lives
By our diplomatic correspondent

Mr Morrison, the Foreign Secretary, made a statement and replied to questions in the House of Commons yesterday about the missing British diplomats, Mr Donald Maclean, 38, and Mr Guy Burgess, 40.

Both statement and answers threw little new light on the increasingly serious affair, and were guarded in the extreme. They were obviously governed by one significant consideration.

"The security aspects of this case are under investigation," said Mr Morrison, "but it is not in the public interest to disclose them." He would consider making further statements, "always provided the security aspect is not prejudiced."

Mr Sandys, Conservative M.P. for Streatham, asked if Mr Morrison was satisfied that Mr Burgess had no Communist associations. The Foreign Secretary replied that there was no "regular week-to-week check" on Foreign Office officials.

Asked if the two diplomats had any connection with Russia, Mr Morrison said he thought it was a matter which should not be prejudged at this stage. He did not reply to a question asking if their disappearance had anything to do with their private lives.

Mr Morrison said he had little to add to the Foreign Office statement of last Thursday. It was established on 29 May that the two men were abroad.

Mr Maclean had been given leave of absence "for private reasons" from 26 May Mr Burgess was on leave "pending a decision as to his future". He had been recalled from Washington owing to his general unsuitability in the position.

On 29 May it was found out that the two men had left Southampton "ostensibly for a week-end cruise". They disembarked at St. Malo on 26 May. "No further confirmed information of their whereabouts has so far been received."

The Foreign Secretary was surprisingly vague about how long Maclean and Burgess have been employed in the Foreign Office. "Certainly a good number of years," he said.

All the information, in fact, is in the current "Foreign Office List". This records that Maclean was appointed to the Foreign Office on 15 October 1935. Burgess was appointed with effect, from 1 January 1947.

The Foreign Office revealed yesterday that inquiries about Mr Maclean and Mr Burgess were started as the result of a telephone call from Mrs Maclean, the diplomat's wife, to the Foreign Office on the night of 28 May or early morning of 29 May. Mr Maclean was expected back from his leave on the morning of 28 May.

It was known that Mrs Maclean was about to have a baby. Mr Maclean's absence from the Foreign Office on the 28 May was thought to be associated with his domestic affairs.

When he left the Foreign Office on the afternoon of Friday, 25 May, he gave no address where he could be got in touch with over the week-end. Mrs Maclean was anxious about her husband's failure to return home and made this very evident in her telephone conversation.

The Foreign Office said yesterday that it had always regarded the missing men's silence, in spite of world-wide publicity, as a serious matter. There was nothing further to go on at present to enable any specific conclusion to be formed.

A Foreign Office spokesman said there was no foundation for a report that Mr Maclean had been ordered not to consort with Burgess out of office hours. The *Daily Telegraph* yesterday did not say that any "order" to this effect had been given to Mr Maclean, but that both had been warned that their out-of-office association was considered undesirable.

He also denied that a Foreign Office official had gone to Paris during the week-end in the case. The Foreign Office position is that the search has been placed in the hands of the appropriate authorities and they are now conducting it.

Two points emerge from Mr Morrison's answers and his insistence on the paramount importance of security considerations.

One is that much more must be known officially than has been revealed about the activities and opinions of the men concerned. The other is that some other country or countries would appear to be involved in the disappearance.

Security matters do not arise in cases of ordinary and innocent disappearance. In such, all known facts would be made public and all countries if necessary asked to help.

From the Foreign Secretary's attitude it could be inferred that there are at least official suspicions that sinister possibilities in this case cannot be ruled out.

There has been no evidence that one or both of them applied for francs or travellers' cheques before they left. This suggests that either they thought they would not be staying long abroad and had enough foreign money left over from other visits, or that they knew that they could obtain funds elsewhere abroad for a longer stay.

The crucial difficulty in the affair is what has happened to the two since they landed at St. Malo. It is significant that there is no mention in any of the three telegrams, two purporting to come from Mr Maclean and one from Mr Burgess, of returning to England.

All the probabilities suggest that both men had to leave the country quickly by the force of urgent circumstances which are not yet known.

Assuming that they are still free men and that their telegraphed messages were genuine in intention, even if not actually written by them, they still are unable or unwilling to tell those acutely anxious about them when they are likely to be back with them.

This position can be explained in two ways: either that they have no intention of returning, for reasons not yet apparent, or that somewhere they are under duress.

14 June 1951
Diplomats may be behind Iron Curtain
Unsolved riddle
By our diplomatic correspondent

The belief is growing that the disappearance of the British diplomats, Mr Donald Maclean, 38, and Mr Guy Burgess, 40, who have now been missing nearly three weeks, may never be explained and that nothing more may be heard of them.

In spite of the keenest search and the widest publicity throughout Western Europe, nothing has been established about the missing men's whereabouts since they were assumed to have landed at St. Malo at 6 a.m. on Saturday, 26 May.

The authorities are being reluctantly driven to consider one possibility which could explain the failure to trace the two men. This is that they are not in Western Europe and may have been taken, voluntarily or under duress behind the Iron Curtain.

The Foreign Office said yesterday that it had no information that Mr Burgess knew Dr. Nunn May, the convicted atomic scientist, or Mr Karl Strauss, who was accused by Sir Hartley Shawcross, when Attorney-General, of being a Czech agent.

Mr Auden, the poet, had been reported as saying that Dr. Nunn May was a "close friend" of Mr Burgess. The Foreign Office commented that Mr Auden had not come forward with any information to help the authorities investigating the affair.

Asked whether Mr Burgess was known to be a Communist, the Foreign Office spokesman said he could not go into that point. As reported in the *Daily Telegraph* yesterday. Mr Sandys (Cons., Streatham) is asking in the House of Commons whether the Government was aware of Mr Burgess's associations with Communist circles.

The serious implications of the diplomats' disappearance are shown in a statement by Scotland Yard yesterday. It said that the Commissioner, while appreciating Press efforts to help the police, "must reserve the right to decline information when it is in the public interest".

He regretted that he could not give any information about the missing diplomats. Inquiries should be made to the Foreign Office.

Mr Stephen Spender, the poet, who is staying in northern Italy, last night described Mr Burgess as having been "a very doctrinaire Communist when at Cambridge" and as having "converted several of his friends", said Reuter.

"But," Mr Spender added, "the fact that he approved of my very anti-Communist book, 'World Within World', would indicate that he had changed." Mr Burgess had a telephone conversation with Mr Spender shortly before his disappearance.

Italian police representatives engaged in the search for the two diplomats yesterday visited Mr W. H. Auden, the poet, for a third time at his home at Forio d' Ischia on an island in the Bay of Naples.

15 June 1951

First Moscow report on two diplomats

27-line account

By our diplomatic correspondent

Moscow newspapers yesterday for the first time mentioned the missing Foreign Office officials, Mr Donald Maclean and Mr Guy Burgess. Pravda, Izvestia and another newspaper printed, without comment, a 27-line report from the Tass agency in London.

One account was headed, "Disappearance of two workers of the English Ministry of Foreign Affairs". The Tass report said that the British Press "for a number of days has been persistently commenting on the disappearance of the two officials". It set out the essential facts and added that the police in a large number of countries "had been mobilised to search". The report said that "the significance which is attributed to the disappearance of Maclean and Burgess is shown in particular by the fact that the British Government discussed the question . . . and the Foreign Minister made a declaration in the House of Commons."

"He pointed out," Tass concluded, "that no confirmation had been received of the diplomats' whereabouts since they landed at St. Malo in France."

There may be a simple explanation why Russian newspaper readers were given the abbreviated and uninteresting report almost three weeks after the British officials disappeared. It was certainly a decision of the Kremlin Politburo to release the meagre details.

If, however, it could be assumed that Mr Maclean and Mr Burgess were somewhere in Russian hands, in Eastern Germany or elsewhere – of which there is no evidence – certain phrases in the Tass report would have a singular piquancy. The reference to Mr Morrison's not knowing where the diplomats are is one of them.

When every possibility, even remote of the mysterious affair has to be considered, it cannot be disregarded that the real intention of the Moscow announcement may be to prepare the Russians for another and more startling one.

If the two officials have been taken to Russia, news of their arrival would lose a great deal of its force if the Russian people had not been told something about them beforehand.

31 August 1951

Diplomats still missing

Report "unfounded"

By our diplomatic correspondent

A report published yesterday, not in the *Daily Telegraph*, that Mr Donald Maclean, 38, and Mr Guy Burgess, 40, the two diplomats who left London on 25 May, had been located, was officially described by the Foreign Office as being "without foundation".

It had been stated that "agents of M.I.5" know where the two men are and what has happened to them since they disappeared.

The Foreign Office said that it had checked that the source quoted in the report (M.I.5) had made no such statements as those attributed to it. The official view still is that nothing has been established about the missing men's whereabouts since they were assumed to have landed at St. Malo at 6 a.m. on Saturday, 26 May.

24 December 1953
Burgess writes to his mother
Letter posted in London
By a *Daily Telegraph* reporter

Guy Burgess, 42, the diplomat who vanished with his colleague. Donald Maclean, 40, in May 1951, has written a letter to his mother, Mrs E. M. Bassett, at Arlington House, Piccadilly. The letter was posted in London.

It arrived in the mail at 6.30 p.m. on Tuesday, among a bundle of Christmas cards. The envelope bore the postmark "London, S.E.1," dated 21 December. Mrs Bassett's name and address were typewritten.

Burgess's stepfather, Lt.-Col. J. R. Bassett, yesterday described the letter as "a wonderful Christmas present." It was a purely personal message "from a son to his mother".

Col. and Mrs Bassett are convinced of the authenticity of the letter. Col. Bassett said it was definitely in Guy Burgess's handwriting. "I have known his writing since he was a boy," he added.

When asked if the contents indicated his stepson's mode of living or his whereabouts, Col. Bassett replied: "I know nothing."

I understand that the tone of the letter is reassuring. It is headed "November", but not more precisely dated, and ends with the signature "Guy" and a last, intimate message.

Since Burgess is believed to have gone to Eastern Europe after making the Southampton–St. Malo crossing with Maclean, the inference is that the letter was brought from the Continent for posting in London. It bore a British 2½d stamp.

The S.E.1 district in which it was posted includes London Bridge and Waterloo stations, both giving access to the Channel ports.

There is, however, another possibility. Two ships from Russian ports, the Dutch-built vessel *Lakhta*, 1,352 tons, and the *Lermontov*, 5,599 tons, were in the Port of London on Monday. The *Lakhta* was still there yesterday.

Both are general cargo vessels owned by Russia and are not infrequent visitors to London. They use the Surrey Commercial Docks, Rotherhithe, the postmark of which is S.E.1.

The *Lermontov* sailed on Tuesday. Members of the crews are allowed ashore by immigration officers if the ships' captains agree.

One possibility is that Burgess's letter was entrusted to a diplomatic courier. Its tone and the fact that its authenticity has not been questioned suggest that the writer is not under any kind of duress.

It was stated at the Foreign Office yesterday that the letter is the first positive evidence received from any source that Burgess is alive.

Mrs Melinda Dunbar, mother of Mrs Donald Maclean, said in Paris yesterday that she had received "absolutely nothing" from her daughter. Mrs Maclean, with her three children, disappeared from her flat in Geneva in September.

28 April 1954
Two Russians tell of Burgess and Maclean
By a *Daily Telegraph* reporter

British security officers are studying reports made by Mr Petrov, former third secretary at the Russian Embassy in Canberra, Australia, and Capt. Khokhlov, the Soviet agent who surrendered to the American authorities in Germany.

These contain facts which agree with those obtained by M.I.5 officers investigating the disappearance of Donald Maclean and Guy Burgess, the British Foreign Office officials, in May 1951.

The disclosures suggest that the route taken by Burgess and Maclean was Paris–Rome–Prague and on to Moscow. The information is not being accepted without careful inquiry.

There is a suggestion that the journey to Moscow was made both by car and plane and that Soviet agents in Paris assisted in smuggling the Britons across the borders. Reference is also made to a woman agent working from Zurich, who has already been the subject of inquiries.

It is believed that Burgess is dealing with propaganda and assisting in the production of an English language magazine. Maclean is assisting in the drafting of Soviet Foreign Office notes and memoranda.

Roger Casement

"Loyalty is a sentiment, not a law."

The Irish-born Roger Casement might for much of his career have been taken as an impeccable avatar of the British Empire. He served it with much distinction over the course of two decades, combining great administrative skill with profound humanitarian instincts. These both found voice in the report he was commissioned to write on the human rights abuses committed in the Belgian Congo – which was being run, with almost unimaginable brutality, as a private fiefdom by Leopold II, the Belgian king. Casement's revelations caused great controversy, and though there was some attempt to suppress his findings, they contributed to mobilising the international pressure that eventually led to Leopold handing over control of the country to the state. As time went by, Casement witnessed further atrocities committed in the name of imperialism, and was horrified by Britain's entry into, and conduct of, the Boer War. These led ultimately to his resigning from imperial service and committing himself to the Irish struggle for independence.

As if his conviction for treason – a term he would have argued with – was not sufficient cause for scandal, the British government also circulated copies of what later became known as the *Black Diary* in an attempt to silence those voices calling for a commutation of Casement's sentence. Purported to have been written by Casement, it documents a busy though discreet homosexual life, with many partners, often young men, most of whom were paid for sex. Though doubt now obtains as to whether the diaries represent an actual record of events or instead a fictional representation of what its author had wanted to have experienced, at the time it caused a huge furore and undoubtedly eroded support for clemency. Roger Casement (he had been stripped of his knighthood and other titles) was hanged at Pentonville prison in London in August 1916. His body was unceremoniously buried in quicklime in a cemetery yards from where he had been executed.

16 May 1916
The trial of Sir Roger Casement at Bow-Street
Charge of high treason

Into the treason trial at Bow-street yesterday there was introduced an element of surprise. Sir Roger Casement did not enter the dock alone; there followed him a reddish-haired, unshaven man wearing a waterproof coat, who during the proceedings stared fixedly at the roof. This man when war broke out was a porter at Paddington.

Police officers had in the morning gone not only to the Tower, where Sir Roger was imprisoned, they had visited Wandsworth prison, where Daniel Julian Bailey was in custody. He, so the prosecution allege, is an Irish soldier who when a prisoner in Germany was seduced from allegiance to his Majesty and accompanied Sir Roger Casement on the submarine which, by way of the Shetlands, came to a lonely shore off Ireland. There a party of three landed – Sir Roger Casement and Bailey and a man named Monteith.

When Sir Roger Casement and Bailey mot at Bow-street Police-station Sir Roger declared that Bailey was innocent, and desired that he should be as well defended as himself.

The charge against the prisoners is:

For that they did, between the 1st day of November 1914, and on divers other occasions between that day and the 21st day of April 1916, unlawfully, maliciously, and traitorously commit high treason within and without the realm in contempt of our Sovereign lord the King and his laws, to the evil example of others in the like case, contrary to the duty and allegiance of the said defendants.

There was a big crowd outside the court, and when Sir John Dickinson took his seat on the bench only a few people had found accommodation in the small space remaining after provision had been made for representatives of the Press.

Sir Roger Casement moved briskly to his place in the dock, his trim figure and well-brushed grizzled hair forming a striking contrast to the unkempt condition of his companion. Sir Roger's attitude was that of a man intensely, nervously, interested. Occasionally he passed notes to his counsel.

It was a remarkable story which the Attorney-General told in opening the case for the Crown. Practically it divided itself into three chapters: The attempted seduction of Irish prisoners; the voyage in the U boat; the arrest. Sir Frederick began with a short recital of Casement's career as a servant of the Crown, ending, appropriately enough, with a letter to Sir Edward Grey expressing in effusive terms his thanks to the King for having conferred the honour of Knighthood upon him. "I read that letter because it may be useful to remember what were the feelings of Casement on June 19, 1911," was counsel's comment.

The scene was changed to the prisoners' camp at Limburg. Introducing himself as the organiser of the Irish Volunteers, Casement was alleged to have invited the Irish prisoners to join the Irish Brigade, which, in the event of Germany winning a sea battle, would be landed in Ireland "to defend the country against the enemy – England." The vast majority received these persuasions with contempt, He was hissed, and on one occasion hooted out of the camp, and a private in the Munster Fusiliers actually struck him. Men loyal to Britain were punished, and the few who yielded to his suggestion were rewarded by being given a green uniform with a harp worked upon it, liberal rations, and a certain degree of liberty. Bailey was said by returned prisoners to be one of these.

Then came the voyage in the submarine, and the story as to this was supplied in a statement made by Bailey. He joined, he said, to get out of the country, and he got out with Casement and a man named Monteith on U20. Near Tralee the three of them were put into a collapsible boat, with a quantity of arms and ammunition. These were buried near where they landed. There were adventures in a motor-car, and police searchings, and in the morning Bailey was arrested. Meanwhile the sloop Bluebell had sighted a suspicious-looking ship flying the Norwegian ensign. The story of how the captain ordered the stranger – the Aude – to follow him into port, and how the latter, after the hoisting of the German flag, was scuttled by her own crew, is already familiar to the public.

The story of Sir Roger's capture, however, was gone into in some detail. The discovery by a farmer of a boat in which was a dagger, and the tracing of footprints, followed by the recognition of Casement by a farm servant at an early hour of the morning, put the police on the track, and the accused was discovered at a place called McKenna's Fort. He described himself as "Richard Brennan, an author," but eventually, after being brought to England, admitted his identity. One other interesting point Sir Frederick Smith mentioned quite casually. Divers have discovered that the Aude carried rifles.

A number of witnesses were called. Nearly all were soldiers, and their stories of what happened in the prison camp were followed with breathless interest by the crowded court. The men who joined the "Irish Brigade" were to be the guests of the Gorman Government, one man said, and there was a promise of being sent to America if Germany did not win. Of 2,500 Irish in the Limburg Camp only fifty-two were reported to have joined the Irish Brigade.

Sir F. E. Smith said: On behalf of the Crown. I support the charge of high treason against the two prisoners Casement and Bailey. The prisoner Casement was born on 1 September 1864. He was in the service of the Niger Coast Protectorate from 31 July 1892. He was appointed to be his Majesty's Consul at Lourenço Marquez on 27 June 1895. On 29 July 1898, he was appointed Consul for the Portuguese Possessions in West Africa south of the Gulf of Guinea He was employed on special service at Cape Town during the war in South Africa – 1899 to 1900 – and received at the conclusion of hostilities the Queen's South African medal. On 20 August 1900, he was transferred to the Congo State, and, in addition, was appointed on 6 August 1901, to be Consul for part of the French Congo Colony. On 30 June 1905, he was made C.M.G., and was appointed, on 6 August 1906, Consul for the State of San Paulo. On 3 December 1908, he was promoted Consul-General at Rio de Janeiro. On 20 June 1911, he was made a knight, and in the same year received the Coronation medal. From 1909 to 1912 he was employed, while titular Consul-General at Rio de Janeiro, in making certain inquiries relative to the rubber industry, and on 1 August 1913, after a considerable career of public usefulness, was retired on a pension.

It is perhaps worthwhile, having regard to the singular later developments of his career, to read a letter dated 19 June 1911, in which he replied to the communication from Sir Edward Grey intimating that his Majesty intended to bestow a knighthood upon him.

He wrote:

Dear Sir Edward Grey – I find it very hard to choose words in which to make acknowledgment of the honour done me by the King. I am much moved by this proof of confidence and appreciation of my service in Putumayo conveyed to me by your letter, wherein you tell me the King has been graciously pleased, upon your recommendation to confer upon me the honour of knighthood. I am indeed grateful to you for this signal assurance of your personal esteem and support. I am very deeply sensible of the honour done me by his Majesty, and would beg that my humble duty might be presented to his Majesty when you might do me the honour to convey to him my deep appreciation of the honour he has been graciously pleased to confer upon me.

Those were the feedings in 1911 of the prisoner towards the country which he had served so long and towards the Sovereign of that country. He was then a man of mature years – he was 47 years old at the time. That letter was written by a man who had had nineteen years' experience of the methods of government of this country. He had participated in them. He was a man of cultivated understanding, and, as we shall have reason to see, he had a considerable knowledge of history and of the relationship between this country and Ireland. With that knowledge he wrote this letter.

For convenience I will make a few observations next about, the second prisoner – Daniel Julian Bailey. He has made a statement, according to which he was born in Dublin. He joined the Royal Irish Rifles in the year 1904, and served with his regiment in India from 1907 to 1913. On the outbreak of the war he was employed as a goods porter at Paddington. He was called up at once as a reservist, and he sailed with the original Expeditionary Force for France, and shared the fortunes of the Force during the first days of the campaign. He was taken a prisoner by the Germans on or about 4 September 1914. I cannot describe the exact movements of the prisoner Casement after the outbreak of the war until the happening of certain events. He drew his pension until 30 September 1914. That pension was afterwards withdrawn. Between the months of September and December the fortunes of the struggle in France were such that a large number of British prisoners were taken by the enemy, and amongst these prisoners were a considerable number of Irish soldiers. These prisoners were distributed quite normally amongst the various prisons in Germany, and no differentiation of treatment took place between themselves and other prisoners until the month of December 1914. Prisoners of war belonging to the various Irish regiments were then removed from the different camps in which they were imprisoned, and were collected into a large camp at Limberg. It became evident from what followed that they had been collected at this place for a special purpose – it was the result of considered calculation on the part of the German Government,

At this time the prisoner Casement was in Germany. The full story of the circumstances under which he went to Germany it is not in my power to tell. It is evident the part he was destined to play was that of a man willing, and it was hoped able, to seduce from their allegiance to their King the prisoners of war who had been collected for the purpose of listening to his addresses and lectures on Irish history and other matters.

They were assembled on more than one occasion, and they were addressed collectively, and in some cases individually, by Casement. He moved about the camp freely and with the full knowledge and privilege of the Germans, Evidence would show that between 3 January 1915, and 19 February 1915, Casement repeatedly addressed these prisoners of war.

On more than one occasion he introduced himself as Sir Roger Casement, the organiser of the Irish Volunteers, and stated that he was forming an Irish Brigade. He invited the Irish prisoners of war to join this brigade.

He pointed out repeatedly, and with emphasis, that in his opinion everything was to be gained for Ireland by Germany winning the war, and that the Irish soldiers who were listening to his address had the best opportunity they ever had of striking a blow for Ireland. He stated that those who joined the Irish brigade would be sent to Berlin; that they would become the guests of the German Government; that in the event of Germany winning a sea battle he would land the brigade in Ireland to defend that country against the enemy – England; and that in the event of Germany losing tire war, either he or the German Imperial Government would give each man in the brigade a bonus of from £10 to £20 and a free passage to America.

This plan was conceived and recommended to the prisoners in 1915 by the man who in June 1911, was begging Sir Edward Grey that his humble duty might be presented to his Majesty. Such were the inducements held out to these unfortunate prisoners. But the vast majority of them treated the rhetoric and persuasions of Casement with contempt. He was received with hisses. On at least one occasion he was booed out of the camp. The Munster Fusiliers were particularly prominent in loyal resentment of the treacherous proposals. One private actually struck, or struck at, Casement, and he was stopped from further violence by the intervention of the escort of Prussian Guards who had been assigned to Casement for his protection. The Irish prisoners were, for this, punished by a reduction in their rations, which even before this event were not excessive.

Corporal Robinson, who refused to join the Irish Brigade, was transferred to another camp for punishment, and in the case of O'Brien, whose reception of the proposals was particularly unfavourable, Casement suggested to the camp commandant that he should be punished.

The few men who were seduced from their allegiance by the arguments and persuasions of Casement were rewarded by being given a green uniform with a harp on the facings, by being left at liberty, and by receiving rations liberal both in quantity and quality.

Amongst the prisoners in Limburg at this time was Bailey. He was observed by witnesses wearing this green uniform with a harp upon the collar and cap. He wore German side arms. Evidence would be given that Bailey joined the so-called Irish brigade, being promoted at once to the rank of sergeant. Witnesses of this were all men who had been wounded and taken prisoner. They had since been exchanged, and were now at the disposal of the Crown for the purpose of giving evidence.

Here occurs, said the Attorney-General, a hiatus in the evidence which the Crown is in a position to lay before the Court, but it is evident that the men who could be seduced from their allegiance were intended to be actually used for raising armed insurrection in Ireland against the forces of the Crown. The treason charge against the prisoners was the treason of adherence to the King's enemies in the enemy country. Of that treason evidence would be given of many overt acts – of attempts to seduce, and, in some cases, of the actual seduction of his Majesty's soldiers from their loyal allegiance to his Majesty, and of plottings and contrivings to effect a hostile landing with stores and arms and armed men in divers spots of his Majesty's Dominions, This part of the story I can usefully complete by reading the statement made by the prisoner Bailey, who was arrested on 21 April.

Mr Artemus Jones (interrupting) said that it was not until just before the case opened that he had been instructed to defend Bailey as well as Casement. He did not yet know whether this was a free and voluntary statement, and it might be inadmissible as evidence.

Sir F. E. Smith said he would accept all responsibility. He then read the statement, which was as follows:

"My name is Daniel Julian Bailey. I was born in Dublin, but have not been there since November 1906. I joined the Royal Irish Rifles in 1904. The regiment left Dublin in 1906 for Aldershot. I went to India in 1907 – Meerut Station. I came to Watford in January 1913, as a reservist. I went to Canada in April 1913, and returned in September to Watford. We moved to Craven Park, Harlesden, London, and I was working us a porter in the goods shed at Paddington Station at the outbreak of the war. I was called up to my depot in Belfast immediately, and went out with the Expeditionary Force. I was taken prisoner on 4 September 1914, and was sent to Sennelager. Then they took me with the other Irish to Limburg, where we were all well treated for a time. I saw Sir Roger Casement about April 1915. He spoke to us about joining an Irish brigade, solely for the purpose of fighting for Irish freedom. I joined, to see if I could possibly get out of the country. I signed on as D. J. Beverley. I was made sergeant straight away. We went (about fifty-six) to Zossen.

"At the end of March 1916, I was sent to Berlin. I was taken by motor-car to a suburb of Berlin. In the car with me was Mr Monteith and some German civilians. We went to an explosives school, and got instruction there from a civilian in the use of explosives. I was only there three hours, and was then taken to Zossen. I remained there for a week or more. I was given civilian clothing, and was taken to the Government offices in Wilhelmstrasse, and got further instructions in explosives. Sir Roger Casement was stopping at the Saxonia, but he did not tell me what I was going to do. I stayed there about ten days. Monteith was there too. On Tuesday, the 11th inst., a car came to the door, and the three of us (Casement, Monteith, and I) were driven to the War Office. They gave me a railway ticket, and we got into another car and went to the Zoological Gardens Station, and got into the train for Wilhelmshaven.

"We were put on a submarine – U 20 – there. She steamed out, and had to return, owing to an accident, to Heligoland. There we boarded U 19, and came round the Shetlands to the West Coast of Ireland. I knew now where I was going, but still got no instructions. I gathered, when near Tralee, that it was in connection with the Volunteer movement. They steamed in as near as they could, lowered the collapsible boat, and put us off. When everything was ready we took in the boat the revolvers and ammunition,

&c., which you have found, and I was ordered to bury them. It was about one a.m., or later, when we were put in the boat. When in the surf the boat was overturned, and we had to wade ashore, and I went back two or three times to fetch in the stuff.

"We buried the arms, &c., not far from where we landed. I followed them, and we stopped in an avenue of whins off the road. We left our coats there, and I was token back by Mr Monteith to Tralee by the road. People were going to Mass when we got there – eight a.m. We went to a bridge outside the town and sat down on the wall. Monteith seemed to be looking for somebody. We went back to the town, into a narrow street, when some placards caught his eye. He went over and knocked at the closed shop, which was above where the placards were. Someone looked out of the shop. We went into this shop, and the "Spark" caught his eye. He bought one, and spoke quietly to the man in the shop. He sent one of the girls away, and we went and got something to eat at Lavin's. We had breakfast there and went back to the shop, and he asked if the commanding officer had come yet. He was told no, but to come inside and wait. Four men came in – not all at the same time – and some conversation took place between Monteith and them out of my hearing.

"I was given the suit I have on by a man who wore glasses. This was the man I was in the motor-car with afterwards. Mr Stock was one of the four in the shop. I did not hear if he was the commanding officer. Later on I was taken cut of the shop by a man with glasses and a girl. When we got to the convent a motor-car came up and slopped. The girl went back and we got in. Mr Stack and the driver wore in it. There was a parcel, which I took to contain clothes, in the car. Later on Mr Stack asked me if I knew where "Mr Rice" was. That name had been arranged by Sir Roger Casement. I said I could not locate the spot. They travelled the car about the roads looking for the place. We got a puncture at the end of a road going to the beach, where we were challenged by the police. They did not get out of the ear before the police came; but then they mended the puncture. They got out near a house at a cross roads, and Mr Stack spoke to someone in the house.

"The sergeant came up again here and searched the car, and we went on straight to a little village, where we were stopped again by a young constable. We turned the car then and went to another small village, where we were again searched by the police. I gave my name as David Mulcahy. The man with the glasses furnished me with this name. A revolver was taken from the man with the glasses. We then went on and the car stopped. Mr Stack and the other man got out and spoke to a man on the road with a bicycle. The latter went away and got a second bicycle, and brought one to a house where I stopped during the night. It was a house by itself – not in a village. In the morning he called again, without a bicycle, and directed me to a castle, where he told me to knock about, and he then left me. I remained there until a policeman came up and arrested me.

"When on the submarine I overheard in conversation from time to time that a small Wilson liner was to be piloted into Fenit pier. It had 20,000 rifles (with five rifles in each case) and over 1,000,000 rounds of ammunition. It was disguised as a timber ship. From what I heard there were ten machine guns ready for action, and bombs and fire bombs. I heard that Dublin Castle was to be raided."

Sir F. E. Smith, continuing, said: From that statement it appears that the three passengers. Casement, Monteith, and Bailey, were put into a small boat and landed on the sands near Ardfert, probably about two o'clock in the early morning of Good Friday, 21 April. On Thursday night, at 9.15, a labourer called Hussey saw a light flashing about half-a-mile away at sea, and it is not impossible that it was not unconnected with what happened afterwards.

Contemporaneous with the attempt of the prisoners to land, a vessel carrying arms approached Tralee. The circumstances were such as would satisfy the Court that those on board the vessel carrying arms were taking part in a common adventure with the prisoners. I will relate what was observed board the sloop *Bluebell*, and the Court will be able to appreciate the general character of the plan formed in order to give effect to the high treason conceived and commenced on the soil of Germany. The *Bluebell* on 21 April was patrolling in the neighbourhood of Tralee, when she sighted a ship flying the Norwegian ensign and with four Norwegian ensigns painted upon her hull, fore and aft. The captain of the *Bluebell* hoisted a signal demanding the name of the apparent Norwegian vessel, and making inquiry as to her destination. The reply was that the vessel was the *Aud*, of Bergen, bound for Genoa. The *Bluebell* informed the *Aud* that she must follow the Government vessel. The captain of the *Aud* asked in broken English: "Where are you taking me?" and the *Bluebell* gave orders that the *Aud* should go ahead. The *Bluebell* proceeded to go ahead, but the *Aud* remained without moving. A round was immediately fired across her bows, and she then signalled, "What am I to do?" She was told she was to follow. She was escorted by the *Bluebell* without further trouble until next morning when, not far from Queenstown, the *Aud* signalled, "Where am I to anchor on entering the harbour?" She was told to follow the *Bluebell* and to wait orders. On nearing the Daunt Rock Lighthouse the *Bluebell* headed for the harbour, but the *Aud* stopped her engines. The *Bluebell* ran back to her, and when about a cable's length away saw a small cloud of white smoke issuing from the starboard side of the after hold. At the same time two German naval ensigns were broken, and two boats were lowered. The *Bluebell* fired one round across her bows whereupon the boats coming towards her hoisted flags of truce, and the men in them put up their hands.

They were then taken prisoners and placed under armed guard. The *Aud* sank almost immediately afterwards about a mile and a quarter south-south-east of the Daunt Rock Lightship.

The Attorney-General, after remarking that the association between the events described was obvious, returned to what took place at Tralee. He said: At about four o'clock in the morning on which these men landed a boat was found a few yards from the shore by a farmer, John McCarthy. In the boat was a dagger. This man also found in the sand a tin box containing pistol ammunition, three Mauser pistols, two handbags containing pistol ammunition, several maps, a flash-lamp, two lifebelts, and a large flag, and also three coats and three caps, which suggested that the party consisted of three persons. In one of the coats was found a railway ticket, dated 19 April, from Berlin to Wilhelmshaven. This was on an unfrequented part of the coast. At this point the flag was displayed in the court. It was of great size, and upon the green background was a yellow castle, with turrets flanking a dome.

Sir F. E. Smith, continuing, described the arrest of Sir Roger Casement. The farmer saw footprints of three men in the sand, and about five o'clock in the same morning three men were seen by a farm servant, after a search in the neighbourhood of what was known locally as Mackenna's Fort. It is not so much what is usually described as a fort so much as an excavation affording a good hiding-place. Casement was discovered there. Asked by the police who he was, the prisoner replied, "Richard Morton, of Denham, Bucks", and described himself as an author and said he had slept at a farmhouse near by, and that he intended to go on to Tralee.

As he was being taken to Ardfert Barracks he was seen by a farmer to drop a paper from his coat. This paper was subsequently picked up and was found to be a code. Some of its terms threw a light on its character, object, and scope.

Some of the contemplated messages were:

Wait further instructions.

Wait favourable opportunity.

Send agent at once.

Proposal accepted.

Proposal received.

Please answer by cablegram.

Have decided to stay.

Communication again possible.

Railway communications have been stopped.

Further ammunition is needed.

Further rifles are needed.

How many rifles will you send us?

How much ammunition will you send us?

Will send plans about landing to _____.

Preparations are made about _____,

Send another ship to _____.

Cannons with plenty of ammunition are needed.

Send more explosives.

Send a vessel if possible.

Such, commented counsel, was the nature of the communications which, it was contemplated by Casement and others co-operating with him in Germany, would develop from the situation in Ireland. At Ardfert Barracks he was charged with landing arms and ammunition, and asked for legal assistance. On 22 April he was brought to England and handed over to an inspector of the Metropolitan Police, to whom he said that he was Sir Roger Casement.

Since the *Aud* sank, divers had been sent down with the object of discovering what was the nature of the cargo. Rifles wore discovered, but not German rifles. They were Russian rifles of the pattern of the year 1905.

The second prisoner, Bailey, was arrested between the Causeway and Tralee on the evening of 22 April.

Inspector Parker, of Scotland Yard, said that at seven o'clock that morning he went with other officers to the Tower of London. He saw Sir Roger Casement, and told him he was a police officer, and held a warrant for his arrest. He said: "Are you Sir Roger Casement?" to which prisoner replied, "I am Sir Roger Casement." He admitted he was born on 1 September 1864, in the county of Dublin; that his father was Roger Casement, and his mother Annie Casement, and that his father had been a captain in the Antrim Militia. Witness then read the warrant over to him.

Proceeding, witness said he conveyed Casement to Bow-street, where he was detained. Witness then went with other officers to Wandsworth Prison, and there saw Bailey. He told him he was a police officer, and that he had a warrant for his arrest. Bailey admitted his identity, and said he was born in Dublin. He made no reply when the warrant was read to him, and he was conveyed to Bow-street, where the two prisoners were charged together. Casement remarked: "Am I allowed to say anything now?" and, after being cautioned, he said, pointing to Bailey: "Well, that man is innocent. I think the indictment is wrongly drawn against him. Is it within my power to pay for the defence of this man? I wish him to be in every way as well defended as myself, and if he has no means to undertake his defence I am prepared to pay for him."

Corporal John Robinson, formerly of the R.A.M.C., now residing in Ross-street, Belfast, said: I have been in the Army since June 1906. At the outbreak of the war I was stationed in Dublin. On 17 August 1914, I left for France, attached to the 13th Field Ambulance. On 24 August I was taken prisoner, having a wound in the head. I was blind for the time being. I was in hospital in Germany for three weeks. In addition to my head wound I had also a wound on the knee and in the shoulder. After leaving hospital I was sent to Sennelager, in the Black Forest. In that camp there were other Irish prisoners of war, and when I had been there about three months an order was given by the commandant that the Irish prisoners were to be put together in one hut for better treatment, and sent afterwards to another camp, where they were also to receive better treatment. They did not like being separated from the other troops, and they were put together with fixed bayonets. Two hundred or 300 of the Irish prisoners were thus collected. The treatment was a little better, but not much. The Irish prisoners got camp work, which was lighter than the work in the forest that was given to the English prisoners. I remained at Sennelager between four and five months. All who were removed to that camp were supposed to be Irish. Sennelager was a new camp when we got there. The accommodation was all right, but the food was rotten.

Casement came to speak to the men. When he first came he was dressed in black, with a soft hat. He was alone, and was "spouting" about the Irish Brigade. There would have been about thirty or forty men listening to him. He said. "Now is your chance to fight for free Ireland." He also said he was glad to see us all there. He wanted us to form a brigade, so that if Germany had a victory at sea he would land us in Ireland. He said that when we landed we would free Ireland from England. Sometimes he got a poor reception: the men used to crush round him and try to push him. They tried to hiss him out of it, and I saw one fellow shove him. When the men pushed Casement the guard came and got him away. I saw him in the camp about four times altogether. There was about a fortnight or a week between each visit. He addressed the men on each occasion. His talk was about freeing Ireland, and how he would get us £10 and so many marks a week if we joined the brigade. If Germany lost the war we were to be sent to America. Casement said the £30 would come through him.

We used to get a paper called the "Gaelic American". Everything was explained in it. The Germans used to give us these papers; they were distributed at the huts. There was also a book called "Crimes against Ireland". I got one from a German. There was a copy for each room. If I am not mistaken it bore Sir Roger Casement's name as the writer. There was also a form with questions which the men had to answer. Each man filled it up, and the Germans collected it.

Mr Bodkin then read a circular which, witness said, had been sent round the camp. It ran as follows:

"Irishmen! Here, is a chance for you to fight for Ireland. You have fought for England, your country's hereditary enemy. You have fought for Belgium in England's interest, though it was no more to you than the Fiji Islands. Are you willing to fight for your own country with a view of securing the national freedom of Ireland? With the moral and material assistance of the German Government an Irish Brigade is being formed. The object of the Irish Brigade shall be to fight solely the cause of Ireland, and in no circumstances shall it be directed to the interests of Germany."

The statement went on to declare that the Irish Brigade should be formed to fight under the Irish flag alone, with a distinctive Irish uniform and Irish officers. It should be fed and efficiently equipped with arms and ammunition by the. German Government, and be stationed near Berlin. At the end of the war the German Government undertook to send those members of the brigade who should desire it to America, with the necessary means of landing. The statement added that Irishmen in America were raising money for the brigade. Those men who did not join the brigade would be removed from Limburg and distributed amongst the other camps. If interested, the men were to see their company commanders. The statement concluded with the words, "Remember Bachelors' Walk! God save Ireland!"

Witness: There were also little forms with questions on them. It was these we had to fill up. Fifty or sixty men joined the Irish Brigade out of about 1,000.

I filled up one of these papers, but if I had agreed to join the Irish Brigade I would not have been here. Because I had not filled up the papers as the Germans wished I was shifted to Giessen Camp. It was a very good camp, and I was treated much the same as at Limburg.

Were the men who agreed to join the Irish Brigade shifted? – No.

Witness knew that Bailey joined the Irish Brigade, and he recognised him in a newspaper reproduction of a photographic group of men wearing the Irish Brigade uniform. On February 8 witness was exchanged, and returned to this country.

Mr Artemus Jones (cross-examining): Did not some of the men want to know about the arrears of money due by the British Government? – No, I never heard that.

Did not Casement say at the beginning that there was no money in it? – Yes; but he said afterwards there was £10 in it.

Did he say if you are going into this business you are going into it with ropes round your necks? – No. I did not hear him say that,

30 June 1916
Death sentence on Sir R. Casement
Closing scenes

After a four days' trial Sir Roger Casement was found guilty of high treason, and sentenced to be hanged. His fellow-prisoner, Daniel Julian Bailey, also charged with high treason, was subsequently placed in the dock, but no evidence was offered by the Crown. A formal verdict of "not guilty" was returned, and he was acquitted. The proceedings were heard in the Law Courts, before the Lord Chief Justice, Mr Justice Avory, and Mr Justice Horridge.

It was a sitting of constant tension, relieved only when the jury were out considering their verdict. Ladies again formed the larger part of an audience which filled the court and its gallery to the limit. Prisoner had resumed his black attire, and was composed throughout the proceedings.

Within an hour of the opening the Lord Chief Justice had begun his summing up. His direction to the jury was masterly, and lasted about three hours. He indicated that if a British subject did an act which strengthened, or tended to strengthen, the enemies of the King, or to weaken, or tend, to weaken, the power of the King and the country to resist or to attack the King's enemies it was high treason, even although the person accused had another or ulterior purpose in view. If Sir Roger Casement knew or believed that what he did would promote civil war in Ireland, and necessitate troops being kept there, that would be weakening the King's power, and assisting the enemy. These broad definitions of the law were applied to the evidence, and the jury retired shortly before three o'clock. Twice during their retirement the jury sent for papers to assist them in their deliberations.

When, fifty minutes later, the judges, jury, and prisoner reappeared, a strained silence succeeded the temporary commotion of unrestrained chatter. Prisoner was seemingly less affected by the verdict of guilty than many of the spectators. He was pale, but calm. When Master Kershaw asked him in statutory language if he had anything to say why sentence should not be passed upon him, he quietly took from his breast pocket a handful of papers, and from these read, without a trace of emotion in his voice, a statement which occupied three-quarters of an hour.

This was in the main a protest against trial in an English court, before an English tribunal, and the claim of a right to be tried by his peers in Ireland, from whence he had been "dragged by the Crown". But it also embraced a long diatribe on Ireland's treatment by this country, references to the Ulster rising, allusion to his own efforts to foster Irish unity, and many passages of uncloaked and extravagant hostility to what he called English rule. If it was treason to fight against such rights as Irishmen were now permitted to enjoy, he was proud to be a rebel. It was a somewhat defiant statement, delivered in a manner making no display of defiance.

At the last word spectators turned their gaze from the magnetic attraction of the dock to the bench, to see that already the black cap was being placed on the head of .each judge by his clerk. Quietly, with his head bent to a written paper, the Lord Chief Justice uttered the momentous words that passed sentence of death on Sir Roger Casement, and committed him to the custody of those entrusted with carrying out his execution. Prisoner maintained his calmness to the end of the ordeal. He even smiled to friends as he turned from the dock and disappeared.

The counsel were:

For the Crown: The Attorney-General, the Solicitor-General, Mr Bodkin, Mr Travers Humphreys, and Mr Branson (instructed by the Treasury Solicitor).

For the accused: Mr Alex. Martin Sullivan, Mr T. Artemus Jones, Professor J. H. Morgan, and Mr P. H. Hooper (instructed by Mr T. Gavan Duffy).

When the proceedings wore resumed Mr Artemus Jones informed the Court that his learned leader, Mr Sullivan, was not in a condition to attend the Court, his medical adviser having forbidden him to go on with the case.

The Lord Chief Justice said he was very sorry that Mr Sullivan was not able to be present. It was obvious that he was labouring under a strain on Wednesday afternoon. His lordship asked Mr Jones to proceed with his statement.

Mr Artemus Jones submitted that the acts of the prisoner in Germany were quite consistent with an entirely different view from that put forward on behalf of the Crown. Sir Roger Casement went to Germany not to help Germany to fight England, but for the purpose of forming an Irish Brigade to strive for some of the things which they had a right to strive for, namely, the protection of themselves if they were oppressed or tyrannised by an armed force in Ireland not controlled by the Executive Government. It was open to the jury to form that view on the evidence. He suggested to the jury that the meaning of the words "aid and comfort" in the statute, passed almost 600 years ago, was something different from the meaning of those words as used to-day. Those words meant to-day the supply of the enemy with information, forces, and material for the purpose of levying war against the King. The jury had to be satisfied that Casement's intention in Germany was to use the Irish Brigade for the purpose of fighting Germany's battle as against England.

The Lord Chief Justice: The words of the statute are, of course, to be interpreted according to law, and, therefore, are not for the jury, but for us. I shall tell the jury that giving "aid and comfort to the King's enemies" means assisting the King's enemies in the war with this country, and that any act which strengthens or tends to strengthen the enemy in the conduct of the war against us would be giving aid and comfort to the King's enemies, and that any act which weakens or tends to weaken the power of this country to resist or attack the enemy equally is giving aid and comfort to the King's enemies.

Mr Artemus Jones, continuing, said prisoner made it abundantly clear in his appeal to Irish soldiers in Germany to join the Irish Brigade that they would go to Ireland to fight for Ireland, and for no other purpose.

The Attorney-General said he greatly regretted the indisposition which at the last moment had deprived the prisoner of the advantage of the closing sentences of Mr Sullivan, who had conducted the case with the ability, propriety, and eloquence which his distinguished position at the Irish Bar entitled them to expect. The case for the Crown was that prisoner, who had been long in the service of this country, and well understood public affairs, on the outbreak of the greatest struggle in which the country to which he had so long belonged had ever been engaged went to the country of our principal enemy, and set himself to seduce the captured soldiers of his Majesty from their allegiance, with the object of using them, in violation of their military duty and at the risk of their lives, in any enterprise which might injure the country to which they owed allegiance. The answer was that they were not to be used to assist Germany in any way, but only on the conclusion of the war for matters concerned with the condition of Ireland. Had the acts for which the prisoner stood arraigned been committed before the war, the defence which had been put forward might have been relevant.

But one circumstance had intervened which altered the whole face of Irish politics. The greatest military Power that the world had ever known was trying to destroy this country and to make an end of the Empire. From the moment that Germany made that tiger spring at the throat of Europe the past was the past in the eyes of every man who did not seek to injure his country. On the outbreak of the war there was an understanding and a convention between the great leaders that while the danger to the Empire existed the terrible state of things in Ireland should be put an end to.

At the very moment when the Irish soldiers had written their names on the battle-fields of France in that glorious retreat which marked the early days of the war, when the Irish soldiers were taken into captivity, prisoner went to Germany and attempted to seduce those men from their allegiance, and arranged that at some period, which was not at the end of the war, to land and create once again the hideous spectre of disunion and disloyalty and Army insurrection. Why did the prisoner ever go to Germany at all? How did he get there? What was the nature of the assurance given and the arrangements made with him before he went to Germany? How was it that when this country was at war with Germany, when the Irish soldiers had been taken prisoners by the Germans we found him for months a free man in Germany, moving without restriction among the Irish soldiers and attempting to seduce them? The question of why he went to Germany had never been answered. If they knew the full story of the circumstances under which he went to Germany, if they knew what negotiations had taken place and the safeguards and plans arranged, the defence would be more difficult than it was to-day.

"If you come to the conclusion," were the closing words of the Attorney-General, "that the Crown has proved its case, however painful the duty you have to perform, it is a duty from which you cannot and dare not shrink. I have discharged my responsibility in this case. I leave you to discharge yours."

After an absence of fifty minutes, the jury re-entered the court, and returned a verdict of guilty.

Master Kershaw (addressing the prisoner, who stood in front of the dock): Sir Roger David Casement, you stand convicted of high treason. What have you to say for yourself why the Court should not pass sentence and judgment upon you to die according to law?

Sir Roger Casement, drawing from his pocket a bundle of papers, read a long statement occupying three-quarters of an hour. In it appeared the following:

My Lord Chief Justice: I may say at once that I protest against the jurisdiction of this Court in my case on this charge, and the argument that I penned in my prison, which I am now going to read, is addressed not to this Court, but to my own fellow-countrymen. There is an objection, possibly not good in law, but surely good on moral grounds, against the application to me here of this old English statute, 565 years old, that seeks to deprive an Irishman to-day of life and honour, not for adhering to the King's enemies, but for adhering to his own people. The law of that day did not permit a man to forsake his Church or deny his God to save his life. The heretic then had the same doom as the traitor. To-day a man may forsake God and His heavenly Kingdom without fear or penalty. If religion rests on love, it is equally true that loyalty rests on love. The law I am charged under is not based on love, but claims allegiance on the ignorance and blindness of the past. I am being tried in truth not by my peers, but by the peers of a dead past, not by the civilisation of the twentieth century, but by the brutality of the fourteenth, by a statute framed not in the language of the land that tries me, but of an enemy land – so antiquated is the law that must be sought to slay an Irishman whose offence is that he puts Ireland first.

Loyalty is a sentiment, not a law. It rests on love, not on restraint. The government of England rests on the strength and nature of law, and since it demands no love it can evoke no loyalty. But this statute is more absurd even than it is antiquated. If it be competent to hang one Irishman, it is still more competent to gibbet Englishmen. Edward III. was King not only of the realm of England, but also of the realm of France, and he was not King of Ireland. Yet has he a hand to-day in putting the noose around an Irishman's neck whose Sovereign he was not; but the Act can strain no strand around the Frenchman's neck, whose Sovereign he was. Did the Kings of France resident here in Windsor or in the Tower of London hang, draw, and quarter as a traitor every Frenchman for 400 years who fell into their hands with arms in their hands? On the contrary, they received embassies of these traitors, presents from them, even knighthoods. They visited with them, jousted with them, fought with them, but did not assassinate them by law.

Judicial assassination to-day is reserved only for one race of the King's subjects – for Irishmen, for those who cannot forget their allegiance to the realm of Ireland. The Kings of England as such had no rights in Ireland up to the time of Henry VIII. save such as raised a mutual obligation between them and certain princes, chiefs, and lords of Ireland. This form of legal right gave no King of England lawful power to impeach an Irishman for high treason under this statute of Edward III. until the Irish Act – Poining's Act – was passed in 1494. But if by Poining's law an Irishman could be indicted for high treason under this Act, he could be indicted only in one way and before one tribunal – by the laws of the realm of Ireland and in Ireland.

What is the fundamental charter of an Englishman's liberty? That he should be tried by his peers. With all respect, my lord, I assert that this Court is to me, an Irishman charged with this offence, a foreign Court; this jury is for me, an Irishman, not a jury of my peers, to try me in this vital issue, for it is patent to every man of conscience that I have a right, an indefeasible right, if tried at all under this ancient statute, to be tried in Ireland, before an Irish Court, and by an Irish jury. This Court, this jury, the public opinion of this country cannot but be prejudiced in varying degree against me, most of all in time of war. I did not land in England. I landed in Ireland. It was to Ireland I came, to Ireland I wanted to come, and the last place I desired to see was England. To the Attorney-General of England there is only England; there is no Ireland; there is only the law of England, no right of Ireland. The liberty of Ireland and Irishmen is to be judged by the power of England. Yet for me, an Irishman, there is a land of Ireland, a right of Ireland, and a charter for all Irishmen to appeal to in the last resort – a charter that even the statutes of England itself cannot deprive us of.

This charge of high treason involves a moral responsibility, as the very terms of the indictment recite, inasmuch as I committed the acts I am charged with, to the evil example of others in a like case. What was that evil example I set to others in a like case, and who are those others? The evil example charged is that I asserted the rights of my own country, and those I appealed to to aid me were my own countrymen, Irishmen.

I did not appeal to Englishmen. I asked no Englishmen to help me, I asked Irishmen to fight for their rights. The evil example was only to every Irishman, who might come with me, and who in "like cases" seeks to do as I do. How, then, since neither my example nor my appeal was addressed to Englishmen, can I be rightly tried by them? If I did long ago make that appeal to Irishmen to join with me in the effort to fight for Ireland, it is by Irishmen, and by them alone, I can be rightly judged. From this Court and its jurisdiction I appeal to those whom I am alleged to have ruined, to those I am alleged to have injured, by my evil example, and I claim that they alone are competent to decide my guilt or innocence. If they find me guilty, the statute may affix the penalty, but the statute does not override or annul my right to judgment at their hands. This is fundamental, a right natural and obvious, a right that it is clear the Crown were aware of when they brought me by force and by stealth from Ireland to this country.

It was not I who landed in England, but the Crown who dragged me here from my own country, to which I had returned with a price upon my head. I do not shrink from the judgment of my countrymen, I admit no other judgment but theirs, I accept no verdict save at their hands. I assert from this dock that I am being tried here, not because it is just, but because it is unjust. Place me before a jury of my own countrymen, be it Protestant or Catholic, Unionist or Nationalist, Sinn Feiner or Orangeman, and I shall accept the verdict, and bow to the statute and all its penalties; but I accept no meaner finding against me than that of those whose loyalty I endangered by my example, and to whom alone I appeal. If they judge me guilty, then guilty I am. It is not I who am afraid of their verdict. Is it the Crown? If this be not so, why fear the test? I fear it not. I demand it as my right.

My lords, the dominion of the English rule, of English law, of English government in Ireland, dare not rest on the will of the Irish people, but exists in defiance of their will. It is a rule derived, not from right, but from conquest. Conquest knows no title and if it exists for the body it fails for the mind. It can exert no empire over men's minds, and judgment, and affections, and it is from this law of conquest, without title to the judgment and affection of my own countrymen, that I appeal.

In England alone is loyalty to be a crime? If loyalty be something less than love and more than law then we had only such loyalty in Ireland. If we are to be indicted as criminals, to be shot as murderers, to be imprisoned as convicts because our offence is that we love Ireland more than we value our lives, then I know not what virtue rests in any offer of self-government held out by England. Self-government is our right, no more to be dealt out to us or doled out to us, or withheld from us by another people than the right to life itself. Ireland among the nations of the world is treated to-day as if she were a convicted criminal. If it be treason to fight against such an unnatural fate as this, then I am proud to be a rebel and shall cling to my rebellion with the last drop of my blood. It is better to fight and die for right than to live in such a state of right as this, where all your rights become only an accumulated wrong and men must beg with bated breath for leave to subsist in their own land, to think with their own thoughts.

My lord, I have done.

Gentlemen of the jury, I wish to thank you for your verdict. I hope you will not take amiss what I have said, or that I made any imputation upon your truthfulness or your integrity if I have said this was not a trial by my peers. I would put it to you, how would you feel in the converse case if an Englishman had landed in England and the Government for its own purposes had conveyed him to Ireland under a false name and had committed him to prison. How would you feel yourselves as Englishmen if that man were to be submitted for trial by a jury in a land inflamed against him and believing him to be a criminal when his only crime was that he had cared for England more than for Ireland?

The three judges having assumed the black cap, the Lord Chief Justice addressed the prisoner: Sir Roger David Casement, you have been found guilty of treason, the greatest crime known to the law, and upon evidence which in our opinion is conclusive of guilt. Your crime was that of assisting the King's enemies, that is, the empire of Germany, during the terrible war in which we are engaged. The duty now devolves upon me to pass sentence upon you. It is that you be taken hence to a lawful prison, and thence to a place of execution, and that you be there hanged by the neck till you be dead; and the Sheriffs of the county of London and the county of Middlesex are hereby charged with the execution of this judgment, and may the Lord have mercy on your soul.

Prisoner left the dock smiling to friends seated in the well of the court.

The Cleveland Street Scandal

"I do not walk slowly as a rule."

Two words are conspicuous by their absence from the *Telegraph*'s highly decorous coverage of this affair: "homosexual" and "brothel". The establishment on Cleveland Street employed Post Office messenger boys, and it was the arrest of one of these in conjunction with a police investigation into a theft that led back here. It swiftly became clear that many patrons were aristocratic and included, it was rumoured, Prince Albert Victor, the Prince of Wales's son. Anxious and horrified in equal measure, the government moved quickly to cover up the scandal. However, Ernest Parke, editor of the radical paper *North London Press*, knew hypocrisy when he saw it and before long linked Lord Euston to "an indescribably loathsome scandal in Cleveland Street". Given contemporary attitudes to, and the illegality of, homosexuality, Euston had no option but to press a libel case – which he won. However, his success did little to dispel the contemporary belief that homosexuality was a peculiarly aristocratic vice that served to debauch otherwise innocent lower-class youths.

27 November 1889
The alleged libel upon Lord Euston

Yesterday, at Bow-street, Ernest Parke, aged twenty-nine, editor end proprietor of the *North London Press*, surrendered before Mr Vaughan on a warrant charging him with having, on 16 November, published in his paper, false and defamatory libel concerning Henry James Earl of Euston, eldest son of the Duke of Grafton.

Mr George Lewis prosecuted, and the defendant was Mr Lockwood, Q.C., M.P., and Mr Asquith, M.P.; Mr Gill, Mr Bernard Abrahams, and Mr Arthur Newton watched the proceedings in the interest of persons not named.

The defendant was allowed to stand in front of the dock.

Mr George Lewis said Lord Euston, for whom he appeared, complained of a libel published by the defendant in the *North London Press* on November 16, 1889, a newspaper which was not registered at Somerset House, as required by the law, but he should prove that the defendant was the proprietor and the editor. The alleged libel charged Lord Euston with having committed a felony, and he believed a copy of the paper was before the magistrate. His worship would observe that the names of certain distinguished criminals were mentioned who had escaped, and it was alleged that Lord Euston was one of those "distinguished criminals" who had escaped. It was perfectly clear that the charge made against Lord Euston, in very distinct terms, was that he had escaped, for the paper went on to say that these men had been allowed to leave the country. If there had been the least inquiry made it would have been ascertained that Lord Euston was living at 4, Grosvenor-place. The libel concluded by warning Mr Matthews that if he did not take action in the matter there would be a heavy reckoning when Parliament met, for there were certain foul crimes which could not be tolerated, unless London was to be regarded as a disgrace to civilisation. The Earl of Euston was charged with having committed a felony of very atrocious character, and that was the libel for publishing which he should ask the magistrate to commit the defendant to take his trial. The circumstances, so far as Lord Euston could tell him, were these: He had never committed any crime of any sort or kind. The statement was utterly without foundation so far as he was concerned. He had never left the country. There had been no warrant for his apprehension; if there had been his lordship was there to be apprehended. It was perfectly untrue that he had gone away from justice. The whole thing was a fabrication from beginning to end. All that his lordship knew of the matter was that one evening, at the end of May or the beginning of June last, he was walking in Piccadilly at eleven o'clock, and some man put into his hand a card having the words "Poses plastiques" upon it, and the name of the proprietor, with the address, Cleveland-street, Tottenham-court-road. Lord Euston did not know what had become of that card. About a week afterwards he went at eleven o'clock at night to this house. A man opened the door and asked for a sovereign. His lordship gave the sovereign, but having heard what the man had to say, threatened to knock him down, and at once left the house. That was all Lord Euston knew about the place.

Mr Edward H. Bedford, solicitor, 8, King's Bench-walk, stated: I identify copy of paper produced, which I purchased on November 16 in the Imperial Arcade, Ludgate-circus.

Mr Walter Shepheard, Printer, 27, Chancery-lane, deposed: I printed the copy of the *North London Press*, of November 16. I printed between 4,000 and 5,000 copies. I have printed the paper since the first week in November. Mr Parke told me that he was the proprietor and editor.

Mr Lewis: Who brought you the manuscript of the article "West-end Scandals?" – I cannot tell. It came late at night. The manuscript should be at our office, and we can find it.

Mr Adams was called, whereupon Mr Lockwood stated that it was not disputed that Mr Parke was the editor of the journal, nor was the responsibility of the article in dispute.

Mr Edward Owen Adams was, however, examined, and he said that he carried on business at 113, New North-road. He was printer and publisher of the *North London Press* until a month ago. Mr Parke was editor and proprietor of the paper.

Lord Euston was then called, and examined by Mr Lewis. His lordship said: My name is Henry James Earl of Euston and when in London I reside at 4, Grosvenor-place; and when not in town either at Euston Hall, Thetford, or Wakefield Lodge, Stony Stratford – my father's place.

Have you seen a copy of the *North London Press* of November 16? – I have.

Did you at once give instructions for a criminal prosecution for libel in respect of the matters contained in that paper? – I did.

Is there any truth, Lord Euston, in the statement that you have been guilty of the crime alleged against you in that paper? – Certainly not.

Is there any truth, so far as you know, of any warrant having been issued for your apprehension? – No.

Is there any truth in that statement that, to avoid arrest, you absconded from England and went to Peru? – None, whatever. I have not been out of England since I came back from Australia in 1881.

Will you state to the Court what you know with reference to this house in Cleveland-street? – All I know is, I was walking one night in Piccadilly—

The Magistrate: How long ago? – I cannot say the date. It was either the end of May or beginning of June. A card was put into my hand, which, upon reading afterwards, I found was headed "Poses Plastiques – Hammond, 19, Cleveland-street." I do not remember whether Tottenham-court-road was on it. About a week afterwards I went there. It was between half-past ten and eleven at night.

Mr Lewis: Was the door opened to you by a man? – Yes. He asked me to come in, and then asked me for a sovereign. I gave it to him. I then asked him when the *poses plastiques* were going to take place. He said, "There is nothing of that sort here. If you want—"

Mr Lockwood: I object to my friend going into this conversation. It is not alleged to have taken place in the presence of Mr Parke, accused of the libel.

Mr Lewis: The libel alleges that the witness was mixed up with crimes committed at Cleveland-street.

Mr Lockwood: I have no objection to my friend saying what Lord Euston "did" at Cleveland-street. (Laughter.)

The magistrate upheld the objection of counsel.

Mr Lewis: That being so (to witness): The man said something to you. – Yes.

Did you then express anger?

Mr Lockwood again objected. As to anything which this gentleman did, my friend is entitled to ask, but not upon anything which he said.

Mr Lewis (to the witness): Did you instantly leave the house? –I did.

How long were you in the house? – Considerably under five minutes.

Two or three minutes? – Yes.

Have you been there since? – No.

Nor previously to that occasion? – No.

Have you any knowledge of any sort or kind, other than that one visit, concerning the house? – No.

You came here prepared to state what did pass? – Yes.

Mr Lockwood: I may say at once I do not propose to enter into any detailed cross-examination of this witness, for inasmuch, as I recognised the fact that it will be your duty to send this case for trial, the wish of my client is to appear as soon as possible before the tribunal which should have to try this case. I have one or two questions now to put.

Were you in the army, Lord Euston? – Yes.

In what regiment? – The Rifle Brigade.

You are not in it now? – No.

When were you gazetted out? – July 1871, I think.

You were afterwards in a Yeomanry regiment? – A volunteer regiment.

Are you in it now? – I am; it is the 1st Volunteer Battalion Northamptonshire Regiment.

You told my learned friend that you at once gave instructions for a prosecution for libel? – I did.

When was this newspaper first brought to your attention? Yesterday week. I drove straight to Mr Lewis's offices, and placed the matter in his hands.

When did you first make the statement which you have made to-day? – I made it some time ago to some friends of mine.

When first, is my question? – About the middle of October.

This thing happened in the month of June? – Yes.

Your first statement in regard to it was made in the month of October? – Yes.

Did you make a statement at the Home Office about it? – No.

At the Treasury? – No.

You have made no statement to any official either at the Treasury or the Home Office? – I have made no communication of any sort or kind to any official either at the Treasury or the Home Office. That I swear.

I take it that your first statement in October was made to some private friend? – Yes.

Is Lord Arthur Somerset a friend of yours? – I knew him.

When did you see him last? – Last summer; some time during the season. I saw him several times in society. I kept meeting him constantly.

Have you not seen him since? – No.

Now, in regard to this occurrence in May or June, you say you afterwards read the card? – Yes.

How long afterwards? – When I got home; when I took my coat off. I don't remember particularly. I did not read it in the street. I shoved it in my pocket, and when I got home I took it out to see what it was.

Just tell me what it was. Was it a printed card? – It was.

It was not in writing? – It was a lithographed card, and at the top the words "*poses plastiques*" were in writing.

Was the gentleman giving out cards to everybody in Piccadilly, or were you specially favoured? – I was walking along, and he shoved one into my hand.

Did he appear to be shoving them into the hands of people promiscuously or to selected persons? – I really did not notice. He shoved it into my hand. I was not walking slowly at the time. I do not walk slowly as a rule.

Indeed. What time was it? – I was walking home about eleven or twelve.

You had not time to stop and read it? – Witness (smiling): I did not think of it.

I don't know what you are laughing at. Then you got home and read it. How long elapsed after you had read the card before you went to the house to see whether the promises of the card were to be carried out? – At least a week.

So, of course, you kept the card during that time? – Yes, I did.

Then you went to the house about the beginning of July? – No; about the second week in June, or thereabouts

What time did you go? – Between half-past ten and eleven at night.

You went alone? – Yes.

Did you bring the card back with you? – I brought it home.

That is bringing it back with you. (A laugh.) What has become of it? – I destroyed it. I was disgusted at being found in such a place, and so I did not want anything more to do with it.

Oh! I see. You destroyed the card. Did you burn it or tear it up? I probably tore it up. I had no fire.

You probably tore it up on disgust and indignation? – Yes; I was very angry with myself at being caught in such a place.

Lord Euston, from what passed in the house you had no doubt in your own mind what the character of that house was? – Not the smallest.

Mr Lewis, in re-examination: You have been asked what passed in the house, and had you any doubt as to the character of the house. What did pass? What did the man say to you? After I had given him the sovereign I asked when the *poses plastiques* commenced, and he said, "There is nothing of that kind here," and added something more.

Did you at once leave the house? – I did.

Up to the moment when he made that statement to you had you any knowledge of the house other than what appeared on the card? – None whatever.

The Magistrate: Nor any suspicion? – No.

Mr Lewis: You had never been there before? – No.

You had never heard of the house before? – No, not from anybody.

You were asked whether you ever mentioned this matter before October. Was it not until October that some public mention was made of this case or thereabouts? – I believe thereabouts.

Since you have heard of it—

Mr Lockwood: I object to my learned friend asking what the witness had heard.

The Magistrate: How came you to make a statement in October? – Because there was some rumour about, so I went to consult my friends about it.

Mr Lewis: About this house, and not about yourself? – About myself.

Then you made the statement to several friends? – I did.

Is what you have told us the entire and absolute truth in connection with your knowledge of the house? – Yes.

Mr Lewis: I will put in the formal order of Mr Justice Field for this prosecution.

Mr Lockwood (re-examining): I want to ask you about the house. Do I understand you to say that you went into a room at the house? – Yes; into a sort of sitting room in the ground floor, on the right.

Did the same man who opened the door go into the room with you? – Yes; I saw nobody else. I showed him the card, and said, "This is what brought me here." He said, "There is nothing of that sort here."

Did it ever occur to you to give information to the police? – No, it did not. In fact, I did not want to be mixed up with it. I was disgusted, and I did not want to have anything more to do with it.

Have you seen the man since? – No.

You remember that some persons were prosecuted at the Central Criminal Court in connection with this house? – I heard of it.

The prisoners were before the magistrates on many occasions? – I think I heard of it then. I was not at the time in London.

It struck you at once that this was the house which you visited? – I thought it must be.

Did you take any step to see whether this man who interviewed you was the man who was being prosecuted at the Old Bailey? – No. I did not want to be mixed up with anything of the sort.

Mr Lewis: And you would have taken no step whatever except for the publication of this libel? – None whatever.

Had anybody made any accusation against you? – No.

Until the publication of the libel? None.

You were asked whether you had given information to the Home Office, Treasury, or police, and you said No. Had you been asked for information you would have been prepared—

Mr Lockwood: I object.

Mr Lewis: Did they ever apply to you?

The magistrate ruled that the question could not be put.

Mr Lewis: Those are the facts of the case for the prosecution

The magistrate cautioned the defendant, and asked him whether he had anything to say in answer to the charge.

Mr Lockwood: I appear, with my learned friend Mr Asquith, on behalf of the defendant, Mr Parke, and, as I stated to you, we shall take no course which will tend to delay this case coming before the tribunal which, of course, we feel must ultimately decide it.

The Magistrate: I take it that the defendant has nothing to say.

Mr Lockwood: I don't suppose he wishes to make any statement.

The Magistrate: It is not necessary for you to make any statement of what you propose to do.

The Defendant: I reserve my defence.

The Magistrate: I commit you to take your trial at the next session of the Central Criminal Court.

Mr Lockwood, on the question of bail, mentioned that when notice was given to the defendant that an application would be made to the judge sitting in chambers to grant leave to file a criminal information Mr Parke attended, and also his solicitor. Later in the afternoon application was made to the magistrate for a warrant. There was not a tittle of ground for supposing that the defendant would not surrender to take his trial. The warrant was applied for late in the afternoon, and the result was that no opportunity was afforded to Mr Parke of being bailed out, and he was kept in custody until Monday morning. He hoped the fact would be taken into consideration that from the first the defendant had shown anxiety to meet this charge, and had not shown the slightest indication of shrinking from meeting it.

The Magistrate: In my opinion this is a case of very great gravity, and I ought to require such bail as shall certainly secure the attendance of the defendant at the trial which takes place next month. I shall require two sureties in £250 each.

The sureties being forthcoming, the defendant left the court, which during the proceedings had been densely crowded.

Bill Clinton and Monica Lewinsky

"I want you to listen to me. I'm going to say this again;
I did not have sexual relations with that woman, Miss Lewinsky."

Bill Clinton's presidency had already been attended by numerous, if unproven, allegations of sexual impropriety by the time allegations regarding his relationship with White House intern Monica Lewinsky broke. The details emerged when Lewinsky submitted an affidavit in a separate investigation into Bill Clinton's behaviour – the Paula Jones case. After the first sensational frenzy the affair went relatively quiet for a number of months until, having secured immunity in exchange for agreeing to testify before a grand jury, Lewinsky turned over a semen-stained blue dress to the Starr investigators. This promised to provide unambiguous DNA evidence of the relationship. Left with little choice, Clinton made his own confession. Though few gave him any chance of surviving his impeachment – the greatest scandal to descend on the White House since Nixon and Watergate – he was eventually acquitted and served the full term of his presidency.

24 January 1998
Clinton "had four lovers" in White House
President hit by new audiotape reports
By Hugo Gurdon

President Clinton had simultaneous affairs with four other women, including three White House staff members, according to the secret tape of his alleged lover Monica Lewinsky, American television reported last night. In a dramatic new development, the CBS network said that Miss Lewinsky complained bitterly on tape that Mr Clinton was cheating on her during their year-long affair but that the other women did not seem to mind.

The 24-year-old unpaid White House assistant allegedly identified the other women in the recorded conversations, but their names have not been made public.

Miss Lewinsky, who is seeking immunity from prosecution, reportedly bewailed the President's other affairs in distressed comments to Linda Tripp, who later took the tapes to prosecutors.

Miss Lewinsky avoided giving sworn testimony in the Paula Jones sexual harassment case, which had been scheduled for yesterday morning, by telling the judge that she would "plead the Fifth Amendment", which allows witnesses to stay silent rather than risk incriminating themselves.

Kenneth Starr, the independent counsel investigating Mr Clinton's alleged abuses of power, is threatening her with criminal charges and jail if she does not give evidence.

Her lawyer, William Ginsburg, went on television saying he wanted a deal for his client, but that she was being "squeezed" by prosecutors who feel that the damning audiotaped evidence gives them the whip hand at long last against Mr Clinton and his friends.

"She has been targeted," said Mr Ginsburg. "Their position is they are not going to give her immunity."

Sources at the independent counsel's office, however, said they had no interest in taking Miss Lewinsky's scalp; their tough line was merely to make sure she was willing to give them all the most incriminating details.

Mr Starr views her as a way of turning Vernon Jordan, Mr Clinton's close friend and confidant, into a prosecution witness.

On 20 hours of taped conversations, some of it secured by the FBI, Miss Lewinsky allegedly suggests that both Mr Clinton and Mr Jordan asked her to lie under oath to conceal her affair. Both men deny the allegation.

Mr Jordan appears now to be the key to more than one compartment of the Whitewater case, which originally began as an investigation into alleged financial scandals involving Mr and Mrs Clinton in Arkansas.

Mr Jordan is entangled in suspected hush money payments to Webster Hubbell, a long-time friend of Mr Clinton whom Mr Starr successfully prosecuted for fraud, but who is now refusing to co-operate with investigators.

If Miss Lewinsky implicates Mr Jordan sufficiently to persuade him to give details of improper payments to Mr Hubbell, it could crack the Whitewater case open, endangering not only the President but also the First Lady.

Mr Clinton's critics and supporters agree that if obstruction of justice and suborning perjury are proved against him, it would be enough for Congress to impeach him and remove him from office.

Prosecutors also now have a legal briefing paper given by Miss Lewinsky to Mrs Tripp, Mr Starr's informant, apparently designed to help her lie persuasively under oath.

Mr Starr may therefore have evidence that Miss Lewinsky perjured herself, suborned perjury from Mrs Tripp and obstructed justice – offences that could put her in jail for five years unless she tells all.

The sex, lies and audiotape scandal, by far the most damaging yet in the Clinton presidency, now moves into a second phase in which the initial uproar subsides and lawyers for each side get down to the details of attack and defence.

Mr Clinton's attorneys want him to say as little as possible, to avoid damning himself and provoking more detailed questions which he dare not answer.

But his political aides warn that failure to get a convincing story out to the public quickly, with evidence to back his denials, could cause a collapse of his popularity and credibility in office. This would make it easier for Congress to begin the process of impeaching him.

His political advisers say his State of the Union Address on Tuesday will be over-shadowed unless Mr Clinton first manages to rebuff the allegations against him with a convincing television performance.

26 January 1998
Clinton "may be forced to quit in days"
Investigator has independent evidence of
White House sex encounter, says report

President Clinton was being given as little as days to survive in office last night after it was reported that he had been caught by more than one person while engaged in a sexual act with Monica Lewinsky, then a 21-year-old work experience trainee, in the White House. The news shocked even his closest supporters, some of whom said senior Democrats might soon urge Mr Clinton to resign and spare the country the trauma of a long investigation.

ABC News reported that Kenneth Starr, the independent counsel investigating the President's alleged abuses of power, had found witnesses to corroborate Miss Lewinsky's claims of a sexual encounter with the President.

If so, Mr Starr appears to have sufficient evidence to prove that Mr Clinton has lied repeatedly on television and has perjured himself under oath.

George Stephanopoulos, a former senior White House aide and one of the young gurus who ran Mr Clinton's 1992 election campaign, said: "I'm heartbroken, with all the evidence coming out.

"If he's not telling the truth, the whole truth and nothing but the truth, he can't survive."

Washington is stunned at the lightning speed at which the presidency is unravel-ling. The end appears to be rushing upon Mr Clinton whereas it took two years for the Watergate scandal to bring down President Nixon.

Only days ago, few people were prepared to write him off, arguing that he was "the Comeback Kid" and one of the most skilled political survivors of the century. He still may beat the odds, but fewer people are betting on it now.

If Mr Clinton were to fall from power, his most likely course would be to resign under pressure from his own party, whose elders would be concerned about damage to the entire Democratic machine if he lingered in office.

William Kristol, a former aide to Vice-President Dan Quayle, said: "Everyone knows he is lying." Leading Democrats, such as Senator Daniel Patrick Moynihan, could form a delegation this week to tell Mr Clinton it is time to go, Mr Kristol predicted.

It is not known whether Secret Service agents or members of the White House staff discovered Mr Clinton and Miss Lewinsky in flagrante delicto. But Mr Starr is said to be no longer dependent upon Miss Lewinsky's testimony.

On 20 hours of telephone tapes handed to Mr Starr by another former White House staffer, Linda Tripp, Miss Lewinsky says she had a long sexual affair with Mr Clinton and that he tried to persuade her to hide it by lying under oath.

Miss Lewinsky, who may have perjured herself by denying in an affidavit that she had an affair with Mr Clinton, is terrified of going to jail and her lawyer was on television yesterday almost begging Mr Starr for a deal to save his client.

"If she gets a promise of immunity, she will tell all," said William Ginsburg.

According to those who have heard all the tapes, Miss Lewinsky suggests that both Mr Clinton and his friend, Vernon Jordan, tried to get her to deceive lawyers acting for Paula Jones in her sexual harassment suit against the President.

Public opinion polls brought more bad news for Mr Clinton, whose staff were reported to be "in crisis mode" and talking of a presidential "meltdown".

It is getting harder each day for them to explain why the President needs to wait to see the evidence before deciding what to say in a public broadcast designed to clear the air.

Having held steady for days, Mr Clinton's overall approval ratings are suddenly collapsing. NBC, the television network, found it had dropped from 57 per cent five days ago to 40 per cent now, and 69 per cent of those surveyed said Mr Clinton had been "guarded or less than honest" in his televised denials.

Despite the extraordinary storm around him, Mr Clinton sought to suggest business as usual yesterday. He watched the Super Bowl last night, and rehearsed his State of the Union address, due tomorrow.

The address is likely to be overshadowed by the scandal, however – Miss Lewinsky is due to be interrogated by Mr Starr's staff in front of the federal Grand Jury on the same day.

It has also been reported that Mr Starr's investigators searched and removed many articles of clothing from Miss Lewinsky's flat which, ironically, is in the Watergate building.

One of the items taken away for DNA testing is a dress stained with dried semen. This information was confined to Internet sites until the weekend, but is now being discussed on every national television news programme.

Hillary Clinton has taken over the management of her beleaguered husband's defence, and it is clear she and her husband do not intend to go without a vicious fight.

James Carville, a veteran of the 1992 election campaign, went on television yesterday, accusing Mr Starr of conducting a "scuzzy, sleazy" investigation, and adding: "There's going to be a war. The friends of the President are disgusted by these kinds of attacks. We are going to fight and we are going to fight hard."

Mrs Clinton has hired two "bare-knuckle political infighters" – Mickey Kantor, a former Commerce Secretary, and Harold Ickes, an adviser and important fundraiser in the 1996 campaign – to bolster the White House team.

27 January 1998
I didn't have sex with that woman
With Hillary at his side, Clinton denies affair
with young aide and telling her to lie
By Hugo Gurdon in Washington

President Clinton defied the advice of nervous lawyers by going on television yesterday to deny angrily that he had ever had an affair with the 24-year-old former staff member Monica Lewinsky. With his wife, Hillary, at his side, the President declared: "I want to say one thing to the American people. I did not have sexual relations with that woman." He also denied that he had asked her to lie.

Just a day before tonight's State of the Union Address, which threatens to be completely overshadowed by the crisis engulfing him, Mr Clinton shook his finger at reporters, narrowed his eyes for emphasis, and repeated earlier denials.

He said: "I want you to listen to me. I'm going to say this again; I did not have sexual relations with that woman, Miss Lewinsky."

He added: "I never told anybody to lie, not a single time. These allegations are false and I need to go back to work for the American people."

Mr Clinton had seemed punch-drunk and indecisive since the scandal erupted last week, but his performance yesterday was much more determined and forceful than anything he has so far managed.

He was clearly tired, but knew that his appearance in the White House's Roosevelt Room could be his last chance to salvage his crippled presidency.

The First Lady, Hillary Clinton, was also clearly aware that the stakes were high and her assured performance drew gasps of admiration from a few of the assembled press.

The couple were speaking at the launch of a new $1bn (£620m) child care programme and Mrs Clinton, impeccably dressed in a yellow suit and pearls, even managed a joke.

Looking toward the back of the room where the press pack waited to pounce, she said: "I'm pleased to see so many people in attendance who care about child care."

Mr Clinton's legal advisers have warned him to avoid questions or elaborate statements, fearing it could incriminate him and help Kenneth Starr, the independent counsel investigating several of his alleged abuses of power.

However, political aides told him he desperately needed a convincing performance to stop his public and political support disappearing.

But his brief, businesslike appearance failed to calm the storm.

His spokesman, Mike McCurry, was besieged at his afternoon press conference by reporters who felt that Mr Clinton's statement posed more questions than it answered.

The President himself had stalked out of the Roosevelt Room as soon as he finished his statement, leaving shouted questions hanging in the air.

Mr McCurry said the President would answer when appropriate the constantly reiterated questions: what, if not sexual, were his relations with Miss Lewinsky? Why, if their relationship was simply that of a powerful employer and a lowly staff member, did he give her several presents, including a dress and a book of poetry, some of it erotic? Why was Mr Clinton taking so long to come out with a full account unless he was hiding the truth?

The President's statement yesterday continued a fight-back begun at the weekend when even his former adherents began to fear that he could be forced out of office within days.

His chief lawyer, Robert Bennett, launched another attack yesterday in Little Rock, Arkansas, attempting to rob Mr Starr of a torrent of new evidence emerging from the Paula Jones sexual harassment case against Mr Clinton.

Mr Bennett asked the Little Rock court to bring forward the date of the trial, currently scheduled for May, arguing that it was hanging over the President, distracting him from his duty to run the country.

If Mr Bennett succeeds it would curtail the evidence-gathering period, prevent more women from emerging to tell their tales and staunch the supply of damning details being gathered by Mr Starr's prosecution staff. The volume of evidence against Mr Clinton is so great that Mrs Jones wants the trial delayed so that her lawyers can collect more and sift through it.

Miss Lewinsky, whose tape-recorded admission of an alleged year-long affair with Mr Clinton sparked the uproar last Wednesday, finally left her mother's flat in the Watergate building yesterday to consult her lawyers.

Her attorney, William Ginsburg, is reported to have secured a promise of at least partial immunity from prosecution for his client. Mr Starr is delaying granting her total immunity until he knows exactly what she is prepared to disclose about Mr Clinton.

On the tapes, Miss Lewinsky suggests that Mr Clinton and his friend Vernon Jordan, a Washington lawyer, put pressure on her to lie and conceal their affair when questioned by lawyers acting for Mrs Jones.

28 January 1998
Hillary hits at "firestorm of lies" by Right
'We know everything about each other ...
and we understand and accept and love each other'
By Hugh Davies and Hugo Gurdon in Washington

Hillary Clinton declared war yesterday, appearing on television to brand the scandal engulfing her husband as a Right-wing conspiracy to destroy the presidency.

Signalling clearly that she was taking charge of what will be a bitter and protracted fight, the First Lady denounced the President's "malicious and evil-minded" enemies.

Chief target of her anger was Kenneth Starr, the independent counsel investigating her husband's alleged abuses of power.

Attempting to build on the finger-jabbing denial which the President made on Monday, Mrs Clinton said false accusations that he had had a sexual affair then incited others to lie about it were a vicious attempt by Right-wingers to oust her husband and "undo the results of two elections".

She said that she and her husband were victims of a "vigorous feeding frenzy" by the media and spoke of "a firestorm" of lies.

Appearing on NBC's Today programme, she said: "I'm not only here because I love and believe my husband. I'm also here because I love and believe in my country."

Monica Lewinsky, a 24-year-old former White House staff member has been caught in tape-recorded conversations claiming to have had a long affair with Mr Clinton, and accusing him and his friend, Vernon Jordan, of putting pressure on her to conceal it under oath.

Mrs Clinton's pugnacious performance on breakfast television was set up after the

President's public credibility began collapsing over the weekend, prompting speculation that he could resign within days.

There was also fear that the scandal would overshadow the State of the Union
Address he was due to deliver to Congress early today.

The First Lady accused Mr Starr of "looking for four years at every telephone
call we've made, every cheque we have written, scratching for dirt, intimidating
witnesses, and doing everything possible to try to make some accusation against my
husband".

Fighting the independent counsel head on may be the only tactic left to the
White House, but it is dangerous. Mr Starr appears to have a mass of evidence and
Miss Lewinsky is close to agreeing to give sworn evidence against the President.

Mr Starr sought to deflate accusations of political bias by postponing Miss
Lewinsky's and Mr Jordan's testimony to a federal Grand Jury, which had been
scheduled for yesterday. But he went ahead with the Grand Jury hearing of Betty
Currie, Mr Clinton's personal secretary, reported to have been the person who let
Miss Lewinsky into the White House late at night.

Miss Lewinsky's lawyer, William Ginsburg, has outlined the evidence his client
is willing to give in exchange for immunity from prosecution. It is said to include an
admission that she had an affair with Mr Clinton, and that she lied about it under
oath when forced to testify in the Paula Jones harassment case against the President.

It is not thought to include firm evidence that the President or Mr Jordan put
pressure on her to lie.

Mrs Clinton's defence of her husband came six years after she appeared with him
on television to sink the claims of Gennifer Flowers, who said she had had a 12-year
affair with Mr Clinton. Her intervention then saved his bid for the presidency in 1992.

Yesterday, her interviewer reminded Mrs Clinton that her husband had at that
time admitted causing pain and wondered if he might make a similar admission.

"No, absolutely not," Mrs Clinton shot back, "and he shouldn't. We've been married for 22 years and I learned a long time ago that the only people who count in any
marriage are the two that are in it.

"We know everything there is to know about each other – and we understand and
accept and love each other."

Mrs Clinton's version of events was that she was awakened in bed by her husband
last Wednesday. He said: "You're not going to believe this, but . . . " It came as "a big
surprise" to both of them.

She refused to say what her husband had told her about Miss Lewinsky. "We've
talked at great length and I think as this matter unfolds, the entire country will have
more information," she said.

Last night Mr Starr hit back at Mrs Clinton's claims of a Right-wing conspiracy.
He issued a statement saying: "That is nonsense. Our current investigation began
when we received credible evidence of serious crimes."

He added: "We are working to complete the inquiry as quickly and thoroughly as
possible."

18 August 1998
Clinton's TV confession to America
3am news: President says "I misled people,
including my wife. I regret that"
By Hugh Davies in Washington

In a desperate gamble to survive in office, President Clinton made a dramatic six-minute confession in a television broadcast from the White House last night, admitting to a "relationship" with Monica Lewinsky, 25, "that was not appropriate". He said: "In fact it was wrong. It constituted a critical lapse in judgment, and a personal failure on my part for which I am solely responsible."

He looked strained, and had bags under his eyes. He said he had answered questions in an earlier grand jury session about "my private life, questions that no American citizen would ever want to answer".

But he had to take responsibility for his actions, "both public and private".

He claimed that his answers under oath in January during the taking of a legal deposition in the Paula Jones sexual harassment lawsuit were "legally accurate". However, he "did not volunteer" information about Miss Lewinsky when asked.

"But I told the grand jury today, and I say to you now, that at no time did I ask anyone to lie, to hide or destroy evidence or take any other unlawful action."

He admitted to giving "a false impression" by lying to Americans about the affair. He admitted that he had betrayed "even my wife". He said: "I deeply regret that."

He said he wanted to protect himself from the "embarrassment" of his conduct. He wanted to protect his family. "Now this matter is between me, the two people I love most, my wife and our daughter, and our God. I must put it right.

"I am prepared to do whatever it takes to do so. Nothing is more important to me personally. But it is private. I intend to reclaim my family life for my family. It's nobody's business but ours."

Polls show that Americans had been expecting an abject apology and full explanation of what happened with the White House trainee. However, he launched a surprising attack on the independent counsel Kenneth Starr for "prying into private lives". He spoke of "the pursuit of personal destruction". He said it was "time to move on". He said: "Our country has been distracted by this matter for too long. I take my responsibility for my part in all this . . . We have important work to do . . . real security matters to face.

"And so tonight I ask you to turn away from the spectacle of the past seven months, to repair the fabric of our national discourse, and to return our attention to all the challenges and all the promise of the next American century."

His day of shame created a drama not seen in Washington since Richard Nixon's Watergate crisis. The confession came in four hours and 26 minutes of humiliating cross-examination by prosecutors at the White House that was fed by cable below the streets of Washington to two television screens watched by 23 grand jurors at a federal courthouse.

Early details became known through leaks in Washington, although exactly what he said about the sexual aspects was not immediately known.

It appeared that Mr Clinton, faced with the certainty of impeachment if he were found to be lying to a jury, chose to tell the truth seven months after he wagged his finger at television cameras and said: "I did not have sexual relations with that woman, Miss Lewinsky."

It was difficult to predict how Americans would react to his version of what 25-year-old Miss Lewinsky called his "fondling" of her while they had oral sex a dozen or more times in a study next to the Oval Office. Much hinged on his broadcast.

There was expected to be a dramatic shift against him in the opinion polls, which so far have shown wide support.

Shortly before Mr Clinton gave his testimony, he knelt in prayer at the White House with the Rev Jesse Jackson.

The scene was an eerie reminder of Nixon's darkest night during Watergate when he urged Henry Kissinger to pray with him.

Mr Jackson offered counsel, despite his own reputation for covering up marital infidelity with the singers Nancy Wilson and Roberta Flack.

The drama of the first president to testify before a criminal grand jury investigating his actions began at 12.59pm Washington time in the Map Room of the White House after two and half hours of legal "prepping".

Mr Clinton had a 30-minute meeting with his national security advisers over the arrest of a key suspect in the African bombings. Then he faced Kenneth Starr and his team of prosecutors.

The trappings of the Chippendale-style Map Room, including the map Franklin D Roosevelt used to follow the course of the Second World War, were hidden from the jury's view. Mr Clinton sat in a high-backed chair against a black backdrop.

It was not known who was operating the camera facing the President – probably a Pentagon technician or a secret service agent.

Miss Lewinsky has said that she and the President made a verbal agreement to keep quiet, but has refused to say whether any of Mr Clinton's friends were used in a "cover-up".

Mr Starr, armed with evidence from 80 witnesses, was looking for much more than an admission of extra-marital sex. Lawyers said he was homing in on a pattern of denial and obstruction that fitted Mr Clinton's history in the Whitewater affair.

Critical to Mr Starr's approach was how he planned to handle his inside knowledge of FBI tests on a dress that Miss Lewinsky says was soiled by the President during one encounter.

A large stain was found on the dress and it is thought that federal forensic experts have supplied Mr Starr with their complete findings.

22 August 1998
Clinton was a "diligent lover" in the Oval Office,
grand jury told
"The adulterer"
By Hugh Davies in Washington

President Clinton is lying if he still maintains that their trysts in the Oval Office were not "sexual relations" in the strict legal sense, Monica Lewinsky has told a grand jury.

Leaks yesterday from five extra hours of her testimony on Thursday indicated that she offered graphic details of the oral sex that they performed, saying that the President was diligent in trying to arouse her. He caressed her breasts and touched her genitals during several prolonged encounters.

Mr Clinton, seeking to avoid a perjury charge for his sworn denial of such activity, confessed to Americans on Monday that he had had an inappropriate physical relationship. However, he insisted that his version of what happened was "legally accurate". Sources familiar with his secret testimony to prosecutors say that, one by one, Mr Clinton was asked if he believed certain sex acts were covered by the definition of sexual relations given during the Paula Jones lawsuit. He replied that intercourse was, but oral sex was excluded.

A friend of Miss Lewinsky said she was so incensed at what appeared to be his determined effort to disparage her and wriggle out of responsibility that she gave the jury every detail she could remember of his actions.

Previously, she had been circumspect about telling too much as she still imagined he cared for her.

So far, Mr Clinton has angrily refused to elaborate on what happened, beyond saying that he recalled about half a dozen encounters with her in the Oval Office. He contended that prosecutors had no right to pry into such private acts. His obvious fear is that if Americans became aware of what exactly he was up to in so revered a room, there would be immense shock.

Those who have heard tapes of Miss Lewinsky's account to her friend Linda Tripp say that, according to her, a certain amount of "depravity" was involved.

When Miss Lewinsky's "woman scorned" evidence comes to light in the report to Congress of Kenneth Starr, the independent counsel, White House spin doctors will probably have to go on a full "damage control" alert.

As worrying for Mr Clinton is the determined effort by Mr Starr to unearth the truth about whether, in a panic, Mr Clinton tried to cover up gifts he had given to Miss Lewinsky by getting Betty Currie, his secretary, to retrieve them from her. Miss Lewinsky said that the President told her that if the gifts were not in her possession, she could not hand them over if asked.

The next day, Mrs Currie phoned her, saying: "I hear you have something for me." She assumed that she meant the gifts, which included a dress and a hatpin, and handed them to her when she arrived unannounced at her flat. Asked about his role, Mr Clinton was vague before the jury. The President said he could not recall telling his secretary to call Miss Lewinsky.

Miss Currie has reportedly testified that Mr Clinton asked her questions about his dealings with Miss Mr Lewinsky. One query was: "We were never alone, right?"

The President was also said to have told Miss Currie that he resisted Miss Lewinsky's sexual advances.

25 August 1998
Has the cookie crumbled for Bill Clinton?
Shift in the political landscape after President's admission
that he toyed with the American people
By Ambrose Evans-Pritchard in Washington

If in doubt, it is always wisest to assume that Bill Clinton will confound his enemies. But this time there is very little doubt. The whole of political Washington now knows that the game is almost up.

The public at large – plump, prosperous, disengaged and slow to anger – is a long way behind the curve. President Clinton's job approval ratings are still holding above 65 per cent, kept aloft by the Dow Jones Index and the asset bubble of the Roaring Nineties.

But this is an anomaly that cannot persist for long. On trust and honesty his ratings have already fallen through the floor. A *Washington Post*–ABC News poll had him down to the Nixonian level of 19 per cent on "character".

There has been a tectonic change in the political landscape after his admission that he toyed with the American people for seven months, stonewalling with implausible claims of executive and attorney-client privilege.

Returning after a year in Britain, I am dumbfounded by the insurgent mood of the Washington media. Indeed, it is downright putschist.

Former cheerleaders for the Clinton White House are on the television every night fulminating against the President, cursing him with the fury of the betrayed.

The bureau chiefs for the great metropolitan newspapers and political weeklies shake their heads wearily at suggestions that Mr Clinton can somehow mount a defence against perjury by quibbling over the nature of sex acts, whether performed with or without cigars.

As for the idea of a fresh Oval Office address to the nation, a new improved apology to show that he is genuinely sorry this time, they smile knowingly at the naivety of such an absurd gambit. Mr Clinton's problems have moved beyond public relations.

US News & World Report, which slept through the first five and half years of the Clinton presidency, is reporting this week that Congress will soon receive a bombshell from the independent counsel, Kenneth Starr. The Starr report will conclude that the President "suborned perjury and obstructed justice". It will "echo the language of the Watergate era – abuse of power and lack of fitness for office".

Newsweek, owned by the Queen Bee of the Beltway Democratic establishment, the *Washington Post* proprietor Katharine Graham, says much the same.

It reports that Mr Clinton's testimony before the grand jury last week "further entangled him in a web of lies".

The magazine implies that the President's secretary, Betty Currie, has exposed him to likely impeachment proceedings by revealing a conspiracy to cover up the affair with Monica Lewinsky.

For good measure, it adds that the descriptions of Mr Clinton's sexual proclivities in the Starr report will make people "want to throw up".

This looks like the end of the road. Reporters for the elite media are being taken aside by those in the know – the FBI, the Starr investigation, the arbiters of power at the Metropolitan Club – and warned that President Clinton could be facing 10, 12 or more counts of criminal conduct, and that is on the Lewinsky matter alone.

The few Democrats who dare to appear on television to defend the White House are already hedging their bets. If the reports are true, they admit, the President will almost certainly have to think of alternative employment.

Their words maintain that there is still doubt about the facts, but their body language says otherwise.

Loyalty is weak. The Clinton administration, after all, once played a cynical game of "triangulation" to distance itself from the Democrats' Leftish rump in Congress.

The Democratic leadership in the House, in turn, regards him as an opportunist, a man without ideology who sold out to the corporate lobbies and adopted the balanced-budget agenda of the bond markets.

Increasingly it is a question of political survival for Democrats facing close races in the mid-term elections this November. The party has already lost both the House and the Senate under this president.

There is now a fear of a wipeout on the scale of the post-Watergate rout of 1974, when Republicans on Capitol Hill paid the price for Nixon's protracted disgrace.

In private the whispers are getting louder every day. If it were done, they plot and scheme, if the knife were to be plunged before Bill Clinton can do any more damage to the party, 'twere well it were done quickly.

Mr Clinton surely knows he can expect little mercy.

Sam Nunn, the former chairman of the Senate Foreign Relations Committee, has already delivered the first blow to the head. In an essay in the *Washington Post* he called on Mr Clinton to remember his duty to the American people.

"This will require personal sacrifice and may even require his resignation, but would fulfil the President's most important oath, to preserve and protect our nation," he wrote.

In other words: be gone from here, you cad, before we have you tarred and feathered and ridden out of town on a rail.

But has Mr Clinton got the message?

Dr Crippen

"He was as docile as a kitten, his habits were excellent,
and I never knew a more honourable man."

Mysterious murder in Camden Town

Last night a terrible discovery was made at a house in Hilldrop-crescent, Camden Town, the body of a woman being found buried in a coal-cellar. All the circumstances point to one of the most atrocious crimes known in the long record of the metropolis having been committed there.

Hilldrop-crescent is a secluded part, lying off the busy thoroughfare of

Camden-road. The house in question is No. 39, a well-proportioned, semi-detached villa, on the west side, containing twelve rooms and a basement, the front portion of which forms a coal-cellar. The residence is heavily bowered with trees and evergreens, now thick with summer leaves.

There for some time past have lived Mr and Mrs Hawley Crippen. Of late there have been very few signs of life at the house, but this has not occasioned much comment among the neighbours, who, with the indifference characteristic of a great city, have had no knowledge of the people residing next door beyond, perhaps, a facial recognition.

Nothing has been seen of Mrs Crippen for some months, certainly not since February. She had many friends. In fact, as one who has taken a chief part in the discovery of a body believed to be hers stated last night, "She had so many friends that her disappearance could not go on for long unnoticed. It is surprising that the inquiries were not set on foot much earlier."

The apparent desertion of the house, the vague replies to inquiries, determined that a keen search should be made for the lady. Mr Hawley Crippen is stated to be an American doctor, and Mrs Crippen an artist of some solid reputation.

For the past few days police officers have been engaged in examining parts of the house, and carrying out excavations. Stray passers-by about eleven o'clock last night witnessed a series of flashlights, followed by minor explosions. The spot whence these emanated was the coal-cellar by the side of the garden path. Every effort was being made to conceal this gruesome part of the work. Canvas had been stretched across, which became displaced by the explosion of the illuminant necessary for the taking of flashlight photographs; whilst the silent workers were compelled to seek relief, however, temporary, from their painful task.

Some little time before, at a depth not stated, a body had been discovered, but those in charge of the operations were unable to say definitely whether it was that of Mrs Crippen, and a little time will elapse before a definite conclusion can be come to.

Mrs Crippen was thought by neighbours to be between 30 and 40 years of age. The house is nicely furnished, and to all appearances there has been nothing to excite the suspicion of the next-door residents, who were wondering what had occasioned the necessity for digging at night time.

The police decline to give any information, but the house is at present in their charge.

The affair became a subject for inquiry by the Criminal Investigation Department, and Chief Inspector Dew was at once put in charge of the operations. The excavations have been carried out by a number of constables, and during the night there were relays going backwards and forwards to the house. Two constables patrolled the crescent.

A neighbour questioned last night, stated that Mrs Crippen had lived there over two years. Her attention had never been particularly attracted to the house. She had often seen the Crippens going in and out, and had noticed them as a fairly young and particularly well-dressed couple. Nothing had ever happened to give her the impression that they were on anything but happy terms. She now remembered that she had not seen them for some little time, but she had taken very little notice of this until a number of strange men came to the house and commenced operations in the cellar.

When asked if she had ever had any conversation with the occupants of the next house, their neighbour replied, "Do we in London ever make it a point be friendly with our neighbours?"

Mr Crippen has not been seen for some time, and the police are making inquiries as to his whereabouts.

15 July 1910
Mystery of the "boy"

Miss Ethel Clara Le Neve, who has disappeared with Crippen, was his typist for many years. Although she has a French name, it is said that she was born in England, and speaks English as a native. A milkman, on the other hand, says that the woman who had latterly been passing as "Mrs Crippen" could speak but very little English, and was of foreign appearance. She and Mr Crippen were in the habit of leaving the house early in the morning and returning late in the evening. The suggestion advanced by Scotland Yard that this woman who latterly lived with Mr Crippen "may be dressed as a boy" is founded upon the fact that the man had been seen for some time accompanied by a "youth" of foreign appearance, whose masculinity was not convincing to people.

The strange fact is vouched for by Miss May, secretary to the Music Hall Artists' Guild, that at the annual dinner of the Music Hall Railway Associations, held on 28 February, Mr Crippen appeared with his typist, and that she was wearing a handsome sealskin coat similar to the one which had been worn by the deceased woman, and also a beautiful brooch which was very like one Mrs Crippen used to wear. The police have in their possession a statement made by Miss Le Neve at the time that Mr Crippen was interviewed by them. Both statements were then regarded as satisfactory.

Shortly after midday yesterday, Professor Topper and Chief Detective-Inspector Dew visited 39, Hilldrop-crescent, and half an hour later a van drew up containing two coffins, which were admitted to the house. This gave rise to the rumour that more than one body had been found. The report was authoritatively denied, and it was explained that the two shells were required because of the shockingly mutilated and decomposed state of the discovered remains. The body had been literally dismembered, placed three feet deep in the earth, and covered with lime. Official photographs of the scene were taken by flashlight, and the remains were then removed for medical examination by Professor Pepper.

Although the cause of death will not be made known until the inquest, it was reported last evening that traces of poison had been found. Up to a late hour the police were still dismantling the interior of 39, Hilldrop-crescent, and digging in the grounds for any further evidence which might be brought to light. They were also making diligent inquiries of all chemists and lime merchants in a wide circuit to assist the elucidation of the mystery. Any local tradespeople having definite information concerning purchases of poison or lime in the beginning of February are asked to communicate with Scotland Yard.

The inquest will probably be opened to-morrow.

On inquiry at a late hour last night at Scotland Yard, it was elicited that no arrest had been made in connection with the crime.

Crippens' antecedents
By our own correspondent in New York

The American police have an excellent description of Hawley Harvey Crippen, and if he lands here he will be arrested just as surely as was Porter Charlton. The newspapers devote great space to the murder of Mrs Crippen because she was a Brooklyn girl, and well known to New Yorkers as Belle Elmore, a vaudeville actress and treasurer of the Music Hall Artists' Guild. Her friends describe her as very good-looking, a fine figure, popular, and clever. She was of Polish descent, and told her friends that her father was a nobleman, who had been driven from his country. He is believed, however, to have run a grocer's shop at Brooklyn. After his death his daughter discovered papers which led her to believe that she was heir to the estates and the title of Baroness Makomaski of Poland. She employed counsel at one time to prove her claim.

Crippen, when he married the woman, was in the service of the Munyon Remedy Company. He employed his wife as his assistant and cashier. They were in the Philadelphia office for a time. In 1898 Crippen was put in charge of the offices of the Munyon Remedy Company in New York, and his wife was cashier here. They made a success of the place, and in 1900 Munyon sent them to London to take charge of his branch office there. They were accompanied by Colonel McIntosh, a veteran proprietary medicine man, who was going abroad to open a branch of the Universal Remedy Company.

Dr. Munyon, of Philadelphia, who was interviewed to-day, said that Crippen had been in his employ for about thirteen years. He described Crippen as a clever medical man of very gentle and kind disposition, and quite incapable of killing his wife. "Mrs Crippen," he said, "was a beautiful woman, just a trifle taller than her husband. She was a giddy woman, who worried her husband a great deal. Crippen told me that his wife had been on the stage in London. Some years after he started with me I saw he was distressed. I attributed it to the annoyance of his wife. Crippen went to New York. He corresponded with me for a long time, and then went to London to practise medicine, and became my correspondent there. I heard from him a number of times, but he never wrote me anything about his domestic affairs. I found it necessary to make a change in London, and another man was selected to fill Crippen's position. I heard from Crippen last six months ago, then I lost track of his whereabouts in London."

Asked if it was true, as rumoured, that Crippen was jealous of his wife, Dr. Munyon replied, "Not that I know of. He had reason to be jealous of her, but Crippen was not the kind of man to let jealousy master him."

Dr. Munyon said that Crippen was about 56 years old and his wife twenty years younger. "I knew Crippen well enough to understand his disposition," said Dr. Munyon. "He was as docile as a kitten, his habits were excellent, and I never knew a more honourable man."

16 July 1910
North London crime
World-wide search for Crippen.

The most systematic and comprehensive search that has marked any police investigation of recent years was yesterday in full operation to discover the murderer of
Mrs Cora Crippen otherwise Belle Elmore, whose supposed remains were found in
the cellar of 39, Hilldrop-crescent, on Wednesday night. Not only are the full forces
of Scotland Yard working at high pressure in the elucidation of the mystery, but the
police throughout the entire country, together with detectives on the Continent and
in America, are now associated to that end. In the circumstances, it is confidently
thought that it can only be a matter of a few days, if, indeed, not more than a few
more hours, before some important development takes place.

Being conversant with the French tongue, Dr. Crippen might readily have thought
of going to France, and thence to America. Both English, French, and German
shipping companies have accordingly been asked to use the closest scrutiny of passengers who may have booked, or who may yet book, for the States from Cherbourg,
Southampton, Liverpool, Dover, or Plymouth. The police still think that Miss Le
Neve may be travelling with the "doctor" dressed as a boy. They can find no other
explanation of the fact, which has been corroborated, that "Dr." Crippen purchased a
boy's suit of clothes and a pair of No. 5 boy's boots from an outfitter's in High Holborn.

Meanwhile the most diligent inquiries were throughout yesterday being prosecuted in London for a due to the missing pair's present whereabouts. In response
to the wide publicity given to their descriptions, hundreds of communications have
poured into Scotland Yard. Hence the many rumours that the "wanted" man and
woman had been seen in at least a dozen different places at the same time. It is
unnecessary to catalogue these reports, seeing that none of them were, up to a late
hour, verified. Many of them were obviously misleading, but some few were followed up by the police. The report, for instance, that Crippen and Le Neve had
been seen at a seaside resort was probably suggested by the fact that the young woman's parents formerly lived at Hove, near Brighton, where they are well respected.
They informed the police yesterday that they had no knowledge of their daughter's
present whereabouts.

Mrs Le Neve, whose present residence is in North London, has explained that her
daughter, Ethel Clare, informed her, a week or two before Easter, that she had been
married to "Dr." Crippen. The marriage was a great surprise, and a matter of considerable suspicion, to the mother. No notification of it is to be found at Somerset
House. The value of Mrs Le Neve's information lies in the fact that when she last
saw her daughter, on Thursday last, Miss Le Neve said that she and Crippen were
"going back to France again soon", and discussed what arrangements could be made
for boarding the French maid at Hilldrop-crescent in their absence. On that occasion she invited her brother Sidney to visit her at Hilldrop-crescent on Saturday. Her
brother went there about 10.45 a.m., when the French maid handed him a note in
his sister's handwriting to the effect that she had been called away.

It is significant that it was on Saturday that Crippen first knew, beyond all
shadow of doubt, that the police had come to the conclusion that his wife had been

murdered by someone. Despite the rumours to the contrary, there is no ground for belief that he has been in London since then. Certainly he has not been to his house in Hilldrop-crescent. Wherever he may be at the present moment, he cannot for long escape the vigilance of the search. All hotel, lodging, and apartment keepers are, therefore, again asked, on behalf of the police, to re-read the descriptions of the missing pair, and, after making allowances for possible disguises, to communicate in the event of their entertaining suspicion of identity, but only where they have confidence that their surmises are correct. The following notice is also being circulated round all cab ranks and shelters:

£1 Reward.
　　If a driver of a cab has picked up any person or luggage from 39, Hilldrop-crescent, Camden-road, N., on or Feb. 1 last, he is requested to communicate at once with the police at the nearest police-station.

It may be said that the police strongly hope that Miss Le Neve will see the wisdom of assisting, rather than mystifying, their investigation. There is no charge against her, and it is recognised that she may have had no knowledge of the crime. It would, therefore, be greatly to her advantage if she came forward, if only to clear herself of the possibility of being "an accessory after the fact".

Further information was obtained yesterday regarding the steps which were taken by Mrs Crippen's friends in London to discover her whereabouts after the receipt of the letter announcing her departure for America, which has since been found to be a forgery. The statement was made yesterday that "Dr." Crippen's son wrote from America to the Music Hall Ladies' Guild, saying that he had no knowledge of his step-mother's death. Below is a copy of the letter:

Los Angeles, Cal, 9 May 1910.
　　Music-Hall Ladies' Guild. – Miss Melinda May.
　　Dear Madam – Received your letter forwarded to me from the county clerk, 23 April 1910, but owing to many misfortunes, sickness, and death of our son, I overlooked your letter until this date.
　　The death of my stepmother was as great a surprise to me as to anyone. She died in San Francisco, and the first I heard of it was through my father, who wrote to me immediately afterwards. He asked me to forward all letters to him, and he would make necessary explanations.
　　He said he had, through a mistake, given out my name and address as my step-mother's death-place.
　　I would be glad if you find out any particulars of her death if you would let me know of them, as all I know is the fact that she died in San Francisco. – Yours very sincerely,
H. OTTO CRIPPEN
1,612, Holmby-avenue, Los Angeles

Inquiries show that Mrs Crippen had two private banking accounts, one of which was with the Birkbeck Bank. This leads the friends of the murdered woman to associate money with the motive of the crime, and one of them went so far as to say that developments will show how someone other than the deceased woman endeavoured to withdraw the money from one account.

That Mrs Crippen was apparently well-to-do was confirmed yesterday to a representative of the *Daily Telegraph* by a young lady, a member of the music-hall profession, who said that she first met Miss "Belle Elmore" about two years ago in a West of England town. Although she was then only doing what is professionally known as a "first turn", so that she could not, therefore, have been in receipt of a large salary, she stayed at the best hotels and spent money freely. Our informant added that she again met Miss Elmore about five or six months ago in Oxford-street. Mrs Crippen was accompanied by the "Doctor", who "looked such a meek and mild little man that he seemed incapable of injuring a fly". This meeting must have taken place but very shortly before Mrs Crippen so suddenly disappeared.

The exact date of Mrs Crippen's murder can only be conjectured. Information of a sensational nature which may have some bearing on the actual committal of the crime is supplied by Mrs Clackner, who occupies an oil shop in Brecknock-road, which lies at the back of Hilldrop-crescent. Mrs Clackner declares that she has more than once heard revolver shots coming from the direction of Crippen's house. Crippen, it should be added, was known to carry firearms.

"Some months ago," said Mrs Clackner, "I was settling myself down in bed to go to sleep about midnight, when I suddenly heard some screams coming from the back of the premises. Everything round about was quiet, and it seemed to me that the screams came from a woman. I jumped out of bed and pulled up the window, and then I heard another scream, which sounded worse than the first, and I also heard a cry, such as 'Oh, don't! Oh, don't!' coming from No. 39."

On the other hand, the immediate neighbours of Mr Crippen are unable to say that they heard any screams at night about the time suggested, and the police are not disposed to attach much importance to the incident.

From inquiries among Mrs Crippen's friends, it appears that the dead woman often complained that the house in Hilldrop-crescent was dull, and that her life there was very lonely.

26 July 1910
Crippen's flight
Hot Atlantic chase

Communication by wireless telegraphy will, it is expected, again be established this evening – probably before nine o'clock – with the Canadian Pacific steamship *Montrose*, upon which "Doctor" Crippen and Miss Le Neve, who are wanted in connection with the Holloway murder, are fleeing to Canada, Inspector Dew, of Scotland Yard, being in pursuit on board the White Star liner *Laurentic*. It is hoped to convey a further message to Captain Kendall, commanding the *Montrose*, either by means of the *Laurentic* or by a passing liner, and possibly via Newfoundland.

Until this evening's wireless report has been received – and pending its publication by Scotland Yard – it is, therefore, impossible to say what has happened on board the *Montrose* since she was last in touch with land. The dramatic possibilities of the situation will be obvious. It needs only to be said that the greatest anxiety prevails in official quarters, not as to the identification of the fugitive couple, but concerning the events which may have followed the disclosure of identification.

In the circumstances, not only Scotland Yard, but the public generally, will await with intense interest the further news which Captain Kendall must now be ready on the first opportunity to transmit. The hope of establishing communication so early with the Canadian-bound boat depends, of course, to a very large extent on the weather and the progress which the vessel and other ships have made. It is possible that nothing will be heard of the *Montrose* until Wednesday.

There is full confirmation of the detailed statement which appeared in these pages yesterday. According to the latest information which has been received, the identification of the two passengers who booked passages under the names of "Mr Robinson and son" has been established beyond any reasonable doubt. In the first place, Captain Kendall was able to establish the fact to his own satisfaction that the "son" of "Mr Robinson" was a woman. Deliberate but unobtrusive scrutiny subsequently assured him that, allowing for the clever but ineffectual disguises, "Mr Robinson and son" answered in every particular the official descriptions published of the missing "Doctor" Crippen and his typist. The confidential communications which followed between the astute Captain and Scotland Yard dissolved any shadow of doubt that remained – at least so far as the London Criminal Investigation Department was concerned.

Inspector Dew has practically received carte blanche instructions to act as he may think fit in the matter of arresting the fugitives, but it is understood that he will endeavour to get into communication with the *Montrose* from the *Laurentic* as the latter vessel overhauls her, with the object of further advising Captain Kendall. The chief fear that is now entertained is that, should Crippen become aware that he and Le Neve are suspected, he may attempt suicide. It is, therefore, hoped that, in the exercise of his powers as commander of his ship – which, in the eyes of the law, is a recognised bit of British "territory", conferring upon its chief navigating officer the full powers of a magistrate and police official – the representative of the Home Office and of Scotland Yard while at sea – Captain Kendall will have already decided to place the couple under close surveillance, if not actual arrest. The mere fact that Le Neve was masquerading as a boy would justify him in this course of action.

No hazardous attempt will be made by Inspector Dew to board the *Montrose* from the *Laurentic* in mid-ocean in order to effect an arrest, but as the vessel upon which he is now overhauling the fugitives is due in Canada at least twenty-four hours ahead, the course of action will be as follows: Inspector Dew will disembark by special police tug off *Rimouski*, at the mouth of the St. Laurence River. He will then await the arrival of the *Montrose*, and, in conjunction with the Canadian police, board her and apprehend the fugitives. Should this plan fail for any reason the arrest will be made off Quebec, the first port of call on the Canadian side, where all incoming passenger and emigrant ships are boarded by the Customs and quarantine officers of the Dominion. In the unlikely case of the *Laurentic* failing to arrive first the Canadian police will act upon full instructions, which have been cabled from the Home Office and from Scotland Yard.

The *Montrose*, it should be noted, left Antwerp for Quebec (2,989 miles) on

Wednesday, and steams twelve knots. The *Laurentic* left Liverpool for Quebec (2,633 miles) on Saturday, and steams eighteen knots. Barring accidents, it is clear that the new White Star liner, holding the record for the voyage to Canada, must overtake the older Canadian Pacific Company's boat, which, distinguished from several other first-class vessels belonging to the company, is chiefly a cargo-carrier.

The question of extradition from Canada offers no difficulties. Under the "Act respecting fugitive offenders in Canada from other parts of his Majesty's dominions", shortly known as the Fugitive Offenders Act, it is clearly laid down that:

A magistrate in Canada may issue a provisional warrant for the apprehension of a fugitive who is, or who is suspected of being, in, or on his way to, Canada, upon such information, and under such circumstances, as would in his opinion justify the issue of a warrant if the offence of which the fugitive is accused had been committed within his jurisdiction, and such warrant may be backed and executed accordingly.

Warrants for the arrest of Crippen and Le Neve have, it is understood, already been applied for. These will be executed in the manner already indicated, and the American "doctor" and his typist will be committed to prison pending the arrangements which will be made for bringing them back to England. Formal police-court proceedings will intervene, but it is unlikely that the full facts of the mystery of 39, Hilldrop-crescent, Holloway, will be inquired into by a Canadian Court. Only such prima facie evidence as is necessary to establish identity and the justification of arrest will be taken. There is, therefore, no reason why Inspector Dew should not have his suspects back in England by 15 August, when the inquest upon the remains discovered at Hilldrop-crescent is to be resumed.

It is recalled by a gentleman who has been associated with this case, and the fact may be here mentioned for the first time, that a sensational incident happened at 39, Hilldrop-crescent on the day that Inspector Dew and Sergeant Mitchell searched the house, not only at the invitation of Crippen, but with his assistance. Crippen, according to this informant, accompanied the police officers to the staircase leading to the cellar where, several days later, the human remains were unearthed, but as they were about to descend the "doctor" made an excuse for allowing the policemen to go first. He himself remained behind at the top of the stairs, and after some moments of awkward search in the semi-darkness he called out with a sinister laugh, "You will never find anything there!" and then, "It's not a nice place to stay in!" At the same time one of the officers noticed that Crippen held something in his hand, which appeared to glint and gleam.

In the light of the later knowledge obtained by the police, that Crippen always carried a loaded revolver, there can be little doubt that he meant more than he said on that ugly occasion, and that if either of the men in the coal cellar below him had delayed over long, or found at that moment the loosened bricks, which later revealed the true nature of the charnel house, they might never have left the secret tomb alive.

It is little wonder that after this incident Crippen determined on instant flight. The details of his escape have been recalled many times, but from information which reached London yesterday from many sources it is possible to fill in some of the gaps of the narrative. On the morning of their disappearance (Saturday, 9 July) Crippen and Le Neve went by an excursion to Margate. The visit is proved by the fact that (regardless of the value of such a short-sighted act as a clue to the police)

Crippen posted a money-order in payment of a bill to one of the largest stores in the West-end. The letter, written from Albion House, bore the Margate post-mark of 9 July. The following day a chair attendant at Ramsgate reported that he believed he had seen Crippen on Ramsgate sands. There can now be no doubt that he did. On the Monday two gentlemen believed that they saw the missing couple on Margate jetty. It has now been definitely ascertained that they left Margate on 11 July on the *Kingfisher* for Boulogne. From the French seaside resort, with which the "doctor" was familiar, he and Le Neve made their way to Bruges. Here it has since been reported to the Belgian police by the manageress of a large hotel that a couple of persons whom she now believes to have been Crippen and Le Neve had late dinner on the 11th, and that the man went away, leaving the girl behind. Crippen, the police believe, journeyed to Paris, and was followed there a day later by Le Neve. The pair than took train to Brussels, in the vicinity of which they spent some days, finally going on to Antwerp.

The itinerary of this remarkable tour has yet to be fully confirmed. One thing, however, is clear, that the flight to America must have been decided upon as the result of the hotness of the pursuit on the Continent. The suggestion that Crippen and Le Neve had escaped to the Continent was made in these pages, and it was generally adopted by the French and Belgian papers, several of which not only published full information, but pictures and photographs as well. Belgium was for Crippen obviously shrinking rapidly into a prison area when he decided to expedite his attempt to get to Canada or America. According to the information of our representative, he originally booked passages by a Canadian-Pacific sailing boat from Antwerp in August. In his alarm, following the hue and cry, he changed his mind and, at the last moment, transferred to the *Montrose*, where in all probability he is now under clone surveillance.

In Liverpool, states a correspondent, Captain Kendall, master of the *Montrose*, is recognised as a particularly smart officer. He has only been on the *Montrose* since April last, but previously he commanded the *Monmouth* and the *Milwaukee*, having been promoted to be captain of that craft from the chief officership of the *Empress of Ireland*. He is a man of resource, as was testified two or three years ago, when, as commander of the *Monmouth*, he picked up the disabled Admiralty vessel *Argo* and towed her successfully into Moville Harbour.

1 August 1910
Arrest of Crippen and Miss Le Neve
Capture on the *Montrose*
By our special correspondents by Cable and Wireless

"Dr." Crippen and Miss Le Neve were arrested on board the Canadian Pacific Company's liner *Montrose* at nine o'clock (Canadian time) yesterday morning. Our Special Correspondents supply the following details of one of most dramatic arrests that have ever been effected.

Wearing the uniform of a pilot, Inspector Dew, accompanied by four officers of the Canadian police, boarded the liner about two miles from Fathor Point.

Crippen was walking on deck. The inspector approached him from behind, and touched him on the shoulder.

Crippen turned round sharply, and there was a mutual recognition between him and the inspector.

"There's your man!" said Inspector Dew to one of the Canadian officers, and Crippen accompanied his captors to a cabin, where he was formally arrested.

"I am rather glad the anxiety is over," appears to have been the only remark he made.

The inspector then went to Miss Le Neve's cabin. She was reading a book, and on looking up at her visitors immediately guessed what their purpose was.

She is said to have uttered a piercing scream, then grew suddenly calm, and submitted to arrest. Subsequently she collapsed completely.

It is stated that the prisoners will return to England by the *Royal George* on August 4.

John Darwin

"When he was younger he used to think that he was God's gift and cleverer than everyone else, and I knew he would never change."

3 December 2007

Missing man resurfaces after five years

By Gary Cleland

A father of two who disappeared while canoeing five years ago and was presumed drowned has walked into a police station more than 250 miles away.

John Darwin's red canoe was found washed up on a beach at Seaton Carew, near Hartlepool, in March 2002. Police and coastguards scoured the coastline looking for him, but no trace of the prison officer, then aged 51, was found.

However, Cleveland Police said that Mr Darwin walked into West End Central Police Station in London at 5.30 p.m. on Saturday.

A spokesman said: "Mr Darwin is fit and well and relatives have been informed of his whereabouts."

The police did not know where he had been since his disappearance.

Mr Darwin, who worked at Holme House prison in Stockton, was last seen near rocks at Seaton Carew on 21 March 2002.

Witnesses reported him entering the sea with his canoe at around 8 a.m., but no alarm was raised until 9.30 that night when he failed to arrive for a night shift.

His wife Anne, a doctor's receptionist, said six months after he vanished: "People die, have a funeral, they have a headstone, there is something to mark the fact that they existed on this planet.

"But without a body, I don't know how we can mark John's life. It's difficult to grieve without bringing things to a close."

7 December 2007

A cold betrayal and a loving family torn apart

Canoeist "is getting memory back"

John Darwin, the mystery canoeist, is "partially" regaining his memory but cannot explain how he came "back from the dead".

Family friends told how the 57-year-old former prison officer, who resurfaced this week after being missing for five years, now remembers being in Panama with his wife last year.

However, he insists he has no memory of the events of 2002, when he went missing, presumed dead, after a canoeing accident in the North Sea.

Family members, who police believe were unaware of any alleged fraud, were said to be "bewildered" by Mr Darwin's behaviour.

It emerged last night that he and his wife, Anne, were known in Panama under an alias of Mr and Mrs Jones.

Mrs Darwin left Panama on Wednesday night, according to the country's immigration department. It could not confirm where she had gone. Detectives were left waiting at Heathrow last night after a false tip-off that she was on a flight to Britain. They intended to arrest her on suspicion of fraud.

Police are also investigating alleged sightings that placed Mr Darwin in Britain several times in the past five years. In one sighting in 2005, a former colleague of the prison officer believed he had seen him, fleetingly, outside the family home in Seaton Carew in Hartlepool. Mrs Darwin told officers that the witness must have confused him for his cousin, who "looked just like John".

Police believe the parents have "betrayed" their whole family, including their sons Mark and Anthony. Officers believe they knew nothing about the alleged deception.

A police source said: "There is nothing to suggest that the sons or the rest of the family are anything other than the victims in this case. They are very upset and you can imagine why. They were told their father was dead and they grieved. Then he reappeared, then he was arrested and finally their mother turns up and says she knew he was alive after all and had been lying to her sons."

Detectives yesterday began questioning Mr Darwin in Cleveland after medical tests indicated he was fit to be interviewed. They will put it to him that he faked his death.

Mrs Darwin has admitted it was time to "face the music" after confessing that she knew her husband was alive and had lived with him in the Central American country, where she moved six weeks ago.

Meanwhile, the mystery of their life together in Panama continued to deepen.

Police are investigating whether Mr Darwin had spent several years there, perhaps using a false passport to travel across the world, before he was joined by his wife.

But a friend of the couple who did not wish to be named revealed that Mr Darwin had flown back to Britain after his wife had found "another man".

The friend said: "She got together with another man and John panicked because she had all the money and he was officially dead. Faced with that, he gave himself in, knowing that he would take her down with him."

Some neighbours said that they had seen Mrs Darwin with a Canadian.

A police source said: "The big question is why did John Darwin walk back into a police station on Saturday?

"One theory is that they had gone through this together but recently split up or the relationship soured. We will be investigating whether there were any other 'love interests' involved."

10 December 2007
Canoeist's wife questioned by police

Detectives were last night questioning the wife of John Darwin, the canoeist who faked his own death, after she returned to the UK having admitted that she had concocted a tangled web of lies.

Anne Darwin was seized in front of fellow passengers and arrested on suspicion of fraud moments after her flight landed at Manchester yesterday.

She was taken to Hartlepool police station for questioning, next door to the magistrates' court where her husband will appear today charged with two counts of deception.

Mrs Darwin's return came after she confessed publicly that her husband had been living secretly in a bedsit next to their home for three years after faking his own death.

Mervyn Donnelly, 64, who lived in the bedsit next door, told the *Daily Telegraph*: "I can't believe it, he was living a few feet away from me and I never suspected a thing.

"If I'd seen him in the passageway I would have thought it was a ghost because, as far as I was concerned, he was dead. If I ever heard a noise in that flat I just thought it must be another tenant."

Mr Darwin may also have had a second bolthole, the *Daily Telegraph* can reveal. Until January 2006, Mrs Darwin owned a terraced house in Easington Colliery, Co Durham, and one line of inquiry will be whether her husband spent time hiding there. The property has since been demolished.

It was also revealed that a man registered himself on the electoral roll at the bedsit under the alias John Jones in 2003, the year after Mr Darwin apparently drowned in the North Sea.

It was under that name it is alleged that he later secured a passport so he could travel abroad. He would also have needed a birth certificate to obtain the passport.

Det Sgt Iain Henderson, of Cleveland police, said he could not disclose whether the investigation would be extended to look at other members of the Darwin family, including their two sons Mark, 31, and Anthony, 29.

In a breathtaking confession at the weekend, Mrs Darwin said her sons had no idea of the plot and wept as she begged for their forgiveness.

She admitted talking about disappearing with her husband because of debts, but claimed she did not realise he would go through with a vanishing act. Mrs Darwin said that when he turned up a year later, she took him in and got "trapped" into going along with the scam to start a new life.

Mr Darwin has given a different account of events, according to a police source. He has been charged with making an untrue statement to procure a passport and obtaining a money transfer by deception in relation to a life insurance policy.

17 January 2011
Out and about at the scene of his crime: this time without a canoe
"I really miss Anne. I want to get back in the situation we were in"
By Steven Swinford

The last time he appeared out of the blue was when he walked into a police station five years after supposedly being lost at sea in a canoeing accident.

This time John Darwin was making no attempt to hide his identity – and even managed a smile – as he returned to the scene of his crime on day release less than halfway through a six-year jail sentence for fraud.

The 60-year-old former prison officer was pictured taking a stroll at Seaton Carew, near Hartlepool, close to the spot where he faked his own death.

Also pictured out and about was his estranged wife, Anne, who appeared to have undergone a makeover as she prepared for release.

Both want rebuild their lives after the crime that gave them global notoriety.

According to sources close to the couple, Darwin has written dozens of letters to his wife while in prison and is determined to win her back.

He is said to have hatched a new plan to make a fortune after his release by publishing his memoirs, called *The Canoe Man: Panama and Back*.

"I want to be able to get back into the situation we were in," he told a friend. "I really miss Anne. I love her but I'm not sure we can get back together."

Whether Mrs Darwin, 59, accepts his advances remains to be seen. She has been working at an RSPCA centre while serving her sentence at Askham open prison in York and appeared happy and healthy, having died her grey hair brown. She has reportedly taken an Open University business studies degree and wants to return to Panama, where she and her husband fled. She was understood to be furious about her husband's decision to write his memoirs.

The couple swindled £680,000 from pensions and insurance companies after Mr Darwin faked his death in the North Sea in March 2002.

He hid out in a tent before returning to the family home in Seaton Carew and living in a secret bedsit for five years.

Even the couple's sons, Anthony and Mark, were not allowed in on the secret and have refused to have anything to do with their parents since they were imprisoned.

A family friend said yesterday: "They have had no contact with them. They weren't even aware that he [John] had been out on day release."

Margaret Burns, Darwin's 83-year-old aunt, said: "I cannot believe that he came back to Seaton Carew, you would have thought he had more sense than that, but perhaps not.

"When he was younger he used to think that he was God's gift and cleverer than everyone else, and I knew he would never change."

In March 2007 Mr and Mrs Darwin left for Panama where they bought a flat. But in December of that year Mr Darwin flew back to Britain and walked into a police station in London, claiming he was suffering from amnesia.

His wife initially expressed delight that her husband had turned up, but confessed to the fraud after a picture emerged showing the couple together in Panama.

When they are released, the Darwins will have nothing. Mrs Darwin has agreed to repay £591,838 – the sum of her remaining "realisable assets". Her husband will repay a token sum of £1 as he has nothing left.

The separation from her sons is understood to have taken a particular toll on Mrs Darwin, and she has written to them many times begging for forgiveness.

After the trial, Anthony said: "I can't ever forgive them for putting us through the torture of mourning."

A friend added: "The most painful thing for Anne has been having no contact with her sons and knowing that might never change.

"She has been struggling to make sense of everything, devastated at the pain she had caused and trying to put John out of her thoughts."

22 January 2011
"Canoe Man" paddles back into view
John Darwin, who faked drowning, is now penniless,
paranoid and terrified of returning to prison
By Neil Tweedie

Easington Colliery is an obsolete town with an obsolete name. The mine that gave it its purpose is long shut but the place remains, lines of drab terraces marching down to the grey North Sea.

Desolation is its chief asset. When the makers of *Billy Elliot* wanted the perfect "It's grim up North" setting, they settled on Easington, Co Durham. The town figures prominently in tables of deprivation, and lays claim to the most obese population in the country. Pound shops rub shoulders with pubs protected by steel window shutters, the standard furniture of broken Britain. No paradise, then. Certainly not the paradise envisaged by John Darwin when he was dreaming of wealth and sunshine.

Say John Darwin in the Co-op and they hesitate, but mention "Canoe Man" and the lights switch on.

"Living here, is he?" says the lady at the check-out. "Well, I won't be bothering to look out for him."

Darwin will be pleased with that. Since his release from prison earlier this week he has been stalked by the media. Desperate not to antagonise his probation officers, he has been forced to lie low.

"John is in such a state at the moment," says Paul Wager, his oldest friend. "He's just done three years in prison and what's freaking him out is the thought that he would have to go back because of insinuations that he is talking to the press. At the moment he is like a fox that's gone to ground and can't get out."

Darwin, who staged his own death to rescue himself and his wife from the imminent collapse of their property empire, is already a kind of folk hero in a town short of things to celebrate.

"The residents of Easington Colliery are aware that he is there, and he is now a kind of local celebrity," says Mr Wager, an artist. "One thing I have picked up there is that John has a lot of support from a lot of those people, working-class people who have formerly worked down the pit. When they look at what the politicians and bankers have got away with, they don't judge him so harshly."

Look south along the coast and you see Hartlepool. Beyond is Seaton Carew, a

Victorian seaside resort assailed by smells wafted over the sea from the petrochemical plants of Teesside. It was from there, on 21 March 2002, that Darwin set off in his red kayak on a one-way journey.

The banks were clamouring for the repayment of debts that he and his wife Anne had run up. A teacher turned prison officer, Darwin had fancied himself as a financier and had taken to betting on the stock market before settling on buy-to-let property as the way to pay for the lifestyle he and his wife, his childhood sweetheart, craved.

But the Darwins soon found themselves in trouble, overstretched by the mounting costs of their mini-property empire and more than £60,000 in debt to credit card companies. The solution was a sell-off of the cheap terrace houses they had collected, and the four-wheel drive they had bought on tick. But they were not about to admit defeat. The insurance and pension companies could rescue them. All John Darwin had to do was die.

So there he found himself, at the age of 51, paddling into the unknown. After ditching his canoe up the coast, he met up with Anne, who drove him to Durham railway station. Darwin hid himself away in Cumbria while men risked their lives to search for him, and his family, including his two sons, Mark and Anthony, grieved. In 2003 a coroner returned an open verdict, concluding that he had got into difficulties at sea and drowned.

Brazenly, Darwin returned to Seaton Carew, living next door to his wife in one of two seafront houses they owned. Anne played the role of widow to perfection, giving nothing away, even to her children. The bearded man occasionally spotted next door was thought by neighbours to be a handyman or boyfriend.

For phase two of the plan, Darwin got himself a false passport in the name of a dead child, John Jones. The Darwins started liquidating their assets, gathered up £250,000 of insurance and pension money paid out for the "death" and began looking for a home abroad, travelling to Cyprus before choosing Panama. Stupidly, they allowed themselves to be photographed in the central American country and their picture used on a property website.

In September 2007, Cleveland Police reopened the investigation. Anne moved permanently to Panama the next month, but their new life was crumbling. In December, Darwin walked into a police station in London and "resurrected" himself, claiming amnesia. His wife followed him back to Britain. In March 2008, Darwin pleaded guilty to deception and was sentenced to six years in jail. Anne hoped to escape, denying deception and money laundering, but was found guilty on all charges. Imprisoned near York, she will be allowed out on licence in March. The couple are said to be estranged.

"After the ordeal they have been through during the past three years, emotions are stretched," says Mr Wager. "I honestly don't think Anne would divorce John, but whether that means she remains separated from him is a different issue."

And the sons who disowned them? "They are still on the sidelines, really. John's brother and sister are certainly on the sidelines – they don't want to know him."

Mr Wager insists that he and his wife will stand by their old friend. "John Darwin and I were babies together. My father and his father were very great friends. He's from a very nice family, they are really nice people.

"John went off the track and had to be punished. But he had a lot of spirit and that spirit was broken by the banks. He was in a corner and had nowhere to go. He was in a desperate situation."

His friend, he says, has barely begun to think about how to rebuild his life. "He is totally isolated. People need to realise that he's very alienated. He's out and no one wants to help or know him, apart from my wife and me.

"Without our support during the past three years I think he would have totally packed up. What is important is that we have to forgive people. What gets me is that paedophiles and rapists get relatively short sentences compared with theirs. Six years was an excessive sentence in my opinion."

Mr Wager does not believe there is some secret fund in Panama awaiting the Darwins' return. "The authorities have gone through everything and there's nothing like that, to my knowledge. He certainly hasn't got anything. He came out of prison with a black bag. He walks with a limp now because he needs a hip replacement. He looks better than he did but he's aged quite a bit since he has been in prison."

Despite his status as a former prison officer, Darwin, it seems, was well-regarded by fellow inmates for what they considered to be a victimless crime. "He had a lot of respect from hardened criminals because he took on the Establishment."

Reports about the benefits Darwin will be able to claim are, say Mr Wager, pointless and cruel. "This is a guy who has worked 30 years of his life, never been unemployed, paid his taxes, paid his national insurance. Hartlepool is full of people who have never worked and are funded."

On the evening of Darwin's release, he held a small celebration, a subdued affair, no doubt. Now 60 and penniless, spurned by his loved ones, John Darwin must rebuild his life when many his age would be enjoying their retirement in the sun.

Ronald Darwin, John's father, now dead, once said of his son: "He had ideas above his station. He had big dreams and ambitions."

Those ambitions have been reduced to a small terrace house overlooking a cold sea, the one he paddled out into in that moment of madness.

29 January 2011
Canoe man's latest vanishing act: the missing Panama spoils
By Jon Swaine in Panama City

They gained infamy for an insurance deception whereby he vanished at sea in a canoe. But while John and Anne Darwin were ultimately exposed and jailed, some of their ill-gotten assets remain as elusive as ever, the *Daily Telegraph* can disclose.

Three years after the "canoe man" conspiracy was uncovered, thousands of pounds worth of assets held in Panama, where the Darwins set up a new life, are unaccounted for.

A brand new 4x4 vehicle worth £25,000, which was parked outside their Panama home when the fraud was exposed in December 2007, has never been recovered.

Mrs Darwin, who claimed £250,000 from her husband's life insurance and pension schemes, had access to two bank accounts in the country that were previously unknown to investigators.

The *Daily Telegraph* has learnt of the new details a week after Mr Darwin was released on licence from Moorland open prison in Doncaster, after serving half of his six-year sentence. Mrs Darwin is due to be freed from Askham Grange jail near York in March.

The couple, from Seaton Carew, near Hartlepool, gained notoriety three years ago when Mr Darwin turned up at a police station claiming to be suffering from amnesia.

He had been declared dead after vanishing at sea in his canoe in March 2002. His wife cashed in the insurance policies and moved to Panama.

He joined her before visa problems forced him to return to Britain. All their assets were frozen in 2008 and Mrs Darwin, 59, agreed to pay back £592,000. Mr Darwin, 60, was said to be penniless and ordered to pay £1. A list of Mrs Darwin's assets included a flat in Panama City, now valued at £62,702, and a 480-acre plot beside the Panama Canal, worth £232,336.

It also included £157,721 in bank accounts in Britain and Jersey, which was recovered, and three HSBC accounts in Panama containing a total of £144,000.

Officers in Panama agreed to help with the recovery effort, which is being led by a court-appointed receiver from Grant Thornton, the accountants.

But 14 months on, no assets in Panama have been seized. Neither of Mrs Darwin's properties has been sold, and none of the cash has been recovered.

She is still listed as the resident of the flat on an up-to-date rota pinned in its lobby. Maria Estevez, an executive at the building's management company, said: "Anne Darwin is the owner."

The brand new Toyota Land Cruiser has vanished. The vehicle was bought with a £25,700 bank draft. It was registered in Mrs Darwin's name. A spokesman for the Crown Prosecution Service said: "Its location is unknown. If you know where the Land Cruiser is, please tell the police." Meanwhile a letter sent by the CPS to Panama's prosecutor general requesting help with the inquiry, which has been seen by the *Daily Telegraph*, lists two additional Panamanian bank accounts.

One of these is in the name of Jaguar Properties Corp, the Panama-based front company used by Mrs Darwin to buy the two properties. After being asked repeatedly to clarify over the past week, neither the CPS nor Cleveland Police could say yesterday whether the account had been examined or may contain money.

The CPS spokesman said: "We have no information about other accounts . . . The confiscation order is against Anne Darwin, not Jaguar Properties."

Lawyers for Mr and Mrs Darwin did not respond to requests for comment.

Revd Harold Francis Davidson, rector of Stiffkey

"He challenged them to arrest him in a lions' cage."

Though he was nominally the rector of Stiffkey, a small village in rural Norfolk, the self-style "prostitutes padre" spent most of his time on the streets of London attempting, he said, to prevent girls falling into vice. Though for a long time nothing could be proved against him, he had difficulty explaining away a number of the very compromising situations in which he found himself. His frequent absences drew complaints both from his constituents and his family, and eventually the Bishop of Norwich instituted an investigation into the rector: the combination of Davidson's existing record of eccentric Gladstone-esque behaviour and a photograph of him in the company of a barely dressed teenager was enough to ensure he was defrocked.

31 July 1937
Ex-rector of Stiffkey dead
Two days after lion mauled him

Mr Harold Davidson, the former Rector of Stiffkey, who was mauled by a lion in a Skegness amusement ground on Wednesday night, died in hospital at Skegness yesterday. He was 65.

In recent years he had been taking part in show-ground performances, including fasting in a barrel at Blackpool.

At Skegness he addressed crowds from inside a lions' cage, and on Wednesday one of the animals attacked him, inflicting severe injuries before being driven off by an attendant. The inquest will be opened at Skegness to-day.

Mr Davidson, who was ordained 35 years ago, had previously been an actor, and he once said that he gave up an income of £1,000 a year to become a curate at £3 a week.

He was rector of Stiffkey, in Norfolk, for 25 years, until, in March 1932, a series of charges was preferred against him in the Norwich Consistory Court.

The proceedings lasted over several weeks, and ultimately five allegations of immoral conduct were found to have been proved.

The sentence of the bishop, Dr. Bertram Pollock, was that Mr Davidson should be deprived of "all ecclesiastical dues and rights and emoluments belonging to the ecclesiastical promotions".

The rector vehemently protested his innocence, and made an appeal to the Archbishop of Canterbury, but Dr. Lang dismissed it. Then Mr Davidson went before the Judicial Committee of the Privy Council and conducted his appeal in person. It failed.

He embarked on a campaign against the Church of England hierarchy which he continued until his death. He adopted extraordinary methods to draw attention to his case, and thousands paid pennies "to see the ex-Rector of Stiffkey".

He appeared on the stage in London and the provinces, and sat in a barrel at Blackpool until the police served a summons on him for obstruction. Crowds streamed past him as he read the summons in his barrel.

Prevented from continuing this exhibition, he was shown to Blackpool crowds fasting in a glass cabinet. A further prosecution followed, and in 1935 he was sent for trial and acquitted on a charge of attempting to commit suicide by starving himself.

He brought an action against the Blackpool Corporation for false imprisonment, and was awarded damages of £382 and costs.

He travelled the country "on show" at fairgrounds, lecturing and holding "receptions". Always he insisted that he had been trying to "rescue" the girls whom he had been found guilty of molesting; that he had a right to be tried by a jury; and that he was only trying to raise money to get his case reopened.

When police went to the Skegness amusement ground with a warrant for his arrest for debt he challenged them to arrest him in a lions' cage from which he was haranguing an audience. It was half an hour before he surrendered and left the cage.

As a variation from starving, he lay on view in a glass case at Blackpool last year with an automatic demon prodding him with a fork.

Mr Davidson once wired to Gandhi inviting him to sit in his barrel at Blackpool, and last year he created a scene at the Church Assembly.

He stood up in front of the public gallery and, shouting for "justice", showered typewritten papers on the delegates.

Right to the last he protested that he was the lawful rector of Stiffkey.

John Drewe and John Myatt

"I took a step back and thought, 'This is a crime,' and I got very frightened."

They were an odd pairing. But between them John Drewe, "a ruthless confidence trickster", and John Myatt, a self-effacing and impecunious art teacher from Staffordshire, pulled off Britain's biggest modern art fraud. Drewe's cunning – he inserted himself into the heart of the art establishment with incredible facility – was matched with Myatt's gift for producing impeccable forgeries of some of the greatest painters of the previous two centuries. When their scam finally unravelled, Drewe, acknowledged as the mastermind, received six years, Myatt just one.

13 February 1999
The art conman who changed history
Even experts were fooled by the criminal who
went to extraordinary lengths to create an image of authority
By Will Bennett

Detectives waiting at Battersea heliport in London were impressed as Professor John Drewe arrived in a helicopter claiming to have links with the Israeli secret service.

The dapper, articulate Drewe was carrying photographs of paintings he said had been stolen by the Mafia, which was trying to sell them in London.

Indeed the paintings had been stolen, although a man Drewe named as being involved was acquitted by a jury. But Drewe's claim to be a professor at a secret Israeli installation trying to recover a stolen plan for a "Stealth" helicopter was pure fantasy.

Detectives now believe that Drewe arranged the meeting with them in 1994 to try to establish himself as a trusted informant in case the art fraud he was already running was uncovered.

It was a typically devious piece of thinking by Drewe and yet the fraud itself, the biggest involving modern paintings this century, was devastatingly simple and has sent shivers through Britain's £2.2bn-a-year art market.

The provenance of works of art, the record of their previous history, is crucial. A prospective buyer wants to inspect it just as the purchaser of a used car wants to see the logbook.

Drewe realised that dealers, auctioneers and collectors would be less likely to question the authenticity of a fake painting if he created a provenance as bogus as the work of art itself.

He inserted false information into the records of the Tate Gallery and the Victoria and Albert Museum in London so that the paintings which he was paying an artist to fake acquired an instant history. Then, distancing himself to lessen the chances of detection, he persuaded others to sell the pictures.

The famous auction houses and plush art galleries to which they were taken in the West End are a world away from Drewe's modest upbringing.

He was born John Cockett in 1948 in Sussex, where his father Basil, a telephone engineer, and his mother Kathleen lived in a farm cottage near Uckfield.

He was educated at Bexleyheath Grammar School, Kent, which he left after passing O-levels. When he was 17 he took a lowly job with the Atomic Energy Authority.

Dr John Catch, his boss at the time, found him clever but arrogant and disinclined to take advice and the teenager left after two years.

Much of the next 20 years of his life is a mystery, although at some stage he changed his name to Drewe, adding the letter "e" to the second half of his mother's maiden name of Barrington-Drew.

Briefly, he taught A-level physics without any qualifications at two schools in Britain and later falsely pretended to have a degree from an American university. In 1979 a mutual friend introduced Drewe to Bathsheva Goudsmid, an Israeli. They moved in together in Golders Green, north London, and she had two children before the relationship ended acrimoniously in 1994.

By the late Eighties, Drewe appeared well-off, driving a Bentley and dining in expensive restaurants. Dozens of paintings, apparently by famous artists, passed through his home.

Drewe told Miss Goudsmid that the pictures belonged to John Catch, using the name of his old boss at the Atomic Energy Authority. He added that Catch was a peer of the realm and a German baron who was going to leave him his £2m fortune. According to Drewe, Catch wanted to sell the paintings but did not want this to become widely known and had asked Drewe to sell them on his behalf in return for a commission.

The reality was that in 1986 Drewe had replied to an advertisement in *Private Eye* magazine offering "genuine fakes, 19th and 20th-century fakes from £150". It had been placed by John Myatt, an impecunious art teacher from Staffordshire.

Drewe told Myatt that he was a research scientist, was paid by the Government to inspect nuclear submarines and gave the impression that he was involved with British intelligence.

Short of money and with his marriage on the rocks, Myatt did not question this and produced paintings in the style of Alberto Giacometti, Roger Bissière, Jean

Dubuffet, Marc Chagall, Graham Sutherland, Ben Nicholson, Nicolas de Staël and others at up to £250 a time.

Drewe paid him between £50,000 and £100,000 over the next few years. Myatt produced a painting about every two months, once taking five days to paint a fake Giacometti nude using household emulsion. Drewe then aged the picture with dust tipped from a vacuum cleaner and varnish and coated the frame tacks with salt to rust them.

Myatt used a mixture of emulsion and lubricating jelly to imitate de Stael's brush-strokes and found that faking Bissières became "a kind of addiction".

At first, the artist thought Drewe wanted the pictures for his home but gradually realised he was involved in fraud. However, he continued because Drewe fascinated and frightened him.

Meanwhile, Drewe smoothly burrowed his way to the heart of Britain's art establishment. He donated £20,000 to the Tate Gallery which was "bowled over".

When he applied for a reader's ticket for the V&A's archives as Dr Drewe, his character reference was written by himself in the name of Dr Cockett.

The archives at the Tate and the V&A contain records of thousands of paintings, including files from now defunct art galleries and dealers. Drewe tampered with this mine of information and inserted photographs of Myatt's paintings into the records, the labels on them being produced on an old typewriter. He even bought archive paper of the right age.

He stole a catalogue of an exhibition held at the defunct Hanover Gallery in London, replacing it with a bogus version which contained some of the fakes.

Drewe forged a receipt purporting to show that a Giacometti had been sold for £1,900 in 1958 and inserted it into the records. The picture had been recently painted by Myatt. He approached the families of the artists being forged for information and, with threats of legal action, bullied a Roman Catholic religious order into providing fake histories. The fake pictures were sold by runners who fell for a series of lies. One was Daniel Berger, who was told that they were being disposed of by a man who did not want his children to know he was selling them.

Clive Bellman fell for Drewe's story that the paintings were being sold to buy archive material in Russia to prove that the Holocaust took place.

Drewe was said to have paid his co-defendant Daniel Stoakes, an impoverished male nurse from Exeter who had been a schoolfriend, a retainer to pose as the owner of a collection of Nicholsons. Stoakes was acquitted.

Numerous experts were fooled by the paintings. Fifteen fake pictures were sold through Sotheby's, Christie's and Phillips.

Peter Nahum, a leading London art dealer and *Antiques Roadshow* expert, bought a fake Sutherland for £5,250. He and the art market middleman Ivor Braka bought a bogus Nicholson. Altogether Drewe cost Mr Nahum about £40,000.

Whitford Fine Arts, a gallery in London's West End, complained after a de Staël sold to them turned out to be a fake but were persuaded to accept four bogus Sutherland sketches in exchange.

The biggest victim was an American gallery owner who became worried about a Giacometti for which he had paid £105,000 and hired a specialist firm to verify it. Ironically the company was run by Drewe, who charged the man £1,140 to authenticate a painting which he had had faked in the first place.

In 1995 Drewe's operation was revealed after almost a decade. Miss Goudsmid, horrified by what she had read in documents left behind by Drewe, contacted the Tate and the police.

Mr Nahum, suspicious about the Sutherland, and the Mayfair art dealer Leslie Waddington, an expert on Dubuffet who was unhappy about sketches he had seen, also went to police.

Drewe denied tampering with the records and claimed the fakes had been sold by arms dealers and countries desperate for hard currency.

Myatt confessed his part in the fraud and gave evidence against Drewe. However, he did not paint some of the fake Nicholsons and police believe that there may be another artist involved.

It is thought that Drewe, now married to a medical practitioner, Dr Helen Sussman, made at least £1m. Only 60 of about 200 fakes which he sold have been recovered in Paris, New York and Britain.

The damage to Britain's art market is containable because only the works of a few artists were involved. But pictures by them will be treated cautiously for years and the embarrassment caused to a business priding itself on expertise is immense.

In one sense Drewe's life has been a tragedy. John Bevan, QC, prosecuting, said: "It was a waste of a clever, hugely retentive brain on a lifestyle which left a trail of victims in its wake."

2 July 1999
"I paint pastiches – not forgeries"

John Myatt has just served a sentence for his part in the largest contemporary art fraud of the 20th century. He tells Colin Gleadell it was a moment of bad judgment that he will always regret.

In the annals of the great art forgers of the 20th century certain names stick out. Han van Meegeren for his Vermeers, Elmyr de Hory for his Matisses, Tom Keating for his Samuel Palmers and Eric Hebborn for his Piranesis. But what about John Myatt, the artist at the centre of the so-called Tate archive fraud, described by Scotland Yard as "the largest contemporary art fraud of the 20th century"? Will he be equally remembered for his Ben Nicholsons?

Only four months ago, when the fraud trial closed, Myatt's paintings in the style of Nicholson, Alberto Giacometti and Graham Sutherland were splashed across every newspaper. But who still remembers his name? The case was more closely identified with John Drewe, who, the prosecution alleged, masterminded the fraud after answering the *Private Eye* advertisement for "genuine fakes" placed by the impoverished Myatt in 1986. Drewe allegedly went on to create false histories of ownership to document Myatt's paintings and plant them in the archives of the Tate Gallery and the V&A.

Myatt's fakes, or "pastiches" as he prefers to call them, were subsequently treated as authentic by art historians, dealers, and sale-room experts. Many were sold, one for more than £100,000. Drewe, still maintaining his innocence, was sentenced to six years, and has lodged for an appeal. But Myatt, who admitted his part in the affair, was given one year, and, on 14 June, was released early from Brixton prison.

At his home in Staffordshire, where I visited him this week, he wears an electronic tagging device on his ankle, which will be removed at midnight on 11 August, his 54th birthday.

Myatt lives in a slightly dilapidated but homely three-bedroomed converted farm-house with his two teenage children (he was divorced from their mother in 1987). On the kitchen table are photocopies of portrait drawings he did of warders, prison-ers, their wives and girlfriends in exchange for HM Prison telephone cards while serving his sentence. They are accurate and precise. "They had to be," he says. "That's what the clients wanted."

He paints, as always, in the living room. On a side table stand the same materials he used for his fakes – "poster paints, for texture, quick-drying household emulsion, acrylics and KY jelly to make the paint flow. Anything I've got," he says. "I chuck it on." On the easel is a "Ben Nicholson" he is doing for a friend.

The only sign of luxury is a digital piano on which he plays anything from Mozart to rock 'n' roll. "I was lucky to keep that," he says. "The police confiscated everything else of value, including all my Ben Nicholson books." Music has been very much part of his life. In the seventies, he worked as a songwriter for Dick Leahy, now George Michael's publisher. It was Leahy, Myatt says, who commissioned his first "pastiches" – in the style of Raoul Dufy. Myatt's musical career peaked in 1979 when he co-wrote the record Silly Games, sung by Janet Kay, that went to number one in the charts. Now he sings in the local church choir, and performs on the piano for the Women's Institute.

Myatt's artistic skills were learnt at art schools in Stafford and Cheltenham before going to Bristol in 1969 to obtain a teaching diploma. Prior to meeting John Drewe, his employment as an artist or teacher had been sporadic, but Drewe offered him more consistent work and pay.

At first the commissions were for simple pastiches in the style of Dutch marine painters or modern masters – Klee, Picasso or Braque. "I thought they were for his house," Myatt said in court. But then, he explains, "I got a phone call telling me to sit down because one of my paintings, a deliberate copy of a cubist portrait by Albert Gleizes, had been valued at £25,000. I got drawn in at a moment of total crisis, when judgment goes through the window. I was going through my divorce, and looking after two children in nappies while trying to work as a supply teacher. I was getting bad-tempered with the kids so I had to stop teaching. Working for Drewe, I realised I could stay at home and look after the children. But there came a point, later on, when I took a step back and thought, 'This is a crime,' and I got very frightened."

In 1994 he stopped painting for Drewe, but two years later the police came knock-ing at his door. He decided then and there to confess, and is now deeply contrite. "I got a sentence," he says, "because I deserved one. I wish it hadn't happened. But now I try not to think about it, and the damage it may have done."

Myatt still does not know precisely what was sold or for how much. He is also vague about what he painted. "About six Ben Nicholson canvases, half a dozen Nicolas de Staëls, three or four large Giacomettis. But if you showed me a Giacometti drawing, I wouldn't know if I had done it."

But, he is quite clear, "what I did were pastiches, not forgeries. I was very surprised they were accepted. Any student could have done them. When I heard the Tate had been given one of my Bissières, I retrieved it and burned it. I could not have handled seeing it on the wall at the Tate." How different from Hebborn, who boasted that his "Old Master" drawings had been bought by museums.

In court, Drewe suggested that Myatt had confessed because he "wanted to be the next Tom Keating". But Myatt is modest about his skills. "I don't think of myself as a de Hory, Keating or Hebborn. My work was not good enough. I didn't take the trouble. My Nicholsons took a couple of evenings; the Sutherlands a couple of hours. Now I would be much more meticulous, but I would also sign the work with my name, and have it stamped."

He looks at the "Ben Nicholson" on the easel and points to a view of water among the abstract shapes. "Now that's not Nicholson. And the rest of the canvas is just Myatt dealing with the same problems as Nicholson. I think I'll put a boat in just there."

The Dreyfus Affair

"'We shall cry "Vive la France" when he passes,' exclaimed a workman.
'No; he is not worth that – the villain!' replied a comrade."

The Dreyfus Affair split France into two camps: broadly defined as the pro-Army, largely Catholic anti-Dreyfusards; and the republican, anti-clerical Dreyfusards. It exposed the anti-Semitism of a large proportion of the country's population, and a level of corruption that went right to the heart of the government. It's also one of the earliest, and most striking, examples of the sway that the press and public opinion can exert, even on a highly complex legal case. At the centre of the scandal was a promising French artillery officer, Alfred Dreyfus, who was accused of handing secret documents to the German army. Dreyfus's family came from the Alsace, one of the disputed border areas between France and Germany: more pertinently, at least as far as his accusers were concerned, he was Jewish.

Three years later, in 1897, evidence unearthed by an investigation led by Georges Picquart, head of counter-espionage, suggested strongly that the perpetrator was in fact another soldier, Major Ferdinand Walsin Esterhazy. But senior officers suppressed the incriminating information and, after a trial lasting just two days, Esterhazy was acquitted. Picquart, however, found himself arrested on a charge of violation of professional secrecy. In 1898, the case exploded when perhaps the most celebrated writer in the country, Émile Zola, published an extraordinary denunciation of those who had been involved in framing Dreyfus.

The Dreyfus affair was an unprecedentedly divisive issue that exposed deep fault lines in contemporary France, and the rancour and bitterness would persist even after Dreyfus was belatedly acquitted in 1906. By this time, Esterhazy had long since sloped off to England, where he lived quietly until his death in 1923. Dreyfus himself was reinstated as a major in the French Army. He served throughout the First World War, and retired with the rank of lieutenant colonel.

24 December 1894
Paris day by day
French officer convicted of treason
By special wire from our own correspondent

Alfred Dreyfus, captain in the 14th Regiment of Artillery, on the staff of the War Office, has been found guilty of having supplied a foreign Power with a certain number of secret documents regarding the national defence, and has been sentenced to transportation to, and imprisonment for life in, a fortress, and also to military degradation. Such is the result of the trial by court-martial, which closed last evening, and although this erewhile brilliant and promising officer was widely believed to have turned traitor to his country this confirmation of the terrible suspicion has produced a great and painful sensation. The man's name is execrated to-day in every household in France, and the cry of disappointment that the death penalty for such a crime should have been abolished is general. Such a case of treason had never been known in this country since Bazaine betrayed it in the terrible year.

As the hour approached when the trial should terminate yesterday the crowd in the Rue du Cherche-Midi assumed formidable proportions, and intense excitement was displayed. When the proceedings were resumed at one o'clock in the afternoon, Maître Demange delivered his address for the defence, which was continued, with a brief interval during which the sitting was suspended, until half-past five. What the learned lawyer said has not been suffered to transpire, but it may be assumed that he merely pleaded for mercy. Only ten minutes sufficed for the reply of Commandant Brisset, representing the Government, and the barrister was then allowed to make a few more remarks. Nothing, however, could be more significant than the extreme brevity of Commandant Brisset's observations on the case. Then, while the officers composing the military tribunal withdrew to consider their decision, the prisoner was removed from the court to the infirmary, running down the staircase and along the passage in the hope of escaping the crowd which had gathered there while awaiting admission to the hall, for now that the decision was to be proclaimed the public were to have access to the court, which had been denied them ever since the preliminary proceedings had been entered on. Presently the veto was withdrawn, and in a moment the hall was filled. The officers were still absent, but Maître Demange was seated in his place, apparently overwhelmed with fatigue and absorbed by painful thoughts. It was seven o'clock when the cry of "Present arms" rang through the hall, and while the small guard saluted the members of the court-martial returned. Dreyfus had not been led back, there being an express regulation, that the prisoner shall not be present while the decision is read out, so that any compromising display of irritation on his part may be avoided.

A solemn silence prevailed as all rose to their feet, and then the President read out the sentence, beginning with the words, "In the name of the French people", at which he and the other six officers composing the tribunal raised their hands to their képis with the military salute. "The first Court-Martial of the Military Government of Paris," he continued, "had met, and the President had put the following question: 'Is M. Alfred Dreyfus, Captain in the 14th Regiment of Artillery, Staff Probationer attached to the Ministry of War, guilty of having in 1894 procured for a foreign Power a certain number of secret documents connected with the National Defence, and of having been engaged in intrigues or in communication with that Power or its agents to induce it to commit hostile acts, or to undertake war against France or to procure it the means of doing so.' The votes having been taken separately, beginning with the lowest grade, and the Colonel presiding having given his opinion last, the answer has been 'Yes' with a unanimity of votes, the accused is guilty." Then a cry of "*Vive la Patrie*" was uttered by someone in the hall amid intense emotion, but the President took no notice of it, and went on with his reading: "Therefore and unanimously the First Conseil de Guerre condemns *le nommé* Alfred Dreyfus to perpetual transportation in a fortress, and condemns him to military degradation." Then followed the reading of the different clauses of the Penal Code on which the sentence was based, and in which it was set forth that in cases where the death penalty was abolished it should be replaced by transportation to a fortress "designated by law outside the Continental territory of the Republic. The persons transported will enjoy there all the liberty compatible with the necessity of guarding them securely." This done, the President asked Commandant Brisset to see that the sentence was at once communicated to the prisoner, in the presence of the guard, and to inform him that he was legally allowed twenty-four hours to apply for a revision of the sentence. "The sitting is at an end," added Colonel Maurel, and he left the court with his colleagues, while the public followed their example.

A few minutes afterwards Dreyfus was in the court, hearing the reading of the sentence by the clerk. He betrayed no emotion. Outside the building, in the Rue du Cherche-Midi, a dense crowd, indignant and menacing, had gathered, and a strong force of police had been told off to clear the road. All wanted to have a glimpse of the prisoner. "We shall cry 'Vive la France' when he passes," exclaimed a workman. "No; he is not worth that – the villain!" replied a comrade. At last Dreyfus was perceived leaving the building on his way to the prison in his artillery uniform. He hurried along so fast that the two officers who led him could hardly keep pace with him. There was a rush in his direction, in spite of the police, and an explosion of fury would have been witnessed if the prison-door had not suddenly closed with a bang, leaving Dreyfus safely within the courtyard. As has been explained, the prisoner can appeal, but in these cases the sentence can only be cancelled if there is a flaw in the procedure. Dreyfus had a consultation with his counsel this afternoon. Transportation to a fortress means removal to the Ducos Peninsula, in New Caledonia, settled by law twenty-two years ago. If, as is taken for granted, the decision is confirmed by the Conseil de Revision, a Military Court of Cassation, Dreyfus will undergo the sentence of military degradation, probably, in the large quadrangle of the Ecole Militaire, his sword being broken and the insignia of his rank wrenched off in presence of the assembled troops, and he will then be removed to the Ile de Ré, pending his departure for New Caledonia, where his wife and family can join him. He can apply for a grant of land, and if his conduct has been good for five years he may be sent to another place. Now an outcry is being raised that such a crime should be punished thus, and not with death. It is defined by the law as "political", and people contend that the law ought to be better provided for dealing with such cases. At a court-martial held in the Gironde, yesterday, a soldier was sentenced to death for spitting in the direction of the President and for flinging his képi at the representative of the Government. This is bad enough, in all conscience, but people are arguing that high treason is even worse, and that there ought not to be two weights and two measures.

The Military Council of Revision will meet on Tuesday to consider the appeal made by Dreyfus against the sentence passed on him.

14 January 1898
Paris day by day
M. Zola to be prosecuted
By special wire from our own correspondent

To-day's first exciting sequel to the Esterhazy court-martial is the arrest of Lieutenant-Colonel Picquart, who was so severely censored by Commandant Ravary in his report, and whose furious attack on Commandant Comte Walsin Esterhazy during the trial has been the subject of so much comment. Already it had been affirmed that Lieutenant-Colonel Picquart had formally solicited, about two months ago, an investigation into his behaviour when he was the head of the Intelligence Department. This, however, was not exactly correct. What happened was this: When he was first examined Général de Pellieus, astonished at the disclosures which he volunteered, exclaimed, "But, Colonel, you have acted in such a manner that you might have to be sent before a council of inquiry." "I am quite ready to appear before one," was the reply. This is by no means the same thing as a spontaneous and formal application, nor, as has been insinuated, did Lieutenant-Colonel Picquart later on return to the subject. Lieutenant-Colonel Picquart is at Mont Valérien, and it is officially announced that, owing to the facts revealed during the investigation and the court-martial, he is to be kept in a fortress until it is decided whether he shall be sent before a council of inquiry. He was taken into custody about half-past six o'clock this morning, at his residence in the Rue Yvon Villarceau.

Whether the initiative thus taken by the authorities will be followed by other action is still a matter of speculation. Already, as will be remembered, an inquiry into the case of the alleged attempt to corrupt the late Colonel Sandherr is in progress, but it has been thought that other measures might also be adopted, apart, of course, from anything in the same direction, upon which Commandant Esterhazy might decide on his own account with the consent of his chiefs. It is, indeed, asserted on usually good authority that the Juge d'Instruction who is investigating the Sandherr affair will be asked to push his inquiry further, and it seems likely that the public will soon be enlightened on this subject. Meanwhile the report that as the accusation against Commandant Esterhazy has completely broken down, another officer, who is now abroad, may be pointed to as an object of suspicion, is gaining ground. Already is discreet reference being made to a military man who got into trouble for debt, and who is said to be now resident in a foreign capital. We are promised, if this surmise be correct, more stories of ladies, loans, and letters, so that persons with a taste for sensational gossip will be kept well supplied with material. It is added, however, that if any charge is formally brought against this officer, it is foredoomed to failure, as he was quartered in a town situated in the neighbourhood of the Eastern frontier, and could not, any more than Commandant Esterhazy, have had access to the special information alluded to in the notorious memorandum.

Distancing all his previous efforts in defence of ex-Captain Dreyfus, M. Emile Zola today provided a big sensation by addressing an open letter headed "I accuse" to the President of the Republic. The epistle overflows a whole page of the newspaper *l'Aurore*, with which M. Clémenceau is connected, and it may indeed be said to have caused intense excitement everywhere. The journal containing the letter was fast bought up on the boulevards, and around the Bourse, and people were knocking against each other in the streets as they read it. Men and women were even bending over the paper as they crossed thoroughfares, at the imminent risk of being knocked down by a 'bus or a cab. Some of M. Zola's passages are worth giving in full, notably the opening and closing ones. He says: "Monsieur le Président – Permit me, in my gratitude for the kind reception with which you on one occasion favoured me, to be anxious about your just glory, and to tell you that your star – so lucky down to the present – is threatened with the most shameful, the most indelible, of stains. You emerged safe and sound from low calumnies, you have conquered hearts. You appear radiant in the apotheosis of that patriotic festival which the Russian alliance has been for France, and you are preparing to preside at the solemn triumph of our universal Exhibition, which is to crown our century of work, truth, and liberty. But what a splash of mud has been cast on your name – I had almost add your reign – by this abominable Dreyfus affair. A Council of War has just dared, by order, to acquit an Esterhazy, thus giving a fearful blow to all truth and justice. And it is now over France, who has the pollution on her cheek, while history will write that it was under your Presidency such a social crime could be perpetuated. Well, as they have dared, I also will dare. I shall speak the truth, for I have promised to speak it if justice, regularly informed, fails to bring it out full and entire. My duty is to speak out. I do not want to be an accomplice. My nights would be haunted by the spectre of the innocent man out there who is expiating, amid the most horrible of tortures, a crime which he has not committed. And it is to you, Monsieur le Président, to whom I intend to cry out this truth with all the strength of my revolt as an honest man. For your honour's sake, I am convinced that you are ignorant of the truth. And to whom, then, shall I denounce the maleficent mob of real culprits, if not to you, who are the chief magistrate of the country?"

M. Zola, after this impassioned preamble, goes on to talk of the influence of Colonel du Paty de Clam. This officer, he says, when only a commandant, conducted the case, and did everything. He was the very incarnation of the Dreyfus affair, and that would not be known until a thoroughgoing investigation had been made of his acts and responsibilities. He acted on claptrap melodramatic lines, with purloined papers, anonymous letters, mysterious midnight women, retailing overwhelming proofs. It was he who conceived plan of dictating the memorandum to Dreyfus, who studied the face of the unfortunate officer in a mirrored room, who was described by Commandant Forzinetti as he went to the cell of the accused with a dark lantern, and threw a sudden flood of light on the face of the sleeping officer in order to surprise him into a confession amid the emotion of an abrupt awakening. M. du Paty de Clam, according to M. Zola, is therefore the first culprit in the terrible judicial error committed. The *bordereau* had been for some time in the hands of Colonel Sandherr, of the Intelligence Department, who had since died from general paralysis. Then flights took place, papers disappeared, as they are still disappearing, and the author of the memorandum was looked for amid staff or artillery officers when it was clear that he was a regimental man. This was an a priori supposition, and the moment suspicion fell on Dreyfus M. du Paty de Clam made the matter his own. There were also the War Minister, Général Mercier, of apparently medio-cre intelligence; the Chief of the Staff, Général de Boisdeffre, who seemed to have given way to religious animosity; and Général Gonse, whose conscience was accom-modating. But, argues M. Zola, it was M. du Paty de Clam who led them all by the nose, who hypnotised them, for he also dabbled in spiritualism and occultism. It would, in fact, be impossible to make people believe in all the traps and snares which he put under the feet of the unfortunate Dreyfus.

As if that were not enough, however, M. du Paty de Clam terrorised Madame Dreyfus, telling her to say nothing while her husband was tearing his flesh and shouting his innocence. And so the investigation was conducted in fifteenth-cen-tury style, based on a childish charge, on an idiotic memorandum, while the famous secrets delivered were valueless, and therefore mere swindles. The novelist next pic-tures the degradation and the expiation, all after proceedings conducted *en famille* by the War Office, while experts were shoved aside in a military manner when they had their doubts about the *bordereau*. M. Zola then emphatically denies the exist-ence of a document connected with the national defence, the production of which would cause war at once.

Coming to the Esterhazy case M. Zola defends Colonel Picquart, arrested to-day, and says that the officer in question conducted his inquiry with the full consent of his chiefs. He came to the conclusion that Esterhazy wrote the *bordereau*, and M. Zola says he was believed by Général Gonse, by Général de Boisdeffre, and even by Général Billot, War Minister, but the staff, knowing that Esterhazy's condemnation would lead to a revision of the Dreyfus court-martial, refused to go on. This, asserts the novelist, was the worst of all, for Général Billot refused to do justice, although he had the power. He, with Général Gonse and the Chief of the Staff, knew a year ago that Dreyfus was innocent, and they kept the terrible secret and slept and had wives and children whom they loved. It was in vain that Colonel Picquart and Senator Scheurer-Kestner supplicated. Nothing was done, and Esterhazy was being informed by veiled women of the so-called plot against him. In this melodramatic episode of the affair M. Zola also recognises the stage management of Lieutenant-Colonel du Paty de Clam, who was backed by the high officers mentioned, all being afraid that the War Office would tumble down before public contempt. And now the result of it all is that the indubitably honest man, Colonel Picquart, who did his duty is to suffer. The Council of War or court-martial has disgraced, according to M. Zola the military system henceforward. The first court may have been lacking in intelligence, but the second was compulsorily criminal. The Army assuredly was to be respected, the army of the people rising to defend the territory, but the sword of the master was to be resented, and its hilt should not be kissed. M. Zola, concludes as follows:

"I accuse Lieutenant-Colonel du Paty de Clam of having been the diabolical worker of a judicial error, unconscionably I am ready to believe, and of then having defended his nefarious doings for the past three years by the most absurd and culpable mach-inations. I accuse Général Mercier of being the accomplice, at least, through weak intelligence, in the greatest iniquity of the century. I accuse Général Billot of having in his hands the certain proofs of the innocence of Dreyfus, and of having suppressed them, thus rendering himself guilty of treason against humanity and justice, for a political reason and in order to save the compromised staff. I accuse Général de Boisdeffre and Général Gonse of being the accomplices in the same crime, the one through religious animosity doubtless, the other, perhaps, through that "esprit de corps" which makes the War Office the sacred and unassailable ark. I accuse Général de Pellieux and Commandant Ravary of having made a flagitious investigation, whereby I mean an inquiry of the most monstrous partiality, whereof we have, in the report of the last-mentioned, an imperishable monument of candid audacity. I accuse the three experts in handwriting, the men Belhomme, Varinard, and Couard, of having drawn up false and fraudulent reports, unless a medical examination shall prove them to be victims of a disease of sight or of judgment. I accuse the officers of the War Ministry of having organised a Press campaign, in order to lead public opinion astray. Finally, I accuse the first court-martial of having condemned a man on a document kept secret, and I accuse the second court-martial of having covered this illegality by order, and of committing in its turn the juridical crime of knowingly acquitting a guilty person. In bringing forward these accusations, 1 know that I am exposing myself to the penalties of the Press Law of 1881, but I am voluntarily running this risk. I do not know the persons whom I accuse, and I bear them no rancour. I ask for light in the name of humanity, my protest is the cry of my soul, and let anybody that dares bring me before an Assize Court, and let the investigation be made in broad daylight. I await that, and beg you to accept, Monsieur le Président, etcetera. – (Signed) Emile Zola." The excitement over this letter continues this evening, and the anti-Dreyfusians have burned fifty copies of the paper containing it on the Boulevard Montmartre.

Both at the Senate and the Chamber, where the election of officials was proceeded with, and an inaugural address was delivered, M. Loubet bring re-elected President of the Upper House, while M. Scheurer-Kastner, significantly enough, was beaten in his candidature for a vice-presidency, there was considerable excitement about the turn that events are taking in connection with the Esterhazy case. At the Chamber, after M. Henri Brisson had delivered his speech, which was pleasant and friendly, but by no means remarkable, he announced that Comte Albert de Mun had asked to be allowed to interpellate the Government as to the measures which it proposed taking with regard to M. Zola's letter. Loud applause burst forth, to be followed by vehement protests, when M. Cochery pointed out that both M. Méline and Général Billot were absent. It was promptly decided that the sitting should be suspended until they arrived and when it was resumed the President of the Council said that the Government understood and shared the emotion and indignation of the House at the accusation brought against the chiefs of the Army. M. Zola's article would be the subject of legal proceedings, although he was aware that this prosecution had been sought, and would prolong a deplorable agitation in the country, which, like the Government, desired calm and peace. Loud applause arose, which was resumed when Comte Albert de Mun exhorted the Minister of War to defend the Army. Général Billot replied that this was the fourth time that he had been called upon within a year to defend a judgment. "With closed doors," cried the Socialist M. Chauvin, amid din. The Army, continued the Minister of War, was above these attacks, but it was very sad to see its honour audaciously assailed in the presence of Europe, which was looking on. Could they compromise the national defence? The Government was ready, and resolved to put an end to this state of things and to defend the honour of the Army, respect for the decisions of the court-martial, and the interests of the country. M. Jaurès, the Socialist champion, now followed with such violent criticism that Général Billot answered that he had renewed and aggravated the attacks of M. Zola. Never had the chiefs of the army been more respectful of law, more faithful to the country, and, in conclusion, he adjured the Chamber to allow the Army to devote itself silently to its sacred mission, the defence of France. M. Cavaignac, a former Minister of War, followed, also in defence of the Army, and after saying that Général Billot could with one word stop the campaign which had been undertaken, he added that there was in the Dreyfus "dossier" a document which he could safely publish. It was the written evidence at the time of the trial that the condemned man had confessed that he had given unimportant papers to a foreign Government in order that he might obtain important ones. Had not the officer who commanded the parade at the degradation of Dreyfus communicated the confession to the Minister of War, and why had he not published it? Why, too, when Général Billot was convinced that the charge against Commandant Esterhazy was baseless had he not stopped this fresh campaign with a clear and precise word. M. Méline replied that if the Government had acted as M. Cavaignac wished it would have opened the revision of the Dreyfus case. "No," retorted M. Cavaignac, "The confession of which I speak is contained in a document which had nothing to do with the trial, and the Government could well have published it." Finally, an order of the day, setting forth that the Chamber approved the statement of the Government, and relied on it to take the necessary measures to put an end to the campaign undertaken against the honour of the Army, was adopted in two portions, and then in its entirety, by large majorities. M. Cavaignac's speech has created a great impression.

Commandant Esterhazy has written to the Minister of War, asking to be pensioned off, owing to ill-health, which has prevented him from discharging his regimental duties for some time. His real object, however, is believed to be that he may have a free hand in dealing with his traducers.

Tom Driberg

"Driberg was not an easy man to know or, some would say, to like."

"Confirmed bachelor", "aesthete", Tom Driberg's largely respectful obituary is pockmarked with a kind of code: discretion is maintained, but something is communicated to those in the know. Anyone charged with the same task now would undoubtedly spend a lot more time on his encounters with guardsmen in public lavatories (as well as, on those occasions when he was caught in flagrante delicto by the police, his attempts to use his influence as a journalist to hush the incident up). They might, too, dwell on the rumours that he was a KGB agent, or an MI5 informant, or possibly both. There is no mention of his friendships with everyone from Aleister Crowley to the Kray Twins, and perhaps the obituaries editor might have chosen someone somewhat more sympathetic to the subject to write the closing sentiments; but then much has changed in forty years.

13 August 1976
Lord Bradwell – obituary

Lord Bradwell, better known as Tom Driberg, who has died aged 71, was an enigmatic personality of exceptional gifts whose decision to enter Parliament in his thirties robbed Fleet Street of a talented practitioner. He was the original William Hickey of the *Daily Express*.

A quirky, fastidious man who combined extreme Left-wing political views with lifelong High Churchmanship, he took a prominent part in church affairs as a layman and became a member of the Church of England's Central Board of Finance. His earliest journalistic experience was on the Oxford undergraduate paper *Cherwell* and the Communist *Sunday Worker*, the twenties forerunner of the *Daily Worker*.

Educated at Lancing, where he was a contemporary of Evelyn Waugh, he became a classical scholar at Christ Church, Oxford, and joined the *Daily Express* in 1927, after working for some months as a film extra, Soho dish washer and pavement artist.

He started on the *Express* as a reporter on three months' trial, but was soon transferred to a gossip column, which he took over entirely in 1933 and which was renamed William Hickey.

After Driberg entered Parliament in June 1942, he continued the column for a year, but was dismissed by Lord Beaverbrook in July 1943, following a speech in which he alleged that Sir Andrew Duncan, the war-time Minister of Supply, was unpatriotically preparing to leave the Ministry to return to industry and a £25,000 a year job.

Subsequently he wrote a political column for *Reynolds News*, the Sunday organ of the Co-operative Society, and which became the *Sunday Citizen* in 1963. That newspaper closed in 1967.

He represented Maldon in Parliament till 1955 but did not contest the General Election that year. In 1959 he returned to the House as Labour MP for Barking, sitting till 1974. He was a member of the party executive from 1949 till 1972 and chairman in 1957. He was made a Life Peer in 1975.

Also 13 August 1976
Judgment belied
Notable record as activist
By H. B. Boyne

Tom Driberg, as everyone at Westminster knew him, gave the impression of being more suited to a contemporary literary life than to the rough and tumble of party politics. But his notable record as a Left-wing activist belied this judgment.

From the time he joined the Labour Party, just before the Dissolution of 1945, he aligned himself with the *Tribune* group. His gifts as polemicist and pamphleteer were freely at its disposal.

A didactic rather than forceful speaker, and something of an aesthete, Driberg made his most effective contributions to the Left-wing cause with his pen.

As a Fleet Street gossip columnist, he must have been the terror of compositors and proof-readers. Even a misplaced comma gave him pain and he hated nothing more than to be made to seem responsible in print for solecisms which he would never wittingly have committed.

This intense preoccupation with style and usage made him an excellent chairman of the Commons Select Committee on Publications and Debates Reports, a post he held in 1964–65. Improvements in the presentation of Hansard and other Parliamentary papers owed much to his care.

Driberg never seemed to hanker after office and, indeed, it is doubtful whether he would have been a great success as a Minister. But he did a competent administrative job as chairman of the Select Committee on Broadcasting of Proceedings in Parliament, which sat during 1965–67.

Driberg's literary output was by no means confined to political subjects. He published in 1956 a biography of his former employer, Lord Beaverbrook, which was diligently researched but enraged its subject.

Other books included a "Portrait with Background" of Guy Burgess and a study of Frank Buchman and the Moral Re-Armament Movement.

Driberg was not an easy man to know or, some would say, to like. It has been said that he would sacrifice a friendship for the sake of a well-turned, wounding phrase.

But I found him invariably courteous and his severest critic could not have accused him of detracting from the dignity of Parliament.

His marriage at 46 came as a surprise to friends who had come to regard him as a confirmed bachelor. Lady Bradwell was the former Mrs Ena Binfield.

Edward VII

"The Prince of Wales cannot be a private man if he wished it."

Edward VII tried the patience of his parents as few sons have before or since, though perhaps it didn't help that he was born to two unyielding Teutonic martinets. "Bertie" was largely uninterested in the comprehensive plan for his education that his father Albert drew up for him, preferring to reserve his energy for lechery and other unseemly forms of vice. In November 1861, in the aftermath of yet another outrage by his son, Albert set off for Cambridge to deliver a stern reprimand. As they walked in the cold, bone-penetratingly damp morning air, Albert contracted a high fever from which he would never recover.

His grieving wife settled into a pattern of profound disappointment at her son and his behaviour: in particular his appearance as a witness in the 1869 Lady Mordaunt Divorce case was a source of great hurt to her. The Baccarat Scandal, otherwise known as the Tranby Croft Affair, only served to confirm his reputation as the "playboy prince".

Edward had been at a house party in September 1890, staying with Arthur Wilson and his family at Tranby Croft in Yorkshire. Also present were two of the prince's advisers, Lord Coventry and Lieutenant General Owen Williams, as well as Edward's friend Sir William Gordon-Cumming.

On the first night, as the men settled into a game of baccarat, Stanley Wilson noticed, or at least he thought he did, Gordon-Cumming illegally adding to his stake. He shared this with the rest of the family, and it was decided that they would keep a close eye on him the following evening. Unaware of his hosts' scrutiny, Gordon-Cumming played once more in a manner that at the very least invited suspicion. After consulting with the royal courtiers, and securing the agreement of the prince, the family confronted Gordon-Cumming and demanded that in exchange for their silence he sign a document declaring that he would never play cards again.

But somehow the secret wriggled out and a horrified Gordon-Cumming, deciding that the Wilson family had leaked the story, demanded a retraction. They refused, and in short order he filed a writ for slander 1891. Aware of the implications of any kind of scandal at a time when knowledge of Bertie's peccadilloes had undermined his popularity with the public, his courtiers pushed to have the case heard in a military court. Their efforts were in vain and June 1891 Bertie was called as a witness, the first time the heir to the throne had been compelled to appear in court since 1411. The trial itself was distinguished by high drama, a skilful attempt by Gordon-Cumming's defence to highlight a number of discrepancies in the prosecution's case, and a somewhat biased summing-up by the judge. Gordon-Cumming lost the case, his career and his reputation; the prince's unpopularity persisted.

3 June 1891
The baccarat case
Evidence of the Prince of Wales

The examination of the plaintiff being concluded, the Solicitor-General, at two minutes after one o'clock, called his Royal Highness the Prince of Wales, who entered the box and was duly sworn.

In examination by Sir Edward Clarke:

Your Royal Highness has known Sir Willian Gordon Cumming for twenty years? – I have.

Am I right in saying for the last ten years at least he has enjoyed your Royal Highness's favour? – Certainly.

He has been a guest at your house? – On several occasions.

And admitted to your companionship and intimacy? Certainly.

And did that friendship – intimacy – continue unimpaired and undisturbed up to 9 or 10 of September last year? It did.

On the afternoon of 8 September, sir, had he travelled down to Tranby Croft with you? – Yes.

And on the evening of the 8th and the evening of the 9th had played baccarat at the times which have been mentioned in his evidence? – Yes.

You, sir, took the bank on both occasions? – I did.

Do you remember on the first evening there was no croupier? – I think not.

In the event, sir, of there being no croupier, the banker himself would be open to receive payment of counters? – He would unless he asked a friend to perform that duty for him.

Then he might ask some friend to do that in order to take the trouble from him of receiving and paying the counters while he was dealing the cards? – Very frequently, but not always.

On the second evening, sir, General Owen Williams, I believe, acted as croupier? – Yes.

Is it a fact, sir, at the end of the second evening's play Sir William Gordon-Cumming showed you his tableau, and a remark passed as to his winnings? – I think so.

And at the time that that tableau was shown and the remark made, I take it that nothing had occurred to give you the smallest suspicion as to his play? – Nothing whatever.

It was not, I believe, sir, until the evening of the 10th that any communication was made to you in regard to the alleged bad play? – No.

May I ask by whom the communication was first made to your Royal Highness? – By the Earl of Coventry.

And before dinner on the evening of the 10th your Royal Highness had heard no statement from any one except Lord Coventry? – From nobody.

May I ask if your Royal Highness remembers whether the statement made to you by Lord Coventry purported to be the statement of an individual, and, if so, whether that individual was named? – Of individuals.

Of whose? – Of three gentlemen and two ladies. I don't know whether it was the next day? – I saw Mrs Wilson the next morning.

Did she make a similar statement to you? – She said very little.

In reference to the statement, there is one point in it respecting which I should like to ask you whether you can charge your memory if any of the three gentlemen said anything of the kind. Do you recollect whether Mr Lycett Green, or Mr Arthur Wilson, or Mr Levett said anything about withdrawing a portion of the statement? – I do not remember that.

The Lord Chief Justice: Is this about withdrawing a portion of the statement?

Sir C. Russell: It is in the précis, my Lord. (To his Royal Highness): You do not remember any such statement being made? – I do not personally.

Now had you, sir, seen those three gentlemen, and heard the statement with reference to these ladies before you were called upon to express any opinion as the signing of the memorandum? – Yes, previous to the signing of the memorandum.

May I ask whether that paper was the suggestion of yourself, or of any one in which you acquiesced? – I acquiesced in the suggestion made by Lord Coventry and General Owen Williams.

The suggestion did not come from you? – No.

I need hardly ask you whether you were greatly distressed by the occurrence? – Yes.

Do you recollect, at the interview which Sir William Gordon-Cumming had with you, in the presence of General Williams and Lord Coventry, his asking you whether you could believe the statement, or something to that effect? – I do not think he asked me that question.

Do you recollect what you said with reference to the story of the witnesses when you heard it? – I have no distinct recollection.

Do you recollect whether Sir William made any reference to the Duke of Cambridge? – I am certain he did.

You are quite clear he did? – I am quite certain of it.

And upon his making that reference, did General Williams say anything? – He said he thought the authorities and the Duke of Cambridge would not have dealt so leniently in the matter as we did.

Did you desire to act in the circumstances of the case as leniently as you could to Sir William Gordon-Cumming? – Most certainly.

The date which appears on that paper was put there after it was signed – in point of fact, it came to you without signature? – The date was put on after it was signed. It was an omission on the part of Lord Coventry.

It was put on the same night? – Yes.

You have been asked whether you have been intimate with Sir William Gordon-Cumming. You have not met him since and have intimated to him that you cannot meet him? – [His Royal Highness was understood to say that it would be more agreeable for him not to do so, but the exact expression employed did not reach the reporters.]

One of the Jury: I should like to ask one question. Are this jury to understand that you as banker on these two occasions saw nothing of the alleged malpractices of the plaintiff?

His Royal Highness, turning to the jury-box, replied: No; it is not usual for a banker to see anything in dealing cards, especially when you are playing among friends in their house. You do not for a moment suspect one of anything of the sort.

The Juryman: What was your Royal Highness's opinion at the time as to the charges made against Sir William Gordon-Cumming?

His Royal Highness: The charges appeared to be so unanimous that it was the proper course, no other course was open to me, than to believe them.

The Solicitor-General: I take it that the answer to the first question is No!

At this point, the examination of the Prince of Wales having concluded, the Court adjourned for luncheon.

10 June 1891
The baccarat case
Verdict for the defendants

The Solicitor-General: I hope you will forgive me interposing. Your Lordship said in court with regard to that letter that a gentleman could not be asked whether he would have a letter of his read, because he could only give one answer to it.

The Lord Chief Justice: He could only give one answer, I agree. With regard to the interview between the plaintiff and Sir Berkeley Levett, Sir William Cumming was in a very painful position, and of course, if he could have got Mrs Arthur Wilson and the others to say, "Well, it was some time ago; we may have made a mistake; we are ready to say we have made a mistake," it was a very desirable thing to do. It would have been a complete answer and a happy end to the whole affair. As to Sir William Cumming sending for Mr Levett, a brother officer, I accept the plaintiff's view that it was a withdrawal, and not a softening, that he required. Who can complain and say the plaintiff was doing anything wrong? Not I. It is very far from being a strong fact against Sir William Cumming; it is the most natural thing in the world. Those were all the circumstances and all the facts of the case that I need say anything about except one, and of that I must say something. Sir Edward Clarke, in the course of his able speech, distinguished between his position as Solicitor-General and as an advocate. I do not. In the course of his speech he said the true solution of this, or nine-tenths of it, was to save the Prince of Wales. He said Royalty is great. He said Royalty has been the parent of the beautiful feeling called loyalty, and loyalty has led people to sacrifice everything for their King and for their Queen, and people lay down their lives for their kings and princes, and thus Sir William Gordon-Cumming came to sign this document to save the Prince of Wales. He put it much better than that but that is what he meant. It is no part of my duty to express an opinion or to presume to express any opinion upon the Prince of Wales or what effect this matter might have upon the estimation in which he is held. I am aware that a white light beats upon a throne, and a light pretty near as strong beats upon the Heir Apparent, and I am quite aware that a man may think in this country, where monarchs and the Royal family are so deeply bound up with traditions and interests of the country, that no sacrifice could be too great to maintain these institutions. I can understand that. What the life of the Prime of Wales is I neither know nor desire to know. What I know about the Prince of Wales, in the very slight acquaintance I have with him, is that he is a courteous gentleman. Beyond that I know nothing. I have not the honour of his intimacy. England is not only a free, but, if I may say so, a very censorious country, and the life of the Prince of Wales, like the life of almost any person of very high rank, but pre-eminently in his case, is subject for public comment and is matter of public knowledge. Where the Prince goes, what he does, how he spends his time are known, through the press and in a hundred other ways, to multitudes and multitudes of people who, perhaps, never saw him; and the acquaintances of the Prince of Wales are so many, and are spread through such different strata of society, that their knowledge, no doubt, filters down through the different layers of which our complicated society is made up, and there is scarcely any person who does not know, or who does not think he knows, something of the life and character of the Prince of Wales It is the penalty that very high rank has to pay for its existence. The Prince of Wales cannot be a private man if he wished it; the Queen could not be a private woman if she wished it. Her life is lived with her subjects' knowledge. Therefore the Prince of Wales is in a general way known first of all for his constant and admirable devotion to public duty – going here, and going there, opening this institution and that institution. For my own part, that might seem grievously boring, and intolerably depressing; but he goes through it like a man, and I daresay that, in a free country, if he spends the morning or afternoon in perhaps making one good speech and hearing a number of speeches which are not very good, he perhaps in the evening likes to enjoy himself. I do not that know that his Royal Highness would not take offence at my saying; but, remembering this fact – that he played baccarat with a number of distinguished people and without betting – if any one went on to say what that would be, I suppose the common opinion of hundreds of thousands of people, that he personally disapproved of the fact that the Prince in one large house introduced baccarat, and that he had played it for a couple of nights, I do not imagine it would have done much harm to the Monarchy or the Prince of Wales or anything else. Some people might say, "Why not read the Bible, or do some interesting and exalting occupation? That would make no real, substantial difference, and that anybody would think the worse of a hard-working man spending the evening in this way among his friends it would be hard to believe. I cannot help thinking that, even if it were otherwise, a man might accept many things. He might accept death, but he would not accept dishonour. Do you believe that an innocent man – a perfectly innocent man – would write down his name on a dishonouring document, on a document which, in fact, stated that he had cheated and taken money out of the pocket of the Prince of Wales by craft and sharping, simply that it might not be known that the Prince of Wales had played baccarat for very moderate stakes? Is not the consequence far too great for the cause? Is it not attributing far too much to this spirit – a good spirit in its way, a noble spirit, I frankly admit – is it not putting an incredible weight upon it to suppose that any gentleman in the circumstances would allow himself not to die but to be called a card-sharper and a cheat for the rest of his life, for fear it should be known that the Prince of Wales had done something of which many people would disapprove? I could quite understand a man giving up his all except his honour – but I cannot understand a man giving away all that life is valuable for and without which it is not worth while to live. You must judge of these acts and all that he has done exactly as you would judge the acts of any person, either in the middle or lower class of society. And now I send you to your duty. You have a very grave and a very important duty. You have sworn to perform it, as God shall help you, according to the truth. You must not, and you will not, I am sure, perform it in any other sense than the single, simple, unalloyed desire that truth and justice should prevail. You must remember that the consequences are not yours, but the duty is, and I send you to do your duty in the noble words of a great man many years gone – I divert them from his purpose to adapt them to this case – when you pass your judgment upon Sir William Gordon-Cumming I pray you recollect your own.

The jury retired at twenty-five minutes past three.

The jury returned after an absence of thirteen minutes, and, having taken their seats,

The Associate said: Gentlemen, are you agreed upon your verdict?

The Foreman: We are.

The Associate; Do you find for the plaintiff or for the defendants?

The Foreman: We find for the defendants.

The verdict was at first received with silence, but thereafter there was loud hissing, which the ushers failed to suppress.

Sir Charles Russell: Your Lordship will give judgment in accordance with the finding of the jury?

The Lord Chief Justice? – Yes.

The jury were then discharged, and the hissing was renewed, no attempt being made to stifle the demonstration.

The Court then adjourned.

A large crowd assembled outside the court, by whom the defendants on making their appearance in the corridor were greeted with hooting and hissing. On account of the pressure and the somewhat menacing demeanour of the assemblage the parties took refuge in leaving Mr Justice North's Court. On leaving later on the hooting and hissing were renewed by the portion of the crowd which had not dispersed.

The Press Association says that its representative interviewed one of the jurymen immediately he left the court, and that the latter stated that there was no doubt from the first moment the jury entered the private room how the verdict would go. As each juryman was asked whether he was for the plaintiff or the defendants, the reply was unhesitatingly given, "For the defendants," One of the jury who sympathised with the plaintiff was struck with the unanimity which prevailed, and, although he would have liked to have found for the plaintiff, he could not conscientiously do so in view of the evidence. It appeared to him that the jury had made up their minds before the summing-up of the Lord Chief Justice.

Edward VIII

"You all know the reasons which have impelled me to renounce the Throne."

Handsome, glamorous and blessed with a social conscience – famously he had been so horrified by the conditions he witnessed on a tour of South Wales that he exclaimed, "Something must be done" (although his sympathy didn't extend to the non-white members of his empire: he described Australian Aborigines as "the most revolting form of living creatures I've ever seen! They are the lowest known form of human beings and are the nearest thing to monkeys") – Edward VIII's reign began with great excitement. But his womanising and recklessness had long been a source of concern to the British Establishment – with dark prescience his father George V had predicted that, "After I am dead, the boy will ruin himself in twelve months."

The old king's sentiments were partly inspired by Edward's relationship with a racy American socialite – and divorcee – called Wallis Simpson. In November 1936 Edward conveyed to the Prime Minister Stanley Baldwin his desire to marry Simpson as soon as her circumstances allowed. The horrified Baldwin replied that the British people would find the idea morally repugnant and would never accept Simpson as their queen. Edward's subsequent suggestion that they could enter into a morganatic marriage (whereby their children would not inherit the throne) was also rejected.

Despite the efforts of Winston Churchill in support of Edward and a degree of sympathy from the public that surprised the Prime Minister (thanks to a compliant Press, the British people had previously been kept in the dark about the relationship), Baldwin held firm. Edward signed the instruments of abdication on 10 December, 1936, becoming in due course the Duke of Windsor. Much of the next thirty-five years of his life was spent in a kind of self-imposed exile, mostly in France; but even if absent in body, his actions – notably an incriminating entanglement with Nazi Germany – ensured he never receded entirely from public view. He died in 1972, Wallis Simpson survived him by another fourteen years.

12 December 1936
Edward VIII sails from England
"It may be some time before I return"

Edward VIII left England in the early hours of this morning in a Destroyer with another Destroyer as escort.

It is believed that he is bound for Italy, where Lord Grimthorpe has offered him the use of his villa at Ravello, near the Bay of Naples.

He left Fort Belvedere by car just before 11 p.m., after bidding farewell to his mother, Queen Mary, his sister, the Princess Royal, and his brothers, King George VI, the Duke of Gloucester and the Duke of Kent.

Shortly after midnight his car drove into Portsmouth Dockyard, and in great secrecy he embarked in the destroyer, which sailed at 1.45 a.m.

An hour before leaving Fort Belvedere King Edward broadcast his farewell message to his former subjects throughout Britain and the Empire. He said:

"Now that I have been succeeded by my brother, the Duke of York, my first words must be to declare my allegiance to him. This I do with all my heart.

"You must believe me when I tell you that I have found it impossible to carry this heavy burden of responsibility and to discharge my duties as King as I would wish to do without the help and support of the woman I love.

"I now quit altogether public affairs and I lay down my burden. It may be some time before I return to my native land."

He was introduced by Sir John Reith as "His Royal Highness, Prince Edward." It is understood, however, that this designation is unauthorised and that a new title will be bestowed upon him by King George VI. after the Proclamation ceremonies have been concluded to-day.

Before making his broadcast King Edward attended a farewell dinner party given by King George at Royal Lodge, Windsor. Other members of the Royal party were Queen Mary, the Duke of Gloucester, the Duke of Kent, the Princess Royal, Princess Alice Countess of Athlone, and the Earl of Athlone.

A few hours before this historic gathering – the only occasion in English history on which a reigning Sovereign and his predecessor have sat together at the same table – the Duke of York had formally ascended the Throne.

At 1.52 p.m. a Royal Commission, appointed by King Edward as his last Royal act, signified, in the House of Lords, his assent to the Abdication Bill.

Queen Mary last night issued a moving message to "The People of This Nation and Empire." In the course of this she said:

"I need not speak to you of the distress which fills a Mother's heart when I think that my dear son has deemed it to be his duty to lay down his charge.

"I know that you will realise what it has cost him to come to this decision; and that, remembering the years in which he tried so eagerly to serve and help his Country and Empire, you will ever keep a grateful remembrance of him in your hearts.

"I commend to you his brother, summoned so unexpectedly, and in circumstances so painful, to take his place.

"I ask you to give to him the same full measure of generous loyalty which you gave to my beloved husband, and which you would willingly have continued to give to his brother."

Also 12 December 1936
How King Edward spoke to the world
Alone beside fire in his old study
By our own correspondent

A farewell dinner party without parallel in British history was held at Windsor Royal Lodge to-night. It was given in honour of King Edward by King George VI.

It was the first time that he had acted as host since the accession. The guests were seven members of the Royal family. In addition to King Edward, the others were:

Queen Mary, the Duke of Gloucester, the Duke of Kent, the Princess Royal, Princess Alice Countess of Athlone and the Earl of Athlone.

King George and the Duke of Gloucester drove from London to Royal Lodge during the evening. Almost immediately they drove over to Fort Belvedere through Windsor Great Park and returned to Royal Lodge with King Edward and the Duke of Kent, who had been with him most of the day.

Shortly after eight p.m. Queen Mary arrived by road, accompanied by the Princess Royal, Princess Alice and the Earl of Athlone. Her car was about a quarter of an hour late, due to fog on the road from London.

Soon after 9.15 p.m. King Edward left the party to go to Windsor Castle to make his broadcast. He was driven to the Castle by a chauffeur.

King Edward was seated in the back, with his hat drawn over his eyes. He was wearing a light coat and a light coloured muffler.

He was driven up the Long Walk and entered by the Sovereign's Entrance at 9.40 p.m.

The car entered the quadrangle of Windsor Castle, and within a minute of King Edward's arrival two lights were switched on in the suite he formerly occupied as Prince of Wales in the Augusta Tower. He was received by the Master of the Household and B.B.C. officials, and then went to the Augusta Tower.

There King Edward sat alone in a swivel chair in a barely furnished room. Before him was a plain oaken table drawn up before the fire. On it was the microphone.

He had not used the room since he was Prince of Wales, when it was his favourite apartment at the Castle.

After the broadcast he chatted and said farewell to a number of the Castle officials and old servants.

He then left by the way he had come, the Sovereign's entrance, and on passing through the Cambridge Gate into the Park he was warmly cheered by a crowd of several hundred, which included many who were attending a dance close at hand.

Instead of covering his face, as he had done on the journey to the Castle, King Edward leaned forward in his seat and doffed his hat in reply to the loud cheers he received. His face was lit up by the headlights of cars, which, had stopped on the Windsor-Ascot road and the flashlights of photographers.

King Edward returned to Royal Lodge and remained there for a time with the King and Queen, Queen Mary, the Duke of Kent and the Duke of Gloucester, who had listened to the broadcast from there. Later he motored to Fort Belvedere before leaving for Portsmouth.

The rest of the Royal family then returned to London.

Also 12 December 1936
Late king's allegiance to the new
"If I can be of service in a private station"

King Edward made his broadcast from the Augusta Tower at Windsor Castle at ten o'clock last night. He was introduced by Sir John Reith, who said: "This is Windsor Castle: His Royal Highness Prince Edward." King Edward said:

At long last I am able to say a few words of my own. I have never wanted to withhold anything but, until now, it has not been constitutionally possible for me to speak.

A few hours ago I discharged my last duty as King and Emperor, and now that I have been succeeded by my brother, the Duke of York, my first words must be to declare my allegiance to him. This I do with all my heart.

You all know the reasons which have impelled me to renounce the Throne. But I want you to understand that, in making up my mind, I did not forget the country or the Empire which, as Prince of Wales and lately as King, I have for 25 years tried to serve.

But you must believe me when I tell you that I have found it impossible to carry the heavy burden of responsibility and discharge my duties as King as I would wish to do without the help and support of the woman I love.

And I want you to know that the decision I have made has been mine and mine alone. This was a thing I had to judge entirely for myself. The other person most nearly concerned has tried, up to the last, to persuade me to take a different course.

I have made this, the most serious decision of my life, only upon the single thought of what would, in the end, be best for all.

This decision has been made less difficult for me by the sure knowledge that my brother, with his long training in the public affairs of this country, and with his fine qualities, will be able to take my place forthwith without interruption or injury to the life and progress of the Empire.

He has one matchless blessing, enjoyed by so many of you and not bestowed on me, a happy home with his wife and children.

During these hard days I have been comforted by her Majesty, my Mother, and by my Family. Ministers of the Crown and, in particular, Mr Baldwin, the Prime Minister, have always treated me with full consideration.

There has never been any constitutional difference between me and them and between me and Parliament. Bred in the constitutional traditions by my Father, I should never have allowed any such issue to arise.

Ever since I was Prince of Wales and, later on, when I occupied the Throne, I have been treated with the greatest kindness by all classes of the people wherever I have lived or journeyed throughout the Empire.

For that I am very grateful. I now quit altogether public affairs and I lay down my burden.

It may be some time before I return to my native land, but I shall always follow the fortunes of the British race and Empire with profound interest and, if at any time in the future, I can be found of service to his Majesty in a private station I shall not fail.

And now we all have a new King. I wish him and you, his people, happiness and prosperity with all my heart.

God bless you all.

God save the King.

Enron

"If they are so profitable, why did they need all that borrowed money?"

In retrospect, the Enron scandal seems like a harbinger of the global financial crisis, which erupted seven years later. There was the same range of toxic debts, creative accounting and a reckless culture of corporate overreach, but few people bothered to learn any lessons from the collapse of the energy giant. The shock of Enron's financial struggles was compounded by the instigation of a criminal inquiry, and every piece of information that emerged only seemed to magnify the scandal's extent. It was, the *Telegraph* concluded, something of a modern morality tale. Eventually, both chairman Ken Lay and chief executive Jeff Skilling were convicted for conspiracy, fraud and insider trading. Lay died before sentencing, Skilling got 24 years and four months and a $45m penalty (later reduced). The former chief financial officer Andrew Fastow was sentenced to six years of jail time and Lou Pai, chief executive of the subsidiary Enron Accelerator, settled out of court for $31.5m.

3 December 2001
Enron files for Chapter 11 bankruptcy
By Dominic White

Enron, the US energy group, last night filed for Chapter 11 bankruptcy protection and hit former suitor Dynegy with a $10bn (£7.2bn) lawsuit for breach of contract.

The lawsuit accuses Dynegy of terminating an $8.4bn merger deal. Enron is also seeking to stop Dynegy from exercising its option over Enron's Northern natural gas pipeline, which is the main artery of its delivery system.

Ken Lay, Enron's chairman and chief executive, said: "While uncertainty during the past few weeks has severely impacted the market's confidence in Enron and its trading operations, we are taking the steps announced today to help preserve capital, stabilise our businesses, restore the confidence of our trading counterparties, and enhance our ability to pay our creditors."

He added that the company would implement "substantial workforce reductions".

The filing was announced as UK banks came under pressure to reveal their exposure to Enron, with Royal Bank of Scotland especially in the spotlight.

Weekend reports suggested that Royal Bank's gross exposure was as much as £600m, although City sources pointed yesterday to a figure closer to £300m. A spokesman for the bank refused to comment on the figures. "Of course we know what our exposure is," he said. "But it is a matter of commercial confidentiality between us and the company."

The Financial Services Authority is now attempting to establish the extent of all British banks' involvement with Houston-based Enron.

A spokesman for the FSA said: "If a bank feels it is going to have a material effect on profits, it might feel the need to make a statement."

Abbey National confessed on Friday that it had made a £95m provision against its £115m portfolio of bonds issued by Enron.

Barclays has been one of the largest arrangers of finance for Enron in recent years but is thought to have exposure of less than £50m as the majority of its loans were syndicated to other banks.

It is expected to clarify its position today in its bi-annual pre-closed-season trading update.

5 December 2001
Criminal inquiry started into Enron trading
By Simon English in New York and Sophie Barker in London

Enron's attempts to resurrect its business were dealt a fresh blow yesterday when it emerged the US Justice Department is opening a criminal investigation into the most dramatic corporate collapse in American history.

The Houston energy trader already faces an inquiry by the Securities and Exchange Commission and numerous lawsuits from investors and employees.

The Justice Department never comments publicly on investigations but is understood to be delving into Enron's unusual reporting practices.

The company has already admitted that financial reports going back several years were wrong, with profits overstated by $500m due to false assumptions about what would happen to trades that had not closed.

Former chief financial officer Andrew Fastow, who was ousted as the crisis unfolded, insisted through a lawyer yesterday that he is not responsible for Enron's woes. He has received death threats, claims his attorney.

Enron shares surged 53 to 93 cents yesterday as news that the company had secured a $1.5bn loan from JP Morgan and Citigroup reached the markets.

The money will allow Enron to keep operating as it tries to save the business under Chapter 11 bankruptcy protection.

The rise makes an opportunistic bid by little-known Standard Power & Light even less likely to succeed. Last Friday, Standard, which has 11 employees and revenue of $1.5m a year, said it wanted to buy Enron for under $1 a share. Wall Street is not taking the offer seriously.

There were further signs yesterday that tighter regulation of the energy market is now likely.

Congress's energy and commerce committee is meeting Enron executives on Thursday to begin an investigation into what the impact of the failure is on the nation's power markets.

Writing in the *Wall Street Journal* yesterday, Joe Berardino, the chief executive of Andersen, the Enron auditors also facing investigation, said accountancy rules are out of date.

"The current financial reporting system was created in the 1930s for the industrial age. That was a time when assets were tangible and investors were sophisticated and few," he wrote.

Meanwhile, Centrica stepped in to buy commercial energy supplier Enron Direct for £96.4m, marking the first stage in the break-up of Enron's European subsidiary.

The higher-than-expected price equates to £197 for each of Enron Direct's 160,000 customers. However, Centrica expects synergies from the deal to make its power stations more efficient.

8 December 2001

Enron chiefs face "insider trading" suit

By Simon English in New York

Embattled Enron executives face allegations that they engaged in insider trading in the months leading up to the collapse of the energy giant.

A lawsuit filed in a Houston court claims Enron directors artificially inflated the share price while netting $1.1bn (£800m) from offloading some of their own stakes in the business.

The lawsuit is filed on behalf of the Amalgamated Bank, which manages $4bn-worth of retirement funds, and accuses 29 executives including former chief executive Jeff Skilling and chairman Kenneth Lay of insider selling. Auditors Andersen are also cited a co-defendant.

Usually when investors win a settlement from a company that has exaggerated its profits, the auditors pay only a small percentage of the award.

Andersen, which had revenues of $9.3bn last year and 85,000 employees, declined to comment specifically on this case but insists the business is strong enough to withstand the crisis.

A spokesman said: "When there are problems in a company and questions are raised about the accounting, it is not unusual for the auditors to be brought into the litigation."

Auditors usually claim in such cases that they obeyed the law but were misled by management. Enron paid Andersen fees of more than $50m a year.

The energy company did not return calls yesterday.

Separately, Zurich Financial confirmed that it had an exposure to Enron of around $100m (£70m) in its investment portfolio, and said it would make provisions against this.

The portfolio owns about $90m of bonds issued by Enron and $10m in equity from the collapsed energy group.

The insurance group also has a minimal exposure of under $10m through a variety of insurance contracts.

French insurer AGF yesterday estimated its gross exposure to the collapsed energy group at under €45m (£28m).

Moody's also reaffirmed its long-term debt rating for JP Morgan Chase, one the lead bankers for Enron, at AA3 – its fourth highest grade.

The credit rating agency said JP Morgan's exposure to Enron was "manageable, given the company's strong and diversified stream of pre-tax income" and "strong base of common equity capital that exceeds $41bn".

Also 8 December 2001

Life was a gas for Enron's power dressers

Energetic and thrusting, Houston's power men rocketed to stardom but then fell to earth

By Simon English

Enron was a power company with a difference. Its Houston skyscraper headquarters was quite unlike those of the staid oil companies such as Shell and Texaco up the road.

The place bustled with young staff in hip clothes. They clearly enjoyed Enron's status as a darling of the stock market and believed the banner in the lobby that read "From The World's Leading Energy Company to . . . The World's Leading Company".

It must have seemed possible. Enron had transformed itself from a sleepy gas company engaged in the dull business of finding energy in the ground and sending it down pipelines. It had become an internet trading giant, seventh in the Fortune 500, with revenues of $100bn and executives who were cocky, very rich and friends with President George Dubbya.

It had come so far, that becoming the world's leading company looked an easy challenge. Since the then chief executive Kenneth Lay hired Jeff Skilling 16 years ago, Enron had been transformed. Skilling was an innovator and a daredevil who approached business the same way he approached leisure. Lay wanted him to shake up the power markets after lobbying so hard to free them from regulation, and today, nobody can say that Skilling failed in his mission.

His corporate adventure junkets were said to be so wild that staff feared that someone would get killed. While rivals worried about gas shortages, Skilling, on the back of a one-page presentation to executives, turned Enron into a bank rather than a supplier. It would guarantee the supply and price of gas to its customers by buying and selling the gas itself. Enron, rather than its customers, would shoulder the risks.

It signed contracts with buyers and sellers, keeping the prices secret and making money on the difference between the two. From there it was a short step to financial contracts linked to the gas supply. Suppliers could hedge against moves in interest rates or the inability of a customer to pay.

If it worked for gas, it would work for all sorts of other things; paper, steel, broadband capacity, the weather. A wine bar that reasoned customers drank more in hot weather became an Enron customer by buying a hedge against a cold snap. There seemed to be no limits.

By inventing new markets and dominating them before lawmakers or regulators even knew what was going on, Enron could make fat profits. It even extended the same principle to its accounting practices. It estimated how much money it would make from a deal over several years, and booked the whole lot in year one.

While there is no evidence yet of fraud or other illegal activity, the books, if not cooked, were certainly warmed.

Expansion continued. Entrepreneurs with risky ventures knew that waiting for a traditional bank to approve a loan could mean a missed opportunity. So they borrowed from Enron instead. If the burgeoning corporation laid off any of these risks with other lenders, it never said so.

Staff who couldn't cope or who expressed concern were forced out. The brightest and hungriest were hired from Harvard alongside leading mathematicians, physicists, even an astronaut.

One rival to Skilling, Rebecca Mark, was given her own business and told to go off and dominate the water market. The new business, Azurix, raised $695m on flotation in 1999 but went wrong almost immediately. Governments and consumers take water more seriously than they do gas and Enron's approach scared them. The shares of Azurix plunged and Mark was out.

Last February, as the first cracks in the Enron structure started to appear, Skilling took over as chief executive from Kenneth Lay, who became chairman.

The shares fell from $80 to $50 by March and the directors had joined the sellers. Lay has sold $100m-worth in the past three years, former chief financial officer Andrew Fastow $30m, Skilling $67m.

These share sales had to be disclosed, but much else wasn't. There was a culture of secrecy, and one analyst who questioned the accuracy of the balance sheet was called an "asshole" by Skilling, who assured the fans that new money-making schemes were round the corner. While they were waiting to see what they were, Skilling shocked them all; the workaholic thrill-seeker quit, saying that life was short and that he missed his children.

One of those schemes has turned out to be trading data transmission capacity on fibre optic cables. Enron borrowed $1bn for this venture and hid the debt behind private partnerships run by Fastow. They traded with Enron but their finances were separate.

The descriptions of these businesses in filings to the SEC defy comprehension. They were called "share settled costless collar arrangements" or "derivative instruments which eliminate the contingent nature of existing restricted forward contracts".

Even Lay seemed confused, telling reporters who asked him about these arrangements "You're getting way over my head". By then, Enron had 3,500 subsidiaries, which would allow a full-time chairman just an hour a year to look at them.

Yet still no one asked the question posed belatedly by Rob Plaza of MorningStar. com: "If they are so profitable, why did they need all that borrowed money?"

When the Wall Street Journal began delving into the offshoots, and the company reduced the value of its own equity by $1.2bn, Fastow was quickly ousted. Trading partners became nervous, the shares fell and kept on falling. By the time a rescue deal from rival traders Dynegy was put forward, the stock was in the junk yard.

Even that collapsed when Enron suddenly admitted to a $690m debt that had to be paid immediately.

Dynegy chief executive Chuck Watson recalled: "We were renegotiating daily because every time I turned around the stock price was falling. It got to the point where there was hardly any equity left in the business."

The debt is now $40bn and Enron is a shambles, trying to salvage something from the wreckage under Chapter 11 bankruptcy protection. Staff have lost their jobs and most of their retirement savings. Criminal and government investigations have begun.

No one emerges with credit from the shabby affair.

The accountants, rather than the analysts that usually take the blame, are the focus of most criticism. Some lawmakers want a scalp – the head of someone at auditors Andersen, paid $1m a week by Enron, would do.

Securities & Exchange Commission chairman Harvey Pitt is among those whose conflicts of interest are being questioned. As a former securities lawyer, he had represented each of the Big Five accountancy firms in his time and was trying to forge a gentler relationship with the profession.

"Somewhere along the way, accountants became afraid to talk to the SEC and the SEC appeared to be unwilling to listen to the profession. Those days are ended," he said in a speech in October.

For their part, accountants have already closed ranks. They blame outdated financial reporting laws for their failure to spot the crisis.

The Bush administration, perhaps grateful for the distraction of Afghanistan, has been silent on what is possibly the greatest American financial scandal ever.

The President received hefty donations from Enron and Lay was the only executive granted a private interview with Dick Cheney when the vice-president was working out energy policy.

John Dingell, of the House Energy Committee, spoke for many when he asked: "Where was the SEC? Where was the Financial Accounting Standards Board? Where was Enron's audit committee? Where were the accountants? Where were the lawyers? Where were the investment bankers? Where were the analysts? Where was the common sense?"

The Expenses Scandal

"Price includes three anchor blocks, duck house and island."

A year before the expenses scandal broke, a Freedom of Information request, granted by an Information Tribunal, had been blocked by the House of Commons authorities. It was, they said, "unlawfully intrusive". Nevertheless, after the High Court ruled in favour of releasing the information the House of Commons authorities had committed to the principle of publishing the expenses, albeit with the more "sensitive" material removed. Before this could be set in motion, however, the records were leaked in full to the *Telegraph*. Two of the more outré expenses claims are included below. The scandal ended the careers of a number of politicians, with some choosing to fall on their own sword, and others waiting to be pushed. However in the long term it has undeniably contributed to the public's increasing distrust of politicians, and disillusionment with the political system as a whole. In the general election of 2010, only 65.1 per cent of the British population bothered to vote.

8 May 2009
The truth about the Cabinet's expenses
The Prime Minister Brown paid his brother more
than £6,000 for "cleaning services"

More than half the Cabinet are facing allegations over their use of Parliamentary expenses after details of their claims were obtained by the *Daily Telegraph*.

They include Gordon Brown, who paid his brother for "cleaning services" at his private flat in Westminster.

Jack Straw, the Justice Secretary, admitted yesterday that he had over-claimed for both his council tax and mortgage bills.

The disclosures show the scale of ministers' claims and the extent to which politicians have exploited the expenses system to subsidise their lifestyles.

The Prime Minister is among 13 members of the Cabinet facing questions over their use of Parliamentary expenses. Yesterday, after being approached by the *Daily Telegraph*, Mr Brown repaid a plumbing bill he had claimed for twice during 2006.

Receipts submitted by the Prime Minister to the Parliamentary authorities disclosed that between 2004 and 2006, he paid Andrew Brown for cleaning at his flat. Andrew Brown, a senior executive at EDF Energy, received £6,577 over 26 months. Last night, the Prime Minister's office said he shared a cleaner with his brother. In a statement, No 10 said Mr Brown "reimbursed him [the brother] for his share of the cost".

The statement is likely to give rise to questions as to why the Prime Minister did not simply lodge receipts directly from the cleaner. He has directly employed other cleaners.

However, the payments to Andrew Brown would not have been disclosed under controversial laws allowing the personal information to be blacked out from the publicly released documents.

The disclosure of the expenses of the Cabinet raises questions about the parliamentary expenses system, coming within weeks of disclosures over questionable claims made by Jacqui Smith, the Home Secretary.

This summer, MPs are due to publish a detailed breakdown of claims. However, the *Daily Telegraph* begins a series of articles today that detail the scandal of members' expenses across all parties. Many of the claims go beyond what members of the public would find acceptable.

The disclosures underline the need for urgent reform of the system amid fears that the spending of taxpayers' money was not being appropriately monitored.

It can be disclosed that: Jack Straw, the Justice Secretary, received a 50 per cent discount on his council tax from his local authority but claimed the full amount. He discovered the "mistake" last summer within weeks of the High Court ordering that MPs release details of their expenses. He has repaid the money. Lord Mandelson, the Business Secretary, claimed thousands of pounds to improve his constituency home after he had announced his resignation as an MP. He sold the property for a profit of £136,000.

Hazel Blears, the Communities Secretary, claimed for three different properties in a single year. She spent almost £5,000 on furniture in three months after buying the third flat in an upmarket area of London.

David Miliband, the Foreign Secretary, spent hundreds of pounds on gardening at his constituency home – leading his gardener to question whether it was necessary to spend the money on pot plants "given [the] relatively short time you'll be here".

Alistair Darling, the Chancellor, changed his official "second home" designation four times in four years.

Geoff Hoon, the Transport Secretary, also switched his second home, which allowed him to extensively improve his family home in Derbyshire before buying a London town house also funded by the taxpayer.

Andy Burnham, the Culture Secretary, Caroline Flint, the Minister for Europe and Paul Murphy, the Welsh Secretary, also bought flats – or the freehold on a property they already owned – and claimed stamp duty and other moving costs. Mr Burnham warned the Parliamentary authorities that his wife might divorce him if expenses were not paid promptly.

In a statement issued last night, Downing Street defended Mr Brown's claims. The statement said: "At all times the Prime Minister has acted with the full approval of the parliamentary authorities. In relation to the cleaning services, Mr Gordon Brown and Mr Andrew Brown employed one cleaner who worked for both of them, the majority of time for Gordon Brown.

"Payment was made directly to her by Mr Andrew Brown for the work in both flats. Mr Gordon Brown reimbursed him for his share of the cost. Of course, Mr Andrew Brown did not receive any financial benefit." Several senior ministers were repeatedly warned by the parliamentary authorities and had claims rejected or withheld.

This newspaper uncovered evidence suggesting that the second homes allowance, which allows annual claims of up to £24,222, has been exploited by dozens of MPs and is in need of immediate reform. In many cases, the House of Commons fees office uncovered serious wrongdoing but the MPs implicated were not independently investigated.

The rules governing the Parliamentary expenses system are notoriously lax and difficult to interpret. The main principle is that the second home must be "wholly, exclusively and necessarily incurred from the purpose of performing your Parliamentary duties".

Some Cabinet ministers appear to have far more straightforward claims than those highlighted today.

Ed Miliband, the Energy and Climate Secretary, claimed only £6,300 a year in rent for a modest home in his constituency. He also claimed utility and council tax bills. Alan Johnson, the Health Secretary, claimed for only his constituency home over the past four years. He also rented a modest property but claimed for food and some furniture. Hilary Benn, the Environment Secretary, claimed only £147.78 in food.

12 May 2009
Clearing the moat at viscount's manor
Douglas Hogg
By Rosa Prince

A former Conservative Cabinet minister included with his expenses claims the cost of having the moat cleared, piano tuned and stable lights fixed at his country manor house on his second home allowance.

Douglas Hogg, Viscount Hailsham and a former agriculture minister, also employed a full-time gardener and " lady", who had a salary package of £14,000 a year to keep house at the estate, parts of which date back to the 13th century.

Among the MP's claims on the house in Lincolnshire, which includes a lodge and outhouses and on which he had no mortgage, were bills for a "mole man", the cost of running his housekeeper's car and a £31 call-out to have bees removed.

His expenses were so extensive that in 2004 he negotiated a special deal with the Commons fees office, which for several years automatically paid him a 12th of the annual allowance each month. In correspondence with officials, the Eton-educated barrister claimed this was necessary as the running costs of his estate were "greatly" in excess of the maximum permitted under MPs' second home allowances, adding: "It will certainly make my life a lot easier." At one stage, Mr Hogg sent a 10-page letter detailing the costs of running his estate over the previous three years.

He explained that he was not claiming for all of the sums involved, adding: "Whilst some items may be disputable as to whether they do or do not fall within the allowance, I would suggest that it is certain that allowable expenditure exceeds the allowance by a sizeable margin and consequently we need not spend too much time on debate." Among the expenditure was nearly £18,000 paid to his gardener, a separate bill of almost £1,000 to have the lawn mowed regularly, and £671.17 for a mole catcher.

He also paid £4,488.48 for "machines and fuel", including a new lawnmower, between £200 and £300 a month for "oil and coal", insurance costs, phone bills, and thousands of in repairs, including £2,115 to have the moat cleared, and £93.41 for tongs.

Also itemised were £40 for piano tuning, £646.25 for "general repairs, stable, etc" and around £200 a year for maintenance to his Aga. His council tax bill for the Band H home came to £2,444.32 in the financial year 2005–06.

After an exchange with the fees office, Mr Hogg agreed to pick up 35 per cent of the housekeeper's salary.

Mr Hogg defended his use of the Additional Costs Allowance yesterday, saying that it was necessary to employ a "lady" and gardener to run the manor house while he and his wife Sarah, a life peer, were in their London town house.

He added that he had acted within "both the letter and the spirit" of the rules while being paid more than £20,000 annually to run the estate.

Mr Hogg's home was featured in the 1954 novel *Katherine*, by Anya Seaton; the Victorian house contains remnants of the original, medieval manor where previous occupants include a sister-in-law of Geoffrey Chaucer; Margaret Beaufort, grandmother of Henry VIII; and Joan Beaufort, grandmother of Richard III.

Mr Hogg's complicated financial arrangements seemed to have caused something of a headache for officials in the fees office.

While his claims were initially allowed by senior officials, later attempts to implement a tougher regime were opposed by the MP.

Asked to provide receipts, he responded, saying that his agreement meant documentation was not necessary.

In December 2003, he wrote: "I am writing this formal letter in the hope that we can resolve this matter by the end of next week.

"I have received the letter dated 4 September 2003 and the pro forma rejection of my October claim dated 20 November 2003 (which was more than a little surprising . . .) I hope that you will agree that the matter cannot be left outstanding for any longer. I would be surprised if any other Member has provided fuller documentary evidence.

"These sums are significant and in the absence of some good and compelling reason I suggest that they should be paid without further delay." Eighteen months later, when the system was queried again, he wrote: "Might I suggest that we continue with the present system. It is a system that was positively suggested by the Fees Office. It is to everybody's convenience.

"I am happy to let you have the supporting documents but to do it in a monthly way as you suggest was positively declined by your colleagues and I was happy to welcome their suggestion."

A week later, he sent a follow-up letter which read: "I very much hope that you will agree that because of the nature of these expenses and because of pre-existing agreements and because of the essential facts and the underlying documentation you will agree to continue the monthly payments which we have previously agreed on.

"It is much more convenient for me. It is much more convenient for you and, as you will see, claims are fully documented."

In 2008, after finally agreeing to submit receipts, his expenses exceeded the maximum allowed under the ACA, but the fees office accidentally paid them in full.

Once this was spotted, he repaid £1,517.

Also in 2008, Mr Hogg moved his second home designation to London, where his costs fell dramatically. Cleaning costs alone fell from £1,213 to £40 a month.

Mr Hogg, who represents Sleaford and North Hykeham, is the son of Lord Hailsham, the former Lord Chancellor. His grandfather also served as Lord Chancellor.

As John Major's agriculture minister between 1995 and 1997, he was criticised for his response to the BSE crisis.

Mr Hogg told the *Daily Telegraph*: "Turning to my own ACA claims; they were the subject of prior consultation with the fees office and I therefore hope and believe that they comply with both the letter and the spirit of the rules.

"I say this with some confidence because as long ago as March 2003 I checked them with the then head of the fees office – both as to the identity of the property in respect of which I was making the claim and as to the expenses themselves – thereafter the fees office has been given all the information that they require and in particular has been kept fully informed of all the expenditure incurred on the property.

"With the agreement of the fees office and reflecting the fact that my allowable expenses exceeded the ACA (a fact which I demonstrated and they accepted and have never questioned) the monthly claim was made on the basis of one twelfth of the allowance.

"It was initially at the suggestion of the Fees Office and subsequently confirmed that I did not submit monthly receipts but rather supplied them with full particulars at the end of the financial year.

"For most of the working week my wife and I are in London.

"We therefore employ a lady to look after the house in Lincolnshire and for similar reasons we pay for the cost of maintaining the garden.

"There are of course other substantial costs involved in running the Lincolnshire property."

21 May 2009
£30,000 for the garden, including the ducks bill
Sir Peter Viggers
By Nick Allen

A Tory grandee included with his expense claims the £1,645 cost of a floating duck island in the garden pond at his Hampshire home.

Sir Peter Viggers, the MP for Gosport, submitted an invoice for a "Stockholm" duck house to the Commons fees office.

The floating structure, which is almost 5ft high and is designed to provide protection for the birds, is based on an 18th-century building in Sweden. The receipt, from a firm specialising in bird pavilions, said: "Price includes three anchor blocks, duck house and island." It was announced last night that following the *Daily Telegraph*'s disclosures, Sir Peter will retire at the next election.

Sir Peter, a qualified jet pilot, lawyer and banker, has been an MP for 25 years and is a member of the Treasury select committee. He lists his recreations in *Who's Who* as opera, travel and trees.

His expenses files reveal that he was paid more than £30,000 of taxpayers' money for "gardening" over three years, including nearly £500 for 28 tons of manure.

He had a similar arrangement with the fees office to Douglas Hogg, submitting an annual list of the costs of maintaining his second home and then dividing them across the year for monthly payments.

Mr Hogg, who has said he will stand down at the next election, included with his expenses the cost of having a moat cleared.

Sir Peter included his duck island. His handwritten list of spending for the financial year 2006–07 amounted to £33,747.19 and included "pond feature £1,645".

In March 2007 he submitted a single claim of £18,522.59 for the final seven months of the financial year, noting that he understood it would be "limited by the annual maximum". The fees office reduced the claim to £10,769.94 accordingly.

It was unclear whether he received money specifically for the duck island. A fees officer scrawled "not allowable" next to it. Sir Peter also submitted a £213.95 electrician's bill including fixing lights on a "fountain" and "hanging lights on Christmas tree". The year before, the annual costs Sir Peter had submitted came to £24,164.96.

He asked for part of that to be paid under a separate office costs allowance.

They included £6,960 on gardening, £1,800 on grass cutting and estate management, £533.23 on garden design, £460 on pest control, and £250 on irrigation.

He submitted "sample invoices" of £782.50 and £750.

In February 2007 officials wrote to Sir Peter asking him to submit claims based on "actual costs" per month. In 2007–08, the costs of maintaining his second home rose to £36,158.93 including £19,000 on gardening and £3,275 for roof and chimney repairs.

He reached the maximum allowed by December 2007.

Sir Peter was educated at Cambridge and served as an industry minister under Margaret Thatcher. He owns a flat in central London and sold his second home last year for £800,000.

In a statement before his retirement was announced, Sir Peter said: "The claims I made were in accordance with the rules, and were all approved by the fees office.

Since then the situation has changed and we must all take account of that.

"My expenses are being examined by David Cameron's scrutiny panel and I await any recommendations they may make." Mr Cameron has made clear that any "excessive" amounts claimed by MPs will have to be paid back.

FIFA

"All World Cups can have a bad smell."

For many years, football's governing body FIFA had been dogged by accusations of profound corruption. The organisation's excesses seemed to be embodied by its preposterous and crass Swiss president, Sepp Blatter, who was as gifted at attracting unwanted attention as he was at riding out the furore that would inevitably follow each of his outrages. At the 2014 World Cup he interrupted a one-minute silence for Nelson Mandela after just 11 seconds; he suggested women's football might be improved as a spectacle if they wore tighter shorts. He and the empire over which he presided smiled through countless allegations of fraud and financial malpractice, until finally an FBI investigation ended his reign of impunity.

28 May 2015
FIFA chief Blatter faces questioning over "deep-rooted corruption"
"Kickbacks and sleaze became a way of doing business at FIFA"
By Claire Newell, Edward Malnick and Luke Heighton

Sepp Blatter, the head of FIFA, could be interviewed "within weeks" as part of a corruption investigation that engulfed football's governing body last night.

Fourteen officials and executives were arrested at the request of the FBI yesterday, some in Zurich, over bribes totalling $150m. FIFA was accused of "rampant, systemic and deep-rooted" corruption.

Mr Blatter, the FIFA president, was warned he could be questioned by the office of the Swiss attorney general. It is conducting its own inquiry into alleged vote-rigging over the Qatar World Cup bid.

The escalation of that inquiry came as the FBI claimed it had uncovered 24 years of "brazen corruption . . . undisclosed illegal payments, kickbacks and bribes" by FIFA officials. The American inquiry alleges that votes for the award of the 2010 World Cup – ultimately given to South Africa – were bought with bribes. In what was labelled the darkest day in the body's history: FIFA was accused of running a "World Cup of fraud" by the head of the IRS Criminal Investigation division.

The FBI said that the "beautiful game" had been "hijacked" by corruption.

Swiss authorities announced that they had opened a criminal inquiry into the 2018 and 2022 World Cup decisions.

US authorities claimed that "bribes and kickbacks" were paid in the awarding of the 2010 World Cup and the 2011 presidential election which was won by Mr Blatter.

Jack Warner, the former FIFA vice president who stepped down in 2011 following corruption allegations, was accused of receiving $10m in bribes.

The revelations came days before votes are due to be cast in the 2015 FIFA presidential election and will bolster calls for the organisation to be reformed and for the 2018 and 2022 votes, won by Russia and Qatar, to be rerun.

Last night, UEFA called for the presidential election to be postponed.

Damian Collins, the Conservative MP for Folkestone and Hythe who has campaigned against corruption in FIFA, said that there was "no question" that the 2018 and 2022 decisions should be rerun. "It's staggering that FIFA is ignoring calls for the votes to be rerun," said Mr Collins. "Several of the individuals involved in making the decision have resigned because of corruption charges and the words from the Department of Justice could not be more damning.

"One former executive committee member has pleaded guilty to criminal offences. Did FIFA know what was happening?" FIFA has faced many corruption allegations in recent years, including over the decision to award the 2022 competition to Qatar.

But the events this week will add to pressure on the president of world football's governing body. There are currently two criminal investigations into FIFA. Yesterday, Swiss police arrested several of its officials at the five-star Baur au Lac hotel in Zurich where they had gathered in preparation for Friday's vote.

The men arrested there included Jeffrey Webb, the head of the Confederation of North, Central America and Caribbean Association Football (Concacaf) and FIFA vice-president and Costa Rica's national football chief Eduardo Li, who was expected to join FIFA's executive committee on Friday.

Eugenic Fugueredo, of Uruguay, the president of South American football's governing body, Conmebol, was also held by Swiss police, as was Rafael Esquivel, the president of the Venezuelan Football Federation.

They were joined by executive committee member Jose Maria Marin, from Brazil, FIFA development officer Julio Rocha of Nicaragua, and the UK's Costas Takkas, an attaché to the president of Concacaf.

Mr Warner gave himself up to police in Trinidad last night and was expected to face an extradition hearing.

The indictment claims that Mr Warner, who was vice president of FIFA until 2011, accepted $10m from the government of South Africa to secure his vote. His two sons have pleaded guilty to charges of wire fraud conspiracy and structuring of financial transactions. It is understood that at least one of the sons was helping the FBI with their investigation.

During a press conference, Kelly Currie, acting US attorney for the eastern district of New York, where the charges were brought yesterday, said that they were "issuing FIFA a red card".

"Today's announcement should send a message that enough is enough," he said.

"After decades of what the indictment alleges to be brazen corruption, organised international soccer needs a new start – a new chance for its governing institutions to provide honest oversight and support of a sport that is beloved across the world, increasingly so here in the United States."

James Comey, the director of the FBI, added: "Undisclosed and illegal payments, kickbacks and bribes became a way of doing business at FIFA."

Loretta Lynch, the US attorney general, said that the corruption "spans at least two generations of soccer officials who . . . have abused their positions of trust to acquire millions of dollars in bribes and kickbacks."

A spokesman for the office of the Swiss attorney general said that FIFA's president "could be questioned in the coming weeks" and that every person who had participated in World Cup votes could be interviewed as part of their inquiry.

In a statement, Mr Blatter said: "Today's action by the Swiss office of the attorney general was set in motion when we submitted a dossier to the Swiss authorities late last year. Let me be clear: such misconduct has no place in football and we will ensure that those who engage in it are put out of the game."

He added: "We welcome the actions and the investigations by the US and Swiss authorities and believe that it will help to reinforce measures that FIFA has already taken to root out any wrongdoing in football."

4 December 2015
FIFA plunged into fresh turmoil as 16 more charged
Vice-presidents Napout and Hawit are arrested

The brazen corruption within FIFA was shown to have plumbed staggering new depths last night after another 16 people were charged with committing a $200m (£133m) fraud in sport's biggest ever scandal.

Football's beleaguered world governing body was back in full crisis mode yesterday when the FBI orchestrated the arrest and indictment of more of its most senior officials following another dawn raid on their hotel rooms as they were preparing to unveil reforms designed to clean up the organisation.

Swiss police staged a repeat of May's swoop on FIFA's luxury Zurich accommodation by arresting two more of its vice-presidents, who were among several high-ranking officials charged by the United States Department of Justice with taking bribes related to the award of television and marketing rights for World Cup and other matches.

Juan Ángel Napout, the president of the South American Football Confederation, and Alfredo Hawit, the head of the North, Central American and Caribbean Confederation, were seized in a raid carried out at 6 a.m. local time at almost the same time as those conducted six months earlier.

That was followed last night by the unsealing of a fresh string of indictments in Washington by America's Attorney General, Loretta Lynch, who branded the level of corruption as "outrageous" and "unconscionable" after huge sums of money destined for disaster relief and development projects were found to have been among that which was embezzled.

Napout and Hawit were named last night in a 236-page DOJ indictment along with 14 other men, including Brazilian former FIFA executive committee members Ricardo Teixeira and Marco Polo Del Nero and Rafael Salguero from Guatemala, who stand accused of a fraud in excess of £133m. That is a third more than the $150m (£100m) alleged to have been taken in the original indictment, which was against 18 individuals.

Three of those were revealed to have pleaded guilty yesterday, including former FIFA vice-president Jeffrey Webb, arguably the most senior of all the men charged having been tipped as the heir apparent to Sepp Blatter. Five more men effectively turned themselves in, including another FIFA executive committee member, Luis Bedoya, taking to 11 the number charged or convicted by the DOJ – an entire football team.

Napout and Hawit were last night fighting extradition to the US, joining several other officials still resisting following their arrest in May. The most shocking detail in the new indictment surrounded Webb and disgraced former FIFA vice-president Jack Warner, who were among those charged six months ago.

The indictment states that they "embezzled or otherwise personally appropriated funds provided by FIFA, including funds intended for natural disaster relief". It was the first official confirmation of allegations that Warner diverted $750,000 (£495,000) in emergency funds donated by FIFA and the Korean Football Association intended for victims of the 2010 Haiti earthquake. He is fighting extradition from Trinidad to the US.

Lynch told a news conference in Washington DC: "The betrayal of trust that is set forth here is truly outrageous, and the scale of corruption alleged herein is unconscionable." Among those charged were members of FIFA's disciplinary and audit and compliance committees, which are meant to police wrongdoing in the game.

Incredibly, the new indictment also details illegal activity alleged to have taken place since May's first wave of arrests, including attempts at covering it up. Hinting at even more action to come, Lynch warned other corrupt officials: "The message of this announcement should be clear to every culpable individual who remains in the shadows, hoping to evade this investigation. You will not wait it out and you will not escape our focus."

Lynch would not be drawn on criticism of the US investigation by suspended FIFA president Blatter, who has repeatedly claimed it was motivated by sour grapes over the country's failure to land the 2026 World Cup. Blatter is facing criminal proceedings in Switzerland over a £1.3m payment to Michel Platini, with both men also facing life bans by FIFA's ethics committee.

The timing of the charges could hardly have been worse for the governing body, which had chosen yesterday to trumpet reforms agreed in the wake of May's meltdown.

Fernando Sarney, the latest Brazilian on its executive committee, said of the mood at yesterday's meeting: "It was like someone had died, that was the atmosphere inside. The feeling was like, 'It's happening again', that it's something we think is personal. It was supposed to be a positive day today with the reforms."

Those reforms were unanimously approved by shell-shocked executives, who put them forward for ratification – pending an independent assessment to satisfy FIFA sponsors – at February's congress. They included the rebranding and expansion of the executive committee into a partially neutered 37-strong FIFA council, service on which would be limited to 12 years and that would feature a minimum of six female members.

Each councillor will be required to pass centralised integrity checks and disclose their remuneration.

Speaking after a press conference to present the reforms, British vice-president David Gill hailed them as "very well thought out" and "very much a step in the right direction".

But FIFA's commitment to transparency did not extend to its acting secretary general Markus Kattner explaining why he signed off on a £1.3m payment by Blatter to Platini, which is the subject of a criminal investigation and an ethics probe in which both face being banned for life.

Acting president Issa Hayatou being presented as one of the faces of reform also jarred considering he was reprimanded by the International Olympic Association in 2011 over allegations that he took bribes and was also named in parliament as having been paid to vote for Qatar to stage the 2022 World Cup.

Hayatou, who appeared to nod off during yesterday's press conference, said: "I would not be here if I was corrupt."

Kattner said FIFA's plan was to be "recognised as a modern, trusted, professional organisation" within three years.

22 December 2015
Blatter and Platini defiant in face of eight-year bans
Game's leaders are cast out over £1.3m payment

Sepp Blatter and Michel Platini's reigns as the two most powerful men in football drew towards the most humiliating and bitter conclusion last night after they were banned from the game for eight years.

Blatter claimed he had been "killed" and "betrayed" by the ethics committee he had established and Platini branded the suspensions "a mockery" as the presidents of FIFA and UEFA were cast out of the sport over a £1.3m payment that is also the subject of a criminal investigation.

Four of the world governing body's ethics judges found insufficient evidence to prove the transaction was intended as a bribe by Blatter to secure Platini's support at its 2011 presidential election. But it still convicted the pair of offering or accepting gifts, conflict of interest and of violating their fiduciary duties, fining Blatter 50,000 Swiss francs (£33,700) and Platini 80,000 Swiss francs (£54,000) on top of their suspensions.

Yesterday morning's verdicts were widely expected and both men had already vowed to fight them to the bitter end, with a succession of appeals set to follow. Blatter confirmed as much yesterday, during an extraordinary press conference in which the man who has led FIFA for 17 scandal-plagued years defiantly signed off with the catchphrase from the film The Terminator. "I'll be back," proclaimed the 79 year old, sporting a plaster on his face following the removal of a blemish.

Blatter commandeered FIFA's former headquarters in Zurich for his news conference, declaring he would contest his guilty verdict at its appeals committee, the Court of Arbitration for Sport and even the Swiss federal court.

He told a packed conference: "I will fight for me and I will fight for FIFA. Suspended for eight years? For what? I am sorry that I am a punching ball. I am sorry that, as president of FIFA, I am this punching ball. I am sorry for football. I am sorry for the 400-plus FIFA team members. I'm sorry about that. I am also sorry about me and about how I am treated in this world of humanitarian qualities."

Blatter – FIFA president since 1998 and general secretary for two decades before that – claimed he had almost died after collapsing last month, adding: "They tried to kill me now. But I was safe till the last minute. I was nearly there."

The Swiss's reign has been beset by scandal, with several of his most senior lieutenants convicted of corruption and more likely to follow amid widening investigations by United States and Swiss law enforcement.

FIFA's process for awarding World Cups has come under particular scrutiny and Blatter made a remarkable admission yesterday when he told *Sky News*: "All World Cups can have a bad smell." He added: "World Cups are not bought or sold. World Cups are given on merit. All World Cups I have been in, now it's always political intervention that have made the difference between one or the other. The World Cup smells of the political intervention. You cannot stop them."

Platini confirmed he, too, would appeal to CAS and take legal action for damages. He said in a statement: "The FIFA ethics commission's procedure against me is a true mockery. It was orchestrated to tarnish my reputation. I'm convinced that my fate was decided before the 18 December hearing and that this decision is just a pathetic manoeuvre to hide a true will of taking me out of the football world."

Blatter and Platini both claimed the £1.3m payment which led to their downfall was made following a verbal agreement between them when the Frenchman was recruited to work for the FIFA president between 1998 and 2002. It was not paid until nine years later, shortly before Platini mandated UEFA members to re-elect Blatter.

The duo's explanation for the transaction was branded "not convincing" by the ethics committee.

A statement from the ethics committee said: "Mr Blatter's actions did not show commitment to an ethical attitude, failing to respect all applicable laws and regulations as well as FIFA's regulatory framework to the extent applicable to him and demonstrating an abusive execution of his position as president of FIFA, hence violating article 13 of the FCE (general rules of conduct)."

It added: "Mr Platini failed to act with complete credibility and integrity, showing unawareness of the importance of his duties and concomitant obligations and responsibilities. His actions did not show commitment to an ethical attitude, failing to respect all applicable laws and regulations as well as FIFA's regulatory framework to the extent applicable to him and demonstrating an abusive execution of his position as vice-president of FIFA and member of the FIFA executive committee."

Platini's hopes of succeeding Blatter as FIFA president at February's election have been effectively ruined, even if he manages to overturn the ban.

Paul Flowers

"Tomorrow morning I lead the Cenotaph do at
11 so I can't get wasted tonight. Just v v merry!!"

Drugs, rent boys, financial irregularities, more drugs, allegations of a political cover-up – the revelations surrounding Methodist minister and former bank chairman Paul Flowers had every ingredient needed for utter public disgrace. And after the first set of allegations it soon emerged that Paul Flowers' conduct had landed him in trouble before. Suspended by the Co-operative Bank, Flowers also received a fine of £400 for the possession of drugs. It was later revealed too that, while deputy head of social services at Rochdale Council, he was involved in rejecting allegations of child sex abuse against the former Rochdale MP, Cyril Smith.

18 November 2013

Drugs shame of former bank chairman

Video shows Methodist minister who oversaw Co-op's £700m loss
allegedly buying cocaine and crystal meth days after giving evidence to MPs

By Hayley Dixon

The former chairman of the Co-operative Bank has allegedly been caught buying crystal meth and cocaine and boasting about taking ketamine and the date rape drug GHB.

The Rev Paul Flowers, a Methodist minister, is said to have bought the illegal substances just days after giving evidence to the Treasury select committee on how the bank lost £700m and came close to collapse while he was at the helm.

He also sent text messages, it is alleged, claiming that a party he organised was turning into a "drug fuelled gay orgy".

Yesterday he apologised for his behaviour, which he blamed partly on the pressures of his former job.

He could face criminal charges after the police said they were examining the allegations.

The former Labour councillor, 63, has been suspended from the Methodist Church, where he has been a minister for 40 years, while investigations take place.

Video footage, obtained by the *Mail on Sunday*, appears to show Mr Flowers in his car discussing the cocaine and crystal meth he wanted to buy from a dealer in Leeds.

He is apparently seen counting out £300 and handing it to a friend before asking: "Ket? No?" When told they cannot get ketamine, a Class C tranquilliser, he replies: "Don't worry, we will cope with what we've got."

Mr Flowers, whose mother, Muriel, died a year ago, said in a statement released through his Church: "This year has been incredibly difficult, with a death in the family and the pressures of my role with the Co-operative Bank.

"At the lowest point in this terrible period, I did things that were stupid and wrong. I am sorry for this, and I am seeking professional help, and apologise to all I have hurt or failed by my actions."

The video was filmed by Stuart Davies, who met Mr Flowers through the gay dating site Grindr last month.

In a series of text messages, Mr Flowers, who resigned from the bank in June after the perilous state of its finances was disclosed, is said to have written: "I was 'grilled' by the Treasury select committee yesterday and afterwards came to Manchester to get wasted with friends."

In another message, he apparently boasted that his plans were "turning into a two-day, drug fuelled gay orgy!!!" On the day he was due to appear before the Commons committee, an appearance that was postponed due to time constraints, he is said to have texted that he was "snorting some good stuff".

Mr Davies, 26, claimed he had heard Mr Flowers "bragging" about his connections in Parliament and his 40 years in the Church, adding: "He seemed to be using his status to get young men off their heads for sex."

Mr Davies claimed he had seen Mr Flowers, a former chairman of the drugs charity Lifeline, taking cocaine, the date rape drug GHB, ketamine and cannabis at a party. He claimed the former banker had discussed how he had been in the Commons the day before for the postponed meeting.

"He took great delight in telling us how he had put one over on them – 'Tory —' he called them – because they'd wanted him back the next day but he had told them where to go," said Mr Davies.

"We asked him how he kept his drug taking secret and he laughed and said that a Labour MP had passed him in the corridors and said, 'Have you got a touch of the old Colombian flu?'" A spokesman for the Methodist Church said: "Paul is suspended from duties for a period of three weeks, pending investigations, and will not be available to carry out any ministerial work. We will also work with the police if they feel a crime has been committed."

West Yorkshire Police said it had "been made aware of the allegations made in the *Mail on Sunday* article and is now making further inquiries".

Mr Flowers was not at his home in Bradford yesterday, where a police officer knocked on the door in the afternoon. He was also absent from Wibsey Methodist Church, where another minister took the Sunday morning service.

The Rev Paul Flowers was heavily criticised for his role in the disastrous series of deals that brought the Co-operative Bank close to collapse. The bank ran up more than £700m in losses in the first half of this year and was forced to fill a £1.5bn black hole in its funding. The losses stemmed from the Co-op's takeover of the Britannia Building Society, payouts to compensate customers mis-sold products and its aborted takeover of 632 Lloyds Banking Group branches.

In 2011, two years after he oversaw the Britannia deal, Mr Flowers told the Mutuals Forum that it would be easy for him to be "fearsomely smug" about how the Co-op had negotiated the financial crisis without support. He also described the Financial Services Authority as "oiks". But when he gave evidence to MPs earlier this month, he found himself humiliated. Appearing before the Treasury select committee, he admitted that his only qualification for chairing the Co-operative was a four-year stint in a bank after leaving school.

Asked about the size of the Co-op's balance sheet, he replied: "£3 billion."

Andrew Tyrie, the committee's chairman, pointed out that the actual figure was £47bn. He also did not know the size of its loan book. Mr Tyrie said: "These are very basic numbers for a chairman of a bank."

20 November 2013
Disgraced bank boss was investigated eight years ago
By Georgia Graham

A disgraced banker caught on camera apparently buying drugs was investigated about his conduct eight years ago, it has emerged.

Paul Flowers, the former Co-op Bank chairman, Methodist minister and local councillor, was forced to refer himself to the Standards Board for England for sending a "joke" message that is alleged to have "sexual connotations" to council colleagues in 2005.

Although councillors who had been sent the message raised their concerns with the Labour-run council at the time, five years later Mr Flowers was selected by Ed Miliband, the Labour leader, for his Business and Industry Advisory Group.

Mr Flowers, 63, has now been suspended from the Party and his church after film footage apparently showed him discussing the purchase of Class A drugs.

He is being investigated by police after being caught on camera apparently trying to buy crystal meth, cocaine and ketamine. He has now said his actions were "stupid" and "wrong".

He was reported to have bought drugs days after giving evidence to the Commons Treasury committee on how the bank lost £700m. When Mr Flowers appeared before the committee he was criticised for apparently lacking a grasp of the basic facts about the bank or the issues surrounding it. He is not expected to be recalled, but the scandal has put more pressure on regulators to increase checks on people appointed to senior banking roles.

Following the drug investigations it has since emerged that in 2011 Mr Flowers was forced to resign from Bradford council after adult content was found on his computer when it was repaired. At the time he cited "personal reasons" and increased duties at the Co-operative Banking Group for leaving the council.

Grant Shapps, the Conservative Party chairman, has written to Ed Miliband telling him the behaviour and actions of Mr Flowers have "shocked and appalled the public". "They have also raised serious questions about the Labour Party to which you have not yet adequately responded," he wrote. Mr Shapps added that people asking "honest" questions about how much the Labour Party knew about Mr Flowers' past were met with a "wall of silence".

Shadow chancellor Ed Balls' office has said that he will not give back a donation from the Co-op Group of £50,000, made in March 2012 when Mr Flowers was bank chairman and a group director.

Len Wardle, the Co-op Group chairman, yesterday resigned, citing "serious questions" raised by the scandal surrounding former banking chairman. Mr Wardle had earlier announced his decision to retire next year, but the Co-op Group said he has now resigned "with immediate effect".

21 November 2013
Labour's "cover-up" over Co-op bank chief
Independent inquiry ordered into the appointment of drug-taking Methodist
By Peter Dominiczak and James Kirkup

An independent inquiry has been ordered into how the Rev Paul Flowers was appointed chairman of a major British bank, amid allegations that the Labour Party covered up concerns about the alleged drug-taking Methodist minister's conduct.

David Cameron yesterday accused Ed Miliband of failing to disclose doubts about Mr Flowers before he was appointed to the board of the Cooperative Bank, which has close links with the Labour Party.

Mr Flowers was a member of Mr Miliband's business advisory group despite serious allegations about his behaviour as a Labour councillor.

The Prime Minister yesterday told the Commons that Labour "knew" about the Methodist minister's past but did "nothing" to raise concerns with the authorities.

The deepening scandal led large charities, including Oxfam and Christian Aid, to announce that they were reviewing their relationship with the bank.

It emerged last night that Mr Flowers quit a drug charity over allegations he submitted £150,000 of false expense claims. He was suspended as chairman of trustees at the Lifeline Project over a "significant" number of allegedly false claims made between 1992 and 2004, it was reported.

In relation to Mr Flowers's appointment to the board of the Co-op Bank, Mr Cameron said an inquiry would be held to find out exactly "what went wrong". It will investigate the near-collapse of the bank earlier this year as well as the appointment, and is expected to be overseen by the Prudential Regulation Authority.

Mr Flowers, 63, who led the bank for three years before stepping down in June, apologised this week after he was filmed allegedly buying drugs including crack cocaine and crystal meth. It has since been disclosed that he resigned as a councillor in Bradford after claims that homosexual pornography was found on his computer.

In 2005, he also referred himself to the Standards Board for England for sending a "joke" message to council colleagues which was alleged to have had "sexual connotations". Although fellow councillors raised concerns with the Labour-run town hall at the time, five years later Mr Flowers was selected by Mr Miliband for his business and industry advisory group.

The Conservatives accused Labour of knowing about Mr Flowers's reasons for leaving Bradford council, but failing to tell the Co-op, which Mr Cameron said was "driven to the wall" by the Methodist minister.

As head of the bank, Mr Flowers was able to approve millions of pounds of donations to the Labour Party. Ed Balls, the shadow chancellor, is facing calls to repay a £50,000 donation approved by Mr Flowers, who has described Mr Balls as a "political friend".

It was also reported that Labour received more than £18m in "soft loans" from the Co-op Bank at a 4 per cent interest rate, well below the 5.6 per cent offered to regular customers.

Mr Cameron told the Commons: "The Chancellor will be discussing with the regulators what is the appropriate form of inquiry to get to the bottom of what went wrong here, but there are clearly a lot of questions that have to be answered.

"Why was Reverend Flowers suitable to be chairman of a bank? Why weren't alarm bells rung earlier?" He added: "What we can now see is that this bank, driven into the wall by this chairman, has been giving soft loans to the Labour Party, facilities to the Labour Party, donations to the Labour Party, trooped in and out of Downing Street under Labour, still advising the leader of the Labour Party. Now we know all along they knew about his past. Why did they do nothing to bring to the attention of the authorities this man who has broken a bank?"

Labour denies that Mr Miliband or any shadow cabinet ministers were aware of the Bradford allegations.

The independent inquiry ordered by Mr Osborne will not begin until a police investigation has concluded.

22 November 2013
Ed Balls "proud" to take £50,000 from Co-op

Ed Balls has said he was "proud" to have taken a £50,000 donation linked to the Rev Paul Flowers, the disgraced former Co-operative Bank chairman, as Labour fought back angrily against Conservative "smears".

The shadow chancellor said his party had done nothing wrong in its dealings with Mr Flowers, who led the bank to the brink of collapse and was accused this week of taking cocaine and using rent boys.

Several disclosures about Mr Flowers's conduct have left Labour's senior figures facing questions about their dealings with him.

It emerged yesterday that:

Mr Flowers had close political links to Sir Cyril Smith, the late Liberal MP accused of child abuse offences, the politician's brother said.

Mr Flowers helped oversee Rochdale social services at the time of an investigation into alleged Satanic abuse, the council confirmed.

Police officers are thought to be preparing to arrest Mr Flowers over alleged drug offences.

The Co-operative Group said it was asking Mr Flowers to return tens of thousands of pounds in wages.

The Government is preparing to set up an inquiry into Mr Flowers's appointment at the Co-op and David Cameron has accused Labour of concealing information about the banker's conduct and history.

Ed Miliband, the Labour leader, yesterday insisted that his party had acted entirely properly over its dealings with Mr Flowers.

The banker was appointed to Mr Miliband's board of business advisers in 2010, and kept his position there even after being forced to quit Bradford council in 2011 for using pornography on his council laptop.

After days of Conservative attacks over the scandal, Labour sought to shift the attention to the Government's dealings with the Co-operative Bank. Mr Balls said ministers should account for regulators' oversight of the bank from May 2010 when the Coalition took office.

During that period, Mr Flowers oversaw a deal to buy more than 600 branches of Lloyds Bank, a deal that helped push the Co-operative Bank deeper into trouble.

Labour also highlighted Conservative dealings with Mr Flowers. Mark Hoban, the Tory financial secretary to the Treasury from 2010 to last year, had 30 meetings with Mr Flowers to discuss the deal, Mr Balls said.

Labour officials also noted that Mr Flowers, who left the bank in the summer, sponsored a drinks reception at the Conservative Party Conference last year.

Mr Miliband said that Mr Cameron was playing politics instead of focusing on ensuring the stability of the bank.

"What the British people have a right to expect from the Prime Minister is not just to engage in smears, unjustified smears, but actually to concentrate on helping the borrowers, the savers, the investors, in this important institution."

The Co-operative Group, which is owned by its members, has historic links to Labour and has provided' the party with extensive financial and political support .

In March last year, Mr Balls's office received a donation worth £50,000 from the group. As chairman of the Co-operative Bank, Mr Flowers was a director of the group at the time. In evidence to a Commons committee this month, Mr Flowers said he had been involved in the decision to make the donation .

In a *Sky News* interview, Mr Balls said that he was a "huge supporter" of the Co-operative Group and was happy to take its support.

"I am proud to have that donation. It has helped me make the arguments I have made in Parliament. They made a donation to me last year which I am very proud of and was properly declared."

Conservative MPs have suggested that Mr Balls should repay the money, a call echoed by Nick Clegg, the Deputy Prime Minister.

Mr Balls said he could not and would not do so: "I have not got £50,000 in my office to give back and I don't think it would be the right thing to do."

In a BBC interview, he denied discussing the donation with Mr Flowers, and insisted the former bank chairman was not involved in the payment. "I have never in my life had a conversation with Paul Flowers about that matter or any other," he said. "Paul Flowers was not involved in that in any way."

Challenged about Mr Flowers's evidence to MPs, Mr Balls cast doubt on the former banker's statements: "He was someone who was buying drugs and engaged with rent boys. He has made a lot of allegations. There is no truth in that at all."

There is no suggestion that Mr Flowers is linked to any of the allegations around Sir Cyril Smith.

Also 22 November 2013
Co-op to strip Flowers of £155,000 pay-off
By James Quinn

The Co-operative Group has moved to strip its former bank chairman, the Rev Paul Flowers, of a £155,000 pay-off and is investigating his expenses claims.

Mr Flowers was not owed any money as a result of resigning as chairman of the Co-op Bank in June but, at the same time, he was asked to stand down as deputy chairman of the group, for which he was paid £62,000 a year.

The Manchester-based mutual, which has been shaken by allegations surrounding Mr Flowers, has now written to him, asking for the repayment of £31,000 paid, covering July to December. The group's board has also agreed to stop a further £124,000 due to him over the next two years.

Sources said Co-op had previously agreed to pay the money as it was a democratically elected position from which he had been asked to resign.

But a Co-op spokesman said: "Following recent revelations, the Board stopped all payments with immediate effect and no further payments will be made. As previously stated, an internal fact-finding review is now under way."

A review of Mr Flowers' expenses claims has also begun amid concerns he may have used some of the mutual's money for his private affairs.

His emails and correspondence during his time at the bank and the group will be scrutinised.

At the same time, the bank is conducting an examination of the actions of its directors and senior managers in the run-up to the discovery of its £1.5bn capital short-fall in June. The findings will be passed to the Financial Conduct Authority, which is examining whether it can bring any enforcement actions against past directors.

Mark Carney, the Governor of the Bank of England, is today due to discuss the situation at the mutual at the Prudential Regulation Authority's board meeting. Although the Co-op is not understood to be on the formal agenda, it is thought the eight-man board will discuss the expected Treasury-led inquiry into the bank's near downfall.

David Cameron, the Prime Minister, is expected to announce an independent inquiry into the situation at the bank within days, under the auspices of the Financial Services Act 2012.

However, the inquiry will have to wait until two ongoing investigations – one by West Yorkshire Police into alleged drug purchases by Mr Flowers and the other by the FCA – have been completed.

23 November 2013
Labour drags Whitehall chief into Co-op
scandal with inquiry warning
By Peter Dominiczak

Britain's most senior civil servant has been dragged in to the scandal over the Rev Paul Flowers after he was warned that an inquiry into the Co-op Bank was being used as a "Trojan horse" for a party political attack on Labour.

George Osborne, the Chancellor, confirmed last night that a full independent inquiry would be held into the bank after Mr Flowers, a Methodist minister, was arrested as part of a drugs investigation.

Labour has written to Sir Jeremy Heywood, the Cabinet Secretary, demanding that the inquiry is not subject to "party political point-scoring".

It was the latest attempt by Ed Miliband's party to hit back after days of disclosures about Labour's links to Mr Flowers.

Mr Flowers was this week accused of taking cocaine and using rent boys while he was chairman of the Co-op Bank.

The *Daily Telegraph* can disclose that during a Co-op conference Mr Flowers boasted about attending all-night parties that were "more than his body could survive", just months before leading the bank to the brink of collapse.

Mr Flowers, the bank's chairman for three years, told delegates at the Co-operatives United World Festival and ICA Expo in Manchester last year that he had been "partying into the wee small hours". His remarks at a public event attended by hundreds of people will add to concerns about why no one reported his behaviour to the authorities.

At the festival, Mr Flowers said: "Can I just say something about this international co-operative year that we have been marking and celebrating over the last few days, some indeed partying into the wee small hours for more nights than we would care to remember – or our bodies can actually also survive."

Mr Flowers apologised after he was captured on film allegedly buying hard drugs including crack cocaine and crystal meth. It also emerged that Mr Flowers was caught drink-driving in Manchester in 1990 after celebrating his 40th birthday.

While serving as the chairman of the Co-op Bank, Mr Flowers was communicating with rent boys using his work email address, it has been claimed.

David Cameron this week accused the Labour leadership of knowing about Mr Flowers' past but failing to tell the authorities.

He announced an independent inquiry to find out how a figure with such a controversial past came to lead a major British financial institution.

Michael Dugher, the shadow cabinet office minister, welcomed the investigation but wrote to Sir Jeremy calling for public assurances that the inquiry would be "genuinely independent".

"There is growing concern over the politicisation by senior Government ministers of recent revelations regarding the Co-operative Bank," Mr Dugher wrote.

"It cannot be acceptable that issues which could affect the deposits of thousands of families and businesses up and down the country are subject to "party political point–scoring and smear."

He added: "We believe, however, that as Cabinet Secretary it is your responsibility to ensure that any such inquiry must be genuinely independent and robust. It must not become some sort of "Trojan horse" for a party political attack.

"We would therefore be grateful if you could provide a public and written assurance that this will be the case."

David Davis, the Tory MP who challenged Mr Cameron for the party leadership in 2005, said yesterday that Mr Osborne and the Treasury had "serious questions to answer" about the oversight at the Co-op Bank.

It was claimed last night that Lord King, the former governor of the Bank of England, had warned that there had been a "political desire" for the Co-op to buy 630 Lloyds branches.

25 November 2013
Shamed bank chief "sent texts about drugs days after disclosures"
By Matthew Holehouse

The disgraced former chairman of the Co-op Bank sent drug-related texts days after being exposed in a Sunday newspaper and pledging to seek professional help, it was claimed yesterday.

Reverend Paul Flowers, a Methodist minister who resigned as the bank chairman in the summer over concerns over his competence, sent the texts on Tuesday, two days after being exposed buying drugs.

Mr Flowers has since been arrested and bailed in connection with a drugs supply investigation. He has been suspended from the Methodist church and the Labour Party. The disclosures of his drug abuse raise fresh questions as to how he became the chairman of a major bank and why he was granted access to Labour's leadership.

Mr Flowers also invited a teenage male prostitute to join him at a garden party thrown by Baroness Thornton, a Labour peer, at her Notting Hill home in July, according to text messages seen by the *Mail on Sunday*.

Baroness Thornton confirmed Mr Flowers attended but there is no suggestion she had any knowledge of his other activities.

Mr Flowers also boasted to the 19-year-old escort of lunching with senior Labour figures. "He told us he often went for lunch with Ed Miliband and Ed Balls, and would speak about meeting important-sounding people in the Commons or for lunches in London," the escort said.

The Labour Party said Mr Flowers had met Mr Miliband on three occasions, including two informal dinners, and had attended events with Ed Balls, but they had never had a formal meeting.

Messages show Mr Flowers would take ketamine, a horse tranquiliser, at eight in the morning and discussed "floating" on the drug the day before leading a Remembrance Sunday service. "Tomorrow morning I lead the Cenotaph do at 11 so I can't get wasted tonight. Just v v merry!!" he wrote. He also discussed using GHB, a date rape drug.

Yesterday it emerged that Steven Bayes, the deputy chairman of the Co-op group's board, was once arrested in a Belfast hotel with his 17-year-old boyfriend for suspected gross indecency but the Public Prosecution Service ruled it was not in the public interest to take further action.

Errol Flynn

"The rest of my life will be devoted to women and litigation."

16 October 1959
Errol Flynn – obituary
Costume actor of many parts

Errol Flynn, the film actor who has died in Vancouver at the age of 50, excelled in the portrayal of colourful extroverts, preferably in costume.

Admired by many filmgoers in several countries, he figured frequently in newspaper reports. His critics averred that his private personality differed but little from his film one.

Born in Hobart, Tasmania, he served as a patrol officer in New Guinea before beginning his acting career in England. He appeared with a Northampton repertory company and at the Malvern Festival.

In 1935 he went to Hollywood, He quickly established himself as a popular favourite in such films as *Captain Blood, Sea Hawk* and *Adventures of Robin Hood*.

In his role in *Objective Burma*, he appeared to fight the war with Japan almost single-handed. This aroused a good deal of comment

He became a naturalised American citizen in 1942. In recent years he had figured in a series of court cases, including one of attacking two girls, aged 16 and 17, of which he was acquitted.

On several occasions he was involved in restaurant and night-club brawls with prominent Hollywood and New York personalities. "The rest of my life," he said jokingly a few weeks ago, "will be devoted to women and litigation."

He married three times. His marriages to Lily Damita, a French film actress, and Nora Eddington ended in divorce. He married Patrice Wymore, the actress, in 1950.

Professor's son
Dashing and reckless
By Campbell Dixon

Son of a slight, sedate professor of zoology, at London University, Errol Flynn was everything that fans expected of a film star, tall, handsome, dashing, reckless and unconventional.

Sensational newspapers printed so many stories of his romances, drinking and general wildness that he was assumed to be just another Hollywood playboy.

This did him an injustice. It is true he was reckless, that he found pretty girls as irresistible as they found him, and that he drank far more than was good for him.

But this was only half the picture. Well over six feet tall, with a powerful physique, chiselled features and a charming voice, he was one of the most attractive fellows you could wish to meet, and one of the most amusing. He had a lively wit, was a brilliant raconteur and, unless provoked, bubbled with high spirits and good will.

About his work he was always modest. If his looks and physique generally condemned him to play dashing officers and adventurers, he cheerfully did his best with them, and his best was very good indeed.

But, as he proved in *The Forsyte Saga*, he also had gifts that might have made him the successor to John Barrymore if he had not also shared some of that great actor's weaknesses.

Colonel Gadaffi

"His teeth are naturally immune to stain."

21 October 2011
Colonel Muammar Gaddafi – obituary
Libyan dictator whose pursuit of terror at home and
abroad ultimately led to his own downfall

Colonel Muammar Gaddafi, the former Libyan dictator who has been killed aged 69, liked to promote himself as an instigator of global revolution; for the four decades of his rule, however, this was carried out through the subjugation of his people at home, and the sponsorship of terrorism abroad.

His grip on power always looked solid. But in February 2011 the uprisings in North Africa, which had already seen the fall of the governments of Libya's neighbours, Egypt and Tunisia, suddenly put his regime in jeopardy.

There were demonstrations in all Libya's principal cities – including the capital, Tripoli. The east of the country, where Gaddafi's power had always been weakest, saw an enthusiastic, if chaotic, revolt, and the port city of Benghazi fell to the rebels. Gaddafi loyalists were widely accused of slaughtering civilians as he attempted to reimpose his authority, and with the backing of a UN Security Council resolution, an Allied force which included the Americans, the British and the French imposed a no-fly zone.

Allied aircraft neutralised Libya's air force and prevented Gaddafi's troops from advancing into Benghazi. Air strikes then began targeting Gaddafi forces all over Libya, as well as the regime's command and control structures.

Critics argued that by effectively acting as the rebel air force, the Allies were grossly overstepping their mandate. But the pattern of the conflict was duly established: Nato aircraft cleared the way for rebels to advance westwards along the coast, Gaddafi loyalists then beat them back. The stop-go nature of the fighting endured for six months, but in August the rebels finally encircled Tripoli, and when they successfully captured the town of Zawiya, with its crucial oil refinery, just 30 miles west of the capital, the resistance of Gaddafi's forces crumbled. On 21 August the rebels entered Tripoli and battle was soon under way at Gaddafi's own compound.

Gaddafi, however, was not to be found, and mystery surrounded his whereabouts for a further two months. Some suggested he had fled abroad, perhaps to Niger, but the authorities there denied the rumours. Finally rebels ringed his birthplace of Sirte, on the coast midway between Tripoli and Benghazi. Despite the hopelessness of their position, forces loyal to Gaddafi waged a bitter last stand.

When rebels finally captured Sirte yesterday morning, leaked reports of his capture began to circulate. Gaddafi had been seized while trying to flee, some rebels said, and had been wounded in both legs. Others said he had been found hiding, like the deposed Iraqi dictator Saddam Hussein before him, in a hole. Nato confirmed that it had targeted several vehicles, one possibly containing Gaddafi, in an air strike at 8.30am. Mobile telephone pictures of a bloodied figure resembling the dictator began to circulate on the internet. Finally, the news came through that he was indeed dead.

It was a suitably chaotic end for a man who could never be easily pigeonholed. Erratic, vain and utterly unpredictable, he always seemed to be enjoying a joke which no one else could see. His image, plastered on walls all over Libya, seemed a parody of Sixties radical chic – the craggy features, longish hair, the eyes half-hidden behind retro blue–tone shades.

Gaddafi would arrive at summits of Arab leaders in a white limousine surrounded by a bodyguard of nubile Kalashnikov-toting brunettes. At one nonaligned summit in Belgrade, he turned up with two horses and six camels; the Yugoslavs allowed him to graze the camels in front of his hotel – where he pitched his tent and drank fresh camel milk – but refused to allow him to arrive at the conference on one of his white chargers. Several of the camels ended up in Belgrade zoo.

At an African Union summit in Durban in 2002, his entourage consisted of a personal jet, two Antonov transport aircraft, a container ship loaded with buses, goat carcases and prayer mats, a mobile hospital, jamming equipment that disrupted local networks, $6m in petty cash, and 400 security guards with associated rocket launchers, armoured cars and other hardware, who nearly provoked a shoot-out with South Africa's security forces.

On his return motorcade through Swaziland, Mozambique, Zambia, Zimbabwe and Malawi, Gaddafi tossed fistfuls of dollars from his car to appreciative crowds, remarking that this way he could be sure they went to the poor.

Gaddafi's political pronouncements were equally outlandish. He told the Algerian regime that it had wasted the one and a half million martyrs who had died in the war against France because it had not continued across North Africa to "liberate" Jerusalem. He once suggested a binational state for Palestinians and Israelis called Isratine.

Under the banner of pan-Arabism, he offered political unity (under his leadership, inevitably) to Syria, Egypt and Sudan (none of which wanted it), then changed tack to pan-Africanism, calling for a united continent (also to be ruled from Tripoli). As a first step, he threw open Libya's frontiers to all African citizens; the result was that four million, mainly Muslim, Libyans became resentful hosts to at least one and a half million impoverished sub-Saharan migrants.

Yet the self-styled "Universal Theorist" and "Guide of the First of September Great Revolution of the Arab Libyan Popular and Socialist Jamahiriya" was no joke. In the 1970s and 1980s, while other tyrants were content to repress their own people, Gaddafi seemed hell-bent on bringing murder and mayhem to the whole world.

After Pam Am Flight 103 was blown up over Lockerbie in 1988, leaving 270 dead – the biggest mass murder in British history – a court found two Libyans guilty of planting the bomb on board. In 1984, WPC Yvonne Fletcher was shot dead in London with a machine gun fired from inside the Libyan embassy. Then there was the bombing of a Berlin discotheque, explosions at Rome and Vienna airports and the bombing of a French airliner over Chad.

In addition, Gaddafi sent arms shipments to the IRA, Abu Nidal, and numerous other terrorist organisations and set out to export revolution to his neighbours, perpetuating regional conflicts in Sierra Leone, Zimbabwe, Chad and Liberia. Domestic opponents – the "running dogs" who opposed his dictatorship – were ruthlessly liquidated. In 1984 bomb attacks on seven Libyan exiles living in Britain left 24 people injured; one Libyan journalist opposed to Gaddafi's regime was assassinated as he walked past London's Regent's Park mosque.

In the mid-1980s "taking out Gaddafi" became an American obsession. In 1986, for example, he survived missile attacks ordered by President Reagan – attacks which he claimed had killed his adopted daughter (in fact evidence later emerged to suggest that she remains alive and well).

Indeed, for all his madcap behaviour, Gaddafi was no fool. He survived at least a dozen attempts on his life and remained the longest ruling revolutionary from the Nasserite sixties. In the 1970s and 1980s he could defy the might of the United States and laugh off UN resolutions, confident that the Arab world, the Third World and the Soviet bloc would back him. But times changed. By the 1990s the Soviet Union was no more, and Arab leaders had had enough of Gaddafi's troublemaking.

As a result, in the late 1990s he made his most audacious move since coming to power: the reinvention of himself as a peace-loving international statesman. In 1999 Libya finally apologised for the shooting of Yvonne Fletcher, and handed over the men suspected of masterminding the Lockerbie bombing for trial. Gaddafi admitted that some of the "liberation" movements he had assisted were not really "liberation" movements at all; it had all been a terrible mistake. In 2004, following a British diplomatic initiative, he publicly renounced Libya's weapons of mass destruction programme.

With Libya's proven reserves of 30 billion barrels of oil as bait, it did not take long for Western leaders to bury the past and beat a path to his tent. The British public was treated to the spectacle of Foreign Secretary Jack Straw praising the colonel's "statesmanlike and courageous" strategy and Prime Minister Tony Blair offering the "hand of partnership" over a glass of camel's milk.

The reasons for Gaddafi's change of heart aroused much speculation. He had certainly been anxious to end the UN sanctions imposed in 1992, which had crippled his country's economy. But it was the 11 September attacks that appear to have been the catalyst.

Gaddafi was the first Arab leader to condemn the attacks (helpfully suggesting that the United States bomb the safe havens of Islamist militants in London); and the most instantly alert to the implications for his own survival.

For Gaddafi came from a generation of revolutionaries that was motivated by Arab nationalism and the "anti–imperialist struggle", not by religious extremism. Suddenly he found himself threatened not only by America's assault on the "Axis of Evil", but also by the underground religious revolutionaries of al-Qaeda. And it was the latter which he saw as the most potent threat.

Muammar Gaddafi was born in a tent near Sirte, Libya, in 1942 (some sources record 7 June as the precise date). He was the youngest child and only son of a nomadic and illiterate Bedouin family of the Gadadfa tribe. It seems to have been the tribal culture and unstructured democracy of Bedouin life that inspired his revolutionary political ideas.

He was sent away to school at nine years old and then went to secondary school at Sebha, where – like many other Arab students at the time – he was inspired by Nasser's call to Arab resurgence through socialism and revolution. Early in his teens he seems to have formed a revolutionary cadre with a group of friends.

Imbibing Greek notions of democracy and Islamic notions of equality while studying History at Tripoli University, he went on to the Benghazi Military Academy. In 1966, having reached the rank of colonel, he did signals training with the British Army at Beaconsfield.

In September 1969 he led a bloodless coup that overthrew the royal regime of the charming but weak British-backed King Idris. Libyans were taught that he led the charge not from the turret of a tank, but at the wheel of a blue Volkswagen Beetle. The battered Revolutionary Vehicle came to occupy pride of place in Tripoli's national museum.

Gaddafi was lucky in his timing. Where Nasser in Egypt and the Ba'athists in Iraq and Syria had to struggle against internal opposition and foreign intervention, Gaddafi was able to remove American and British bases and Italian civilians (who were forced to dig up their dead and take them with them) almost without a murmur. World oil supplies were tightening, and he was able to divide the oil companies and enforce nationalisation and higher prices. Henry Kissinger, eager to see a firm anti-communist in position, actually welcomed his arrival.

Gaddafi established a Revolutionary Command Council with himself as commander-in-chief of the armed forces. Two years later he formed the Arab Socialist Union as the only political party in Libya, though it was not until 1976 that the true nature of his "revolution" became clear.

Changing the country's name to "Popular Socialist Libyan Arab Jamahiriya", he implemented his Third Universal Theory of governing laid out in his Green Book

(1976), an indigestible jumble of economic and political theories which became the official law of the land.

Conventional political institutions, including the government and head of state, were abolished (Gaddafi had no official title), to be replaced by a "direct democracy" of popular congresses served by people's committees. The result was a system of administrative chaos counterbalanced by a centralised regime of terror and absolute political control.

Opportunistic, idealistic and mercurial, Gaddafi launched a series of attempts to take his revolution forward at home and abroad. While his economic policies – banning wages and private ownership – had disastrous results, he remained genuinely popular because oil revenues enabled him to supply even the poorest peasants with education, health care and imported food.

Meanwhile, state–controlled media elevated him to the status of demi-God. "His teeth are naturally immune to stain, so that when he releases a full-blown smile, the naturally white teeth discharge a radiation pregnant with sweet joy and real happiness for those lucky ones who are fortunate to be around him," fawned the *Al Zahf Al Akhdar* newspaper.

Abroad, though, his campaigns ended in failure. For the first decade he spent most of his time trying to achieve union with Egypt, Tunisia and the Sudan, followed by Morocco, Tunisia, Niger and Chad. All came to nought, as did his failed invasion of Chad in 1972. It may possibly have been in frustration that, in the 1980s, he became such a ready sponsor of anti-Western terrorism.

In Libya much was made of Gaddafi's many cultural achievements. He was the author of a book of allegorical short stories, and the inventor of a car, the Saroukh el-Jamahiriya (Libyan rocket), launched in 1999 on the 30th anniversary of the Libyan revolution. When Tony Blair paid his visit in 2004, the two leaders apparently swapped ideas about their own versions of the "third way". Gaddafi illustrated his version by drawing a circle with a dot in the middle, the dot being himself.

Libya's new status in the world was graphically illustrated in August 2009, when the Lockerbie bomber Abdelbaset Ali Al Megrahi, who had been serving life in a Scottish prison and been diagnosed with terminal prostate cancer, was released from prison by Kenny MacAskill, the Scottish justice minister, ostensibly on "compassionate grounds".

Megrahi returned to Libya to be greeted by scenes of jubilation, with some of the crowd waving the Scottish Saltire. Gaddafi, apparently oblivious of the huge embarrassment he was causing in Scotland, publicly embraced the bomber.

In 2000 or thereabouts, Gaddafi himself was said to have contracted cancer. In Libya the question of who would succeed was taboo, but still the subject of intense behind-the-scenes debate, some suggesting that he would hand power to Saif al-Islam Gaddafi, his son, who had been groomed to present a moderate image to the West – an image that was swiftly dispelled when his father's regime came under threat in early 2011.

Muammar Gaddafi had two wives, Fatiha, whom he married in 1968, and with whom he had a son, and Safiya, whom he married in 1969 and with whom he had a daughter and six sons.

Serge Gainsbourg

"We were a public couple. We went out a lot.
The trouble was, I didn't always make it back ... "

4 March 1991
Serge Gainsbourg – obituary

Serge Gainsbourg, the controversial French singer, composer and film director, who has died in Paris aged 62, was best known in Britain for his *"succes de scandale"*, *Je t'aime moi non plus*, the heavy-breathing duet recorded with his then girlfriend, the English actress Jane Birkin.

Je t'aime achieved huge popularity in 1969, despite – or perhaps because of – being banned by the BBC and denounced by the Vatican. Peter Cook recorded a spoof version featuring "Serge Forward and Jane Firkin".

Gainsbourg was one of the many French popular performers whose reputation as a "serious" songwriter dissolved in the Channel. In France he was celebrated for his contribution to popular *varietés*, for his film scores and for his *louche* personality.

A notoriously heavy drinker, Gainsbourg maintained an awesome intake of alcohol and tobacco. After a heart attack in 1973, he continued to smoke three or four packets of *Gitanes sans filtres* a day.

Gainsbourg was fond of telling interviewers that he was in a better state than his doctors. Indeed, he outlived three of his cardiologists.

According to the doctor who was treating him at the time of his heart attack, Gainsbourg stopped smoking only for three days, while he was in intensive care, "because he believed, foolishly, that his *Gitane* would cause the oxygen cylinder to explode".

It was often supposed that Gainsbourg took drugs, but in truth he was naturally outrageous, and undertook most of his more contentious projects as he was approaching pensionable age. He was finally banned from live television after a series of drunken appearances on chat shows – culminating in the occasion when he made an obscene suggestion, in broken English, to the American pop singer, Miss Whitney Houston.

For 10 years Gainsbourg, who had no driving licence or chauffeur, kept a 1928 Rolls-Royce which, he said, he used occasionally "as an ashtray".

Although he became best known for his collaborations with pop musicians in the 1970s, Gainsbourg acquired a considerable knowledge of the decadent movement. His house in the Rue de Verneuil, Saint Germain, was furnished in the style of the apartment of des Esseintes in Huysmans' *A Rebours*, and was a shrine to decadence: next to paintings by Dalí and Francis Bacon, and originals of Chopin's letters, there were pictures of Screaming Jay Hawkins and the Sex Pistols.

In his later years, Gainsbourg – in private a gentle, polite man – cultivated, with increasing success, the public image of the "dirty old man of Europe".

In the 1960s – after his divorce from his Italian wife, Francoise Antoinette Pancrazzi, who described him as an aesthete tormented by his own ugliness – he developed a reputation as an unlikely Don Juan. His supposed conquests included Brigitte Bardot.

Having developed, with *Je t'aime*, the taste for putting a nation into shock, Gainsbourg set out – with some success – to repeat the experience. In 1979 there was outrage from French traditionalists, led by *Le Figaro*, when he recruited a group of Jamaican reggae musicians and recorded a highly idiosyncratic version of *La Marseillaise*.

The song was re-titled *Aux Armes et Caetera*, and provoked riots when concerts were disrupted by veteran paratroopers.

Six years previously there had been opposition to the release of Rock Around the Bunker, his collection of songs about the Third Reich. The LP included a reading of *Smoke Gets in Your Eyes*, which some listeners considered to be in questionable taste.

Record buyers who were familiar with Gainsbourg's family history, however, chose to see this and other of his more controversial releases as an indication of the singer's having been born with "a skin too few". As a child, Gainsbourg, the offspring of Russian Jewish refugees, had been made to wear the yellow star, and on several occasions had narrowly escaped death.

The son of a night-club pianist, he was born Lucien Ginzburg in Paris on 2 April 1928 and brought up in the Pigalle. He changed his name for one he considered to be more aristocratic while still acknowledging his Russian origins.

He trained as a painter but by the early 1950s he came under the influence of the jazz musician, Boris Vian. Gainsbourg began to work as a singer and pianist in the nightclubs of Saint Germain des Pres.

Towards the end of the decade he began a career as a film actor, playing villains in low-budget European co-productions of varying artistic merit. Gainsbourg's own performances in such pictures, typically set in ancient Rome, drew a mixed response from critics.

Of one showing, when he was obliged to flee his public at a cinema in Barbes Rochechouart, he recalled that "they were shouting at the screen in Arabic: 'Die, you bastard!'"

In the 1960s Gainsbourg, whose own recordings tended towards the cynical, specialised in writing mainstream pop for such luminaries as Juliette Greco and Petula Clark. Increasingly, however, he indulged his fondness for mischief, notably in 1966 when he wrote the highly suggestive *Les Sucettes* ("Lollipops") for the young France Gall.

France Gall, only 16, had won the Eurovision Song Contest the year before with a Gainsbourg song, and had no idea of the new song's "hidden agenda".

In the mid-1960s, Gainsbourg wrote BB and other "bubble-gum pop" hits for Brigitte Bardot. Then in 1968 he met the coltish Jane Birkin, who had already acquired some valuable experience of minor scandal (as a result of her nude nymphet role in Antonioni's film of *Blow Up*).

Birkin lived with Gainsbourg for more than 10 years before leaving him in the early 1980s. "We were a public couple," Gainsbourg recalled. "We went out a lot. The trouble was, I didn't always make it back . . . "

After Birkin left him, Gainsbourg lived with his "little Eurasienne" wife – Caroline von Paulus, whom he addressed as "Bambou". They had a son, Lucien, known as "Lulu". On his last album Gainsbourg prefaced a song: "When I die, at least throw a few nettles on my tomb, my little Lulu."

As his career progressed into the 1980s, Gainsbourg discovered that his capacity to outrage was increasingly hindered by public tolerance. But nevertheless he achieved his aim in 1984 with *Lemon Incest*, an unusually sensual reading of Chopin's *Etude No 3 in E Major, Opus 10*.

The video for the song showed Gainsbourg in bed with his 14-year-old daughter, Charlotte, who subsequently embarked on a successful career as a film actress.

By the time he released *You're Under Arrest*, in 1987, Gainsbourg was visibly suffering the effects of his four decades of hard living. In 1989 he was rushed to hospital for a six-hour emergency operation on his liver.

Although an enthusiastic Anglophile, Gainsbourg never made concessions to the English-speaking market. Apart from *Je t'aime*, none of his witty, urbane songs ever achieved significant success in Britain.

His films, like *Je t'aime, moi non plus* (made in 1976, starring Gerard Depardieu), or *Equateur* (1983), were mainly screened in pornographic cinemas in Britain.

Perhaps surprisingly for a man widely supposed to be on terms of only nodding acquaintance with his face flannel, Gainsbourg also directed advertisements for Lux soap and Woolite.

Though he enjoyed moments of spectacular public disgrace, Gainsbourg was also celebrated for his extravagant acts of kindness and generosity. Bardot described him as "the best and the worst. He struck me as a little Jewish Russian prince reading Andersen and Grimm, who came face to face with the tragic reality of life: a Quasimodo, touching or repugnant depending on his mood".

Gainsbourg was appointed an officer of the French Order of Arts and Letters. The Minister of Culture, Jack Lang, called him "one of the greats of French music and poetry".

George Graham

"I have made no money from transfers."

George Graham was an Arsenal legend twice over: first as a player, when as an elegant midfielder he'd spearheaded the club's march to the league and cup "double" in 1971; and latterly as the manager who built a relentless and well-drilled side who enjoyed great success both at home and abroad. But by 1994 the stern disciplinarian's magic touch appeared to be waning. Though they had won the European Cup Winners' Cup earlier that year, his ageing, increasingly one-dimensional, side were struggling to keep up with their domestic rivals. But nonetheless there was disbelief and no small measure of sympathy when the allegations about Graham emerged. After serving his ban from football the Scot would go on to manage both Leeds and – to many Arsenal supporters' dismay – Tottenham Hotspur, but despite winning the League Cup with Spurs he never settled at either club, and hasn't worked as a manager since 2001.

12 December 1994
Graham involved in investigation
By Christopher Davies

A number of accusations about "rake-offs" from transfers – particularly involving Scandinavian players joining English clubs – have resurfaced following reports at the weekend that George Graham, the Arsenal manager, had been under investigation by the Inland Revenue.

Tax officials are reported to be investigating a secret payment of £285,000 to Graham as part of the £1.57m transfer of John Jensen from Brondby, the Danish club, in 1992. The deal was conducted by the Norwegian agent, Rune Hauge, who was not available for comment at his home or office in Norway yesterday.

Graham is reported to have deemed the payment an unsolicited gift and therefore not taxable. He is said subsequently to have told the Inland Revenue about it and it is believed that a settlement has been agreed.

Speaking at Arsenal's London Colney training ground yesterday, Graham emphatically denied that he had taken cash. He said: "The only thing I have to say about these stories is that I have not profited from any transfers and I think it's important that is made clear."

It is alleged that there are discrepancies with other Scandinavian transfers. The Jensen deal is one of many under investigation by the Premier League. Graham Kelly, chief executive of the FA, said: "The Premier League are looking into various alleged issues. The papers of the relevant transfers were passed on by the Football Association and we await their findings.

"The activities of agents are permitted under FIFA laws from June last. They will be licensed from 1 January and in theory it will be much cleaner and easier to police agents activities."

Those licensed will have to deposit a bond with world football's ruling body, who hope they can monitor country-to-country transfers closely.

The Arsenal board met at Highbury yesterday when the allegations were discussed, but managing director Ken Friar maintained that as far as the club were concerned, the Jensen deal had been conducted in the normal way with Brondby paid in full.

"We will be co-operating with the Premier League inquiry which is due to take place shortly," he added. "We will make no further statement ahead of the inquiry."

An Inland Revenue spokesman said: "It is common knowledge that we are in the middle of an ongoing investigation into football. We are principally looking at Premier League clubs and substantial sums of money are involved."

22 February 1995
Arsenal sack Graham over cash "bung" for transfer
By John Ley

George Graham was sacked as manager of Arsenal yesterday for failing to "act in the best interests of the club".

Graham, 50, has been the subject of a Premier League inquiry into allegations that he accepted a cash "bung" as part of transfers of foreign players to the club.

Arsenal's board of directors, having received the details of the league's findings, decided that it could not stand by one of the most successful managers in the club's history.

The Premier League will, in the next 24 hours, release the interim report of its inquiry, but the club pre-empted this, sacking Graham seven hours before last night's Premiership game against Nottingham Forest, which Arsenal won 1–0.

Graham wasted little time in responding to his dismissal and said that he would be seeking legal assistance to "vigorously contest" his sacking.

He believes he was entitled to expect better treatment after his long association with the club, and called "for a full and open inquiry by the Football Association".

In response to claims by Mr Peter Hill-Wood, the Arsenal chairman, that Graham did not "act in the best interests of the club", the former manager, through his solicitors, also called upon the FA to hold an inquiry into the manner of his dismissal.

"I have made the welfare of Arsenal my sole objective for the eight years I have been the manager and my track record shows my success," he said.

"Before that I played for Arsenal for seven years and so I can demonstrate more than 15 years of total commitment to the club. The allegations are nonsense. I deeply regret that this kangaroo court judgment should have been reached in such a hole-in-the-corner way. My record of loyalty and service demanded better treatment.

"I believe this matter should be investigated by the Football Association. What is the future for football if the standards of justice inside the game can be ignored in this way?"

Graham, who earned a reported £300,000 a year, will not receive compensation for the remainder of his contract, which was due to run until May 1997.

There has been speculation about his position since the first allegations in November that he accepted a £285,000 payment from the £1.1m transfer deal that brought Danish international John Jensen to Arsenal in 1992.

Graham claimed the money was a gift from the Norwegian agent Rune Hauge and said that he returned the money to Arsenal. "I have made no money from transfers," he insisted.

Since the allegations, Arsenal have failed to publicly back their manager who, during his tenure as manager, won six major trophies.

The club announced its decision to sack him in a statement by Mr Hill-Wood. He said: "Arsenal have been informed by the FA Premier League inquiry of the results of their investigations into alleged irregularities concerning certain transfers, and the board have concluded that Graham did not act in the best interests of the club.

"The board have therefore terminated Mr Graham's contract as manager."

The chairman said it was sad that Graham's distinguished career with Arsenal should end this way, and he paid tribute to Graham for the success that he had brought to the club.

Graham had managed Arsenal following a playing career in which he won a League Championship and FA Cup winners' medal with the club as a player in 1971.

While the reaction of supporters was mixed, the general feeling at last night's match was one of disbelief.

"I am very shocked," said Mr Gerald Smith, 39, of Palmers Green, north London. "People forget what a state the club was in before George came. Whatever he has done, surely he could have been punished without getting the sack."

Not all supporters were critical of the sacking. Fiona Sealey, 30, of Ruislip, west London, said: "We need a change. It is a shame how this has all come about but anyone who has seen us at home this season knows something had to be done.

"I am sorry for George. He has taken us back to the top but it was time for him to move on."

Also 22 February 1995
Graham vows to fight sacking
Highbury board take tough action after Premier League
reveal findings of inquiry into irregular transfer dealings
By Henry Winter

A magnificent managerial career that commenced nearly nine years ago, and took in six trophies at home and abroad on the way, ended in utter disgrace for George Graham yesterday.

A candle lit recently for Graham by an Arsenal fan in Milan cathedral has been extinguished. But Highbury's decision to terminate their manager's contract, following allegations that Graham received an illegal payment in the 1992 John Jensen transfer, met with bitter resistance from the 50-year-old Scot last night.

Graham called Arsenal's verdict a "kangaroo-court judgment" which he would "contest vigorously".

Highbury's most successful manager, whose name was chanted during last night's FA Carling Premiership home victory over Nottingham Forest, lamented that he had been ill-treated by a club he had made great again.

In the famous ground which his money-spinning trophies had helped transform, Graham would have found many friends last night, even if those in the boardroom had donned black caps earlier in the day. The mood, initially muted, was definitely pro-Graham, particularly as a team he built – and selected – won with the scoreline synonymous with Graham triumphs: 1–0.

"One Georgie Graham," the Clock End and North Bank sang in harmony. When Forest's fans commenced the airborne taunt of "Where's your manager?", the Clock End hardcore rose to their feet to remonstrate angrily.

By the end, Highbury's feel-good factor had resurfaced. "I said to the players before the game that we owe this one to George," said Stewart Houston, Graham's No 2, who is expected to remain as caretaker for the rest of the season. "Tonight you saw their reaction to that.

"When I told the players the news about George's dismissal at the pre-match meal, their reaction was stunning. It was a strange, eerie feeling, as if they had had a loss – which it is. It is a loss to this football club."

Peter Hill-Wood, Arsenal's chairman, who had described the day as one of the worst of his life, said of Houston: "I don't know who else we'd look for. He's got all the qualities but he's untried."

Of Graham, the man he dismissed, Hill-Wood said: "What we had to do was

inevitable. I think the Premier league inquiry was handled properly and fairly."
Responding to Graham's vehement assertions that the allegations were "nonsense",
Hill-Wood said: "The evidence that came to us would indicate that George isn't
right."

Despite the decision by Hill-Wood's board to end Graham's Highbury career, the
Premier League said yesterday that the commission of inquiry investigating allegations of financial irregularities concerning Graham and others will still report their
interim findings tomorrow morning.

Rumours at Arsenal intimated that the terminating of Graham's contract, following 'bung' allegations, would pre-empt Premier League action. But Rick Parry, chief
executive of the Premier League, insisted in a statement: "As part of the inquiry process, representatives of Arsenal FC and George Graham have been seen within the
last week and presented with details of the findings of the FA Premier League commission of inquiry relevant to them.

"On the basis of the information received, Arsenal FC have decided on the course
of action announced earlier today. The commission will now, as required, report
those findings to the board of the FA Premier League."

Earlier, Hill-Wood said: "I have been in touch with Rick Parry two or three times
today and I think he is happy with the action we have taken. I don't think the Premier
League will take any further action.

"The whole uncertainty of the past two to three months has had an effect on the
club and players. We have to forget the past and we have good enough players to
come through."

Who will manage those players is, predictably, a matter of considerable debate following the demise of Graham, the ninth manager to part company with a Premiership
club this season. Houston is the man in possession, but Pat Rice, Arsenal's respected
youth-team coach, was installed as 5–2 favourite.

Houston is second favourite, followed by Liam Brady, Steve Coppell, David
O'Leary, David Pleat, and Mick McCarthy. Interest in Walter Smith, the Rangers
manager, was denied by Arsenal.

Last night's game, in which Graham's final signing, Glenn Helder, shone throughout, concluded one of the most extraordinary days in the club's eventful history.
It began with a brief statement. "Arsenal Football Club have now been informed
by the FA Premier League inquiry of the results of their investigations into alleged
irregularities concerning certain transfers and the board have concluded that Mr
Graham did not act in the best interests of the club. The board have therefore terminated Mr Graham's contract as manager."

It concluded with Houston standing Graham-style in the dugout, although the
programme carried a page of notes from the departed, disgraced Graham. They
made interesting reading. "Rumours of my impending resignation have proved
somewhat premature . . . "

But the candle for Graham had been snuffed out.

Hugh Grant

"This all seems very odd. It doesn't seem at all like Hugh."

Hugh Grant's brush with scandal came when, in the aftermath of the overwhelming success of *Four Weddings and a Funeral* his star was firmly in the ascendant. Ultimately the incident, whilst humiliating, did little to affect his career; his relationship with Elizabeth Hurley survived too, though they would separate amicably in 2000. It did, however, instil in him a lasting disdain for the press and its voracious attempts to intrude into the private lives of the rich and famous, something that has undoubtedly inspired his work at the campaign group Hacked Off.

28 June 1995
Hugh Grant on prostitute charge
By John Hiscock in Los Angeles

Hugh Grant, the British star of the film *Four Weddings and a Funeral*, was arrested in Hollywood yesterday and charged with indecent conduct with a prostitute in a public place after meeting her on Sunset Boulevard.

Grant, 34, whose girlfriend is Elizabeth Hurley, the actress, was arrested by vice squad police, who alleged that he drove up to a prostitute at about 1.30 a.m.

Officer Lorie Taylor, of Los Angeles Police, said: "Grant was observed to drive a vehicle up to a prostitute and allow her to enter. They drove a short distance to a residential street and engaged in lewd conduct.

"Vice officers walked up on the car and observed the act. Both the prostitute, described by police as a black woman named Divine Brown, 23, and Grant were taken into custody," said Officer Taylor.

Officer Cory Palka said Grant was "extremely embarrassed" when the two officers introduced themselves, but was "very nice and very co-operative".

Grant was released on bail. He and Brown, who was charged with soliciting, are due to appear in court on 18 July.

Eduardo Funes, a police spokesman, said that Grant would not have to appear. He could be represented by a lawyer.

"It's a misdemeanour charge, which carries a custodial sentence," he said. "You could be sent to jail for up to six months or have a $1,000 fine, or both.

"It's up to the judge. It depends on whether there is a track record."

The area in which police allege that Grant stopped is a notorious haunt of prostitutes, both male and female. It is also heavily patrolled by undercover police.

After his arrest, he said: "I did something completely insane. I have hurt people I love and embarrassed people I work with. For both things I am more sorry than I can say."

A friend of Grant's said last night: "This all seems very odd. It doesn't seem at all like Hugh."

Grant, one of the film industry's most in-demand actors, is in Hollywood to promote his new film *Nine Months*, advertised on posters along Sunset Boulevard.

Yesterday's press conference about *Nine Months* was cancelled abruptly, although some journalists had flown in from as far away as Britain for it.

Grant, who read English at New College, Oxford, before becoming an actor, won the Hollywood Foreign Press Association's Golden Globe award this year for *Four Weddings and a Funeral*.

He was virtually unknown outside Britain until he was cast opposite Andie MacDowell in that film, which was nominated for an Academy Award for Best Picture.

Known for his beguiling smile and self-deprecating wit, Grant is now starring in *The Englishman Who Went Up a Hill But Came Down a Mountain*.

After minor roles in repertory, Grant wrote and performed in satirical revues before James Ivory, the film director, spotted him and cast him in *Maurice*, an adaptation of E. M. Forster's sombre novel about homosexual lovers.

He later appeared in *Remains of the Day* and *Bitter Moon* before being picked for *Four Weddings and a Funeral*, a low-budget production that turned out to be Britain's highest earning film and helped to turn him into an international star.

1 July 1995
Grant and Hurley have lunch and a cigarette ...
By Paul Stokes and Robert Hardman

With just a dog and the international media for company, Hugh Grant and Elizabeth Hurley spent their first day together yesterday since the actor was arrested for a "lewd" act with a Los Angeles prostitute on Tuesday.

The gaze of the world's press was unforgiving when the couple decided to have a light lunch in the garden of their rented farmhouse at West Littleton near Bath.

Neither had much to say as they picked at a salad and the meal was abandoned after 10 minutes. Both reappeared and walked to the greenhouse where they watered the plants. He did most of the talking, she listened intently. At one point, an arm reached out for her waist but then hesitated and withdrew.

Earlier, Miss Hurley lit a cigarette and inhaled before passing it to her chastened companion who finished it.

Such is the interest in the potential collapse of showbusiness's most photogenic partnership that the minutiae of these banal garden scenes were being transmitted around the world. And for all the sadness within, there was a sense of farce in the country lanes around Littleton House.

Miss Hurley, 29, had arrived the previous evening at the house that the couple took on a 12-month lease in February. Her journey had involved a high-speed chase down the M4 from London with a dozen motorcycles and four cars in hot pursuit.

Grant, 34, arrived at around 1.15 a.m. in one of two black Mercedes with impenetrable windows. "This is when the crockery starts flying," remarked a police onlooker.

Photographers were in place from first light while cars and outside broadcast vehicles lined the roads through the village as the media circus grew throughout the day. A caterer was quickly on the scene with a mobile snack van.

The activity soon aroused the territorial instincts of Miss Hurley's Alsatian, which started barking. "Shut up," a man's voice retorted from inside. "Yes, shut up," came the female rejoinder.

A florist's van arrived with a £30 bouquet of flowers addressed to Miss Hurley. Sent from Bristol, it was signed with a single kiss and said: "Don't be sad, you will never be alone." One peep through the curtains would have assured her of that.

Also breaking up the solitude were the occupants of a van carrying a £450 Slumberland bed. It had been ordered within hours of Grant's arrest on Tuesday. A spokesman for Bensons Bed Centre in Bristol said that Miss Hurley had requested "a kingsize bed for the spare room". Its presence suggested that reconciliation still has some way to go.

This weekend, West Littleton holds a "Village Gardens Open" event. It is thought unlikely that the star of *Four Weddings and a Funeral* and the £1m face of the new Estee Lauder line will be opening up their grounds, which are adorned with guard dog warning signs.

For Grant, the trouble is likely to start again tomorrow. A Sunday newspaper is claiming that it has signed up Divine Brown, the prostitute he hailed on Sunset Boulevard. She is alleged to have given "a full and detailed account" of her story.

Last night, a spokesman for the Los Angeles City Attorney's Office said that Miss Brown had been jailed for prostitution twice before.

The office has already filed the criminal complaint against Grant. He faces a six-month sentence, although a fine and probation are more likely if he is convicted. "He would also be required to take an Aids test and undergo Aids education," said the spokesman.

It is not known how Grant, who has already apologised for "insane behaviour", will plead. In the meantime, the siege of West Littleton has only just begun.

12 July 1995
I have been abominable, Grant confesses on TV
Hurley joins her boyfriend for film premiere after he pays
tribute to her on American chat show
By John Hiscock in Los Angeles

Hugh Grant's girlfriend, Elizabeth Hurley, flew to be with him at the premiere of his latest film yesterday, hours after he had given a television interview praising her for her support after his arrest with a prostitute.

Questioned about Miss Hurley on *The Tonight Show* with Jay Leno – an appearance scheduled before his arrest and designed to coincide with the release of *Nine Months* – Grant said: "I've done an abominable thing and she's been amazing about it.

"And, contrary to what I read in the paper today, she's been very supportive and we're going to try to work it out."

Grant, 34, seemed nervous as he walked on to the stage and was scarcely put at his ease by Leno's opening question: "Let me start with question number one. What the hell were you thinking?"

The star of *Four Weddings and a Funeral* fidgeted with his tie before answering.

"I keep reading new psychological theories and stuff like that. You know, that I was under pressure or I looked tired or I was lonely or I fell down the stairs when I was a child.

"But I think you know in life pretty much what the good things are to do and the bad things. I did a bad thing and there you have it."

The audience was immediately won over by the actor's stammering charm and his answer about Miss Hurley brought prolonged applause.

Grant said the public reaction had been fantastic. "There have been tons of letters from everyone from film stars I have never even met to interesting letters from people who have really suffered themselves, who have epilepsy and are paralysed. That really brought it home to me that my problems aren't that bad."

Grant said he never thought his arrest would attract such "a circus". He added: "I can see there's juice in it. If I hadn't been the person that perpetrated this whole thing then I suppose I would be enjoying it as much as anyone else. But it's pretty miserable being on the other side of the equation. In a curious kind of way I think I need to suffer for this."

When he told his father what had happened, he said his father replied: "Look here, old boy, I was in the Army and I know about that sort of thing."

Grant said: "He was cool, really cool."

When asked by Leno whether his arrest for "lewd conduct" with the prostitute Divine Brown would affect his career, Grant replied: "There are so many bad things about it. One of them was the embarrassment I caused the people I've been working with on this film.

"It's there on my list of horrors but it's not top of the list because much higher than that is the stuff I have done to people I care about like my family and girlfriend."

After the show, audience members were keen to forgive Grant his indiscretion. "I really feel sorry for him," Rachel Parenza, 22, said. "He seems to genuinely acknowledge that what he did was wrong and that he wishes he had never done it. I guess the guy deserves a break."

Grant's arrest and his scheduled appearance in court next Tuesday appear not to have damaged his box-office appeal. The rich, powerful and plain curious of Hollywood turned out in force for the premiere of Nine Months at Century City.

Extra police were on duty to hold back the crowds and a spokesman for 20th Century Fox said: "Apart from the Oscars, it's the biggest event of the year so far in Hollywood.

"We've been inundated with inquiries about this from press and television people around the world."

In the film, Grant plays a successful child psychiatrist who is appalled to discover that he is to become a father. The co-stars in the film, Tom Arnold, Julianne Moore and Robin Williams were also on the guest list for the premiere.

Preview audiences have reacted favourably to Nine Months and Daily Variety, the newspaper of the film industry, predicted that the film, which it describes as "intermittently amusing and emotionally predictable", will be a hit.

Grant was allegedly caught on a speed camera in his car driving at 98mph on the M5 in April but will deny a speeding charge, his solicitors told Exeter magistrates court yesterday.

The case was adjourned for a week to fix a trial date.

13 July 1995
Guilty Grant prepares for classes on Aids danger
By John Hiscock in Los Angeles

Hugh Grant will have to spend "a few hours at most" at an Aids education course as part of his sentence for lewd conduct with a Hollywood prostitute.

The actor was fined £700, put on two years' probation and ordered to take the course after he had pleaded no contest – the equivalent to a guilty plea – to the charge.

The city attorney's office spokesman Mike Qualls said Grant could decide where to take his Aids counselling.

"There are a variety of different programmes in which he can enrol," he said. "Some involve one-on-one counselling while other programmes have group therapy. It will probably involve a few hours at the most.

"There is a county health officer who sits in the courtroom all day to counsel prostitutes and Mr Grant can see her if he wants. He can even do it in England.

"All he has to do is send a certificate to the court by 13 November stating he has gone through the programme."

Grant was reunited with his girlfriend Elizabeth Hurley for the premiere of his latest film *Nine Months*.

In contrast to her appearance at the British premiere of *Four Weddings and a Funeral* – where a smiling Miss Hurley wore a dress held together with safety pins – the 29-year-old model was pale and expressionless.

The couple did not speak and they ignored the fans, reporters and photographers lining the barricades outside the cinema.

Not all the reviews of *Nine Months* have been favourable. The *Los Angeles Times* critic said: "Rather than act, Grant has chosen immersion in movie star mannerisms.

"He winks, raises his eyebrows, flutters his lids, fools with his hair, rubs his nose, forces a grin and then starts over again. His performance doesn't edge into self-parody, it embraces it wholeheartedly".

Bill Grundy and the Sex Pistols

"Our children were waiting for *Crossroads* when
suddenly they heard every swearword in the book."

If anyone had told you in 1976 that the man who called himself Johnny Rotten would one day be cheerfully advertising Country Life butter, you'd have been excused for questioning their sanity. The majority of the nation struggled to get to grips with punk: their reactions to it teetering nervously between fear, disdain and amusement. Bill Grundy displayed all of these emotions during the short segment of the *Today* show featuring the band, which he began by making a taunting comparison between their music and that of Bach, Mozart and Beethoven, and ended by sententiously expressing his desire to never see them again. What he perhaps didn't realise at the time was that he had destroyed his own career, and simultaneously, if unwittingly, made theirs.

2 December 1976
Four-letter words rock TV
By Ann Morrow

Happy family viewing was somewhat disrupted last night when parents found their children exposed to foul language used by a punk rock group called the Sex Pistols on the *Today* programme.

The switchboard at Thames Television was jammed with calls from enraged viewers complaining about the liberal use of four-letter words on this normally pleasant topical half-hour, which begins at 6 p.m.

An apologetic statement later regretted the remarks. Because the programme was live it was impossible to foresee the language that would be used – a risk that is inevitable in live television.

A Thames statement later said: "We apologise to callers to the company and will make an apology tomorrow on the *Today* programme for this most unfortunate incident." An apology was made at the end of the programme.

When the group appeared – its members are celebrated for their bizarre style – the interviewer, Bill Grundy, who is not easily shocked, asked them if they would like to say something.

They did. At first it was under their breath but then became more audible.

One of the girls said she was pleased to be on the programme. Mr Grundy said he was pleased, too. At this, one of the punk "gentlemen" called him a "dirty old man" and "a dirty old bastard". These were the less offensive words used.

One parent Mr Leslie Blunt, said: "Our children were waiting for *Crossroads* when suddenly they heard every swearword in the book. Surely a button can he pressed to stop this filthy language."

Pressing the fade-out button on a television programme is ultimately the producer's responsibility. A Thames spokesman explained: "It is a very difficult decision. Of course, you can fade out but if somebody says a four-letter word it happens so quickly and it is then too late to do anything about it."

A full inquiry will be started today. And one of the questions will be: could the show have been stopped?

3 December 1976
Ban on Grundy in TV "dirty talk" row
Grundy suspended
By Peter Knight

Bill Grundy was suspended for two weeks by Thames Television last night as the row continued over obscene words used by the Sex Pistols pop group when interviewed by him in the *Today* programme on Wednesday.

Thames also reprimanded those responsible for the Sex Pistols' appearance on the programme, which comes on at 6 p.m. and is seen by many children. The TV company has been flooded with protests from parents.

The suspension on Mr Grundy applies to the *Today* programme only. He was due to present tonight's edition.

A Thames spokesman said last night: "Our director of programmes. Mr Jeremy Isaacs, has expressed his views firmly to all on the *Today* programme, describing last night's incident as 'a gross error of judgment' caused by 'inexcusably sloppy journalism'."

Mr Grundy spent 2½ hours with senior Thames executives inquiring into the appearance of the Sex Pistols. Afterwards the Thames spokesman said that some viewers who had protested about the obscene words used by the group had said they felt sorry for Mr Grundy.

"He was clearly embarrassed by these people and some viewers appreciated what he was trying to do – to show what a disagreeable lot of lads they were."

But Mr Ray Mawby, Tory MP for Totnes, who is lodging a formal protest with the Independent Television Authority, said it appeared Mr Grundy was inciting the group.

Mr Mawby added: "This is disgraceful. A man who is employed in this capacity ought to know the rules and ought to know better than to do this."

Before being told of his suspension by Thames, Mr Grundy said: "The object of the exercise was to prove that these louts were a foul-mouthed set of yobs. That is what it proved.

"I ended the programme by saying: 'I don't ever want to see you again', and I meant it."

The group had been invited to appear in the programme to talk about "punk rock" music, a recent development in pop music which is based on outrage and shock effects.

When Mr Grundy heard the leader of the group use a four-letter word he asked him to repeat it, which he did. Other members of the group then began calling Mr Grundy names and swearing at him.

But Mr Grundy denied yesterday that he had encouraged the group to use bad language on the programme. He said: "There is no way I can be accused of that. When they started swearing I sat back and said 'Okay, you can't shock me'."

He said he was the father of six children and did not approve of bad language, although he thought that violence was worse.

Other *Today* staff questioned by Thames executives yesterday included Mr Tom Steel, 33, who became executive producer only about a month ago, and the programme's studio producer, Mr Michael Housego,

The announcement of Mr Grundy's suspension came soon after Rank Leisure Services announced it was notifying promoters of the Sex Pistols' current tour that it was cancelling the group's appearance at Bournemouth next Tuesday.

Rank Leisure said the decision was "taken after full consideration of the group's appearance on television and the manner of their stage presentation.

"Rank Leisure Services takes the view that this is not of the type of presentation with which the company wishes to be associated."

Sex Pistols have also been banned from one of the north's leading entertainment centres – the Preston Guild Hall.

Their booking for the centre's Charter Theatre on 10 December was cancelled by the entertainments manager, Mr Vin Sumner, who said: "In view of what has happened, there is no way I am accepting this booking now."

Sex Pistols have been given the go-ahead for a concert at the University of East Anglia in Norwich today.

But the Students' Union has warned the group there must be no repetition of bad language.

Aiden Lines, union president, said: "The group has signed a £750 contract with the union and we cannot cancel the concert because it would cripple us financially.

Malcolm McLaren, 28, manager of the Sex Pistols, said last night: "Mr Grundy's intention to expose the Sex Pistols as loud mouthed yobs is misdirected. They have never pretended to be anything else.

"They are working-class spivs, dole-queue kids. They dress loudly and they are loud mouthed.

"They are yobs and proud of it. They are certainly anti-everything Mr Grundy stands for.

"We do not apologise for anything that was said and we hope that TV will not always remain closed off from life as it is lived on the streets."

The BBC issued a statement which said: "In response to Press inquiries concerning the group Sex Pistols, Radio One points out that their single 'Anarchy in the UK' is not being played in its daytime programmes."

The *Today* programme upset some viewers on Tuesday when Eamonn Andrews interviewed Fiona Richmond, who has written about her sex experiences for a magazine.

Although no bad language was used in the interview, some viewers were upset by Miss Richmond talking about her experiences. While the language was in no way explicit, it was clear that Miss Richmond was referring to her affairs with men around the world which formed the basis of her articles.

4 December 1976
Sex Pistols record "shunned" by packers
By a *Daily Telegraph* reporter

The Sex Pistols, the leading exponents of the punk rock cult, who used obscene language on television earlier this week are being banned from appearing at concerts on their first nationwide tour.

At least seven engagements have been withdrawn, there are doubts about others, and women packers at EMI's Hayes record factory have refused to handle their latest record, *Anarchy in the UK*.

Thames Television was inundated with protests following an interview with Bill Grundy on the *Today* programme, in which obscenities were used.

Mr Grundy was later suspended from appearing on any Thames programme for two weeks.

Yesterday the Sex Pistols, whose lead singer rejoices in the name of Johnny Rotten, found that their television outburst had left them out in the cold.

Major concerts on their Christmas tour were cancelled at Norwich, Lancaster

University, Preston, Torquay, Guildford, Newcastle, Bournemouth and, possibly, Bristol.

At the University of Norwich a decision to cancel the Sex Pistols concert was taken after a meeting of the Students' Union and university authorities. A spokesman said the university was responsible for the "safety and security" of people.

Mr Leslie Hill, managing director of EMI Records, said yesterday that the group's record "had commercial potential".

"I do not think there is anything objectionable about it. The record industry is often a controversial business."

The Sex Pistols have a £44,000 contract with EMI, which owns 50 per cent. of Thames Television. EMI is releasing *Anarchy in the UK.* to coincide with the group's seasonal tour.

The record, which begins with the words "I am an antichrist, I am an anarchist", goes on to exhort listeners to "destroy". But it has now been banned by the BBC and many record shops are believed to have sent back the record to their head offices.

Neil Hamilton

"Neil's a British bulldog. We are not contemplating
a future outside politics."

The allegations of misconduct against the right-wing (he was pro-capital punishment, anti-child benefits) minister Neil Hamilton, who had hitherto been chiefly noted for his combination of levity and Euro-scepticism, came at a time when John Major's Conservative government seemed soaked in scandal of almost every kind. Hamilton lost his seat in the Tory immolation at the 1997 election, and suffered the indignity of being asked to stay away from the party conference by the new leader, William Hague. Since leaving Parliament he has managed to indulge his propensity to seek attention by appearing in a succession of reality television programmes, and his suspicion of Europe by standing as a UKIP candidate. He has not enjoyed conspicuous success in either avenue.

21 October 1994
Pressure on second minister to resign
By George Jones

Mr Neil Hamilton was fighting to keep his post as Corporate Affairs Minister last night after the Conservative Party was plunged into a new row over standards in public life. Mr Tim Smith, a junior Northern Ireland Minister, had earlier fallen victim to the so-called "cash for questions" saga when he resigned after admitting that he had received money from Mr Mohammed Al-Fayed, the Harrods chairman.

Mr Smith, MP for Beaconsfield, acknowledged that the payments had been for tabling questions and initiating a Commons debate, before he became a Minister, and said he had not declared them at the appropriate time.

But Mr Hamilton refused to resign, despite pressure from senior Tories that he should seek to clear his name from the backbenches.

He categorically denied that he had received any payments and issued a writ for libel against the *Guardian* newspaper which alleged that the two MPs had accepted money, through a Westminster lobbying company, from Mr Al-Fayed at the height of the Lonrho and House of Fraser controversy.

Although Mr Major appealed to MPs to stand by the principle that "people are innocent until they have been shown to be guilty", Tories appeared divided over whether Mr Hamilton should keep his job. They made their views known to the executive of the Tory backbench 1922 committee last night.

One said that Mr Hamilton's position was made more difficult by his responsibilities for business ethics. He said he had told the Government Chief Whip that Mr Hamilton "should do the decent thing, resign and fight to clear his name from the backbenches".

Another suggested that Mr Hamilton should "stand aside" for the sake of the party until the matter had been resolved.

But a strong alternative being expressed was that, since Mr Hamilton had rejected the allegations, he should stay.

The allegations against the two MPs were the latest twist in the "sleaze factor" which has dogged the Government for 12 months.

Two other MPs, Mr Graham Riddick and Mr David Tredinnick, were earlier accused of being prepared to accept payments of £1,000 for tabling questions.

The Government's efforts at damage limitation were overshadowed by controversy over the way Mr Major was first told of the latest allegations. Although they appeared in newspapers yesterday, Mr Major told MPs that the Cabinet Secretary, Sir Robin Butler, had already investigated the matter on the basis of "privately" received information.

He said it was clear that the allegations originated from – but were not delivered directly by – Mr Al-Fayed. But Mr Major surprised the House when he added: "I made it absolutely clear at that time that I was not prepared to come to any arrangement with Mr Al-Fayed."

MPs saw this as a hint that Mr Al-Fayed might have sought something, through an intermediary, in return for making the allegations privately. Downing Street later refused to elaborate on the Prime Minister's remark but said there was no implication of blackmail against the Government.

Labour MPs waved £10 notes as Mr Major entered the Commons chamber for question time. Tories listened in silence as Mr Tony Blair, the Labour leader, said the allegations were evidence that the Government had become "tainted".

Mr Major said he would not tolerate anything other than the highest standards but he was not prepared to take action on the basis of unsubstantiated allegations. He said he had received "concrete assurances" from Mr Hamilton that the allegations were without foundation. "He has written to me explicitly refuting the allegations that he was paid any money either to ask questions or undertake any activity whatsoever on behalf of Mr Al-Fayed."

Mr Ian Greer, the political lobbyist alleged to have paid the MPs to table questions, said the claims were "wholly untrue". Peter Carter Ruck and Partners, solicitors acting for Mr Greer and Mr Hamilton, said libel writs had been served on the *Guardian* on behalf of both men.

Mr Hamilton, MP for Tatton, Cheshire, said in a statement "There is no truth in the allegations in today's Guardian that I received payments from Ian Greer on behalf of Mohammed Al-Fayed in return for asking Parliamentary Questions or for any other action.

"As Minister of Corporate Affairs I have from the outset scrupulously excluded myself from consideration of any matters concerning House of Fraser on account of my earlier interest in issues involving the Al-Fayeds as a backbencher."

Downing Street disclosed that the Commons Committee on Members' Interests had already investigated an allegation that Mr Hamilton and his wife, Christine, had received a free holiday at the Ritz Hotel in Paris owned by the Al-Fayeds. The Committee accepted Mr Hamilton's explanation and the Cabinet Secretary did not feel the matter should be reopened.

Mr Smith, who quit at lunchtime after offering his "profound apologies" to Mr Major, said he became involved with Mr Al-Fayed in 1986, agreeing to further "legitimate concerns", tabling questions and calling a late-night debate. He said: "Mr Al-Fayed paid me fees. I ended this relationship with him in 1989. Shortly before then I made an appropriate entry in the Register of Members' Interests.

"But, I acknowledge, I did not declare all the necessary information in the Register of Members' Interests until close to the end of my consultancy and I should have done so before then."

The payments were declared in his tax returns, he said.

26 October 1994
Major sets up "sleaze" inquiry
Hamilton sacked as Prime Minister cites further allegations
By George Jones

A far-reaching inquiry into standards in public life was announced by the Prime Minister last night as allegations of "sleaze" claimed another casualty with the enforced resignation of Mr Neil Hamilton as the Corporate Affairs Minister. Mr Major also said he had reported Mr Mohamed Al-Fayed to the Director of Public Prosecutions for what a senior Tory MP described as "attempted blackmail".

Mr Major told a tense Commons that the DPP had been sent a note of a meeting he had with an "informant", in which Mr Major was allegedly offered a deal by Mr Fayed, the Harrods chairman, over allegations of wrongdoing by ministers.

Mr Michael Howard, the Home Secretary, also confirmed that he was involved in the investigation, conducted by the Cabinet Secretary, Sir Robin Butler, into Mr Al-Fayed's allegations.

After being cleared by Sir Robin, Mr Howard said that he had "never been guilty of any impropriety in the conduct of any of my responsibilities as a minister or MP".

Mr Major's attempt to defuse the charges of "sleaze" engulfing the Government by setting up an independent inquiry headed by an Appeal Court judge, Lord Nolan, were overshadowed by the mysterious and acrimonious circumstances surrounding the sacking of Mr Hamilton.

The Cabinet Secretary found no evidence to disprove Mr Hamilton's denial that he had taken payments from Mr Al-Fayed to table parliamentary questions.

He also appeared to have accepted Mr Hamilton's explanation that he had not declared a €4,000 stay at the Ritz Hotel in Paris, owned by Mr Al-Fayed, because he thought he had been invited as a private guest.

Mr Major told MPs that other "unconnected allegations" had been made since Sir Robin had completed his investigations. The combined allegations had "disabled" Mr Hamilton from carrying out his ministerial responsibilities and he had agreed to resign.

Friends of Mr Hamilton disputed that version. They said that Mr Hamilton had been sacked and was hurt and angry over his treatment.

In a letter to Mr Major last night Mr Hamilton revealed his bitterness. He said it was "sad and deeply disturbing" that he had been forced from office because of a "foully motivated rumour and media witch-hunt".

He vowed to clear his name, saying that he had not been paid by Mr Al-Fayed, "nor have I acted for him in return for favours".

Despite his obvious anger, he added: "I have been honoured to serve in your Government and, as you know, you will be able to rely upon my support in the future."

In his reply, Mr Major said he was sorry at the way events had turned out and confirmed that he had been "entirely prepared to accept" that Mr Hamilton had acted properly.

He added: "However, I must be concerned at the general perception of the Government and capacity of ministers to carry out their work without damaging distractions.

"It was for that reason I felt it in the best interests of the Government you should stand aside."

The confusion surrounding the real reasons for Mr Hamilton's departure increased when Mr David Hunt, the Public Service Minister, said that the allegations over which he was finally forced to stand down were unfounded.

"It is the culmination now of some fresh, additional, unfounded allegations that sadly caused Neil and the Prime Minister to feel that he should resign," he told *Channel 4 News*. Downing Street refused to specify the new allegations against Mr Hamilton and said it was unlikely that another formal inquiry would be launched as he was no longer a member of the Government. But officials said they were not connected with the earlier charges and had been passed to Mr Major on Monday night after he received Sir Robin's report.

Mr Hamilton pulled out of a long-standing lunch engagement in Sussex when he was summoned to the office of the Chief Whip, Mr Richard Ryder, at midday to be told of the new information. Also present at the meeting was his ministerial boss, Mr Michael Heseltine, the President of the Board of Trade.

Senior Tories said that Mr Major, who did not meet Mr Hamilton yesterday, was "irritated" by the way he had defended his decision to try to stay in office, particularly his joke about registering a gift of a ginger biscuit.

Ministers also described as "ill judged" a statement issued by Mr Hamilton's office earlier yesterday, in which he likened his decision to issue a libel writ to the Prime Minister's decision last year to launch libel proceedings against *Scallywag* magazine over allegations of an affair with a Downing Street caterer.

"There is no reason whatsoever why a minister of the Crown should not remain in office whilst undertaking libel proceedings," said the press release issued on Mr Hamilton's behalf to local newspapers. "Indeed, the Prime Minister did just that – and quite rightly so."

In a further attempt to clear the air Mr Major published a five-page report from the Cabinet Secretary into the allegations by Mr Al-Fayed, which had been passed to Mr Major on 29 September by an unnamed informant.

Sir Robin said that the intermediary made it clear that Mr Al-Fayed wanted a meeting with the Prime Minister, principally because he wanted a highly critical Department of Trade and Industry report into his takeover of Harrods "revised or withdrawn".

The intermediary also said that Mr Al-Fayed was considering passing on to others a number of allegations against ministers.

Sir Robin said Mr Major replied that it would be impossible for him to see Mr Al-Fayed in those circumstances. "You added that, if ministers had been guilty of wrongdoing, you were not going to make any sort of deal, regardless of the cost to the Government's reputation."

During the Commons exchanges on Mr Major's statement, Sir Peter Tapsell, MP for Lindsey East, asked if the DPP would be examining whether Mr Al-Fayed "will be prosecuted for attempted blackmail".

To the surprise of MPs, Mr Major replied: "A note of my meeting [with the informant] has been passed to the DPP."

Although Mr Tim Smith resigned last week as junior Northern Ireland Minister after admitting that he had not declared payments from Mr Al-Fayed at the appropriate time, Sir Robin found that the other allegations against ministers were either false or entirely unsubstantiated, as well as being denied by the ministers concerned.

But Mr Major told MPs action was "imperative" to meet public disquiet about standards in public life. He said the Nolan committee would be established on a permanent basis and would look at the standards of conduct of all holders of public office, including MPs, civil servants and members of quangos.

Opposition leaders welcomed the inquiry. But Mr Tony Blair, the Labour leader, dismissed the plans as "decision making on the run" and said that important issues had been ignored too long. Mr Blair also expressed concern that the wider inquiry might be used to sweep the "cash for questions" allegations against Tory MPs from public view.

Mr Major made clear that he believed the Commons Privileges Committee should continue to investigate those charges in private not public, despite a threatened Labour boycott.

Many Tory MPs were in a despondent mood last night over the unfolding "sleaze" saga. They were alarmed that the Prime Minister's statement – particularly the counter-allegations against Mr Al-Fayed – suggested that the whole affair was much deeper than had been admitted.

There were further suggestions at Westminster that more than three ministers had been named in the original allegations.

The sacking of Mr Hamilton infuriated Right-wing Tories. They alleged that he had been forced out of office by pressure from Left-of-Centre ministers. Appeals from two prominent Right-wing ministers, Mr Michael Portillo and Mr Peter Lilley, for the Government to stand by Mr Hamilton were to no avail.

There was criticism among Tories over the way Mr Major had abandoned Mr Hamilton five days after saying that he was not prepared to take action on the basis of unsubstantiated rumours and that people should be regarded as innocent until proved guilty.

Some said that the Prime Minister had again laid himself open to charges of indecisiveness and that it would have been better for Mr Hamilton to leave the Government at the same time as Mr Smith resigned last week.

Last night Labour kept up its attack on the Government over standards in public life, alleging during a Commons debate on "creeping privatisation of the NHS" that the chairmen of 66 NHS trusts were either prominent members of the Tory Party or had made a donation to it.

Also 26 October 1994
Why Hamilton was forced to go in the end
A minister's fight to stay in office
By Philip Johnston

Business has been brisk this week at the office of the Register of Members' Interests, tucked away at the end of the committee corridor in the Commons.

MPs have been appending anything that could be construed as falling within the 10 categories of registrable interests, ranging from paid directorships to overseas visits.

One minister said yesterday that he had been trawling his memory to recall anything from his days as a backbencher that may return to haunt him.

"Few of us can say, hand on heart, that we have never been a guest of someone or taken a weekend here of there or attended a function that should properly have been registered," he added.

Mr Neil Hamilton, who resigned as Corporate Affairs Minister yesterday, must now rue the day that he failed to send his registration slip to the members' interest committee noting a stay at the Paris Ritz in 1987, courtesy of Mohamed Al-Fayed.

As he strenuously denied receiving any payments from Mr Al-Fayed to ask questions in the Commons – and issued a writ for libel against the *Guardian* for saying he had – it was the Ritz episode that kept the dogs at his heels.

Despite the resignation of Mr Tim Smith, the other minister named by Mr Al-Fayed as a recipient of the Harrods owner's largesse, it was clear from the outset that Mr Hamilton intended to fight his corner.

He argued that the "cash for questions" allegations were unfounded and he was entitled to defend himself while remaining in office.

His stay at the Ritz was well known. It had been reported in the *Guardian* more than a year ago and the Commons members' interest committee had decided not to conduct an investigation.

Over the weekend, Mr Hamilton's Right-wing colleagues at Westminster sought to shore up his position. Sir George Gardiner, MP for Reigate and secretary of the 92 Group of Right-wingers, assured him of strong support.

After a period when it looked as if Mr Hamilton would not survive – especially when Mr David Hunt, Chancellor of the Duchy of Lancaster, cut the ground from beneath him on a television interview – opinion at Westminster began to swing back in his favour.

Mr Michael Portillo, the Employment Secretary and the Cabinet's leading Right-winger, came out publicly to defend Mr Hamilton's right to stay in office.

Other colleagues were also willing to defend him. Mr John Townend, chairman of the backbench finance committee, said it was the mainstay of British justice that a man was innocent until proven guilty.

Tuesday dawned and Mr Hamilton was preparing to continue with his ministerial engagements. He travelled to Sussex for a meeting with East Sussex County Council, arriving in Bexhill-on-Sea exhibiting his renowned wit, but what in retrospect appears to have been gallows humour.

Just as he joked last week about registering the gift of a biscuit from a school, he commented wryly on the unusual interest of the media in local industry.

He was then due to attend the annual meeting of the Sussex Chamber of Commerce at Gatwick Airport's Ramada Hotel – but did not appear.

Back in London, there was consternation in the Government over a press release from Mr Hamilton's office at Westminster, which sought to draw a parallel with his predicament and that of Mr Major, when he issued a writ for libel against *Scallywag* magazine for alleging an extra-marital affair.

"There is no reason whatsoever why a Minister of the Crown should not remain in office whilst undertaking libel proceedings," said the statement. "Indeed, the Prime Minister did just that – and quite rightly so."

Friends of Mr Hamilton said the statement was not intended for release yesterday, had not been approved by the Minister and was a briefing note on which a press release to constituency newspapers was to be based later in the week.

Suddenly, Westminster was again awash with "Hamilton to go" rumours but official sources said yesterday morning: "No government changes are expected."

But the story was to take another bizarre twist. Unknown to Mr Hamilton, further allegations had been made against him to the Prime Minister on Monday night after he had effectively been exonerated by the Cabinet Secretary's report on the Al-Fayed claims.

Mr Hamilton's sudden departure from Sussex was in answer to a summons from the Chief Whip, Mr Richard Ryder. Around 1 p.m., he arrived at the Chief Whip's office at 12 Downing Street, where Mr Michael Heseltine, President of the Board of Trade and Mr Hamilton's superior, was also waiting.

Here, for the first time, he was told of other allegations against him – but not of the detail. With Mr Major due in the Commons within two hours to announce an inquiry into standards in public life, Mr Hamilton was left with no option. In short, he was fired.

1 October 1996

Tory drops libel fight over sleaze

Major faces new cash-for-questions furore

By Ben Fenton and George Jones

The Government faces renewed allegations of parliamentary sleaze involving Tory MPs last night after the spectacular collapse of one of the most high-profile libel actions in recent years.

Neil Hamilton, the former corporate affairs minister, had sued the *Guardian* over allegations that he received payments to ask questions on behalf of Mohamed Al-Fayed, the owner of Harrods.

The paper claimed that Ian Greer, a parliamentary lobbyist, was the intermediary for the payments and he also sued the paper in a joint action with Mr Hamilton, MP for Tatton, Cheshire.

But the two men dropped their action minutes before a legal deadline and the trial, due to start today, was abandoned. Mr Greer and Mr Hamilton agreed to pay what the paper said was a "substantial contribution" – £7,500 each – to its costs.

Both men issued statements denying any admission of the paper's accusations and cited technical legal problems for the decision to drop the case.

Alan Rusbridger, the *Guardian*'s editor, said that research carried out as part of the paper's defence showed that its original allegations were "just the tip of the iceberg". He added: "This research, together with documents which were disclosed to us by 10 Downing Street as part of the legal process, made it apparent that [Mr Hamilton and Mr Greer] didn't have a leg to stand on."

Mr Rusbridger said his paper would be "publishing a lot more". Today's *Guardian* claim that more Tory MPs were involved in the scandal will cause consternation in the party and is likely to threaten the stability of the Government. Labour demanded a full inquiry by Sir Gordon Downey, the parliamentary commissioner for standards.

The latest developments could not have come at a worse time for John Major as the Tories prepare for their last conference before the election.

Although the Prime Minister and senior colleagues have been spared the embarrassment of appearing in the witness box, the Tory "sleaze" saga has been revived on the eve of Tony Blair's speech to the Labour conference in Blackpool and six days before the Tories meet in Bournemouth. Mr Blair will seize on the claims that other Tory MPs took cash for questions to justify Labour claims that the Government is no longer fit for office.

There will be dismay among many Tories, who had felt that they were recovering from the damage caused by the row over standards in public life and the Scott inquiry into arms for Iraq.

Ministers fear that it will undermine the Government's slow recovery in the opinion polls.

Mr Hamilton, a noted parliamentary wit and Euro-sceptic, had taken a high profile in seeking to clear his name after resigning from the Government. Sources close to both plaintiffs claimed that paying £7,500 to the *Guardian*, which they said had costs of £400,000, was nominal and indicated that the newspaper had not won a full victory.

But Mr Rusbridger said: "The point was not to wring huge sums of money from these men, but to establish the principle that they were paying our costs so they could not claim [the deal] had any honour in it for them at all.

"Perhaps we should put this in perspective: yesterday they were suing us for £2.5m and today they are paying us £15,000."

Mr Hamilton had always maintained his innocence and helped to push through a change in the law of parliamentary privilege to allow him to defend himself in court.

He said that a "conflict of interests" had arisen between "myself and my co-plaintiffs".

Mr Hamilton, 46, said he could not afford the enormously increased costs of briefing new lawyers in addition to the £150,000 he had already paid.

"Furthermore, I am not prepared to prolong indefinitely the appalling emotional stress which my wife has already suffered as a result of this article."

Mr Rusbridger said it was "one of the most astonishing legal cave-ins in the history of the law of libel".

"These are men who for two years have blustered about their innocence. One has persuaded his fellow Conservative backbenchers to amend the 1689 Bill of Rights. He has gone cap in hand to his fellow MPs to fund his action and, as recently as three weeks ago, was vigorously promising to expose journalistic 'corruption and fantasy'.

"Yet at the courtroom door both men have thrown in the towel and paid the *Guardian* a substantial contribution to their costs.

"The only possible explanation is that both knew the evidence the *Guardian* had compiled to defend the case would have blown the action out of the water and revealed a pattern of parliamentary sleaze more far-reaching than we had ever imagined."

Mr Greer said: "This matter has gone on long enough and is fast turning into a media circus.

"My lawyers have advised me not to litigate, so we have taken a difficult and sensible commercial decision. I totally refute that this sensible decision is an admission of the allegations."

The case was set to run for at least three and a half weeks, involving Richard Ferguson, QC, for the plaintiffs, and Geoffrey Robertson, QC, for the newspaper.

It is thought that the "conflict of interest" arose last Friday when Peter Carter-Ruck and Partners, the solicitors who had been acting for Mr Hamilton and Mr Greer for two years, received the transcript of a telephone conversation between the MP and Michael Heseltine.

In the course of the call, the Deputy Prime Minister demanded to know if Mr Hamilton had ever received money from Mr Greer. Mr Hamilton said he had not. But sources close to the case say that this was "at variance" with a statement made by Mr Greer.

Shortly after the telephone conversation with Mr Heseltine Mr Hamilton resigned from the Government.

With Mr Carter-Ruck's firm and counsel saying that they was no longer able to continue, the two plaintiffs employed other solicitors, but soon afterwards decided that they could not afford to restart the case.

Mr Major and Mr Heseltine had been subpoenaed to give evidence about why Mr Hamilton was forced to resign a week after he strenuously denied the *Guardian*'s allegations.

The paper had also said that Mr Hamilton failed to disclose a £3,600 bill he ran up at the Ritz hotel in Paris, where he stayed in 1987 as a guest of the owner, Mr Al-Fayed.

At first Mr Hamilton had said that he did not intend to resign. Tim Smith, a junior Northern Ireland minister named in the same story on 20 October 1994, stepped down the day after the allegations.

When Mr Hamilton did resign, under pressure from Mr Major, he said that he would carry on a legal battle to clear his name.

This involved forcing a change in the law because the Bill of Rights forbade the courts to question parliamentary activities.

Mr Hamilton said yesterday that he would continue to fight to clear his name by referring the allegations made by Mr Al-Fayed to the Commons committee for standards and privileges.

Because the issue is unresolved he must now give up hope of returning to office.

Jonathan Aitken, the former Treasury Chief Secretary, still has a libel action against the *Guardian* outstanding. The paper accused him of allowing Said Ayas, a Middle Eastern businessman, to pay for a stay at the Ritz in Paris in 1993.

2 October 1996
Tory MP admits taking £10,000
By Ben Fenton, Colin Randall and George Jones

Neil Hamilton, the Tory MP who dropped a libel action aimed at clearing his name of allegations that he received money from Ian Greer, a lobbyist, to ask parliamentary questions, admitted last night receiving two payments totalling £10,000 from Mr Greer.

Mr Hamilton, who is now relying on an investigation by Sir Gordon Downey, the Parliamentary Commissioner for Standards, to save his reputation, said he had received the money in 1988 and 1989 as "commissions" for introducing firms to the lobbyist.

He did not name the two companies but said they were not connected with Mohamed Al-Fayed, the Harrods boss. The *Guardian* had alleged that Mr Hamilton and other Tory MPs had accepted cash from Mr Greer to generally represent the interest of Mr Al-Fayed.

The former corporate affairs minister admitted that in 1994 he had told Michael Heseltine, then President of the Board of Trade, he had no financial relationship with Mr Greer.

In a statement last night, Mr Hamilton repeated that he did not regard these two payments as a "financial relationship".

Mr Hamilton resigned as a minister in October 1994, five days after the *Guardian* alleged the cash-for-questions relationship and also after separate allegations were made about his business affairs.

On the BBC *Newsnight* programme last night, Mr Hamilton said the two commissions were for £4,000 and £6,000.

He described as "preposterous" new allegations in the *Guardian* yesterday that he had received cash-filled envelopes from Mr Al-Fayed between 1987 and 1989. He admitted that he had a free holiday at the Ritz Hotel in Paris, owned by Mr Al-Fayed, in 1987, but denied being extravagant in running up a bill for extras of £2,000 in six days.

Mr Hamilton also said that he had a short holiday in 1989 in a flat in the grounds of Mr Fayed's castle in Scotland.

A spokesman for Ian Greer Associates said two commissions had been paid to Mr Hamilton but this was the extent of their financial relationship.

It is thought that the disclosure by Downing Street of a document which showed that Mr Hamilton had denied any financial relationship with Mr Greer to Mr Heseltine in 1994 was the indirect cause of the breakdown of the libel action, which was formally ended in the High Court yesterday.

This denial had not been previously known to the legal team representing the two plaintiffs.

In a separate development, IGA said last night that during the last two elections Mr Greer had passed on thousands of pounds into the constituency "fighting funds" of 25 MPs: 21 Tory, two Labour and two Liberal Democrats.

A total of £29,000 was paid to Tory MPs in 1987, £18,000 from Mr Al-Fayed.

The Labour MP Chris Smith received £200 in 1992. Doug Hoyle, chairman of the Parliamentary Labour Party, got cash in 1987 and 1992.

In most cases the money was paid directly to the constituency associations so the MPs might not have been aware of its provenance. Such donations are perfectly legal although MPs cannot spend more than £6,000 on election expenses.

But a Conservative Central Office internal memo, disclosed to the *Guardian* as part of the evidence in the libel action, shows the party was extremely wary of the information being made public.

Sir Paul Judge, then director-general, wrote: "Despite our not being involved directly, this issue clearly does have the potential to embarrass the Party."

He added: "The list contains a number of prominent names including Michael Portillo, Gerry Malone and Michael Hirst. It is clear that the *Guardian* could generate considerable 'sleaze' by portraying these payments to the fighting funds candidates [sic] as being designed to buy influence."

Sir Gordon Downey said yesterday that he would carry out a full investigation of the original affair and the new allegations, which named three other Tory MPs.

"These are serious allegations and, in a sense, whether they are true or not, allegations will tend to colour people's views about Parliament," he said.

"To that extent, I regret it. I will regret it even more if there is foundation for the allegations, of course."

Labour and Liberal Democrat politicians urged the Prime Minister to disclose all necessary documents.

Also 2 October 1996
Two words shattered £800,000 libel case
Newspaper rejects suggestions that
Hamilton settlement was "score draw"
By Ben Fenton

It takes a legal earth quake edging off the Richter scale to bring a libel action – two years and about £800,000 in preparation – crashing to the ground less than 24 hours before it is due to start.

To those unfamiliar with the intricacies of the law of libel, it has been hard to understand precisely why the action against the *Guardian* by Neil Hamilton MP and Ian Greer, the political lobbyist, collapsed in a heap.

It seems that the fault line was prised open by a little Latin phrase: Duces tecum.

Last Thursday Charles Gray, QC, arrived at the High Court to represent Mr Major, Michael Heseltine, the Deputy Prime Minister, Richard Ryder, Chief Whip at the time of the Hamilton resignation, and Sir Robin Butler, the Cabinet Secretary.

Each had been served with a formal witness order, issued by the *Guardian* last month, called a *Subpoena duces tecum*. Loosely translated, it means "Under penalty, you shall bring with you . . . " and is a command not only to attend the trial to give evidence in person, but also to have available all relevant documents.

Until a few years ago, the parties to a civil action had to wait until the trial was running before they saw the witnesses and their documents, which often led to adjournments as the new material was studied by both sides.

Now, the judge can order the witness to appear before the jury is empanelled, so that the surrendered evidence can be studied by both sides.

After Thursday's hearing, and at the order of Mr Justice Bell, Mr Gray released selected documents from the Cabinet Office and 10 Downing Street.

They covered the days between the *Guardian's* original allegations about Mr Hamilton's receipt of cash-for-questions, published on 20 October 1994, and his enforced resignation as corporate affairs minister five days later.

None of these documents which, now that the case has been formally concluded, will theoretically remain secret for at least 30 years, had been seen by either Geoffrey Robertson, QC, for the *Guardian*, or Richard Ferguson, QC, for Mr Hamilton and Mr Greer.

The documents did not reach both parties, by messenger, until well after dark last Thursday and had an immediate effect.

It appears that the details of questions put to Mr Hamilton by Sir Robin and Mr Heseltine and his answers were at odds with the version of events known to his lawyers. The particular question that caused the most problems seems to have been whether Mr Hamilton had ever received money from Mr Greer.

Mr Greer was immediately prompted to tell Peter Carter-Ruck, the head of the firm of solicitors representing both men, that what the MP said two years ago raised a "conflict of interest" between the plaintiffs.

Mr Carter-Ruck and Mr Ferguson said they could not continue with the case but agreed to stay on to arrange a settlement with the newspaper, which was explained yesterday to the trial judge and formally approved. Negotiations for a final settlement took place over the weekend.

The newspaper, which at first said it wanted to go to trial and "destroy" the plaintiffs, agreed to settle for £15,000, and the deal was announced on Monday.

The *Guardian's* editor, Alan Rusbridger was angered by the way in which Mr Hamilton and Mr Greer interpreted the end of the action as – to quote one of those briefing journalists on their behalf on Monday – "a score draw".

In an article, the editor said: "Last night, press statements by both Mr Greer and Mr Hamilton falsely claimed that the *Guardian* had made the first settlement offer.

It was the last of hundreds of lies both men have told in the course of the case – to the public, the lawyers and (it may be) to each other."

The decision by Mr Hamilton and Mr Greer that they could no longer afford to fight to clear their names left the way open for them to be buried in an avalanche of mud from their original attackers.

The *Guardian* ran stories over three pages yesterday. Even so, a front-page editorial said that the law bound it to returning the *duces tecum* papers to their owners so the version of events it was publishing was "incomplete".

It was "a glimpse of a revealed pattern of greed and deception which should be of grave concern to the Prime Minister and all those concerned for parliamentary democracy", the paper said.

In several thousand words, the *Guardian* heaped new charges on Mr Hamilton and Mr Greer and drew others into the crosshairs of its campaign. The former minister was cast as a man who frequently popped into the Park Lane offices of Mr Al-Fayed to pocket brown envelopes personally filled with £50 notes by the Harrods chairman.

The statements of three of Mr Al-Fayed's former and present employees were repeated, alleging that Mr Hamilton and Mr Greer turned up in person to collect their cash.

Mr Greer was portrayed as an ace of lobbyists, developing "networks" of MPs to pursue by parliamentary and political means the interests of his high-paying clients.

Three Tory knights – Sir Michael Grylls, Sir Peter Hordern and Sir Andrew Bowden – were added to the pairing in October 1994 of Mr Hamilton and Tim Smith MP as the executors of Mr Al-Fayed's commercial will within the halls of Westminster.

They were all said to have received money from Mr Al-Fayed through Mr Greer, although Sir Peter always declared his paid interest and Sir Andrew denied yesterday receiving any money.

The *Guardian* left its readers with the impression that they were viewing only the tip of a grimy iceberg and that if the procedures introduced at the recommendation of the Nolan committee worked effectively, the whole edifice would tip up and expose itself to view.

And all because of two little Latin words.

3 October 1996
Neil didn't chicken out, says MP's wife
Christine Hamilton talks to us
By Elizabeth Grice

Threat of financial ruin, not failure of nerve, was what stopped Neil Hamilton from pursuing his libel action in the High Court, his wife Christine claimed last night.

"We did not chicken out, certainly not," she said. "We just could not afford another £60,000 or £70,000 to brief a new legal team. We are at the limit of our borrowing capacity.

"It was an enormous let-down. We felt cheated because we believed court was the proper forum to have allegations against Neil tested on oath."

Mrs Hamilton was passionate in her husband's defence but said that there had been times over the past two years when she wished she had married a bus driver.

"We have gone through some tremendous highs and lows," she said. "After coping with such a welter of lies there were times when I thought 'Let's just cut and start again and go to Timbuktu'.

"But we are determined to see it through. We've got the stamina, mentally and physically. Neil's a British bulldog. We are not contemplating a future outside politics."

Mrs Hamilton, although clearly a woman of cast-iron nerves, says she is "soft and sensitive" to pain when her husband is attacked. "I get more upset than he does. But it doesn't help me to help Neil if I show it.

"People have the mistaken idea that politicians are immune to criticism. It was a devastating moment when I saw the *Guardian* front page on Tuesday morning."

She is angry that "so much nonsense" has been written about their holiday at Mohamed Al-Fayed's Scottish castle. It was a converted stable, she points out, where they stayed two nights on their way to Cape Wrath.

"It's all been made out to be corrupt. But it was 10 years ago and the climate has completely changed about what it is proper to declare. Hindsight is a wonderful thing."

Her husband's two payments totalling £10,000 from the lobbyist Ian Greer were not, she said, the subject of any deceit or late admission and were unconnected with the Fayed allegations.

"They were right up front in Neil's witness statement. We wanted it all to come out in court. We have nothing to hide." Asked whether she wished she had never heard of Mr Al-Fayed and Mr Greer, she replied: "I don't feel that about Mr Greer, but of course I wish I had never heard of Al-Fayed."

Throughout their ordeal, she said, her husband had never lost his sense of humour. "I love him for all sorts of reasons and one is his sense of fun.

"Life needs characters. Neil is a character. There are a lot of colourless people in Parliament but when those who are not colourless are treated in this way, is it surprising?"

Keith Hampson

"I have always led a normal heterosexual life."

13 May 1984
Minister's aide resigns after gay club incident
Bailed MP says: "I was fed up and drank too much"
By Christopher House, George Jones, Christopher Elliott, Paul Williams and Carole Dawson

Dr Keith Hampson, Conservative MP for Leeds North-West, resigned last night as Parliamentary Private Secretary to Mr Heseltine, Defence Secretary, after being arrested for an alleged indecent assault in a London club which features male strippers.

His resignation came just hours after Mr Heseltine was informed of the alleged incident involving Dr Hampson, his Parliamentary Private Secretary since last June.

In a statement made to the *Sunday Telegraph* at 4.15 yesterday afternoon, Dr Hampson said: "To avoid embarrassment to Michael Heseltine and the Government I have resigned as Parliamentary Private Secretary.

"This is because of personal problems resulting from one night a week or so ago when I was totally fed up and drank far too much."

The resignation was immediately accepted by Mr Heseltine and both he and colleagues were shaken by the situation.

Mr Heseltine is understood to have been saddened by the resignation of Dr Hampson, whom he had known for years. But given the sensitive nature of his appointment as aide to the Defence Secretary, it was considered that Dr Hampson had no alternative.

A report on the alleged incident has been submitted to Mrs Thatcher, who is spending the weekend at Chequers. Although Whitehall sources insisted last night that Dr Hampson had no access to secret information, his resignation will lead to questions about security.

There is concern in Whitehall that Mr Heseltine was not informed until yesterday morning – nine days after Dr Hampson's arrest.

The Government is certain to face questions from MPs on why neither Mrs Thatcher nor Mr Heseltine was informed sooner.

They may be questioned about the security clearance given to PPSs, as it is understood that Dr Hampson was not positively vetted before taking up his post.

No 10 Downing Street is understood to have learnt about Dr Hampson's arrest late on Friday.

Events moved swiftly after Mr Heseltine learned of the alleged incident. Dr Hampson was at Conservative Central Office yesterday morning and afternoon interviewing candidates for vacancies in the party's research department.

He issued his statement of resignation after a series of hurried telephone calls involving Mr Heseltine and senior party officials.

After his arrest Dr Hampson was given police bail pending the outcome of a report to the Metropolitan Police solicitors. He has not been charged with any offence.

The incident is alleged to have occurred in the Gay Theatre in Berwick Street, Soho, at 10.30 p.m. on Thursday, 3 May. The theatre gives continuous two-hour shows.

Dr Hampson, aged 40, who is married, is alleged to have indecently assaulted a police constable from Scotland Yard's Club Squad, who was on routine surveillance duty in plain clothes. The officer was with a woman police officer, who was also in plain clothes.

Dr Hampson was arrested and taken to West End Central police station where the Club Squad is based. He was interviewed by senior police officers and later released.

A statement from Scotland Yard said: "We can confirm that a man was arrested in the Gay Theatre in Berwick Street, W1, on Thursday, 3 May, for an alleged indecent assault on a male."

The statement said he was freed "pending a report on the incident to the Metropolitan Police solicitors.

"He has not been charged, therefore we cannot confirm or deny his name."

The incident might be deeply embarrassing to the Government given the sensitive nature of Dr Hampson's appointment as aide to Mr Heseltine. Although Parliamentary Private Secretaries are not members of the Government, their appointment has to be approved by the Prime Minister and is generally regarded as the first rung of the ministerial ladder.

Dr Hampson had access to Mr Heseltine's private office in the Ministry of Defence and attended briefings with ministers and officials. His main role was to liaise between Mr Heseltine and Tory backbenchers, acting as the minister's "eyes and ears" within the House of Commons.

Defence officials emphasised last night that Dr Hampson was not given classified documents or information during his work with Mr Heseltine. It was said that he was excluded from discussions on secret matters in the Ministry.

Mr Ted Leadbitter, Labour MP for Hartlepool, who has taken a special interest in security matters, will write to the Prime Minister today asking why it took so long before she and the Defence Secretary were informed.

He wanted to know whether they considered they had been kept properly informed.

Dr Hampson has represented Leeds North-West since the General Election last June.

He has been Parliamentary Private Secretary to Mr Heseltine since June last year. Previously he was PPS to Mr Tom King, then Minister, Local Government and the Environment. He was a personal assistant to Mr Heath, the former Prime Minister, in the 1966 General Election and also assisted him in the 1970 election in his Bexley constituency.

Before entering Parliament Dr Hampson was a lecturer in American history at Edinburgh University. He is on the liberal, or "wet" wing of the Conservative Party.

At the last election Dr Hampson had a majority of 8,537 over the SDP candidate.

The news stunned party workers in Dr Hampson's Leeds North-West constituency.

Mr Raymond Curry, the constituency party chairman, said last night: "This is news to me. I am surprised and I am sure everyone else will be. I can't make any specific comments about it until I have talked to Keith. He is very popular."

19 October 1984
Tory MP "thought WPC in gay club was in drag"
"Muddled impression" after pints of "brain damage"
By Guy Rais

Mr Keith Hampson, 41, Conservative MP for Leeds North-West, who is accused of indecently assaulting a plain-clothed policeman in the Gay Theatre, a club in Berwick Street, Soho, denied on oath yesterday that he had any homosexual tendencies.

"I have always led a normal heterosexual life," he told the jury at Southwark Crown Court.

The jury of nine men and three women is expected to give its verdict today.

Hampson, a doctor of philosophy, resigned as Private Parliamentary Secretary to Mr Heseltine, Defence Secretary, after his arrest.

His first wife was killed in a car crash in 1975 three months after their marriage. His second wife, Susan, a journalist on the *Financial Times*, is expecting their first child.

Hampson, of Markham Street, Chelsea, denied a charge of indecently assaulting PC Stuart Marshall on 3 May contrary to Section 15 of the Sexual Offences Act, 1956.

Mr Roy Amlot, prosecuting, said after watching a naked man "prancing" on the stage to music in the Gay Theatre Hampson indecently assaulted PC Marshall in the dimly lit lounge area of the "small and seedy" club.

PC Marshall had been on a routine visit to the club, accompanied by WPC June Maudling.

It was alleged that Hampson had put one hand on PC Marshall's buttocks, and with the other stroked his groin area.

Giving evidence in a firm voice after sitting in the dock beside a prison officer, Hampson described events on the night he took a trip to Soho.

The previous week had been taxing and on the day in question he had been working on a draft speech for Mr Heseltine for the Institute of Strategic Studies.

They had had "a terribly late night" in the House and he had spent all day working on the speech. Shortly after 6 p.m. he was feeling a bit fed up and went to the Marquis of Granby in Smith Square next to the Conservative Central Office where he used to drink with some of his chums.

He stayed there for about two hours with four friends. "We were drinking what we call 'brain damage' – pints of Bass. My wife was not expected home until about 11 p.m."

After dropping one of his friends off at a tube station he returned to the Ministry of Defence where he did some more work until about 9.15.

He then decided to go to the West End to see a licensee and his wife at a public house off Shaftesbury Avenue. They were not in, and he had one drink and left hurriedly as his car was on a double yellow line. The time was then 9.45.

"Soho is a lively place and I decided to stay there and fill in time."

Asked by Mr John Mathew, QC, defending, if he had ever been to sex-oriented establishments in Soho before he replied: "At times, yes," and recalled going to a strip club where there were girl strippers on his 40th birthday.

Hampson said he drove around the one way system before finding a parking spot fortuitously in Berwick Street.

He noticed a sign which simply said "Male Revue" adding "It wasn't a moment for major thought. If you are fairly merry, or out on the town you do live dangerously, and I thought I'd go in and see what was doing. I had never been in one before."

He was asked to pay £5, but when he hesitated because he only intended staying half an hour he was allowed to pay only £2.

When he first walked into the basement it was almost pitch-black. He "blundered" into a row of seats and he took one in the middle. After he had been there a few minutes he noticed a couple of men come in and a woman – who later turned out to be a police officer – wearing what he thought was a rubber trench coat.

"My impression was very muddled and I thought 'God, what's a woman doing here in drag. I was quite fascinated and I turned round a couple of times to stare at her."

Hampson said that by that time the five pints he had drunk began taking effect and he left to go upstairs to the lavatory.

Afterwards, "to get value for money he thought he would round things off" and go down again. The woman interested him because he thought she must be "a chap in drag".

Hampson said he went back and stayed at the back where he could see the woman much better. He was standing to the right of the man he later knew was a police officer, who was "sort of leaning back against the wall." The WPC was on his opposite side.

He bent down and began staring at her. "I never denied that my hand fell against the policeman's thigh but he simply grabbed me."

Asked if he recalled his left hand touching the officer's thigh, he replied: "I think inadvertently my left hand did touch his thigh."

Everything then went in rapid succession. "He grabbed my left forearm, and said he was a police officer."

Mr Mathew: Did you at any stage bring your right hand across to his right thigh, move it across to his private parts and grasp it and move it up and down?

Hampson: I am not aware of that at all.

After he was taken upstairs "I was feeling pretty devastated. I thought 'My God' what are people going to say finding me in a place like this?"

Mr Mathew ended his questioning asking: Did you take any action towards that PC with any indecent thoughts in your mind?

Hampson: No, of course not.

Cross examined by Mr Amlot who asked him why he had gone to the bar Hampson replied: "It was a sense of devilment sometimes one gets into."

Asked why he was so curious about the woman he replied "I was a bit light hearted and not rational or sober about it."

Mr Amlot: It's possible you touched his penis?

Hampson: No, absolutely not.

Earlier Mr Amlot said the club was one of the small and seedy establishments that officers from the clubs section of Scotland Yard were required to keep an eye on.

PC Marshall said he had been attached to the clubs squad for about three months when he visited the Gay Theatre on 3 May.

"I was in plainclothes, wearing a blue jacket, blue jeans and a pair of training shoes. We arrived just after 10 p.m. and were checking for offences under the Sexual Offences Act."

He said he spoke briefly with the club's manager, then went downstairs where there was a small stage and some seats.

"On the stage was a male in his early twenties who was dancing naked. There were approximately seven people scattered around in chairs and two people standing at the back. Music was being played on a cassette on the stage."

The club was dimly lit. "It was a bit like a cinema, it took a while for your eyes to get used to it."

He stood at the back, where he was joined by his female colleague.

"I saw the man I know now to be Dr Hampson seated two rows from the back in the end seat.

"He turned round and looked directly at me. He then stood up and left the room going towards the stairs.

"Dr Hampson returned to the room and walked directly in front of me and stood on my right-hand side, approximately three or four inches away from me. He was watching me. He then put his left hand at the back of my right thigh and raised it on to my right buttock.

"Simultaneously his right hand went on to the front of my thigh on my right leg. He moved towards me then and grasped my groin area – my penis and testicles."

PC Marshall said the incident happened after he had been in the basement room for about a minute and a half and he subsequently told Hampson he was a police officer.

"I showed him my warrant card and asked him to accompany me upstairs. He agreed to do so." Hampson was arrested and cautioned, but made no reply. He was the taken to West End Central police station.

Cross-examined by Mr Mathew PC Marshall said he knew the club had been raided by police a number of times. Once in March nine or 10 people were arrested and men had also been arrested for alleged indecent assaults on police officers.

WPC Maulding was his partner in the clubs; squad, and they had both kept observation on the club before.

He denied he had deliberately dressed to look like a homosexual. He had worn very tight blue jeans, an open-necked shirt, black jacket and training shoes. He had a chain around his neck and his hair was brushed back.

Mr Mathew: Obviously, the object of you going dressed like that was to fit in with the scene in the gay club.

PC Marshall: I was in plain clothes and that is the clothes I would wear any day.

Mr Mathew: You must at least have been expecting that someone might make a homosexual overture towards you?

PC Marshall: I did not expect a homosexual overture.

Mr Mathew: Were you hoping somebody would, so you could make an arrest?

PC Marshall: No, sir.

He denied a suggestion that WPC Maudling had very close cropped hair and said he could not remember whether she was wearing a long trenchcoat.

Mr Mathew: She might have given the appearance of a man dressed as a woman – a man dressed in drag?

PC Marshall: I don't think so, sir.

PC Marshall agreed that the moment he told Hampson he was a police officer, Hampson was obviously very shocked and said "Oh my God."

PC Marshall denied a suggestion by Mr Mathew that he had made "a precipitous arrest".

WPC Maudling said: "I was wearing a brown-collared check patterned dress and lady's fawn overcoat mac, which was knee-length."

She said that she had been standing about three feet from PC Marshall. Hampson had stood on the other side and looked at PC Marshall.

Mr Mathew: He may have been looking at you.

WPC Maudling: I never saw him looking directly at me. I saw him looking at PC Marshall.

Mr Mathew: A woman tends to be a little bit of a curiosity in this type, of club, doesn't she?

WPC Maudling: People do look at you, yes.

She said she saw Hampson put his right hand onto her colleague's thigh and move it up to his groin.

Hampson's wife Susan, called as a character witness for the defence, said she had known him for two years before they were married five years ago "and there is a baby on the way".

"Has he ever displayed any homosexual inclinations of any sort," asked Mr Mathew.

"No," replied Mrs Hampson firmly.

"Any homosexual friends between the two of you?" – "No."

Reminding her that she had sat in court and heard the evidence Mr Mathew asked her why she thought her husband had gone to such a club; "Do you think it was out of curiosity? – "Yes, Keith may have wondered what it was like."

Lord Tonypandy, former Speaker of the Commons, said in a letter read to the court that the allegation was "so totally out of character that I just cannot understand what happened."

He had found Hampson to be "an honourable man whose word is his bond and it was a very great shock when I heard of his court case."

Mr Peter Cash, a principal at the Department of the Environment, described his "absolute astonishment" when he learned of Hampson's arrest and said he had never seen him exhibit any homosexual tendencies.

Mr Gerald Fowler, director of the North East London Polytechnic and a former Labour Minister of State for higher education, said that when Hampson was single he had lived in the flat next-door. "He had a strong interest and a natural interest in young ladies."

Mr David Hunt, Parliamentary Under Secretary, Energy, said: "I find the suggestion that he may or may not be a homosexual to be ridiculous."

The judge said it was clear that Mr Hunt had meant to say he found the suggestion that Hampson may be a homosexual to be ridiculous.

Julia Langton, political correspondent of the *Guardian*, said she had known Hampson for years and had twice been on holiday with him. She was astounded by the news of his arrest, as it was "wholly out of character".

The trial was adjourned until today.

20 October 1984
DPP to decide on retrial for sex case MP
By Guy Rais

The jury hearing the cease against Dr Keith Hampson, 41-year-old Conservative MP for Leeds North-West, failed yesterday to decide whether he was guilty of indecently assaulting a police constable.

After deliberating for five hours, the jury of nine men and three women told Judge

Gerald Butler, QC, that there was no possibility that they would reach a verdict, either unanimously or by a majority of at least 10–2.

After discharging the jury, Judge Butler asked the prosecution to consider carefully whether there should be a second trial.

Emphasising that any retrial should be held as soon as possible, he added: "Although it is not a matter for me in any way, I nevertheless think it right to suggest, in all the circumstances, the prosecution might care to consider the future course of this case particularly bearing in mind the widespread and massive publicity it has attracted.

"I simply ask: Can the prosecution be satisfied that this defendant can have a fair retrial?"

Mr Roy Amlot, for the prosecution, said: "In the usual way, careful consideration will be given – and no doubt as soon as possible – as to whether a retrial is necessary or not in this case."

Sir Thomas Hetherington, Director of Public Prosecutions, is likely to decide within the next few days

Although some observers, thought the judge's remarks suggested that he did not favour a retrial, it would be unusual for the Director of Public Prosecutions to decide against a new hearing simply because a jury failed to agree. Because lack of a verdict might be considered unsatisfactory for Dr Hampson, the Director may take the view that it would be best for the case to be re-heard to get a definite result.

Hampson, of Markham Square, Chelsea, denied indecently assaulting PC Stuart Marshall who was on duty in plain clothes in what was described as the "small and seedy" Gay Theatre Club in Berwick Street, Soho, last May.

The prosecution alleged that Hampson, touched PC Marshall's right buttock with his left hand and grasped his private parts with his right hand.

Hampson vehemently denied the offence, saying he accidentally brushed the policeman's thigh as he tried to get a better look at a person he thought was a man in drag.

In fact it was Woman Police Constable June Maudling who also was in plain clothes.

In evidence Hampson denied he was a homosexual. He had been drinking on the night in question and had never been to the club before. He had gone to Soho to fill in time before his wife arrived home at about 11 p.m.

In his summing up Judge Butler reminded the jury that Hampson was a map of exemplary character.

"He is an MP and a man who, at the time, was high in the affairs of government. But he appears in the dock as an ordinary citizen, subject, as all of us are, to the laws of the land," he said.

The judge recalled evidence that Hampson's first wife had died in tragic circumstances and that he subsequently remarried. "It is plainly a happy marriage.

"Many highly regarded, and high-ranking people who know him well told you not only of his integrity and good character, but also said that to suggest he was a homosexual, or had homosexual tendencies, was, absurd and unthinkable, He has told you that he is not a homosexual."

Of the Gay Theatre, the Judge said: "If I were to suggest to you that 'sleazy' fairly described it, maybe you would not disagree with me."

The jury should remember that "the history of mankind is littered with debris of men who have acted more stupidly than anyone would have thought possible at the time".

The jury were absent for just over three hours when they were recalled to court by the judge who told them he would be ready to accept a majority verdict. He stressed they should still try to reach a unanimous verdict.

After two more hours the foreman of the jury told the judge that, however long they continued, they would not be able to reach even a majority verdict.

Judge Butler told the jury that it was no reflection on them that they had not reached a verdict.

26 October 1984
Sex case MP cleared as retrial is dropped
By Guy Rais

Dr Keith Hampson, 41, Conservative MP for Leeds North-West, was formally cleared yesterday of indecently assaulting a plain clothes policeman in a Soho homosexual club.

The prosecution announced at Southwark Crown Court that it was dropping the case following a jury's failure to agree at the first trial a week ago.

Judge Gerald Butler, QC, said he would direct that a verdict of not guilty be recorded. "That, of course, has the same effect as if the defendant had been tried and acquitted."

At the two-day trial a jury of nine men and three women failed to reach a verdict after five hours of deliberation and was discharged.

The decision not to have a retrial was taken ultimately by the Attorney-General, Sir Michael Havers. Dr Hampson, who was not in court to hear the decision, later spoke of his "relief" at the outcome.

At yesterday's two-minute hearing, Mr Roy Amlot, who led the prosecution at the trial, read a statement to Judge Butler.

It stated: "Following the disagreement last week the question of a retrial has been given the most anxious consideration by the Director of Public Prosecutions, the police, myself and ultimately the Attorney-General, who has taken the final decision on our advice.

"We have, of course, given very considerable weight to your observations after the failure of the jury to agree.

"It is a fact that the widespread and massive publicity given to the case could make it difficult to find a second jury to approach the matter with an open mind, but we would never allow that fact to be a reason by itself for not proceeding with a retrial. That would be a most unfortunate precedent.

"However, in the exceptional circumstances of this particular case, it has been decided that the interests of justice do not require a second trial. I therefore offer no evidence upon the indictment."

Judge Butler said: "I have no doubt that the .prosecution gave the most careful consideration before reaching its decision. I for my part am satisfied that in the particular circumstances of this case it is right to give my agreement."

Dr Hampson's counsel, Mr Edward Jenkins, made no comment.

It was Judge Butler who had raised doubts after the trial last week that Dr Hampson could have a fair retrial in view of what he called the "widespread and massive publicity" the case had attracted.

Mr Amlot then replied that careful consideration would be given to the question of a retrial. Although he did not make any reference to the judge's comment at that time, Judge Butler's doubts clearly weighed heavily in the Attorney-General's final decision.

Dr Hampson, of Markham Square, Chelsea, who resigned as Private Parliamentary Secretary to Mr Heseltine, Defence Secretary, after his arrest, denied indecently assaulting PC Stuart Marshall, who was on duty at the Gay Theatre club in Berwick Street, Soho.

The prosecution alleged that Dr Hampson touched the police constable's right buttock with his left hand and grasped his private parts with his right hand.

This Dr Hampson strongly denied, saving he: accidentally brushed the PC's thigh as he tried to get a better look at a person he thought was a man in drag, but who in fact was WPC June Maudling, also in plain clothes and on duty.

He also vehemently denied he was a homosexual and said on the night in question he had been drinking after a long day at the House of Commons. It was his first visit to the pub and he had gone to Soho to fill in time before his wife returned home.

After hearing the court's decision, Dr Hampson spoke of his relief at being cleared. Hand-in-hand with his wife, Susan, who is expecting their first child, Dr Hampson said before boarding a flight for America: "It has been a long ordeal. "I have always maintained that I was innocent of the charge and this outcome is a vindication of my position. Susie and I hope that we can now get on with our work now that the matter is over."

The court's decision lifted doubts over the future of Dr Hampson continuing as an MP. It is understood that his constituency executive will now drop any possibility of further action.

A constituency spokesman said they were "delighted for him and his family. We hope it is an end of the matter, and doubt very much if anything more will be said."

The Gay Theatre club where Dr Hampson was arrested closed its basement premises shortly after the arrest according to the prosecution, a nude male dancer was "prancing" about the small stage in the basement on the night in question.

It has since re-opened and as recently as five days ago two men were charged with gross indecency while in the audience at the club and each fined £60.

At present there are four unlicensed homosexual clubs in Soho, and police have no powers to close them.

They present male strip shows which require a music and dancing licence, and although owners can be taken to court for not having a licence, the courts have no statutory powers to ban the clubs.

Similarly, although proprietors can be taken to court for running a disorderly house, and performers and members of the audience can be accused of gross indecency, the clubs can still stay open.

Clubs were excluded from having to be licensed when the Sex Establishments.

Act came into force. Senior police officers believe that a change in the law giving the courts power to close premises would greatly help to curb acts of gross indecency.

Within the West End there are some six properly registered and licensed clubs catering for homosexuals. They are described by police as well run and give no trouble.

Ian Harvey

"He fell below that standard."

21 November 1958
Mr Harvey, M.P. on indecency charge
Guardsman case

Mr Ian Douglas Harvey, 44, Conservative M.P. for Harrow East and Joint Parliamentary Under-Secretary for Foreign Affairs, was accused with a guardsman, aged 19, at Bow Street yesterday, of offences of indecency. They were remanded on bail until 10 December.

There were two charges against both men. The first against each was of "being a male person, committing an act of gross indecency with another male person at St. James's Park on 19 November."

The second charge was of "behaving in a manner reasonably likely to offend against public decency at St. James's Park on 19 November" contrary to the St. James's and Green Parks regulations.

Mr Harvey, of Orchard Rise, Richmond, Surrey, was described as an advertising agent and M.P. Appearing in the dock with him was Guardsman Anthony Walter Plant, of the 2nd Bn. Coldstream Guards, Wellington Barracks.

Each was granted bail in his own recognisance of £25 after Det. Sgt, R. Fowler, replying to Sir Laurence Dunne, the magistrate, said that in Plant's case his own recognisance was satisfactory.

Sgt. Fowler said he was instructed to ask for the remand so that the police might be represented. There was no objection to bail.

Mr Harvey arrived at Bow Street more than half an hour before the court was due to sit. He and Guardsman Plant were in court less than two minutes. Guardsman Plant was in uniform.

They appeared in the dock together. Mr Harvey mounted the steps into the dock first, followed closely by Guardsman Plant.

Mr Harvey left the court by taxi 29 minutes after the end of the hearing. He was in the comer of the back seat, with the collar of his overcoat pulled up above his ears. He tried to shield his face from Press photographers taking flashlight pictures.

Guardsman Plant was driven away in the rear of an Army vehicle, accompanied by an Amy officer who sat beside the driver. The guardsman shielded his face with a pair of white gloves as photographers tried to take shots of him.

Both men were arrested at 11.50 p.m. on Wednesday and were charged at Cannon Row police station. Mr Harvey was given bail. The guardsman remained in custody at Cannon Row.

11 December 1958
Ex-minister "fell below standard"
Ian Harvey plea
By a *Daily Telegraph* reporter

Ian Douglas Harvey, 44, former Conservative M.P. for Harrow East and until his resignation Joint Parliamentary Under-Secretary for Foreign Affairs, was fined £5, with £4 4s costs, at Bow Street yesterday on an indecency charge.

A 19-year-old Guardsman who appeared with him was similarly dealt with. Both pleaded guilty to "behaving in a manner reasonably likely to offend against public decency at St. James's Park on 19 November," contrary to the St. James's Park and Green Park regulations.

Mr Geoffrey Lawrence, Q.C., for Harvey, said had resigned his office and seat in Parliament "because as a junior minister and member of the House of Commons he recognised that the only standard of behaviour was the highest possible. He fell below that standard. He has sought no personal excuse. He realised at once that the standard must at all costs be maintained."

Harvey arrived at the court about half an hour before it was due to open. He paused a few moments for photographers. He also posed for photographs afterwards.

In the dock beside him stood Guardsman Anthony Walter Plant, 2nd Bn., Coldstream Guards, Wellington Barracks. There were two charges against each of them. The first was "committing an act of gross indecency with another male at St. James's Park on November 19." This was not proceeded with.

Mr Alastair Morton, prosecuting, said there was no reason why the case should not be disposed of, "as cases of this sort normally are, under the by-law." The two men were seen by a police officer and a park-keeper in some shrubbery at 11.45 p.m. in St. James's Park.

They ran away when torches were shone on them. When charged and cautioned neither made any reply.

Mr Lawrence said: "I will make no attempt to put any gloss on the facts. They speak for themselves" Harvey expressed apologies "of the utmost sincerity" to all who had been affected by what he had done.

No one reached the public position he had reached without some considerable distinction in his earlier career. Before the war he was in business, but served in the Territorial Army. He was mobilised at once in 1939.

He became adjutant in an anti-aircraft regiment in the Royal Artillery, and was later sent to the Staff College at Camberley. He saw active service in Holland and Germany. Afterwards he served on several local authorities before becoming M.P. for Harrow East in 1950.

"His political career began with the utmost promise when in 1956 he became Parliamentary-Secretary, Ministry of Supply." He was appointed Joint Parliamentary Under-Secretary for Foreign Affairs at the beginning of 1957.

"That was the level of public service he had reached when he committed this offence."' What followed was swift and irrevocable. He resigned his office and withdrew from the House of Commons because he considered it his duty to do so.

"It is difficult to lay too much emphasis on the personal disaster of a case of this kind." He had every promise of greater success and distinction in the future.

"For him it must be the end of his hopes, at any rate in the sphere of public life. Nothing remains for him when this case is over but the obscurity of private life, to which he has already sought to withdraw."

He would have to pay the price to the end of his life. "He admits his guilt, and in the days since his arrest he has not flinched from the consequences."

"I think it is some tribute to his character that there is no evasion, there has been no evasion, of the consequences of what he has done. He cannot, of course, be unmindful of the trouble and distress of mind which this failure to keep the standard he knows he should have done has occasioned.

"I do not mean only his family and friends, but his constituents, his colleagues and the country itself." That was why he wanted to express his sincere apologies. "No penalty which overtakes him in this court can be a measure of his personal disaster."

Mr Paul Wrightson, for Plant, said inquiries showed Plant was "not addicted in this way. Although he is 19 he is rather naive and young for his age."

On the night of the incident he had seen his fiancée home and was returning to barracks when he met Harvey. He had said he went with him "out of curiosity".

Plant had served nine months of a three-year engagement in the Army. The Army authorities assessed his character as very good.

Before joining the Army be worked for a firm for three and a half years. The character they gave him was of the highest.

After the lines had been announced by the magistrate, Mr Reece, the two men left the dock. Harvey walked away with his solicitor. Plant was driven off later in a police van.

A War Office spokesman said afterwards that as far as the Army was concerned there would be no further charge against Plant.

Sebastian Horsley

"I can count all the lovers I've had on one hand – if I'm holding a calculator."

19 June 2010
Sebastian Horsley – obituary
Painter with a talent for self-promotion who had
himself crucified and indulged in drugs and prostitutes

Sebastian Horsley, who was found dead on Thursday, aged 47, relentlessly pillaged the misery of his upbringing and the sexual idiosyncrasies of his adulthood to promote himself as a "dandy" and "artist".

To secure his reputation as the former, he chose to wear red velvet suits, top hats, waistcoats and tails. But his claim to be an artist who "leaves my footprints in Bacon's snow" rested on slenderer evidence. His paintings, large-scale oils for the most part, drew on Baudelaire's *Les Fleurs du Mal* or featured the sharks among which he had swum as a young man, and were neither the subject of universal acclaim nor endless gallery displays.

In fact Horsley's greatest talent was for self-promotion. The pinnacle of his career in this regard came in 2000, when he travelled to the Philippines and was crucified ("Christ, after all, had profound style"), fainting when the nails were driven in and falling when his footrest fell away. It was a gruesome and ignominious end to what some had viewed as a stunt in extremely poor taste, but Horsley's name was trumpeted around the world, and even, he seemed to suggest, to the heavens. "I'd been rejected by a god I didn't believe in," he noted.

Of his mother he noted that "motherhood wasn't her thing". As for his father: "He didn't give a toss about me. And I hated him. But I hated Stepfather even more. He was a tosspot. I'd come home to find him in bed with Mother, and Father in bed with someone else. Clearly everyone in my life who should have been vertical was horizontal."

Sebastian went to Pocklington school and then applied to Edinburgh university before landing up at St Martins School of Art in London, where he graduated in 1983.

Instead of plunging straight into Bohemia, however, he made money on the stock market, though as Northern Foods had been worth £2bn at its peak, making ends meet was not a concern.

Thereafter Horsley withdrew to his skull-festooned Soho flat, making sorties to give interviews or visit his tailor. Things did not always go to plan. He was refused entry to the United States in 2008 on grounds of moral turpitude. That seemed to be a reference to his drug habit.

But Horsley delighted in revealing the seamy quality of his sex life too, sometimes in a column for the *Erotic Review* which was eventually dropped for its unflinching gynaecological or scatological detail. He claimed to have slept with more than 1,000 prostitutes, noting: "I can count all the lovers I've had on one hand – if I'm holding a calculator."

Perhaps inevitably, he seemed deeply bored most of the time, taking refuge from his life of ease in narcotics. He described injecting heroin as "the kiss of the archangels, breathtaking, heart-stopping, brain-burning pleasure".

In 2007 he produced what he called an "unauthorised autobiography", *Dandy in the Underworld*. In it he claimed to have had an affair in the early 1980s with the gangster Jimmy Boyle, a relationship that, he said, stemmed from "my desperate search for a father figure". Whether true or not, it made for a good story.

Perhaps the best description of Horsley, who became friends with Nick Cave after trying to steal the singer's girlfriend, was provided by the author Will Self, who said he was "simultaneously anachronistic, grotesque, stylish and affected".

Earlier this month *Dandy in the Underworld* was transferred to the stage. Milo Twomey, who plays Horsley, said that in part it sought to answer public curiosity about the artist. "People say: 'What is there to him? A twat in a hat'."

Sebastian Horsley married, in 1983, Evelynn Smith. They separated a decade later and she died in 2003. In an interview earlier this month Horsley suggested that, at 47, he was "two-thirds dead". He was wrong. An apparent drug overdose killed him eight days later. "I haven't really had a life," he noted in that interview. "I've just sat in a room and died. That's what we all do."

Ben Johnson

"I can only say at this moment it is a tragedy, a mistake or sabotage."

27 September 1988
Ben Johnson is stripped of his gold medal
Drug test failed by winner of fastest ever 100 metres
By Charles Laurence and Colin Gibson in Seoul and Brian Oliver

Ben Johnson, the fastest man on earth, was stripped of his Olympic gold medal in Seoul early today after being found guilty of using drugs to win last Saturday's 100 metres race. Johnson, 26, from Toronto, shattered the world record in winning the Olympic title, watched by millions of television viewers across the world.

The medal was officially withdrawn from Johnson on the unanimous recommendation of the International Olympic Committee's chief executive board. A spokesman for the IOC said the board had considered a suggestion that the anabolic steroid, stanozolol, had been administered by a third party, but had rejected this because it did not fit the "drug profile".

A decision whether to upgrade the silver and bronze medal holders has not been confirmed, but the IOC spokesman said this was likely.

Senor Juan Antonio Samaranch, president of the IOC, said: "This is a blow for the Olympic Games and the Olympic movement, but shows that the IOC was right in the firm stance that it has adopted to keep sport clean.

In one of the most astonishing chapters in Olympic history Johnson, also the world 100 metres champion, now faces a life ban and international disgrace.

Reports last night suggested that the Jamaican-born athlete who ran the 100 metres in 9.79 seconds to win Saturday's race, had already left South Korea.

His business advisers, however, say Johnson will be appealing on the grounds "that his urine sample was mishandled by officials".

His manager Mr Larry Heidebrecht said early today in Seoul that the news of Johnson's drug test was a "shattering disappointment" and that the athlete had "absolutely never taken drugs".

He said Johnson was the most tested athlete in recent history and no traces of drug-taking had ever been found. "I can only say at this moment it is a tragedy, a mistake or sabotage."

Mr Heidebrecht claimed he was investigating "peculiar things" that may have led to the drug test report.

"Ben is certainly not guilty of anything. He has absolutely never taken any drugs of any kind. He has kept to the same training and he has proved in numerous meetings that he can break records without using drugs or any other form of unauthorised training."

Mr Heidebrecht refused to say where Johnson was this morning, but one report said Johnson had gone to Seoul's Kimpo airport and was planning to catch the first available plane out of South Korea.

Mr Heidebrecht said: "All I can say is that he will be going home fairly shortly."

Police and soldiers sealed off the 17th floor of the Hilton Hotel in Seoul where Johnson, his mother and coach Charlie Francis were staying. Telephone calls to their rooms went unanswered.

Mr Roger Jackson, the Canadian Olympic Association president said: "We met until 2.30 in the morning reviewing all the evidence that was before us.

"The reports were consistent with the evidence we have been given. They suggest that an anabolic steroid had been used."

Mr Paul Duprey, the president of the Canadian Athletic Board, was called to the IOC's hotel in the centre of Seoul for urgent talks late last night.

Mr Lyle McCosky, Canada's assistant deputy minister of sport, also attended the meeting. The incident is a great embarrassment to the Canadians who led the fight against drugs in international sport.

Mr McCosky said Canada had strong views about drugs in sport and had "tried to bring about a level playing field and common strategy throughout the sport world".

He added: "Our policy is if any athlete is found to be confirmed positive on drug use, then the Canadian Government would withdraw all financial support for the rest of his life. The whole thing would be painful for Canada".

Now that Johnson has been disqualified, he will automatically be banned for life by the International Amateur Athletic Federation (IAAF) and forfeit the world record he set in Seoul.

But his previous world mark of 9.83 seconds, set at the world championships in Rome, is expected to remain in the record book as the Canadian's dope test there proved negative.

It is believed that Johnson's gold medal will go to the runner up, Carl Lewis, the American who held the Olympic title until Saturday. Britain's Linford Christie would move up to the silver.

The American Calvin Smith, who came fourth, would get the bronze.

Johnson has long been rated a phenomenon among sprinters because of his exceptionally fast start.

After his 100 metres victory over Carl Lewis at last year's world championships in Rome, Lewis alleged that many track and field athletes took drugs.

Although he stopped short of accusing Johnson directly, the implication was that Lewis believed Johnson had been involved in drug abuse.

Lewis yesterday retained his long jump title – the first man ever to do so – and will seek a repeat victory in the men's 200 metres final tomorrow.

On Saturday Johnson won the fastest 100 metre race in Olympic history, clocking four-hundredths of a second faster than his own world record

After the race, Johnson said the most important thing on his mind was beating Lewis. Later, he had second thoughts. The medal, he decided, was most important.

"Anybody can break a world record," he said. "But the gold medal is mine."

Johnson attributed his extra burst of speed to a training regimen that had enabled him to lose 1.5 kilograms in weight since the world championships in Rome last year while maintaining the strength to work with the same 132 kilogram weights in training.

He spent 2½ hours in the sophisticated doping control centre at the Olympic stadium on Saturday evening.

The International Olympic Committee introduced the most stringent drugs testing in sporting history for the Seoul Games, using British-made equipment which is the best in the field.

Before the 16-day Games opened a week ago, officials said they anticipated 15 positive tests among the 10,000 athletes.

In the first week, six athletes were expelled after failing tests, and another was sent home for failing a dope test in a pre-Olympic event.

Four were weightlifters (two Bulgarians, a Spaniard and a Hungarian) and the other two, an Australian and a Spaniard, had been competing in the modem pentathlon.

Swedish officials sent home Jon Christensen last Wednesday following the disclosure of results of a test taken at a weightlifting competition before the Olympics.

Bulgaria, stung by the loss of two gold medals, pulled their entire weightlifting team out of the Olympics last Saturday.

Also 27 September 1988
End of road for good ambassador says Christie
By Michael Calvin in Seoul and John Harlow

Linford Christie, third in the 100 metres final, said he was "shattered" by Johnson's disqualification.

Christie is a good friend of the Canadian. "I'm really surprised. Ben has been a good ambassador for the sport for some time.

"He has been tested every time he has run so it would be wrong for me to speculate about whether he has been cheating for a long time.

"For anyone caught it's the end of the road. There's obviously a certain amount of sadness involved."

Christie was helped in his starting technique by Johnson, whose rival Carl Lewis resisted initial requests to comment.

However, in the aftermath of Saturday's final Lewis reflected: "Johnson was just not the same person on Friday and Saturday. That race was shocking. I don't know how he does it, maybe he has a hypnotist. He got something to stimulate him in the final."

Mr Joe Douglas, Lewis's manager, said: "We now know that athletes will be chasing a tainted world record.

"That is the position the game has come to. The achievements of Carl Lewis stand by themselves."

David Jenkins, the former British Olympic runner currently facing charges in the United States that he ran a steroids smuggling ring, said on Channel Four that he felt it was unfair that Johnson should be persecuted further when he had already "crucified himself".

Jenkins, who argues that there is nothing wrong with athletes taking drugs under medical supervision, said the Canadian runner had been pushing back the frontiers of human ability.

"When he stood on the podium everyone was full of admiration, but now everyone is trying to find severe punishments for him."

But Steve Ovett said that it was right that Johnson should lose the $10m it was estimated he would earn over the next four years.

He said the Olympics committee should ban any athlete who uses steroids for life which would prevent many, especially Eastern Europeans, from returning to the international circuit within 18 months.

He agreed that this would not affect Johnson. "His career, his sporting life, is dead and buried.

"I cannot see the logic in using drugs myself. If one morning I saw my medical cabinet full of half-empty pill bottles I would throw all my medals in the bin.

"Drugs in sport is part of a wider problem of drugs in society and it is up to the individuals, and especially the cultural leaders, to stand against them."

Canadian 110 metres hurdler Stephen Kerho said: "I'm hurt and very much disappointed. I'm a proud Canadian and this does nothing for Canada's international image."

"He is supposed to be the fastest man in the world. Now we know why," Guam judo fighter, Ricardo Bias said.

Also 27 September 1988
Canada cancels hero's welcome
By Eric Dowd in Toronto

The hero's welcome Canada had planned for the return of Ben Johnson was cancelled last night.

Canadians had been ecstatic about his gold medal win, with a record television audience watching his triumph.

In homes and bars throughout the country, people leapt around excitedly and embraced each other. Many took to the streets in the early hours, honking their car horns and waving the national flag.

Newspapers carried headlines such as: "Canada has world's fastest man", "Johnson brings home the gold", "Ben we love you" and "A proud day for Canada".

Mr Mulroney, the Prime Minister, telephoned Johnson to congratulate him and the Toronto Star newspaper said that Johnson had given Canadians "a burst of national pride".

But in Toronto, where Johnson lives with his family, people were wondering if he would dare fly straight back or whether he would wait until the storm had abated.

A crowd gathered outside the home of his sister Clare, who refused to make any statement. Johnson's brother-in-law eventually emerged and told reporters: "I don't believe it."

The city authorities gave Johnson a huge parade and reception in the civic square when he broke the world 100 metres record in Rome last year. They planned something even bigger for "our boy" on his return from Seoul.

On the city streets, Canadians were clearly angry about the shock news from Korea. One said: "If he took drugs, he deserves to lose his medal."

Other comments included: "He was stupid" and "He knew it was wrong."

Johnson has always refused to say how much he earns. But he is thought to have made at least £250,000 from endorsements in the past year.

He had contracts with Mazda, the car manufacturer, Kyodo, a Japanese distributor of oil and gas, Visa Cards, Johnston's Wax, the manufacturers of Johnson outboard engines for motor boats, Diadora, the Italian sportswear manufacturer, and a grocery chain food supplements company

His contract with Diadora, for which he endorsed a wide range of clothing, from track suits to socks, was expected to bring him £1m if he won Olympic gold.

Also 27 September 1988
Record breaker whose achievements
were dogged by suspicion
Seoul '88
By Ken Mays

Ben Johnson, 27, was born in Jamaica, moved to Canada 12 years ago and has been a consistent member of the Canadian national team ever since.

Johnson first came to Olympic attention with his 100 metres bronze medal at the 1984 Games in Los Angeles and was the Commonwealth champion in Edinburgh two years ago.

He assured that his name would go into the record books when he broke the world record at the World Championships in Rome last year, but already suspicions were beginning to dog his achievements.

He held three world best times for low-altitude running between 1985 and 1987, but he could not get under Jim Hines altitude time in Mexico.

In 1986 he lost only once and recorded 10 sub 10.10 sec times while last year he was unbeatable as his speed improved.

He had a magnificent string of victories in 21 straight races everywhere from Perth to Tokyo but this year has had a mediocre season with several defeats, especially to Calvin Smith and never looked good until the Seoul final.

His success was put down to his ability to get away from the blocks and the speed with which he did it in the World Championships has been under close scrutiny ever since.

His performance in Rome was regarded as one of the greatest of all time where he passed the 60 metres mark in 6.38, by far the best time recorded at that point.

He had broken the American domination of the event and they clearly did not like it. His American arch-rival, Carl Lewis, campaigned against the use of drugs in sport with heavy hints about Johnson.

Lewis said gold medallists at the World Championships "definitely used drugs". He said: "A lot of people have come out of nowhere and are running unbelievably. I just don't think they are doing it without drugs.

Even after Saturday's Olympic final, Lewis said of Johnson: "He was not the same person Saturday as he was Friday [in the first two rounds]. I don't know whether he has a hypnotist or something, but he did something to stimulate himself for the final."

28 September 1988
How Johnson pulled a fast one
As the world's fastest sprinter flies home in disgrace,
what made him cheat – and how many others are breaking the rules?
By Colin Gibson in Seoul and Tim De Lisle in London

If it is the taking part and not the winning that matters in sport, nobody told Ben Johnson. To win the gold medal in the fastest, briefest, and one of the most prestigious events in the Olympic Games, he was prepared to risk his reputation, his career, his million-dollar income, even his life.

The drug he was found guilty of taking was the anabolic steroid stanozolol. One of the most dangerous drugs in the medical armoury, it is prescribed in extreme cases of anaemia. Its side-effects are various and serious.

They were spelt out in Seoul yesterday by Professor Robert Dugal of the Central Institute of Research in Montreal, who is both the last man to have dope-tested Johnson before the Olympics and, in the words of a colleague, "the state-of-the-art expert" on drug abuse in sport.

Stanozolol, Dugal said, can cause jaundice and cancer; and the latest data "suggest that there could even be major psychological disturbances".

It is none the less popular with athletes. Two years ago stanozolol was unknown in sport: since then, 15 athletes have been caught using it. They take it because it builds up muscle and increases the amount of haemoglobin in the blood, which in turn increases the intake of oxygen.

In general it does more for field athletes – javelin-throwers, shot-putters and so on – than for their counterparts on the track. But in the 100 metres, as Johnson showed on Saturday, the would-be champion needs to explode out of the starting-block like a bullet, which means he needs muscle.

Yesterday, as Johnson headed for his Toronto home and his gold medal headed for Carl Lewis's sideboard, his manager, Larry Heidebrecht, was still protesting his innocence. He had "absolutely never taken drugs of any kind". The drink he had after the race might have been spiked; the urine sample itself might have been interfered with; the method of detection was unreliable.

The protestations cut little ice with the International Olympic Committee, or with Johnson's compatriot, Professor Dugal, who insisted: "There is ample evidence indicating that a steroid was used on a number of occasions, and recently."

The fastest man on earth had pulled a fast one, and paid the penalty.

He took the drug in order to win. Yet he knew that if he won – or finished second, third or fourth – he would have to take a dope-test. There are two schools of thought, not necessarily incompatible, as to why he thought he could get away with it.

The first is that he underestimated the testing procedures. "Some athletes thought stanozolol was undetectable," Dugal says. "They were wrong. Male hormones naturally produce certain steroids and they are evident in urine samples. When an artificial steroid is administered, it suppresses the production of normal steroids. That was the case here."

The other possibility is that Johnson thought that by stopping his use of the drug shortly before the Games, he could make sure that there was no trace of it in his urine.

"Athletes know the cycle of anabolics," Dugal says. "They go on them for two or three weeks and then interrupt the dosage for the weeks of competition. This appears to have been the case here."

Johnson had long been suspected of taking steroids. After winning the bronze medal at the 1984 Olympics, his physique appeared to change and he became unbeatable.

In 1986–87 he won 21 100 metre races in a row, including the World Championship in Rome. There were mutterings about how he did it among his fellow athletes, and veiled accusations from his arch-rival Lewis; but, as his manager argues, Johnson took a lot of dope-tests and passed them all.

This year, up to last Saturday, he had been less successful, and another theory abroad in Seoul is that he took an extra dose of stanozolol after losing last month to Calvin Smith in Cologne and then to Lewis in Zurich.

It certainly seems that he took the steroid some time after last February, when he was tested negatively in Montreal by Robert Dugal. The drug is likely to have come from Mexico, perhaps via California. At Tijuana, just across the border from San Diego, there are more laboratories producing steroids than US Customs agents can keep track of.

That Johnson was not tested in the seven months up to last weekend was a matter of luck. After the Canadian national championships in Ottawa in August, two of the first three athletes in each event were tested. They were chosen by a roll of the dice, and the dice were on Johnson's side.

He was not tested in Vancouver before the Canadian Olympic team left for Seoul, when four weightlifters were positively tested and dropped from the team; and he was not tested after his qualifying races in Seoul, because at the Olympics – unlike, for instance, routine meetings in Britain – tests are conducted only after a final.

Perhaps he just thought his luck would hold. Athletics officials and experts disagree as to how many athletes take drugs – Prince Alexandre de Merode, head of the IOC medical commission, puts it at six per cent; a recent British report on drug abuse put it at 10 per cent.

Either way, it is clear that a number of Johnson's fellow competitors have got away with it this time. His was the seventh positive dope-test of these Olympics. The IOC said before the Games that it expected 15. Even if only one per cent of the 9,300 competitors are taking drugs, five in every six of them will get away with it.

Where does this leave the Olympic movement? The feelings of the athletics world were expressed yesterday by Sir Roger Bannister, the track hero cent of a more innocent age who went on to become a doctor and chairman of the Sports Council at the time when it first acted against steroids.

"It's tragic for Johnson and Canada, and I suppose for the Olympics, but I hope good will come of it. It has taken 18 years for the governing bodies of the sport to refine the testing and reach a stage of certainty.

"In my view this is a more serious blight on sport than politics or commercialism, though in a sense it is connected to both. I hope it is now clear to young athletes that not only is it cheating, but the authorities will catch you, and also it is medically dangerous. No medal is worth it."

Dr David Kelly

"He is a professional scientist, not somebody who should be a ping pong ball for politicians."

In May 2003, the BBC's defence correspondent Andrew Gilligan sat down in a London hotel with Dr David Kelly, a 59-year-old weapons expert at the Ministry of Defence, to discuss the drafting of what has subsequently come to be known as the "dodgy dossier" – the briefing document purporting to reveal evidence of weapons of mass destruction possessed by Saddam Hussein. Kelly, on the understanding that he would not be revealed as the source, confided his unhappiness at some of the claims made in the draft he'd seen, particularly the suggestion that Iraq was capable of launching a biological and chemical strike within 45 minutes of receiving the order to do so. This, allegedly, was an addition that Kelly said was made by Alistair Campbell, Tony Blair's director of communications. A week later Gilligan made a broadcast suggesting that the government's dossier had been "sexed up". The government furiously denied any involvement in assembling the intelligence used within the dossier. It was subsequently claimed that they authorised the leaking of Kelly's name as Gilligan's chief source – with the aim of undermining the credibility of the BBC journalist and his story. Dr Kelly was highly disturbed to find himself at the epicentre of a press scandal, and even more so to learn that he had been asked before two House of Commons committees, one of which would be public. On 15 July he appeared before the Foreign Affairs Select Committee. Manifestly distressed, Kelly spoke in a voice so soft that, even on one of the hottest days of the year, the air conditioning had to be turned off so that he could be heard. Three days later, Kelly slit his wrists. The Hutton Inquiry was set in motion to investigate the events leading to Kelly's tragic death. It established that he had been the BBC's prime source, and concluded that although once it became clear that this was the case the MoD had been obliged to make his identity known; however, he did criticise them for not alerting Kelly to the fact that they had leaked his name to the press. Nevertheless, unsubstantiated rumours of something more sinister have persisted, rumours that even a subsequent coroner's report have not fully dispelled.

16 July 2003
I was not main source of
Iraqi dossier story, says MoD man
By Andrew Sparrow

An attempt by Downing Street to blame an obscure official for the leak about the "sexing up" of its Iraq dossier backfired yesterday.

MPs on the Commons foreign affairs committee declared that it was "most unlikely" that David Kelly was the source after they heard him give evidence.

In a letter to Jack Straw, the Foreign Secretary, they also complained that Mr Kelly had been "poorly treated" by the Government.

Dr Kelly, an adviser in the MoD's proliferation and arms control secretariat, was named last week as the suspected source of Andrew Gilligan's report on BBC Radio 4's *Today* programme about the "sexing up" of the dossier on Iraq's weapons of mass destruction published last September.

Gilligan met Dr Kelly for lunch in a London hotel a week before he broadcast his radio report, and the two men discussed the dossier. Downing Street and the MoD think that Dr Kelly was Gilligan's source.

They believe that identifying him will show that the BBC's story was unreliable, because Dr Kelly was not senior enough to have first-hand knowledge of how the final draft of the dossier was compiled.

Although Dr Kelly contributed to the document, he only wrote the historical sections, not the material based on up-to-date intelligence. Yesterday Dr Kelly told the committee that he confessed to his MoD bosses that he had met Gilligan because he thought he might have "contributed" to the story.

In particular, Gilligan said his source had told him that there was a 30 per cent probability of Iraq possessing chemical weapons. Dr Kelly said that was "the sort of thing" he might have said.

Gilligan said he was told by his contact that Alastair Campbell was to blame for the fact that the controversial claim that Iraq could deploy WMD in 45 minutes was inserted at the last minute. Mr Campbell, the Prime Minister's communications chief, strongly denies this.

Dr Kelly told MPs he discussed Mr Campbell's name with the journalist but, when Gilligan's exact words were put to him, he said: "I cannot recall using it in that context. It does not sound like anything I would say."

Although Dr Kelly was at times evasive, he insisted that he did not believe he was the "main source" of the BBC story.

He was more decisive when Richard Ottaway, a Tory, put it to him that he could not be the central source because he did not know that the 45-minute allegation was included late or that it came from a single source. "Correct," Dr Kelly replied.

Sir John Stanley, a Tory MP, said Dr Kelly was being "exploited" by the MoD "to rubbish Gilligan and his source". Donald Anderson, the Labour chairman of the committee, asked Dr Kelly if he felt "used".

Later Mr Ottaway said: "The MoD have been blown out of the water. They put out a statement saying they did not know whether he was the single source, but it was pretty clear from what Dr Kelly said that he was not. This is a diversion tactic that has failed."

The committee has asked Gilligan to return tomorrow to give further evidence, in private.

19 July 2003
Death of the dossier fall guy
MoD scientist named as a mole in
Iraq weapons row is found dead
By George Jones

Tony Blair was plunged into the biggest crisis of his premiership last night after a leading Ministry of Defence adviser who became caught up in No 10's vitriolic battle with the BBC was found dead in woodland near his Oxfordshire home.

Dr David Kelly had been named as the likely source of the BBC allegation that the Government "sexed up" intelligence reports on Iraq's weapons of mass destruction.

His suspected suicide shocked Westminster and Whitehall as the Government faced up to the prospect that Dr Kelly could have been driven to his death by the attempts to identify him as the mole.

His wife Janice told a friend that he was "very, very stressed and unhappy about what had happened and this was really not the kind of world he wanted to live in".

Iain Duncan Smith, the Conservative Party leader, demanded that Mr Blair cut short his world trip and return to take charge of the crisis.

Senior MPs said Alastair Campbell, the Prime Minister's communications director, and Geoff Hoon, the Defence Secretary, could be forced to resign if the Government was blamed for forcing Dr Kelly into the spotlight.

Dr Kelly, 59, disappeared after going for a walk on Thursday evening. A body was found yesterday morning. Police said the death was "unexplained" but they were not seeking anyone else in connection with it.

Although a formal identification had not been made, police said the body and clothing matched the description of Dr Kelly.

Mr Blair was given the news as he flew to Japan after receiving a hero's welcome from a joint session of the United States Congress. As he stepped off the Boeing 777 in Tokyo he looked shaken. Officials said he was "very distressed for the family".

After he held hurried satellite telephone consultations with ministers in London, the Ministry of Defence announced that an independent judicial inquiry would be held into the circumstances leading to Dr Kelly's death. It will be headed by Lord Hutton, a senior law lord and former lord chief justice of Northern Ireland. The inquiry is expected to take about six weeks and will be narrowly focused on the events surrounding Dr Kelly's death, not the Government's use of intelligence material on weapons of mass destruction before the Iraq war.

Although Downing Street urged people not to rush to judgment, attention was increasingly turning to Mr Campbell's role in the affair.

The inquiry is certain to centre on how he and Mr Hoon thrust Dr Kelly, a civil servant, into the spotlight.

Dr Kelly had become caught up in a bitter and personal battle that Mr Campbell was fighting with Andrew Gilligan, a BBC reporter.

Mr Campbell, who flew back to London from Washington last night, has denied the central charge that he was responsible for inserting in an intelligence dossier on Iraq the claim that weapons of mass destruction could be deployed at 45 minutes' notice.

However, Gilligan insisted that that was what he had been told by a senior intelligence source who was an expert in weapons of mass destruction.

As the row intensified, the Ministry of Defence disclosed that one of its weapons advisers had owned up to briefing Gilligan. In an unusual move, Mr Hoon challenged the BBC to confirm whether he was their source.

After Dr Kelly's name was leaked to the press he came under intense media scrutiny.

On Tuesday he was called to give evidence before the Commons foreign affairs select committee, which has been investigating the way in which the Government used intelligence material in the approach to the war.

Friends said he was angry and deeply unhappy about the way he was questioned by the MPs. Dr Kelly said he was not the source and the committee concluded that he probably was not. The MPs criticised the Ministry of Defence for using him as a "fall guy".

Richard Ottaway, a Conservative member of the committee, said that spin doctors had used Dr Kelly as a distraction from the row over weapons of mass destruction. He said that political machinations could have resulted in Dr Kelly's death.

Also 19 July 2003
Death of a "mole"
Hounded and unhappy, he walked out to a lonely death in the woods
By Michael Smith, Toby Helm, Andrew Sparrow and Ben Brogan

David Kelly was never afraid to talk to the press. He had made 17 different visits to Iraq as a United Nations inspector, and was one of the world's leading experts on Saddam's biological weapons.

He routinely briefed journalists on the inspectors' findings and it was scarcely surprising that reporters wanting to know more about the issue should seek his advice.

But despite the obvious enjoyment he found in his work, it was not easy. Dr Kelly led a number of the inspections, inevitably coming under intense pressure from the Iraqi regime, which routinely tried to prevent the inspectors doing their work.

But that was as nothing to the pressure he came under after telling his boss that it was possible that he was the source for part of the BBC *Today* report by Andrew Gilligan that the Government had "sexed up" intelligence to make the case for war.

The MoD has been careful to portray the admission as given voluntarily. But it came only after a colleague noticed that he was taking an undue interest in the Commons foreign affairs select committee's grilling of Gilligan about his source and raised the issue.

Dr Kelly had reason to be concerned. He had met Gilligan a few weeks earlier and had discussed the issues the story raised. He had also spoken on the telephone to Susan Watts, the science editor of the BBC's *Newsnight* programme, who broadcast a similar report to Gilligan's a few days later.

More tellingly, he had made similar points to his colleagues in private conversations. It had been only a matter of time before someone put two and two together and now someone had.

The response of Dr Kelly's bosses in the Ministry of Defence, which employed him, and the Foreign Office, where he actually worked as an adviser on Iraqi biological weapons, was, according to official sources, the model of probity. He was interviewed by his line manager and the MoD's head of personnel on Friday 4 July and was reprimanded for breaking Civil Service rules by having unauthorised contact with a journalist, the MoD said. "That was the end of it," a spokesman said.

But that was not the end of it. Dr Kelly told one colleague that the questioning was "quite brutal". He admitted meeting Gilligan for lunch at the Charing Cross Hotel on 22 May.

Was it at his instigation? No. What had he told Gilligan about the 45-minute claim? Nothing. Had he told him it was from a single source? No. That was classified information. Had he told Gilligan that? No. Had he mentioned Alastair Campbell? No, he was raised by Gilligan. What did he say? He couldn't remember.

Chief among those demanding answers was Geoff Hoon, the Defence Secretary, who saw Dr Kelly as a way of getting rid of Gilligan, a constant thorn in the MoD's side, defence sources said.

The MoD said that although ministers were notified, the procedure was decided by civil servants and the MoD's permanent secretary. However, MoD officials told the *Daily Telegraph* privately that the issue quickly took on a political dimension. "The MoD these days does nothing without Downing Street's clearance. No 10 will have known about David Kelly immediately and will have taken a keen interest in how he was handled."

It was true that Dr Kelly had never been threatened with dismissal, sources said. But he had been threatened with prosecution under the Official Secrets Act, and, more worrying for someone just a year from retirement, he was also told he might lose his pension.

Even by the MoD's account, Dr Kelly was told to go away for the weekend and "think about what the options were". When he returned to work on the Monday the questions, and the pressure, resumed. Dr Kelly was pressed to say things about Gilligan that he was not prepared to say, the sources said.

The following day, the MoD issued a cryptically worded statement: "An individual working in the MoD has come forward to volunteer that he met Andrew Gilligan of the BBC on 22 May. It was an unauthorised meeting. It took place one week before Mr Gilligan broadcast allegations against the Government about the WMD dossier on the *Today* programme."

The statement did not name Dr Kelly. Rather it sought to portray the official involved as someone relatively junior with little involvement in the compilation of the dossier. In fact, Dr Kelly was of course an authority on the issue and when Jack Straw, the Foreign Secretary, appeared before the foreign affairs committee in September to discuss the dossier, it was Dr Kelly who was at his side advising him.

The MoD said the scientist was consulted before the statement was released. An MoD spokesman said his superiors discussed with him whether to make his name public.

"We flagged up the fact that it was likely that his name would get into the public domain, and that both committees might want to talk to him," a spokesman said.

Having issued the statement, the MoD insisted the BBC come clean and admit that the as yet unidentified official was its source. The BBC, realising perhaps that it had already talked too much about its source, refused to discuss the issue.

Meanwhile, Downing Street sources were making clear that Mr Campbell remained angry at what he saw as a BBC slur against him personally and was determined to prove the official was its source.

Mr Hoon wrote to Gavyn Davies, the BBC chairman, naming Dr Kelly and challenging him to confirm he was Gilligan's source. The BBC stood firm. At this point Dr Kelly's name was leaked to the press.

Tom Baldwin, a political writer for *The Times* and a close friend of Mr Campbell, denied yesterday that it was leaked to him, although it was certainly obtained first by *The Times* and in his report Baldwin cited Downing Street sources for Dr Kelly's identification.

One minister who works closely with Mr Campbell denied that "he will have sought to throw Kelly to the wolves". But he confirmed that Downing Street and Mr Hoon would have discussed how to handle his case.

The MoD insisted that it did not leak Dr Kelly's name. "We began to receive inquiries about him from the media on 9 July. We gave him advice as to how best to handle it. It was not a question of us saying we've got the bastard let's throw him to the wolves."

Whoever was responsible, what is not in doubt is that Dr Kelly felt betrayed. "He had been promised that they would not name him," a colleague said. "The MoD told him they would not say he was Mr Gilligan's source."

Whatever they had promised him, by the next day both Downing Street and the MoD were saying precisely that. At the morning Downing Street briefing where the Prime Minister's spokesman speaks on direct behalf of his boss, journalists were told unequivocally that Dr Kelly was definitely Gilligan's source.

It was not long before both the foreign affairs committee and the intelligence and security committee said they wanted to talk to a by now very unhappy Dr Kelly, who had been taken to an MoD "safe house".

The MoD insisted that he was being protected from the press and would not be going home "for quite a while". He resurfaced to face the foreign affairs committee on Tuesday, looking tired and thoroughly demoralised.

Prof Chris Payne, a family friend who was at Oxford with Dr Kelly, saw the hearing on the news. "I said to myself, 'Poor bugger, he must be feeling the stress. I must give him a ring at the weekend and meet up for a drink'."

Prof Alistair Hay, a close colleague, was dismayed at his friend's appearance. "His whole demeanour was one of someone who had been beaten by the process," he said. "He is a professional scientist, not somebody who should be a ping pong ball for politicians."

But that is precisely what he had become and to make sure that he did not say anything else inconvenient to the press, he was accompanied by two quite obvious minders, who sat behind him throughout the proceedings.

They were almost certainly Ministry of Defence policemen. After the hearing was over, they bundled Dr Kelly off as quickly as they could.

Once the MPs had decided to take at face value his assurance he was not the main source, they concentrated on delivering pithy sound-bites for the cameras.

The Labour MP Andrew Mackinlay demanded ferociously that Dr Kelly provide a list of all the journalists he had spoken to in the last six months.

Dr Kelly replied quietly that he would provide it to the MoD. "No, I am asking you now," Mr Mackinlay said. "This is the high court of Parliament and I want you to tell the committee who you met."

It was Mr Mackinlay's list, due to be delivered to the committee yesterday, which Dr Kelly had spent the past week compiling, the MoD said. "His line manager, the Head of the Proliferation and Arms Control Unit was talking to Dr Kelly putting the list together," a spokesman said. No doubt there were more questions to be asked. What had he said to that journalist? Who had authorised this conversation?

By now the pressure of living in the MoD "safe house" was getting to him. He was a family man, happiest at his home in the Oxfordshire village of Southmoor where his wife Janice was a local historian.

Tom Mangold, a television journalist and close friend, said Mrs Kelly had told him her husband was deeply unhappy and furious at how events had unfurled.

"She told me he had been under considerable stress, that he was very, very angry about what had happened at the committee, that he wasn't well, that he had been to a safe house, he hadn't liked that, he wanted to come home."

Ted Kennedy

"A pink hairbrush lay on the front passenger seat."

In 1969 Ted Kennedy looked set to inherit the presidency his elder brother John had held before his assassination and to which his elder brother "Bobby" had aspired before he too was brutally gunned down. Handsome, tall and charismatic, and a gifted orator, Ted also shared his siblings' taste for vice – in his case women and drink. And it was a combination of these two temptations that led to the incident that would blot his chances of achieving the glittering prize that had seemed destined to be his. It later emerged that in the nine hours before he reported the accident to the police he found time to walk back to his motel, complain to its manager about a rowdy party, take a shower, have a nap, read the paper and consult with a friend and two lawyers. Tragically, divers later suggested that they would have been able to drag Mary Jo out of the sunken vehicle if they had been called immediately. With the scandal raging, Kennedy made a 13-minute televised address in which he denied driving drunk and rejected rumours of "immoral conduct" with Kopechne. He was, he said, haunted by "irrational" thoughts immediately after the accident, and wondered "whether some awful curse did actually hang over all the Kennedys". Though he acknowledged his failure to report the accident right away was "indefensible", his belated honesty was not enough to secure any sympathy from the wider public. It was widely rumoured that his connections had ensured he received the comparatively light sentence of two months in jail, suspended. But they would not be enough to resurrect his chances of standing in the 1972 presidential election.

21 July 1969
Kennedy may face crash summons
By Mabel Elliott in Edgartown, Massachusetts

Senator Edward Kennedy is expected to receive a summons today to appear in court for failing to report the accident in which his car plunged into Nantucket Sound, killing a woman passenger, Miss Mary Kopechne.

If an application is granted to the chief of police the summons will be presented personally to the senator, who is 37. If the senator is found guilty he faces a minimum sentence of two months' imprisonment and a maximum of two years.

The eight or so hours between the time his car plunged into Nantucket Sound from a bridge on Chappaquiddick island and Mr Kennedy reporting distraught and shocked at the police station at Martha's Vineyard have not yet been officially accounted for by police or friends.

The body of Miss Kopechne, 28, attractive blonde secretary to the late Senator Robert Kennedy was found in the back seat of the submerged car.

The police chief, Mr Dominic Arena, told me yesterday: "It was about 8 a.m. on Saturday morning we were told of the accident by two boys fishing off the bridge. They said they had spotted a car in the water.

"I put on swimming trunks and dived into about 8 ft of water. The girl's body was in the back of the car.

"Her face was upwards and she was wearing a white blouse, slacks and sandals. A pink hairbrush lay on the front passenger seat.

"I had been told this was the senator's car. I phoned my office and said 'Get hold of Ted Kennedy at once.' I was told he had just walked in. It was then about 8.30 a.m. A doctor said the girl had been dead 'some hours'."

The police chief added: "When I saw Mr Kennedy he was extremely distressed. I told him he need not make a statement, but he said he wanted to co-operate fully.

"There will be no post mortem examination. The medical examiner said there was no doubt whatever that Miss Kopechne had died from drowning."

Samples of her blood are being analysed to discover whether there was any alcohol content. The senator, with the dead girl and six or seven other guests including four women, had been attending a party on the island at a house rented by his cousin Mr Joseph Gargan.

The senator told police he could not remember how he escaped from the car after it hit the water. But he did remember "diving repeatedly" to try to save the girl.

The events of the next hours appear confusing to both Mr Kennedy and the police. Wet through but uninjured, he said he returned to the party cottage and sat in the back of a friend's car.

On his way from the accident he must have passed at least two houses in which the occupants were up and burning lights.

The ferryman did not get a call during the early hours but Mr Kennedy said he returned to Edgartown and went to his hotel.

How did he cross the 500-yard strip of water? Was he taken in a private boat?

The manager of the Shiretown Inn here where Mr Kennedy was staying for the annual yacht regatta refused to say whether he returned during that night.

But a member of the staff could not recall seeing him after he left for the party on Friday evening.

One of the five women guests was Miss Rosemary Keogh, who shared a flat with the dead girl in Washington. They were staying in a motel here and Mr Kennedy was believed to be driving Miss Kopechne back there when the tragedy occurred.

In his statement the senator left blank his passenger's surname identifying her as "Miss Mary". Police said he did not appear to remember her surname at that moment.

In his statement to the police, Senator Kennedy said: "On 18 July at approximately 11.15 p.m. I went over to Chappaquiddick. Later I was driving my car on Main Street to get the ferry back to Edgartown.

"I was unfamiliar with the road and turned right instead of bearing hard left I descended a hill and came upon a narrow bridge.

"The car turned over and sank into the water and landed with the roof resting on the bottom. I attempted to open the door and a window of the car but had no recollection of how I got out.

"I came to the surface and repeatedly dived down to the car in an attempt to see if the passenger was still in the car. I was unsuccessful in the attempt. I was exhausted and in a state of shock.

"I recall walking back to where my friends were eating. There was a car parked in front of the cottage and I climbed into the back seat. I then asked someone to bring me back to Edgartown."

The statement released by the police in Senator Kennedy's name does not give the name of the person.

Under Massachusetts law a manslaughter charge is mandatory in cases where someone leaves the scene of an accident involving a fatality and where negligence is proved.

Mr Kennedy would have 24 hours to answer the charge. A summons would necessitate his appearance in court. Mr Walter Steele, district prosecutor, told me he was inquiring into the possibility of immunity because the accident occurred while the Senate was in session.

All the guests at the party have now left the island. Mr Paul Markham, a close friend of the Kennedy family and a former US attorney, represented the Senator at the police station.

Mrs Joan Kennedy and their children were said to be at their Cape Cod summer home with him yesterday.

The police chief said he did not ask Mr Kennedy whether he had been drinking at the party. A breathalyser test, he added, was out of the question because of the time lag.

Holidaymakers in this resort island in the Atlantic have been shocked by the tragedy. Senator Kennedy has many friends here.

One said he made a habit of attending the regatta and on several previous occasions had brought Mrs Kennedy with him.

Lord Lambton

"I have no excuses whatever to make. I have behaved
with credulous stupidity."

The resignation of Lord Lambton as a junior minister initially seemed fairly innocuous; it was thought it might be due to the stress caused by a dispute over the use of his title. However, once it became clear that prostitutes, drugs and other high-profile figures – notably Earl Jellicoe, the Lord Privy Seal – were involved, a certain amount of panic suddenly seemed in order. The combination of call girls and a defence minister carried the ugly promise of some form of breach of national security. But a subsequent investigation determined that any indiscretions on Lambton's part were personal rather than professional. Lambton himself offered a range of reasons to explain his visit to the prostitutes, variously citing his sense of "the futility of the job" and lack of demanding tasks as a junior minister, and his obsession with the battle over the use of an aristocratic title that had been used by his father, which he sought to soothe by engaging in frantic activities such as gardening and debauchery.

23 May 1973
Lambton quits for "personal reasons"
By H. B. Boyne

The resignation of Mr Antony Lambton, 50, from his £8,500-a-year post as Defence Under-Secretary, RAF, was announced from 10 Downing Street yesterday. His letter to the Prime Minister merely said: "I am afraid that for personal and health reasons I wish to tender my resignation from your Government. It has been an honour to serve under you for the past three years."

Mr Lambton's intention to resign immediately was conveyed to the Prime Minister, who was in Paris on Monday evening. Yesterday Mr Heath was informed of the terms of his letter and accepted the resignation.

Soon after his return from Paris last night Mr Heath had a talk with Mr Francis Pym, Government Chief Whip, to whom Mr Lambton had confided his decision. They doubtless discussed the question of a successor.

Some hours later the Prime Minister's office issued the text of his reply to Mr Lambton's letter. Notable for the omission of any of the expressions of regret which are normal in such circumstances, it read:

"Thank you for your letter of 21 May telling me that for personal and health reasons you wished to tender your resignation.

"In accepting your resignation, I should like to thank you for the work you have done as a member of the Government during the past three years."

The manner in which Mr Heath began and ended his letter was not disclosed.

The resignation did not come as a complete surprise to some of Mr Lambton's colleagues in the Government. He had told them of his intention to give up his Berwick-upon-Tweed seat at the end of the present Parliament and commented that he did not see much point in remaining a Minister when he was not going to stand again.

But they were puzzled by the suddeness of his decision to resign, especially at a moment when the Prime Minister was out of London.

While Mr Lambton's health has not been entirely robust for some years, there has been no sign of a recent deterioration.

A "personal" reason, some thought, might be the controversy over his desire to retain the courtesy title of "Lord," though he disclaimed the Earldom of Durham after his father's death in February 1970, for the purpose of remaining in the Commons.

Despite a recommendation by the Committee of Privileges, the Speaker, Mr Selwyn Lloyd, ruled that the courtesy title should be used in Parliamentary proceedings and documents.

But pressure has recently been renewed for a debate on the committee's report and decision by the House that "Lord" should give way to "Mr".

It is hard to see why the prospect of this reverse should induce Mr Lambton to give up his Ministerial post and renounce all political ambitions.

In official government nomenclature, as distinct from Parliamentary papers under the Speaker's control, he has been "Mr" all along.

MPs are left to assume that there must be some other compelling personal reason why he has suddenly decided to resign.

Elected MP for Berwick in 1951, Mr Lambton quickly established himself as a Foreign Affairs specialist, and was denounced as a "cheeky young pup" by a fellow Conservative in a Commons debate in December 1953 for his spirited defence of Mr Eden's policy in Egypt.

But after two years as Parliamentary Private Secretary to the Foreign Secretary, Mr Selwyn Lloyd, he suddenly resigned in 1957 in protest against the Government's Suez invasion.

He was responsible for an important new definition of obscenity in a private member's Bill in 1957. This made the test of obscenity one of intention on the part of the author.

Seven years later he was one of a number of MPs who defended the book "Fanny Hill" in a Commons motion against police prosecution.

One of Mr Macmillan's fiercest critics between 1959 and 1964, Mr Lambton denounced him in 1962 as "a temporary leader who has brought the party to its present disrepute, who appears likely to lead it to a temporary oblivion rather than admit that the once bright spark of his leadership has gone."

Mr Lambton married Miss Belinda Blew-Jones in 1942 when he was 20 and she 19, after a week's engagement. He worked in a munitions factory in Durham after being invalided out of Sandhurst in 1941, earning £2 2s 6d per week.

His family has been by personal tragedies for centuries – said to be the consequence of a curse that nine generations of Lambtons were doomed not to die in their beds.

Mr Lambton's brother killed himself in 1941 while suffering from temporary imbalance of mind.

Mr Lambton has a son and five daughters. The heir to the disclaimed Earldom of Durham is Mr Lambton's son, Mr Edward Richard Lambton, who was born in 1961.

News of Mr Lambton's resignation came as a complete surprise to most people in his constituency, Berwick-upon-Tweed.

Mr Maurice Hill, his agent for 10 years, said: "There was never a hint of this, even during the preparations for the constituency association annual meeting this week.

"He has been a damn good MP who has served this area extremely well. He has made the 600-mile journey from London and back many many times a year and really put himself out to help people."

Maj. O. B. Younger, the local association's chairman, said: "The dispute over the title of Lord Lambton has undoubtedly been a great aggravation to him. It has been very unpleasant at times and must have got him down."

24 May 1973
Lambton drugs charge shock
Minister photographed with call girl

Summonses alleging the possession of cannabis and amphetamines were taken out against Mr Antony Lambton last night only a few hours after he had confessed in a statement that he had resigned as Defence Under-Secretary, RAF, on Tuesday as a result of being secretly photographed with a prostitute.

In a second statement, made "from somewhere in Scotland" after the drug summonses had been issued, 50-year-old Mr Lambton said police called at his London home on Monday "appearing to believe that I was a heroin addict".

He allowed them to inspect the veins of his arms and legs for injection scars but they were unmarked.

Then police searched Mr Lambton's house. He said he showed them "a small parcel of 'soft' drugs that I had confiscated from a friend many months ago."

The summonses against Mr Lambton were issued at Marylebone court following instructions to the police from the Director of Public Prosecutions.

They had not been served late last night and no date for the court hearing had been announced.

Investigations involving other public figures were intensified yesterday as rumours grew that more Ministers may be implicated in a vice ring scandal.

A suggestion on Independent Television News last night that the resignation of another Minister, of senior rank, might be imminent was noted without comment in Government circles. One Conservative backbencher said: "Various names are being bandied about. It would be unfair and imprudent to mention them, hut in a situation like this nothing can be ruled out until we know the facts."

Mr Heath is to make a statement in the Commons this afternoon on the Lambton affair and other allegations.

It is his intention to disclose everything that can be made known without prejudicing the course of justice, says our political correspondent.

The general assumption in the House is that there will have to be some form of judicial inquiry into the question whether security has been endangered. Conservative MPs expect Mr Heath to make clear that he requires impeccable standards of personal conduct from Ministers, regardless of their seniority.

Mr Lambton's first dramatic statement was issued yesterday morning following days of rumours about a vice ring supplying prostitutes for "top people".

In the statement Mr Lambton dismissed stories of a "high life" vice ring, blackmail and security leaks. But he admitted a "casual acquaintance with a call girl and one or two of her friends."

He said police had told him that the husband of one of the girls had taken some secret photographs showing him with the girl.

"This is the sordid story," Mr Lambton's statement went on. "There has been no security risk and no blackmail.

"I have no excuses whatever to make. I have behaved with credulous stupidity."

As Defence Under-Secretary for the RAF, Mr Lambton was responsible to Lord Carrington, Defence Secretary, for a service of the highest military importance, says our political correspondent.

He must have had access to top secret information of great use to a potential enemy and, like all other Ministers and senior civil servants, he must have been warned of the security risk inherent in his position and of the necessity for the utmost circumspection in his private affairs.

25 May 1973
Heath sets up security test
Jellicoe quits in call-girls scandal

Mr Heath announced yesterday that he had asked the Security Commission to verify that there had been no security breaches in the "call girl" affair which a few hours earlier resulted in the resignation of a second Minister, Earl Jellicoe, Lord Privy Seal and Leader of the House of Lords. Like Mr Lambton, who resigned as Defence Under-Secretary on Tuesday, Lord Jellicoe has admitted an association with prostitutes.

The Commission was set up in 1964, mainly to advise the Prime Minister on security lapses in Whitehall. Its present chairman is Lord Justice Diplock.

In his statement to MPs, Mr Heath said that on 9 April the Security Service had reported to Mr Carr, Home Secretary, and himself that police inquiries on other matters had disclosed allegations about an association of a prostitute and a Minister.

The Security Service was told to satisfy itself that there was no danger to national security in the affair. On 13 April, Mr Heath was told that the Minister concerned was Mr Lambton, and that the affair was also thought to involve dangerous drugs.

Early this month other people said to be involved with prostitutes, including Lord Jellicoe, 55, were named to Mr Heath.

On Monday this week, Mr Lambton was interviewed by police in connection with his association with prostitutes and the alleged possession of drugs. Next day he resigned and on Wednesday a drug summons was issued against him.

Lord Jellicoe's resignation resulted from an interview with Mr Heath on Tuesday when he was told that there were call-girl allegations affecting him. Mr Heath said he had been kept fully informed of events in the affair and on the information available there were "no grounds for supposing that any other Minister, or any member of the public service, is involved".

It was generally noted, says our political correspondent, that this statement fell short of guaranteeing that the name of no other MP or peer will crop up during the Security Commission's inquiry or through police investigations.

But Conservative MPs were considerably relieved that Mr Heath ruled out further Ministerial involvement as at least two senior members of the Government, in addition to Lord Jellicoe and Mr Lambton, had been subjects of widespread speculation.

In his letter of resignation to Mr Heath, Lord Jellicoe said there was "unhappily justification" for reports linking his name with a ring of call girls. He had had some "casual affairs" which he "deeply regretted". He was resigning because disclosure of his conduct would be of grave embarrassment to the Government.

Like Mr Lambton, Lord Jellicoe said his involvement with the girls had not resulted in blackmail or breaches of security. Mr Heath, in reply, said Lord Jellicoe's decision to resign "accords with the best traditions of British public life".

Also 25 May 1973
Vice "link with duke"
By T. A. Sandrock

Vigorous police inquiries into a vice ring for "top people" are continuing, despite Mr Heath's statement that no security risks were involved.

Among those reported to police as being involved in the ring is a duke. He is not associated with the Government, and there is no question of a security risk as far as he is concerned, but I understand police are considering whether they need to take action in his case.

Scotland Yard's Serious Crimes Squad have received two rolls of tape reported to have been recorded in the bedroom of Nora Levy, the call girl over whom Mr Lambton resigned.

It is supposed that bedroom photographs and tapes were to have been used for blackmail or for filtering into the pornographic trade.

But police learned yesterday that Mrs Levy had asked a man friend to help her recover the photographs taken in her flat from the man who took them. She feared that Mr Lambton would be blackmailed, and that if this happened, it would "blow open a profitable vice ring".

Det. Chief Supt Albert Wickstead, who is in charge of the Serious Crimes Squad, flew to Durham yesterday to serve summonses alleging drugs offences on Mr Lambton. They are returnable at Marylebone on 13 June.

Nick Leeson

"He is a delightful man, very charming, and comes from a smashing family. Everyone who knows him is shocked."

People liked and trusted Nick Leeson, which was probably part of the problem. He didn't look like Gordon Gecko or Patrick Bateman, and so when it emerged that his actions had brought down Britain's oldest merchant bank, people were shocked. But in retrospect some of this surprise was misplaced. Leeson had actually been sent to Singapore in the first place because, after fraud was discovered on his application, he was denied a broker's licence in the United Kingdom.

Initially, his fraudulent, unauthorised and speculative trading paid off, earning large profits for the bank, and a huge bonus for himself. But his run of good luck ended, and he was soon forced to start drawing on Barings' error accounts to hide his rapidly spiralling losses. In 1992 the account was £2 million in the black, by the end of 1994 this had galloped up to £208 million. Perhaps, if things had worked out differently, if one of his gambles had paid off, he might have been able to earn back everything he'd lost and pretend that nothing had happened, but when the Kobe earthquake struck on the morning of 17 January 1995, his bet that the Japanese stock exchange would not shift significantly overnight left him dangerously exposed. A series of desperate trades, based on the expectation that the Nikkei would recover, resulted only in more losses and once losses reached £827 million, double the bank's trading capital, Leeson knew the game was up. He fled to Singapore, leaving only a devastated bank – which would be declared insolvent before the end of February – and a note reading 'I'm Sorry'.

28 February 1995
Rogue trader from council house flees with his wife
By Michael Fleet

An international search was under way last night for Mr Nick Leeson, the "rogue trader" whose high-risk gambling brought down Barings.

He was thought to have crossed the border into Malaysia, possibly on a false passport. Another theory is that Mr Leeson and his wife, Lisa, may have fled on their yacht.

Mr Leeson, 28, is a product of a modest council house on an estate in Watford, Herts, and an education which saw him fail A-level mathematics.

He became one of the rising stars of international finance after moving away from a dreary home life in suburbia. At 18, he left Parmiters School, Watford, to join Coutts & Co, the Queen's bankers, as a junior clerical officer.

At school he had been known as a diligent if unspectacular student who enjoyed sport, playing football for the first XI, but he had to study hard to gain eight O-levels.

One of those was an A grade in mathematics but when he went on to take the subject at A-level he failed it, having to make do instead with a C in English literature and a D in history.

Mr Paul Kitchiner, the deputy head teacher of the grant-maintained comprehensive, remembered the young Leeson as a hard-working boy who became a prefect. "He did well at maths up until O-level but could not maintain that into the sixth year, which was a disappointment to him as he should have done better.

"He had always had an interest in banking and joined Coutts & Co straight from school."

Mr Leeson impressed Coutts at an interview in June 1985 and was taken on by the general banking division. Three years ago he moved to Singapore with Barings.

From then on, the Nick Leeson seen in the Far East was very different from the one who grew up in Watford. In England he was regarded as quiet and unpretentious. In Singapore he was described as arrogant, cocky and outgoing.

His mother, Anne, died in 1987, leaving his father, William, a widower with four children, one of whom, a daughter, still lives at the family's house in Haines Way, north Watford.

The house had its curtains drawn yesterday. Neighbours were hostile to questions, particularly after Mr Leeson's father was involved in a fracas with a photographer on Sunday.

Mr Leeson senior is a plasterer who gets work around the country, but finds time to enjoy a drink at the local public house, the Hare, at weekends.

One regular said Mr Leeson was proud of his son's achievements and the salary, reportedly £200,000 a year, he commanded.

He remembered meeting the money man when he was setting out on his career. "He was a pleasant lad and obviously brainy. His dad was chuffed at what he had done. He was in here on Sunday when news of all this broke. I didn't speak to him then but it has obviously all come as a shock."

Mr Les Baker, a family friend, called by to leave a note of support and declared his faith in Nick Leeson. "My grandchildren went to school with him and we all got on well together. He is a delightful man, very charming, and comes from a smashing family. Everyone who knows him is shocked."

The trader was married in March 1992 to Miss Lisa Sims, then a 21-year-old clerk at Barings and the daughter of a printer from West Kingsdown, Kent.

Mr Alex Sims said his son-in-law was quiet and reserved, a far cry from the image of City whizkids.

Mr Sims said: "I can't believe this is happening. Nick is such a quiet lad, and I mean really quiet. He doesn't have any hobbies as such. He is dedicated to his work. I don't believe for a moment he is the only one involved in this. It seems he is being made some sort of scapegoat and having everything blamed on him."

Mr Sims said he had been trying to contact his daughter and son-in-law without success. "When I saw that all this may involve some sort of fraud my knees went weak.

"I had given up smoking last year but this has been so traumatic I have started again. I know Nick is innocent and that all this will work out in the end.

"He has been painted as a council house yuppie, but that's not really him. He is honest and hard working.

"Nick and Lisa had a wonderful lifestyle but they weren't extravagant or flashy. They were very comfortable and had no money troubles, so I know Nick wouldn't have done anything deliberately illegal.

"If he is responsible for what has happened, it must have been a genuine mistake.

"He grew up as a normal lad who decided he was going to do well in life. He was well educated and is well spoken and is not the sort who normally become dealers. Generally they are loud, brash and flash but Nick was none of these things."

In Singapore, Mr Leeson has a home in an expensive apartment block in the Orchard district. Yesterday four days' worth of newspapers were piled on the mat. Mr Leeson also owns a yacht which was moored off the coast and which investigators believe he may have used to leave Singapore.

Friends and colleagues talked of him as having been one of the most respected money men in the region. One futures trader at a Japanese house working in the Singapore International Monetary Exchange said: "Before this thing happened, we thought he was very brilliant, the most confident trader around town.

"He seemed to be able to move markets. Every day, we would monitor what he was doing."

Rumours were that last year his bonus was at least £1m and possibly as high as £2.5m.

Mr Leeson did not fit the physical image of a brash young trader, being both chubby and balding, but a television journalist working in Japan who knows him said he was inclined to be extrovert when out with friends.

"He is somewhat gung-ho and is the type to sometimes make a lot of noise in restaurants," said Mr Tim Charlton.

3 March 1995
Fugitive bank trader arrested
Leeson in jail after seven days on run

By Tim Butcher in Frankfurt and Hugo Gurdon in Singapore

Mr Nick Leeson, the financial dealer whose multi-million pound debts broke Barings Bank, was in jail last night after being arrested at Frankfurt airport. He and his wife, Lisa, flew economy class from Borneo, ending a seven-day international hunt.

Mrs Leeson, 24, was freed without charge after questioning and her lawyer said she was on her way to London.

The couple had booked out of the Shangri-La resort hotel near Kota Kinabalu in northern Borneo with more than $10,000 in cash. They paid cash for their tickets, written in their own names.

They had no onward tickets to London, but German officials quoted Mr Leeson, who comes from Watford, as saying that was where they were heading.

Extradition proceedings were immediately started by Singapore authorities who want to interview Mr Leeson, 28, about an alleged passport forgery after last weekend's collapse of the City's oldest merchant bank.

Mr Leeson was expected to go before an examining magistrate in Frankfurt today. Officials in London said he would not be extradited to Britain.

News of Mr Leeson's arrest brought applause from his former colleagues in the derivatives market in Singapore, many of whom lost huge bonuses as a result of the Barings collapse. "We are delighted he got nicked," said one dealer.

German police were tipped off that the Leesons, who disappeared from their flat in Singapore last Thursday, were on Royal Brunei flight BI 535 from Brunei.

A news organisation monitoring flights from southern Asia told the German immigration police at 4.30 a.m. that the couple had boarded the Frankfurt flight from Brunei via Bangkok and Abu Dhabi.

An arrest warrant, issued in Singapore by the Commercial Affairs Department, the island's fraud squad, was faxed to German police with two A4-size photographs of the Leesons, with passport details.

The plane was sealed off after touching down at 6.23 a.m. and five officers checked the passports of all passengers as they disembarked.

"They were among the last to leave the Airbus and they gave us no problems as they told us who they were immediately," said Chief Insp Michael Brall.

Rumours had spread that Mr Leeson had put to sea in his yacht, that he had hidden himself on an Indonesian island and there was at least one reported sighting of him in Canada.

The reason for his return to Europe remained unclear, as he refused to speak to the press.

Mr Leeson, wearing jeans, an open blue shirt, glasses, and carrying a book and a small backpack, was taken to an office in the airport where he was interviewed for several hours. He did not initially ask for a lawyer and spent some time talking to Mr Trevor Kayless, vice-consul from the British consulate general in Frankfurt.

To comply with German national law, he was formally arrested at 11.30 a.m., but not charged. The police then had the right to hold him for 36 hours.

The permission of a magistrate is required for him to be held beyond tomorrow night.

The faxed warrant that arrived early yesterday was a Singapore document, which has jurisdiction only in Singapore. It said that Mr Leeson was charged with offence S468 of the penal chapter 224.

Interpol was quoted as saying that he was wanted for "forging an accounting document worth ¥7bn [£45m]".

An international warrant was being sent from Singapore which could be used as the basis of an extradition claim. If Mr Leeson is convicted of fraud in the strict island state, he could face seven years in jail and fines on each charge.

6 March 1995
"Leeson claimed he was close to a breakdown"
Trader apologised in alleged resignation
By Hugo Gurdon and Philip Sherwell in Singapore

The disgraced Barings banker, Mr Nick Leeson, claimed he was close to a nervous breakdown in a purported letter of resignation faxed to his bosses in Singapore after fleeing to Malaysia, it emerged early today.

In a hand-written note on one side of paper from the Regent hotel in Kuala Lumpur the trader, now in a German jail awaiting proceedings for extradition to Singapore, tendered his resignation and gave his "sincere apologies for the predicament that I have left you in".

The alleged fax, published by the *Business Times* of Singapore, appears to contradict claims by Mr Leeson's wife, Lisa, that the couple had gone on a holiday for his birthday and were unaware of the crisis he had left behind.

Since returning to Britain, Mrs Leeson has said her husband only realised four days after leaving Singapore that anything was wrong when he read a local English language newspaper at their hotel in Kota Kinabalu.

The fax, dated 24 February, is addressed to Barings' local directors, Mr James Bax, head of Singapore operations, and Mr Simon Jones, finance director of Baring Futures, (Singapore). It continues: "It was neither my intention nor aim for this to happen but the pressures, both business and personal, have become too much to bear."

He said he had received medical advice and that the pressure had "affected my health to the extent that a breakdown is imminent".

The fax went on: "In light of my actions, I tender my resignation with immediate affect and will contact you early next week to discuss the best course of action.

"Apologies, Nick."

In the days before he fled Mr Leeson was engaged in further gambles to recoup losses. It was then that he claims to have been advised by doctors that he was on the point of a breakdown.

The fax from Kuala Lumpur was sent on the day he checked out of the Regent and flew with his wife to a beach hotel in Borneo.

At least six senior managers at Barings branches around the world warned London over the past three years that Mr Leeson's concentration of power in Singapore was dangerous.

A source with a close knowledge of how Baring Futures was set up in the island state disclosed yesterday that Mr Bax, was not the only insider alerting London to potential disaster.

"I could find a good half-dozen people who contacted managers in London about the importance of always keeping Chinese walls between the two sides of the business," said the source.

Mr Leeson had a mini-empire in the Singapore office which allowed him to trade massive sums and to oversee the monitoring of those trades.

Senior Barings management decided a month before the bank's collapse that Mr Leeson should be asked to reduce his holdings in futures contracts.

According to today's *Financial Times*, minutes of a meeting of the Barings' asset and liability committee in London on 26 January recorded: "Leeson to be advised that position should not be increased, and when possible reduced".

That same day, Mr Leeson allegedly made his biggest purchase of loss-making futures contracts.

8 March 1995
Leeson made plans to scatter to Four Winds
By Philip Sherwell and Hugo Gurdon in Singapore

Mr Nick Leeson and his wife Lisa hatched secret plans early last month to flee Singapore, even as the Barings trader was multiplying his bets on Japanese stocks in an attempt to salvage spectacular losses that broke the bank only two weeks later.

The couple originally wanted to be out by the end of March, according to documents held by the Four Winds removal firm.

But as the financial crisis escalated, they twice brought forward their departure date.

On the final occasion, by which time the Leesons had already skipped town, a friend called a removals company to fix the date for 1 March, just two days after the trader's bonus – expected to exceed £1m – was to be paid. But Barings crashed on Sunday, 26 February.

Taken with the letter of resignation which the disgraced trader purportedly faxed to his bosses from Kuala Lumpur on 24 February, these new revelations appear to shatter Mrs Leeson's claims that the couple had no idea about the impending disaster when they disappeared for five days.

Mrs Leeson had telephoned the removal company's Singapore office in the second week of February for a quotation for shipping their possessions to England.

"I went round on the afternoon of 15 February to the Leesons' apartment. Lisa was there. She was very personable, a nice girl," said Ms Diane Massimiani, assistant manager of Four Winds.

"She said she wanted the stuff shipped to Kent, probably in mid or late March."

The Leesons' removal arrangements came as a surprise at Barings head office in London. "We had no plans for him to come back and he had not given us any indication that he was coming back," a spokesman said last night.

Mrs Leeson placed the first call to Four Winds shortly after Barings Group treasurer Mr Anthony Hawes had flown to Singapore to reassure financial authorities that it could meet Mr Leeson's spectacular stock market commitments.

On Friday 17, by which time Barings had dispatched more than £480m to cover the down payments on Mr Leeson's 20,000 futures contracts, Four Winds sent the couple a removal estimate, understood to be for about £1,000. At the start of the next week, Ms Massimiani says she received a call from Mrs Leeson to say they would probably want to move sooner, but gave no date.

It was during this fateful week that Barings sent another £113m to its Singapore office. But on Thursday 23, realising the scale of the looming catastrophe, Mr Leeson abruptly left Singapore and fled to Kuala Lumpur.

His wife Lisa joined him in the Borneo holiday resort of Kota Kinabalu the next day. Meanwhile in Singapore on Friday 24, Ms Massimiani received a telephone call from a well-spoken Englishwoman who said she was a friend of Lisa and asked if the move could be brought forward to Wednesday, 1 March, just five days later.

The friend said the couple were away and would return on Tuesday night.

"On Tuesday afternoon I looked at the name and suddenly realised who the lady I had been dealing with was," said Ms Massimiani. "We immediately decided to cancel the order." Mrs Leeson has since said they went away for the weekend to celebrate her husband's birthday. They only discovered from a newspaper on the Tuesday that Barings had collapsed, and decided to return to Britain.

But not only were the Leeson's removal dates confused. So, too, were their flight plans.

Mr Leeson spent the night of Thursday, 23 February, in the Regent Hotel in Kuala Lumpur, where he checked in alone. Although there are frequent direct flights from the Malaysian capital to Kota Kinabalu, Mr Leeson instead arrived there with his wife late on Friday afternoon on a flight from the Philippines' capital, Manila.

Leeson allegedly practised the signature of a Wall Street trader in order to commit forgery, according to a telex sent to German police in support of Singapore's request for Leeson's extradition.

Leeson is accused of having forged two documents to show that Barings Futures had received ¥7.8bn (about £46m) from one of Wall Street's biggest trading firms, and that the money was in Barings' account, allowing continued high-stakes trading.

9 March 1995

"Scapegoat" Leeson hits back at Barings

Trader will help fraud office if he is sent to Britain

By Robin Gedye in Frankfurt

Nick Leeson has been made the scapegoat for a "wide circle of people" in Britain and Singapore who were also responsible for the collapse of the bank, lawyers representing him said yesterday.

They said they would seriously consider taking the highly unusual step of co-operating with the Serious Fraud Office in building a case against him if it meant he could be extradited to Britain before Singapore.

Mr Stephen Pollard, his British lawyer, cited newspaper reports in Germany that six members of Barings board had been questioned by the Serious Fraud Office.

"We will certainly be speaking to the SFO with a view to helping them with their inquiries.

"The SFO will have to decide whether there is enough evidence against Mr Leeson to form the basis of a crime in England."

Mr Pollard said that anyone "who still believes that Nick Leeson, acting on his own as a rogue trader, brought Barings bank down is being fairly unrealistic.

"Some very interesting information Mr Leeson has given us indicates that he has been made a scapegoat for others involving a much wider circle of people in Britain and Singapore."

Mr Pollard said suggestions that Mr Leeson earned money himself through the deal were totally incorrect.

"Everything he did was in the interests of the bank. There is no suggestion there is any personal gain to Mr Leeson in any matters relating to this dreadful outcome."

Mr Leeson, 28, who has spent six hours talking to Mr Pollard in prison in the past two days, has been accused by the Singapore authorities of forging papers showing a $50m payment to his trading unit from an American investment firm.

Barings bank executives have refused to comment on reports that $800m was transferred from London to back Leeson's derivatives gambling in the build-up to the crisis that brought down the bank.

Mr Leeson's lawyers said there was very little connection between the allegation of forgery in Singapore's extradition request and the real story behind the collapse of Barings.

Mr Eberhard Kempf, Mr Leeson's German lawyer, suggested the forgery allegation was used because it was the only relevant and easily identifiable crime in the extradition treaty between Germany and Singapore.

"On the one hand, there is the real story of the crash of Barings and Mr Leeson and on the other the story of falsification and they have very little in common," he said.

Mr Pollard refuted suggestions that his client had wanted to go into hiding and insisted he had gone on holiday with his wife to escape "the increasing pressure at work and in his private life.

"There was absolutely no question of flight or of abandoning their flat. Mr and Mrs Leeson left Singapore for Malaysia on 23 February for a holiday. They travelled under their own passports with their own money.

"Knowing there had been problems in the bank which might have led to his sacking, Mr Leeson left Singapore determined to offer his resignation which he did in a letter dated 24 February."

Mr Pollard said that when Mr Leeson left Singapore he had no idea that his actions could possibly lead to any form of criminal charges.

"They flew to Kuala Lumpur and travelled on to their holiday destination. It was not until he saw a chance headline in an English language newspaper on 26 February that Mr Leeson learned of the merchant bank crash. At no time did he suspect it would turn into the situation that has evolved.

"He was thrown into confusion and shock by what he saw in the paper and telephoned his mother-in-law in Britain and a friend in Singapore," Mr Kemp said.

"Acting on information that the Singapore police were looking for him, he decided to fly to Britain at the earliest available opportunity."

Mr Pollard said his client had wanted to return to a country where he felt more comfortable and could expect a fairer hearing than in Singapore. The danger of arrest in Frankfurt was something he was prepared to risk.

"The earliest flight was one to Frankfurt where Mr Leeson hoped to contact a lawyer in Britain to ask him to meet him at London Airport when he arrived."

Mr Pollard said he wanted to clear up a number of misconceptions about his client who had seemed to be "in remarkably good spirits, calm, confident" and who had not lost his sense of humour. "He is coping well with prison conditions, which are good and for which he is grateful."

Reports that Mr Leeson was close to suicide or distressed were incorrect. "There is no question that he is suffering in any way mentally or in any other respect.

"I would also like it to be known Mr Leeson does not own a Porsche but used to drive a Rover which he sold as it was getting too expensive to run with Singapore tax.

"He was lent a Mercedes by a friend and did not own a yacht although Barings had a boat, on which he went about five times for purposes of corporate entertainment."

Suggestions that Mr Leeson led a luxurious lifestyle were "well wide of the mark". Mr Pollard said he was earning about £4,300 a month plus a housing allowance.

Mr Leeson's wife, Lisa, 24, is expected to visit him today.

24 November 1995
Nine months and eleven charges later, the Leesons are back in Singapore
By Philip Sherwell in Singapore

The disgraced former Barings trader Nick Leeson was back in Singapore yesterday for the first time since he and his wife Lisa left without warning on 23 February.

Leeson was there to make his first court appearance in Singapore at the start of what will be the biggest fraud case in the country's history.

Looking nervous Leeson stood in the dock this morning as a court official read out every trading detail of the 11 forgery and fraud charges arising from the downfall of Britain's oldest merchant bank, Barings.

He was told he would not have to enter a plea to the charges which cover the intricate financial ruses he is alleged to have used during the first two months of this year as he attempted to cover soaring trading debts.

Leeson wore a white shirt and tie and dark trousers, as he stood in a court room packed with public and press. He faced a battery of seven prosecution lawyers and was represented by the Cambridge-trained John Koh.

His wife was not in court. She is staying in a Singapore hotel under a false name and has made no comment since returning to the city.

Stephen Pollard, Leeson's British lawyer, who attended the hearing said: "Lisa does not intend to say anything at this stage. We are at an extremely sensitive time and we don't want to do anything to jeopardise the case. They are both coping extremely well considering the pressure they are under."

Leeson's extradition from Germany came nine months to the day after he and Mrs Leeson disappeared from Singapore with Barings on the brink of collapse as a result of the catastrophic losses he ran up during his time as chief futures trader there.

After they arrived in Singapore, Leeson was driven away for questioning. His wife took a taxi with Mr Pollard, to show him the condominium block where the couple had lived.

The cab stopped briefly outside the complex and she pointed up at the block where the Leesons had enjoyed the comfortable expatriate life in a £4,000-a-month apartment.

Leeson is expected to be tried, and possibly sentenced, before Christmas. If he pleads guilty and strikes a plea bargain deal as expected, the trial might last only a few days, legal sources say.

Although he faces a maximum jail term of 14 years, the sources say that he may be sentenced to between two and five years if he co-operates with Singapore's criminal investigations into former Barings executives.

On the 12-hour overnight flight from Frankfurt, the party was cordoned off in the jumbo jet's upper business class deck after German police handed over Leeson to three officers from Singapore's Commercial Affairs Department (CAD), the investigation wing of the Ministry of Finance.

Looking jet-lagged and wearing a back-to-front blue baseball cap, a green sweatshirt over a light-blue Manchester City soccer jersey, baggy grey jogging pants and white training shoes, Leeson, 28, was escorted out of Singapore airport by the plain-clothes CAD officers.

He was not handcuffed to his escorts.

He smiled for the cameras but made no comment as he emerged into a melee of photographers and reporters.

Germany agreed to extradite Leeson for trial on eight charges of fraud and three of forgery arising from six desperate weeks in February and January this year when he tried to conceal and recoup his soaring losses on the Osaka stock market.

Meanwhile, Leeson has secured a £450,000 book contract and there is talk of a £3m film deal.

He has said that the money raised will go to meet legal costs.

Investigators have this week been studying newly recovered tapes of telephone conversations that Leeson held with his wife in which they talked of leaving Singapore during the calamitous few weeks before Britain's oldest merchant bank sank with debts of £860m. Barings, like other security firms, routinely taped conversations from the trading floor as a safeguard.

Senior officials from the CAD, known in Singapore as the "Mounties" of white-collar crime investigators because "they always get their man", were questioning Leeson last night at the department's headquarters.

His Singaporean lawyer, Mr Koh, an ex-CAD deputy director, has discussed a deal with his former colleagues after Leeson dropped his opposition to extradition last month. He said that his client was "in a pretty positive frame of mind".

After claiming for several months that he faced a "show trial", Leeson's extradition turnabout came in the wake of the scathing official Singapore report into the Barings fiasco which accused two former senior executives of the bank of colluding to cover up his financial misdemeanours.

Now Leeson, who had been convinced he would be made a scapegoat for the whole affair, is willing to co-operate with the CAD's criminal investigations into other ex-Barings employees in return for a reduced sentence.

Mr Koh is expected to concentrate his efforts on mitigation, emphasising Leeson's voluntary return, his readiness to answer all questions, and the fact that he has not benefited financially from his crimes.

Taking into consideration that he already has spent almost nine months in prison in Frankfurt and with remission of up to a third for good behaviour, Leeson is likely to spend a much shorter time in a Singapore jail than he feared.

2 December 1995
Leeson is sentenced to six and a half years in jail
By Philip Sherwell in Singapore

The former Barings trader Nick Leeson was jailed for six and a half years in Singapore today on two counts of cheating linked to the collapse of Britain's oldest merchant bank.

Judge Richard Magnus said Leeson, 28, had "spun a web of deceit" and created "a superficial reality designed to beguile" both Barings and the Singapore futures exchange.

The judge said he had used his position as general manager of Barings futures "to trade his honesty and integrity".

Leeson, from Watford, Herts, had pleaded guilty yesterday to two "cheating" charges involving about £120m but, in imposing today's sentence, the judge said he was also taking into consideration another nine fraud and forgery counts covering £170m which the prosecution had decided not to pursue.

Leeson had been driven into the court complex in a police van smiling broadly, and walked into court looking relaxed. When the sentence was announced he looked up at the ceiling and was escorted out of the dock with his head bowed.

The jail term was backdated to the start of March when Leeson was detained by German police at Frankfurt airport. He had fled from Singapore a week earlier and had been hiding at a luxury resort on the island of Borneo.

With remission of up to a third of the sentence for good behaviour, he would be expected to serve almost another four years in a Singapore prison.

Mr Leeson's lawyers had been hoping for a shorter sentence in the light of his detailed co-operation with white-collar crime investigators since his extradition from Germany last week.

He had faced a maximum sentence of eight years: seven for cheating the futures exchange by submitting false reports with which he gained a £70m refund on Barings down payments, and one year for deceiving Barings auditors into believing that a trading loss of nearly £50m was actually a debt owed to the company.

The judge handed down sentences of six years for the first offence and six months for the second, to run consecutively. He has been sharing a Spartan modern cell with two other inmates facing fraud charges.

By staging a swift open-and-shut trial, Singapore has avoided the embarrassment of a drawn-out courtroom saga which could have endangered the city-state's reputation for financial probity. In interviews with investigators this week, Leeson traded names and details about the Barings debacle in the hope of receiving more lenient treatment. His next appearance before a Singapore judge could be as a state witness if the authorities decide to prosecute former Barings executives currently under investigation.

His wife Lisa was not in court to hear the sentence imposed. She flew back to Britain on Thursday.

After today's hearing, Leeson's British and Singaporean lawyers went straight into talks with their client to discuss a possible appeal against the level of sentence.

Also 2 December 1995
"Boy Wonder" who led Barings down the road to ruin
The council estate boy fell in love with life as a wheeler and dealer

Any Hollywood film starring Hugh Grant as the fallen financial trader, Nick Leeson, was "highly improbable", his Singaporean lawyer said in court yesterday.

But earlier this year, Leeson and his wife, Lisa, achieved a sort of celebrity status when the collapse of Barings made them the world's most sought-after couple.

They were ensconced at a luxury Shangri-La resort near Kota Kinabalu in Borneo when news broke that the Queen's bank (founded in 1762 and run by the Barings dynasty ever since) had gone bust thanks to the disastrous punts of an unknown 28-year-old British futures dealer based in Singapore.

On the evening of Thursday, 23 February, Leeson had been called in to a meeting with his bosses to discuss a gaping financial discrepancy in his trades. After 10 minutes, he said he had to take his wife to hospital and left.

A few hours later, the Leesons arrived in the Malaysian capital, Kuala Lumpur, from where the next day he sent a faxed resignation and apology, before they flew to Kota Kinabalu.

John Koh, Leeson's defence lawyer, insisted he had not fled Singapore to escape justice, but out of panic. But a removals company in the city was asked to make quick plans to ship the couple's belongings back to England during February and there are said to be taped telephone conversations in which the Leesons discuss leaving Singapore.

By the time they next surfaced, the German police were waiting for them as they arrived in Frankfurt on 2 March on a flight from Borneo, hoping to make a connection to London.

In Singapore, the Commercial Affairs Department's investigators were searching Barings' offices and the Leeson's abandoned £4,000-a-month condominium for clues about the collapse.

Nick Leeson, the council estate boy made good, had fallen in love with his life as a high-flying wheeler and dealer amid the hustle and bustle of the Far East.

In his lurid, striped Barings blazer, he was a well-known figure on the boisterous trading floor of Simex, the Singapore futures exchange, and was known as a man with the Midas touch. Fellow brokers had no idea it was all an illusion, and that his Account 88888 was amassing losses.

Dubbed the "turbo-arbitrageur", he flourished in the hard-working, hard-playing existence. While Mrs Leeson was a reclusive character who preferred to stay at home, her husband enjoyed the raucous atmosphere in the expatriate quayside haunts.

Leeson was born in Watford in February 1967. He left school at 18 after A-levels and went to work at the bank Coutts & Co for two years before moving on to the American financial institution Morgan Stanley.

In 1989, he took a job at Barings in London where he met his future wife, Lisa Sims. They married in March 1992 and shortly afterwards moved to Singapore, where he was initially responsible for settling trades.

But he was a rising star and in 1993 was appointed general manager of Barings with the unprecedented responsibility of controlling both the trading floor operations and the back-office settlements. It was this dual role that allowed him to mask his losses for so long.

He may not have belonged to the blue-blooded dynasty that ran Barings, but his bosses seemed willing to stand by him as long as they thought he was turning in spectacular profits.

In Singapore, they nominated him for registration with the futures exchange, even though in London, Barings knew that the Securities and Futures Authority had turned him down because he had unsettled county court debts to his name.

And they also turned a blind eye to the occasional drunken incident at the prestigious Cricket Club so long as he was the goose laying the golden eggs.

But the paper profits hid the reality of the ruinous losses of his speculative and apparently unauthorised trading. By the end of December 1994, he had run up a deficit of nearly £50m on Japanese Nikkei futures. The final reckoning came when the Kobe earthquake on 17 January sent the Nikkei tumbling. Leeson was locked into huge deals on the Osaka exchange and his losses soared.

But London continued to fund his gambles, apparently unaware that their "Boy Wonder" was about to sink Britain's oldest merchant bank.

According to Mr Koh, Leeson stands to make no financial gain from the fiasco, with book proceeds going to agents, the ghost-writer and lawyers.

He had borrowed against two London houses in his wife's name to pay the Singaporean investigators' legal costs of about £70,000.

And in London, a writ had been served on him to strip him of any possible gain which might accrue. "The likelihood of his profiting from his notoriety is remote," said Mr Koh.

Libor

"Dude, you're killing us."

28 June 2012
Interest rate was rigged by Barclays
Bank fined £290m for distorting cost of
loans paid by millions of customers
By James Kirkup and James Hall

Mortgage holders, credit card users and small businesses may have been charged too much for their loans after one of Britain's biggest banks admitted systematically rigging financial markets.

Barclays was fined a record £290m yesterday for repeatedly distorting basic financial data which are used to set interest rates on millions of loans and other transactions around the world.

Bob Diamond, the Barclays chief executive, said he will give up his multi-million-pound bonus over the scandal but faced calls to resign last night amid claims that his bank's actions posed a threat to the global market system.

As MPs suggested that a criminal inquiry should be held, financial regulators warned other major British banks may also have been involved in attempts to manipulate data about interest rates. Up to 40 global banks face being named and shamed as part of the investigation.

The scandal relates to the London Interbank Offered Rate (Libor), the interest rate that banks pay on money they borrow from one another.

The Libor rate is one of the basic pieces of information on which trillions of pounds of financial transactions are based. It helps determine the interest rate that is applied to loans, including some mortgages, credit cards and business loans.

Libor is calculated on information about rates supplied by 15 of the world's biggest banks, which are under strict obligations to provide accurate figures.

British and American regulators yesterday concluded that, between 2005 and 2009, Barclays traders and managers repeatedly made "false reports" in order to push Libor and other interest rate measures higher or lower than its true rate. The manipulations helped increase traders' profits and protected Barclays' reputation. They also raise the prospect of consumers and businesses paying the wrong rate of interest.

Market rules dictate that bank staff who report interest rates for calculating Libor are supposed to be isolated from traders who have a financial interest in the rates.

The Financial Services Authority and the US Commodity Futures Trading Commission found that Barclays staff systematically broke those rules.

The contents of various communications were made available in the FSA's report and provide an insight into the casual exchanges made between traders and rate-submitters. In one request for a change to the Libor, a trader said: "Please feel free to say 'no'. Coffees will be coming your way either way, just to say thank you." The Barclays submitter wrote: "Done, for you big boy."

In a telephone conversation a trader complained to a manager that a Barclays employee was submitting "the highest Libor of anybody". He added: "He's like, 'I think this is where it should be'. I'm like, 'Dude, you're killing us'."

The trader said he had "begged" for a low rate and the submitter had said he would "see what I can do".

After an employee lowered the Libor on request, a trader said: "When I retire and write a book about this business your name will be written in golden letters."

An external trader emailed another trader at Barclays to state: "If it [Libor] comes in unchanged I'm a dead man." The Barclays trader said he would "have a chat" and the submission was later lowered.

The external trader responded: "Dude. I owe you big time! Come over one day after work and I'm opening a bottle of Bollinger."

The FSA also highlighted suspicious extracts from instant messaging conversations with external traders, which included admissions such as: "If you know how to keep a secret I'll bring you in on it."

From 2005 until the summer of 2007, Barclays' attempted manipulation was driven by traders trying to increase profits on their own deals using complex financial instruments. But when the credit crunch began in August 2007, regulators found, the bank's senior management began to direct the false reporting activities.

During the first years of the crisis, Barclays frequently paid higher interest rates than other banks due to concerns about its financial position. Regulators found that in order to protect Barclays' reputation, the bank's senior management instructed staff to make artificially low Libor submissions "routinely".

Lord Oakeshott, a former Liberal Democrat Treasury spokesman, described the bank as "a casino that was rigging the wheels and loading the dice". He added: "If Bob Diamond had a scintilla of shame, he would resign."

Andrew Tyrie, the chairman of the Commons Treasury select committee, said Barclays had put at risk the integrity of the financial markets, with potentially serious consequences for British consumers. "This is tantamount to lying," he said. "This could have affected hundreds of thousands of homeowners by forcing them to pay more for their mortgages."

Ray Boulger, of John Charcol, a mortgage broker, estimated that about 250,000 mortgage customers have loans with rates linked to Libor. Mark Harris, of Savills Private Finance, said that among the individuals most likely to have been affected would be buy-to-let investors and those buying very expensive homes. Chris Leslie, a Labour shadow Treasury spokesman, suggested that a criminal investigation may be necessary.

Barclays said that the fines related to actions in the past which fell "well short" of its standards. Mr Diamond, who had a pay package worth more than £17m last year, said: "I am sorry that some people acted in a manner not consistent with our culture and values." The bank has disciplined several staff and the settlement is expected to see more employees leave.

29 June 2012
Barclays "rigged rates to protect itself"
Diamond gives detailed account as £3.2bn wiped off bank's value
By Harry Wilson, Jonathan Russell and Philip Aldrick

Barclays' chief executive Bob Diamond has admitted for the first time that the bank made a conscious decision to falsify Libor in order to protect the bank at the height of the financial crisis.

The revelation in a letter to Andrew Tyrie, chairman of the Treasury Select Committee, will put increasing pressure on Mr Diamond to reveal whether the decision was taken at board level.

"Even taking account of the abnormal market conditions at the height of the financial crisis, and that the motivation was to protect the bank, not to influence the ultimate rate, I accept that the decision to lower submissions was wrong," he stated.

In the most detailed account so far on how the Libor rates were manipulated, Mr Diamond said fixing of Libor was carried out by individual traders and, separately, by the bank itself.

He said traders attempted to influence the rate in order to benefit their own desks' trading positions, and that the bank made the decision in order to protect shareholders' interests.

The Libor scandal saw £3.2bn wiped off the bank's value yesterday in the biggest one day fall in its share price for more than three years.

The bank's value fell by 15.5 per cent yesterday as the growing public and political outrage led to mounting speculation that Mr Diamond and Barclays' chairman, Marcus Agius, could be forced to stand down within days. However, Mr Diamond reportedly told executives at Morgan Stanley that he would not resign.

Politicians and investors joined the chorus of disapproval of the bank's admission that it attempted to manipulate the Libor borrowing rate for several years.

Investors were last night reported to be demanding a meeting with the bank's senior independent director, Sir Michael Rake. Martin Taylor, a former chief executive of the bank, described the findings against Barclays as showing a "policy of systematic dishonesty".

"It's hard to believe that a policy which seems so systematic was not known to people at or near the top of the bank," Mr Taylor added.

David Cameron said Mr Diamond had "serious questions to answer". The Prime Minister said: "I think the whole management team have got some serious questions to answer. Let them answer those questions first."

Business Secretary Vince Cable warned that, should Mr Diamond or other managers be found to have been involved in the interest rates manipulation, they could be disqualified from working in the finance sector.

"That certainly is a sanction open to us, yes," he said, while claiming that discussions over Mr Diamond's departure were "premature".

In the letter Mr Diamond appeared to try to defend elements of the practice by pointing the finger at other banks.

Addressing the market turbulence at the height of the financial crisis he wrote: "The unwarranted speculation regarding Barclays' liquidity was as a result of its Libor submissions being high relative to those of other banks. At the time, Barclays opinion was that those other banks' submissions were too low given market circumstances."

He also said the bank raised concerns about the Libor setting process with authorities including the Financial Services Authority, Bank of England and US Federal Reserve: "Barclays has co–operated fully with the authorities in their investigations . . . and the authorities have extensively praised the level and speed of our co–operation."

The former chancellor Alistair Darling said Barclays created a culture that tolerated and may even have encouraged market abuse, as he urged the FSA to launch a broader investigation.

Speaking to the *Daily Telegraph*, he called for an overhaul of the way Libor is scrutinised. "Quite clearly, there was a culture here that tolerated – if it didn't encourage – this sort of behaviour," Mr Darling said. "The FSA needs to carry out a further investigation to find out who was responsible for this, who knew what was going on, as well as to track those people who manipulated or attempted to manipulate the figures. Because until that's done confidence won't be restored."

The Libor rigging has already cost the bank £290m in fines and Mr Diamond said the bank was carrying out reviews of employee conduct which could lead to pay being clawed back and dismissals.

Mr Diamond, along with three other Barclays executives, including Chris Lucas, the bank's finance director, have already said they will not take a bonus for this year as a result of the scandal.

However, pressure is growing for a criminal investigation of the bank's actions. George Osborne, in an emergency statement to Parliament, said the Serious Fraud Office was considering further action.

Barclays is unlikely to be the only bank found to have manipulated Libor, which is used to set the rate on loan and derivative contracts worth more than $500 trillion (£320 trillion). Shares in other major British lenders, including state-backed banks, Lloyds Banking Group and Royal Bank of Scotland, fell amid fears they could be drawn in. Twelve banks disclosed they were being investigated over Libor rigging.

Also under scrutiny will be Mr Agius's role as chairman of the banking industry's lobby group, the British Bankers' Association, which is responsible for Libor. Mr Diamond has been called to appear before the Treasury Select Committee. In his letter to Mr Tyrie he said he would be happy to attend.

2 July 2012
"Truly sorry" Barclays chair resigns
By Rowena Mason and Philip Aldrick

The interest rate rigging scandal has claimed its first scalp among the senior management of Barclays with the bank's chairman set to announce his resignation today.

Marcus Agius is expected to say he is "truly sorry" for the scandal, which has dealt a "devastating blow" to the bank. Meanwhile, Lord Turner of Ecchinswell, the head of the Financial Services Authority, said "more heads will roll" at badly behaving banks.

Yesterday it emerged that Barclays stepped up its efforts to rig interest rates after

Bob Diamond, its chief executive, personally spoke to the deputy governor of the Bank of England. Bob Diamond had a conversation with Paul Tucker about how much Barclays was claiming it had to pay to borrow money during the financial crisis in 2008.

After Mr Diamond spoke to Mr Tucker, Barclays staff came to believe the Bank of England wanted them to falsify this data – which was used to calculate Libor, the interest rate that banks pay to each other.

The bank's traders then escalated their secret attempts to manipulate the markets and make it appear that the bank was paying less to borrow money than was actually the case, documents show. Sources at both banks said this was the result of a "misunderstanding" and insisted that Mr Tucker had not sanctioned Barclays' actions.

At the time, the Bank of England was keen to see a lower Libor rate, as that would have been a positive sign in the depths of the credit crunch.

The disclosure increases the pressure on Mr Diamond, who has now been put at the heart of discussions about the fixing of Libor.

When he gives evidence to MPs this week the bank chief will also have to explain why his employees were left with the understanding they had the Bank of England's blessing.

As the board of Barclays called an emergency meeting last night, there were calls for a criminal inquiry into the bank by Vince Cable, the Business Secretary, and Lord Blair of Boughton, the former Metropolitan Police commissioner.

Mr Diamond is also facing calls to step down over his failure to spot the scandal, which may have caused banks to charge mortgage holders, credit card users and businesses too much for billions of pounds in loans.

Barclays was last week fined £290m for its role in the affair. Other high street banks are expected to face heavy penalties for similar wrong-doing.

Mr Diamond is likely to face calls to issue a full apology when he is questioned by the Treasury committee on Wednesday. Sources confirmed he would be asked exactly what he talked about with Mr Tucker, the second most senior figure in the Bank of England, during the crucial phone call about Libor in October 2008.

MPs will be especially keen to know how a confused message was passed on to Barclays traders, who ended up "escalating" the rate-rigging scandal soon afterwards.

Although the bank chief may have to give evidence under oath, he is expected to stonewall many questions for legal reasons. John Mann, an MP on the Treasury committee, said Mr Diamond would face tough questions about the conversation.

"I'm certain that issue will come up," he said. "We will certainly want answers as to if Bob Diamond has been hands-on and it will be surprising if he wasn't. We want to know exactly what he was doing."

Both Barclays and the Bank admit that a conversation took place about Libor but deny there was any instruction to lower the rate. They claim that traders misunderstood directions from their superiors about how they should deal with Libor.

The Financial Services Authority accepted the explanation that instructions from the bank's executives were misinterpreted by more junior employees. "No instruction for Barclays to lower its Libor submissions was given during this telephone conversation," the FSA said.

"However, as the substance of the telephone conversation was relayed down the chain of command at Barclays, a misunderstanding or miscommunication occurred. This meant that Barclays' submitters believed mistakenly that they were operating under an instruction from the Bank of England as conveyed by senior management to reduce Barclays' Libor submissions."

US regulators believe that a member of Barclays' senior management team was responsible for the message that the bank's data needed to be lower.

One trader emailed his boss at the time to say: "Following on from my conversation with you I will reluctantly, gradually and artificially get my Libors in line with the rest of the contributors as requested. I disagree with this approach as you are well aware. I will be contributing rates which are nowhere near the clearing rates for unsecured cash and therefore will not be posting honest prices."

At the time of Mr Diamond's conversation with Mr Tucker, the Bank of England was keen to see Libor reduced, as a higher rate was a sign that the credit crunch was strangling lending between the banks.

However, the Bank of England last night insisted it was "nonsense" to suggest that it was aware of any impropriety in the setting of Libor.

A spokesman added: "If we had been aware of attempts to manipulate Libor we would have treated them very seriously."

Several other companies are also expected to settle with the regulators, after George Osborne, the Chancellor, disclosed that the Royal Bank of Scotland was among the dozen banks or so under investigation.

It emerged over the weekend that RBS has sacked up to 10 traders in connection with Libor fixing.

4 Jul 2012
Diamond and senior aide forced to quit
By Harry Wilson

Bob Diamond, chief executive of Barclays, and one of his most senior lieutenants were forced to resign after the bank came under pressure from both the Bank of England and the Financial Services Authority to remove senior executives over Libor rigging.

Mr Diamond's dramatic resignation came yesterday morning, followed just hours later by that of Jerry del Missier, one of his closest colleagues and the bank's chief operating officer.

The resignations followed conversations on Monday evening between Sir Mervyn King, Governor of the Bank of England, Lord Turner, chairman of the FSA, and Marcus Agius, chairman of Barclays, in which Britain's two most senior regulators made it clear they thought Mr Diamond should go.

Mr Agius yesterday refused to comment on the conversation and said Mr Diamond and Mr del Missier had both reached their own "individual separate decisions" to leave the bank.

Mr del Missier's resignation comes less than a month after he was promoted by Mr Diamond to lead a major shake–up of the bank in light of new banking regulations coming into effect.

"Bob and Jerry's actions are important steps as we begin to move forward from the very difficult events of the past week," said Mr Agius.

He added: "I think it is a measure of these two leaders that they took their decisions, choosing to put the future of Barclays ahead of their own careers."

George Osborne welcomed Mr Diamond's resignation, saying he had done the "right thing for the bank".

"I hope it's a first step to a new culture of responsibility in British banking," the Chancellor added.

But in the City the news of their departures was greeted with dismay, with Investec banks analyst Ian Gordon describing it as "mob rule" in a note to clients.

Following Mr Agius's own resignation as chairman of Barclays on Monday, the bank had to add in its statement on Mr Diamond's resignation that he would now stay on as a "full-time" chairman to oversee the search for a new chief executive. Mr Agius said the process would be "quick" and that the bank would look at both internal candidates as well as potential successors from the wider banking industry.

Lord Turner offered a scathing critique of banks at the FSA's public meeting yesterday. He spoke of the "cynical greed of traders asking their colleagues to falsify their Libor submissions".

Separately, Sir Michael Rake, who on Monday was made deputy chairman of Barclays, came under fire at easyJet.

Its 38 per cent shareholder Sir Stelios Haji-Ioannou called for an EGM to remove Sir Michael as the airline's chairman, citing his time-consuming role at Barclays.

7 July 2012
SFO begins criminal inquiry over Libor
By Louise Armitstead

The Serious Fraud Office (SFO) has formally opened an inquiry into the Libor scandal that will investigate individuals and banks for evidence of criminal activity.

The organisation said its director David Green had "decided formally to accept the Libor matter for investigation". The decision will throw Barclays back into the spotlight after the bank agreed to pay £290m to settle with financial regulators in the UK and US over attempted Libor rigging.

Danny Alexander, Chief Secretary to the Treasury, said: "I want the Serious Fraud Office to follow the evidence wherever it goes, to bring prosecutions if they possibly can."

Separately, Germany's financial watchdog BaFin started an investigation into allegations of Libor manipulation at Deutsche Bank, according to Reuters.

Deutsche's shares fell more than 4 per cent. BaFin declined to comment on the reports, except to say: "We are making use of our entire spectrum of regulatory instruments, so far as this is necessary."

There were also reports that the steering committee that sets the euro–denominated interbank-lending rate, Euribor, is planning to hold an emergency meeting on Monday to discuss the implications of the scandal.

This week Bob Diamond, who resigned as chief executive of Barclays on Tuesday, repeatedly told MPs that the bank was just one of a series of global institutions embroiled. He said Barclays was being unfairly targeted because it was the first to settle. One MP called Barclays a "rotten, cheating" bank.

Barclays' board met on Thursday to discuss whether it could legally claw back part of Mr Diamond's controversial pay awards in the wake of the scandal. It is also deciding how to respond to the Treasury Select Committee's request for letters sent to Barclays by the Financial Services Authority, questioning the bank's aggressive culture. On Monday the TSC will question Marcus Agius, who resigned as chairman of Barclays on Monday but was reinstated a day later as executive chairman following Mr Diamond's departure.

Regulators found that Barclays staff had tried to affect the rate at which banks lend to each other between 2005 and 2009. Initially the traders were acting in their own interests. Later, at the height of the financial crisis, they wanted to dispel rumours Barclays was having funding issues.

13 July 2012
Barclays' customers close accounts over "appalling" Libor–fixing scandal
By Harry Wilson

Barclays is facing growing protests over its attempts to rig Libor with some customers withdrawing money in response to the bank's admission that it tried to manipulate the world's key borrowing rate.

Leicester City Council has said it will withdraw the £6m it holds on deposit with Barclays, warning it had been "appalled" by the bank's behaviour.

The latest blow for Barclays came as analysts at Morgan Stanley estimated the costs of Libor–related litigation for Britain's biggest banks.

Analysts said Royal Bank of Scotland could face the largest claims of any UK bank with a potential bill of £680m, compared to £625m for Barclays, £224m for HSBC, and £38m for Lloyds Banking Group. The cost across the 12 global banks implicated in the scandal could hit $22bn (£14.3bn). Other analysts such as Liberum Capital have forecasted that the costs could be even higher.

Reacting to the scandal, Leicester deputy mayor Rory Palmer said the council felt "uncomfortable" holding its money with Barclays.

"I have been appalled by what Barclays did and we'll not be investing our money with them. I think the people of Leicester would share that discomfort, so we are taking steps to end our association with Barclays," Mr Palmer told the *Leicester Mercury*.

He said it would be "a couple of weeks" before the council would be able to withdraw its money.

"The money will be put into other banks. We have a financial responsibility to invest taxpayers' money wisely and there is also a moral responsibility," he added.

The news came after the Japan Bank for International Co-operation dropped Barclays as a manager on its sale of a five-year bond, in what appeared to be the first time the bank had lost a major piece of business as a result of the scandal.

Barclays has faced a series of protests in recent weeks over Libor rigging. Ahead of former Barclays chief executive Bob Diamond's appearance before the Treasury select committee last week, several members of the Move Your Money UK campaign withdrew their savings from the bank.

Neil Winkcup, 46, a chartered engineer, said he had removed his money because he was "disgusted by Barclays' morals and greed".

Mr Diamond has engaged a public relations team and top white-collar defence lawyer Andrew Levander of Dechert following his grilling at the hands of MPs.

The former Barclays boss said suggestions from MPs that he misled them had had a "terribly unfair impact upon my reputation" and branded the allegations as "unfounded".

17 July 2012
Diamond gave Libor-fix order, says former right-hand man
Barclays boss "rang del Missier to discuss conversation with the Bank"
By Louise Armitstead and Philip Aldrick

Bob Diamond was rounded on by his former right-hand man and three top City regulators yesterday as he was accused of giving the direct instruction to lower the Libor rates at the heart of the rigging scandal.

Jerry del Missier, former chief operating officer at Barclays, told the Treasury Select Committee that Mr Diamond had clearly told him in October 2008 to "get our Libor rates down".

The disclosure came as the former Barclays boss was branded as being "less than candid" with MPs over the Libor scandal.

Mr Diamond's testimony from last week – that Mr del Missier asked traders to lower Libor in October 2008 after "misinterpreting" an email – was crushed by Mr del Missier's claims that the order was relayed to him in a telephone conversation.

Mr del Missier, the third of the three senior directors ejected from Barclays to be grilled by MPs over the scandal that cost the bank £290m in fines, confirmed that he had given the low-balling orders.

"I passed the instruction on to the head of the money market desk," he said. "I relayed the content of the conversation I had with Mr Diamond and fully expected the Bank of England views would be fully incorporated in the Libor submission. I expected that they would take those views into account." But he added: "I took the action on the basis of the phone call that I had had with Mr Diamond."

MPs pointed out that his evidence did not fit with Mr Diamond's. Mr del Missier replied: "I only know what I clearly recollect from the conversation."

Mr del Missier also revealed that Barclays' compliance team had been told "in a note" about the board-level order to lower Libor submissions.

An hour later, Lord Turner, chairman of the Financial Services Authority told MPs that Mr Diamond's evidence to them was another example of the "pattern of behaviour" at Barclays which he summarised as "trying it on, gaming the system".

Andrew Bailey, head of banking supervision at the FSA, said Mr Diamond had been "highly selective" in his description of Barclays' relationship with the regulators.

Mr Bailey said he went to a Barclays board meeting in February where he read the "riot act" and he expressed concerns with the tone from the top. Last week Mr Diamond told MPs that the regulators had been "happy".

The series of conversations over lowering Libor submissions from October 2008 have become pivotal, not just to the Libor scandal but to the reputations of Mr Diamond, Barclays and Paul Tucker, Deputy Governor of the Bank of England.

Mr del Missier said he could not shed any more light on the now infamous telephone conversation between Mr Tucker and Mr Diamond when the pair discussed Barclays' borrowing levels. But he told MPs that Mr Diamond had not just emailed him a summary of the call, he also rang to discuss it.

Mr del Missier said: "[Mr Diamond] said that he had a conversation with Mr Tucker . . . that the Bank of England was getting pressure from Whitehall around Barclays, on the health of Barclays as a result of Libor rates, and that we should get our Libor rates down and that we should not be outliers."

Grilled over whether he knew the action was illegal, he said: "At the time it did not seem an inappropriate action given that this was coming from the Bank of England."

He later acknowledged that it was illegal in US law.

26 July 2012
£9m pay-off for Libor scandal exec
Barclays' Jerry del Missier gets "golden goodbye"
By Alistair Osborne and Jamie Dunkley

The former Barclays Bank executive at the centre of the interest-rate rigging scandal that cost the lender £290m has walked away with a pay-off of almost £9m.

Jerry del Missier, the bank's former chief operating officer who resigned three weeks ago, is understood to have negotiated the deal with Barclays' outgoing chairman Marcus Agius in the days before he quit.

The pay-out looks certain to trigger another political storm over bankers' pay.

Mr del Missier was one of Barclays' highest-paid executives, receiving a salary and bonus package for 2011 worth £6.7m plus a further £10.8m from share awards from previous years.

He became co-head of the investment bank in January 2011, when former chief executive Bob Diamond was promoted to the top job, but emerged as a leading figure in the Libor rigging scandal.

Only last week Canadian Mr del Missier conceded to MPs on the Treasury select committee that he had told Barclays traders to lower the bank's Libor submissions in the autumn of 2008.

That followed a controversial telephone call between Mr Diamond and Paul Tucker, the Deputy Governor of the Bank of England.

Mr del Missier revealed how Mr Diamond had clearly told him in October 2008 to "get our Libor rates down".

"I passed the instruction on to the head of the money market desk," he said. "I relayed the content of the conversation I had with Mr Diamond and fully expected the Bank of England views would be fully incorporated in the Libor submission. I expected that they would take those views into account."

Grilled over whether he knew the action was illegal, he said: "At the time it did not seem an inappropriate action given that this was coming from the Bank of England."

Mr del Missier's £8.75m pay-off is thought to be the price for him dropping claims to as much as £40m of potential share awards still outstanding, which are subject to claw back provisions.

News of his golden goodbye package came as Barclays was rocked by its fourth major resignation in less than a month, with the departure of Alison Carnwath, head of the bank's remuneration committee.

Ms Carnwath, who outraged shareholders by approving a £17m pay package for Mr Diamond including a £2.7m annual bonus, said she was "no longer able to devote sufficient time" to the bank.

"I cannot give the time Barclays seems to want from its non–executives at the moment and the demands are only going to get worse. You can't be half-in and half-out," she said last night.

Ms Carnwath was the lightning rod for a shareholder rebellion over Mr Diamond's pay at April's AGM, when 32 per cent of investors refused to back the bank's remuneration report and more than a fifth opposed her re-election to the board.

She said last night she found the shareholders' response "pretty annoying", claiming she had disagreed with the decision to award Mr Diamond a £2.7m bonus but failed to persuade other directors.

The board eventually agreed to impose stricter targets on part of the bonuses for Mr Diamond and finance director Chris Lucas. Sources close to the bank say Ms Carnwath's resignation was unexpected.

Barclays was also last night seeking to put distance between itself and donations made to US Republican presidential candidate Mitt Romney's election campaign by some of the bank's executives. Barclays' head of UK and European government relations, Cyrus Ardalan, is said to have written to MPs stressing that any fund-raising or political activity was carried out in "a personal capacity".

Alexander Litvinenko

"The bastards got me. They won't get everybody."

Alexander Litvinenko's murder was at once redolent of a bygone era (the Russian secret services accused of targeting a dissident) and oddly contemporary (it's hard to imagine George Smiley ever sitting down to a plate of sushi). An investigation much delayed by debates about the admissibility of evidence finally concluded in January 2016 that Litvinenko was killed as part of an FSB operation, probably sanctioned by Vladimir Putin.

20 November 2006
Ex-KGB colonel "poisoned by Russian agents"
"He looks like a ghost. A month ago he was a fit young man"
By John Steele

Detectives are trying to piece together the recent movements of a former Russian security agent and critic of President Putin who is seriously ill in hospital after being poisoned.

In an episode reminiscent of the Cold War, Alexander Litvinenko, 43, a former KGB colonel living in exile in London, fell ill at the start of the month after meeting a contact in a London restaurant.

He is said to have been investigating the recent murder of a woman journalist in Moscow.

Mr Litvinenko started feeling sick after he was passed documents, possibly containing the names of the killers, in a sushi restaurant. His condition deteriorated last week and tests are said to have shown he had been poisoned with thallium, an odourless, tasteless substance.

Scotland Yard launched an investigation on Friday and its officers have asked the sushi bar, Itsu in Piccadilly, for any CCTV images.

Mr Litvinenko and his friends suspect the Russian government and say he was probably poisoned during his restaurant rendezvous.

There was no suggestion yesterday that Mr Litvinenko's contact, an Italian academic, or anyone working at the restaurant, was involved.

Reports so far have not suggested anything as dramatic as the murder in 1978 of the Bulgarian dissident Georgi Markov, who died after being shot in London with a ricin-tipped pellet from an umbrella gun.

However, the incident comes only weeks after the murder of the Russian journalist, Anna Politkovskaya, a fierce critic of Russia's role in Chechnya. Last week, before his condition worsened, Mr Litvinenko said a contact had approached him to say they should talk and they arranged to meet at the restaurant. "He gave me some papers which contained some names, perhaps names of those who may have been involved in the murder of Anna Politkovskaya, and several hours after the meeting I started to feel sick," he said.

He was said to be in a serious but stable condition in University College Hospital last night.

A clinical toxicologist, John Henry, who examined Mr Litvinenko, said he believed he was given a potentially lethal dose of thallium. "It is tasteless, colourless, odourless. It takes about a gram, a large pinch of salt like in your food, to kill you.

"He is quite seriously sick. There's no doubt that he's been poisoned by thallium and it probably dates back to 1 November when he first started to get ill."

Mr Litvinenko's friend, Alex Goldfarb, who has visited him in hospital, said: "He looks terrible. He looks like a ghost actually. He lost all his hair. He hasn't eaten for 18 days. He looks like an old man. A month ago he was a fit, handsome young man."

One report suggested that Mr Litvinenko had suffered kidney and bone marrow damage and was vomiting regularly. Scotland Yard confirmed it was investigating the "suspicious poisoning" but no one has been arrested. It declined to comment on suggestions Mr Litvinenko was under armed guard.

Mr Litvinenko is a controversial figure in Moscow, having alleged that members of the Federal Security Service (FSB) – the main successor to the Soviet KGB – had plotted to kill the tycoon Boris Berezovsky.

Mr Berezovsky, who visited Mr Litvinenko last week, said he suspected Russia's intelligence services.

Mr Litvinenko's contact at the restaurant, Mario Scaramella, visited the British Embassy in Rome once he realised he was the last person to have seen Mr Litvinenko.

He was interviewed by intelligence officials before leaving and, it is believed, going into hiding.

An Italian political source and close friend of Mr Litvinenko said: "Mario is very scared. He is worried that the Russians and the Chechens are after him.

"He has obviously been made some sort of scapegoat.

"Mario is very well connected and has a lot of sources within the intelligence agencies but he did not have any involvement in the attempt on Litvinenko's life.

"The last time I spoke to him he felt very worried and threatened. He feels he has been set up."

Mr Scaramella is an environmental professor who has lectured in the United States and in his home city of Naples. He was also a consultant on the Italian government's Mitrokhin Commission, which investigated the KGB's activities in Italy.

21 November 2006
Two Russians and a hotel meeting:
was this when the poison trap was sprung?

The plot could easily have come from a John le Carré spy thriller. The shadowy world of the Cold War has descended on 21st-century Britain with the poisoning of a former Russian counter-intelligence agent. As Alexander Litvinenko lies close to death in a London hospital, the questions surrounding his poisoning swirl around him. Who is he? What has he done to suffer such an attack? And how might it all be linked to the brutal world of the new Russia? Ben Fenton examines the theories.

Alexander Litvinenko, a fit 43-year-old former lieutenant-colonel of the FSB, Russia's equivalent of MI5, first began to feel ill on the evening of 1 November.

Unlike some English people, when former Russian spies who believe there is a price on their head suffer from unexpected stomach pains, they do not immediately suspect the sushi.

They think of when and where they might have been poisoned.

Through the encroaching nausea and pain, Mr Litvinenko spoke of his suspicions to his close friend Alex Goldfarb, the man who helped him reach the relative safety of Britain six years ago.

The ex-spy, a minor thorn in the side of Vladimir Putin's government for almost a decade, had been to two meetings that day. There were no other events Mr Litvinenko could think of that might have caused his illness.

The second meeting, a lunch at the Piccadilly branch of the Japanese restaurant chain Itsu, was with an Italian named Mario Scaramella, who provided the Russian, proud holder of a British passport for only a month, with details of a threat to both their lives.

This led back to the murder in Moscow last month of the investigative journalist Anna Politkovskaya, responsibility for which Mr Litvinenko had laid firmly and very publicly at the door of the FSB.

And that was one of several reasons why the former spy was very much persona non grata with his former masters. Ironically, Mr Litvinenko laughed off the threat that so worried Mr Scaramella, who has since disappeared from the public gaze. But it was the first of his two meetings that is currently of more interest to Scotland Yard.

It was held at an unknown central London hotel in the morning of 1 November with two Russians who, although not suspects, may yet have important information to give as witnesses. One was well known to Mr Litvinenko. He was a tall and burly former member of the KGB's ninth directorate, the arm of the feared Soviet intelligence service which supplied bodyguards for political figures. His name was Andrei Lugovoy.

During his time as a state employee, Mr Lugovoy had worked for Boris Berezovsky, then deputy head of the Russian security council, as part of his personal protection team and accompanied him on at least one perilous trip to negotiate with Chechen rebels.

He had also worked on the payroll of Mr Berezovsky, a billionaire who was an ally of Mr Putin and is now an enemy of the president.

At the hotel meeting, Mr Lugovoy was accompanied by another man, named Vladimir, who Mr Litvinenko did not know.

His friend Mr Goldfarb said that through the agony of his illness, Mr Litvinenko could not recall details of the meeting.

"Like all of us, he assumed that he would not be the target of any attack because he lived in Britain." But Mr Litvinenko also had his background as an FSB man to fall back on. Oleg Gordievsky, the KGB defector and friend of Mr Litvinenko, said: "He told me he was safe because he would see an assassin coming a mile off. You might say that he was a victim of his own pride."

Alexander Valterovich Litvinenko was born in Voronezh in southern Russia. He left school at 18 and was drafted into the army. He served for 20 years, rising to the rank of lieutenant-colonel.

At 26 he joined the counterintelligence agency of the KGB. From 1991 he worked for the Central Staff of what by then was known as the FSB, specialising in counter-terrorism and organised crime.

In a press conference in Moscow in November 1998, he claimed he had been asked to organise the assassination of Mr Berezovsky.

He was arrested the following March and imprisoned in the FSB prison at Lefortovo in Moscow. He was acquitted in November 1999 and re-arrested before the charges were again dismissed in 2000.

A third criminal case began but Mr Litvinenko slipped out of the country, claimed asylum in Britain and was convicted in his absence.

But is Mr Litvinenko really a victim of the Russian intelligence services rather than, perhaps, of some internal feud?

Certainly, the FSB's reach into Russian society has spread in the six years since President Putin came to power and democracy in the world's largest country has grown commensurately weaker. Yet if a plot was hatched in Moscow to poison Mr Litvinenko in London, many Russians believe a threshold has been crossed.

"It is difficult to know why Litvinenko was targeted but the theory is that this is a statement of intent to those who speak out against the regime," said a Russian commentator with close links to the intelligence services.

"Those critics who feared for their lives always had the option to flee abroad. But the message now is: We can get you anywhere."

If the theory is right, it certainly seems effective. While many analysts that follow the FSB have grown more circumspect in what they say of late, Mr Litvinenko's poisoning appears to have left them terrified.

But there must be a strong note of caution here. Many experts sneered at the idea that Mr Litvinenko was a target of official action. In Moscow, Putin loyalists said that he was too small a fry to have bothered the regime.

"I am at a loss to understand who may be interested in eliminating Litvinenko who presents no threat to us at all," Gennady Gudkov, a parliamentary deputy who sits on the State Duma's security committee, told the independent radio station Ekho Moskvy.

Certainly, Mr Litvinenko had not done much for his credibility by claiming that the FSB was behind the Sept 11 atrocities or that senior al-Qa'eda officials were agents of Russian intelligence.

But occasionally he had scored hits on his old bosses. Firstly, in 1998, shortly after he was sacked from the FSB he held a press conference, flanked by masked officers employed by the FSB, to reveal a plot to murder Mr Berezovsky.

If that was greeted with scepticism, Mr Litvinenko's next claim that the FSB was behind a series of bombs that exploded in Moscow apartment blocks in 1999, blamed on the Chechens, won far greater acceptance. It was a key to the Russian justification for its brutal second war in Chechnya.

Another sceptic was Nigel West, the British intelligence expert, who said yesterday he would be most surprised if the FSB had tried to kill Mr Litvinenko because it would fly in the face of 65 years of Soviet or Russian practice.

"Neither the FSB nor the KGB has ever killed a defector on foreign soil and their predecessors, even under Stalin, did so only once in the case of Walter Krivitsky in Washington in 1941. Even then there were doubts as to whether he might have committed suicide."

There are two precedents for the use of poisons by Soviet bloc agents to assassinate dissidents.

The first is the case of the Bulgarian Georgi Markhov, killed with a ricin pellet fired from a device in an umbrella. The second concerns three Romanian dissidents working for the American-funded Radio Free Europe in Vienna. Agents of Romania's foreign intelligence service broke into their office and sprinkled plutonium dust in their desks. All three died months later from lung cancer.

Thirty years later, this John Le Carré world of espionage is just as dirty as ever. Only the characters, and the poisons, change.

22 November 2006
Poisoned Russian on hit list, says man he met in sushi bar
By Nick Pisa in Rome

The Italian who met Alexander Litvinenko at a Piccadilly sushi bar on the day before the Russian fell sick from poisoning emerged from hiding yesterday to give his version of their rendezvous.

Prof Mario Scaramella, 38, said he told the former KGB man of death plots against Russians living in Britain and that both their names were on a hit list.

Prof Scaramella, who describes himself as a defence consultant, said he did not eat at the restaurant and just drank water while Mr Litvinenko helped himself to fish from a buffet and was brought soup by a waiter.

The professor stressed he had nothing to do with the poisoning and pointed the finger of blame at the Russian secret services. He said the original arrangements for the meeting had been by email and it was agreed that they would meet on 1 November in central London.

Prof Scaramella was surrounded by four bodyguards as he arrived for his press conference at Palazzo Madama, the Italian upper house of parliament, in Rome.

He said: "I was in London to meet Mr Litvinenko because I wanted to discuss with him some alarming news.

"The information I had received was very disturbing and contained details of plots against Russians both in Italy and Great Britain.

"I called him and we arranged to meet as we always do in Piccadilly Circus. I have met him several times. He is a very good source of mine and has contacts in Russia.

"I was with him for maybe 30–45 minutes. We were downstairs and there were no other people there.

"I had already had lunch in the Pizza Hut so I had nothing to eat. I don't eat fish that is that fresh – and had a glass of water.

"Mr Litvinenko had some fish from a buffet and some soup was brought to us.

"He personally took his food from the buffet. I paid for the bill. As I recall, it was about £17."

Prof Scaramella added: "I told him that I had . . . been given a list of names and lots of facts from a contact.

"The information was a list of people. It was a hit list and on that list was his name, my name and Paolo Guzzanti [head of an Italian commission investigating KGB activities in Italy].

"It was unbelievable and there were also names of people in Britain on it. I asked him to make a call to his people in Russia to evaluate it.

"Mr Litvinenko told me not to worry about it. The arrangement was that I would call him later that night or the following morning.

"When I called him back the next morning his wife said that he was very sick but she laughed it off saying half of London was ill."

Prof Scaramella, who has been the target of an attempted assassination by the Camorra, or Naples Mafia, in 2004, also said Mr Litvinenko had mentioned he had been at another meeting.

"When we arranged the meeting he said to me that he was in London to see some people in the morning and that he would be free to see me in the afternoon," the professor said. "When he arrived he did not mention who he met but I understand the authorities are investigating the possibility he was poisoned at this meeting."

He said the hit list had come from "from someone who lives out of Russia" but refused to elaborate.

When asked if he was scared and what steps he had taken to increase his personal security he said: "I don't want to answer that question."

He added: "These people are very dangerous. We are talking about people involved in the murder of [Russian journalist] Anna Politkovskaya."

He also described how there was a strong connection between the Russian Mafia and the former KGB as well as its replacements, the FSB and SVR. He said he thought the poisoning of Mr Litvinenko was an attempted "political assassination".

When asked about radioactive thallium he said: "I know that in Russia money, especially dollars, is coated with such a material so that it can be tracked."

24 November 2006
"The bastards got me. They won't get everybody"
Poisoned spy's last words of defiance

Alexander Litvinenko fought to the very end. "I want to survive, just to show them," he is reported to have said, hours before he slipped into unconsciousness.

Mr Litvinenko was in pain and so weak he could not move his limbs but he was reported to have told his friend, Andrei Nekrasov: "The bastards got me. But they won't get everybody."

"Sasha [Litvinenko] was a good-looking, physically strong and courageous man," said Mr Nekrasov, a film-maker. "But the figure who greeted me looked like a survivor from the Nazi concentration camps."

That visit to his hospital bedside on Tuesday is understood to have been the last time 43-year-old Mr Litvinenko could communicate properly.

Yet he was still able to crack jokes, suggesting his poisoning was proof that his very public opposition to the Kremlin had hit home. "This is what it takes to prove one has been telling the truth," he said.

The one-time lieutenant colonel in the Russian secret service who claims he was poisoned by his former colleagues was being treated in a darkened room under police guard at University College Hospital, London, with all visitors carefully screened.

There was continuing confusion last night over the cause of his poisoning after the hospital ruled out heavy metals such as thallium and said radiation was unlikely.

Although three times the usual quantity of thallium was found in his system, it would not have been enough to bring on such extreme symptoms and the hospital has found no sign of radioactivity.

Dr Paul Travers of the Anthony Nolan Trust, a register of bone marrow donors, said: "The symptoms of hair-loss, gut problems and bone marrow failure are classic examples of the body struggling to cope with rapidly dividing tissues, either through cancer or chemotherapy."

Another medical source said such a rapid decline was likely to have been the result of cyto-toxic drugs, which kill cells, such as those used in chemotherapy, or a radioactive isotope, which has since left the system.

The source added: "There is no antidote to what is happening so in many ways it doesn't really matter what caused it, all the doctors can do is react to the symptoms."

Despite opposition to the Kremlin, Mr Litvinenko was a patriot who dreamed one day of going back to Russia – even though he had been looking over his shoulder ever since defecting to Britain in 2000.

As an outspoken critic of the state Russia was in, he realised his life and those of his family – his wife Marina and 12-year-old son – were at risk. He kept his address a secret, changed his phone number regularly and met contacts at public locations.

He was investigating the murder of the journalist Anna Politkovskaya, another opponent of the Kremlin. It was after being handed documents about the case that he was taken seriously ill on 1 November.

He first became an agent under the Soviet-era KGB, in the late 1980s, after transferring from the Russian military. It is now known as the FSB, the Federal Security Service, specialising in organised crime and counter terrorism.

A decade later he voiced concerns about corruption in the FSB and exposed an alleged plot to assassinate the then powerful tycoon Boris Berezovsky, who now also lives in exile in London.

Around that time he fell out with Vladimir Putin, then head of the FSB and now president of Russia. He was sacked, arrested and charged with corruption. Eventually acquitted, he fled to the UK where he was granted asylum.

Here, he became a relentless critic of Mr Putin's regime, co-authoring several books. One, *Blowing Up Russia: Terror From Within*, accused Russian agents of co-ordinating a series of apartment block bombings in 1999 that left more than 300 dead – attacks Moscow blamed on Chechen rebels.

Mr Litvinenko denounced the war in Chechnya as a crime, called for Russian troops to be withdrawn and said compensation should be paid to Chechens.

On the morning of November 1 he had met Andrei Lugovoi, a former KGB agent who now runs a security firm in Moscow, and a man called Vladimir, at the Millennium Hotel in Grosvenor Square, London.

Mr Lugovoi used to work for billionaire Mr Berezovsky, who also employs Mr Litvinenko.

Mr Lugovoi said he was visiting Britain to watch a football game and denied any involvement in the poisoning.

In the afternoon Mr Litvinenko met Italian investigator Mario Scaramella at the Itsu sushi restaurant in Piccadilly, who gave him information about the murder of Miss Politkovskaya.

Mr Scaramella has also denied any involvement.

Alex Goldfarb, a friend of the dead man, said he had seen a copy of the "hit list" handed to Mr Litvinenko by Mr Scaramella, which included both their names and an "elaborate conspiracy led by Russian intelligence".

Intelligence expert Glenmore Trenear-Harvey, who knew Mr Litvinenko, said his accusations about the FSB were believable.

But he added: "There is a Don Quixote quality about him, always tilting at windmills.

"I believe the FSB when they say he was not important enough to assassinate, but if he was getting close to the killers of Anna Politkovskaya they could have taken things into their own hands."

25 November 2006
Spy poisoned by radiation
Victim accuses Putin of murder from deathbed
By Ben Fenton, John Steele and Duncan Gardham

A radiation alert was declared by the Government last night as it was disclosed that a former KGB colonel who died in London had been poisoned by a rare and deadly substance.

Alexander Litvinenko, in his last statement before his death on Thursday night, accused President Vladimir Putin of Russia of being responsible for his murder.

Security chiefs fear that state-sponsored agents were responsible for the death of Mr Litvinenko, whose body was ravaged by polonium 210, a radioactive isotope rarely used outside military and scientific establishments.

Scientists found a "significant, large" amount in his urine. Traces of polonium were also found in Mr Litvinenko's home and a restaurant and hotel he had visited in London. They may have been detected in blood, urine or sweat.

If evidence of Russian involvement emerges, it threatens to plunge relations between London and Moscow to the kind of low last seen during the Cold War.

Security chiefs are alarmed at the possibility that Russia may be prepared to strike at critics abroad with little heed of its public image.

Scotland Yard stopped short of confirming a murder inquiry but the affair is causing increasing alarm. The Government's Cobra security committee met several times on Thursday and yesterday.

John Reid, the Home Secretary, chaired a meeting at lunchtime, after which the Government asked the chiefs of its Health Protection Agency (HPA) to hold a news conference to reassure the public about polonium 210 risks.

The HPA chief executive, Prof Pat Troop, said the finding of polonium in Mr Litvinenko's body was "unprecedented". Such poisoning had never been seen in Britain and the HPA knew of no other case around the world.

But she insisted it was not dangerous to the wider public and would only be lethal if it were ingested or breathed in.

Scotland Yard sources said a "major operation" had been launched to check for traces of polonium 210 at five London locations – a sushi restaurant and a hotel bar, where Mr Litvinenko met associates on 1 November; his home in Muswell Hill; and two hospitals. Last night, it was confirmed that traces were found at the Itsu restaurant in Piccadilly, the Millennium Hotel, Grosvenor Square and at Mr Litvinenko's home. Cordons were set up.

Police are working with Government nuclear scientists and it is unclear when a post mortem examination of Mr Litvinenko's body will be allowed. Specialists from the Government weapons laboratory at Porton Down confirmed that "monumental doses" of polonium were found in his urine. Dozens of people who came into contact with Mr Litvinenko since he fell ill on 1 November, including his wife, Marina, his son, Anatoly, his family and friends, bar and hotel staff and medical teams, will be spoken to by doctors.

But the HPA stressed that residual traces of polonium 210 would easily be washed away by normal hygiene.

In emotional scenes outside University College Hospital, where Mr Litvinenko died, his statement was read by a friend. It said of Mr Putin: "You have shown yourself to be as barbaric and ruthless as your most hostile critics have claimed. You may succeed in silencing one man, but the howl of protest from around the world will reverberate, Mr Putin, in your ears for the rest of your life.

"May God forgive you for what you have done, not only to me, but to beloved Russia and its people."

Walter Litvinenko said: "My son was killed by a little tiny nuclear bomb. But the people who killed him have big nuclear bombs and those people should not be trusted.

"He was very courageous when he met his death and I am proud of my son.

Marina [his wife] and Sasha [Alexander] were so happy in London, but the long hand of Moscow got them here on this soil."

The *Daily Telegraph* can disclose that Mr Litvinenko told two academic interviewers this year that he was trained by the KGB and was second in command of a unit that committed "extra-legal killings".

Mr Putin said: "As far as I understand from the medical statement, it does not say this was the result of violence, this was not a violent death.

"There's no grounds for speculation of this kind. I hope the British authorities would not contribute to instigating political scandal: it has nothing to do with reality."

27 November 2006
Minister attacks Putin and "murky murders"
By Duncan Gardham and George Jones

Tensions between Britain and Russia over the death of Alexander Litvinenko, the former KGB agent, burst into the open yesterday when a Cabinet minister condemned the "murky murders" clouding Vladimir Putin's regime.

Peter Hain's hint at possible Kremlin involvement in Mr Litvinenko's death from radiation poisoning four days ago came as John Reid, the Home Secretary, said the police were now treating the death as "suspicious".

Until now police have referred to it as an unexplained death although they previously said they suspected deliberate poisoning. A formal request has been submitted to Moscow for any information that might help the police.

While Downing Street and the Foreign Office have carefully avoided suggesting direct Russian involvement, Mr Hain, Northern Ireland Secretary and a contender for Labour's deputy leadership, delivered an outspoken attack on Mr Putin.

Mr Hain, interviewed on BBC Television's *Sunday AM* programme, said relations between London and Moscow were "tricky" following Mr Litvinenko's death.

He criticised the Russian leader's "huge attacks" on liberty and democracy. "The promise that President Putin brought to Russia when he came to power has been clouded by what has happened since, including some extremely murky murders," Mr Hain said.

He referred to the earlier shooting outside her apartment of Anna Politkovskaya, a prominent journalist critical of President Putin's human rights record in Chechnya. Mr Hain said the attacks on democracy and individual liberty in Russia had overshadowed President Putin's success in "binding a disintegrating nation together" and achieving stability from an economy which had been collapsing into "Mafioso-style chaos".

"It's important he retakes the democratic road in my view," Mr Hain said. His remarks do not appear to have been sanctioned by Downing Street and are likely to embarrass Mr Blair, who has courted Mr Putin as an international friend and ally.

A Downing Street spokesman said last night: "While there is an ongoing police investigation and Health Protection Agency investigation, we don't have anything to say on this."

Mr Hain is an outspoken minister, who is prepared to go further than other Cabinet colleagues and officials in speaking his mind. Government officials insisted last night, however, that they would not point the finger of suspicion without evidence of Russian involvement. Mr Litvinenko, who was granted asylum in this country and had recently become a British citizen, died from suspected poisoning with the radioactive element polonium 210.

His friend, Alex Goldfarb, welcomed Mr Hain's comments. He said it was "long overdue" that western governments raised concerns about "the twist of Russia towards an uncontrollable and unaccountable police state which poses a danger to the rest of the world".

The Government's emergency planning committee, Cobra, met over the weekend to discuss the implications of his death, which is threatening serious diplomatic repercussions.

The Foreign Office has spoken to the Russian Ambassador, Yuri Fedotov, asking authorities in Moscow to make available any information that might assist the police.

Shortly before his death on Thursday, Mr Litvinenko blamed his mysterious poisoning on Putin. The Russian president has dismissed the accusation.

The weekend papers canvassed various conspiracy theories – including suggestions that he had been murdered by dissident Russians seeking to discredit Mr Putin.

Police are trying to piece together Mr Litvinenko's movements on 1 November, the day he was taken ill.

They have focused their attention on the Itsu sushi restaurant in Piccadilly, where he met Italian investigator Mario Scaramella for lunch. Investigations are also continuing at the Millennium Hotel in Grosvenor Square where Mr Litvinenko met two former KGB colleagues, Andrei Logovoi and Dimitry Kovtun.

Searches have taken place at the hotel's Pine Bar and a room on the fourth floor. Traces of radioactivity have been found at both the hotel and sushi restaurant, along with Mr Litvinenko's home in North London, but police are still trying to work out in which order and by whom the traces were deposited.

The Health Protection Agency has asked anyone who ate at the Itsu restaurant or the Pine Bar at the Millennium Hotel to contact NHS Direct, but said the risk of having been exposed to the substance remained low.

Mr Reid refused to be drawn on the progress of the police investigation, apart from confirming that murder was a possible line of inquiry. "As at this stage, they're saying to me that they now regard the death as suspicious. That wasn't the case yesterday, for instance. "They're now saying, however, that they keep all possible options and avenues open," he said.

The Tories will be seeking a Commons statement from the Government today. David Davis, home affairs spokesman, called on the Russian authorities to co-operate with police inquiries.

28 November 2006
Deadly radiation trail leads to the
London office of another Putin critic
By Duncan Gardham and Ben Fenton

Traces of radiation have been found at the offices of the billionaire Russian exile Boris Berezovsky and a security firm which employs the former commander of Britain's special forces.

Polonium 210, the rare radioactive element thought to have killed the former KGB spy Alexander Litvinenko, has been found at Mr Berezovsky's offices and those of the private security firm Erinys.

Erinys employs Major-General John Holmes, a former commander of the SAS and former director of British Special Forces, at its offices in Grosvenor Street, Mayfair.

The company employs 16,000, largely ex-Forces personnel in Iraq to guard oil installations and has connections around the world, including Moscow.

Mr Berezovsky, one of Russia's first "oligarchs", made his wealth in automotives and oil before falling out with President Putin and being granted asylum in Britain.

As police sealed off part of his offices in Down Street, Mayfair yesterday, he was described by a friend as "extremely nervous".

The friend added: "He is deeply shocked by Alexander Litvinenko's death and fears he could be next."

Police confirmed that radiation had been found at the two addresses but were still unable to explain the sequence of events that led them to the two sites.

A source said: "We are still trying to piece together Litvinenko's movements, who he met and where."

The Health Protection Agency said it had received 450 calls over the weekend and asked three members of the public who may have come into contact with Mr Litvinenko and are showing possible symptoms of radiation poisoning to take further tests.

The symptoms include sickness, vomiting and bleeding gums. The people involved have been asked to take urine tests.

Forty members of the medical staff at University College Hospital and Barnet General, where Mr Litvinenko was treated, have also been sent for tests after the HPA conducted assessments.

It is understood that close members of Mr Litvinenko's family, including his wife, Marina and 12-year-old son, have also been offered the tests, which can take up to a week.

Prof Pat Troop, the chief executive of the Health Protection Agency, said they had not identified when and where Mr Litvinenko ingested the poison, adding that working out the time of poisoning on the basis of the radioactivity found in his body was "not a precise calculation".

Police were continuing searches of the Pine Bar and fourth floor rooms at the Millennium Hotel in Grosvenor Square, where Mr Litvinenko met Andrei Lugovoi, a private security specialist from Moscow, and Dmitry Kovtun.

They have now completed checks at the Itsu sushi restaurant in Piccadilly where Mr Litvinenko met an Italian intelligence adviser, Mario Scaramella, for lunch.

At that lunch he was handed a list of possible targets provided by an informant in France, which included himself and Mr Berezovsky. It is thought that Mr Litvinenko may have gone to Mr Berezovsky's office with the list to photocopy it.

Erinys said yesterday that Mr Litvinenko had visited its offices on an unrelated matter and it had later called the Metropolitan Police.

Workers at other offices in the block said the premises on the fourth floor have been sealed off since Sunday.

In a statement composed before his death on Thursday, Mr Litvinenko, who had recently become a British citizen, pointed the finger at Mr Putin.

John Reid, the Home Secretary, said the Russian authorities had been asked to provide "all necessary co-operation" with the investigation.

In an emergency statement to MPs, he said the Russian ambassador was called to the Foreign Office on Friday.

"He was asked to convey to the Russian authorities our expectation that they should be ready to offer all necessary co-operation to the investigation as it proceeds," Mr Reid told the House of Commons.

At the weekend the Northern Ireland Secretary Peter Hain criticised the "very murky murder" of the journalist Anna Politkovskaya, an opponent of Mr Putin.

Yesterday Tony Blair's official spokesman said: "The Prime Minister and other ministers have repeatedly underlined our concerns about some aspects of human rights in Russia. In terms of this particular case, we have to proceed carefully."

Mr Reid would not confirm that the incident would be discussed when Mr Blair and President Putin meet next week. "To some extent it will depend on developments," he said.

29 November 2006
Murdered spy saved my life, says Berezovsky
By Duncan Gardham

Boris Berezovsky, the billionaire Russian exile, yesterday broke his silence over the death of his friend Alexander Litvinenko to say the former spy had saved his life.

Litvinenko, then a lieutenant-colonel in the KGB successor the FSB, was arrested by the Russians after claiming that he had been told to organise the assassination of Mr Berezovsky.

The businessman, who was one of the most powerful men in Russia, fled to Britain where he was granted asylum. He organised Litvinenko's escape through Turkey.

Yesterday the Russian oligarch said he was "deeply saddened" at the loss of his friend.

"I credit him with saving my life and he remained a close friend and ally ever since," he said. "I will remember him for his bravery, his determination and his honour. All of my thoughts are with his bereaved wife Marina, his son and the rest of his family."

Mr Berezovsky's comments came as police announced they were searching for radioactivity at another hotel, the Sheraton in Park Lane, as they try to trace Litvinenko's trail across London on 1 November, the day he was taken ill.

Mr Berezovsky employed the former secret agent and visited him as he lay dying from radiation poisoning in University College Hospital last week.

Traces of polonium 210, the radioactive element thought to have killed Litvinenko, were found at Mr Berezovsky's office in Mayfair after the spy apparently visited him to show him a "hit list" he had been given with both their names on.

On his death bed, Litvinenko had accused Vladimir Putin, the Russian President, of killing him.

Mr Berezovsky did not repeat the allegations yesterday but said: "Many of Mr Litvinenko's friends and I have already publicly expressed our views about what we think might have happened. Therefore I believe the most helpful course we can take is to let the police get on with their work.

"I have complete faith in the British authorities and the police. They are conducting a thorough and professional investigation and we should now wait for the results." The Health Protection Agency said eight people from more than 1,100 who called a national helpline were being treated for possible symptoms of radiation poisoning.

A further 40 health workers have been referred for tests but the results will not be known for several days.

Radiation has been found at the Itsu sushi restaurant in Piccadilly where Mr Litvinenko had lunch with Mario Scaramella, an Italian investigator, and at the Millennium Hotel where he met two former KGB officers, now back in Moscow.

The office of a security firm which employs Major-General John Holmes, the former director of British Special Forces, has also shown signs of radiation along with another address in the same street, as has Litvinenko's home in north London. Mr Scaramella flew back to Britain yesterday to talk to police.

"I have always said I am willing to help them and that is why I am here," he said.

Litvinenko's brother, Maxim, also flew to London from Italy, where he has already spoken to officers from the Italian special branch DIGOS.

London's inner north district coroner Dr Andrew Reid said an autopsy and examinations of Litvinenko's body would be carried out to investigate the cause of his death.

Tony Blair, speaking in Copenhagen after talks with the Danish prime minister, discussed Mr Litvinenko's death for the first time, saying there would be no barriers in the way of a full investigation.

"I haven't spoken to President Putin but I will do so at any time that is appropriate," he said.

The Kremlin has dismissed reports of its involvement as "nonsense".

30 November 2006
Flights take poison trail to Moscow
By Matt Barnwell and Duncan Gardham

The finger of suspicion over the Alexander Litvinenko poisoning was pointing at Moscow last night after the discovery of radioactivity on passenger jets that flew regularly to the seat of Vladimir Putin's government.

In his deathbed message, Mr Litvinenko accused Mr Putin, the Russian president, of being behind his poisoning. The trail of the three grounded British Airways aircraft now suggested a clear link back to the Russian capital.

Tony Blair has said that no "diplomatic or political barrier" will be allowed to stand in the way of the Scotland Yard investigation into Mr Litvinenko's death.

But a potential crisis looms if the evidential trail does lead back to Moscow.

The discovery of radioactivity on BA jets was the latest dramatic development in an investigation that now spans the globe. Friends of Mr Litvinenko, a former KGB agent, claim he was poisoned by Russian secret service agents because of his criticism of Mr Putin's regime.

The earliest of the dozens of flights that are now part of the Scotland Yard investigation was between Moscow and Heathrow on 25 October – several days before Mr Litvinenko was allegedly poisoned with a radioactive toxin in London.

A total of 47 flights made by the grounded jets between London and Moscow between that date and 28 November are now involved in the alert – considerably more flights than to any of the other nine destinations they have visited.

The inquiry is being carried out by Britain's leading anti-terrorism unit at Scotland Yard.

Mr Litvinenko met two Russians at the Millennium Hotel in Grosvenor Square on 1 November, the day he fell ill after being allegedly poisoned by the radioactive element polonium 210. One was Andrei Lugovoi, the former KGB agent, and the other Dmitry Kovtun, a business associate.

Both have denied any involvement in the poisoning. The only other man known to have met Mr Litvinenko that day, the Italian academic Mario Scaramella, last night declared himself free of radiation following tests in Britain.

It is unclear whether either Mr Lugovoi or Mr Kovtun have been tested. They have both since returned to Russia.

Mr Scaramella, who met Mr Litvinenko at the Itsu sushi bar in Piccadilly, returned to London from Italy to undergo medical checks and to assist the police investigation.

He insisted yesterday that he was neither "under investigation nor a suspect" in the case.

He is staying at a secure location close to London and is being interviewed by Scotland Yard detectives.

There were claims yesterday that Mr Litvinenko had raised suspicions over Mr Scaramella on his deathbed but the Italian said: "Scotland Yard's position on this is clear – it's just another one of these absurdities that is being said about me."

Reacting to the discovery of radioactivity on BA jets, Mr Scaramella's lawyer, Sergio Rastrelli, said: "I have seen the reports but Mario flew to London on easyJet so that is further evidence that he has nothing to do with this."

A friend of Mr Litvinenko said last night that the former spy had been trying to lure his killers back to Britain.

Alex Goldfarb told the *Daily Telegraph* that Mr Scaramella had been named only to try and draw the suspects back to London. He said: "The discovery of radiation on flights to Moscow confirms what we have been thinking all along.

"Alexander suspected Russians may have been involved and wanted to lure them back to Britain. The police have known this from day one.

"I am not convinced about anything in this case but Mario does come with some very good references and I assume there would be some signs of radioactivity around him.

"On the balance of probabilities this discovery means it is more likely that Alexander's killers came from Russia."

Lord Lucan

"I have just got away from being murdered."

9 November 1974
Police seek Earl after nanny is murdered
By John Weeks

Police were trying to trace the Earl of Lucan, 39, last night – 24 hours after his children's nanny had been found battered to death in the Belgravia house where his estranged wife lives.

The body of the nanny, Mrs Sandra Rivett, 29, had been stuffed into a canvas bag at the house in Lower Belgrave Street.

It was discovered after the Countess of Lucan, 35, the Earl's wife, ran into the street late on Thursday shouting "Murder". Lady Lucan, who had several head wounds, was "progressing satisfactorily" last night in hospital.

Lord and Lady Lucan's three children – Lady Frances, 10, Lord Bingham, 7, and Lady Camilla, 4, were in the house on Thursday night.

Lord Lucan, who has lived apart from his 35-year-old wife since last year, has a home nearby in Eaton Row, Belgravia.

Police forced their way in late on Thursday, but Lord Lucan was not there. Lady Lucan's car, a Daf, was missing, but was found later in Chester Square.

Det. Chief Supt Roy Ransom, who is leading the inquiries, spent several hours yesterday at the bedside of Lady Lucan getting details of the attack and murder.

Mr Derrick Whitehouse, 44, head barman of the Plumbers' Arms public house, Belgravia, said yesterday: "On Thursday night Lady Lucan staggered into the bar with deep cuts about her head.

"She was bleeding badly and the blood was pouring down her face. She was shouting and screaming and told us 'I have just got away from being murdered. He's murdered my nannie. My children, my children'."

People living near Lady Lucan in Lower Belgrave Street said they: heard no noise coming from her house and the first they realised that something was wrong was when police and a fleet of ambulances arrived outside. Police went into the house and found Mrs Rivett's body in the basement. They also found a piece of blood-stained lead piping, believed to be the murder weapon.

Mrs Rivett, who was estranged from her husband, Roger, had lived with Lady Lucan and the children in Lower Belgrave Street for only a few weeks.

Friends described her last night as "a vivacious redhead" and "a girl who always liked a laugh". Earlier this week she had drinks in the bar of the Plumbers' Arms.

Police revealed that Lord Lucan had telephoned his mother, the Dowager Countess of Lucan, at her home at Lords View, St John's Wood at midnight on Thursday and spoke to her for several minutes.

Last year, when he and his wife decided to live apart and there was talk of divorce, Lady Lucan said: "It is hard to believe we should break up when we have been together ten years and could have lasted another ten.

"My husband and my children are my whole life. I am still fond of my husband."

The present Earl of Lucan – Richard John Bingham – is the seventh holder of the title which dates from 1795. His family motto is "Christ is my hope".

He succeeded to the title in 1964 – a year after he married Veronica Duncan, daughter of the late Major C. M. Duncan, MC, and Mrs J. D. Margrie.

Lord Lucan is fond of playing backgammon and is a frequent visitor to the Claremont Club. He is also a keen competitor in power-boat racing and an enthusiastic bobsleigher.

Educated at Eton, he was a lieutenant in the Coldstream Guards and is currently a lieutenant in the Regiment's reserves.

In 1966, the film director, Vittorio de Sica, saw Lord Lucan playing at the baccarat tables at Deauville and tried to persuade him to play opposite Shirley Maclaine in a film called *Woman times Seven*.

Lord Lucan went to Paris where he had a screen test, but it is said that when he faced the cameras he "froze up".

His great-great grandfather, the third earl, ordered the charge of the Light Brigade at Balaclava in 1854.

14 November 1974
Dawn search by frogmen for Lucan's body
By T. A. Sandrock and John Weeks

A search of isolated coves and beaches on the Sussex coast is to begin at dawn today for the missing Earl of Lucan. Police frogmen will be assisted by members of a special police task force and by coastguards.

The search is planned both east and west of Newhaven, in areas worked out after a study by experts of wind and tide tables.

Although there is no definite evidence that Lord Lucan has taken his life fears are growing that he is now dead.

A co-ordinated search will also be made along the cliffs, with particular attention paid to caravan sites closed for the winter.

A car he is known to have used was found abandoned at Newhaven after a double attack in which Lady Lucan was badly injured and her children's nanny killed.

All inquiries have failed to establish whether he crossed to France on the Newhaven–Dieppe ferry.

The Earl of Lucan, 39, is wanted on charges of murdering the nanny, and attempting to murder his 35-year-old wife. Warrants have been issued for his arrest.

Lady Lucan left hospital yesterday. She was driven in a police car from St George's Hospital, Hyde Park, to the High Court for a hearing concerning custody of the couple's three children.

Lady Lucan arrived at the court, escorted by four detectives assigned to guard her, just after the private hearing had finished. A court official handed a paper to her.

At the hearing were Mr Norman Turner, the Official Solicitor, and Mr William Shand Kydd, Lord Lucan's brother-in-law. Mr Shand Kydd's wife Christine was also there.

Mr John Aspinall, one of Lord Lucan's closest friends, said last night his concern about his children was the most likely cause of Lord Lucan's worries.

"The case of his children, when he lost custody was a terrible blow to him," Mr Aspinall said on ITN's *News at Ten*.

Police are already investigating the reports that a possible motive for the attack at Lady Lucan's home in Lower Belgrave Street, Belgravia, stemmed from disagreements between Lord Lucan and his estranged wife over the welfare and care of the children.

A year ago there were proceedings concerning the children, Lady Frances, 10, Lord George Bingham, the heir, 7, and Lady Camilla, 4. Then Lady Lucan was granted custody of the children with the ruling that Lord Lucan should have reasonable access to them.

The Earl was represented yesterday in the Family Division hearing before Mr Justice Rees, who had conducted the earlier proceedings.

Lady Frances and Lord Bingham are staying with an aunt in Northamptonshire. They attend the local school.

From the court Lady Lucan wearing a green coat, pillbox hat and dark glasses, was driven to Gerald Road police station. She saw Det. Chief Supt Roy Ranson, who is leading inquiries into the attacks, and other Murder Squad officers. She clarified her earlier statements about the murder and the attack on herself.

Then, again escorted by her bodyguard, she was driven directly to her home.

Callers at the house, where lights were blazing on three floors, were mostly turned away last night by a shirt-sleeved policeman who opened the door about six inches on a chain.

He was supported by an armed officer standing against the wall down the hall. Press inquiries were rebuffed by a blank: "Lady Lucan has no comment to make".

One personal friend who emerged from the house said he expected Lady Lucan to remain there for the night. She would remain under armed guard.

The scene of the crime – the kitchen – was clearly visible from the street through open venetian blinds. It is a 12-foot square room, with dishwasher, refrigerator, a few odd dishes and the dog's dinner on the floor.

Police seeking the Earl have so far failed to establish whether he is abroad. He did not have a passport with him when he disappeared and he did not obtain a temporary travel document.

There is no trace of the Earl having travelled on a cross-Channel ferry any time between Friday, when his bloodstained car was found abandoned at Newhaven, and Sunday.

Interpol has been alerted. Addresses abroad which Lord Lucan might visit are being checked.

He may be very short of money. Murder Squad detectives can find no trace among his friends of anyone lending him money. Yesterday they began checking on what funds might be available to him in Britain and abroad.

A cablegram from America delivered on 11 November to the Earl's home in Eaton Row, Belgravia, offering him and his family use of a five-bedroomed house in Haiti, was also being checked.

There was no signature or sender's address and London police have asked the

Federal Bureau of Investigation to try to trace it. Inquiries indicate that the cablegram may be a hoax.

Police are considering a partial reconstruction of the murder, based on information from witnesses. Yesterday, police scientists carried out further tests on floor coverings and wallpaper in Lady Lucan's house.

The inquest on the nannie, Mrs Sandra Rivett, 29, was opened yesterday at Westminster coroner's court. Evidence of identification was given by her husband. Roger, of Coulsdon, Surrey.

Medical evidence established that death was caused by blows to the head with a blunt instrument. The inquest was adjourned until 1 December.

17 June 1975
Lord Lucan hit my head and tried to strangle me, says wife
"He thrust three fingers down my throat and we started to fight," inquest told

The Countess of Lucan, 37, said yesterday that her husband tried to strangle her at her Belgravia home on the night last November when her children's nannie was murdered.

Looking pale, she said at a Westminster inquest: "He thrust three gloved fingers down my throat, and we started to fight . . . it is very difficult to remember . . . but he attempted to strangle me and gouge out my eye . . . "

Lady Lucan was giving evidence at the inquest on her nannie, Mrs Sandra Rivett, 29, found beaten to death in the basement of the Lucan family home in Lower Belgravia Street on the night of 7 November.

Shortly afterwards the 40-year-old Earl, who is estranged from his wife, disappeared from his flat in Elizabeth Street, not far away. A widespread police search failed to find him.

A warrant was later issued in his absence, charging him with murdering the nannie and the attempted murder of his wife.

Lady Lucan, wearing a black velvet coat over a check suit with a white cloche, told Dr Gavin Thurston, the Westminster coroner, and the nine-member jury that her husband left her in January 1973. "We never lived together again."

On the night of the murder she was watching television in her bedroom with her elder daughter, when Mrs Rivett offered to make tea.

But the nannie did not return and when Lady Lucan went to investigate she heard a noise in the downstairs cloakroom.

"Somebody rushed out and hit me over the head. Three more blows followed. I screamed and the person said 'Shut up'. I recognised the voice of my husband."

Lady Lucan said that after the attack her husband looked at her injuries and put a towel on her bed, where she lay down. When he went to the bathroom she ran to a nearby public house for help.

Speaking in a firm voice, Lady Lucan told the coroner her name, Veronica Mary, and said that she was married in 1963. Soon afterwards her husband succeeded to the title.

There were three children, Lady Frances Bingham, 11, and two younger ones. She agreed with the coroner that the "marriage situation" deteriorated.

Mr Thurston asked: "Did he have any occupation, any work?" She replied: "He was a professional gambler." This meant he was out a great deal in the evening.

Her husband left her in January 1973, and went to live in Eaton Row Mews House which backed onto Lower Belgrave Street, and was about three houses away. They never lived together again.

The children lived with her until 21 March that year and after that they lived with Lord Lucan at 72a Elizabeth Street, about 300 or 400 yards from Lower Belgrave Street.

"The children came back to me on 1 July as a result of a court action. My husband had access."

The coroner: What was your husband's attitude towards the children as regards his affection? – Very affectionate.

Would it be fair to say they were still a very great part of his life and very important to him? – They were very important to him, yes.

Lady Lucan said that during the 12 months after she had been given custody of the children in July 1973, her husband used to take the children out every other weekend.

"In the early days I used to see him, but in the later days the nannie handed over the children," said Lady Lucan.

The coroner: When did you last see your husband, and I am not speaking of 7 November? I saw him to speak to, it must have been about 18 July on my son's sports day.

When did you last see him without speaking to him? – On 24 October when I looked out of the window and saw him.

What was he doing? – He was sitting in his car. I noticed he was wearing dark glasses, or glasses.

Lady Lucan added that her husband, in a dark blue Mercedes, was about to drive away. Asked if her husband had a key to the house, Lady Lucan said she thought so.

Did you have any idea or feeling you were being followed by anybody during the last half of 1974? – No.

Did you get a regular allowance from your husband? – Yes.

How much were you allowed? – £40 per week. Lady Lucan said payment was erratic but she got the total in the end.

The coroner asked if her husband could have threatened her in any way. Lady Lucan said "No."

Did your husband know Sandra Rivett? – He met her when he collected the children and brought them back.

That was all, as far as you are aware? – As far as I'm aware, yes.

Did you know much about your husband's financial situation? – I have read a bit about it. I read an article in the *Daily Express* which suggested he was in financial difficulties but I don't know from my personal knowledge.

Lady Lucan said her husband had been healthy and had had no serious illnesses.

Mrs Rivett, a cheerful woman, came to the family through a friend, said Lady Lucan. Asked if the nannie had many men friends, she replied: "I know two she talked to. I knew she was separated from her husband."

The two men had not been to the house and Mrs Rivett had not asked if one could come.

Mrs Rivett was about the same height as herself, 5ft 2in, but when she had tried on a dress given to Lady Lucan it had not fitted her. The nannie was of a rather fuller build.

On Thursday, 7 November, Mrs Rivett was at home in the evening, although Thursday was usually her day off.

"Her current boyfriend had his day off on Wednesday, so she asked if she could change hers to Wednesday as well so that she could go out with him."

Inside the house that evening were herself, her three children and Mrs Rivett. The front door had a Yale lock. Usually a brass chain was put on the door after 6 p.m. but it was not there that evening simply because she had not thought to do it. The back door was bolted.

Lady Lucan said she and her daughter spent the evening in her bedroom watching television from about 8 p.m. At about 8.55 p.m. Mrs Rivett looked in and asked Lady Lucan if she would like a cup of tea.

She explained to the coroner: "I have the habit of getting myself tea at that time. It was not a very usual thing for her to put her head around the door and say: 'Would you like a cup of tea?' I had been doing this since our separation."

Lady Lucan said that after a time she went down to the ground floor to see what had happened to the tea and looked down the stairs to the basement. There was no light on in the basement.

"Did you call out?" asked the coroner.

Lady Lucan said she had called out the nannie's name.

What did you do then? – I heard a noise.

What sort of noise? – Just a noise of somebody, or something, in the downstairs cloakroom.

That is where there is a wash basin and lavatory? – Yes.

And what happened next? – I walked towards the sound.

And what happened then? – Somebody rushed out and hit me on the head.

Was there more than one blow? – About four.

Did you hear anybody speak at that time? – At the time I was hit on the head, no. Later I did. I screamed.

And then what? – The person said 'Shut up'.

Did you recognise the voice? – Yes.

Who was it? – My husband.

What did you do then? – He thrust three gloved fingers down my throat and we started to fight.

What happened during the fight? – It is very difficult to remember what happened. During the course of it he attempted to strangle me from in front.

Lady Lucan said that somehow or other she got between his legs on the ground and then her husband desisted. She asked him if she could have a drink of water and they went into the cloakroom and she had a drink from the tap. Then they both went upstairs.

Lady Lucan said her daughter was still in the bedroom with the television. The coroner asked if Lord Lucan had said anything about a towel and she replied: "We went together and together we looked at my injuries. I think I said 'I do not feel very well' and he laid the towel on the bed and I got on it.

"The towel was placed on the pillow. My daughter was sent upstairs as soon as we went into the bedroom and the television was switched off."

The coroner: Did he say anything about helping you further? – Very vaguely. I understood he was going to get a cloth to clean up my face. He would have gone into the bathroom for this.

What did you do then? – I heard the taps running and I jumped to my feet and ran out of the room and down the stairs.

Lady Lucan said she ran to the Plumbers' Arms, about 30 yards away, and was later taken to St George's Hospital where she stayed for just under a week.

Cross-examination was opened by Mr Michael Eastham, QC, for the Dowager Countess of Lucan, who asked: "The separation was in January 1973, but even before that you entertained feelings of hatred for your husband?"

There were objections and the coroner said it was a very strong way of putting it.

Mr Eastham referred to a letter to Mr William Shand-Kydd in which Lord Lucan said he was not guilty and that Lady Lucan was deliberately making it look as if he was.

The letter to Mr Shand-Kydd, who is Lady Lucan's brother-in-law, started "Dear Bill" and was dated November 7.

In it, Lord Lucan referred to "the most ghastly circumstances" and added: "When I interrupted the fight at Lower Belgrave Street and the man left Veronica accused me of having hired him.

"I took her upstairs and sent Frances to bed and tried to clean her up. She lay doggo for a bit and when I was in the bathroom left the house.

"The circumstantial evidence against me is strong enough. Veronica will say it was all my fault. I will lie Doggo."

He had continued: "Veronica has demonstrated her hatred for me in the past and would do anything to see me accused.

For George [his son] and Frances to go through life knowing their father had stood in the dock for attempted murder would be too much. When they are old enough to understand explain to them the dream of paranoia and look after them."

After reading the letter, the coroner said that from the use of the phrase ghastly circumstances," Lord Lucan himself was under stress.

It was then agreed that cross-examination should be opened by Mr Brian Watling, Treasury Solicitor, with Mr Eastham closing.

Mr Watling for the Commissioner of Police then asked Lady Lucan: "When you were struggling with your husband it is right you grabbed hold of him?" Lady Lucan said that was so.

By his private parts? – Yes.

What effect, if any, did that seem to have on him? – He went back, moved back.

Did he say anything to you at that stage? The coroner then interposed and told counsel that he did not propose to allow Lady Lucan to answer the question.

In answer to further questions Lady Lucan said that she felt the object with which she had been hit was slightly curved. She had told police the object felt "bandaged".

Mr Eastham told the coroner he was aware that questions aimed at discrediting witnesses were not allowed at inquest proceedings, but he wanted to ask questions directed to establishing the relationship between Lord and Lady Lucan. The purpose would be to assist the jury when they considered what had happened on the night of 7 November. "That involves the inescapable and unpleasant duty of suggesting that what she is saying she knows to be untrue," said Mr Eastham.

"There is a tape of what this lady said about her husband which has been used in other proceedings," continued Mr Eastham.

Counsel said he had a heavy responsibility on his shoulders because the only case he could put forward was based on what Lord Lucan had said to his mother and to Mrs Susan Maywell-Scott and in what he wrote in letters.

Mr Eastham said he would undertake to the coroner to limit his questions as far as he could but it was essential that he got out sufficient evidence for the jury to properly realise the issue they would have to consider.

Mr Eastham said the reference to paranoia would be totally inexplicable to the jury without further evidence.

Mr Bryan Coles, for Lady Lucan, said the proceedings concerning Lord and Lady Lucan had been held in camera in the family division. The jury then retired while the coroner heard further submissions by Mr Eastham.

When they returned 15 minutes later Mr Eastham said to the coroner: "In view of the ruling you have given in the absence of the jury I do not think I can assist the jury at all and I do not wish to ask the lady any questions."

The coroner asked Lady Lucan if, when she came to the top of the stairs and called Mrs Rivett's name she had seen anybody else. Did anybody rush past?

Lady Lucan: "I saw nobody else, nor at any other time that evening."

She then left the box after giving evidence for nearly two hours.

Woman Det. Con. Sally Bower said that on 20 November, she took statement from Lady Frances Bingham, then aged 10. Lady Lucan was also in the house at the time.

"I think she was telling the truth as she saw it," said Woman Det. Con. Bower. "She was quite clear and composed."

Lady Frances, in the statement read to the coroner by the police officer, said that on 7 November she had tea with her brother, George, her sister, Camilla, her mother and Mrs Rivett in the nursery at about 3.30 p.m.

After tea she played in the nursery and then watched television. Later she went to her mother's room and asked her where Mrs Rivett was. Her mother said she had gone to make tea.

"After a while Mummy said she wondered why Sandra was so long. It was before the news came on at 9 p.m.

"I said I would go downstairs to see what was keeping her but Mummy said 'No', she would go down."

The statement added: "Mummy left the room to go downstairs. She left the bedroom door open, but there was no light in the hall. Just after Mummy left the room I heard a scream. It sounded as though it came from a long way away.

"I thought perhaps the cat had scratched Mummy and she had screamed. I was not frightened. I went to the door and called 'Mummy', but there was no answer.

"But about 9.05 p.m. when the news was on television. Daddy and Mummy appeared in the room. Mummy had blood over her face and was crying."

Her mother told her to go, but Lord Lucan did not say anything to her. "I didn't say anything to either of them. I only caught a glimpse of her.

"As far as I can remember Daddy was wearing a pair of dark trousers and overcoat. I was sitting on the bed when they came in the door. I did not hear any conversation between Mummy and Daddy."

She said she went to her bedroom, went to bed and read a book – "I didn't hear anything from downstairs."

After a while she heard her father calling for her mother. She got up and "saw Daddy coming from the bedroom on the floor below. He went downstairs. That was the last I saw of him. He never came up to the top of the house, either, to look for Mummy or to say goodnight to me."

Lady Frances said in the statement that she was very surprised to see her father home that night. Camilla had told her father that Mrs Rivett had boy friends and went out with them on her day off. Her father had asked her when Mrs Rivett had her day off.

Mr Arthur Whitehouse, formerly head barman at the Plumber's Arms, said that on the night of November 7 a woman he now knew to be Lady Lucan came in. She was head-to-toe in blood from a severe wound in the head.

She started to shout: "Help me, help me. I have just escaped from a murderer." She also shouted: "My children, my children, he has murdered my nannie." She did not give any name.

Dr Michael Smith, a police surgeon, said that in a canvas sack in the basement of the Lucan home he found a body. There were bloodstains on the floor and in his opinion death had taken place only shortly before.

Sgt Donald Baker said the house was almost in darkness and he used a small hand torch to find his way round. At the far end of the hall towards a door leading to the breakfast room, he noticed what appeared to be fresh blood on the wallpaper.

At the foot of the stairs leading to the breakfast room he noticed a large pool of blood with two or three footprints in it. The first light he and a colleague came to was from a bed-side lamp in a bedroom where a bloodstained towel was lying on a pillow.

In the nursery above were the three children. Lady Frances was standing beside the bed. He made a more thorough search of the basement.

"I turned on the light and eventually saw what I thought was a tent bag on the floor. The top of the bag was folded over and there were bloodstains on it. The cord was not drawn.

"As I opened the bag, I saw what appeared to be the top of a man's thigh in black tights. I took out an arm from the bag. It was very white and I could feel no pulse."

He was satisfied no one had climbed over the walls at the rear of the house.

Dr Hugh Scott, then casualty officer at St George's Hospital, London, said that when he examined Lady Lucan she was very distressed and badly injured from scalp wounds. She was also suffering from cuts inside the mouth and complaining of a pain in the leg.

There were about seven scalp cuts from the top of the head to the hairline on the right side of the forehead. Dr Scott said that a piece of lead piping found by the police at the Lucan home could have caused the wounds.

It would be difficult to explain them as the result of a fall. It was a possibility, but very unlikely, that the injuries were self inflicted, he said.

Small lacerations on the palate at the back of Lady Lucan's throat could have been caused by a finger. Dr Scott was asked by Mr Webster if there were any similarities between the lacerations on Lady Lucan's head and those on Mrs Rivett.

He replied: "I certainly can see some."

He thought it possible that the instrument that had caused the lacerations to Lady Lucan could also have caused those inflicted on Mrs Rivett.

PC Christopher Beddick was on duty at the St John's Wood home of the Dowager Lady Lucan, who was looking after the three children, when shortly after midnight the phone rang.

She said: "Where are you? Are you all right? . . . Yes they are all safe here and are asleep . . . Well look, the police are here, do you want to speak to them?"

PC Beddick said the phone went dead and she hung up and said to him: "That was my son. He won't speak to you now. He will phone you in the morning."

Before Lady Lucan began to give evidence the coroner said to the nine-member jury: "We are here in a position where we have a person who has been killed and, we shall hear from the evidence, where somebody has been named as responsible. If this is so, what should one do?

"You will note that Lord Lucan disappeared and was last seen at 1.30 a.m. on the morning of November 8 last.

"I have deliberately delayed this inquiry for a long time in the hope of something more concrete turning up.'

Dr Thurston said he had also considered the position of a wife in these circumstances. While in certain circumstances a wife need not give evidence adverse to her husband, there were exceptions and one which was well established was where a man has assaulted his wife.

These circumstances arose in connection with the present case and he added: "After a great deal of very anxious consideration I have decided I shall call Lady Lucan in connection with part of the matters of which you will hear."

The first witness Mr Thurston called was Mr Roger Rivett, a security officer, of Brighton Road, Coulsdon, Surrey, who said that he had left his wife, Sandra Eleanor, towards the end of April 1974. That was the last time he had seen her alive, but he had been told that she had been working as a children's nannie.

The inquest was adjourned until today.

18 June 1975
Earl said Lady Lucan accused him of hiring killer
Friend's wife tells of meeting with wanted
peer on night of nannie's murder

The last person known to have seen the Earl of Lucan before his disappearance said yesterday that Lord Lucan had said his wife accused him of taking out "a contract" to kill her.

The allegation was made yesterday by Mrs Susan Maxwell-Scott, 38, of Grant

Hill, Uckfield, Sussex, who saw the 40-year-old Earl on the night his children's nannie was murdered last November.

Mrs Maxwell-Scott, wife of one of Lord Lucan's gambling friends, Mr Ian Maxwell-Scott, was giving evidence at the Westminster inquest on Mrs Sandra Rivett, 29, who was beaten to death at the Countess of Lucan's Belgravia home last November 7.

After describing a late night visit to her country home by Lord Lucan soon after the murder, Mrs Maxwell-Scott told of a conversation she had with him about events at his estranged wife's home.

Lord Lucan said that by an "unbelievable coincidence" he had been passing the house when "on looking through the Venetian blind in the basement he saw a man attacking his wife . . . the man whom he had seen run off.

"He said his wife was very hysterical and cried out that someone had killed the nannie and almost in the same breath she had accused him of having hired the man to kill her. He said she frequently accused him of having a contract to kill – an idea from an American TV movie . . . "

When proceedings resumed yesterday, Det. Sgt Graham Forsythe said a blood-stained canvas bag was found in the darkened basement of Lady Lucan's home.

"There was a woman's arm hanging from the sack. The rest of the body was enclosed by the sacking. The flesh was warm to the touch but I could not feel any pulse. There was a large pool of blood in front of the sack.

He had gone with other officers to Lady Lucan's home at about 10.20 p.m. on November 7. He found blood splashes on the ceiling and walls in the hall.

Lying on the floor he found a piece of piping which appeared to be bound with some kind of adhesive medical tape. It was heavily bloodstained.

At the bottom of the basement stairs he found some broken cups and saucers in a pool of blood. There were no lights on in the basement.

He saw a light bulb lying on a cushioned chair, and there was no bulb in a light fitting near the kitchen door in the basement.

At 11.01 p.m., said the detective sergeant, he and other officers went to a house in Eaton Row. "I went there specifically looking for the whereabouts of Lord Lucan. This arose from information I had received from other colleagues."

Det. Sgt Forsythe said that unable to get in he broke an upstairs bedroom window. The search was fruitless but he left a guard there and returned to Lower Belgrave Street. When he arrived, he added, the Dowager Countess of Lucan was already there.

He told her that her grandchildren's nanny was dead and that her daughter-in-law had been attacked and was in hospital. The Dowager Countess replied: "Oh dear."

The officer asked: "Does you son live here?" She replied that the couple had separated, adding: "The children made wards of court and Veronica is to continue medical treatment for her mental complaint."

"I said, 'What was that?' and she said, 'manic-depressive, not violent, verbally. In the original court case, it was thought that she was dangerous to the children.

"'I knew something was wrong because John telephoned me a short while ago and told me to come here' . . . "

The officer added: "I said, 'What time was this?' and she replied, 'about 10.45 p.m'. I said, 'What did he say?' and she said. 'There has been a terrible catastrophe at 46. Ring Bill Shand-Kydd [Lady Lucan's brother-in-law] immediately.'"

The Dowager Lady Lucan went on to say: "He said he had been driving past the house and he saw a fight going on in the basement between a man and Veronica.

"He went in and joined them. He said Veronica was shouting and screaming. He sounded very schocked."

She told the officer she had asked Lord Lucan where he was going and he replied, "I don't know." He then rang off.

"Did he say what was wrong?" asked the officer. She replied: "I tried to find out, but he just told me to get the children out as soon as possible."

The Dowager Countess told the officer her son had a blue Mercedes car which he probably kept at Elizabeth Street.

Det. Sgt. Forsythe said he obtained an order at Bow Street magistrates' court under the Bankers Book Evidence Act to inspect Lord Lucan's accounts at Coutts Bank in the Strand; Lloyds in Pall Mall; the Midland at Newgate Street, and National Westminster in Bloomsbury Way. They were overdrawn to a total of £14,177, he added.

The individual accounts were: Coutts overdrawn by £2,841; Lloyds, overdrawn by £4,379; Midland, overdrawn by £5,667, and the National Westminster, overdrawn by £1,290.

Professor Keith Simpson, pathologist, said Mrs Rivett's body was doubled up inside the canvas bag. Her clothing was undisturbed but heavily soiled with blood.

From the conditions he found he considered death took place before the body had been encased. Mrs Rivett had been a healthy woman. There was no sign of any recent intercourse or a sexual assault.

There were three blunt injuries to the face, one above the right eye, a second near the mouth and the third over the left eyebrow. There were four splits in the scalp on the front side of the head above the ear, and two other splits near the neck.

There was also heavy bruising on the tops of both shoulders, and at the back of the right hand was some superficial bruising likely to have resulted from the hand being used for protection.

On the front of the right upper arm there were four in-line bruises which could have been caused by the rough grip of fingers. There had been a great deal of blood, mostly from the nose and mouth.

There was surface and deeper bruising to the brain, and the injuries to the side of the head must have caused more than dazing, said the professor. These injuries, together with the bruising of the brain which followed them, had caused death.

There had also been much inhalation of blood, and it was this which had made it clear that no further kind of asphyxia followed.

Prof. Simpson, shown a piece of lead piping, said it was similar to one he had seen earlier except it was not wrapped in surgical plaster strip.

The one he had seen weighed about 2¼lb and the splits to the skull and shoulders were consistent with such an instrument being used. The injury to the eye and mouth was more likely to have been caused by a fist or hand slap.

Prof. Simpson said Lady Lucan's head injuries could have been inflicted by an instrument similar to that which caused Mrs Rivett's.

The Dowager Countess Lucan declined the coroner's invitation to sit while giving evidence. She affirmed, and gave her address as Lord's View, St John's Wood, London.

She said she used to see her son at fairly regular intervals, about once every 10 days.

Her son had "strong and passionate feeling" towards his children, she said. The coroner: "Was it a disappointment to him that he did not have custody of them." – "Yes."

When did you last see your son before this incident? – I am not prepared to say for certainty, but I think probably the best I can say is that it was on the Sunday before the 7th of November.

How was he? – He was in a state of great anxiety about the children, but not noticeably or more obsessionably so than was to be expected.

Dealing with the events of 7 November, the Dowager Lady Lucan said she first received a telephone call from her son when she returned to her flat after attending a meeting. She could not be positive about the time, but it was about 10 p.m. She did not think it was as late as the police had said.

Answering the coroner, she said she did not hear any call-box ticks. What did he say? – He said it was John speaking and he said there had been a terrible catastrophe at number 46 and said "Veronica is hurt and I want you to collect the children as quickly as possible."

He also said, and he might have said this first, "Ring Bill Shand-Kydd, and he will help." He also said the nannie was hurt and I said "Badly?" and he said "Yes, I think so."

And that was the whole of the conversation? – Yes.

We have heard how you returned to your home and then there was a second telephone call. – Yes. It was well after midnight. We had got the children in bed first. I must add that in the first telephone call he said "I interrupted a fight in the basement."

He used those words? – Yes.

As regards the second telephone call, what did he say to you? – He said: "Have you got the children?" I said: "Yes, they are here in bed and asleep," and he said: "That's all right." I asked him what he was intending to do and I got nowhere.

I also said I had the police with me and would he like to speak to them. He hesitated and then said: "No, I don't think I'll speak to them now. I will ring them in the morning and I will ring you, too."

At that stage, said the Dowager Countess, her son rang off. Answering the coroner, she said that on the second telephone call, her son sounded very much more "on all fours". The first time he had sounded in a highly shocked condition.

Asked if Lord Lucan told her how he came to see the fight in the basement, she replied: "No. He said he was passing, but did not indicate whether he paused or whether it was so obvious on passing. I know he did frequently go past the house and look at it. It was very near his flat."

She told Mr Brian Watling, Treasury Counsel, she had answered questions about whether Lord Lucan had told her he had interrupted a fight in the basement or seen one, and she said it was a subjective impression at the time, and it was her subjective impression now, that her son had interrupted a fight. She thought the upshot of the two statements was the same.

Mr Watling asked whether she had contacted Mrs Shand-Kydd and told her Lady Lucan was in hospital. The Dowager Countess said she had, but when she began to describe Mrs Shand-Kydd's reaction, there were objections from Mr Bryan Coles, counsel for Lady Lucan.

Later, the coroner requested that the Press should not report the Dowager Lady Lucan's full reply to Mr Watling's question.

Questioned about statements she had made to the police the Dowager Countess told her counsel Mr Michael Eastham, QC, that her impression was from the conversation with her son that he had said he was passing the house, not driving past.

She said she very much regretted she had not pressed the point, when during the second telephone call, her son hesitated before saying he did not wish to speak to the police. She said during the first telephone call, her son muttered quite a bit. He used the words "blood and mess". They were not part of a coherent statement, but expressions of horror and disgust.

Shortly before November she had lent her son £4,000 towards the costs of the custody proceedings.

The Dowager Countess concluded her evidence after being in the witness box for just over an hour.

Mrs Susan Mary Maxwell-Scott, of Grant Hill, Uckfield, Sussex, told the inquest that she and her husband had been friendly with Lord Lucan for a long time. Her husband had known him before they were married 17 years ago.

"He was always a first friend of my husband and I came to know him well when we moved to the country and he and Lady Lucan used to come and stay with us."

Mrs Maxwell-Scott continued: "On Thursday, 7 November, I was at home with my two youngest children and the dog. My husband was in London. He had originally intended to return but then phoned to say he was spending the night in London. He phoned about 10 p.m.

"After I had had a bath I turned the light out about 11 p.m. I had taken some supper to bed and read a book. The next thing I heard was the front door bell. I was asleep, dozing, I think, but I cannot have been sleeping very heavily or I would not have heard it.

"The first time it went I vaguely wondered whether to do anything at all and there was a second, a shorter apologetic little ring, and I thought I had better get up and see who it was.

"I went to my bathroom which overlooks the front door, turned on the light and looked out of the window. I saw Lord Lucan standing beneath the window looking up towards me in the light.

"I did not notice the car: I was just looking at Lucan. I said 'Hello' through the window and went down to let him in. He started off about apologising for arriving so late and I took him into the drawing room and offered him a drink. I gave him a Scotch and water. I had to fetch the glass from the kitchen and we sat down."

Asked by the coroner how Lord Lucan looked she replied: "He looked a little dishevelled. When I have seen him he is normally very tidy. He was fashionably dressed – wearing a light blue polo neck silk shirt, grey flannel trousers and a sleeveless brown pullover, no coat.

"While he was sitting down I noticed a patch on the right side of his trousers at the hip. I asked him what was the matter and then he told me what had happened at his wife's house."

Mrs Maxwell-Scott said that Lord Lucan told her he had been walking past his wife's home on his way to change for dinner.

"The word 'walking' is rather important," interposed the coroner.

"Yes," replied Mrs Maxwell-Scott. "I am almost certain he used the word. He could have said 'passing' and I assumed he was walking."

Mrs Maxwell-Scott said Lord Lucan told her that on looking through the Venetian blind in the basement he saw a man attacking his wife.

Mrs Maxwell-Scott continued: "Lord Lucan told me that he opened the front door, he had a key, and went down to the basement. As he entered the hall he slipped in a pool of blood. He was not telling it like a story.

"This is my best attempt to tell you what he said to me. The man whom he had seen attacking his wife ran off. Whether this was on hearing Lucan coming down the stairs or whether it was on seeing Lucan, I am not clear. Lucan said the man made off. Lucan, perhaps unfortunately, refrained from chasing the man but went to his wife."

He did not say where the man ran off – No. He said the man made off. Perhaps through the back door, I don't know.

He went to his wife – Yes. She was covered with blood and was very hysterical.

Did he say anything further about what his wife had said? – Yes. He said first she was very hysterical and cried out to him that someone had killed Sandra, or the nannie, then, almost in the same breath, accused Lucan of having hired the man to kill her.

This, Lucan told me, was a thing she frequently accused him of. A contract to kill.

Mrs Maxwell-Scott said Lord Lucan told her that he had tried to calm his wife down. He had taken her upstairs and persuaded Lady Lucan to lie down while he got some wet towels to mop up the blood on her.

"Did he tell you what he did next," asked the coroner.

"He said he went to the bathroom and started soaking towels, prior to wiping the blood and while he was there, Lady Lucan left and ran downstairs and out of the house," said Mrs Maxwell-Scott.

Mrs Maxwell-Scott said Lord Lucan went on to tell her that after leaving the house himself, he telephoned his mother, the Dowager Countess, and asked her to look after the children.

Mrs Maxwell-Scott said at one time Lord Lucan looked at his watch and said something about the time. She thought it was about 12.15 a.m. He then telephoned his mother.

"He said, 'Mother, this is John,' and then asked about the children. I gathered the answer must have been satisfactory because he said something like 'good' or 'I am glad'."

Mrs Maxwell-Scott said Lord Lucan then said something on the telephone to the effect that he would keep in touch. He asked Mrs Maxwell-Scott for some writing paper so that he could write to Mr Shand-Kydd.

Mrs Maxwell-Scott said that Lord Lucan did not say what he wanted the notepaper for, but he wrote some letters and asked her if she could post them.

She said she tried to persuade him to stay the night, but he said after "slightly agreeing" that he had to get back to clear things up. When he said "get back" he did not mention London.

Lord Lucan left at about 1.15 a.m. and she then went to bed. She thought his car was a dark saloon.

She told the coroner that Lord Lucan asked if she had any sleeping pills, saying he was sure he would have difficulty in sleeping. She found four Vallium pills, tranquillisers, the best she could find, and he took them.

She told Mr Watling that Lord Lucan indicated he had seen the sack at his wife's home but had not examined it.

Mr Watling: When Lord Lucan left that house, he knew or had been told that the nannie had been killed and his wife badly attacked.

You are no doubt aware that no one has seen Lord Lucan since he left your house at 1.15 that morning? – Nobody has said they have seen him.

Is it right you are, in fact, a trained lawyer, a member of the Bar? – I was called to the Bar nearly 18 years ago, but I never practised.

Your father was a lawyer? – My father was a lawyer.

Is it right that Lord Lucan at no time described to you that man he had seen attacking his wife? – Not entirely right. Lord Lucan did not see him clearly enough to describe him.

Did he describe the man to you at all? – He said he was large.

She agreed with Mr Eastham that in a roundabout way, they had spoken of the nannie, and he had said that no one would have wanted to kill her.

Saying she thought Lord Lucan had used the words "unbelievable nightmare experience" when speaking of that night, Mrs Maxwell-Scott added that she did not think he was hysterical but shocked.

"It was quite incredible that he should have had anything to do with it."

The hearing was adjourned until today.

19 June 1975
How did countess know nannie was dead, asks jury
Lead piping found in car Earl of Lucan had borrowed

The foreman of the jury at the inquest on the Lucan family's nannie asked yesterday how the Countess of Lucan had known that Mrs Sandra Rivett had been murdered.

He was referring to evidence given earlier by Lady Lucan about the night last November when she was attacked at her Belgravia home and the body of Mrs Rivett, 29, was later found in the basement.

The foreman said to Dr Gavin Thurston, the Westminster Coroner: "We have heard nothing at all from Lady Lucan about the nannie being murdered.

"We heard about her going to the barman at the Plumbers' Arms and saying to him: 'He has murdered my nannie.' How did she know the nannie had been murdered?"

The coroner replied: "That is quite right. I suggest we hear the rest of the evidence and then I hope to be able to satisfy you on that."

The jury was told later that piping similar to the one alleged to have been used to attack Lady Lucan and her nannie was found in a car which the Earl of Lucan borrowed and abandoned at Newhaven.

Bloodstains found in the car matched the blood groups of both Lady Lucan and Mrs Rivett.

Mr Michael Stoop, a retired company director and member of the Clermont Club, was the first witness yesterday. He said he had known Lord Lucan, another member of the club, for about 15 years.

On October 21 or October 23 he was at a club dinner when Lord Lucan asked if he could borrow a car. "I suggested he should borrow my Mercedes as my Ford was dirty and an old banger," said Mr Stoop.

Lord Lucan had said he would borrow the Ford, a Corsair. "I imagine it was just his natural manners that he accepted the Ford. He didn't want to deprive me of my better car."

Mr Stoop said he arranged to leave his Ford with the keys inside outside his garage for Lord Lucan to collect. The next time he saw the car was when he got it back from the forensic laboratory.

He was shown a letter which he identified as one he had received at St James's Club on November 11.

The letter, in Lord Lucan's handwriting, read:

"Dear Michael, I have had a traumatic night of unbelievable coincidences. I won't bore you except when you come across my children, please tell them you knew me and all I care about is them.

"The fact that a crooked solicitor and a rotten psychiatrist destroyed me between them will be of no importance to the children. I gave Bill Shand-Kydd (Lady Lucan's brother-in-law) an account of what really happened, but judging by my last efforts in court no one, let alone a 67-year-old judge, would believe – and I no longer care, except that my children should be protected.

"Yours ever, John."

Mr Stoop said as far as he could remember the letter had been in a largish, business-type white envelope. He did not notice whether there was a postmark, and he thought he had thrown the envelope away.

Answering Mr Brian Watling, Treasury Counsel, he said he had offered Lord Lucan his Mercedes because the Ford had only been insured for himself. But Lord Lucan said he would insure the Ford. Mr Stoop added that there was no piece of lead piping in the car when he lent it.

Mr Michael Eastham, QC, retained by Lord Lucan's mother, asked if, when he received the letter, he knew what had happened and that Lord Lucan was missing. Mr Stoop said he did, and he had got in touch with the police within five minutes of receiving it.

Mr Eastham: Are you sure you did not look at the postmark, because it is rather important to establish? – I am afraid I did not.

Mr Eastham referred to the letter Lord Lucan had written and. because of an earlier ruling by the coroner, asked Mr Stoop to reply "Yes" or "No" to a series of questions.

Mr Eastham quoted: "The fact that crooked solicitor and rotten psychiatrist destroyed me between them" and asked the witness if he understood it to refer to certain court proceedings about the children.

Mr Stoop said he did and that he understood the same proceedings were referred to when the letter stated: "to judge by my last effort in court no one, let alone a 67-year-old judge, would believe that".

Mr Eastham asked if he understood the phrase: "I no longer care except that children should be protected." The witness replied: "I cannot deal with that by a simple 'yes' or 'no'."

Mr Eastham: "I know you cannot, but I am in a difficulty. May I put it this way. If I asked you against what or whom the children were to be protected could you answer?"

The coroner disallowed the question and Mr Eastham asked that the previous answer about not being able to give a yes or no should be recorded.

Mr Ian Lucas, a senior fingerprint officer at New Scotland Yard, said a print found on the interior driving mirror of a Ford car recovered by police at Newhaven, Sussex, and a print found in Lord Lucan's flat had probably been made by the same person.

He had received no prints which could be traced directly to Lord Lucan.

Answering Mr Watling, Mr Lucas said that all the prints found in the basement of Lady Lucan's home had come from police officers, one of Lady Lucan's children, or the victim.

Mr Watling: So, whoever attacked Mrs Rivett left no fingerprints? – I did not find any.

Dr Margaret Pereira, a principal scientific officer at the Metropolitan Police Laboratory and an expert in blood-grouping, said that she took samples of blood from the kitchen floor at Lady Lucan's home.

All were of human blood. Two stains belonged to Group B – Mrs Rivett's group. Another gave a reaction to Group A – Lady Lucan's grouping.

Later she took samples from other parts of the house and two samples of hair. Group A bloodstains were found primarily on the ground floor and Group B primarily in the basement.

She said the lead piping found at Lady Lucan's home was "grossly distorted". It was nine inches long, weighed 2lb 3½oz, and was covered with adhesive stretch bandage.

The piping was heavily bloodstained and the staining gave reactions to Group A and Group B.

She also examined a piece of piping found by police in the Ford car recovered at Newhaven. It was covered in stretch bandage, was 16½in long and weighed 4lb 1oz, but there were no bloodstains.

The heavy Group B was in the basement and to get this blood on her shoes it was very probable that Lady Lucan had walked through the basement.

She found extensive blood on parts of the car when it was at Newhaven and most of it gave a reaction for AB, either a separate group representing about three per cent. of the population, or a mixture.

Mr Eastham said both the victim and Lady Lucan had bled extensively and he asked the witness to assume that Lord Lucan had run down the basement, and slipped in a pool of blood.

Dr Pereira agreed that Lord Lucan would then have extensive blood on his own clothes and that if he went on to assist his wife up the stairs she would expect that he would have extensive blood on him.

And part of the blood in the motor car then would be AB? – Yes.

She said that Group B bloodstaining found on Lady Lucan's clothing could have come from her assailant if he had been saturated with blood of that group or if the attacker himself had been of that group.

Answering Mr David Webster, for the Rivett family, Dr Pereira said that if Lady Lucan's assailant had first put Mrs Rivett's body in the sack in which it was found, that could account for the assailant carrying Group B blood. Blood found on the piping at Lady Lucan's home could have come from both Lady Lucan and Mrs Rivett.

Dr Pereira said that some of the bloodstaining found at Lady Lucan's home could have been transferred from one part of the house to the other by someone walking through it, such as a police officer.

"Anyone with big feet," she added, amid laughter.

Dr Pereira said that greyish blue wool fibres found on a blood-stained bath towel, on a washbasin in the basement and on the lead piping were indistinguishable from each other. They could have originated from the same source.

Dr Robert Davis, senior scientific officer at the Metropolitan Police forensic science laboratory, said that in his opinion, the piece of lead piping found at Lady Lucan's home and the piece found in the car at Newhaven had come from the same length of pipe. Corrosion inside them indicated they had once been used as water pipes.

Mr Charles Henry Genese, director of a money-lending company at Bexleyheath, Kent, said Lord Lucan called at his office on September 11 last year and wanted to borrow some money, up to £5,000.

"He was perfectly open about his financial commitments," said Mr Genese. "He told us his gross income was in the region of £12,000 a year. He was reasonably open in that he told us that maintenance, school fees, bank overdrafts, rates and household expenses were on a par if not more than his income.

"He was living at what I knew to be a rather high standard."

Mr Genese said Lord Lucan told him he had put some silver up for sale by auction and from the proceeds later in the year would be able to pay off what he had borrowed.

"First of all we said we could not possibly lend him any amount because of his financial position. We did say that if he provided us with an acceptable surety we would consider it.

"Some three or four days later he phoned and said he had a surety – we knew the person concerned and said we would lend him £3,000. The interest was £120 a month equivalent to 48 per cent. per annum for a period of six months, but he could pay off in any given time."

Questioned by Mr Bruce Coles, for Lady Lucan, Mr Genese said he was looking to the surety for the payment of the sum outstanding. He was satisfied that he was going to be paid.

Mr Andrew Demetrio assistant restaurant manager at the Clermont Club, Berkeley Square, said that about 8.30 p.m. on 7 November Lord Lucan telephoned and booked a table for four people.

A party of four turned up and said Lord Lucan was coming and they wanted a fifth chair at the table for him, but the Earl never came.

Mr William Brian Edgson, an employee at the Clermont Club, said that at about 8.45 p.m. Lord Lucan came to the outside of the club. He seemed his normal self.

Lord Lucan left the club after a minute or two. Mr Edgson said that he himself had driven from the club to Lower Belgrave Street. In daytime it would take about 10 minutes because of West End traffic, but the time would be shorter in the evening.

Det. Insp. Charles Hulls, who gave evidence after the jury returned, said that at 10 p.m. on 9 November he went to 46, Lower Belgrave Street and switched off the lights in the basement.

"I stood in complete darkness at the bottom of the stairs. I then moved backwards and forwards two or three paces a few times and from my position I tried to look at the pavement outside.

"I could not see through the Venetian slats in the blind, which were pointing upwards. The blind was fully down but half closed with the high side of the slats on the outside.

Det. Insp. Hulls said unsuccessful attempts had been made to try to recover the envelope which had contained the letter sent by Lord Lucan to Mr Stoop. He understood that Mr Stoop had screwed up the envelope and thrown it into a wastepaper basket at his club. The inspector said dustbins at the club had been emptied without the envelope being found.

Det Chief Insp Henry Gerring said that from outside 46 Lower Belgrave Street, all he could see through the slats in the basement venetian blind "was the red glow of the light on the kettle".

"When the light on the breakfast-room table was switched on, I could make out the figure of Mr Hulls in the area at the foot of the stairs. Then, only by stooping with my head between two and three feet from the ground, I could make out Mr Hulls' figure."

When the kitchen lights were switched on, he could see Mr Hulls at the foot of the basement stairs, and about three or four of the bottom steps. Walking past the house and looking through the slats in the blind, he could see only the kitchen and not the foot of the stairs.

Det. Chief Insp. Gerring said that at 1 a.m. on 8 November, the only signs of struggle he saw were on the first floor and not below that level, although a picture was lopsided on the side of the stairs going downwards.

Mr Watling said: "We have heard that Lord Lucan was able to let himself into the house with a key. Have you been able to trace any other person who has a key to the Yale lock on the front door of the house?"

Chief Insp. Gerring said he had not. There were no signs of forcible entry.

"Have you been able to find any trace of a third person in the house that night?" – "None whatsoever."

The coroner then told the jury that this was the whole of the evidence, and that he would begin his summing-up this morning. The jury was then released for the day and the coroner sat in camera to hear legal submissions.

The hearing was later adjourned until today.

9 December 2015
Witness emerges to give new twist to Lord Lucan mystery
Member of wealthy 1970s gambling set claims peer killed himself
hours after nanny was murdered
By Patrick Sawer

The decades-long mystery of Lord Lucan's fate took an unexpected twist yesterday when it was disclosed that a witness has come forward to claim that the peer killed himself within hours of murdering his family's nanny in 1974.

Amid dramatic courtroom scenes, it was claimed a member of Lord Lucan's gambling set has contacted a private detective to tell him he has evidence that following the murder of Sandra Rivett at the family home in Belgravia on 7 November 1974, Lucan took his own life and had never left the country.

If true, it would end years of rumour and speculation about Lucan's fate.

There have been repeated "sightings" of the peer in Australia, Ireland, South Africa and New Zealand, and even a claim he fled to India where he lived as a hippy called "Jungle Barry".

The new claim emerged during a procedural hearing in the High Court to determine whether a death certificate should be issued for Lord Lucan, which would allow his son, George, now Lord Bingham, to adopt his father's surname and title.

Lord Bingham said he looked forward to the court making a decision. He said last night: "It's been 41 years and its time to put it to bed."

David Vann, a pet dealer and amateur detective who has spent years investigating the peer's disappearance, earlier told the court he had been approached via email by someone he regarded as a "credible witness". Mr Vann said his correspondent had been a member of the Clermont set of wealthy gamblers, who had come forward because he was fed up with the "myths" and "theories" being peddled about the aristocrat's fate.

"I have received an email that may be of relevance to this court from a gentleman who used to frequent the Clermont Club at least three times a week and has information that Lord Lucan killed himself on 8 November 1974," said Mr Vann.

He later told the *Daily Telegraph*: "The person who has written to me is very annoyed about the fact that all these theories about Lord Lucan's death have been put about to protect people, many of whom are now dead. He says in the email that it was all over by 5 a.m. [of 8 November]. This man was a member of the Clermont set and is in a position to know." Mr Vann added: "My correspondent has never spoken publicly on the matter before, nor has he contacted the police. He has approached me because he believes I have acted credibly in the past on this issue."

Mr Vann, who also uses the name Ian Crosby, is a controversial figure. In 2009, he was prosecuted by officials from the Vale of Glamorgan for cruelty to tortoises and iguanas at his home in Llantwit Major, after which he was banned from trading or owning pets for five years. He has always maintained his innocence.

He says the email about Lord Lucan went missing after Vale of Glamorgan officials seized his files, including all the documents and correspondence relating to the Lucan investigation. The email resurfaced recently after the documents were returned.

Lord Lucan disappeared after Miss Rivett, nanny to his three children, was found murdered at 46 Lower Belgrave Street. The nanny's attacker also turned on Lady Lucan, beating her severely before she managed to escape.

In 1999, Lord Lucan was officially declared dead by the High Court but a death certificate has never been issued. Sitting in the Chancery Division of the High Court, Master Teverson invited Mr Vann and any other parties in possession of evidence relating to Lord Lucan to submit it to the court, ahead of a full hearing to be held in February.

Bernie Madoff

"I only hope that he lives long enough that his
jail cell becomes his coffin."

13 December 2008
Wall Street trader held over "£50bn fraud"
By Tom Leonard and James Quinn in New York

It is already being talked of as potentially the biggest fraud in corporate history.

Even by the standards of New York's recent financial turmoil, the charges levelled at Bernard Madoff are eye-watering: a $50bn (£33bn) swindle perpetrated by one of the most celebrated traders on Wall Street.

Mr Madoff, 70, a former chairman of the NASDAQ stock exchange and a supposed pillar of the financial community, has been accused of defrauding hedge funds of billions with nothing more sophisticated than a glorified pyramid scheme called a "Ponzi".

The news has rocked the hedge fund world as some investors face losing all their money in a scam that, if confirmed, would have what one expert described as a "monumental impact".

Funds with some exposure to Madoff include Bramdean Alternatives Ltd, which is headed by City "superwoman" Nicola Horlick. In the alleged fraud outlined by the US government, Mr Madoff promised huge returns to investors in his asset management business, only to lose their money on the markets. He then allegedly paid them back with money from later investors.

Prosecutors allege Mr Madoff ran his fraudulent operation secretly from a separate floor of the Manhattan offices of his trading firm, Bernard L Madoff Investment Securities. They claim his scheme unravelled after clients wanted to redeem some $7bn and Mr Madoff realised he could not find the money.

In a criminal complaint filed by the FBI and the US Attorney's office, Mr Madoff allegedly told colleagues that his investment advisory business was "all just one big lie" and that his firm was "basically, a giant Ponzi scheme". According to the *Wall Street Journal*, he was arrested on Thursday after he was turned in by his two grown-up sons.

Mr Madoff has been charged with a single count of securities fraud and faces up to five years in prison and a fine of up to $5m (£3.3m).

He also faces a separate civil lawsuit filed by the US Securities and Exchange Commission (SEC), which accuses him of defrauding his clients in an ongoing $50bn fraud.

"Our complaint alleges a stunning fraud that appears to be of epic proportions," said Andrew Calamari, associate director of enforcement at the SEC's New York office. The complaint alleges Mr Madoff has been released on $10m bail.

Questions are likely to be asked how an alleged fraud of this scale escaped the notice of the financial authorities.

Madoff Securities International Ltd, of London, in which Mr Madoff was a major shareholder, said that its activities were not involved with the US firm under investigation.

15 December 2008
Wall St wizard and the missing $50bn
The background to what is being described as the
biggest financial fraud in New York history
By Tom Leonard

As Bernard Madoff's delighted clients swapped investment stories at the golf course in Palm Beach, they sometimes joked that if he was a fraud, he'd take down half the world with him.

In this, at least, they were perceptive. The fallout from the news that the celebrated Wall Street investor was behind an alleged $50bn swindle – a "Ponzi" scheme in which early investors were paid with the money put in by later ones – has swept through the worlds of international business, moneyed society and philanthropy. Potentially thousands of investors, including hedge funds, banks and wealthy individuals, have had huge sums wiped out at a stroke in what could be the biggest fraud in Wall Street history.

A Jewish charity in Boston has shut down and sacked its staff, a group of hedge funds in Connecticut has said it is closing. ("I'm wiped out," said its chairman simply.) And banks as far afield as Paris, Zurich and Tokyo are anxiously calculating the cost of their exposure to Mr Madoff. Geneva-based banks and investment funds alone are estimated to have lost more than $4.22bn. Even Nicola Horlick, the "superwoman" of the City of London, has been hit – her Bramdean investment company reportedly investing nearly £21m with Mr Madoff. Like others, she could only splutter her fury over the weekend at the "systemic failure" of US regulators.

She may have a point. It is claimed that Mr Madoff's Manhattan-based investment advisory business was never inspected by regulators after he subjected it to oversight two years ago. Mr Madoff, 70, was a generous political donor and had advised the Securities and Exchange Commission how to regulate markets. According to Bloomberg News, for whatever reason, the SEC hadn't examined his books since he registered the unit in September 2006.

A dozen SEC inspectors are now poring over his records, trying to find out what went wrong. There are plenty of theories, but the bottom line is that Mr Madoff seems to have fooled a lot of people who should have known better. Supposedly "sophisticated investors" included Fred Wilpon, the main owner of the New York

Mets baseball team; Norman Braman, a big Florida car dealer who once owned the Philadelphia Eagles American football club; and Ezra Merkin, the chairman of General Motors' financing arm. Carl Shapiro, a Boston philanthropist and former women's clothing magnate, has lost at least $145m, it was reported yesterday. The alleged fraud had "swept up some of the most prominent and wealthy Americans, along with many people who thought they were embarking on a comfortable retirement and have now been left destitute", said Brad Friedman, a lawyer involved in representing more than 30 investors with losses they believe could exceed $1bn.

The big names, it appears, would have been among an A-list of investors that Mr Madoff used as a marketing tool to pull in others. He hired unofficial agents and fostered an aura of exclusivity by targeting wealthy country clubs across the US with "invitation only" policies. Refusing to take some people on as investors only added to his appeal – Barbara Fox, president of a Manhattan estate agency, told the New York Times she "literally begged him" to take her on, but he turned her down.

At lunch or on the links, members would talk of him in hushed, admiring tones – Magic Mr Madoff and his Amazing 10 per cent Returns, even in a bear market. In clubs such as the Palm Beach Country Club in Florida and the Old Oaks in Purchase, New York, some called him "the Jewish bond" because his fund always managed to pay 8 to 12 per cent every year. He also had unofficial agents – friends and colleagues – helping him link up with the wealthy of Dallas, Chicago, Boston and Minneapolis. In Minneapolis, investors from two country clubs alone are thought to have sunk $100m into his operation.

Even his agents invested heavily. Richard Spring, a former securities analyst from Boca Raton, told the Wall Street Journal he had about $11m – 95 per cent of his net worth – invested with Mr Madoff. "That's how much I believed in him," he said. Mr Madoff never wanted people to give him too much money straight away. "Bernie would tell me, 'Let them start small, and if they're happy the first year or two, they can put in more'," he said.

It helped enormously that many of these investors were just like Mr Madoff – rich, elderly Jewish New Yorkers who divided their time between the city and Florida.

It helped, too, that he and his wife, Ruth, were well liked on that social circuit. They are keen golfers and Mr Madoff belonged to half a dozen clubs. They were known as a friendly, understated couple who were not interested in social climbing. Perhaps they felt they didn't need to be – the Madoffs have at least three homes, including a $9m duplex apartment close to Central Park on Manhattan's Upper East Side, another in Roslyn, New York, and a beachfront house in Montauk, Long Island. There may still be a yacht moored down in the Bahamas. Mr Madoff has a 55ft fishing boat called Bull, on which he loved to take friends and staff.

Mr Madoff, a native New Yorker who went into finance aged 22 with $5,000 raised from a summer job as a beach lifeguard, was a prominent and generous member of the city's Jewish community. He set up a charitable foundation and was a pillar of Wall Street, where he became chairman of the Nasdaq stock exchange.

There was, as countless hapless investors have testified, little about him to arouse suspicion and so much to inspire trust. The lucky few who were allowed to invest with him believed they were being let in on a big secret – which was half right. The secret was that there was no Midas touch to the Madoff investment strategy. His magic, according to the prosecution line, was more that of the Wizard of Oz. Behind the façade of the impressive art-laden offices of his legitimate trading firm, there was a tiny, private office on a separate floor where he kept the accounts to his other business "under lock and key".

Ponzi schemes – named after a notorious 1920s American fraudster – can only last as long as there is a steady stream of new investors and enough money to keep paying the old ones. From what prosecutors say Mr Madoff allegedly told colleagues, his grip on the operation finally came loose this month when investors asked to redeem $7bn and he struggled to find it.

Prosecutors have yet to say where all the money went and how much, if any, is left. Did he spend it? Did he lose it on the markets? Is it under his bed?

Anything seems possible in this case. Nor will they spell out exactly how long it lasted, although they have said it was years and some have speculated that it may have been decades. However, it certainly unravelled fast.

His arrest at 8.30 a.m. last Thursday by two FBI agents who turned up at his Manhattan apartment came just hours after he had allegedly come clean about everything to his sons, Andrew and Mark, said one of their lawyers. Mark, 42, ran the proprietary trading business and Andrew, 40, was one of its directors. Their lawyers insist that neither, who had worked their lives in the family business, had any knowledge of what their father was doing.

According to prosecutors, he had told two staff – understood to be his sons – that he was "finished", that his business was "just one big lie" and "basically, a giant Ponzi scheme" that had been insolvent for years.

Charged with a single count of securities fraud, as well as a separate civil fraud lawsuit, he has been freed on $10m bail.

As the blame game deepens over responsibility for the mess, it has emerged that Mr Madoff has weathered several investigations. In 1992, he faced regulatory scrutiny after the SEC sued two Florida accountants for allegedly raising $441m while selling unregistered securities. The SEC determined that the money had been accounted for and didn't accuse Mr Madoff of wrongdoing.

And his uncanny ability to give a steady 10 per cent or so return to investors had raised eyebrows at least once before. But hedge fund managers never like to discuss their strategies and Mr Madoff's reticence – "it's a proprietary strategy. I can't go into it in great detail", he said seven years ago – was never seen as that unusual.

It is only now that those investors are realising the Wizard of Oz really was too good to be true.

18 December 2008
Madoff under house arrest
By James Quinn

Alleged fraudster Bernard Madoff has been placed under house arrest and will be electronically tagged after failing to meet the original terms for his $10m (£6.5m) bail.

Mr Madoff, 70, who is accused of defrauding investors of up to $50bn through a giant Ponzi scheme, will remain on bail. His wife Ruth will have to surrender her passport, and the couple will have to put up two further properties to secure the bail in addition to their $7m Manhattan penthouse.

Judge Gabriel Gorenstein ordered the changes after Mr Madoff apparently failed to produce four co-signatories to his original bail.

Meanwhile, Securities and Exchange Commission (SEC) chairman Christopher Cox admitted that the regulator's own lack of oversight of Mr Madoff's fund management business is "deeply troubling".

Mr Cox admitted the financial watchdog had been made aware of "credible and specific allegations" regarding Mr Madoff's alleged wrongdoing as far back as 1999, but had failed to act. He has ordered a root-and-branch review of the SEC's actions by the regulator's inspector general.

Of particular focus will be former SEC employee Eric Swanson, who has since married Mr Madoff's niece Shana.

Mr Swanson has said that he did not participate in any inquiry relating to the Madoff funds but said he will co-operate with the investigation. It has emerged that former New York Attorney General Eliot Spitzer invested with Madoff.

20 December 2008
Betrayed by their best friend
Bernard Madoff wooed the jet set,
but few knew how much was at stake
By James Quinn

On Wednesday afternoon, an estate agent called Dorothy Levy took a call in her office in Palm Beach, the Floridian playground of the super-rich. A friend, a wealthy doctor, needed to sell his house and move into a rented condo, and quickly.

At around the same time, an elderly man left Manhattan's Pearl Street courthouse and walked briskly towards the waiting black 4x4. As he walked, head down, baseball cap on, he said nothing to the waiting reporters. This was Bernard Madoff, accused of masterminding what could yet prove to be the biggest fraud the world has ever seen. The doctor? Just one of the thousands of victims of this scandal.

Since the story broke on 11 December, Levy has taken a number of calls from members of Palm Beach's small but select community, dominated by Jewish retirees who, in many cases, left their entire life savings in Madoff's seemingly capable hands.

The 70-year-old was a pillar of the community, living – when he was not in New York, or at his beachfront house in the Hamptons – in a wood-clad, tropically styled house on North Lake Way. Just two weeks ago, according to Bloomberg, he stopped off at the Everglades barber shop in the town for his "usual" – a $65 haircut, a $40 shave, a $50 pedicure and a $22 manicure.

Madoff, a self-made man who started his investment business with $5,000 earned from working as a lifeguard and installing refrigeration systems, lived a stone's throw away from the perfectly manicured lawns of the Palm Beach Country Club, the community's heart. The club has a joining fee of $300,000 and requires prospective members to provide a history of charitable giving. It was fertile terrain when hunting for clients. One such was Carl Shapiro, a textiles magnate whose son-in-law, Bob Jaffe, worked as a recruiter and gatekeeper for Madoff. When word of the accusations against Madoff broke, Jaffe called Shapiro and told him to turn on the news. He saw the man he had known for 48 years, and thought of as a son, leaving court after being indicted over what federal officials called "the world's largest Ponzi scheme". For Shapiro, who had invited Madoff to sit at the family table at his recent 95th birthday party, it was like "a knife in the heart" – not least because he had poured money into the fund in recent months, at Madoff's personal request.

Shapiro lost $400m of his own money and $145m from a charitable foundation. He is far from alone: the known number of casualties is growing by the day, cutting a scythe through the Jewish elite on both coasts. The impeccably connected Madoff looked after funds for Hollywood mogul Jeffrey Katzenberg, who is reported to have lost millions, and a children's charity set up by Steven Spielberg, which had more than half its assets with his firm. On the East Coast, the tycoon who owns the New York Mets baseball team was hit heavily, as were many charities, including the foundation set up by Holocaust survivor Elie Wiesel, and Yeshiva University, America's oldest Jewish university, for which Madoff was treasurer of the board of trustees.

The list goes on: politicians, such as former New York governor Eliot Spitzer, whose family foundation lost money; European banks such as Santander and RBS; financiers such as Arpad Busson, the billionaire hedge-fund manager and philanthropist – and the fiancé of actress Uma Thurman – whose firm had $230m under Madoff's management, and Nicola Horlick, the City "superwoman", whose Bramdean Alternatives had $31m at stake. And spare a thought for the family of hedge fund boss Walter Noel, the co-founder of the Fairfield Greenwich Group, which has a scarcely credible $7.5bn in jeopardy: four of his five daughters are married to men who work for the firm.

There could even be more victims to come. The investors who have come forward – many of whom had no idea their money was being managed by Madoff due to the complex scheme he operated, by which certain funds fed into others – have so far claimed losses of $35bn, still some $15bn shy of the $50bn total that Madoff is alleged to have mentioned to his two sons, Mark and Andrew. That alleged confession was triggered after investors whose fingers had been burnt by the financial crisis asked Madoff for their money back – they wanted $7bn, but there was only $300m in the bank. The system of sucking in new money to pay existing investors, which federal investigators allege had gone on since at least 2005, could not continue.

Madoff's group of companies is now under federal control, with investigators from the FBI, the Securities and Exchange Commission (SEC), and the US attorney-general's office camped in the firm's headquarters, the so-called "Lipstick Building", poring through reams of paperwork. Guards are positioned at the entrance to stop angry investors. Others are understood to be watching over Madoff himself, as he bides his time until his next court date, under house arrest in his $7m apartment on New York's Upper East Side. Having failed to convince his sons – or any of his friends – to co-sign bail papers with his brother Peter and wife Ruth, Madoff has been fitted with an electronic tag, and must not leave his two-floor apartment between 9 p.m. and 7 a.m.

In the meantime, the issue for investigators is how and whether such a crime could have been committed by just one man. "Speaking as a Jew on Christmas, I would be less shocked if Santa Claus showed up to my house than if Bernie Madoff pulled off this fraud alone." Ron Geffner, a partner at law firm Sadis & Goldberg told *Fortune* magazine.

"It's hard to imagine that given the amount of assets that he managed that people would not have been aware. If nothing else, employees, no matter what floor they were on, would have known that somewhere within the firm money was being lost."

Another body that should have realised that something was amiss was America's main financial regulator, the SEC. Despite several tip-offs, it failed to detect that anything was wrong. Wall Street veteran Harry Markopolos, who first alerted the SEC to Madoff in 1999, was treated, as he put it this week, as "the boy who cried wolf".

Eighteen months ago, a firm called Aksia looked into Madoff's fund on behalf of its clients and did not like what it saw. It discovered that the main fund through which all the money was invested was being audited by an unknown accountancy firm, Friehling & Horowitz. Based in Rockland county, in upstate New York, its staff consisted of a 78-year-old retiree living in Florida, and an accountant and a secretary in a 13ft by 8ft office.

Aksia also questioned the nature of the operations on the 17th floor of the Lipstick Building, where staff at Madoff's share-dealing arm were not allowed to venture. Christopher Cox, the SEC's outgoing chairman, has said that a preliminary investigation into how and why his staff had not pursued Madoff was "deeply troubling" and admitted that he was "gravely concerned by the apparent multiple failures" of the agency to investigate the allegations. Barack Obama has claimed that the US has been "asleep at the switch" when it comes to financial regulation.

Many of the victims, however, are not waiting for the government. Already the lawsuits are flying, as investors seek to recoup some of their losses. The New York Law School is suing Ezra Merkin, his Ascot Partners hedge fund and auditors BDO Seidman, over money it has lost; other accounting firms are likely to be drawn into the legal crossfire, with KPMG, Ernst & Young and PricewaterhouseCoopers among the auditors of funds that channelled money into Madoff's pot.

Whatever the outcome of such cases, the high-rollers of Palm Beach and elsewhere have been left reeling. For an awful lot of once very wealthy people, this is shaping up to be a Christmas to forget.

30 June 2009
Madoff jailed for 150 years
Madoff offers no excuses as victims have say in court
By James Quinn

Bernard Madoff has been sentenced to 150 years in prison for orchestrating an "extraordinarily evil" and "unprecedented" $65bn (£40bn) fraud that duped 13,500 investors out of their life savings and shocked the investment world.

Madoff, who ran a "staggering" Ponzi scheme that promised inflated investment returns but simply handed one investor's money to another, will die in prison as a result of being given the maximum possible sentence for the 11 counts of fraud, mail fraud and money laundering he pleaded guilty to in March.

Judge Denny Chin, sentencing, told 71-year-old Madoff that although the sentence was in many ways "symbolic" it was designed to reflect the "scope, duration and enormity of the fraud" and that "symbolism is important to deter future crimes and as retribution".

He also expressed surprise at the lack of support for Madoff, revealing that "not a single letter" was submitted in his support, not even from his wife Ruth or sons Andrew and Mark.

The judge ignored last minute pleas from Madoff's lawyer Ira Sorkin to hand down a 12-year sentence, and ignored a pre-sentencing report prepared by the US Probation Service (USPS) which recommended he be given 50 years. "Mr Madoff's crimes were extraordinarily evil. The breach of trust was massive," said Judge Chin, who also intimated that Madoff had not been as helpful with investigators as he might have been.

"I simply do not get the sense that Mr Madoff has done all that he could or told all that he knows." Madoff, who appeared in court dressed in a grey suit, white shirt and black tie, remained silent as the 150-year sentence was read out, while dozens of his victims cheered and applauded. "I only hope that he lives long enough that his jail cell becomes his coffin," said Michael Schwartz, whose mentally disabled brother's trust fund was wiped out by Madoff. Victim Sheryl Weinstein, whose family knew Madoff, branded him a "beast". Miriam Siegman explained she had resorted to using government-issued food stamps and scavenging from bins. Madoff sat listlessly as nine victims described the impact of the fraud on their lives.

He spoke briefly to apologise for his crimes, and at one point turned to face his victims and said: "I live in a tormented state knowing the pain and suffering I have created. I cannot offer you an excuse for my behaviour. I don't ask for any forgiveness."

Madoff also used his final public appearance – unless he is successful on appeal, which he has 10 days to file – to attempt to shield his family from any suggestions of wrongdoing, saying that he had lied to his wife and two sons for decades. The US Attorney's office yesterday stressed that its investigations continue into the fraud, and that it will pursue any individuals who are found to have assisted him.

Peter Mandelson – Part One

"I can scarcely believe I am writing this letter to you."

Known, with varying degrees of affection, as 'The Prince of Darkness', Peter Mandelson is admired and loathed in equal measure. His first notable success was to, along with other modernisers, make Britain's great party of the left electable again – as the re-branded New Labour. Next, as one of the first 'spin doctors' he was instrumental in Tony Blair's rise to Downing Street. Ruthless as he was, it was perhaps unsurprising that he made powerful enemies along the way. Most damagingly, his relationship with Gordon Brown was almost destroyed in the aftermath of his decision to back Tony Blair's campaign for the party's leadership. In a story that is almost too good not to be true it is said that when Mandelson once asked the chancellor if he could borrow 10p to ring a friend, Brown passed him a coin and replied: 'Have 20p – then you can call them both.'

It was Mandelson's close relationship with Blair that earned him a place at his administration's top table after 1997; and this proximity also ensured that he would be given a second chance as a minister after scandal ended his first spell in government. But it was not enough to save him when he became embroiled in another contretemps. Mandelson would return to the cabinet almost a decade later (after a spell as a European Commissioner) though to almost everybody's surprise, it was Gordon Brown who brought him back into the fold. The Dark Lord (a new nickname bestowed on him after his enoblement) would find himself on the fringes of power once more in 2010, after Labour lost the general election of that year; however, perhaps he could console himself that at least this time his defenestration could not be blamed, on any kind of personal indiscretion on his part.

22 December 1998
Mandelson in £373,000 loan storm
By Polly Newton

Peter Mandelson was at the centre of a political storm last night after it emerged that he had accepted a loan of almost £375,000 from Geoffrey Robinson, the beleaguered Paymaster General, to buy his London home two years ago.

The Trade and Industry Secretary was forced to issue a statement denying any wrongdoing. Mr Robinson's financial affairs are the subject of a DTI inquiry.

The Tories claimed that he faced a clear conflict of interest.

Only £40,000 of the loan has so far been repaid, though Mr Mandelson said he was "in the process of repaying the remainder in full with the help of my mother".

Although Mr Mandelson was quick to defend his conduct, he admitted that "with hindsight" it would have been better to make the facts of the loan for the house – in fashionable Notting Hill, west London – known at an earlier stage.

But Tony Blair was said last night to be satisfied that Mr Mandelson was "properly insulated" from any decision relating to the Robinson inquiry.

Mr Robinson said in a statement: "Peter Mandelson, a friend of long standing, asked me for help in 1996. I was in a position to help through a loan and did so with the understanding that it would be repaid in full in due course. That is all there was and is to it."

Mr Mandelson, who takes a ministerial salary in the region of £90,000, was adamant that there had been no breach of the ministerial code.

He said he had no intention of resigning over the disclosures, which follow an investigation by the *Guardian*. "There is no conflict of interest, therefore the matter does not arise," he told BBC2's *Newsnight*.

But John Redwood, the Tory trade and industry spokesman, demanded to know why he had accepted the loan and why he still held it at a time when Mr Robinson's financial affairs were under inquiry.

"I want to know why Mr Mandelson accepted a loan of such a mind-bogglingly large sum and the terms and conditions under which it was given.

"How can Mr Mandelson be Britain's top company regulator when he has this kind of relationship with people undergoing scrutiny by his own department?"

He found it "very odd" that Mr Mandelson had taken on the sum at a time when he could be assumed to be on a backbench MP's salary of about £40,000. The normal limit on borrowing was three times a person's income.

Mr Mandelson said that while his department was conducting the inquiry into Mr Robinson's affairs, he had removed himself from any potential conflict of interest by telling Michael Scholar, Permanent Secretary to the DTI, that he would not be involved in the investigation.

Of his failure to inform Mr Blair of the loan until last week – when the Prime Minister was pre-occupied with the bombing raids on Iraq – he said: "I didn't feel that I needed to disclose something which was a personal arrangement made between myself and Geoffrey Robinson two years ago, before the election had taken place."

Had he believed there had been any conflict of interest, he would have informed Mr Scholar.

"Having satisfied myself that no conflict of interest arose in this matter, I didn't believe I needed to refer to it," he said.

The loan, which Mr Mandelson described as "a personal arrangement", was agreed in October 1996, when Labour was in opposition. At the time, he was a key adviser to Mr Blair; Mr Robinson, a millionaire businessman, was a backbencher.

In his statement, the Trade Secretary said: "I have since repaid £40,624.68p and the loan now stands at £332,375.32p. In addition to this loan, I obtained a mortgage from a building society."

The loan was always intended to be a short-term arrangement and he was "in the process of repaying the remainder of the loan in full with the help of my mother".

He said: "In September 1998 the Permanent Secretary of the DTI advised me that the department was considering allegations concerning Geoffrey Robinson's business affairs. We agreed that I should not be involved in this process. Since that conversation, I have played no part whatsoever in the department's consideration of the matter.

"Because I was satisfied that any conflict of interest had been properly dealt with, I did not disclose the existence of the loan to the Permanent Secretary as I had agreed with Geoffrey Robinson that it would be a personal matter between us. However, when it became clear that the loan was in the public domain I immediately told the Permanent Secretary and informed No 10. At all times I have protected the integrity and professionalism of the DTI.

"Geoffrey Robinson asked for confidentiality and I respected that. I do not believe that accepting a loan from a friend and fellow MP was wrong. There is no conflict of interest.

"In the case of the register of members' interests and the ministerial code you have to identify a potential conflict of interest before the need to declare a financial interest arises. I removed myself from any such conflict of interest and insulated myself from any contact with Geoffrey Robinson's affairs and thereby removed the need for any declaration."

Downing Street said Mr Blair was "confident that Peter Mandelson has been properly insulated from any decision relating to Geoffrey Robinson".

A Conservative source described the disclosures as "a devastating insight into the extent of cronyism at the heart of new Labour".

The ability of Mr Mandelson to buy a £475,000 house has long been the subject of speculation at Westminster. Even now, he has no obvious source of income beyond his ministerial salary. The controversy has erupted amid growing speculation that Mr Robinson's resignation is imminent. He has faced a series of investigations and last month had to apologise to the Commons for breaching rules on disclosure of interests.

He also faced fresh allegations about his business links with Robert Maxwell.

24 December 1998
Blair shattered by loss of Labour's chief
propagandist and paymaster
By George Jones

Tony Blair suffered his most shattering blow since becoming Prime Minister yesterday when Peter Mandelson, his closest political ally and a principal architect of New Labour, resigned from the Government over a £373,000 loan from Geoffrey Robinson.

Mr Robinson, who lent the money to Mr Mandelson to buy a house, also quit as Paymaster General, claiming he was the victim of a "highly charged political campaign".

The dramatic fall of two ministers closely associated with the modernisation of Labour stunned Westminster. Labour MPs said it was the worst 48 hours experienced by the Government but praised Mr Mandelson for sparing Mr Blair further embarrassment.

After 24 hours of attempting to brazen out the row over the secret loan, Mr Mandelson decided to step down to prevent the Government being engulfed in the kind of accusations of misconduct and "sleaze" that overwhelmed the Tories.

In an emotional letter to Mr Blair, Mr Mandelson said: "I can scarcely believe I am writing this letter to you." Later, in a series of interviews he appeared red-eyed and severely chastened, emphasising that he had paid a high price for his home in Notting Hill Gate.

He admitted that his action allowed the impression to be created that New Labour had fallen below high standards in government. "I had to do something radical to restore people's faith in this Government, their confidence in ministers and also their regard for my own integrity," he said.

Mr Mandelson's resignation was announced by Downing Street at 12.30 p.m.

The Prime Minister immediately appointed two loyal, high-flying "Blairites" to plug the gaps in his Cabinet. Stephen Byers, Treasury Chief Secretary, replaces Mr Mandelson as Trade and Industry Secretary. His job as Treasury number two is taken by Alan Milburn, the health minister.

Responsibility for the Millennium Dome will pass back to Chris Smith, the Secretary of State for Culture, Media and Sport.

Although Mr Mandelson spent Tuesday insisting that he had done nothing wrong and would not resign, both he and Mr Blair realised that his position was becoming untenable and was creating increasing difficulty for the Government's image.

At around 10 p.m. on Tuesday, Mr Mandelson telephoned Mr Blair at Chequers, saying he found the whole affair "pretty wretched" and was considering quitting.

Mr Blair advised Mr Mandelson to "sleep on it". Yesterday morning, Mr Mandelson called Mr Blair again to say that he had made up his mind to resign.

Officials said he wanted to demonstrate that he would not seek to cling on to office in the same way that ministers had under the previous Tory government. Mr Blair made no attempt to dissuade Mr Mandelson.

Initially Downing Street had backed Mr Mandelson's assertions that he had not broken the code of conduct for ministers. However, after receiving a further report from Sir Richard Wilson, the Cabinet Secretary, Mr Blair accepted that Mr Mandelson has been compromised by taking the loan and keeping it secret.

Downing Street made clear that Mr Blair believed Mr Mandelson should not have accepted the money in the first place. Having taken it, he should have told both the Prime Minister and the permanent secretary at the DTI, Michael Scholar.

In his resignation letter, Mr Mandelson insisted he had not done anything wrong or improper. But he accepted "with all candour" that he should not have entered into the arrangement two years ago with Mr Robinson.

He also acknowledged that he should have told Mr Scholar about the loan when Mr Robinson's business affairs came under scrutiny by the DTI.

"I am sorry about this situation. But we came to power promising to uphold the highest possible standards in public life. We have not just to do so, but we must be seen to do so," he said.

Mr Blair wrote back emphasising that they had been personal friends and the closest of political colleagues. "It is no exaggeration to say that without your support and advice we would never have built New Labour."

While acknowledging a "misjudgement" on Mr Mandelson's part, he praised him for putting the reputation of the Labour Party and the Government first. Mr Blair held out the prospect that Mr Mandelson could return to office in the future, saying he would "achieve much, much more with us".

Friends of Mr Mandelson said he now planned a good Christmas break but intended to make a political comeback, probably in a party role in next year's mid-term elections.

John Prescott, the deputy Prime Minister, refused to comment on allegations that details of the loan surfaced as a result of a feud between Mr Mandelson and Charlie Whelan, the press secretary to Gordon Brown, the Chancellor.

"There may well be tensions between different groups. That is not giving proof at all that such a serious allegation was made by an individual of one team against another," he told *Channel 4 News*.

It was clear that Mr Mandelson faced continuing questions from the Tories over details of the deal and whether or not he had disclosed its existence to the Britannia Building Society when taking out a mortgage on the new house.

Last night a spokesman for Mr Mandelson admitted that the mortgage application form "may not reflect" how he paid for the house. He said that Mr Mandelson would be writing to Britannia to clarify the matter.

Peter Lilley, the deputy Tory leader, said: "He has spent over 18 months deceiving people about his financial position." The whole affair had badly dented the Government's reputation, he added.

Mr Blair took advantage of Mr Mandelson's downfall to secure the resignation of Mr Robinson, who had been at the heart of a succession of sleaze stories because of his business activities and offshore trusts.

The Prime Minister had been planning for some weeks for the minister to step down during the Christmas recess.

Mr Robinson said he had been subjected to a persistent – "and I believe unfair" – set of allegations about his business affairs.

Jack Cunningham, the so-called "Cabinet Enforcer", admitted it had not been a good day for the Government. "There is no doubt that it has caused damage to the Government. It would be ridiculous to pretend otherwise."

Peter Mandelson – Part Two

"Once again his behaviour falls well below
that expected of a senior minister."

22 January 2001
Calls for inquiry over Mandelson citizenship row
By David Millward

Peter Mandelson faced calls yesterday for an investigation into his intervention on behalf of an Indian businessman who was seeking British citizenship.

The businessman provided £1m to help the Millennium Dome's Faith Zone.

Mr Mandelson's approach to the Home Office on behalf of Srichand Hinduja, who is facing corruption charges in India, re-ignited controversy over the Dome and Labour's links with businessmen.

"We have a rich businessman in the middle of a corruption scandal who gets a British passport in record time after donating £1m to the Dome," said Norman Baker, Liberal Democrat MP for Lewes.

"We need a clear statement on who lobbied the Home Office on the Hindujas' behalf and when."

Mr Hinduja and his brothers, Gopichand and Prakash – who all became British citizens in 1999 – were questioned again yesterday by Indian authorities investigating an arms scandal, in which they deny involvement.

The Labour Party confirmed that Mr Mandelson, when he was minister responsible for the Dome, asked his private office to inquire whether the Home Office would be sympathetic towards a second application for a British passport by Mr Hinduja, having rejected a first.

In a statement to a Sunday newspaper, Mr Mandelson said: "To the limited extent that I was involved in this matter, I was always very sensitive to the proprieties. The matter was dealt with by my private secretary. At no time did I support or endorse this application for citizenship."

The Hindujas, who made their fortune in banking, communications and oil, have lived in Britain for many years and their reputation for philanthropy drew them close to politicians.

The Blairs attended a Hinduja Diwali party in November 1999 and Cherie Blair modelled a churidar kameez designed by one of Srichand Hinduja's daughters.

Last night, a spokesman for Mr Hinduja said that he had asked Mr Mandelson "informally" in the summer of 1998 if the Home Office would consider his application for British nationality.

He said Mr Mandelson had confirmed that he was eligible to apply, but said all further dealings had been directly with the Home Office.

24 January 2001
Mandelson forced to come clean
Blair backs ally in Hinduja passport row
By George Jones

Tony Blair ordered an all-out effort to shore up the position of Peter Mandelson last night after Downing Street admitted that it had not told the truth about the Northern Ireland Secretary's involvement in a passport application by the wealthy Hinduja brothers.

Downing Street dismissed suggestions that Mr Mandelson should resign.

Officials denied that he had done anything "improper" by contacting a junior Home Office minister in 1998 about the Hindujas' prospects of acquiring British citizenship at a time when they were offering to donate £1m to the Millennium Dome.

Mr Mandelson, in a series of television interviews last night, also denied that he had exerted any pressure on the Home Office to grant the nationality application.

However, Norman Baker, the Liberal Democrat MP for Lewes, whose Commons questions first disclosed Mr Mandelson's involvement, thought otherwise.

"There now appears to be a clear link between the Hindujas gaining British nationalities and being asked for money to fund a zone in the Millennium Dome," he said. "If these allegations are true, I believe that it would be unwise for the Prime Minister to reappoint Peter Mandelson to the Cabinet if Labour are re-elected."

Michael Ancram, the Tory chairman, piled the political pressure on Mr Mandelson and called for him to be stripped of his role in Labour's election campaign.

He said that, for the second time in three years, Mr Mandelson was shown "to have been less than candid in his explanation of his dealings with colleagues in relation to money or influence".

"Once again his behaviour falls well below that expected of a senior minister," he said.

There was considerable embarrassment that Mr Mandelson – who was forced to resign from the Government two years ago over a secret £373,000 home loan – was again at the centre of controversy.

With an election thought to be only four months away, Mr Blair cannot afford to lose Mr Mandelson, his close political ally, who is drawing up Labour's campaign strategy with Gordon Brown.

Although there is no evidence of any impropriety, the timing of events put the Government's reputation for truthfulness under the spotlight.

In February 1988, when Mr Mandelson was Mr Blair's Cabinet "enforcer" and the minister responsible for the Dome, the Hinduja brothers indicated that they were interested in supporting the project.

In June that year, they contacted Mr Mandelson to ask whether their application for British citizenship – which had been turned down once – would be reconsidered in the light of a change of Government policy in favour of granting passports to long-standing residents. Mr Mandelson then contacted Mike O'Brien, the Home Office minister responsible for immigration, about their request.

Five months later, in October 1998, the Hinduja brothers agreed to donate £1m towards the Millennium Dome's Faith Zone. In March 1999, Srichand Hinduja resubmitted his application for a British passport, and received one six months later – a third of the time a typical decision takes.

On Monday, Alastair Campbell, the Prime Minister's official spokesman, angrily denied suggestions that Mr Mandelson had intervened personally to secure British citizenship for Srichand Hinduja.

Yesterday, Mr Campbell said he had been wrong to tell reporters that Mr Mandelson's sole involvement was a call from his private secretary at the Cabinet Office to the Home Office. He said that Mr Mandelson now recalled having asked his officials to set up the telephone call with Mr O'Brien after meeting the Hindujas at a function.

Mr O'Brien recalled that the conversation consisted of Mr Mandelson querying how the Hindujas' application for citizenship might have been considered in the light of changes to immigration rules.

"Mike O'Brien has confirmed that Peter Mandelson did not make representations on behalf of the brothers or make representations on any potential application and did not support or endorse it," said Mr Campbell.

Later, Mr Mandelson appeared to contradict Downing Street's account. "There is no question of my forgetting about anything," he said. "I was not asked until today.

"My concern was to treat them [the Hinduja brothers] courteously throughout and without giving them any sort of preferential or favourite help at all. The facts speak for themselves. I acted in an entirely proper way."

Downing Street embarked on a determined damage limitation exercise, claiming that it was only on Monday, when Government officials were back at their offices, that they were able to clarify Mr Mandelson's role in what has become known as the "passport for favours" affair.

Officials would not say who had disclosed Mr Mandelson's personal involvement – though it is understood that Mr O'Brien had recalled the telephone conversation and sought a correction.

They admitted, however, that there had been discussions late on Monday night between Mr Mandelson, Mr O'Brien and Downing Street and a decision was taken to make a clean breast of it the following morning.

Mr Campbell said Mr O'Brien had confirmed that Mr Mandelson did not make representations on behalf of the brothers or make representations on any potential application and did not support or endorse it.

The Hindujas are Asian businessmen who have close connections with Labour, but whose business dealings have attracted controversy.

India's Central Bureau of Investigation is seeking to charge Mr Hinduja and his brothers Gopichand and Prakash in connection with the Bofors arms commission scandal. They all deny any wrongdoing.

25 January 2001
No way back for Mandelson

Blair taunted as his closest ally is forced to quit for
second time in two years after lying over passport row
By George Jones

Peter Mandelson's political career came to a sudden and dramatic end last night when he resigned from the Cabinet for the second time in just over two years, leaving serious questions about Tony Blair's judgment.

He quit in disgrace after admitting giving "wrong" information about his involvement in the passport application of an Indian businessman who gave £1m to the Millennium Dome.

Downing Street signalled that Mr Mandelson would also be stepping down from his role of joint co-ordinator with Gordon Brown, the Chancellor, of Labour's campaign for the election.

Alastair Campbell, the Prime Minister's official spokesman, who played a key role in Mr Mandelson's resignation, said the former Northern Ireland Secretary was "clearly looking to wind down his political activity".

Although Downing Street acted with ruthless efficiency to secure Mr Mandelson's resignation during the morning, his departure was highly damaging to Mr Blair only months before the general election is expected.

His departure will also be a serious blow to Labour's election campaign and to supporters of the euro, as Mr Mandelson was one of the strongest Cabinet supporters of early entry to the single currency.

But his departure is likely to strengthen the position of Mr Brown, who has long resented Mr Mandelson's closeness to the Prime Minister.

William Hague, the Conservative leader, infuriated Labour MPs by using Commons question time to accuse Mr Blair of a "monumental error of judgment" in bringing Mr Mandelson back into the Cabinet in October 1999, only 10 months after his resignation over a secret home loan.

He mercilessly taunted a subdued and tired looking Mr Blair, saying that Mr Mandelson's career in government epitomised the spin and arrogance of New Labour in power.

Mr Blair, his voice breaking with emotion at times, paid tribute to Mr Mandelson for his "tireless efforts" in promoting peace in Northern Ireland.

Mr Mandelson was a "bigger man" than many of his critics, he said, and in the "broad sweep of history" his contribution in Northern Ireland "will be far greater than what has happened in the last 24 hours, tragic though that is".

Minutes before, a clearly dejected Mr Mandelson had made his last appearance in the Commons as Northern Ireland Secretary, answering questions on Ulster affairs despite announcing his resignation an hour earlier outside No 10.

Although he denied acting improperly over the passport application from Srichand Hinduja, his resignation became inevitable when Downing Street said that he had given contradictory and misleading accounts of his role after being approached by the billionaire businessman three years ago.

Mr Mandelson, who awoke yesterday to tabloid newspaper headlines branding him a liar, said he wanted to escape the "media pressure and exposure" that had dogged his career.

He wanted "to lead a more normal life, both in politics and, in the future, outside", causing speculation that he might stand down as MP for Hartlepool at the election.

Mr Mandelson's fate was sealed when he was summoned to Downing Street for urgent talks with Mr Blair and Mr Campbell to "establish the facts" of the passport issue.

Mr Campbell left the meeting to brief political correspondents shortly after 11 a.m., virtually accusing Mr Mandelson of misleading him.

He said there were "difficulties and contradictions" in Mr Mandelson's version of events. He also disclosed that over the weekend Mr Mandelson had assured him he had not been personally involved in contacting the Home Office about the passport application – a claim contradicted by Mike O'Brien, who was immigration minister at the time.

Downing Street officials dismissed reports that Mr Campbell, who insisted that he was still friends with Mr Mandelson, had demanded his resignation or suggested that he would quit if Mr Mandelson did not go.

Mr Blair made clear in the Commons that Mr Mandelson had resigned because he had not told the truth to Mr Campbell.

He said: "I accept that the reply of the Northern Ireland Secretary through his office to inquiries from a newspaper at the weekend was misleading and resulted in the House of Commons and the lobby being misled – and I accepted his resignation on that basis."

Mr O'Brien, minister of state at the Home Office, conceded that his decision to disclose that Mr Mandelson had telephoned him about the Hinduja passport had triggered the events which brought about his resignation.

"I feel very sad that I had to make it clear that that conversation did occur," he said.

Mr Blair told MPs that he believed the successful passport application from Mr Hinduja had been handled in "accordance with the proper criteria".

But he announced that a former Treasury solicitor, Sir Anthony Hammond, QC, had been asked to review the case to ensure that the application "was properly dealt with in all respects".

Many Labour MPs, while acknowledging that it had been a bad day for the Government, were relieved to see Mr Mandelson go.

They drew parallels with the circumstances of his resignation as trade and industry secretary in December 1998 after failing to disclose a £373,000 home loan from Geoffrey Robinson.

Against the advice of colleagues, Mr Blair brought Mr Mandelson back into the Government after only 10 months on the backbenches.

This defied the convention that disgraced ministers are not reappointed until they have been re-elected at a subsequent election.

Mr Mandelson has been Mr Blair's closest ally and was central to the creation of New Labour and its victory in 1997. Yesterday a clearly disappointed Mr Blair decided that he had become a liability.

Unusually, there was no exchange of letters between them, setting out the context of his resignation.

Mr Mandelson's brief statement to reporters and Mr Blair's tribute in the Commons were the only public record of his departure.

Srichand Hinduja said that he was "sad" to see Mr Mandelson go.

"I wish to reiterate that I have never at any time linked our support for the Millennium Dome with our request to Mr Mandelson for information in 1998," he said.

Also 29 January 2001
Master of spin trapped in his own web
How Mandelson dug his way deeper into disaster
By George Jones

Immediately after Peter Mandelson resigned last Wednesday, Tony Blair lavished praise on him, saying the former Northern Ireland Secretary was a "bigger man than many of his critics". He condemned William Hague in the bitterest terms for attacking Mr Mandelson.

Yet three days later, New Labour's spin machine was launching a pre-emptive strike to destroy Mr Mandelson's credibility.

At a briefing with Sunday newspaper journalists on Friday, Alastair Campbell questioned Mr Mandelson's state of mind, agreeing it was similar to that of Ron Davies, the former Welsh Secretary, who resigned after a "moment of madness" on Clapham Common in 1998.

Mr Campbell claimed yesterday he had been "misrepresented". But the journalists present stood by their reports, and said they believed he was making a deliberate intervention.

Downing Street had got wind that Mr Mandelson was no longer prepared to go quietly. He was intending to use a Sunday newspaper article to fight back, claiming he had been unfairly forced to resign by a Downing Street "kangaroo court".

So Mr Campbell got his retaliation in first by briefing the political correspondents that Mr Mandelson was "curiously detached".

It resulted in yesterday's headlines about Mandelson and Blair "going to war". This was a far cry from Mr Mandelson's first resignation from the Cabinet in December 1998. Then, according to Westminster legend, Mr Campbell wept, the Blairs invited Mr Mandelson and his Brazilian lover, Reinaldo da Silva, to Chequers and there was an exchange of warm letters.

This time, the traditional resignation letters were dispensed with – a hint that neither man was prepared to disguise his own anger.

In a belated attempt to play down this new rift, it was disclosed yesterday that Mr Mandelson had fulfilled a long-standing invitation to attend a family birthday party at Mr Campbell's home.

But Mr Mandelson has not spoken to Mr Blair since his resignation – and yesterday Cabinet colleagues were queuing up to rubbish his prospects of making a comeback.

Mr Mandelson has been well and truly cast aside by New Labour, with a speed and ferocity which confirms its reputation as one of the most ruthless and calculating political machines this country has seen.

But Mr Mandelson, above all, knows where the New Labour skeletons are buried. He remains a highly volatile figure and – if his sense of resentment turns into a desire for revenge, he could inflict damage on the party.

However, in his rambling and, at times, incoherent account in yesterday's *Sunday Times*, Mr Mandelson goes some way to vindicating Mr Blair's decision to demand his resignation.

His own version of events raises serious questions over his own probity and behaviour as a minister – and reveals the real reason for his sacking.

Mr Mandelson admitted that when the Liberal Democrat MP Norman Baker started asking parliamentary questions last month about his involvement in the Hinduja passport application, his initial reaction was to try to persuade the Home Office to cover it up.

When he heard about Mr Baker's question, he made clear to his civil servants that he did not want to be involved in the answer.

Mr Mandelson wrote: "I stated that my contact with the Home Office had been casual and fleeting, as well as confidential, and I did not see why my involvement needed to feature.

"The Home Office responded that it wouldn't be possible to answer the question in this way and that they would have to refer to the contact."

He admitted that he now accepted that this had been "a mistake".

To its credit, the Home Office was straightforward, telling MPs that Mr Mandelson "made inquiries" about how an application might be viewed, but stating that he had not made representations that an application be granted.

Mr Mandelson also revealed that Jack Straw, the Home Secretary, told him on Wednesday, 17 January, that the Home Office had a record of his conversation in June 1998 with one of its ministers, Mike O'Brien, about the Hinduja passport approach.

Yet three days later on Saturday, 20 January, when contacted by the *Observer* newspaper, Mr Mandelson was economical with the truth. He appeared to forget what Mr Straw had told him, and maintained that the matter had been dealt with by his private secretary.

Later that weekend, when contacted by Alastair Campbell, Mr Mandelson again emphasised that his officials, and not he personally, had contacted the Home Office. The next morning, Mr Campbell briefed political journalists to that effect, and this was repeated by Chris Smith, the Culture Secretary, in the Commons that afternoon.

On Monday evening, Mr O'Brien, still a Home Office minister but no longer responsible for immigration, alerted Downing Street that Mr Mandelson's version was inaccurate – and they had spoken about the Hinduja citizenship matter.

On Tuesday morning, Mr Campbell corrected himself – he admitted that he had given wrong information and that Mr Mandelson had made a call to Mr O'Brien.

Mr Campbell attempted to pass it off as a memory lapse by Mr Mandelson, because the call had been short and he could not recollect it.

But that strategy was blown out of the water when Mr Straw contacted Mr Blair later that day to say that he had specifically reminded Mr Mandelson of the O'Brien phone call only days earlier.

From that moment, Mr Mandelson's fate was sealed. For the second time within two days, Downing Street had given misleading information about Mr Mandelson's involvement.

No wonder Downing Street panicked when it saw Wednesday morning's tabloid newspaper headlines branding Mr Mandelson a "liar" and accusing him of telling "porkies". Mr Mandelson was summoned to No 10 and within hours he was returning to the backbenches for the second time this Parliament.

Mr Mandelson now claims civil servants who worked for him in the Cabinet Office in 1998 supported his original version – that the "original inquiry" to the Home Office was made by his then assistant private secretary.

It will be for Sir Anthony Hammond's inquiry to establish the facts – whether the Home Office or Cabinet Office recollections were correct. But that will not save Mr Mandelson, nor result in him being brought back into Government for a third time.

He was forced to resign because he did not give truthful answers about a matter the Home Secretary had told him about only days before.

Mr Blair's patience snapped – particularly as he had taken a big political risk by bringing Mr Mandelson back into the Cabinet after he quit because of his embarrassing lapse of memory over the £373,000 home loan from Geoffrey Robinson.

Mr Mandelson insisted yesterday he did not lie. But his evasions led to Downing Street virtually doing so on his behalf and plunged the Government into its biggest crisis since the loan row.

The master of spin, one of the architects of New Labour, was finally trapped in one of his own carefully constructed webs. As he wrote yesterday: "This relatively trivial error was turned into a huge misjudgment that led to my resignation." That will be his political epitaph.

Diego Maradona

"I have spent three months with my personal physical trainer
at a secret hideaway in the mountains."

One touch to control the ball, another to nudge it into position and a third to send it rocketing past a helpless keeper. It looked as if Maradona was back to his best. His 15-month ban for testing positive for cocaine, his fluctuating weight, his drift away from European football – none of that mattered now. He was fit, firing and, it seemed, in top form. Surely the Argentinian great would go on to light up the 1994 World Cup, just as he had sparkled in Mexico eight years before. Only a handful of observers – watching him charge towards the camera to celebrate the goal, every nerve in his face tensed, his eyes almost popping out of his head – were left with an uneasy feeling that something was up.

24 June 1994
Fate of the "hand of God" now rests in God's hands
Robert Philip at the World Cup

"It rests," said the king with an innocently boyish grin, "in the hands of God." Diego Armando Maradona stood on the ivory sands of Nantucket Island, enjoying the feel of the warm waves swirling gently back and forth across his bare toes.

At his back, the ice-blue waters of Cape Cod sparkled under an evening sun; to his front, a tangle of television crews, hand-held cameras and boom-microphones jousting for position, were arranged before him in a wide and respectful arc.

Such royal audiences are rare, and as his majesty is not above taking the odd pot-shot at irksome reporters with an air rifle, the first questioner understandably chose a path bordered with sycophancy.

"Following your brilliant display against Greece, do you think you can become the MVP [most valuable player] at World Cup 94?"

"With respect to Greece," answered Maradona through his interpreter, "they are not one of the most powerful teams. But I think I surprised many people.

"The critics who know everything said I was finished. They said that I was over-weight and unfit. That I was too old, too slow. But I have spent three months with my personal physical trainer at a secret hideaway in the mountains, far from the prying eyes of Buenos Aires.

"I have lost 30 pounds and am now fitter than I have been for many years. I was satisfied to play well and score against Greece, but Saturday's match with Nigeria will be a better test for me. This should tell the world whether I can be the Diego Maradona of '86 again. I have done everything I can. Now it rests in the hands of God. . . ."

Maradona, his reputation diminished by tales of cocaine abuse and sexual peccadilloes, is using USA '94 as one final opportunity to rebuild his image as both a footballer and sporting icon.

. . . The World Cup has seen the very best and worst of Maradona since 1978, when Cesar Luis Menotti astounded the nation by omitting the 17-year-old won-derboy from his ultimately triumphant squad. In '82, he was sent off for a spiteful groin-high lunge at the Brazilian Batista in Barcelona.

We need not delve too deeply into '86, save to mention that many then regarded him as the greatest player the world had ever seen, and in 1990 he spilled the petu-lant tears of a child following Argentina's defeat by West Germany in the final.

"Good memories, bad memories," is how Maradona described his cheq-uered World Cup past. "But this is the biggest sporting event of all. It is difficult for America to comprehend, but the World Cup is bigger, far bigger, than the Olympic Games. When it is next held in France in 1998, my time will have passed. Therefore I must make the most of this chance I have been given here in the United States to prove that Diego Maradona deserves to be looked upon with the same respect given to Pele."

Filled with remorse, it is difficult not to feel moved by Maradona's touching sin-cerity. "Football gave me everything. It took a small child born into poverty and made him a king. Then they took away the king's crown and now he has very little.

I love football with all my heart and would give everything I have to turn back the clock. Only God can do that. Diego Maradona is in his hands."

With that, Maradona resumed his stroll along the shore, though he could not resist one final act of mischief. "You must tell America," he told the cameras over his departing shoulder, "how happy I am to be in a country where they play football with their hands."

I July 1994
End of World for Maradona
By John Hiscock and Andrew Graham-Yooll

Diego Maradona, Argentina's brilliant but flawed soccer captain, was thrown out of the World Cup last night, his career in ruins, after taking a banned drug.

Tests showed that Maradona, 33, who was banned in 1991 for 15 months for taking cocaine, had taken five different forms of ephedrine, which is available over the counter in nasal sprays.

His expulsion was announced after the results of a second set of tests received from a Los Angeles laboratory proved positive. FIFA, the international football body, gave the news at a packed Dallas hotel.

Instead of playing in a record 22nd World Cup game against Bulgaria last night Maradona was lying low in his hotel, under siege from the world's press.

Senor Guillermo Canedo, chairman of the FIFA World Cup organising committee, said: "Until the case is settled he is suspended from all footballing activity."

Senor Julio Grondona, president of the Argentina Football Association, said the ephedrine was in a nasal spray or drops not prescribed by the team doctor.

Ephedrine, used in remedies for colds and hay fever, is widely abused in sport. It affects the central nervous system, increasing mental alertness and aggression and reducing fatigue.

Prayers for the national team were said in Argentina's churches last night, while radio stations cancelled all other programmes to discuss the crisis.

Maradona was accused of arrogance and of ruling the Argentinian squad by whim. He insisted on taking his entire family with him and a large retinue of "doormats" (the name given to the people he habitually walks all over).

Also I July 1994
Disgrace stops Maradona from regaining summit
World Cup drugs ban ruins Argentinian idol's chance of redemption
By Roddy Forsyth

The hopes which FIFA entertained of presenting an unblemished World Cup finals to the greatest virgin football audience in the world went badly awry yesterday when the organising committee of the tournament announced in Dallas that Diego Maradona had been expelled from the competition for drug abuse.

Maradona had been the subject of a random test after Argentina's 2–1 victory over Nigeria last Saturday in Boston and it was subsequently found that he had taken five prohibited substances, described by FIFA's chief medical expert, Dr Michel D'Hooghe of Belgium, as "a cocktail of drugs".

Maradona is the first player to be sent home from the finals in such disgrace since Scotland's Willie Johnston was found to have taken a banned drug, which he claimed was a treatment for hay fever, in 1978.

Sepp Blatter, the general secretary of FIFA, explained at a press conference in Dallas the procedures which had led FIFA into an emergency session to decide Maradona's fate. he had taken five banned substances, the Argentinian Football Association had voluntarily expelled him from the finals, and FIFA would set up an inquiry into the affair once the finals were completed. No punitive action would be taken by FIFA in the meantime against Argentina and the result of the match will stand.

The impression was that the world governing body of the sport was anxious to defer an inquest into an ugly incident in order not to sour the mood of what has generally been seen to be a vigorous and exciting competition.

Joao Havelange, the Brazilian president of FIFA and a contentious figure at the best of times, was conspicuously absent from the proceedings until near the end of the press conference. He sat looking ashen and drawn until he was eventually asked for his thoughts on the matter: "I was praying that the result would be different because I love these players as I love my children and my grandchildren. But the medical facts are established and we cannot lie," he said.

On Sunday night, 24 hours after he had been tested, Maradona was in jovial mood at the Argentinian headquarters at Babson College, a few miles outside Boston.

Maradona laughed and joked with reporters in Italian and Spanish and when I asked him how he had achieved his remarkable fitness, a phenomenon which has been widely remarked on by everyone who has seen his performances in the opening games, he replied: "It may have surprised many people but it hasn't surprised me, after all I have been training for three months and you would expect to see some effect. My play so far is a big satisfaction for me but the most important thing is winning."

But yesterday a new light was cast upon his physical revival when it was revealed that the drugs found in his urine specimen are all associated with treatments to bring about weight loss.

The sadness of it all is that he had a World Cup record within his grasp. Had he played last night against Bulgaria he would have set a record for appearances in the finals. It should have been his 22nd game.

Blatter said that just as in the case of Johnston, the positive drug test would not cause any result to be altered. When he was reminded that Johnston had been tested after Scotland had lost 3–1 to Peru, while Maradona had been caught out after a victory for his side, Blatter replied: "The principle is the same in both cases: the result – win or lose for the player's team – should not be affected.

"The Nigerians have been kept informed and they have made no complaint about our decision nor have they suggested that the result of the game should be reviewed or altered."

David Will, the Scottish lawyer who was on the committee that dealt with Maradona, said that no rules had been established by the time of the Johnston incident. "That one caught everybody by surprise, too, and it was really dealt with on an ad hoc basis.

"We have had less than 24 hours to react to this but the result would only have been altered if both of the Argentinian players who took the drug test had shown a positive result and had been using the same substances."

Maradona said on television in Buenos Aires last night that he would never play again. "It's finished for me. I had paid my dues and now they have hit me on the head and cut my legs off," he said.

Also 1 July 1994
The logic of his lunacy
Why did Diego Maradona think he could cheat the drugs tests?
By Robert Philip

Diego Maradona knew he had but one last chance. One last chance to restore his tarnished reputation, to win his nation's complete forgiveness, to parade before us all the blessed talent which had made him the most brilliant footballer of his generation. For he was never just a player, he was an artist.

Sadly for the 1994 World Cup finals and tragically for Maradona himself, the many years of serious drug abuse had wrecked him both mentally and physically. No longer able to perform as he did in his dazzling youth, he had to resort to stimulants.

When he scored a typically spectacular goal against Greece in the final moments of Argentina's opening group match of USA '94 last Tuesday, the Argentinian ran towards the nearest TV camera and leered out at us like a crazy man.

As with the unforgettable image of Canadian sprinter Ben Johnson, the fastest cheat in history, crossing the 100 metres finishing line at the 1988 Seoul Olympics – arms raised in triumph, eyes glazed by anabolic steroids – the memory of Maradona's contorted features in his moment of apparent ecstacy, will forever come back to haunt us.

For in our understandable anxiety to restore this often-disgraced little idol to his former glories, we fondly chose to imagine he was running on adrenaline. It now appears likely he was flying on ephedrine.

As an aerosol used to relieve the symptoms of asthma and hay fever, ephedrine may not carry the same stigma as cocaine (the use of which brought Maradona a 15-month ban from football in 1991), but like Willie Johnston, who brought shame upon all Scotland when he was sent home for using a stimulant during the 1978 World Cup finals in Argentina, there can be no excuses and no pardon. He will now be ostracised from football for life.

While we may feel sorrow at a career wasted and fear for his personal future, there can be no sympathy for those such as Maradona: the icons who become pariahs.

We must also consider the possibility that Maradona's every moment of football sorcery – the mesmerising individual goals against England and Belgium at the 1986 World Cup in Mexico, the banana shots, bicycle kicks and boomerang crosses which were his trademark at Barcelona, Napoli and Seville – was achieved with the aid of chemical stimulants. The children who worshipped him will never know if these were the deeds of an athletic genius or of an unscrupulous fraud.

On Buenos Aires breakfast television yesterday, one visibly distressed news-reader finished the morning bulletin with the plaintive appeal: "Diego Armando Maradona . . . why, why, why?"

Why, just like Ben Johnson at the Seoul Olympics six years ago, did Maradona believe he was smart enough to fool the sophisticated drug-testing machinery which is now available to the organisers of every major sports event? Why, with a criminal record for cocaine use, did he attempt anything quite so stupid when he must have known the eyes of the world would be turned upon his every move on and off the pitch? Why did he risk what was left of his status when there was every possibility of detection?

In Boston last week, documentary film-maker Raul Santiago who visited the Argentinian training camp to record footage for his latest project, *The King of Football*, offered money as the main reason for Maradona's unexpected return to international football after the official announcement of his "retirement" in the summer of last year.

"He is like an old heavyweight boxer who has lost his title and wants it back. Maradona will be 34 soon and knows he is running out of time. He needs money badly, but the only place he can make the kind of money he is looking for is in the new Japanese football league. So far they have refused to touch him because of his cocaine record, but if he performs in this World Cup as he did in '86, he knows they just might have a change of mind."

For a man who has been the subject of transfer fees totalling more than $20m, Maradona has little to show for his 17 years in professional football; he has probably spent some of his fortune on cocaine, some of it on women (legend has it he once hired out the services of an entire Barcelona brothel for a night), and some of it on food, drink and hotel accommodation for the vast, leech-like entourage which accompanied him around the globe. The rest of it, to quote Groucho Marx, he has squandered.

Born in the Villa Fiorito slum of Buenos Aires, Maradona never learned to live with either the wealth or celebrity which followed his explosive arrival into international football in 1978 when, as a 17-year-old, he was hailed as the natural successor to Pele. But where the Brazilian made a conscious effort to maintain body and mind, not to mention his reputation as a sporting god, the Argentinian was dogged by a personal cloud of scandal wherever he went.

He left Napoli in disgrace after being tested positive for cocaine, he departed Seville amid similar controversy, and gained further notoriety for the infamous "Hand of God" goal against England at the '86 World Cup. Yet there were occasions, increasingly infrequent, when he came close to usurping Pele's position as the greatest player the world has ever seen.

And despite the cocaine abuse, despite the sexual peccadilloes, despite taking pot-shots with an air-rifle at particularly persistent journalists, there was always much to like about Maradona, for here was a boy emperor who never really wanted to grow up. In the foyer of the team hotel in Sydney last November, when Argentina was preparing for a World Cup play-off match against Australia, he threw a tantrum of a kind that any parent of a three-year-old would recognise. It had been prompted by manager Alfio Basile's refusal to allow him a night out at the circus.

And just last week, standing on the sands of Nantucket on Cape Cod following the game against Greece, Maradona ended a television interview with the mischievous observation that he was "very happy to be in America where they play football with their hands".

Speaking with apparent sincerity, Maradona, who has always coveted the affection bestowed upon Pele, had earlier voiced his remorse concerning previous misdemeanours. "Football gave me everything. It took a small child born into poverty and made him a king. Then they took away the king's crown and now he has very little."

He claimed to have spent the three months leading up to USA '94 with his personal fitness trainer at a "secret hideaway in the mountains, far away from the prying eyes of Buenos Aires", where he had shed 30 pounds. "I love football with all my heart and would give everything I have to turn back the clock. Only God can do that. My future rests in the hands of God."

We now know he was lying. His future lay in the hands of the nearest chemist.

Robert Maxwell

"I do not discount anything, absolutely anything.
I cannot say if he fell in or if he was thrown in."

5 November 1991
Maxwell is found dead in sea
Mystery of disappearance after early morning stroll on yacht
By Alastair Mccall, Anton La Guardia, Martin Newland and Clare Hargreaves

The body of the newspaper publisher, Mr Robert Maxwell, was recovered from the Atlantic last night after he was reported missing from his yacht, *Lady Ghislaine*, which had been cruising off the Canary Islands.

His naked body was identified on Gran Canaria by the ship's captain, Angus Rankin, and later by his wife, Betty, and his eldest son, Philip.

Mrs Maxwell, dressed in black, looked at her husband for a moment then stepped forward and said: "He's a colossus lying here, as he had been in life," according to Spanish Air Force officers.

Mr Maxwell, 68, disappeared between 4.30 a.m. and the yacht's arrival some five hours later in Los Christianos, on Tenerife, during which time it had covered around 60 miles.

Confusion surrounded initial details of Mr Maxwell's disappearance and last night it was still a mystery how he had fallen overboard from the 450-ton, 55-metre *Lady Ghislaine*. He was alone on the ship apart from its 11 crew.

"Right now, all the questions are unanswered," said Sr Angel Delgado, Tenerife's civil governor, who is co-ordinating the investigation.

News of Mr Maxwell's disappearance led to the suspension of trading in shares in his companies, Mirror Group Newspapers and Maxwell Communication Corporation, but not until after a period of hectic trading in them.

Lady Ghislaine moored at 9.45 a.m. yesterday but it was not until lunchtime that Mr Maxwell was reported missing by his crew.

The Los Christianos harbourmaster said: "*Lady Ghislaine* dropped anchor outside the harbour about 9 a.m. Around lunchtime, the captain told me they could not find Mr Maxwell.

"He said the crew realised around 11 a.m. that he had gone missing and said he must have gone overboard at sea, because nobody left the boat during the morning.

"The captain came with a translator and another member of the crew. They looked worried. I told my superiors and the search began very quickly."

A spokesman at the local station of the Guardia Civil said the captain and crew were being questioned.

Three helicopters and a fixed-wing plane were involved in the search for Mr Maxwell, which began at 2 p.m. local time. The search was complicated by the large distance the yacht had covered between the time when Mr Maxwell was last seen and its arrival in port.

A floating body was found by a Fokker aircraft at 5.46 p.m., 20 miles south-west of Maspalomas, the southern tip of Gran Canaria. It was winched on to a helicopter and taken to Gando airport, Las Palmas, on Gran Canaria.

An air force source there said that when the body was lifted from the sea it was naked.

He added: "We don't know if this man was clothed when he fell into the water. His clothes could easily have been washed off his body by the waves. The body showed signs of having been buffeted by fairly high seas."

A soldier who saw the body in the sea suggested that the cause of death may not be drowning. He said: "Normally one can assume that a body which is floating has not died by drowning. A body which has drowned would normally sink through having swallowed excessive amounts of water."

A post mortem examination is expected to be carried out today at the island's forensic institute. British embassy officials were flying from Madrid to the Canaries.

Mr Maxwell, 68, had been taking leave on *Lady Ghislaine* suffering from a heavy cold. He joined the vessel in Gibraltar on Sunday.

His break also followed a strenuous 10 days, in which he had been at the centre of allegations that he had links with Mossad, the Israeli intelligence agency. Mr Maxwell had dismissed the claims as "ludicrous".

Lady Ghislaine sailed for Madeira from Gibraltar and cruised around the Canaries over the weekend. On Monday night the ship was sailing around Tenerife before dropping anchor off Los Christianos.

Mr Bob Cole, Mr Maxwell's press officer, said he was last seen at 4.25 a.m. by a member of the crew, walking on deck. Ten minutes later he telephoned the bridge from his cabin and asked for the air conditioning to be turned down.

At 11 a.m. a business call to the ship from New York was transferred to Mr Maxwell's state room, according to Mr Cole. There was no reply and as a result the captain and a member of the crew went to his cabin, but found no trace of the newspaper proprietor. Four searches of the ship failed to reveal his whereabouts.

Mr Charles Wilson, Mirror Group editorial director, said that Mr Maxwell's walk on deck at 4.25 "was pretty normal" for him. "He was a light sleeper, often up and about throughout the night."

Reaction among Mirror Group employees 'has been one of deep shock', he said. "Mr Maxwell is the man who saved the *Daily Mirror*."

Mr Wilson said he could only assume that Mr Maxwell had slipped and fallen overboard. "His disappearance is simply a mystery," he said.

When asked about recent controversies surrounding the publisher, Mr Wilson said: "What normal people consider pressure was meat and drink to Robert Maxwell.

"His last conversation that I can find was with his son Ian, who spoke to him at 11 o'clock last night when they had a normal business and family conversation and he was in a perfectly good mood."

An hour earlier, Mr Maxwell had been involved in discussions to secure the release of treasured Jewish archives from the Lenin Library in Moscow.

Rabbi Feivish Vogel, director of Lubavitch UK, said they discussed the latest setback in attempts by the Chabad-Lubavitch movement to rescue 12,000 volumes and a number of ancient manuscripts. "I found him to be as robust and as helpful and positive in this last call as in all our other calls to him. There was no trace of anything," he said.

Mr Maxwell headed a publishing and printing organisation that reached across the world. Mirror Group employs 2,876 people, while the Maxwell Communication Corporation employs 14,360.

Even as news of his disappearance was being assimilated by his staff, moves were made to steady the companies' affairs, with an announcement that one of his sons Mr Ian Maxwell, 36, would be acting chairman of Mirror Group, and another, Mr Kevin Maxwell, 33, would occupy a similar position at Maxwell Communication.

Mr Kevin Maxwell said last night that his father had touched millions of lives and the family was determined to continue his tradition. "We are committed to continue in the path that Dad set. He was a maverick, an entrepreneur, and over more than 40 years he created a wonderful publishing business," he said.

"We are confident that our thousands of employees and our literally millions of readers will notice his passing. He was a giant."

Mr Ian Maxwell said it was a "sad day" not only for his family but for all those who worked for his father.

"As we stand here in the front entrance of Mirror Group Newspapers, a company which he acquired with great pride in 1984, it's a particularly sad moment because this paper has lost its publisher, and its chairman and its saviour," he said.

6 November 1991
"An attractive monster with a touch of genius"
The life, times and mythology of a tycoon
By Maurice Weaver

At a charity reception the Prince of Wales found himself talking to Robert Maxwell. The newspaper publisher's large head, wreathed in smiles that never reached the eyes, seemed to block out the rest of the gathering.

His voice, resonant as a growl in an empty cave, reverberated around a barrel chest. The charm was chilling. When Maxwell moved on the Prince turned to a Mirror Group editor and asked quietly: "Tell me – what is he really like to work for?"

The answer goes unrecorded. But the question spoke volumes enough.

Maxwell, the flamboyant entrepreneur, industrial gladiator, war hero, millionaire Labourite, immigrant turned would-be squire, was a figure who defied all the normal yardsticks by which people are assessed. Even a prince, it seems, could not quite get the measure of him.

Magnus Linklater, now editor of the *Scotsman*, was a Maxwell employee – for a few brief months as editor of the ill-fated *London Daily News*. He recalls a publisher with a low boredom threshold, an intolerance of sloth and foolishness, an actor's need for adulation and attention, a schoolboy's ability to bully.

"I got a telephone call in London at eight o'clock one morning. The voice said: 'Why aren't you here?' I asked where. 'Blackpool. Labour Party Conference. Get here by lunch.' Bang – the phone went down."

Linklater made it, just, and lunched with Maxwell and Neil Kinnock.

"Afterwards Maxwell took me to his hotel – he seemed to have taken an entire floor of the Imperial. As we walked in, a group of people who had been waiting in an ante-room stood up expectantly. He swept through, waved a hand and said: 'Later.' In the next room was a TV team. 'Later.' In the next a trade union deputation. 'Later.' Some had been there for hours, stacked up." It was ultimate tycoonery, nourishment for the hungriest of egos, symbolic of a man who never doubted that others would, and should, bow to his requirements.

Joe Haines, one-time Press officer for Harold Wilson and a Maxwell lieutenant for years, recalls in a biography of his boss what occurred when Maxwell, a poor delegator who always kept a finger on the minutiae of management, was asked to replace 10 senior managers' company cars. "Instead of authorising the purchase of the cars," says Haines in his biography of the man, "he asked whether all the managers were necessary, found out that they were not and abolished the jobs of six of them."

Maxwell mythology, born of such yarns that are told and retold in the canyons of Fleet Street and the City, expanded alongside the business empire and the physical girth of the emperor himself. They are the bricks that constituted an awesome and apparently indestructible human edifice.

Maxwell's intellect, his inner fires and his physical constitution were all exceptional.

For those who knew him, worked for him or were merely aware of his reputation, the very idea that such a phenomenon has ceased to exist remains hard to accept. Asked to describe Maxwell, Janet Hewlett-Davies, a one-time employee, once said: "He is an attractive monster with a touch of genius."

Stephen Clackson, news editor of the *London Evening Standard* and another former employee, recalls management conferences at the *Daily Mirror* embracing triumph, despair and sometimes the ruthless demolition of a wanting executive. "It was like Grand Opera," he says. Charles Wintour, former *Standard* editor and later editorial consultant to Maxwell at the *London Daily News*, remembers Maxwell's telling question in the back seat of a limousine en route to a business meeting. "Charles," he murmured, "what is our edge in these negotiations . . . ?" Those who seek to explain this hunger for success and power invariably go back to the cradle. Maxwell's was hewn from rustic wood. Born Jan Ludvig Hoch on 10 June 1923, one of the seven children of a poor Jewish agricultural worker in a primitive

Czech village, he experienced the early frustrations of a clever child baulked by poverty and a rudimentary education system.

His grandfather, Yaacov Schlomovitch, a local wheeler-dealer, was an early influence and by the time he was in his mid-teens young Hoch was selling trinkets in the street in Bratislava. He was there when the war, which was to shape his destiny, began.

At the age of 16 he joined the Czech resistance and tells the story of being captured and sentenced to death, escaping the firing squad only because of his youth. Soon after this he escaped his native country, never to see his parents again (his father was shot by the Germans, his mother died in Auschwitz) and made his way to join the British-run Czech Legion in France.

A knack for languages quickly gave him mastery of French and English and in 1941 he successfully volunteered to join the British Army, in the (now Royal) Pioneer Corps.

The Anglicisation of Jan Ludvig Hoch had begun. First, the name. He changed it to Ivan du Maurier (after his favourite brand of cigarettes).

Then to Leslie Jones. Then to Robert Maxwell. He switched to a county regiment, the 6th North Staffords. His energy and natural leadership abilities earned him promotion to corporal, sergeant and finally a commission. In January 1945, in Belgium, his bravery under fire won him the Military Cross – pinned on by Field Marshal Montgomery.

More promotion followed and the famous Cap'n Bob, to be satirised by the magazine *Private Eye*, was born.

He met his wife, Betty, the daughter of a French Protestant silk manufacturer, when she was working as a wartime interpreter in Paris. Both say it was "love at first sight". They would have nine children though two died – daughter, aged eight, from leukaemia and a son, aged 21, in a car crash.

When the war ended, the dashing Captain Robert Maxwell, MC, led his detachment in the victory parade through Berlin. He became head of the Foreign Office Press Section in Berlin – a crucial secondment which introduced him to the newspaper industry and to influential figures in European publishing. It set the pattern for his life. What would he do next? "I'm going to England," he told an Army friend, "to be a squire."

In fact, he went to London and launched a business career – import-export, buying and selling, bartering, polishing his English, mastering more languages (he spoke nine and associates speak in awe of his ability to switch in mid-breath from negotiating in Russian to haggling in German).

Gradually his activities focused on scientific publishing and in 1951 he borrowed £13,000 to buy a small, loss-making publishing company which he renamed Pergamon Press. It blossomed.

Encouraged by his success, Maxwell looked for other challenges. He found one in an ailing wholesale book company called Simpkin Marshall. He set about turning it into a central clearing house for books, borrowing heavily to finance new warehousing capable of holding 9 million volumes. Its subsequent financial collapse severely shook the publishing industry, which never fully forgave Maxwell. In another man it might have been professionally terminal; Maxwell turned his back on the wreckage and applied himself to Pergamon.

He went on to seek fame by standing for Parliament, holding Buckingham for Labour from 1964–70. His maiden speech on the day a new Parliament was opened in 1964 was long remembered for its flamboyance and length. "Let's just be thankful," quipped one MP, "'that he waited until the Queen sat down." The family moved to Headington Hill Hall, near Oxford, leased from Oxford City Council – "the finest council house in England", he joked.

Then it all seemed to fall apart. Found guilty of having tried to sell Pergamon to the American Leasco corporation by exaggerating its profitability, Maxwell was deemed by Board of Trade inspectors to be unfit "to exercise proper stewardship of a publicly quoted company". A less determined man might have been finished but, after a time in the wilderness, Maxwell clawed back, finding new challenges in the seventies and eighties in printing (the British Printing and Communications Corporation) and publishing (Mirror Group Newspapers, bought in 1984).

It was a tough union-dominated world to which the maverick style of the man now dubbed "the bouncing Czech" was well suited. Infuriated by a protracted strike at BPCC plant in West London he sent in a demolition squad and threatened to take the place apart. "These are the first negotiations I have attended with 14lb hammers as one of the bargaining points," protested John Mitchell, secretary of Sogat's militant London machine room branch. At the *Mirror* building in Holborn, Maxwell pursued the chapel fathers (shop stewards) to their basement conference room and, on finding the door locked, burst it open with his shoulder. It was not the way British management usually operated but it had its effect. There was always the enigma of the Socialist plutocrat. On the one hand was the entrepreneur who literally battered companies into profitability by shedding jobs, slashing costs and squeezing contractors till they squeaked – a man, moreover, who always ran his businesses through impenetrable overseas trusts.

On the other hand was the jolly fellow who sought popular admiration. By dabbling in the finances of soccer, a fad that passed, he not only satisfied a genuine love for the game but found a useful vehicle to present himself, bobble-hatted and scarf-wrapped, as a man of the people. His favourite mode of travel was by helicopter which he landed on his office roof. He had a chauffeur-driven Rolls and the ocean-going yacht, the *Lady Ghislaine* (named after a daughter) which was at the centre of yesterday's events. He was an inveterate "collector" of famous acquaintances and his table was as known for its VIP chatter as its gargantuan helpings. Biographies – some sympathetic, some hostile – were sprinkled with pictures of Maxwell hob-nobbing with the great and the good at home and abroad.

As a politician on the hustings his suave manner was a hit on many a doorstep; his early ownership of the *Mirror* saw him in macho shirt sleeves chatting chummily to machine minders; flying personally to famine-stricken Ethiopia to deliver the fruits of a reader appeal, he produced a moving display of high-profile concern.

His newspaper group was publicly floated this year. A year earlier he had launched the *European*, hailed as the first European national newspaper. It was a characteristically expansive move, a bid to exploit the perceived merging of national interests and identities, but the hoped-for circulation and advertising revenues have failed to materialise.

Maxwell always kept his private life low key. His seven surviving children, now adults, have all done well in business or the professions and two have joined their father's businesses. Ian, who as a young man was once fired by his father for failing to collect him from Orly airport in Paris, is acting chairman of Mirror Group Newspapers and Kevin is acting chairman of the Maxwell Communication Corporation. He is said to have asked both for their CVs and interviewed them at length before giving them the jobs. Both are widely respected as civilised managers.

Their father, once described as "a wild man from the mountains", was never accorded such a tribute. His was a bloody-knuckled battle to the peak. His business methods were frequently a subject of criticism and recently the object of a savaging by the BBC Panorama programme. Legal writs blew about him like confetti. Employees and former employees sometimes accused him of boorishness and unfair, even unethical, treatment.

In the United States, his last hunting ground, he seemed to revel in the more free-and-easy climate of an extrovert meritocracy. The man he most wanted to match, it is said, was Rupert Murdoch to whom he lost the battle to buy both the *News of the World* and *Today*, and whose global empire he coveted.

Certainly, he embraced the American culture with characteristic brio, exchanging the cloak of the English gentleman for the role of the back-slapping, cigar-chomping trans-Atlantic high roller. The Czech seemed to be bouncing all over again.

He exalted in the image of the "people's billionaire" who bought companies like most people did train tickets and rejoiced in the part of the newspaper magnate, phones and aides always at his elbow.

The flagship of his American acquisitions was New York's brash but ailing *Daily News*. It plastered Maxwell's picture, bullish in a baseball cap and grinning from ear to ear, across its front page above the bold headline: "Cap'n Bob Bites the Big Apple". But the American adventure was costly, incurring borrowing debts that put the international financial world on red alert.

Maxwell was in New York last month when the last controversy erupted around him. A prominent American investigative journalist, Seymour Hersh, published a book, *The Samson Option*, in which Maxwell and Nick Davies, foreign editor of the *Daily Mirror*, were said to have had connections with Israeli intelligence. The accusations were raised in the House of Commons by two MPs and brought outraged denials from the proprietor and his reporter.

Robert Maxwell's single-minded pursuit of power and monetary wealth made him many enemies. His dreams of acceptance by the establishment of his adopted country never materialised. Even in the entrepreneur-friendly ambience of the Thatcher-Major regimes his business reputation rendered him persona non grata. Lord Maxwell of Headington was unlikely to have donned ermine.

To the end the true ownership of his vast and byzantine business empire remained shrouded in mystery. While he put "Britain first" on the front page of the *Mirror*, the foundation which controlled his businesses remained based in the tax haven of Liechtenstein. The man who boasted "I am the proprietor – 100 per cent" when he marched into the *Mirror* building later claimed that a nominee of his wife's family controlled the foundation.

Given Liechtenstein's reputation for discretion even Maxwell's death may not unlock that secret.

8 November 1991
Family challenges official account of publisher's death
Did he fall into the sea after an accident or a heart attack?
Conflicting theories emerge
By Colin Randall in Tenerife

The family of Mr Robert Maxwell yesterday challenged the official Spanish account of his death by insisting that an accidental fall preceded his heart attack.

Mr Maxwell's widow, Betty, believes her 68-year-old husband fell from his favourite spot near the starboard stern of the main deck and that heart failure was caused either by the shock of the fall or a desperate struggle for survival in the water.

After a post-mortem examination in Gran Canaria on Wednesday, a judge reported that the preliminary findings indicated natural death before the fall into the sea.

The body was released to the family yesterday after embalming and preparations were made to load the 31-stone coffin on to the Maxwells' Gulfstream jet, but it was found to be too big.

Instead the family chartered a Challenger aircraft from Zurich, which was due to arrive in Las Palmas early today. Mrs Maxwell, her son Philip and daughter Ghislaine were then due to take off with the coffin en route for Jerusalem, where Mr Maxwell will be buried.

Mr Keith Hazell, British Consul in the Tenerife capital of Santa Cruz, said yesterday after speaking to Mrs Maxwell on board the yacht that the family was convinced that an "element of accident" as well as natural causes contributed to his death.

In an indication of the family's concern at the judge's findings, Mrs Maxwell asked Lt Col Alonso Gonzales, head of Tenerife's civil guards, to visit the publisher's motor yacht, the *Lady Ghislaine*, to hear her theory.

The family say that in the period immediately preceding his death, Mr Maxwell suffered "sensations of asphyxia" associated with acute pulmonary oedema, the lung condition from which he had suffered for several years.

He had been seen by crewmen stepping from his suite to take the air on the main deck several times during the night. His last known communication was a telephoned complaint to the bridge at 4.45 a.m. about the air conditioning.

At the Mencey Hotel, where Mr Maxwell dined alone on the eve of his death, restaurant staff recall seeing the publisher gasping for breath during his meal.

Mr Jercio Rodriguez Quimtana, the head waiter, said he remarked on Mr Maxwell's "agitated respiration" to a colleague but attributed it to the fact that he had consumed two beers in quick succession.

Mr Hazell said Mrs Maxwell was absolutely satisfied, as were the authorities, that foul play was not involved in her husband's death.

In the first public comment by members of the Maxwell family gathered in Tenerife, the publisher's daughter, Ghislaine, 29, appeared on the main deck of the yacht named after her to read a short prepared statement to journalists.

Dressed in a red tartan suit and white blouse, and wearing gold ear-rings shaped as cowboy boots, she spoke in a low voice, first in Spanish and then in English.

She said: "I want to take this opportunity to thank all the many hundreds of people who have sent messages of support to us at this very, very sad time."

Miss Maxwell also expressed gratitude to the press "for their courtesy and consideration to my mother and to us".

Asked about the events of Tuesday, she would say only: "All these things will be revealed." She then retreated inside the yacht without further comment.

Despite the preparations of Miss Maxwell, her mother and her eldest brother, Philip, to leave the yacht and fly to Israel for the funeral, the yacht is expected to remain in the Canary Islands.

But Mr Hazell said that with the conclusion of initial inquiries by the Spanish authorities, the vessel was no longer under any legal obligation to remain in Tenerife.

13 November 1991
Maxwell judge does not rule out murder or suicide
By Colin Randall in Tenerife

The Spanish judge investigating the death of Mr Robert Maxwell said last night that she had not ruled out murder or suicide.

Judge Isabel Oliva, working in candlelight during a power cut at her court house in the Tenerife town of Granadilla, said: "I do not discount anything, absolutely anything. I cannot say if he fell in or if he was thrown in."

But she made it clear there was '"nothing suspicious" concerning the 11-strong crew of Mr Maxwell's motor yacht, the *Lady Ghislaine*.

The judge has so far taken statements only from Captain Gus Rankin, 45, British master of the yacht, in addition to Mr Maxwell's widow, Betty, and his eldest son, Philip.

The other 10 crewmen – eight Britons, an American and a Dane – have made statements to Spanish police and will do the same before the judge today and tomorrow.

The crew were also questioned yesterday by insurance investigators from London. Mr Roger Rich and Mr Paul Cox, from Marine Associates Management, are making inquiries linked with £20m policies on the publisher's life. This follows the second post-mortem examination, carried out on the insurers' instructions, shortly before Sunday's funeral in Jerusalem.

Sen Julio Claverie, a Tenerife lawyer, representing the Maxwell family's interests in the Canaries, said Mrs Maxwell and Mr Philip Maxwell had given orders that the two men should receive full co-operation.

Judge Oliva hopes analysis of samples taken from Mr Maxwell's body, from vital organs to bone marrow, will be completed this week.

She said last night: "The preliminary results did not show anything. You cannot discount any possibility."

The judge said nothing in the initial post mortem report supported suggestions, attributed to Judge Luis Gutierrez on neighbouring Gran Canaria, that the publisher may have struggled for survival for up to four hours in the sea.

Earlier, a forensic scientist attached to the investigation had said there were "concrete suspicions" that death may not have been from natural causes.

Yesterday the mother of Miss Liza Kordalski, a hostess on the luxury yacht, said she had been quizzed by a man claiming to be working for Maxwell interests.

Speaking at her home in Cardigan, Dyfed, Mrs Marie Gregory, 56, said: "I've had one investigator round here already. He wanted to know everything about Liza and the family. He asked about any jobs she had before."

Her 29-year-old daughter was among the last to see Mr Maxwell alive. "Liza saw him just before lights out, about midnight. She'd looked after him all evening. The crew were upset they weren't up and about to save him."

A report yesterday told of a small yacht allegedly seen "shadowing" the *Lady Ghislaine* as she lay at anchor off Poris de Abona on the day before his death.

Bill Bond in Madrid writes: The Spanish Catholic daily *Ya* yesterday quoted one of three pathologists who took part in Mr Maxwell's first post-mortem examination as saying that they had been under a lot of pressure which had made their work difficult.

The newspaper quoted Dr Maria Jose Melian as saying that because of heavy outside pressures "we had to make known one or other cause of the death".

4 December 1991
Sons resign in Maxwell debt crisis
Mirror pension cash was switched
By Sonia Purnell

Two of Robert Maxwell's sons resigned from the board of Mirror Group Newspapers last night amid disclosures that "significant" assets of its pension fund had been lent or transferred to private companies controlled by their father.

The resignations came as huge debts threatened to push the publishing empire built up by Mr Maxwell to the brink of collapse.

Mr Ian Maxwell, MGN's chairman, and his brother, Kevin, stepped down from the board within hours of resigning as directors of Maxwell Communication Corporation.

Mr Kevin Maxwell announced his resignation as chairman of MCC at a meeting at which bankers were given details of the financial crisis.

In one of a series of developments that followed the death of Robert Maxwell at sea last month, dealings in shares of publicly quoted MCC and Mirror Group Newspapers were suspended on Monday. It is understood that checks made during the weekend uncovered a series of payments from MCC to Maxwell private interests during the summer.

The payments took the total of the private interests' liabilities from the previously estimated £800m to well over £1bn. One banker said the total could now be almost £1,500m.

This would mean almost certain bankruptcy for at least some of the privately owned Maxwell businesses. Part of the problem relates to shares owned by the MCC and *Mirror* pension funds and used to secure loans made to Maxwell private interests. It is thought that up to £200m has been pledged in this way.

Last night Mirror Group Newspapers said that Mr Ernest Burrington, who was appointed deputy chairman three years ago, and managing director last year, has taken over as chairman.

A statement said: "It has been reported to the board of MGN in recent days that a number of transactions have been carried out between private companies controlled by the late Robert Maxwell and both MGN and its pension fund.

"The precise amounts are still unclear but are of an order that is material to the MGN group. In particular, it has been reported to the board that a significant part of the assets of its pension fund were loaned under securities lending agreements or transferred to private companies controlled by the late Robert Maxwell, apparently without due authority.

"The extent of these assets is unclear. The board will use its best endeavours to ensure that MGN will maintain the benefits of all scheme members in service, deferred pensioners and current pensioners.

"The board is investigating fully all these transactions as a matter of urgency.

"Because of increasing conflicts of interest, Ian Maxwell, chairman and publisher of MGN, Kevin Maxwell and Michael Stoney, who has a major management involvement in the Maxwell private companies, have today resigned from the board of MGN and its subsidiaries and have also ceased their executive duties in the MGN group.

"Ernest Burrington has been appointed chairman and Alan Clements and Sir Robert Clark have been appointed joint deputy chairmen."

Shortly after his appointment as chairman, Mr Burrington, former editor of the *People*, said: "Mirror Group is a great newspaper organisation with a sound track record. It will survive this crisis.

"It surely will continue, and the board has every confidence we will overcome our current difficulties."

At yesterday's meeting with Mr Kevin Maxwell, the banks agreed to leave their loans to the private companies in place until Friday.

The Maxwells told them they had found a "white knight" – an external but friendly investor – to make a substantial cash injection.

It is understood the investor is interested in the family's 51 per cent stake in the Mirror Group and 68 per cent stake in MCC, which owns the American publishers Macmillan. Few details of a proposed deal were given to the bankers who are expecting more on Friday.

Mr Richard Stone, of the accountants Coopers & Lybrand Deloitte, and an adviser to the banks, said: "I can only say the banks have held their position until Friday while the company and its management firm up on their proposals."

If the bankers are not satisfied with the Maxwells' proposals, they are likely to call in the receivers.

Mr Kevin Maxwell said: "When or if the private interests were to have their bank support withdrawn, then the public companies will need to look at provisions or write-offs relating to the inter-company debt."

He was satisfied that all the transactions between the Maxwell private and public companies had been authorised and recorded properly. But he added: "My brother and I were board colleagues with my father for many years. But clearly we didn't know everything that was going on and my father had a style of business based on 'need to know'."

After his meeting with the bankers, Mr Maxwell said that his departure from the MCC board was in the best interests of shareholders and employees as it would avoid "increasing conflicts of interest".

He said: "The board and shareholders must not think that any inquiries into the company's affairs will be impeded by my obvious loyalty to my father.

"Most families have a strong sense of loyalty and our family equally shares that.

"It is a question of not wanting personalities and emotions to get in the way.

"These inquiries are looking at the relationship between the private companies and public corporations.

"It is not appropriate to have a seat on the board at the present time but I hope to be back."

Mr Maxwell denied that he had resigned under pressure from bankers to his family's public and private interests.

The new chairman of MCC is Mr Peter Laister, former chairman of Thorn-EMI.

Mr Laister was appointed MCC deputy chairman a couple of months ago and has been on the board since 1985. Mr David Shaffer, president of Macmillan, becomes group managing director.

It is understood that Price Waterhouse will today be appointed as investigating accountants to examine the affairs of MCC.

Speaking from America yesterday Mr Shaffer, 48, said that MCC's long-delayed results, and the decision on whether to pay a dividend, would be announced within a week.

Mr Maxwell referred to the debate on whether MCC should pay a dividend as "a classic example of where there could be a conflict on interest". Paying a dividend would obviously help the Maxwell family's finances, but many analysts argue that the company cannot and should not pay one.

Talking of his attitude to assets, Mr Kevin Maxwell said: "There are no sacred cows. Where you need your bankers to agree to a standstill, you can't impose your wishes on them but put forward responsible proposals.

"We consider the European and the *New York Daily News* first-class newspapers with first-class prospects. We've put forward a business proposal but we're not being emotional about this or, by definition, our stake in Mirror Group Newspapers.'

5 December 1991
Yes, he was a crook
Robert Maxwell has now been revealed as a fraudster on a massive scale.
How he bullied his way to a multi-million pound swindle
By Neil Collins

There is no longer any point in pretending. Robert Maxwell was a fraudster on a grand scale, who used the formidable array of weapons of the British legal system to prevent anyone revealing the truth while he was alive. Those who tangled with him often regretted it, while many more decided not to, because the time and cost of engaging his battery of lawyers was too much for them.

As his legacy unwinds this week, the liabilities of his private companies appear to be more than £1,500m, nearly twice the first estimate, and far more than the most optimistic valuation of the assets. It is becoming clear that, in the classic mould of fraudsters, Maxwell was unworried by any need to tell the truth, and could see no distinction between things that belonged to him and those which belonged to others.

As a result, he defrauded shareholders, creditors and pension beneficiaries on a grand scale over a quarter of a century. Far from being an eccentric, larger-than-life figure of fun who perhaps cut a few corners but achieved much, he has left a trail of misery among the thousands on whom he trampled, and the real cost of his perfidy will be measured in hundreds of millions of pounds lost by creditors, shareholders and pensioners.

Indeed, it now looks as though Owen Stable, QC, and Sir Ronald Leach were rather restrained in their famous conclusion that Maxwell "is not in our opinion a person who can be relied on to exercise proper stewardship of a public company". At the very least, their investigation into Pergamon Press in 1971 for the Department of Trade is vindicated.

It is probable that the origins of the fraud go back many years, but only this year did it become so massive and blatant as to be impossible to ignore. We know now that Maxwell's troubles were far worse than anything he had previously faced, and that the net was rapidly closing. Even if he did not commit suicide, he had every motive to do so. Despite his legendary ability to bluff and bluster, escape from financial disaster this time was surely impossible.

Two major frauds committed this year have come to light: the transfer of shares which were not in Maxwell's power to move, and the switch of cash from the accounts of the public companies into those of his private interests.

The shares were "borrowed" from Maxwell's quoted investment trust, First Tokyo Indexed, and from the pension funds of his public companies, Maxwell Communications Corporation and Mirror Group Newspapers. The Mirror Group fund appears to have suffered most. On some estimates its pension fund is worth £400m less than it ought to be – a truly shocking figure, considering that the whole fund was supposedly worth £530m in May.

All three funds are essentially collections of shares, most of which are bought and stored away, often for many years. Lending such shares, for a fee, is an accepted, indeed, essential, part of City practice. Stock lending enables market-makers to sell and deliver shares they do not own, and thus maintain a two-way market.

But the stock lender is supposed to be taking a market risk – if he has lent the stock he cannot sell it himself – not a credit risk. The stock lender should have complete confidence that he can get the stock back. In all three funds here, it looks as though huge amounts of shares had been replaced with what was little more than IOUs from the Maxwell private companies. Many of the shares "borrowed" were sold by Maxwell, and the proceeds used either to pay off private debt or to buy shares in Maxwell Communications, a company which by the end of the week is likely to be worthless. Either way, the IOUs look like bad debts.

Pension funds are supposed to be set up in such a way as to prevent this happening, with separate fund managers and trustees. In this case, both functions were effectively captives of the organisation and with one man in charge of all aspects – Robert Maxwell.

His dominance of his empire was such that no lowly employee in the pensions office would have dared question his master's voice.

Similarly, it seems that Maxwell did not trouble himself with any distinction between his money and that of his companies. It would have been simplicity itself for him to order employees to switch money between obscure accounts, without troubling to say whether the recipient account belonged to Maxwell or Maxwell Communications.

Those investigating say that money belonging to both Maxwell Communications and the Mirror Group appears to have been switched this way, a particularly alarming development for those who have assumed that the *Mirror's* assets were 'ring-fenced' from Maxwell. As a result, there is now a question mark over the true value of the *Mirror* shares, which had risen strongly since Maxwell's death on hopes of a takeover, until Monday's suspension.

None of this was suspected by the bankers from N. M. Rothschild and Bankers Trust when they started detailed work on the private companies last Monday week. They thought the liabilities totalled around £800m, and were confident that the assets, including majority shareholdings in both public companies, were worth more than that. As they worked through, they were shocked at what they found.

By Sunday night they had uncovered enough financial horrors to justify asking for the share quotations to be suspended. By Monday, it was clear that Kevin and Ian Maxwell would have to resign to avoid the conflict of interest between private and public interests that their father had so blithely ignored. By yesterday the Serious Fraud Office was in. Last night the bankers were still adding up the private company liabilities, but indicate that the total has passed £1,500m.

Collectively, the companies which represent the Maxwell family are spectacularly bankrupt.

As Maxwell's empire has imploded this week, there has been a constant chorus of "we always suspected something was wrong" from employees, analysts and observers. Many had found out the hard way that Maxwell was an expensive man to cross for those who played by the rules.

He, of course, did not. Any employee with the courage to question the reign of terror or the great man's judgment risked dismissal. City analysts fared no better. Derek Terrington, a media analyst then at stockbrokers UBS Phillips & Drew, wrote a circular on the flotation of Mirror Group Newspapers last May. The price, described by Maxwell as a bargain even a one-eyed Albanian could see, was 125p, but Terrington's circular was headed "Can't Recommend a Purchase". Terrington was right, and the price collapsed immediately, but the acronym had incensed Maxwell, who forced UBS to withdraw the circular, and Terrington has since left the firm.

Inside the Maxwell publishing empire, it is the semblance of business as usual. This week, while the world was collapsing around them, the managers of Maxwell Business Communications, a Maxwell Communications subsidiary, were announcing the purchase, for £200,000, of Communications News. In a press release, Tony Doyle of MBC said the purchase marked 'a new aggressive development phase' for the company.

As one ex-employee remarked: "It always was like Alice in Wonderland working for Maxwell. Now they seem to have stepped through the looking glass completely."

The Metropolitan Police

"You were all part of an evil conspiracy which at times converted the
Obscene Publications Squad into a vast protection racket."

29 February 1976
Ex-Yard chiefs on corruption charges
12 arrested
By Peter Gladstone Smith

Eight former Scotland Yard detectives and four serving detectives were arrested
yesterday and charged with conspiring corruptly to receive money and other considerations. This was the outcome of a three-year inquiry into allegations of bribery and
corruption over sales of pornography in Soho.

Among those charged were ex-Cdr Kenneth Drury, 55, former head of the Flying
Squad, and ex-Cdr Wallace Virgo, 58, former head of the Murder Squad. Most of
the arrests were made shortly after dawn at the homes of the detectives in the Home
Counties and Hereford.

They were carried out by a squad of 24 Yard detectives under Deputy Assistant
Commissioner Gilbert Kelland, who headed the inquiry ordered by Sir Robert Mark
after he became Commissioner four years ago.

Mr Drury left his home in Bexley Lane, Sidcup, Kent, with a paper bag over his
head and was taken into Cannon Row police station covered in a grey blanket.

With two others Mr Drury was charged with conspiring corruptly to receive money
and other considerations from James William Humphreys, former Soho strip club owner.

Humphreys, 45, is serving an eight-year prison sentence for an attack on his wife's
lover. He was described by a judge as "the emperor of pornography".

Mr Drury retired on full pension in May 1972, when he faced a disciplinary
inquiry over a holiday in Cyprus with Humphreys. The inquiry did not find him
involved in any serious offences over the holiday but dealt with minor disciplinary
matters, including unauthorised statements to the Press.

The remaining nine men are charged with conspiring corruptly to receive money
and other considerations from persons trading in pornography.

One of them, ex-Cdr Wallace ("Wally") Virgo, had overall charge of the Obscene
Publications Squad at Scotland Yard for a period. When he retired in March 1973,
he was the Metropolitan Police's longest-serving CID officer, having joined the force
in February 1937. He served in the Irish Guards and was awarded the Queen's Police
Medal and the Good Conduct Medal.

Another former Murder Squad detective accused was ex-Det. Chief Supt William
("Bill") Moody, 50. He retired on health grounds in July 1974.

In 1970 Mr Moody headed an investigation into allegations of bribery and corruption against a detective inspector and a detective sergeant. The two detectives
were convicted and sentenced to terms of imprisonment.

Three former operational chiefs of the Obscene Publications Squad are among
those charged.

One is Ex-Det. Chief Insp. George Fenwick, 46, also formerly head of No. 9 Regional Crime Squad. He retired in February last year after more than 20 years' service

The others are Det. Insp. Clive Alan Miles, 41, who was suspended from duty last May, and ex-Det. Insp. Leslie Frank Alton, 47, who retired in August 1974.

Another senior member of the squad charged is Det. Insp. Charles O'Hanlon, 38, who later served with the Drugs Squad. He was suspended in May 1974.

Two of the former detectives accused were away from their homes when the Yard squads called. They walked into Scotland Yard at noon accompanied by their solicitors and were taken to Cannon Row. Most of the accused arrived in cars at Cannon Row direct from their homes. They were charged and released on police bail to appear at Bow Street tomorrow.

A statement issued by Scotland Yard after the arrests said they were authorised by Sir Norman Skelhorn, Director of Public Prosecutions, after obtaining the fiat of Mr Samuel Silkin, Attorney-General.

Some of the charges cover alleged corruption over a period of nearly 14 years.

The charges were: Between 1 January 1960 and 31 December 1974, conspiring corruptly to receive money and other considerations from persons trading in pornography: Ex-Cdr Wallace Virgo, 58, of Horse Lane Orchard, Ledbury, Hereford; Ex-Det. Chief Supt William Moody, 50, of Ellesmere Road, Weybridge, Surrey; Ex-Det. Insp. Leslie Frank Alton, 47, of Harefield Avenue, Cheam. Surrey; and Ex-Det. Con. Bernard Peter Brown, 43, publican. Coldharbour, Dorking, Surrey.

The same charge between 1 January 1969, and 31 December 1974; Det. Insp. Charles Edward O'Hanlon, 38, of Milner Drive, Sandy Lane, Cobham, Surrey; Det. Insp. Clive Alan Miles, 41, of Homefield Road, Radlett, Herts; Ex-Det. Chief Insp. George Edward Fenwick, 46, of Arundel Avenue, East Ewell, Surrey; Ex-Det. Con. Michael Leonard Chamberlain, 33, of Victoria Gardens, Biggin Hill, Kent; and Det. Insp. David Cyril Jones, 41, of Sunna Gardens, Sunbury-on-Thames.

Between 1 January 1970 and 31 December 1972, conspiring corruptly to receive money and other considerations from James William Humphreys: Ex-Cdr Kenneth Ronald Drury, 55, of Bexley-Lane, Sidcup, Kent; Ex-Det. Insp. Alistair David Ingram, 42, of Avondale Avenue, Hinchley Wood, Esher, Surrey; and Det. Insp. John Bryan Legge, 36, of Minster Drive, Croydon, Surrey.

1 March 1977
Porn Squad Chief "Got £60,000 Bribes"

Wallace Harold Virgo, 50, former Commander of the Metropolitan Police and holder of the Queen's Medal, received £60,000 in porn bribes and was one of six officers in the Obscene Publications Squad involved in a "deplorable web of corruption", an Old Bailey Court was told yesterday.

Mr David Tudor Price, prosecuting, alleged: "It was his reward for allowing the trade in pornography to flourish in the West End of London."

The six former officers are variously charged in a total of 27 counts of bribery and corruption involving £87,485 from pornography dealers.

Alfred William Moody, 50, a former Detective Chief Supt who retired in 1974, was the "principal architect of this criminal behaviour", said Mr Tudor Price.

The accused are: Virgo, of Ledbury, Hereford, who retired in March 1973; Moody, of Ellesmere Road, Weybridge, Surrey and Leslie Frank Alton, 47, former Det. Insp. of Harefield Avenue, Cheam, Surrey, who retired in August 1974; Bernard Peter Brown, 43, former Det. Con., who retired in November 1972, now a licensee of the Plough Inn, Coldharbour, Dorking; David Gareth Hamer, 34, a Det. Sgt of Courtwood Lane, Addington, Surrey, who is suspended from duty; and Rodney Lawrence Tilly, 45, a retired Det. Sgt, of Edelsborough, Bucks, now licensee of the Rule and Square public house.

They plead not guilty that between 1 January 1964 and 24 October 1972 they conspired together and with others to accept money and other considerations from pornographic traders as inducements for showing favour.

Mr Tudor Price told the jury that each of the accused was attached to the Obscene Publications Squad, and it had been their duty to seek out and expose operations in the porn trade.

"The offences show, unfortunately, that for many years members of the Squad, including these defendants, were doing exactly the reverse.

"They were protecting known pornographers, deliberately promoting them. In the nine years from 1964 to 1972 it was Moody who was the principal architect."

During that period, said Mr Tudor Price, Moody had risen from Det. Sgt to the "exalted rank of Detective Chief Supt". Moody had not started the activities and it began some time before he came on the scene, but it was "then organised in a way it was never organised before".

Virgo was in the Squad in 1964 to 1966. After further service in other parts of the force he returned in 1970 to the West End with the very high rank of Commander of the Metropolitan Police.

Mr Tudor Price: "He could, if he had chosen to do so, have stamped out the evil and corruption and exposed it. The Crown say that on the contrary he did the opposite and joined it and took for himself payments of an unprecedented size in the years he was responsible for the Squad, and as Commander of the Police and holder of the Police Medal, the highest award for police service, he received a total sum of £60,000."

Mr Tudor Price said that during the period of the conspiracy no shop could open in the West End to sell obscene books unless it purchased a licence.

Proprietors who paid their "licence" and the regular payments that followed were allowed to trade unhindered and were actively helped to do so by warnings of impending raids.

"If prosecution was instituted, the real owner's identity was protected and he was allowed to put up a substitute – someone else would go to court in disguise and would be fined.

"And, in some instances, pornography seized from traders was actually sold back at half the normal market price."

Mr Tudor Price added: Quite apart from the cash payments, these officers had entertainment lavished upon them. They were able, during their service in the squad, to enjoy a lifestyle a great deal beyond their own means."

Matters came to light in the middle of 1972 after a Sunday newspaper published a general exposé of the porn scene and made specific allegation of police corruption.

Early in 1972 a man called James Humphreys who was actively engaged in the trade from the end of 1969 onwards, went on holiday overseas with a senior police officer who was in no way concerned with this case.

This matter was the subject of Press comment and publicity and inquiries started. In November 1972, a senior uniform branch officer took over responsibility for the Obscene Publications Squad and the CID was phased out.

Early in 1973 two diaries belonging to Humphreys came into police possession. "These diaries gave rise to still further inquiries and as a result a senior police officer began an inquiry into the whole matter which resulted in the present proceedings."

Mr Tudor Price told the court that Mr Ronald Mason, 59, a "leading pornographer" would give evidence. He added: "He was only able to operate, and grow rich, through the assistance of corrupt officers."

The case was adjourned until today.

3 March 1977
Yard chief "went to sulk in lavatory until he got £50 bribe"
By C. A. Coughlin

Ex-Commander Wallace Virgo, 58, holder of the Queen's Police Medal, who, it is claimed, was paid £2,000 a month in bribes, sat in a lavatory sulking when he wasn't given an extra £50 "for a drink", the Porn Squad bribes trial was told yesterday.

"He told me I had to respect his position," former strip club owner James William Humphreys, 48, told the jury at the Old Bailey. "I know it sounds nonsense, but it really is true," he added.

The previous week he had paid Virgo £2,000, Humphreys claimed.

He said the incident happened in a restaurant where he was lending another officer £300. He had to borrow £50 back because Virgo who was also there, went and sulked in the lavatory.

"He expected me to follow him and give him £50."

Soho pornographer Mr Ronald Eric Mason, 59, told the trial of the favours he enjoyed for the alleged payment of bribes to officers of the Obscene Publications Squad.

Mr Mason said his original payments from the early 1960s were £175 a month. When he met Virgo and another accused, ex-Det. Chief Supt Alfred William Moody, the sums increased by £50 a month – "because the guvnor had to be taken care of".

Over the years the money went up from £225 a month to £300, to £400, to £600 and ultimately to £1,000 a month by 1967–68. He made the payments every month to Moody.

Mr Mason said that in return "we were given a warning of an impending raid so that the amount of stock would be depleted. And 'the chairman' would be looked after to the best of the officer's ability in the sense that if it was possible you could go missing instead of being prosecuted.

"It would be impossible to find him and if necessary he would be allowed to change his name and continue as chairman in the same shop or on many occasions in another shop.

"We had a system by which notice of an impending raid would be given by telephone by use of the phrase 'W. H. Smith', which would indicate that the shop should be cleared of hard porn and dressed as near as possible to look like W. H. Smith."

Mr Mason had explained to the jury that "the chairman" was the name of the person on the leases of his shops. It could well be the name of any barrow boy in Berwick Street market who had no active connection with the shop, but would merely lend his name to the lease for a weekly salary.

In the dock are Virgo, of Ledbury, Hereford; Moody, 50, of Ellesmere Road, Weybridge, Surrey; ex-Det. Inspector Leslie Alton, 47, of Harefield Avenue, Cheam; former Det. Con. Bernard Brown, 43, licensee of the Plough Inn, Coldharbour, Dorking; Det. Sgt. David Harmer, 34, of Courtwood Lane, Addington, Surrey; and ex-Det. Sgt. Rodney Tilley, licensee of the Rule and Square, Edelsborough.

They all plead not guilty to conspiring together between 1 January 1 1964 and October 1972 and with others to accept money and other considerations from dealers as inducements to show favour.

The jury have been told that Virgo received a total of £60,000 in bribes.

Humphreys, 48, now serving an eight year prison sentence, admitted under cross-examination by Mr Robin Simpson, QC, defending Moody, that since his arrest in Amsterdam in 1973, he had made a "very great many" allegations against police officers apart from those in the dock.

He had done so after his Old Bailey trial in 1974 which had resulted in his eight year sentence. He had complained about 42 police officers in all.

Questioned by Mr Donald Farquharson, QC, for Virgo, Humphreys said he had heard of Ronald Mason, but did not know him. He agreed that at one time he and Mason were two principal merchants in the pornographic book trade. Humphreys agreed he got £500 a week from two strip clubs he had run for 12 to 14 years. He could not assess how much he made from his wholesale trade in international pornography. He had not been involved in running brothels.

Humphreys said he had a house in Greek Street Soho, in partnership. They rented the flats to some Maltese who put prostitutes in them. When it was suggested that his wife Rusty had been convicted of brothel-keeping in respect of the Greek Street address, Humphreys said: "She had nothing to do with it whatsoever but the building was in her name."

He agreed his business turnover must have been enormous and estimated his income about £100,000 a year. No proper books were kept.

Mr Farquharson. May I take it you made false tax returns? – No.

But did they record your income? – No.

Humphreys agreed that he had a large empire to protect.

Counsel: And as all your activities were criminal, or on the border line of crime, you came into contact with the police? – My activities were anti-social, not criminal, and I came into contact with the police every day.

Mr Farquharson: If you wanted to protect these enormous interests that yielded such enormous benefits to you there were two courses open to you. You could either corrupt the police if they were dishonest or falsely accuse them of corruption if they were not?

Humphreys: I do not agree with that. I agree with the first but of the second part I could not accuse them of corruption and still run the business.

Humphreys, asked whether at any time he had made conditions about the basis on which he would give evidence in the trial, said he had asked for an inquiry into the case for which he was jailed for eight years. This was the only condition he made and he understood the Home Secretary had granted that.

Counsel: Are you saying it was a condition of your giving evidence that there should be an inquiry into your case? – No, I was just given an assurance that the Home Secretary was looking into my case.

If you had not had that assurance would you have given evidence in this case? – I don't think I would have done, no.

Questioned about his payments to Virgo, Humphreys said he had paid him £2,000 a month and £2,000 extra each Christmas. They began in 1970.

He agreed that these allegations against Virgo rested solely upon his word. There were no notes or documents to support it.

The trial was adjourned until today.

6 March 1977
Porn kings and the "professionals"
By Ronald Payne

The most remarkable sight in Number 1 Court at the Old Bailey last week was the box wherein sat the accused.

It was entirely peopled by Scotland Yard detectives. The six, all denying that they corruptly received money for favours to pornographers, arranged themselves in order of seniority, with the grave figure of Commander Virgo, retired, on the right of the line, and the most junior on the left.

Serious and composed police officers in dark suits, some wearing glasses to help cope with the massive documentation, they followed the case dispassionately, like the professionals they are. All are veterans of many appearances in court in the course of their police work.

But a further remarkable feature of this trial, expected to last eight weeks, is that if the accused are professionals, the first witnesses for the prosecution appeared hardly less so.

Both James Humphreys and Ronald Mason were described early on as the two most important merchants of pornography in London. Humphreys is actually serving an eight-year sentence for wounding. Both he and his fellow accuser of the police have long experience of the courts and their protocol.

They also claim to be friends and acquaintances of police officers and have absorbed something of a police manner of giving evidence. Their testimony contained all those polite "Yes, sir", "No, sir" and "With respect, sir", phrases so familiar in official witnesses.

Mr David Tudor Price, for the prosecution, accused Commander Wallace Virgo of taking nearly £60,000 in bribes. He and the five other accused were, in the melodramatic words of prosecuting counsel, "part of an evil web of corruption".

The sums of money mentioned were dazzling. Bundles of notes were handed out to Detective Superintendent William Moody at a rate of £2,000 a month, with a bonus of another £2,000 at Christmas, claimed the prosecution.

Complicated rendezvous were arranged so that members of the Obscene Publications Squad might receive and share out the takings. They were being paid not to take action which they ought to have taken to stamp out pornographic sales.

Both the pornographers spoke in the witness box, in their semi-official manner, of getting "licences", that is to say, highly unofficial licence to sell their wares undisturbed by the law.

Indeed it came to the point where Mr Justice Mars-Jones found it necessary to remind the jury that the word licence was being used in rather an unusual sense in this court.

If the box of accused was full, the benches which accommodate the defence barristers were packed as a football terrace. For each of the six police officers is represented by a counsel and juniors.

For this reason they had to sit respectfully, though appraisingly, listening to the questions of their fellow lawyers while waiting for an opportunity to cross-question the two main witnesses of the week in the interests of their own client. And when the questioning began in earnest, there emerged a growing body of information about the rise of the porn trade from the early fifties onward.

The activities of the principal purveyors produced an unedifying picture of London life in which fortunes could be made from small shops in Soho which provided hard and soft porn (at first, under the counter).

Ronald Mason, who describes himself as a 59-year-old retired businessman living in Guernsey, was particularly revealing in his attitudes. He stoutly condemned as "degrading and filthy", certain pictures of sexual activities appearing in the current number of a magazine on general sale. This magazine, he said disapprovingly, had a circulation of a quarter of a million.

He recalled that one of his employees called Vinn had been sent to prison in the old days for selling copies of *Lady Chatterley's Lover*, "which W. H. Smith now sells openly". Counsel had to agree that that was most unfortunate.

The remarkable Mr Mason told Mr Donald Farquharson, Q.C., that he found it hard to draw a line between hard and soft porn. At this point the Judge reasonably pointed out that such questions about his views on definitions were hardly the affair of a court considering police corruption.

But Mr Mason reported that the sellers in Soho had their scruples, and that he had refused to handle books about juvenile sex and had only started in blue movies late in the sixties.

"Pornography is no longer anti-social because it has been accepted by society," he roundly declared. And although it may seem that such comments are far removed from consideration of whether a group of senior police officers did, or did not, receive bribes, such factors are important, for they reveal the moral climate out of which the charges developed.

Crisply proceeding through the evidence Mr Justice Mars-Jones surveyed the scene through his half-moon glasses, quizzically looking as though nothing could surprise him. He listened at length to the sociological revelations of James Humphreys, the first witness.

His hair curly, his suit suitably smart, Mr Humphreys showed little reluctance to talk about the money he made selling dirty magazines and offering the facilities of strip clubs and sex boutiques. He lived in style in an international porn world of frequent travel and contact with such unlikely characters as Frank the Scan (meaning, of course, Scandinavian) and Charlie the Fat from Miami.

From his international connections Humphreys made money to live like a king. In one year he bought three Rolls-Royces, not to mention a Mercedes for his wife Rusty; he owned a yacht, a villa on Ibiza and a farm in Kent.

Mr Humphreys, though giving an impression that he was pleased with his business success, said that he did not keep books. Even so, he agreed that he had an income of about £100,000 a year, though his tax returns did not record that income in detail. "I can't give a figure," he affirmed.

This large financial empire based on pornography and so ill recorded in business detail did need to be protected, admitted Mr Humphreys under questioning. He looked hurt at the suggestion that his activities were either criminal or on the borders of crime.

"My activities were anti-social," he declared.

The prosecution asserts that in the cause of protecting his interests he paid out £60,000 in bribes. The money, Humphreys said, came from the profits of his shops, which amounted to some £216,000 in three years.

Mr Mason told of payments to police officers of up to £1,000 a month. But be was less forthcoming about the amount of money he made from the sale of what he described as "filth".

Consorting happily with police officers, by his own account in court, Mr Mason said he had been given a C.I.D. tie to wear. This was to enable him to visit a collection of porn seized in police raids so that he could purchase it for up to £500 at reduced rates.

Towards the end of his evidence he remarked that there were many ways of telling a story. "With that, Mr Mason, I would most respectfully agree," said Mr Simpson, Q.C.

Not a word has yet been spoken by the Scotland Yard six, busy making notes in the box. As the jury left court for the weekend they must have been wondering what lay in store when the long court reassembles at the Old Bailey tomorrow.

12 May 1977
Ex-Porn Squad chief guilty of taking bribes
By C. A. Coughlin

Ex-Commander Wallace Virgo, of the Metropolitan Police, holder of the Queen's Police Medal and 25 commendations, was found guilty at the Old Bailey yesterday of accepting bribes totalling £2,050 from Soho pornographer James Humphreys.

Virgo, 59, of Walled Garden, Horse Lane Orchard, Ledbury, Herefordshire, was the commander in charge of the CI Department at Scotland Yard, which included control of the Obscene Publications Squad.

He was acquitted on two other charges of corruption relating to Humphreys and is awaiting verdicts on two more charges including the main conspiracy count.

Another senior officer ex-Det. Chief Supt Alfred William Moody, 51, of Ellesmere Road, Weybridge, Surrey, was found guilty of corruptly accepting bribes of £14,575 from Ronald Eric Mason, 59, another Soho pornographer.

He was acquitted of corruptly accepting £200 from a man named Ivor Cook.

These verdicts returned by the jury on the 47th day of the trial, were unanimous. They have many more counts to consider against other detectives connected with the Obscene Publications Squad.

They spent their second night at a secret London hotel and will resume their deliberations today.

The other accused are ex-Det. Insp. Leslie Frank Alton, 47, of Harefield Ave., Cheam; ex-Det. Con. Bernard Peter Brown, 43, of the Plough Inn, Coldharbour, Dorking; Det. Sgt David Gareth Hamer, 34, of Courtwood Lane, Addington, Surrey; and ex-Det. Sgt Rodney Lawrence Tilley, 45, of the Rule and Square public house, Edelsborough, Bucks.

All except Tilley deny conspiring together and with others corruptly to accept money from pornographic traders and individually they variously deny accepting specific sums.

14 May 1977
Top Yard men in porn racket get 12 years
By C. A. Coughlin

Two senior Scotland Yard detectives who controlled an "evil conspiracy which turned the Obscene Publications Squad into a vast protection racket" were each jailed for 12 years at the Old Bailey yesterday.

Four other detectives in the plot received jail terms ranging from 10 years to three years from Mr Justice Mars-Jones, who estimated that at least £100,000 a year had been paid in bribes to porn squad officers.

The two men sentenced to years were ex-Commander Wallace Harold Virgo, 59, holder of the highest award for police service, the Queen's Police Medal, and with 25 commendations, and ex-Dept. Chief Supt Alfred William Moody, 51, who has been commended 19 times.

The judge ordered Virgo to pay up to £15,000 towards his defence costs and Moody up to £10,000.

Also sentenced to jail were ex-Det. Insp. Leslie Frank Alton, 49, 10 years and ordered to pay up to £5,000 defence costs; ex-Det. Con. Bernard Peter Brown, 43, for seven years; Det. Sgt David Gareth Lee Hamer, 54, for four years; and ex-Det. Insp. Rodney Lawrence Tilley, 46, for three years.

Virgo last night instructed his solicitor to appeal against sentence and conviction.

Mr Justice Mars-Jones told the six detectives: "Thanks to the diligence and persistent inquiries of honest police officers you have been finally brought to book.

"You were all part of an evil conspiracy which at times converted the Obscene Publications Squad into a vast protection racket.

"It became an organisation for the collection and distribution of bribes from law breakers in return for immunity from prosecution, or wholesale interference with the due process of law if a prosecution could not be avoided.

"All this was done on a scale which beggars description.

"I need hardly tell you that the offences on which you have been convicted are among the most serious that any police officer can commit.

"Society rightly demands complete integrity from those who are employed to uphold and enforce the law. They expect those who tail in that duty to receive condign punishment."

To Moody the judge said "You were the main architect of this conspiracy and you also corrupted many other officers including junior officers, young detective constables."

To Virgo the judge said: "You were the most senior officer involved in this plot and you were able to defend the Obscene Publications Squad against attacks by the Press and other interested parties.

"In your position of high authority you were able to put your own men into the squad and to ensure you got your share which I am pretty sure must have been the lion's share. I take into account you are older than the others and are not enjoying good health."

The judge said Alton was almost in the same class as Moody and had taken over an efficient working machine. He managed to squeeze a little more treacle from it by blackmail and presented the worst image for a police officer in Soho than any other.

The final verdicts were returned by the jury of seven men and five women on the 49th day of the trial after an official retirement of just on 24 hours, although they were sent out at 2.20 p.m. last Tuesday and spent three nights in a London hotel.

Apart from Tilley, who pleaded guilty to conspiracy, the jury found the other five all guilty of conspiring between 1 January 1964, and 24 October 1972, together and with others corruptly to accept from persons trading in pornography, sums of money and other considerations both as inducements to show favour and as reward for showing favour in dereliction of their duties as police officers in the Obscene Publications Squad.

The jury also found the accused individually guilty on the following specimen charges:

Virgo: Corruptly accepting £2,000 from Soho pornographer James William Humphreys, 48, in 1970, and corruptly accepting £50 from him in January 1971.

Moody: Corruptly accepting £14,000 between 1 July and 15 September 1969 from pornographer Ronald Eric Mason. 59; corruptly accepting £175 from him in 1965; and corruptly accepting £400 from him the same year.

Alton: Corruptly accepting £1,500 from Brian Young and another man in 1966; corruptly accepting £300 from Mason between July and December 1966; corruptly accepting £1,000 from him in between June and December 1967; and corruptly accepting £500 from Dennis John Riley in 1968.

Brown: Corruptly accepting £500 from Riley in 1968; corruptly accepting £200 from Benjamin Gibbons in July 1968; corruptly accepting £80 from John Murray in 1968; and corruptly accepting £40 from Terence Nichols in 1970.

Hamer: Corruptly accepting £50 from John Mansfield in December 1968.

Tilley: Corruptly accepting £40 from Nichols in 1970.

When the convicted detectives had left the dock the judge listened to submissions from counsel as to how much the accused men should pay towards their legal costs.

The judge commented at one stage during the argument relating to Moody: "This is a case where there is evidence of thousands and thousands of pounds being taken in bribes by your client and no one has yet found out where it has gone.

"I am going to make sure that if there is any of it around then it is going to be used to pay for his defence."

The judge commended Assistant Commissioner Gilbert Kelland, Chief Superintendent Donald Williams and Chief Inspector Ronald Hay and the team working under them for an "outstanding piece of investigation".

He told them: "It was a difficult, delicate and distasteful task on which you were asked to work in 1974.

"Your efforts have been crowned with success and the cancer of corruption which poisoned the Obscene Publications Squad for so long has been exposed and excised.

The judge paid tribute to the Commissioner for the Metropolitan Police, Sir Robert Mark, who retired recently, and said he had done a great service with his determination and vigour when he started the investigation in 1974.

He also praised the Press for bringing the corruption to light and persisting in making investigations in the face of scurrilous comment.

He said: "The whole county owes the Press a debt for what they have done to bring to light the appalling state of affairs which existed in the Obscene Publications Squad.

Moody, of Ellesmere Road, Weybridge, Surrey, joined the police on demobilisation from the Royal Naval Air Service in 1947 and between 1948 and 1950, was the police welterweight boxing champion.

He resigned from the police in 1974 and has a disability pension for an injured neck.

Virgo, who owns a large house in Horse Lane Orchard, Ledbury, Herefordshire, served in the Metropolitan Police for 36 years by the time he retired in March 1973, on an inflation-proof pension of about £4,000 a year.

He had been a detective since 1947 and was awarded his Queen's Police Medal in June 1961. It is likely he will now lose this.

In 1967, he was seconded to the Home Office Prison Department as liaison officer in charge of prison security.

In 1970, as a commander he became head of the Yard's CI Dept, and had overall responsibility for nine crime squads, including the porn squad.

Two of the sentenced ex-detectives are licensees of public houses – Tilley of the Rule and Square, Edelsborough, Bucks, and Brown, of the Plough Inn, Coldharbour, Dorking.

Of the two remaining convicted men, Hamer, of Courtwood Lane, Addington, Surrey, was suspended from duty in July 1975, and Alton, of Harefield Avenue, Cheam, Surrey, retired on pension in August 1974.

Kate Moss

"There is a world of difference between people imagining you're a bit racy and the reality and seediness of being seen to be so."

The furore that ensued after supermodel Kate Moss was caught on camera taking cocaine was a perfect illustration of how one allegation of impropriety can lead very quickly to others: a single indiscretion, and suddenly it's open season. In her case, the shock that accompanied the news that a model who dated a rock star also took drugs was followed by lurid claims about her sexual proclivities. Moss's modelling became, if anything, even more successful after the waves created by the scandal had died down, but her relationship with Doherty did not, sadly, endure.

17 September 2005
Kate Moss in cocaine apology to save contract
By Richard Alleyne

Kate Moss, the model who was photographed in a national newspaper apparently snorting cocaine, was given "a second chance" yesterday by one of the world's biggest clothing retailers after she apologised.

Moss, 31, was said to have put her career, worth up to £4m a year, in jeopardy after pictures showed her taking the drug with her boyfriend Pete Doherty, the musician and drug addict, at a studio in west London.

The fashion and cosmetic houses Chanel, Christian Dior, Robert Cavalli, Burberry and Rimmel have all refused to comment about their contracts with the model, who two years ago denied taking illegal drugs.

But the store H&M, which is using Moss for its autumn clothing collection, designed by Stella McCartney, has decided to stay with the model after she and her agent apologised for the incident.

A spokesman for the chain, which has more than 1,100 stores in 22 countries, said: "We met Kate and her agent and she has told us she regrets the incident and has apologised to us. We are going to give her a second chance.

"We take issues like this very seriously. There were a lot of discussions about it yesterday before it was decided to carry on with the campaign."

The model, who has a two-year-old daughter from a previous relationship with the magazine publisher Jefferson Hack, has maintained her profile in a fickle industry since being spotted at JFK airport in New York aged 14. But fashion sources fear that the latest scandal may finally be the beginning of the end.

In a series of photographs in the *Daily Mirror*, Moss is seen apparently snorting cocaine and was allegedly talking openly about using skunk – a super-strength strain of cannabis – with friends of Doherty.

The newspaper said that she also produced a "mammoth stash" of cocaine from her handbag and chopped it out on a CD cover and allegedly snorted five lines of the drug in 40 minutes.

Hilary Alexander, the fashion director of the *Daily Telegraph*, said: "The problem is that she is hanging around with Pete Doherty, who has a sleazy and seedy image. That is what is likely to do her the most damage."

Moss, from Croydon, south London, is attending New York Fashion Week with Doherty, who was kicked out of his previous band for drug abuse. When challenged about the reports, she allegedly told reporters to "f*** off".

She is due to be a guest editor for a forthcoming edition of French *Vogue*, which is said to include a free copy of a duet sung with Doherty.

19 September 2005
Cocaine and sex claims pile pressure on Kate
By Richard Alleyne

Kate Moss's modelling career was put in further jeopardy yesterday after more revelations emerged about her private life, including further allegations of drug-taking and sleazy sexual behaviour.

The new claims were made as the fashion world gathered for the opening of London Fashion Week, and included reports that the model took cocaine while attending a function with Nelson Mandela.

The allegations are likely to place extra strain on her relationship with the fashion and cosmetic firms that employ her to front their products.

They have also increased concerns about her suitability as a role model for teenagers.

Much of Moss's success and longevity as a model since she was discovered 17 years ago have been attributed to her aloofness and control over her image. She never speaks to the press about her private life and is rarely seen looking anything but her fashionable best.

But since a national newspaper secretly photographed the model allegedly snorting cocaine at a west London recording studio last week with Pete Doherty, her drug-addict boyfriend, further allegations about her private life have emerged.

Yesterday the *News of the World* reported that the face of Chanel, Christian Dior and Burberry had instigated sex with her girlfriends after taking cocaine. It claimed that while sober she would never be attracted to women, but the use of the drug removed all her inhibitions.

The report also claimed that her use of cocaine had moved on from recreational to serious addiction. It is alleged that Moss, 31, was high on the class A drug while attending a charity dinner for the Nelson Mandela Children's Fund in Barcelona.

At the moment her employers, which also include the jeweller H Stern and the cosmetics company Rimmel, have remained loyal to the model. The clothing store giant H&M seriously reprimanded her for her behaviour and continued with a campaign featuring Moss only after she apologised for her behaviour.

Rita Clifton, the chairman of the international brand consultancy Interbrand, said: "Moss is popular for her unusual beauty, but what distinguishes her is that she is accessible and down to earth.

"The other thing that has made her valuable is this 'edge of darkness' feeling about her. The problem is that her image is sliding too much to the latter. There is a world of difference between people imagining you're a bit racy and the reality and seediness of being seen to be so."

In November 1998, Moss's hectic lifestyle and the break-up of her relationship with the actor Johnny Depp took their toll on her health and she checked into London's Priory Clinic, suffering from exhaustion. When she emerged the following January, she announced that she had spent the last decade modelling "drunk". "For years I never thought there was anything wrong with it," she told *Vogue*. "We all used to get drunk at the shows. I just thought I was having a really good time, which I was. But it got too much. There was no normality."

Since rehab and the dissolution of her eight-year contract with Calvin Klein, Moss reinvigorated her career, with the grander status of style icon, appearing less and less on the catwalks. In September 2000, the US magazine *Business Age* ranked her the fifth highest paid model in the world, with estimated earnings of £14.8m.

Her love life has been almost as well documented as her career. She has been linked with the photographer Mario Sorrenti, the Spacehog guitarist Antony Langdon, Rolling Stone Ronnie Wood's son Jesse, Evan Dando of the Lemonheads, the artist Jake Chapman and the actors Billy Zane and Leonardo DiCaprio.

She has a daughter, Lila Grace, born in September 2002, with the *Dazed & Confused* editor Jefferson Hack. The couple split in March 2004.

Her close friends include Anita Pallenberg, Marianne Faithfull, Stella McCartney, Alexander McQueen and Matthew Williamson.

She has recently been in a relationship with the rock star Doherty. It was during a recording session with his band Babyshambles that the pictures of her taking drugs were taken by the *Daily Mirror*.

A spokesman at Storm, the model agency that represents Moss, said: "All the allegations are being dealt with by lawyers and we are not at liberty to say anything further."

22 September 2005
Police chief orders inquiry into Kate Moss drug claims
By Richard Alleyne and Hilary Alexander

Britain's most senior police officer entered the row over the alleged drug use by Kate Moss yesterday as two fashion houses announced they were, at least temporarily, severing connections with her.

Sir Ian Blair, the Metropolitan Police Commissioner, said he had been involved in the decision to begin an investigation into the model's alleged activities and said he was particularly concerned about the impact on "impressionable young people".

Sir Ian, who previously condemned the scourge of middle-class cocaine use and said a few examples would have to made, said he had been disappointed when another celebrity, James Hewitt, had escaped with a caution for possession of cocaine.

He said: "We have to look at the impact of this kind of behaviour on impressionable young people and, if there is evidence, something should be done about it.

"I can remember being asked a question about a previous individual who was given a caution. I think that was a wrong decision."

His comments were made as Chanel and Burberry joined H&M, the retailer, in distancing themselves from Moss.

Chanel issued a statement saying it had "no plans in the near future" to employ the model when its current campaign ends next month and Burberry said it had shelved plans to use the model in the autumn.

A spokesman for Burberry said: "Since last week we have been in discussions with Kate Moss's representatives. Kate has worked successfully with Burberry on a number of assignments over the years.

"At the current time we had one project scheduled with Kate for this autumn and in the circumstances both Kate and Burberry have mutually agreed that it is inappropriate to go ahead.

"We are saddened by her current circumstances and hope she overcomes her problems as soon as possible. We wish Kate all the best."

Moss's career as a model, during which she has reputedly amassed a fortune of £40m, has been increasingly uncertain since the *Daily Mirror* published pictures of her apparently snorting cocaine. Reporters also recorded her allegedly talking openly about using cocaine and other drugs.

Her boyfriend Pete Doherty, the Babyshambles singer, was also involved in the incident at a west London recording studio. The couple have allegedly broken up.

For a few days fashion houses and cosmetic firms remained loyal and supportive of the model until further allegations emerged about her prolific use of the drugs alongside lurid claims about her sex life. H&M, the chairman of which is on the board of an anti-drugs charity, dropped the mother-of-one from an advertising campaign on Tuesday. Fashion experts believe her loss of earnings could be as much as £1m.

Only Rimmel, the cosmetic firm, which has a two-year contract with the model, Christian Dior, and H Stern, the New York jeweller, have stuck with her.

Scotland Yard said the investigations into the allegations were at an early stage and that it was looking at the story and speaking to the newspaper before proceeding.

The specialist crime directorate is said to be looking into the incident. A spokesman for Moss's modelling agency, Storm, said: "We are not commenting at this stage."

At London Fashion Week yesterday friends of the model were rallying around her.

Sadie Frost, the ex-wife of the actor Jude Law and part-owner of the fashion label Frost French, said: "Kate is a good friend and has always been supportive of us.

"We have worked with her on many occasions and she has always been fantastic. She has been set up and used as a scapegoat."

23 September 2005
Kate Moss apologises as Rimmel expresses "shock and dismay"
By Richard Alleyne

Kate Moss, the beleaguered model whose career has been hit by allegations of drug abuse and sexual promiscuity, apologised yesterday for bringing disgrace to herself and her family.

Moss, 31, has been reeling from one blow after another since pictures of her were published in a national newspaper allegedly showing her snorting lines of cocaine.

The mother of a two-year-old girl has endured an outpouring of allegations about her wayward lifestyle which have all but destroyed her previously untouchable image.

As lucrative contract after lucrative contract has been cancelled, Moss was forced to issue a statement to salvage the remnants of her career. "I take full responsibility for my actions," she said.

"I also accept that there are various personal issues that I need to address and have started taking the difficult, yet necessary, steps to resolve them.

"I want to apologise to all of the people I have let down because of my behaviour which has reflected badly on my family, friends, co-workers, business associates and others. I am trying to be positive, and the support and love I have received are invaluable."

The apology came after Rimmel, the cosmetic firm that – unlike some of her other clients – had stuck by the star throughout the furore, bowed to pressure and said her contract was under review. It also issued a stinging rebuke to the model.

A spokesman said: "Rimmel London is shocked and dismayed by the recent press allegations surrounding Kate Moss's behaviour. We are currently reviewing her contract."

Senior figures at Rimmel were said to be deeply concerned by the example Moss was setting after lurid accusations about her drug taking and party lifestyle were published.

Yesterday Moss suffered a further blow as the *Sun* newspaper published new allegations about drug-fuelled parties at her country home near Lechlade, Glos, including claims that crack cocaine was smoked openly.

Moss's lawyer, Gerrard Tyrell, issued an unequivocal denial that she had been involved with crack cocaine, saying: "The allegations that you put to me are specifically denied by my client."

Moss has maintained a public silence since the drugs storm began and she was conspicuously absent from her friend Sadie Frost's fashion show on Wednesday.

Moss has suffered setbacks during her career in the past and come back, most notably after she booked herself into the Priory in London after her break-up with the actor Johnny Depp. She re-emerged a few months later and after admitting to spending most of her previous career drunk, went from strength to strength.

Moss has a daughter, Lila Grace, with Jefferson Hack, a magazine publisher. The couple split in March 2004.

29 September 2005
Moss "starts intensive therapy at US clinic"
By James Burleigh

Kate Moss, the model whose career has recently been hit by allegations of drug abuse, has checked herself into a £2,250-a-night US rehabilitation clinic favoured by the rich and famous, it was reported last night.

Moss, 31, is understood to have been admitted to the Meadows in Wickenburg, Arizona, after the publication earlier this month of pictures allegedly showing her snorting lines of cocaine led to her being dropped from several highly lucrative modelling contracts. Last Friday, she issued a statement taking "full responsibility" for her actions and apologising.

She is believed to be undergoing an intensive 30 days of treatment and will not be allowed any visits or to communicate with the outside world – not even with her daughter, Lila Grace, whose third birthday is today.

A source close to the model, told the *Sun*: "Kate knows she has to take action and there is no better place than The Meadows."

News of the World

"This was a gross, gross breach of journalistic standards. Really terrible. We are only just beginning to see the scale of what was going on."

In June 2014, Andy Coulson was found guilty of a conspiracy to intercept voicemails. He was given a sentence of 18 months, of which he served five. Rebekah Brooks, who it was revealed had been Coulson's lover between 1998 and 2007, resigned from her position on 15 July 2011. "As chief executive of the company, I feel a deep sense of responsibility for the people we have hurt and I want to reiterate how sorry I am for what we now know to have taken place. I have believed that the right and responsible action has been to lead us through the heat of the crisis. However, my desire to remain on the bridge has made me a focal point of the debate. This is now detracting attention from all our honest endeavours to fix the problems of the past. Therefore I have given Rupert and James Murdoch my resignation. While it has been a subject of discussion, this time my resignation has been accepted."

Brooks, however, remained on the payroll, with Rupert Murdoch suggesting she might want to "travel the world on him for a year". The *Guardian* reported that she had received a £10.8m pay-off. At her subsequent criminal trial her defence of incompetence – that she was unaware of the illegal acts being carried out at the paper she edited – was accepted and she was acquitted of all charges. In October 2015 she resumed working for Rupert Murdoch as CEO of the renamed News UK.

Another five former employees at News International received short jail sentences, some of which were suspended. The *News of the World*'s place in the Murdoch stable was taken by the *Sun on Sunday*. It retains its predecessor's interest in celebrity exposés. Murdoch himself was taped claiming that investigators were "totally incompetent" and acted over "next to nothing". He said that his papers' actions were simply "part of the culture of Fleet Street".

6 April 2011
Journalists arrested over hacking
By Victoria Ward and Tom Whitehead

Two senior tabloid newspaper journalists were arrested yesterday on suspicion of mobile phone hacking.

Neville Thurlbeck, the *News of the World*'s chief reporter, and Ian Edmondson, a former assistant editor who was recently sacked over the affair, were questioned after presenting themselves at separate London police stations.

The arrests came as Sienna Miller, the actress, won a High Court order for access to the mobile phone records of third parties that may assist her claim for damages.

They were the first since Scotland Yard reopened its investigation into claims of hacking at the newspaper. Mr Edmondson, 42, was sacked in January after emails were found that allegedly suggested he was aware of the hacking.

Transcripts of voicemail messages obtained by private investigator Glenn Mulcaire were said to have been sent via email under the heading "This is the transcript for Neville", a possible reference to Mr Thurlbeck, 50.

The men were held on suspicion of conspiring to intercept communications and unlawfully intercepting voicemail messages. They were released on police bail to return in September. It is understood that their homes were also searched. Both deny any wrongdoing.

Only one News of the World journalist has been prosecuted over the scandal. Clive Goodman, the newspaper's former royal correspondent and Mulcaire were both jailed in 2007. The names and contact details of up to 3,000 public figures, including actors and politicians, were found in notes kept by Mulcaire.

The News of the World has already settled civil claims running into millions of pounds after being sued by hacking victims including Max Clifford, the publicist, and Gordon Taylor, the former head of the Professional Footballers' Association.

News International said in a statement: "News International has consistently reiterated that it will not tolerate wrongdoing and is committed to acting on evidence. We continue to co-operate fully with the ongoing police investigation."

Miss Miller, 28, won a High Court order requiring Vodafone to hand over data from other people's phone records. The order was granted by Mr Justice Vos, who said that Vodafone had been given data by police in 2006 to identify customers whose voicemails had been accessed.

Meanwhile, Keir Starmer, QC, the Director of Public Prosecutions, risked reopening a row with Scotland Yard over why the original inquiry was narrow. The Metropolitan Police's acting deputy commissioner, John Yates, has insisted officers had followed guidance by prosecutors that an offence was only committed if a voicemail was accessed before its intended recipient had listened to it.

But Mr Starmer told the home affairs select committee yesterday that any advice provided "did not limit the scope and extent of the criminal investigation".

Last night Chris Bryant, the Labour MP who believes his voicemails were hacked, said Mr Yates's job appeared untenable. He called on him to "consider his position" and resign from the Met.

9 April 2011
News of the World admits phone hacking
Murdoch newspaper will offer payouts to
celebrities and politicians
By Caroline Gammell

A former Cabinet minister and a leading actress were among eight people to be offered apologies and money by the News of the World yesterday because their phones were hacked.

Tessa Jowell, the former Olympics minister, and Sienna Miller, the actress, along with six others, will receive unreserved apologies from the Sunday tabloid, which said intercepting their phones was "a matter of genuine regret".

The admission of culpability is expected to prompt a flood of other complaints, and will raise further questions over the handling of the original police investigation, led by the Metropolitan Police's Assistant Commissioner John Yates.

There were even suggestions from legal experts that News International could face a criminal prosecution under the Regulation of Investigatory Powers Act 2000 if it is found to have "connived" or "consented" with the commission of the hacking, or if it was down to neglect on the part of senior executives, though proving this would be difficult.

News International is understood to have set aside £10m to cover legal costs and compensation. It expects about 30 legitimate cases to be brought.

News of the compensation was first publicised by the BBC's business editor Robert Peston, who has close links to Rupert Murdoch's empire.

Miss Miller and Miss Jowell are understood to have received a maximum payout of £100,000 each, while others have received lesser amounts. Kelly Hoppen, the designer, David Mills, Miss Jowell's estranged husband, and Andy Gray, the sports pundit sacked by Sky, are among those to be offered compensation. Joan Hammell, a former aide to Lord Prescott, Nicola Phillips, assistant to the publicist Max Clifford, and Sky Andrew, a sports agent, will also be offered money and an apology.

News International said the hacking occurred between 2004 and 2006. "Past behaviour at the *News of the World* in relation to voicemail interception is a matter of genuine regret," it said. "It is now apparent that our previous inquiries failed to uncover important evidence and we acknowledge our actions then were not sufficiently robust.

"It was our discovery and voluntary disclosure of this evidence in January that led to the reopening of the police investigation."

The current investigation, involving 45 officers, has led to the arrest of the paper's chief reporter Neville Thurlbeck and former head of news Ian Edmondson.

News International said it would continue to defend all cases it believed were "without merit".

Other people who have taken legal action against the paper over alleged hacking include the actor Jude Law, the footballer Paul Gascoigne, the actress Leslie Ash and the comedian Steve Coogan.

Mark Lewis, who represents several clients, welcomed the apology. However, he said: "It is a limited step. It only refers to hacking between 2004 and 2006 which relates to a small number of victims."

Lord Prescott, who is among those who claims his phone was hacked, used Twitter to proclaim that News International had admitted "mass criminality". He repeated his assertion that the Government should delay its decision over Mr Murdoch's takeover bid of BSkyB until the police inquiry was complete.

There was also criticism of the initial police investigation in 2006, which found no evidence of wrongdoing beyond that of Clive Goodman, the royal editor who was jailed in January 2007.

Chris Bryant, a Labour MP who called for a judicial review into the first police investigation, said the payments were "a damage-limitation exercise".

"This proves that everything News International has said about this case to date was a pack of lies," he said. "It wasn't just one rogue reporter. No one ever did a thorough investigation. Senior figures must have been aware of what was going on and they should resign."

12 April 2011
I know nothing about payments to police, says chief executive
By Tom Whitehead

Rebekah Brooks, the chief executive of News International, yesterday denied knowing about any specific payments to police by the company's journalists.

She was giving evidence to the Commons home affairs committee inquiry on phone-hacking.

She appeared to row back on comments she made as editor of the *Sun* in 2003 over payments to police.

Mrs Brooks said she had no intention of giving the impression that she knew of any specific cases when she told MPs in 2003 that the newspaper had paid the police for information in the past.

Giving evidence to the culture committee on 11 March 2003, she said: "We have paid the police for information in the past." She wrote to Keith Vaz, chairman of the home affairs committee, yesterday in response to questions over her original comments. She said: "As can be seen from the transcript, I was responding to a specific line of questioning on how newspapers get information.

"My intention was simply to comment generally on the widely held belief that payments had been made in the past to police officers. If, in doing so, I gave the impression that I had knowledge of any specific cases, I can assure you that this was not my intention."

News International has also written to another nine claimants in the phone-hacking scandal asking them to provide further evidence.

On Friday, eight people who had made claims against the *News of the World*, including Sienna Miller, the actress, received apologies from the newspaper.

In a separate move, the two most senior people heading the phone-hacking investigation made a public truce yesterday in a joint statement.

John Yates, the Metropolitan Police's acting deputy commissioner, and Keir Starmer, QC, the Director of Public Prosecutions, insisted they were working closely together to focus on the case.

The statement follows a widely reported split between the pair over the legal advice to officers during the original investigation in 2006.

Scotland Yard has endured repeated criticism over its handling of its original phone hacking inquiry, which led to the conviction of Clive Goodman, the *News of the World*'s former royal editor, and Glenn Mulcaire, a private investigator, in 2007.

Mr Yates has insisted officers had followed guidance by prosecutors that an offence was committed only if a voicemail was accessed before its intended recipient had listened to it.

But Mr Starmer last week contradicted evidence from Mr Yates when he said advice given by the Crown Prosecution Service "did not limit the scope and extent of the criminal investigation".

Their statement said: "We have both written to, and appeared before, the relevant parliamentary select committees providing detailed evidence on this matter to give an account of our best understanding of what took place five years ago.

"Neither of us had responsibility for this case at the time it was originally prosecuted.

"We have therefore both sought to interpret, as best we can, the original documentation and the recollections of those involved."

The Met began a fresh investigation into phone-hacking in January after receiving "significant new information" from News International.

Last week, detectives investigating the allegations arrested the paper's chief reporter and its former head of news.

Neville Thurlbeck, 50, and Ian Edmondson, 42, were held by Scotland Yard detectives on Tuesday when they voluntarily attended separate police stations in south-west London.

16 April 2011
There could be many more phone-hacking victims, claims Met
By Mark Hughes

The number of victims who had their phones hacked by the *News of the World* may be "substantially higher", the Metropolitan Police has admitted after it began trawling through nearly 10,000 records of private investigator Glenn Mulcaire.

Previously Scotland Yard had said information found in records kept by Mulcaire, who was employed by the newspaper, showed he had 91 voicemail PINs – suggesting 91 potential victims.

But the High Court has heard that the new police investigation expects to find many more victims. And that could open the door for more celebrities to take legal action against the *News of the World*.

The disclosure came as it emerged that the actress Sienna Miller may have had her emails hacked into. Miss Miller, it was revealed yesterday, has been offered £100,000 to halt her case against the newspaper. She is yet to accept or reject the offer.

But while the *News of the World* waits to hear whether Miss Miller will settle, it could now have to defend itself against scores of other claims.

Yesterday the High Court heard that 40 detectives working on the new investigation – codenamed Operation Weeting – are trawling through 9,200 pages of records seized from Mulcaire.

They are looking for direct dial numbers (DDNs), the number dialled by a mobile phone user to access voicemails. Yesterday Jason Beer, QC, for the Metropolitan Police, told the court: "There are, within the Mulcaire archive, records of DDNs where, on the face of it, there is no good reason for these to appear. That is strongly indicative of interception."

Asked whether the number of numbers is larger than the 91 PINs, Mr Beer added: "The number of DDNs is substantially higher than that."

The *News of the World* issued a public apology over phone hacking last Friday, offering to pay damages to anyone who could prove that their phone was hacked by one of its journalists. "Since the admissions last Friday, the Metropolitan Police has been flooded with enquiries. The number of people beating a path to the Met's door has increased very substantially," Mr Beer said.

The court also heard that the *News of the World* had offered to settle the case with Miss Miller. Her lawyer said that her former partner Jude Law, the actor, may start proceedings against the paper.

Civil cases are being brought by 20 people, including Paul Gascoigne, George Galloway and Tessa Jowell.

But yesterday the judge, Mr Justice Vos, ruled that there should be four test cases which will determine how much damages should be paid to future claimants. The test cases, the court heard, are likely to be those of the football pundit Andy Gray, football agent Sky Andrew, Miss Miller and Kelly Hoppen, the interior designer.

Mulcaire and the *News of the World*'s royal correspondent, Clive Goodman, were jailed in 2007 after they admitted hacking into voicemails. In January this year a new investigation was launched. So far three *News of the World* employees have been arrested.

5 July 2011
Milly Dowler phone "was hacked by newspaper"
Murder inquiry hampered after missing teenager's voicemail
messages were accessed and deleted

The parents of the murdered teenager Milly Dowler spoke of their anguish yesterday after learning that private investigators working for a tabloid newspaper allegedly hacked into their daughter's mobile phone.

Sally and Bob Dowler said that they had been given "false hope" that their daughter could still be alive after the investigator working for the *News of the World* allegedly intercepted and deleted voicemail messages on her phone.

A lawyer speaking on their behalf described the alleged hacking as "heinous" and "despicable" as he announced that the family were pursuing a claim for damages.

Last night a Labour MP claimed that investigators had also targeted one of the parents of Holly Wells and Jessica Chapman, the victims of the Soham murderer Ian Huntley.

The hacking of Milly Dowler's phone would represent the most significant twist in the scandal surrounding the *News of the World*, which has previously been confined, in most cases, to celebrity victims.

In what was described as a "shocking development" by sources at No 10, it is claimed that intimate messages on the 13-year-old's phone – some from worried family members – were listened to and then deleted in order to free space on the messaging system shortly after she went missing in March 2002.

The deleting of the messages led family members to believe that the teenager could still be alive. It could also have erased evidence that would have assisted police.

Details of the alleged hacking were found in nearly 10,000 pages of notes seized by Scotland Yard detectives from Glenn Mulcaire, a private investigator who worked for the *News of the World*. Officers from the Metropolitan Police are now said to be speaking to detectives in Surrey who worked on the Milly Dowler investigation, some of whom raised concerns about potential phone hacking at the time of the inquiry.

Yesterday it was also disclosed that police have contacted Sir Richard Branson, the entrepreneur, and Colin Stagg, the man wrongly accused of killing Rachel Nickell, to inform them that they may have been victims of phone hacking.

News International, which owns the *News of the World*, last night faced a growing political backlash as senior Labour figures called for Rebekah Brooks, the chief executive, to step down. Mrs Brooks edited the *News of the World* when the alleged hacking took place. During her time at the newspaper, she campaigned for the introduction of Sarah's Law. The scheme, proposed after eight-year-old Sarah Payne's murder 11 years ago, lets parents check if anyone with access to their children has a paedophile background.

Politicians said that the allegations raised fresh concerns over the bid by Rupert Murdoch's News Corporation – which owns News International – to take full ownership of BskyB. Labour figures questioned the suitability of Mr Murdoch as the prospective sole owner of the television company.

The Milly Dowler allegations date to April 2002, less than a month after the teenager went missing in Walton-on-Thames, Surrey, on 21 March. It is alleged that the newspaper gained her mobile telephone number and began listening to her voicemails just days after she disappeared. When the message inbox became full they allegedly deleted the messages in order that they could hear any newer messages that were left. This, it is alleged, had the effect of leading Milly's family to believe that, because they could leave voicemails when previously they were unable to, the teenager was still alive and was deleting them herself.

At one point during the investigation into her disappearance, the *News of the World* ran an article which, it is suggested, hinted at the fact the newspaper had access to her voicemails.

A story published in the newspaper on 14 April 2002 told of a woman who had apparently been posing as the youngster when applying for jobs. The story claimed the woman gave a recruitment company Milly's number and continues: "The agency used the number to contact Milly when a job vacancy arose and left a message on her voicemail after the 13-year-old vanished."

A statement from the family's lawyer, Mark Lewis of Taylor Hampton, said the Dowlers were distressed at the revelation. He said that they had been contacted by the Metropolitan Police last month during the Old Bailey trial of Levi Bellfield, who was convicted of Milly's murder two weeks ago.

He also questioned why it had taken Scotland Yard officers so long to tell the Dowlers, given that the information is alleged to have been found in files the force has had for more than five years.

The family statement said: "It is distress heaped upon tragedy to learn that the *News of the World* had no humanity at such a terrible time. The fact that they were prepared to act in such a heinous way that could have jeopardised the police investigation and give them false hope is despicable."

Bob Dowler, Milly's father, refused to speak about the allegations. He said: "We are not giving any interviews about this."

Tom Watson, a Labour MP, said in the Commons yesterday that the alleged hacking was a "despicable and evil act".

He also alleged that one of Kevin and Nicola Wells or Leslie and Sharon Chapman, the parents of the two girls murdered by Ian Huntley, had also had their phone messages hacked into.

A News International spokesman said: "We have been co-operating fully with Operation Weeting since our voluntary disclosure in January restarted the investigation into illegal voicemail interception.

"This particular case is clearly a development of great concern and we will be conducting our own inquiries as a result."

Scotland Yard refused to comment, but a senior police source said: "This was a gross, gross breach of journalistic standards. Really terrible. We are only just beginning to see the scale of what was going on."

[Further investigation has reported that the deletion of Milly Dowler's voicemails was later shown almost certainly not to have been because of hacking.]

8 July 2011
Goodbye, cruel World
Britain's biggest-selling newspaper is closed down

Britain's biggest-selling newspaper was shut down last night by the Murdoch family in a surprise move designed to bring an end to the phone-hacking scandal engulfing the *News of the World*.

James Murdoch, the chairman of News International, which owns the newspaper, announced that the final edition would be published this weekend, citing the "inhuman" alleged behaviour of some staff as prompting the decision.

The 168-year-old newspaper will donate all this weekend's revenues to good causes and would not accept any paid advertising, he said.

Hundreds of staff now face an uncertain future. However, Rebekah Brooks, the chief executive of News International and former editor of the *News of the World*, has been allowed to keep her job despite widespread calls for her to be sacked.

Last night she faced angry scenes at the paper as she broke the news to journalists. There were reports she had to be escorted from the offices by security guards for her protection.

Rupert Murdoch and his family sacrificed the tabloid as they fought to salvage their company's attempt to take over BSkyB, the satellite broadcaster, after the scandal resulted in growing political pressure for the Government to block the deal.

Last night politicians warned that shutting the newspaper would not shut down the scandal, which they said would only end when those responsible for the hacking were brought to justice.

The historic announcement of the closure followed several days of allegations that investigators working for the newspaper had hacked into the mobile phones of military families, the victims of the 7/7 attacks and murder victims, including the teenager Milly Dowler.

It was made hours after the Metropolitan Police disclosed that more than 4,000 people had been identified as potential victims of private detectives employed by the paper.

The *News of the World*, the biggest selling English-language newspaper in the world, is currently at the centre of two police investigations, one into the alleged hacking, the other into payments allegedly made to police officers.

After widespread public revulsion at the scandal and condemnation from MPs, dozens of companies had announced they were withdrawing advertising from the paper. The share price of News Corp, the parent company of New Limited, had also been badly affected.

James Murdoch last night said that the paper had lost the trust of its readers after the allegations.

He told staff: "The good things the *News of the World* does have been sullied by behaviour that was wrong. Indeed, if recent allegations are true, it was inhuman and has no place in our company."

The company's investigation into the claims had been inadequate, he said, and its insistence that hacking was confined to one rogue reporter was wrong. "The *News of the World* is in the business of holding others to account. But it failed when it came to itself. Wrongdoers turned a good newsroom bad and this was not fully understood or adequately pursued.

"As a result, the *News of the World* and News International wrongly maintained that these issues were confined to one reporter. Having consulted senior colleagues, I have decided that we must take further decisive action with respect to the paper. This Sunday will be the last issue of the *News of the World*."

Mr Murdoch also conceded that he and other executives had made serious mistakes in their handling of the crisis. "The paper made statements to Parliament without being in the full possession of the facts.

This was wrong," he said. "The company paid out-of-court settlements approved by me. I now know that I did not have a complete picture when I did so. This was wrong and is a matter of serious regret." In a television interview, however, he refused to apologise, simply repeating that the scandal was "regrettable".

More than 200 staff reacted with anger at the announcement, claiming they were innocent victims of the behaviour of a previous regime. Sub editors at sister newspaper the *Sun* walked out in protest.

Mrs Brooks, who is said to have been in tears as she announced the paper's closure, was faced with a "lynch mob mentality" from staff. David Wooding, the associate editor, said: "The problem is, all these decent hard–working distinguished journalists are carrying the can for the sins of the previous regime. I don't think they could have done any more to cleanse the *News of the World*." Mrs Brooks was the editor of the *News of the World* when some of the most controversial incidents – including the hacking of the murdered schoolgirl Milly Dowler's phone – took place. It was reported last night that she offered her resignation on Wednesday evening but it was rejected by the Murdoch family. Mr Murdoch last night staunchly defended Mrs Brooks, insisting that she was not culpable for the hacking allegations.

Last night, senior Labour figures demanded that she step aside and take "responsibility" for the situation. Ed Miliband, the Labour leader, said of the closure: "It's a big act but I don't think it solves the real issues. One of the people who's remaining in her job is the chief executive of News International who was the editor at the time of the hacking of Milly Dowler's phone." Mr Miliband said people were right to be appalled by the allegations, adding: "What I'm interested in is not closing down newspapers, I'm interested in those who were responsible being brought to justice and those who have responsibility for the running of that newspaper taking their responsibility and I don't think those two things have happened today."

In a statement, Downing Street said: "What matters is that all wrongdoing is exposed and those responsible for these appalling acts are brought to justice.

"As the Prime Minister has made clear, he is committed to establishing rigorous public inquiries to make sure this never happens in our country again."

Glenn Mulcaire, the private investigator used by the News of the World, said there had been a "committee" of journalists at the paper who commissioned phone hacking. The admission, made to a victim of sexual assault who was secretly filming their conversation, dispels the notion that phone hacking was encouraged by one rogue reporter. His lawyer later released a statement saying that his use of the word "committee" was a "colloquial expression and did not mean that an official committee had been set up".

9 July 2011
Hacking scandal hits No 10
Cameron defiant as former press aide is arrested
over "illegal payments to police"

David Cameron yesterday struggled to distance himself from the News of the World hacking scandal after he faced questions over his decision to hire Andy Coulson as his director of communications.

In a press conference minutes before Mr Coulson, the paper's former editor, was arrested by police, the Prime Minister repeatedly stressed that the appointment was "his responsibility" but declined to apologise or acknowledge a mistake had been made.

He admitted that the relationship between politicians and the media had become too close.

He said the current system of press regulation needed to be overhauled and announced two inquiries, one into phone hacking and one into the conduct of the media.

Mr Cameron's intervention came 24 hours after the announcement that the News of the World would close, and on the day detectives arrested both Mr Coulson and a former reporter at the News of the World over allegations of phone hacking and illegal payments to police.

Mr Coulson was editor when most of the alleged hacking is said to have taken place but was given a "second chance" with the job for Mr Cameron.

The Prime Minister said that James Murdoch, the chairman of News International and the son of Rupert Murdoch, had "questions to answer" after he admitted making mistakes in his handling of the scandal. He also indicated that Rebekah Brooks, the chief executive of News International and also a friend, should have resigned.

Media regulators suggested they may intervene to stop BSkyB being run by News

Corp, the Murdoch family's main company, on the grounds that the directors are not "fit and proper".

Mrs Brooks told staff at the paper that it had to be shut down because worse revelations about its activities were imminent. She was stripped of her role investigating the scandal.

Ed Miliband, the Labour leader, faced growing questions over his hiring of a former News International employee accused of wrongdoing, which he denies.

Mr Cameron sought yesterday to seize control of the scandal which has dominated the news agenda for a week. The Prime Minister indicated that the alleged criminality at the newspaper would lead to major changes in the entire media industry.

"Because party leaders were so keen to win the support of newspapers we turned a blind eye to the need to sort this issue, get on top of the bad practices, to change the way our newspapers are regulated," he said.

The Prime Minister described the *News of the World* scandal as a "wake-up call", adding: "Over the decades, on the watch of both Labour leaders and Conservative leaders, politicians and the press have spent time courting support, not confronting the problems.

"Well, it's on my watch that the music has stopped and I'm saying, loud and clear – things have got to change."

Mr Cameron's pledge to intervene in the crisis has been criticised by opposition politicians because of his decision to bring Mr Coulson into Downing Street.

Yesterday he repeatedly refused to apologise for that decision, saying he had received "assurances" from Mr Coulson that he had no knowledge of phone hacking at the newspaper.

Asked at a press conference if he had "screwed up" by employing Mr Coulson in the wake of his resignation from journalism, Mr Cameron said: "People will decide." He added: "I decided to give him a second chance but the second chance didn't work. The decision to hire him was mine and mine alone."

He said a company had run a "basic background check" on Mr Coulson before he was employed while the Tories were in opposition. He had received no "actionable" information about the former editor and was unaware of "specific" warnings.

Mr Coulson resigned from Downing Street in January after News International passed new evidence to the police on alleged phone hacking. Mr Cameron said yesterday he had spoken to and met Mr Coulson since then. He said: "I think he did his job for me in a very effective way. He became a friend and he is a friend."

Downing Street sources said that the Prime Minister was currently giving Mr Coulson the "benefit of the doubt" until any evidence emerged proving that the assurances he gave were misleading.

Mr Miliband demanded that Mr Cameron apologise for the decision. The Labour leader said: "His wholly unconvincing answers of what he knew and when he knew it about Mr Coulson's activities undermine his ability to lead the change that Britain needs."

Mr Cameron said that a reported resignation offer from Mrs Brooks, also a good friend, should have been accepted.

13 July 2011

Hacking scandal executives face threat of police inquiry

Rupert Murdoch expected to appear before Parliament next week

By Mark Hughes, Robert Winnett and Christopher Hope

Senior executives at News International could be investigated by police after the company was accused by detectives of deliberately attempting to thwart the first phone-hacking investigation.

Deputy Assistant Commissioner Sue Akers, the officer leading Scotland Yard's new inquiry, yesterday suggested to MPs that the scope of the investigation could be widened beyond journalists at the *News of the World* to include the "criminal liability of directors".

Broadening the inquiry could implicate more senior managers at the defunct tabloid's owners, including James Murdoch, the chairman of News International, and Rebekah Brooks, its chief executive.

The Metropolitan Police yesterday accused News International of "lying" during the original investigation into phone hacking at the *News of the World*. Senior officers told MPs that Mr Murdoch's company had deliberately undermined a criminal inquiry, a move that could leave senior executives facing prosecution.

Peter Clarke, a former deputy assistant commissioner of the Met, said: "If at any time News International had offered some meaningful co-operation instead of lies, we would not be here today."

It also emerged that Rupert Murdoch was set to make an unprecedented appearance before Parliament.

The chairman and chief executive of News Corporation, the parent company of News International, has been asked to appear at next week's hearing of the Commons' media committee, along with his son, James, and Mrs Brooks.

The company said in a statement: "We have been made aware of the request . . . to interview senior executives and will co-operate. We await the formal invitation."

Steve McCabe, a Labour MP, asked yesterday whether the police were looking at taking any action under Section 79 of the Regulation of Investigative Powers Act (Ripa) 2000 which covers the "criminal liability of directors".

Ms Akers replied: "[The CPS] will decide in due course if it comes to that what the most appropriate charges are, and I am sure they won't confine themselves to one particular part of Ripa."

Section 79 of the Act says that directors can be prosecuted if an offence "is proved to have been committed with the consent or connivance of, or to be attributable to any neglect on the part of a director".

Last week, James Murdoch admitted agreeing "out-of-court settlements" to phone-hacking victims, although he says that he did not have the complete picture when he did so. Alan Johnson, a former home secretary, suggested this could lead to prosecution under the Act.

There were also increasing calls in the United States for the authorities to investigate News Corp for possible breaches of the Foreign Corrupt Practices Act, under which it is a crime to bribe foreign officials to obtain or keep business.

Mr Murdoch held crisis talks yesterday with his family and aides, *The Times* reported. Les Hinton, his senior lieutenant in New York, flew in to London and joined Mrs Brooks at Mr Murdoch's home.

Mr Murdoch was also joined by his daughter Elisabeth, whose television production company Shine was bought by News Corp last year.

Ms Akers also disclosed that more than 12,000 names and phone numbers of victims had now been recovered but only a small minority had been informed. She was appearing before MPs alongside four former and current senior officers to answer questions about the alleged failure of the original inquiry.

Mr Clarke, a former head of the anti-terrorism branch, was handed the hacking investigation in December 2005 after members of the Royal household suggested their voicemails were being listened to.

Although two men, Glenn Mulcaire and Clive Goodman, were jailed it appears that the criminality ran deeper. Mr Clarke said he was concentrating on more than 70 alleged terrorist plots.

Any failings were due to the obstruction of News International, he claimed. He said: "This is a major global organisation with access to the best legal advice, in my view deliberately trying to thwart a police investigation."

News International declined to comment on the allegations. Mr Clarke was backed in his attack by Assistant Commissioner John Yates, who was asked to investigate whether a *Guardian* article in July 2009 disclosed any new information.

After eight hours' consideration he decided it did not. He was asked to examine the possibility of a further investigation after reports in the *New York Times* in 2010, but it was decided not to proceed.

The current investigation, Operation Weeting, only began in January this year after three emails were handed by News International to the police.

Mr Yates said: "It is a matter of great concern that for whatever reason, the *News of the World* appears to have failed to co-operate, in the way that we now know they should have with relevant police inquiries up until January this year."

Several Labour MPs called on Mr Yates to resign yesterday. But Scotland Yard sources claimed that a political witchhunt was under way to punish Mr Yates for investigating cash-for-honours allegations.

There were furious scenes in the committee room as MPs questioned some of the most senior police officers in Britain over whether they had accepted money from newspapers – or suppressed investigations amid threats their private lives would be exposed. The claims were vehemently denied.

18 July 2011
Scotland Yard chief quits with parting shot at Cameron
Commissioner heaps pressure on Prime Minister
with barbed reference to Andy Coulson's No 10 role

Sir Paul Stephenson last night resigned as Commissioner of the Metropolitan Police, putting more pressure on David Cameron over his personal links to the phone-hacking scandal.

A clearly angry Sir Paul said he was stepping down after criticism over his decision to employ as a personal adviser Neil Wallis, the former deputy editor of the News of the World who was arrested on suspicion of phone hacking.

In an emotional statement yesterday evening he insisted he did not want to "compromise" the Prime Minister but pointedly said Mr Wallis had not been associated with phone hacking at the time Sir Paul employed him in October 2009.

He said that by contrast the full scale of phone hacking at the News of the World had begun to emerge when Andy Coulson, who went on to become David Cameron's director of communications, resigned as editor.

Sir Paul said: "Let me turn to the reported displeasure of the Prime Minister and the Home Secretary of the relationship with Mr Wallis.

"At the time [I had] no reason for considering the contractual relationship to be a matter of concern. Unlike Mr Coulson, Mr Wallis had not resigned from the News of the World or, to the best of my knowledge been in any way associated with the original phone-hacking investigation."

Sir Paul added that he had felt unable to mention his relationship with Mr Wallis to the Prime Minister, because Mr Wallis had used to work for Mr Coulson.

He said: "Once Mr Wallis's name did become associated with Operation Weeting, I did not want to compromise the Prime Minister in any way by revealing or discussing a potential suspect who clearly had a close relationship with Mr Coulson."

Sir Paul said that while he was resigning with his personal integrity intact he was concerned his relationship with Mr Wallis was proving an unwelcome "distraction" to the "enormous challenge" of policing London in the run-up to the Olympics.

He said: "The heroism and bravery of Met officers . . . is in danger of being eclipsed by the ongoing debate about relationships between senior officers and the media. That can never be right. If I stayed I know the inquiry outcomes would reaffirm my personal integrity. Therefore, although I have received continued personal support from both the Home Secretary and the mayor, I have with great sadness informed both of my intention to resign."

He said that he had no involvement in the original phone hacking investigation in 2006. "I had no reason to believe this was anything other than a successful investigation. I was unaware that there were any other documents in our possession of the nature that have now emerged."

Sir Paul met Mr Wallis later that year and employed him as a PR adviser between October 2009 and September 2010. Sir Paul said he had kept his connection to Mr Wallis secret from Mr Cameron, Theresa May, the Home Secretary, and Boris Johnson, the Mayor of London, to avoid exposing them to criticism.

He added that he had been unable to divulge the relationship earlier because it would have affected the integrity of the police's current investigation into phone hacking. Mr Wallis was arrested on Thursday. Mr Cameron, who was informed of Sir Paul's resignation after taking off on a trade visit to Africa, said he understood and respected the decision.

He added: "What matters most of all now is that the Metropolitan Police and the Metropolitan Police Authority do everything possible to ensure the investigations into phone hacking and alleged police corruption proceed with all speed, with full public confidence and with all the necessary leadership and resources to bring them to an effective conclusion."

Last night Labour attempted to put more pressure on Mr Cameron over the phone hacking scandal.

Yvette Cooper, the shadow home secretary, said: "It is striking that Sir Paul has taken responsibility and answered questions about the appointment of the deputy editor of the *News of the World* whereas the Prime Minister still refuses to recognise his misjudgment and answer questions on the appointment of the editor of the *News of the World* at the time of the initial phone hacking investigation."

Sir Paul's decision will put added pressure on John Yates, the Assistant Commissioner, who has been widely criticised for his failure to reopen the phone hacking investigation.

Mr Wallis's connection with Sir Paul first emerged last Thursday.

Yesterday there was further embarrassment when a Sunday newspaper disclosed that Sir Paul had accepted up to £12,000 in luxury hospitality from Champneys, one of the country's leading health spas, when he was recovering from an operation. Sir Paul and his wife had spent 20 nights with full board at the spa.

The revelation was embarrassing because the spa's PR representative was Mr Wallis.

In a 15-minute statement, broadcast live from the press room in New Scotland Yard, Sir Paul insisted there was "no impropriety" in relation to his use of the spa. He said he did it so he could return to running the Met full time.

19 July 2011
Police examine laptop found in bin near Rebekah Brooks's home
By Raf Sanchez and Andrew Hough

Detectives were last night examining a laptop computer, papers and a mobile phone found in a dustbin near Rebekah Brooks's London home.

The items were discovered in a bag in an underground car park at Chelsea Harbour, a few yards from where the former News International chief executive lives with her husband, the horse trainer Charlie Brooks.

The bag was understood to have been found by a cleaner who handed it to security guards yesterday afternoon.

Mr Brooks then tried to claim the bag but was unable to prove it was his. The guards called the police, who took the bag and its documents away for analysis.

Detectives were understood to be examining CCTV footage to see how the bag made it into the car park.

A spokesman for Mr Brooks said the bag had been dropped off by a friend who left it in the wrong place, possibly causing a cleaner to throw it away, He said the bag and all its contents belonged to Mr Brooks and not his wife, adding: "They are absolutely nothing to do with Rebekah Brooks or the police investigation."

The latest disclosure came after the former *News of the World* editor's lawyer said she had suffered "enormous reputational damage" following her arrest over allegations of phone hacking and corruption. The 43 year old was questioned for nine hours by detectives on Sunday after agreeing to attend a police station.

After she was released on bail, pending further investigations, her lawyers issued an angry statement denying that she had any link to phone hacking or alleged illegal payments to police officers and alluding to legal action. They criticised the police handling of the case, claiming that, during her time in custody, officers "put no allegations to her and showed her no documents connecting her with any crime".

Mrs Brooks was the 10th person to be arrested since the Metropolitan Police reopened its phone-hacking inquiry in January.

"The position of Rebekah Brooks can be simply stated – she is not guilty of any criminal offence," said Stephen Parkinson, of the law firm Kingsley Napley. "The position of the Metropolitan Police is less easy to understand.

"Despite arresting her yesterday and conducting an interview process lasting nine hours, they put no allegations to her and showed her no documents connecting her with any crime.

"They will in due course have to give an account of their actions and in particular their decision to arrest her with the enormous reputational damage that this has involved."

Sources close to Mrs Brooks, a former editor of the *Sun*, had said she was only contacted by the police on Friday evening and was not aware she was to be arrested until she met officers at lunchtime on Sunday.

Her arrest raised questions about her appearance before the Commons culture, media and sport committee, scheduled for today. Commentators said she may be able to decline to answer MPs' questions, citing the ongoing police investigation, with some querying the unusual timing of her arrest.

Mr Parkinson said his client remained willing to answer questions. "It is a matter for Parliament to decide what issues to put to her and whether her appointment should take place at a later date," he said.

Mrs Brooks has denied any knowledge of the alleged hacking cases during her time as editor of the *News of the World*.

[Rebekah Brooks, and the others charged with her, were later acquited of all charges in 2014.]

Also 19 July 2011
Yates steps down as allegations engulf Scotland Yard
I quit but I have done nothing wrong, says counter-terrorism chief

Britain's chief counter-terrorism officer became the latest victim of the phone hacking scandal yesterday, resigning amid claims that he helped a *News of the World* executive's daughter get a job at Scotland Yard.

Assistant Commissioner John Yates, who faced criticism for failing to reopen the Metropolitan Police's inquiry into hacking sooner, was being investigated by the Independent Police Complaints Commission over his links to Neil Wallis, the former deputy editor of the Sunday tabloid.

It also emerged last night that Alex Marunchak, a former executive editor at the paper, was employed by the Metropolitan Police for 20 years as a translator. Between 1980 and 2000 Mr Marunchak, a second generation Ukrainian, combined his day as job as a journalist with working as a part-time interpreter for Scotland Yard when they arrested suspects from Russia and Ukraine.

Mr Yates's resignation followed that of Sir Paul Stephenson, the Met Commissioner, on Sunday evening.

In his resignation speech, an emotional Mr Yates said he was stepping down due to a "huge amount of inaccurate, ill-informed and on occasion downright malicious gossip published about me personally".

The IPCC also announced investigations yesterday into Sir Paul, Andy Hayman, the former assistant commissioner, and Peter Clarke, the former deputy assistant commissioner, for alleged failings in the phone hacking case.

Mr Yates will also face an IPCC investigation for failing to reopen the hacking inquiry in 2009.

Theresa May, the Home Secretary, also announced three separate investigations into the scale of corruption at the Met and the force's relationship with the press.

Speaking in South Africa yesterday, David Cameron said there were "very big questions about potential police corruption".

Mr Yates twice refused to reopen the phone-hacking case despite claims that the original investigation had failed to establish the true extent of illegal activities.

Further pressure was heaped on him following the arrest last week of Mr Wallis, who was employed as a communications adviser to Mr Yates and Sir Paul after stepping down from the News of the World. He won the £1,000-a-day contract during the period that Scotland Yard was facing calls to reopen the phone hacking case. Mr Yates and Mr Wallis are friends who have known each other for 12 years, while Sir Paul had eight meetings with him in three years.

That relationship came under further scrutiny last night when it was alleged that Mr Yates helped Mr Wallis's daughter, Amy, 27, get a job with the force. The police staff position, which Miss Wallis was understood to still hold, was not under Mr Yates's specialist operations command.

Sources told the Daily Telegraph that Mr Yates had been due to be suspended yesterday following a meeting of the Metropolitan Police Authority's professional standards committee. Sources close to Mr Yates said that until that decision he had intended to stay in his job because he had "done nothing wrong".

But following the MPA's decision to suspend him and refer the allegations to the IPCC, he tendered his resignation. Afterwards Boris Johnson, the Mayor of London, said that it was right for Sir Paul and Mr Yates to stand down.

He added: "I believe that both decisions are regrettable but I would say that in both cases the right call has been made. There is absolutely nothing that has been proven against the probity or the professionalism of either man.

"But in both cases we have to recognise that the nexus of questions about the relationship between the Met and the News of the World was likely to be distracting to both officers in the run-up to the Olympic Games."

The Home Secretary also said she was "sorry" that Sir Paul had taken the decision to stand down and expressed "gratitude" to Mr Yates for his work in counterterrorism.

Sir Paul's position as commissioner will be filled temporarily by his deputy, Tim Godwin. Bernard Hogan-Howe, the former chief constable of Merseyside, will become acting deputy commissioner.

Assistant Commissioner Cressida Dick will take Mr Yates's role as head of counter–terrorism, moving from her role in charge of serious crime.

Reacting to the news of the investigations into two of the force's most senior officers,

Scotland Yard released a statement saying: "The Metropolitan Police was informed by the Metropolitan Police Authority, after their meeting this morning, that they had decided to make a referral to the Independent Police Complaints Commission.

"We weren't aware that there was complaint against the Commissioner prior to this notification. We understand the IPCC are now considering the referrals of Sir Paul Stephenson, John Yates, and two ex-officers."

20 July 2011
Murdoch eats humble pie
News Corp boss attacked with shaving foam as
MPs question him about phone hacking scandal
By James Kirkup

Rupert Murdoch admitted yesterday that he had known nothing of his company's phone-hacking scandal or the secret payments which helped to conceal it from the world.

The most powerful media baron in Britain and perhaps globally made the confession as he experienced "the most humble day" in his 80 years.

Questioned by a Commons select committee about phone hacking at the *News of the World*, the News Corp founder conceded that he had "lost sight" of the tabloid's management.

He had "been lax" in not asking staff about the paper's actions, which included intercepting voicemails of the murdered schoolgirl Milly Dowler.

Mr Murdoch also had to endure the indignity of a physical attack, when a self-described comedian, Jonnie Marbles, evaded security to strike him with a "pie" of shaving foam.

Mr Murdoch and his son, James, spent three hours giving evidence to the culture, media and sport committee, facing repeated questions about their knowledge of the wrongdoing that closed the paper and now threatened their global empire. Both offered profuse apologies. Rupert Murdoch said the Dowler hacking had sickened and angered him more than anything in his life. He understood the "ire" of victims and would "work tirelessly to merit their forgiveness".

The company he founded had been caught with "dirty hands". "This is the most humble day of my life," he said.

Despite the unprecedented show of contrition, the hearing and another, separate Commons committee session with police chiefs and lawyers connected with phone hacking, threatened to deepen the scandal further.

The second, home affairs committee, rushed out a damning report late last night accusing Scotland Yard of a "catalogue of failings" in its investigation and criticising "deliberate attempts by News International to thwart the various investigations".

In other revelations:

James Murdoch conceded that the company may still be paying legal fees and other money to Glenn Mulcaire, the private investigator who was jailed in 2007 for hacking phones for the *News of the World*.

Rebekah Brooks, the former News International (NI) chief executive, said that George Osborne, the Chancellor, had been the driving force behind David Cameron hiring Andy Coulson, the former *News of the World* editor.

A former director of public prosecutions said that "blindingly obvious" evidence of hacking and other crimes had lain in a secret NI file for four years before the company told police.

The law firm Harbottle and Lewis accused NI of refusing to release it from a confidentiality clause so that it could defend itself against allegations that it helped cover up the scandal.

Much of the MPs' questioning focused on NI's £700,000 payout to Gordon Taylor, the former head of the Professional Footballers' Association whose phone was hacked.

As head of NI in Europe, James Murdoch authorised that deal, which obliged Mr Taylor to remain silent about the hacking and the payment. He denied suggestions that the payment was meant to keep the scandal secret. But the committee also heard that his father had not learned of the payment until 2009.

Asked who had first informed him of the phone-hacking issue, Rupert Murdoch replied: "I forget."

MPs asked him about his contacts with journalists and editors involved in the scandal. He denied direct knowledge, saying of several senior staff now implicated: "I never heard of them." Mr Murdoch's answers left him facing questions about his responsibilities as chairman and chief executive of News Corp, the global parent company of NI. News Corp shares were up nearly 6 per cent at close of trading in New York, following discussions among its directors about possibly replacing him as chief executive.

Mr Murdoch insisted his company was too big for him to focus on the details of the *News of the World*. "This is not an excuse," he said. "The *News of the World* is less than 1 per cent of my company."

Tom Watson, a Labour MP, repeatedly challenged him about his personal responsibility. James Murdoch tried to stop Mr Watson, but the MP insisted: "Your father has responsibility for corporate governance. It's revealing, what he didn't know, or people didn't tell him."

Rupert Murdoch said he was not "hands off" but added: "The *News of the World*, perhaps I lost sight of, because it was so small in the general frame of our company."

Mr Murdoch insisted that he remained in charge. Yet when asked if he accepted personal responsibility for the wrongdoing, he said: "No."

Responsibility lay with his managers, he said. Mr Watson asked if he was acknowledging that he had been lied to. He replied: "Clearly."

Mark Oaten

"He's a very troubled man living a very dangerous double life."

The timing of Mark Oaten's downfall was particularly damaging to the Liberal Democrats since it occurred as the party was trying to replace the popular Charles Kennedy. Kennedy had stood down following public revelations about his drinking problem – something that had long been the subject of Westminster whispers. Oaten was one of the men vying for the vacant leadership, but the exposé about his private predilections destroyed his chances, and he chose not to stand for re-election to his parliamentary seat in 2010. In 2011 he accepted the position as executive of the International Fur Trade Federation.

23 January 2006
Scandal-hit Lib Dems in freefall meltdown
Party clings to Campbell after Oaten gay sex shame

Sir Menzies Campbell appeared last night to be the Liberal Democrats' only hope of restoring their battered credibility after Mark Oaten's resignation plunged the party into its worst crisis for a generation.

Mr Oaten, 41, who is married with two children, quit as home affairs spokesman on Saturday night after claims that he paid for sex with a 23-year-old male prostitute.

Last night, there were signs that grassroots activists – shocked by the revelations – would rally to Sir Menzies, at 64 the oldest of the leadership contenders, as a steady hand to see them through the crisis. Sir Menzies, thought by some to be too old, was already the bookmakers' favourite to succeed Charles Kennedy in a contest that ends on 2 March.

He is now the 5–4 odds on favourite.

William Hill, the bookmaker, said that since Mr Oaten's resignation not one bet had been laid on the other candidates, Simon Hughes and Chris Huhne.

One pro-Campbell MP said last night: "In this situation, you either opt for a leap in the dark, as the Tories did with David Cameron, or you go for an experienced hand."

However, supporters of Mr Huhne, 51, the Treasury spokesman, said the momentum was with their man and gains for Sir Menzies would be a temporary phenomenon.

Mr Oaten, who last week pulled out of the leadership race because of lack of support, is understood to be fighting to save his marriage.

He quit on Saturday night after being confronted by the *News of the World* with allegations about his private life.

The resignation, on the heels of Mr Kennedy's ousting over drink problems, coincided with the Lib Dems' worst polls in five years.

A Mori poll for the *Sun* put the party on 15 per cent, down from its general election height of 22 per cent and its average of 20 per cent between 2001 and 2005.

The triple misfortune has plunged the Liberal movement into its deepest crisis since the 1970s when Jeremy Thorpe quit as leader of the Liberal party following allegations of a homosexual affair.

Sir Menzies, the acting leader, sought to rally the Lib Dems, calling on members to show "unity and purpose".

With his party in shock over the loss of a rising star, Sir Menzies told *Sky News*: "The task is to draw the party together and move forward.

"No party is entirely subject to what happens to any one individual. The party is much bigger than that. My task as acting leader is to secure a sense of unity and purpose.

"We have a strong political agenda. We have a sense of purpose, we have a great deal to do and a great opportunity in which to do it."

Mr Huhne, MP for Eastleigh – the neighbouring constituency to Mr Oaten's Winchester seat – said the resignation was an "extremely regrettable" loss.

But he told BBC1's *Sunday AM*: "Those of us who enter public life realise that we are going to be subject to a higher degree of scrutiny than those who don't."

Mr Hughes, 54, is the party president and considered second favourite for the leadership. He was making no public comment last night, with aides saying it had been left to Sir Menzies to issue the party's response.

Mr Hughes felt obliged to respond last week to rumours about his own sexuality by formally denying that he was homosexual.

The *Daily Telegraph* understands that Mr Oaten, no political friend of Sir Menzies, had planned to endorse Mr Hughes this week despite the party president's Left-leaning instincts.

Lib Dem MPs accept that Mr Oaten, who invited cameras into his family home before launching his leadership campaign, exposed himself to charges of hypocrisy by his alleged behaviour.

Only last week he lambasted the Government's new strategy on prostitution as "a missed opportunity". Last night, a senior Tory MP took grim satisfaction that the "holier than thou" Lib Dems had been shown up.

But he acknowledged that Mr Oaten was always the leadership candidate they had feared as he "took and held Winchester so he knows how to appeal to Tory voters".

Also 23 January 2006
What possessed him to take such a risk?
Oaten showed a reckless disregard for the skeletons in his cupboard,
further damaging his party's hopes of regaining credibility
By Caroline Davies and Brendan Carlin

Mark Oaten's utter recklessness in pitching for the Liberal Democrats' leadership knowing that his private life would be subject to the most intense scrutiny has dumbfounded many in the party.

The result for its reeling rank-and-file is nothing short of catastrophic – two high-profile resignations in two weeks, two nails hammered in so hard they threaten to splinter and crack any remote hopes the Lib Dems may have nurtured about one day overtaking the Conservatives to break Britain's two-party mould.

Charles Kennedy's demise was tortuously slow. Mr Oaten's fall has been vertiginous.

Just 13 days ago the 41-year-old member for Winchester sought to underscore his "family man" credentials, ushering television cameras into his Hampshire home in Bramdean on the eve of his leadership bid to film him having a meal with his wife Belinda and their two daughters.

Yesterday the house was empty, its inhabitants, according to neighbours, having packed and fled the predicted media onslaught in the wake of sordid allegations.

The claims, in the *News of the World*, are made by an unnamed 23-year-old "rent boy" who says the prominent MP regularly visited him over a period of six months after making contact through a gay sex website in 2004, that Mr Oaten paid £80 a time for homosexual sex, encouraged him to perform "an unspeakable act of degradation" and on one occasion paid £140 for "three-in-a-bed" gay sex.

Mr Oaten's alleged visits were said to have ceased after the man eventually recognised him. "He's a very troubled man living a very dangerous double life," concluded the male prostitute.

By Saturday evening, the former lobbyist and SDP councillor had resigned his front-bench position as home affairs spokesman and was publicly apologising for "errors of judgment in personal behaviour" and "embarrassment caused" to family, friends, constituency and party.

At Westminster, there is intense speculation over what prompted Mr Oaten to pursue his high-risk leadership bid when he knew there were such easily exposed skeletons in his cupboard. Was it sheer arrogance, total denial, or ambition so overriding that he was prepared to risk the party's already damaged reputation?

If he harboured any fears of exposure they were well concealed as he followed Sir Menzies Campbell in announcing his candidacy on Mr Kennedy's resignation, proclaiming: "I believe I am a 21st-century Liberal and I am determined to lead a 21st-century Liberal Party."

The fall-out from his resignation is all the more immense following so closely on Mr Kennedy's admission of a drink problem and the messy behind-the-scenes battle to get him to stand down as leader. For many it further taints the party, attaching to it the sleaze tag akin to that which helped to sink the Major government.

Journalists have a nose for scandal and are always on the scent. Just last week Simon Hughes, 54, the unmarried MP for Bermondsey and another leadership candidate, was asked directly in an interview if he was homosexual. "The answer is no, as it happens," he responded. "But if it was the case, which it isn't, I hope that it would not be an issue."

What next, mumble the party's shocked MPs. A revelation, perhaps – preposterous as it is – that Sir Menzies, the 64-year-old athletic acting leader, abused steroids during his reign as Britain's fastest sprinter, a title he held from 1967 to 1974? The way the Lib Dems are going, nothing seems impossible.

These latest developments undoubtedly considerably bolster Sir Menzies's strong bid to be leader. He was lashed to the helm yesterday as his party lurched through this latest controversy, grimly trying to maintain course. "No party is entirely subject to what happens to any one individual," he assured television viewers. "The party is much bigger than that and my task as acting leader is to restore a sense of unity and purpose."

From a historical perspective the Liberals should be used to dealing with scandal – of a sexual or other nature. The party's leaders, or would-be leaders, have often led energetic private lives.

As far back as 1886 another leadership contender, one Charles Dilke, an unmarried high-flier, was brought down by his association with a number of women – one housemaid reported at the time: "He taught me every French vice" – but principally because his association with a Mrs Virginia Crawford which was cited in the Pall Mall Gazette's divorce reports. He kept his seat, but William Gladstone never gave him office.

Gladstone, the "Grand Old Man", himself engaged in twice-weekly nocturnal rescue missions where he would visit street prostitutes and invite them to Downing Street for "Bible readings", afterwards self-flagellating to rid himself of impure thoughts and writing about it all in his diaries. A discreet press enabled him to serve four terms as prime minister during a 63-year political career which saw him leaving office at the age of 85 in 1895.

Herbert Asquith's propensity to shower his mistresses with love letters was again treated with much tolerance, even when it was discovered that between 1912 to 1915 he was furiously writing three times a day to his mistress Venetia Stanley, often during crisis Cabinet meetings, illuminating her on the country's most secret matters and strategic plans for the armies of the Western Front. She broke off their affair and married one of his Cabinet colleagues.

David Lloyd George's seemingly insatiable sexual appetite earned him the soubriquet "the old Goat". Described by the *Encyclopaedia Britannica* as "incapable of fidelity", he was said to have had as many as six mistresses on the go at once during his time as chancellor, then prime minister. Even a tryst on the Cabinet table refused to outrage a tame press.

Just once, in 1909, the *People* newspaper ventured to accuse him of an affair with a Mrs Catherine Edwards, the wife of a Montgomeryshire doctor. He sued for libel in the High Court – and won.

By the 1970s the press was less willing to turn a blind eye. Jeremy Thorpe, who led the Liberals from 1967 to 1976, was a high-profile scalp following lurid allegations of a homosexual entanglement as a young MP with Norman Scott, a stable lad and former male model.

Mr Scott's evidence of a passionate night spent together – always fiercely denied by Mr Thorpe – was delivered in graphic detail during the trial of a man, Andrew Newton, for shooting Mr Scott's great Dane, Rinka, on Exmoor. Mr Thorpe resigned as leader.

He subsequently lost his seat after Mr Newton claimed to have been hired by Mr Thorpe to kill Mr Scott. This saw Mr Thorpe sensationally facing trial in 1979 for conspiracy to murder. He was acquitted, but finished politically.

Paddy Ashdown – now Lord Ashdown – survived his brush with extra-marital sex and the tabloid newspaper soubriquet "Paddy Pantsdown" after it was revealed in 1992 that he had enjoyed an affair some years before with his then secretary Tricia Howard.

This revelation was prompted by the theft, from his solicitor's office, of papers warning that he might be cited in Mrs Howard's divorce proceedings which found their way to the *News of the World*. If anything, his popularity increased, and he remained leader until 1999, when he handed over the reins to Mr Kennedy.

"Chatshow Charlie" as the new laid-back leader became known, was fighting a different devil. Known to be "fond of a drink", it became a mainstream issue when he was confronted by Jeremy Paxman on *Newsnight*.

His admission to a "drink problem" was eventually forced by evidence given to his former PR Daisy McAndrew, now ITN's chief political correspondent, of a delegation of the party's most senior MPs delivering Mr Kennedy the ultimatum that he must seek treatment. With the threat of a mass walkout by his frontbench team, he was forced to quit.

Ironically it was Mark Oaten who stood at his side as Mr Kennedy announced his resignation. To add to the turmoil, the Lib Dem leader in the Lords, Lord McNally, admitted he too had been an alcoholic in the 1980s.

The Lib Dems won 62 seats in the last election – the highest number for 80 years. Gone were the days when, in the 1960s, it was joked that the entire party could travel to the Commons in a single taxi.

But in the immediate aftermath of the Kennedy debacle, opinion polls show their support slumped to just 15 per cent – their lowest for five years. Polls now are likely to show a further decline. In the matter of a few short weeks, they have found themselves fighting for the survival of their party as a credible force in British politics.

Joe Orton

"It's all explained in the diary. You'll find all the answers there."

"Not for a long time have I disliked a play so much," wrote the *Daily Telegraph* drama critic about one of Joe Orton's scripts, characterising him as someone who had "discovered . . . that he could always get a laugh by being callous about a corpse, and so now he's always doing it". But whatever else he thought about the play's merits, it had undeniably left an impression on him: "I feel," he said, "as if snakes had been writhing round my feet." It was this dark quality that underlay the success of Orton's plays over three intense years, but it's possible that his life, and the relationships that comprised it, were darker still.

Orton met Kenneth Halliwell, who was seven years his senior, at RADA, and they began a relationship that was strange and yet seemingly robust enough to sustain their being both lovers and artistic collaborators. They were convinced of their "specialness" and accordingly refused to work for long periods. When desperately short of money they reluctantly spent six-month stretches at Cadbury's; otherwise they relieved the boredom they'd deliberately courted with bouts of tomfoolery that occasionally collapsed into a kind of art. Their infamous and surreal assaults on the contents of several of Islington's libraries landed them in jail, where unexpectedly Orton had an artistic breakthrough: "Being in the nick brought detachment to my writing. I wasn't involved any more. And suddenly it worked."

As Orton became more successful, so Halliwell drew into himself, becoming depressed and paranoid. He seemed to receive each new triumph by Orton as an insult to himself. The last person who spoke to Halliwell was his doctor, who had called to arrange a visit to the psychiatrist. "Don't worry," Halliwell told him, "I'm feeling better now. I'll go and see the doctor tomorrow morning."

10 August 1967
Joe Orton: Playwright and
flatmate found dead
By T. A. Sandrock

Joe Orton, 34, the playwright, whose play *Loot* has run almost 400 performances at the Criterion Theatre was found dead yesterday with severe head injuries in his bed-sitting room in Noel Road, Islington.

His room-mate Kenneth Leith Halliwell, 41, a freelance writer, was also found dead, probably from an overdose of drugs. The two had shared the room for eight years.

Police are satisfied that no one else was involved and are treating the case as murder and suicide. Orton was found on a bed clothed only in a pyjama jacket. Halliwell was lying naked on the floor. Police took possession of some small bottles.

A preliminary post-mortem conducted by Dr. F. Camps indicated that Orton had been attacked with a hammer found near the bed.

Examination of the room suggests that Halliwell carried out the attack and that the first blow, police believe, stunned Orton sufficiently to prevent him moving. There appeared to have been several blows struck while he lay unconscious.

In May 1962, the two men pleaded guilty at Old Street to theft of and damage to library books, and each was sentenced to six months' imprisonment.

It was stated that they had decorated their flat from ceiling to floor with art plates taken from the library books. They also damaged some of the books by sticking nude photographs in them.

Valuable art plates had been taken out and extraordinary commentaries written at the front of the books. In the front of one book a monkey's head had been pasted in the middle of a rose.

A probation officer said both men were extraordinarily self-centred and were jealous of other people's success. There was obviously a very strong emotional relationship between them.

While in prison Orton wrote two plays, *Loot* and another called *Entertaining Mr Sloane*, the story of a lodger being seduced by his landlady and also being wanted by her homosexual brother.

Orton, whose proper Christian names were John Kingsley, was born in Leicester where he attended primary and secondary schools. His father still lives there in a council flat.

Afterwards; in his own words, he had a variety of jobs and got the sack from every one. He appeared as a juvenile in Leicester's Little Theatre productions and then with the aid of a grant from Leicester education committee went to RADA.

But, as he told a reporter who interviewed him in Leicester last week: "I had the writing itch. While in London I served a short prison sentence for stealing a book but the experience came in useful to me when I started play writing."

He had returned to Leicester to see *Entertaining Mr Sloane*, at the Phoenix Theatre – the first time it had been shown in his home city. He said: "I was delighted with the production."

In a BBC radio interview Orton, who was married and divorced, said: "I want to go on writing plays but you can never tell how long it will last. My accountant has told me not to spend too much money in the next two years.

"By then everything will have been settled and the payment of the film rights for *Loot* will have been settled and I shall know just how I stand financially." He was being paid £100,000 for the film rights of *Loot*, a prize-winning play which ends its run at the Criterion on 26 August.

It went on as usual last night. Added significance was given to a black-edged "In Memoriam" notice for one of the characters in the play which is pictured on the front of the programme.

In June two new Orton plays opened at the Royal Court Theatre under the title "Crimes of Passion". Despite his success he continued to live in his small Islington flat with his friend.

He had also written a script for a Beatles film, which Brian Epstein, the Beatles' manager, did not find acceptable.

Friends in the theatre said there had been several quarrels between Orton and Halliwell in public. One said: "Halliwell was very edgy about their friendship. But everything seemed to be going Joe's way with a new play on the stocks and film scripts in the offing."

Det. Supt Walter Patton and Det. Chief Inspector Arthur Maxwell took charge of yesterday's inquiries. Neighbours told the police that the two men lived in the top floor flatlet.

The bodies were removed to St. Pancras mortuary. An inquest will be opened this morning at St. Pancras.

A neighbour said: "You often saw them on fine nights sitting on the steps reading a book. About the only change one has noticed is that the older one seemed to have taken to wearing a toupee recently.

"None of the telly people who are buying houses in the street at prices from £15,000 to £18,000 seemed to have known them."

Joe Orton killed by frenzied flatmate
Suicide after murder
By a *Daily Telegraph* reporter

Joe Orton, the playwright, was hammered to death by his flatmate Kenneth Halliwell in "a deliberate form of frenzy", a Coroner's jury at St. Pancras, London, was told yesterday at the inquest on both men.

The jury returned a verdict that Halliwell, 41, murdered Orton, 34, author of the prize-winning play *Loot* which has just finished a run of about 400 London performances in London, and then took his own life.

Orton was found dead, with severe head injuries, on a divan bed. A heavily blood-stained hammer was lying on a counterpane covering his body. Halliwell's nude body, with blood splashes on the chest, was lying beside the bed.

Prof. Francis Camps, the pathologist, said it looked as if Orton "did not really know what was hitting him". He had not put up any defence.

Orton had been struck at least nine blows, which suggested "a deliberate form of frenzy". It was his opinion that Halliwell died of acute barbiturate poisoning after "an enormous overdose".

Dr. Douglas Gordon Ismay, of Great Cumberland Street, Marylebone, said Halliwell, a freelance writer, had been seeing him since April. In May, Orton, whose real Christian names were John Kingsley, and Halliwell had gone on holiday to Morocco.

When they came back Halliwell had continually been to see him saying that he was very depressed. "He talked about taking his own life and said that he had been thinking about it for some while."

This had led to trouble between the two men and that there was a suggestion that they would break up after sharing flats together for 10 years.

Dr. Ismay said he had seen Halliwell two days before he died. "Towards the end of the interview he said that he had been taking large quantities of hashish while on holiday and had actually been eating it. This rather disturbed me.

"I spoke to him several times over the phone that same evening and he seemed much happier because of the arrangements I had made for him to see a psychiatrist.

"Halliwell knew what he was doing absolutely but he was emotionally disturbed. A crisis had been building up for some time."

Dr. Ismay agreed with the deputy coroner, Dr. John Burton, that Halliwell's apparently happier state of mind could have been caused by his having finally decided what to do about his relationship with Orton, and that he had planned to murder him and then commit suicide.

Det. Supt. Walter Patten produced a note and diary found at the flat in Noel Road, Islington, where the two men had been living and where they had been found dead on 9 August. It was signed "K. H." (Kenneth Halliwell) and said: "It's all explained in the diary. You'll find all the answers there."

Orton was on his divan bed with the covers pulled up to his chest. A heavily bloodstained hammer was found on the counterpane. Halliwell was lying nude on the floor beside the divan.

Nearby was an opened tin of grapefruit juice, a glass with the remains of some juice in it and, in the kitchen, a bucket containing numerous empty capsules.

Dr. Burton said: "The conclusion must be that Orton was killed by Halliwell, who had then taken his own life. The evidence is fairly overwhelming."

The verdict raised the question of the disposal of Joe Orton's estate. He had recently sold the film rights of the play *Loot* for £100,000 and had considerable success with other works.

Orton and Halliwell had both made wills in each other's favour. The likeliest course is the division of Orton's estate among his family.

The Pankhursts and the Suffragettes

"We don't do this because we like it. It is the only way.
We have no other way of making ourselves heard."

By the late 19th century, the campaign to extend the franchise to women had become steadily more organised and co-ordinated. In 1903 Emmeline Pankhurst founded the Women's Social and Political Union, feeling that the existing alternatives were insufficiently radical, and the movement embarked in a markedly more militant direction. Where before agitation had been confined to the distribution of leaflets and presenting petitions, now the women – sneeringly described as Suffragettes by the *Daily Mail* – began to employ methods such as hunger strikes (inspired by exiles from Tsarist Russia) and arson: scandal had been transmuted into an effective political tool. But it was a tool that had to be used repeatedly if their cause was to be kept in the public eye (over a thousand women would be arrested in the first two decades of the 20th century), and for all its ability to galvanise, it had little value as a means of persuasion. Finally, in 1918, women over 30 (as long as they met minimum property qualifications) were given the right to vote. This was as much because of the efforts of more constitutionally inclined pressure groups as well as a recognition of the contribution women had made to winning the war, yet the electrifying impact of the Suffragettes should neither be underestimated or forgotten.

15 October 1908
Suffragist campaign
Leaders at Bow-street

The centre of interest in the Suffragist proceedings was yesterday transferred to Bow-street Police-court, where it had been decided that all cases arising out of Tuesday night's demonstration should be heard. Before the doors were opened a crowd had collected outside the building, and subsequently it assumed considerable proportions, particularly during the dinner hour. There was a good deal of more or less ironical cheering, and eventually a large force of police was brought out to clear the street.

The magistrate was Mr Curtis Bennett, who first had before him:

Mrs Pankhurst

Miss Christabel Pankhurst

Mrs Drummond

– who had been arrested on warrants in consequence of their failure to appear in answer to summonses calling upon them to show cause why they should not find sureties to be of good behaviour.

Mr H. Muskett (Wontner and Sons) prosecuted.

The defendants had been detained in custody all night. Immediately they were placed in the dock, Miss Pankhurst said they were informed that, under Section 17 of the Summary Jurisdiction Act of 1879, they were entitled to he tried which way they liked, and they deemed to be tried by a jury.

The Magistrate: That section does not apply. We will go on.

Miss Pankhurst then applied for an adjournment, in order that the defendants might be legally advised and represented, and the magistrate said he would consider that question later on.

Mr Muskett said the defendants were all prominent leaders in the agitation which had been disturbing the metropolis for so long, and they were brought up upon warrants for having disobeyed a summons to appear on Monday afternoon, charging them with having been guilty of conduct likely to provoke a breach of the pence. It was alleged that they had circulated, and caused to be circulated and published, a certain handbill calling upon members of the public to "rush" the House of Commons on Tuesday evening. When process was issued, it was only known to the police authorities that the conduct of which the defendants were alleged to have been guilty was likely to lead to a breach of the peace, but now it was known as a fact that an actual breach of the peace had occurred owing to the incitement to riot, for which the prosecution said these ladies were responsible. The fact that between thirty and forty persons were to come before the Court that morning in connection with the demonstration was sufficient evidence of the fact that a serious breach of the peace had occurred. In the latter part of September it came to the notice of the police authorities that a demonstration was to be made by these ladies and their sympathisers on the second day of the present session of Parliament, and Superintendent Wells was directed by the Commissioner of Police to see Mrs Pankhurst at the office of the Women's Union, in Clement's Inn, and caution her as to what the probable results of any such demonstration would be. He saw her on 2 October. and she handed to him a printed bill which she said was about to be circulated, and the wording of which was of a comparatively harmless nature:

Votes for Women – Men and women, come to the House of Commons on Tuesday, 13 October at 7.30 p.m., and support the women who are demanding justice.

The Superintendent duly administered a caution, and left. On 8 October Inspector Jarvis had occasion to attend at the offices of the union, and he saw Mrs Drummond, who was a very active agitator, and Miss Christabel Pankhurst. That young lady said to the inspector, "What about the 13th? Have you seen our new bills?" and she produced a handbill which, in substance, formed the foundation of the present charge. It was worded:

Votes for Women – Men and women, help the Suffragists to rush the House of Commons, on Tuesday, 13 October at 7.30 p.m.

With regard to it, Miss Pankhurst said that the words "to rush" were not in sufficiently large type, and they were going to have them made much more distinct. On Sunday last a meeting of these ladies took place in Trafalgar-square, causing an enormous amount of additional labour to be thrown upon the shoulders of the police.

Superintendent Wells saw Mrs Drummond distributing the bills complained of, and he received from her one, in which the words "to rush" appeared in larger type than on the bill shown to Inspector Jarvis. Mrs Drummond was asked for the names of those responsible for the issuing of the leaflet, and she said the responsible officers of the Women's Union, who were the hon. secretaries, Mrs Pankhurst and Mrs Tuke, the hon. treasurer, Mrs Pethick Lawrence, and the national organiser, Miss Christabel Pankhurst. At this meeting speeches were delivered by Mrs Pankhurst and her daughter and others, inciting the people who were present in the square to carry out the programme of rushing the House of Commons. The magistrate would agree that such conduct as that could not be tolerated in this country, and the authorities accordingly set the law in motion. It was not necessary to adduce any legal authority for the general proposition, which was submitted on behalf of the Commissioner of Police, namely, that all persons who were guilty of such conduct as was attributed to these three ladies might, and ought, to be ordered to find sureties for their future good behaviour. It could not be allowed with impunity that persons should incite other people to riot. Superintendent Wells then went into the witness-box, and spoke as to what took place upon the occasion of his visit to the offices of the Women's Union. He was given a copy of a letter which had been addressed to Mr Asquith, and Mrs Pankhurst said their action would depend upon the reply they received to it. If it was a satisfactory reply, there would be nothing but a great cheer for the Government, but if it was unsatisfactory there would be a demonstration, and they would try to get into the House of Commons. Witness said, "You cannot get there, because the police will not allow you unless you come with cannon." Mrs Pankhurst said no lethal weapons would be used, and no breaking of windows would form part of the programme, but witness pointed out the great danger of bringing so large a concourse of people into the vicinity of Parliament. Mrs Pankhurst replied, "Mr Asquith will be responsible if there is any disorder and accident." Witness, however, expressed the opinion that the suffragists would be responsible. They then discussed the window-breaking matter, and Miss Pankhurst said that although it was not in their programme, they could not always control the women of their union. This was the substance of the interview reported to the Commissioner.

In the course of the meeting in Trafalgar-square on Sunday last Mrs Drummond was distributing the handbills complained of. She was an active leader of the suffragists, and she wore a uniform with the word general or generalissimo on the cap. (Laughter.) Witness told her that she and Mrs Pankhurst would be prosecuted.

Mr Muskett: Did a very large demonstration take place last evening in the vicinity of the House of Commons?

Witness: Yes: the traffic was wholly disorganised for four hours, and for three hours the streets were in great disorder. At ten o'clock I had to clear them.

Did this entail the employment of a very large body of police to maintain order? – A very large body indeed. Ten persons were treated at Westminster Hospital, and seven or eight constables and sergeants were more or less injured.

In cross-examination by Miss Pankhurst, witness said the defendants did not give a definite undertaking to appear in answer to the summonses on Monday afternoon, but they left him under the impression that they would do so. The crowd in Trafalgar-square on Sunday was quite orderly.

Miss Pankhurst: Are you aware that any member of the Government was there?

Witness: I don't know whether I should answer that question.

Miss Pankhurst: I think it has a bearing on the case.

Witness: I saw one.

Miss Pankhurst: Did you see Mr Lloyd George?

The Magistrate: I think you must be satisfied with the answer that he saw one.

Miss Pankhurst: At a later stage I shall have to require the presence of Mr Lloyd George as one of our witnesses. (To witness): Did we incite the people to do personal violence or damage to property? – You did what I complain of – you brought a disorderly crowd to the neighbourhood of Parliament.

What do you understand by the word "rush"? – To make an improper entry.

Miss Pankhurst: It would not necessarily mean that a great deal of violence should be used or weapons carried.

Replying to further questions, the superintendent said he did not hear the speeches made by Mr John Burns at the time of the Trafalgar-square riots.

Miss Pankhurst: The law breaker is now sitting in judgment upon others who have done far less than he did himself. (To witness): Were you in Trafalgar-square when Mr Will Thorne, M.P., made a speech on the question of unemployment? – No.

Did you hear him call upon the people to rush the bakers' shops? – It was reported to me.

Doesn't it occur to you that his action is more reprehensible than ours? – It has occurred to me that he might be prosecuted the same as you are.

You have seen Mr Gladstone's statement to the effect that the police are responsible for these proceedings? – No; you have kept me so busily engaged that I have not had time to read the papers. (Laughter.)

Miss Pankhurst: I tender you our most humble apologies, but we are really not responsible. Can you tell me whether Mr Gladstone and other members of the Government were consulted before these proceedings were taken? – I cannot.

Can you tell me whether anything has been determined as to the length of the sentences to be imposed upon us? – No.

Are you aware that in a London drawing-room Mr Horace Smith asserted that in sentencing one of our colleagues to six months' imprisonment he was only doing what he had been told to do? – No.

What can you tell me as to the demeanour of the crowd last night? – Bad; rowdy.

But not violent or menacing? – They were violent in a measure. Two or three policemen were badly hurt.

There has been no loss of life, and practically no injury to property? – There were two or three windows broken.

Miss Pankhurst: But no serious consequences have followed, having regard to the enormous number of people. Thank you, Mr Wells.

In answer to Mrs Pankhurst, witness said he had recognised from the first that this was a political movement with a political object, "but," he added, "you are getting beyond it now." He knew that in previous franchise agitations responsible statesmen had advised the people to do the same as the Suffragists were doing. He agreed that at the time of Mr John Burns's arrest there was a great deal more violence shown by the crowd than at any of the Suffragist demonstrations. The police had been exceptionally considerate with regard to the women.

Mrs Pankhurst: We make no complaint against the police.

Mrs Drummond (cross-examining): You recognise that this is a political movement?

Witness: Yes, you want something that you can't get. (Laughter.)

Mrs Drummond: I should like to ask Mr Wells if he doesn't think we are going to get it? – I cannot answer that.

Miss Pankhurst: The fact that these proceedings are taken by the Commissioner of Police is no proof that the Government is not pulling the strings in the background? – I cannot say one way or the other.

Inspector Jarvis read extracts from his notes of the speeches made by the defendants in Trafalgar-square on Sunday. Miss Pankhurst said:

I want you all to be there on the evening on the 13th, and I hope that that will be an end of this movement. On 30 June we succeeded in driving Mr Asquith underground. He is afraid of us, and so are his Government. We want you to help the women to rush their way into the House. You won't get locked up, it is only the women who get locked up, because you have the vote. If you are afraid we will take the lead, and you will follow us. We are not afraid of imprisonment.

Witness added that Mrs Pankhurst spoke in a similar strain.

In cross-examination, witness admitted that he might be mistaken in thinking that the defendants promised to appear in answer to the summonses. He had always regarded the Suffragists' word as reliable. Unless the defendants had been very much disguised they would never have got to the meeting at Caxton Hall on Tuesday evening. It had not occurred to witness that by breaking the law the Suffragists might, become law-makers as Mr John Burns had done.

Miss Pankhurst: Do you remember the speech made by Mr Lloyd George in Swansea the other day? He incited his supporters there to fling the women out ruthlessly. Don't you agree with me that that was incitement to violence?

Witness: I cannot express an opinion.

Inspector Shepherd gave format evidence as to the defendants being present at Queen's Hall on Monday afternoon at the time originally fixed for the hearing of the summonses against them.

This was the case for the prosecution, and Miss Pankhurst again applied for an adjournment, which was granted, the magistrate offering to accept bail in two sureties of £50 for each of the defendants.

Miss Pankhurst: I think there will be no difficulty about that.

Mrs Pankhurst: You can take our word.

The Magistrate: I must have bail as well.

Miss Pankhurst: Very well, you have both. (Laughter.)

Mr and Mrs Pethick Lawrence became bail for Mrs Pankhurst, and sureties were also at once forthcoming for the other two defendants.

The cases of the men and women arrested on Tuesday night were next disposed of. As each of the female defendants entered the dock she demanded to be tried by a jury, and the magistrate had to explain that, this was not possible.

Ada Wright was charged with obstruction, and Police-constable 2 AR stated that she attempted to break through the police cordon, shouting, "I shall enter the House."

Defendant: We don't do this because we like it. It is the only way. We have no other way of making ourselves heard.

Defendant was ordered to find a surety in £10 to be of good behaviour for twelve months; in default one month's imprisonment.

Clara Codd and Selina Martin were similarly charged and dealt with. The former was said to have forced her way to the Clock Tower entrance to the House, and demanded to see Mr Asquith; while, according to Police-constable 125 B, Martin was in Whitehall shouting "Votes for women. Stick to me, boys." (Laughter.)

Giving evidence against Mary Ann Redhead, also charged with obstruction, Police-constable 236 L said she climbed on a coping in Whitehall Court, and addressed a large and boisterous crowd. She was very disorderly. The defendant was ordered to find a surety, with the alternative of two months' imprisonment.

Kathleen Tanner, who tried to break through the police cordon in Parliament-square, was dealt with in a like manner.

Mabel Capper was stated by Police-constable 291 L to have clung to the railings outside Scotland Yard, shouting, "Never mind the police, people." The magistrate said she must find a surety in £10 or go to prison for a month.

Defendant (laughing): One month, please.

A similar decision was given in the case of Ada Lamb who tried to break through the police lines.

The next nine defendants were all remanded at their own request, in order that they might, have legal advice. Mr Frost, solicitor, stating that he had just received instructions to appear for them. They were:

Lettice Annie Floyd

Winifred Bray
Elizabeth Billing
Florence Williams
Mary Leigh
Grace Hodgson Boutelle
Amy Shallard
Janet Coates
Maud Brindley.

Mr Pethick Lawrence became bail in each case. Mrs Leigh is the woman who was sentenced to imprisonment at this court for breaking Mr Asquith's windows.

Eleven men, who had been arrested for obstruction and assaults, were next dealt with.

Henry Justus Collett, a well-dressed young fellow, was alleged to have shouted to the crowd in Broad Sanctuary, "Back with the police. Break through them." He was ordered to find a surety in £10; in default, one month.

Harold Peak was fined £5 or one month for striking Police-constable 357 D in the face with his fist when he was requested to go away.

John Thomas Butler was sentenced to three months' hard labour for striking and kicking Police-constable 77 L.

Albert Gurtner, Henry Chase, Frederick George Paine, and Robert Henry Brown were each charged with obstructing the police, and were ordered to find sureties.

Patrick Madden was sentenced to two months' hard labour for assaulting Police-constable 652 Y. The constable stated that the prisoner and the crowd were so violent that he had to use his truncheon.

Albert Bond and Richard Bond, brothers, and James Aylward were each bound over in their own recognisances for obstruction.

For assaulting Police-constable 33 D R in Tothill-street, Alfred Smith was ordered six weeks' hard labour.

The remaining female defendants were remanded without any evidence being given, in order that Mr Frost might appear for them on a future occasion. Their names are:

Gertrude Llewellyn
Kathleen Browne
Marian Wallace Dunlop
Gertrude Mary Ansell
Mary Ann Mitchell Aldbow
Ellen Smith
Jane Grey
Ada Flatman.

They are all charged with obstruction. Mr Pethick Lawrence's bail was accepted for them.

The last case was that of Charles Wilmott Mawson Cookson, a motor mechanic, who was charged with obstructing and assaulting the police. It was alleged that while two women were being taken to the station the prisoner shouted, "Cowards! Down with the police! We're nine to one," and also that he struck a sergeant on the ear.

The magistrate said it was possible that it was some other man who assaulted the sergeant, but in his excitement the prisoner created an obstruction, and he would have to find a surety in £10 for his good behaviour.

23 November 1911
Suffragist riot
223 defendants

Tuesday night's demonstration – the first outcome of the renewal of militant tactics on the part of the Suffragists – resulted in 223 arrests being made, a record number for one night, and scenes which have become familiar daring previous active periods of the campaign were re-enacted at Bow-street Police-court yesterday. From an early hour in the morning the streets in the vicinity of the court presented an animated appearance, and a large force of police was on duty keeping the crowds of sightseers on the move. For some time an almost continuous stream of private motor-cars and taxi-cabs brought up the ladies who were to surrender to their bail, and it was noticed that practically all of them carried bags and parcels, apparently containing clothing and other necessities. Accommodation was found for the defendants and their belongings in various rooms in the police-station, and the neighbouring restaurants were kept busy supplying tea and coffee and other refreshments. The court itself was quickly filled with witnesses and prominent supporters of the movement, amongst whom were Miss Christabel Pankhurst and Mr Pethick Lawrence. Very few of the general public succeeded in obtaining admission, and a long queue waited patiently outside for the greater part of the day.

There was considerable delay before Mr Marsham, the special magistrate in attendance, took his seat on the Bench. Mr Muskett, who, as usual, represented the Commissioner of Police, at once proceeded to make some general observations by way of preface. He said words rather failed him to describe adequately the disgraceful and discreditable scenes of organised disorder which took place on Tuesday night in the vicinity of the Houses of Parliament, the Strand, and other parts of the West end, resulting in the arrest of 223 persons, who were charged with various offences. Arising in the "A" division alone, no fewer than 189 charges had been preferred, made up as follows: Sixty-four obstruction; 114 wilful damage in the shape of window-breaking; three assaults upon the police; and eight stone-throwing, where no actual damage was done.

There was, continued Mr Muskett, practically little new to be said with regard to this class of case, he had only to call attention to one or two matters which apparently led up to these disorderly scenes, which occupied the attention of thousands of policemen from eight o'clock until after ten. He ventured to stigmatise as a disgraceful and unworthy production a leaflet which was widely distributed in the course of last week, and which bore the signature, in print, of Mrs Pethick Lawrence. It ran in these terms:

Votes for women. A deputation of women will proceed to the House of Commons to interview Mr Asquith and Mr Lloyd George on Tuesday, November 21, at eight o'clock, to protest against a bill to give votes to all men being introduced by the Government after excluding all women from the vote. As the leader of this deputation I call upon men and women in their thousands to go to Parliament-square on

Tuesday to see fair play by protecting the women from being brutally victimised by police in uniform and in plain clothes, as they were on Black Friday, November 18, 1910, when, as the result of the ill-usage they received, one woman died and many were seriously injured. Also to take note of those constables who exceed their duty and of hooligans obviously acting under their encouragement, so that they may be prepared to offer evidence, if necessary, in any subsequent police-court proceedings.

It was probably within the magistrate's knowledge, if he was one of those judicial persons who read the newspapers, that on Friday last a deputation from the various bodies in sympathy with this movement was received by the Prime Minister and the Chancellor of the Exchequer in Downing-street. It appeared that, inasmuch as those Cabinet Ministers were prepared to meet this deputation, it became necessary to alter the wording of the leaflet, and accordingly a second leaflet was issued, the opening paragraph of which read:

Votes for women. A demonstration will be made outside the House of Commons on Tuesday next to protest against the announced intention of the Government to carry a bill next session giving the vote to every man and not including any women.

This was addressed to the public, and signed by Mrs Pethick Lawrence, who continued:

I was present at the women's deputation to Mr Asquith and Mr Lloyd George when they refused to grant our demand that the Government should substitute for the Manhood Suffrage Bill a measure giving equal rights to men and women. The W.S.P.U. will therefore make a demonstration to protest against the Government's unjust policy.

It was in accordance with that call to arms that these disorderly scenes took place. A very large meeting was held at Caxton Hall, and for some hours afterwards the police were engaged in various streets in the West-end in coping with a very serious state of disorder, which would be described in detail. Mr Muskett added that in some instances the damage done exceeded £5, and such cases would necessarily have to be committed for trial at the sessions.

At the end of a sitting lasting about five hours, only thirty-seven charges had been disposed of. They all related to cases of window-breaking in the Strand, where alone, it is stated, damage to the amount of over £500 was done. The evidence showed that quite a number of the defendants were armed with hammers, whilst others had bags of stones. The most successful stone-throwers appeared to have been two young ladies named Wentworth and Willcox, who, in the course of a rush along the Strand, succeeded in breaking five large shop windows, valued altogether at £59. In addition to the usual equipment of a hammer and stones, Miss Wentworth was provided with a formidable-looking catapult. In default of paying fines, and the amount of the damage, nineteen of the defendants were sentenced to terms of imprisonment, the remainder being committed for trial or remanded. The following were the cases disposed of yesterday:

Mary Aldham, breaking a window at Charing-Cross Post Office with a hammer, fined 20s, and £2 10s damage, or fourteen days' imprisonment.

Kate Nobled, cracking a window at the same office with a stone, fined 20s, and £5 damage, or one month. Prisoner said she was not guilty; she did it as a protest.

Ethel Lewis, similar offence, fined 10s, and £5 damage, or twenty-one days'.

Janet Augusta Boyd, breaking a window at Somerset House by throwing a stone, fined 10s, and 3s damage, or seven days'. She said she did not consider she was guilty, because she was doing it for a good principle.

Edith Elizabeth Downing, similar offence, fined 10s, and 1s damage, or seven days'.

Vera Wentworth and Cecilia Willcox were charged with breaking five windows in the Strand. It was stated that they ran along the street throwing stones, and owing to the enormous crowd that assembled it was some time before the police could effect their arrest. The following windows were smashed: Lockhart's, damage £14; A.B.C. shop, damage, £15: Lyons' depots (two), damage, £12 and £10; London and South-Western Bank, damage, £8. At the police station Miss Wentworth dropped a large hammer and a catapult was found in her possession. She had been charged on five previous occasions. Both the defendants were committed for trial, Mr Pethick Lawrence and Dr. Garrett Anderson becoming bail for them.

Hester Mitchell, breaking windows at two shops in the Strand (Appenrodt's and Davies and Co., harness manufacturers), fined 10s, and £4 damage, or twenty-one days' in each case. She was carrying a hammer and five stones.

Kathleen Eleanor Roy Rothwell, breaking a window at Dunn's, the hatters, in the Strand, doing damage to the extent of £20, remanded. Defendant said she did not want bail. It was stated that on the way to the station she dropped a bag containing fourteen flint stones.

Margaret Small, breaking a window at the shop of Mr Fredk. Cleaver, tailor, 111, Strand, fined 10s, and £4 damage, or fourteen days'.

May Riches Jones was charged with breaking a window at the post office in Bedford-street, Strand, doing damage to the extent of £4. Mr Muskett said this lady was only twenty-one years of age, and he was not anxious that she should be sent to prison. In reply to the magistrate, the defendant said she came from Birmingham with the intention of breaking a window as a protest against the Government's action. She refused to be bound over. Mr Marsham ordered her to pay a fine of 5s and the amount of the damage, or seven days.

Ada Wright, breaking a window at the telegraph office, 447, Strand, sentenced to one month's imprisonment without the option of a fine, it being stated that she had a very bad record.

Maude Fussell, breaking a window at the post office, 458, Strand, damage £5, sentenced to one month's imprisonment.

Kathleen Houston and Marjorie Hasder, each of whom was stated to have been carrying a hammer, were charged with breaking a window at the West Strand Post Office. Houston was sentenced to one month's imprisonment, and Hasder was fined 10s and £2 10s damage, or fourteen days.

Lizzie Crow and Ethel Lawry, breaking a window at the post office, 447, Strand. Crow fined 10s and 15s damage, or fourteen days', and Lawry fined 5s and 15s damage, or seven days'.

Annie Ainsworth and Katherine Broadhurst, similar offence, each fined 10s and 5s damages, or seven days'. Ainsworth was carrying a hammer wrapped in brown paper.

Maude Brindley and Margaret Rowleatt, breaking a window at the West Strand telegraph office, each fined 20s and £2 10s damage. In the case of Brindley the alternative was twenty-one days', and in the other fourteen days'.

Frances Rowe, Violet Jones, and Telgrade Atheling, breaking three windows at the premises of the National Bank, 180, Strand, doing damage to the extent of £30, committed for trial, bail being allowed.

Evelyn Taylor, Helen Archdale, Aleen Connor Smith, and Violet Hudson Harvey, charged with breaking several windows at Grand Hotel Buildings, were remanded.

Olive Whurry, breaking a window at Clun House, Surrey-street, Strand, damage £10, committed for trial, on bail.

Margaret Haly, throwing a stone at a window at the *Globe* newspaper office, fined 10s, or seven days'.

All the remaining defendants were released on their own recognisances until this morning, when the hearing will be resumed, to be continued during the remainder of the week if necessary.

The magistrate remarked that he hoped that Mr Henlé, a barrister representing some of the ladies, would advise his clients to be wise enough to be bound over.

Mr Henlé: I hope to persuade the Court that a mistake has been made in these cases, and I can hardly advise my clients to be bound over if they are innocent.

2 March 1912
Suffragist raid on West-end windows
Enormous damage

Shortly before six o'clock last night a carefully organised hand of Suffragists carried out such a window-breaking campaign in the principal streets of the West-end as London has never known.

For a quarter of an hour or twenty minutes nothing was heard in the Strand, Cockspur-street, Downing-street, Whitehall, Piccadilly, Bond-street, or Oxford-street but the fall of shattered glass and the angry exclamations of the shopkeepers, who were the principal victims of the women's "demonstration".

Half an hour from the commencement of the assault, 121 women were lodged in the neighbouring police-stations, and in that brief period several thousands of pounds' worth of damage had been done. Many of the finest shop-fronts in the world had been temporarily destroyed, and splinters of glass had been scattered over their valuable contents.

Though it is safe to assume that much of the loss is covered by insurance, the proprietors of the businesses will undoubtedly suffer extensively. At any rate, the best plate-glass will be at a premium for some time to come.

In all 121 arrests were made. The women were taken to the various police-stations in the following numbers:

Cannon-row	10
Bow-street	22
Vine-street	55
Marlborough-street	26
Marylebone-lane	8
Total	121

All the prisoners at Bow-street were bailed out shortly after ten o'clock by Mr Pethick Lawrence.

The attack was begun practically simultaneously in all the streets mentioned. It was one of the busiest periods of the day – the half-hour before the shops closed for the night. Suddenly, women and girls who had a moment before appeared to be on peaceful shopping expeditions produced from bags or from muffs hammers, stones, and sticks, and began an attack upon the nearest windows, to whatever unfortunate owner they might belong.

It was not many minutes before hundreds of windows lay in fragments. The unexpectedness of the attack created consternation amongst the shopkeepers, res-taurateurs, and others, and with such rapidity did the women move that there was no time to warn those carrying on business in other parts of the thoroughfares of what was in store for them.

Information was immediately conveyed to Bow-street Police Station. New Scotland Yard, Vine-street, and other police-stations, and all the reserve constables were hurried out into the streets. In other parts of London shutters were immediately put up upon the receipt of the news, but a number of firms in the City who were oblivions of what had happened were unprepared, and also suffered damage to their premises.

The most daring incident of the raid was the excursion of Mrs Pankhurst and two of her confederates to Downing-street for the purpose of smashing the Prime Minister's windows. Just after half-past five a private motor-car, which was closed, drove at a rapid pace into the street, and as it reached the Prime Minister's residence three women jumped out and immediately began throwing stones at the house. Two windows were broken on each side of the door downstairs, four panes in all. The police patrols in the street were taken completely by surprise, but they quickly grasped the situation, and before the women could do any further damage the constables seized their arms. All three were taken in the direction of Cannon-row Police-station. But their powers of mischief were not yet exhausted. As Mrs Pankhurst was being led past the Home Office she suddenly wrenched her arm free, and threw a stone through one of the windows. About the same time another woman broke two windows at the Local Government Board offices, and quietly waited to be arrested.

When Mrs Pankhurst was searched at Cannon-row three stones were found upon her. She told the officer in charge that she had intended throwing them through the windows at the Prime Minister's house.

At the Home Office a clerk who was sitting writing had an almost miraculous escape. He was near the window when a heavy stone flew over his head, and the broken glass fell on his shoulder. At 10, Downing-street, a stone narrowly missed one of the office-keepers.

The driver of the car which carried Mrs Pankhurst and her friends to Downing-street said that he was also the owner of it, and let it out for hire. He received a postcard from a man named Marshall, whom he knew, ordering him to be at Turpin House, York-buildings, Adelphi, about five o'clock. He went there and picked up four ladies, none of whom he knew. He was told first of all that they wanted him to drive them somewhere in the neighbourhood of Whitehall, and his first instruction was to go to Charing-cross District Railway Station. There a young lady got out, and he was then entered to drive to 10, Downing-street. "I thought this rather strange," he said, "but I went there, and, before I pulled up, out the three of them jumped like lightning and commenced to chuck stones. I did not know they were Suffragists, and I think it is very unfair for them to drag me into a thing like this."

It seems that before the stones were actually thrown at the Prime Minister's house one of the women rang the bell and waited for a response. When the door was opened, she handed to the servant a letter addressed to the Prime Minister. Two stones were then thrown through the door, whilst others crashed through the windows on either side.

Hammers, rather than stones, were the favourite weapons in the other streets. Their utility for the purpose was proved by the rapid destruction their owners executed. Between St. Clement Danes and Charing-cross the array of broken windows soon presented a remarkable spectacle. The southern side of the Strand was the one singled out for attack; the other side, with a few exceptions, escaped. Fifteen minutes before the hour pedestrians in the Strand were startled to see women, the majority of whom were girls, suddenly draw hammers from beneath their costumes and strike plate-glass window after window swiftly. The shop owned at Charing-cross by the Association of Diamond Merchants offered a tempting front, diamonds of priceless value being displayed to public view. A young woman struck viciously at the plate glass with a hammer, but her strength was less than her will, and she failed to penetrate the massive frame. At the same moment there was a crash at the neighbouring picture establishment of Mr R Deighton, in the Grand Hotel buildings, and the huge window was shattered from top to bottom, a large hole having been made in the centre. The same shop suffered in the raid last autumn. Last night the weapon used was a bottle wrapped in paper.

No attempt was made by the women to escape; they calmly waited to be arrested. The jewellers' shops seem to have been specially selected, for a side window of Messrs. S. Smith and Son was punctured, and some yards further east Vaughan's jewellery establishment was broken by a couple of girls, who, after similarly treating the Kodak premises next door, ran away. A policeman gave chase and brought them back, and they then accepted the situation philosophically.

Across the road, Charing-cross Post Office came in for rough treatment. A woman produced a hammer, and three panes above the letter-boxes were reduced to splinters. She was taken to Bow-street, whither she was followed by all the women arrested in the Strand. It was noticed that the Suffragists respected a milliner's shop outside the Hotel Cecil, but attacked a tobacco shop. Among other premises damaged were two of Lyons's refreshment shops, one "ABC" and one of Appenrodt's branches.

On the south side of the Strand windows wens smashed at the following shops: Railway office in Grand Hotel-buildings, the Wigan Coal and Iron Company, National Provincial Bank of England (three), and at the shops of the Irish Linen Company (two), Aerated Bread Company, Morgan and Ball, Clements, Savoy Tailors' Guild (two), Litsica, Marx, and Co., Walk-Over Shoe Company, Kodak, J. Lyons and Co. (three), Vaughan, Palfrey and Bowen, Browning, Samuels (Ltd.), F. Cleaver, Starkie, A. Baker and Co., Salmon and Gluckstein, Bewlay and Co., Thresher and Glenny (four), W. W. Rouch and Co., J. Greenwall and Co., G. H. Elkan and Co., Allen, Chappie and Mantell, Clay and Co., F. C. Bayley, Downs and Co., S. Smith and Son, H. Appenrodt, Deighton, and J. Turner. On the north side, West Strand Telegraph Office, London and North-Western Railway, H. Appenrodt, Case, and B. B. Wells. Included in the list were a silversmith's and three jewellers' windows.

Hundreds of policemen began to arrive in response to the insistent whistles of their comrades, who were outnumbered and powerless at the start. In their helplessness they appealed to all and sundry for assistance, and the women were pursued by crowds of interested spectators. Many of the tradesmen, on hearing the sound of breaking glass, rushed out of their premises, and in several instances prevented damage by seizing the women and handing them over to the police.

When the police were seen to be on the alert the women resorted to artifice. Many of them walked calmly along with hammers and stones concealed in their muffs until they found some window which still remained intact. They then produced their weapons, and sought to remedy the omission of their predecessors. Others drove up openly in cabs, alighted with the air of potential purchasers, and even while the shopwalkers were inquiring their needs they proceeded to astonish these unoffending personages by instituting a ferocious attack upon their expensively dressed windows.

While the raiders were carrying out their work in the Strand other parties were equally active in Piccadilly, Regent-street, and the neighbourhood, and the windows of a large number of leading West-end tradesmen were deliberately broken. In every case the damage was done with a hammer suddenly produced from a muff and hurled at the sheet of plate-glass. In many cases the windows were of large size and a complete hole was made in them. In others the glass, by reason of its thickness, was only cracked, but it was none the less rendered useless for its purpose.

Throughout the whole length of Coventry-street, Regent-street, as far as Oxford-street. along Bond-street, and in the greater part of Piccadilly, the women continued the wreckage, apparently indiscriminately, scores of valuable in leading shops and other establishments suffered severely, some seven or eight windows being broken. Messrs. Swan and Edgar, at the corner of Regent-street and Piccadilly-circus, suffered severely, some seven or eight windows being broken. The Regent-street post office and Messrs. Hope Brothers' establishment were amongst many others to which the women gave their attention.

Oxford-street and Bond-street presented scenes of damage almost from end to end. The large shops of the leading firms suffered most. In Oxford-street, Waring's was assailed and many of the large windows smashed, while other firms who suffered considerable damage included Messrs. John Lewis and Co., Messrs. Peter Robinson, Messrs. D. H. Evans and Co and Messrs. Marshall and Snelgrove. In Oxford-street alone the damage is estimated at over £1,000. In most cases the windows are starred, as if the damage were caused by the smart tap of a hammer which lacked the force to cause a complete fracture. Several of the large panes have been struck in several places. Immediately after the raid the shutters were put up at many shops, and those which had escaped the attention of the women were guarded by commissionaires and police. Joiners had a busy time between seven and eight barricading broken windows in cases where no shatters are used. One of the firms in Oxford-street which escaped was Selfridges.

In Bond-street few shop windows remain intact. Both Oxford-street and Bond-street were densely crowded during the evening, and the police patrols were strengthened to deal with the pedestrian traffic.

In Cockspur-street and Trafalgar-square, where the great shipping firms have their offices, the damage was great. In some cases the brilliantly illuminated models of liners on view inside the windows were injured. A window worth £100 was ruined at the Hamburg-America offices, and the Grand Trunk Railway Company, next door, also suffered.

The outrages were responsible for the compulsory closing of practically every shop of importance in the leading West-end thoroughfares several hours before the usual time.

It is not possible to estimate with any degree of accuracy the full extent of the damage caused, but it is believed that the depredations of the women in the Vine-street area alone represent damage amounting to between £2,500 and £3,000. It is stated that the firm of Swan and Edgar, in Piccadilly, suffered to the extent of £250.

4 March 1912
Suffragist raid
124 charges: £5,000 damage

There was a remarkable scene at Bow-street Police-court on Saturday, when Mrs Pankhurst, leader of the militant Suffragists, who engaged in a window-smashing campaign in the West-end on Friday evening, was sentenced to two months imprisonment by Mr Curtis-Bennett. The court was crowded with tradesmen, their assistants, and others who had been summoned as witnesses, and when the magistrate strongly denounced the conduct of "people such as I see before me", and declared that if the law was not strong enough to cope with such a movement it must be amended, his remarks were loudly applauded. This appeared to exasperate the few women present, one of whom shouted out, "Tyrants". The reply was a burst of laughter, whereupon Mrs Pankhurst turned with a dramatic gesture, and exclaimed, "I should advise these gentlemen to communicate with the Government."

Altogether there were 124 defendants charged with committing wilful damage. In the majority of cases the value of the broken windows exceeded £5, making it necessary that the accused should be committed for trial, and involving the taking of depositions – a tedious process. The result was that although the sitting of the Court was prolonged until six o'clock, only nineteen of the women had then been dealt with.

The remainder were brought up in batches and formally remanded, some until to-day, others until to-morrow, and the remainder until Wednesday. With about half a dozen exceptions, they all refused to be bailed, and they were subsequently removed to Holloway Prison in vans and cabs.

It was remarked that in passing sentences of imprisonment the magistrate did not specify the second division, so that presumably on this occasion the women will be treated as ordinary prisoners, without being called upon to perform hard labour.

From an early hour in the morning considerable crowds assembled in Bow-street to witness the arrival of the defendants, most of whom came in taxis and private motor-cars, bringing with them considerable quantities of luggage. They were made as comfortable as possible in the library and other rooms in the police-station, and supplies of tea, coffee, and light refreshments were brought in from a neighbouring restaurant.

A long queue of Suffragists waited outside the court for several hours, but owing to practically all the available accommodation being required for witnesses very few succeeded in gaining admission. Amongst those who did were Mrs Pethick Lawrence and Miss Christabel Pankhurst, who occupied seats in counsel's box.

Mrs Pankhurst, Mrs Marshall, and Mrs Mabel Tuke were first charged with committing wilful damage at No. 10, Downing street.

Mr H. Muskett, who prosecuted on behalf of the Commissioner of Police, said that probably the most outrageous and disgraceful scenes which had so far characterised the Suffrage movement took place on Friday evening between a quarter to and a quarter-past six. During that time damage to the estimated amount of £5,000 was committed. No new considerations could be brought before any court of justice with regard to these cases, and he submitted that the time had now come when it was impossible to deal with them save by the imposition of the maximum term.

Police-constable 576 A deposed that he was standing near the front door of the Prime Minister's residence when a motorcar drove up. The three defendants alighted from it, and at once threw several stones at the windows, breaking four small panes of glass. Witness arrested Mrs Pankhurst, who said nothing, but handed him three stones.

Police-constable 51 A R, who apprehended Mrs Marshall, stated that on the way to the station she took a stone from her muff and threw it at a window at the Colonial Office. She then dropped another stone, and remarked, "I won't throw any more. That is all I have got."

Cross-examined by Mrs Marshall, witness said on one of the stones there was written, "We demand the minimum vote" – (laughter) – and on another "Justice for Women".

It was stated that the damage done at 10, Downing-street amounted to 9s, and at the Colonial Office to £2.

Mrs Pankhurst, addressing the magistrate, said the last time she was before him she stated her reasons for taking part in this agitation, and she did not propose to repeat them. At that time she hoped what they were doing would be sufficient to make the Government realise that women who paid taxes were entitled to the protection and privilege of the vote on the same terms as men. Since then the Government had left them with no possible doubt as to their petition. They had not the vote because hitherto they had not been able to bring themselves to use the methods which won the vote for men.

Within the last fortnight a member of the Government had challenged them to do much more serious things than they had done on this occasion. Mr Hobhouse, at Bristol, said women had not proved desire for the vote because they had done nothing that characterised the men's agitation that led to the burning of Nottingham Castle and pulling down the Hyde Park railings. During the last few days the Government had provided them with evidence that where the women had failed so far was that they had not done enough.

Last week she wrote to the Prime Minister with regard to the referendum, asking him to see a deputation. He refused with contempt. This week the Government, headed by the Prime Minister, had been going, cap in hand, to the Miners' Federation to try and persuade them to come to terms. What the women had done was a fleabite compared with what the miners were doing. They were paralysing the whole life of the community. They had votes, but they were not content to rely upon constitutional means.

If women had the vote they would be constitutional, but since they had not the vote they were learning their lesson. She hoped this would be enough to show the Government that the women's agitation was going on. If it was not, as soon as she came out of prison she would go further. She would go as far as was necessary to show the Government that women who helped to pay the salaries of Cabinet Ministers – "who help to pay your salary, sir" – were going to have some voice in making the laws they obeyed and spending the money they contributed to.

She wanted to make it perfectly clear that, although they did not desire to go one step further than was necessary, they were prepared to take all steps that were necessary, and face the consequences. She herself was quite ready to go to prison and pay the price, however high the price might be. They thought it worth while. They were fighting for the freedom of their sex, and what happened to them as individuals did not matter, but what would come of what they did mattered very much. The individual might disappear, but the cause was going on.

Mrs Tuke said she resented "absolutely to her soul" the indignity of the position in which women lived to-day without the vote.

Mrs Marshall said that was the sixth time she had been in the dock, and she might be there sixty times, but they would never cease to fight. They had tried every possible means, and at last they had had to break windows, and she wished she had broken more. Many women worked under far worse conditions than miners. England was absolutely on the wane, and she was determined to show that women could stop this downhill trend. Although men had up to the present done as well as they could, they could not get on any longer without women.

The magistrate said there was no doubt the defendants thoroughly recognised that they were breaking the law, and that they gloried in it. They had brought London into a state which could not be allowed to continue in any civilised country in the world – (cheers) – and if the law as it at present stood was not sufficient to cope with such a movement the law must be amended. (A Voice: "By women".) It was intolerable that people should commit attacks on private citizens who were carrying on their avocations, and that their property should be damaged by people such as he saw before him. The women had had every chance given to them from the first, and he himself had endeavoured to point out that the very steps they were taking were steps which, if their cause was a good one, would destroy it, and that if they wanted to succeed, and it was a cause which was worthy of succeeding, they should adopt measures of conciliation and not damage. He felt it his duty in this case to pass upon each of the defendants sentences of two months' imprisonment. (Cheers.)

After the defendants had left the dock Mrs Marshall was brought back and sentenced to a further term of twenty-one days' imprisonment upon the second charge of committing damage at the Colonial Office.

Mrs Marshall (sarcastically): Any more?

The Magistrate: Not at present.

Later in the day Mr Marshall, solicitor to the Women's Social and Political Union, asked the magistrate to reduce the sentence in the case of Mrs Tuke, pointing out that she had not been convicted before, and that the damage done by her was very small.

Mr Curtis Bennett thanked Mr Marshall for drawing his attention to the matter, and altered Mrs Tuke's sentence to twenty-one days' imprisonment.

An application by Mr Pethick Lawrence for a reduction of the sentences passed on Mrs Marshall was, however, refused.

5 March 1912
Suffrage campaign
Miss Pankhurst's threat

There was evidence of disapproval of the militant tactics of the Women's Social and Political Union, at their meeting, at the London Pavilion, yesterday afternoon. A large part of the speech of Miss Christabel Pankhurst was inaudible, in consequence of interruption. Letters were road from Mrs Pankhurst and others, Mrs Pankhurst asking that, it should be proved to the authorities that the supply of militant women was inexhaustible.

Mrs Pethick Lawrence declared that the movement had become a revolution, for which the time was ripe, and any who tried to stop the movement did so at their peril. She regarded the holes in the windows as eloquent mouths. ("Shame on you!") They had asked for bread and been given stones, and stones came home to roost like chickens. Mrs Pankhurst was not there because she had been sentenced to two months' imprisonment. ("It ought to have been two years!") Who incited the women to commit the damage to the windows? Mr Hobhouse, who told them they had not gone so far as men had in the past. They must coerce the Government, as Mr Asquith had stated the Government would coerce the coalowners, and the method they bad adopted of attacking private property was the only way. They would do what was necessary to achieve the political emancipation of the women of this country. (Cheers.)

Dr. Ethel Smyth, in the course of her speech, remarked, "I do not know, and I do not care, whether we have done right or wrong," and it drew the retort, "That shows you ought not to have a vote."

Miss Pankhurst stated that militancy was the only method feared. They knew there was not the smallest intention to enfranchise the women this session, and they had got to carry the position by storm, "by fire and sword," she added, "if you will." If necessary they would adopt fire, the method of 1832 at Nottingham. If heavy sentences were going to be imposed, like those on Saturday, they might as well be hanged for a sheep as a lamb. (Cheers.) Penal servitude might be the punishment, but not for nothing. (Cheers.) They would do their bit, even if it was burning down a palace. (Cheers.)

"Is your organisation," a man asked, "encouraging the use of revolvers to-night in Parliament-square?"

Miss Pankhurst: No; I contradict that rumour.

"Do you approve of smashing innocent tradesmen's windows?"

Miss Pankhurst: Yes; they are not innocent in this matter.

"How can you expect a tradesman to support 'Votes for Women' if you break his window?"

Miss Pankhurst: They ought to have given us the vote long ago.

In conclusion, she slated that if window-breaking was regarded as contemptible, other methods they might have to try would not be so regarded. "If such methods," she added, "are not sufficient, we will terrorise the whole lot of you."

Women's defence.
Interview with Miss Pankhurst

At the offices of the Women's Social and Political Union yesterday, a representative of the *Daily Telegraph* had a conversation with Miss Pankhurst on the subject of the recent outrages. The leader of the militant Suffragists hotly defended window-smashing, refused to believe that the practice was incensing and alienating the public, and was ready to go to prison again in defence of her beliefs.

"We are smashing windows," she said, "to bring our agitation home to the public, and make them understand the meaning of our campaign as they have never understood it before. People who have had their windows broken are saying, 'Why smash our windows? We have done nothing!' Don't you see that we have a ground for quarrel with them for not doing something? They are electors, and therefore they ought to bestir themselves to get votes for women. Men have done worse things than smash windows in the past. They found window-smashing ineffectual, and during the Reform riots of 1832 they destroyed Nottingham Castle by fire."

"But you don't intend to burn down castles, do you?"

"When we see that men succeeded in getting the vote by these methods, is it wonderful that we should come to the conclusion that our peaceful methods are useless? Shopkeepers are saying, 'Something must be done!' What? You can't restrain women by imprisonment. The only way is to carry a Votes for Women Bill. Meanwhile, it is necessary to smash windows to show we are in deadly earnest. We are, symbolically speaking, letting in fresh air and light upon a grievance about which many people are ignorant."

"It is said that you are purchasing revolvers to use against the police?"

"That I entirely and utterly deny."

"And that you are going to destroy the priceless valuables at the British Museum and other places?"

Miss Pankhurst laughed. "That only shows," she said, "that panic reigns supreme It only shows that the public are beginning to realise that we are in deadly earnest. Stone-throwing is a much better understood and more generally approved method of getting our rights than deputations to Parliament-square. We think that this matter must now be carried by storm. The Government won't listen to reason."

"So the smashing is to go on?"

"There can be no stopping until the vote is won."

"As to the *Daily Telegraph* leader," concluded Miss Pankhurst, "we are quite accustomed to that kind of strong language. As to your suggestion about strengthening the law, the law has no terrors for us. We are glad that you recognise that these methods cannot be allowed to go on; but they can only be stopped by strengthening the law by giving votes to women. As to our unfitness for the vote, no people ever were thought fit for it who did not make themselves a terror to society."

Disturbance in prison
Riotous day at Holloway

The prospect of a sojourn at Holloway Gaol did not serve to damp the spirits of the women taken there on Saturday afternoon. Soon after they had been shut in their cells for the night they began to make their presence heard. By two in the morning they were singing and shouting, and it was with great difficulty that they were induced to be even a little reasonable, a result which was only achieved in some instances by the actual physical exhaustion of the demonstrators.

One woman managed to get her bedstead across her cell, and wedged it against the door. For a long time the efforts of the warders were fruitless, and the inmate of the cell sat on the bed jeering at them till at length the door was forced.

Later in the morning the prisoners were paraded in the yard for exercise. Those on remand in consequence of their refusal to find bail, pending the adjourned hearing of the charges against them, were, in the ordinary course, not with convicted prisoners. Among the latter was Mrs Pankhurst, and the "remands", not seeing her, asked where she was. No answer was vouchsafed to their questions, and they began to scream her name. Again they got no response, and they changed their tune to the "Marseillaise", which they attempted to sing with a cheerful disregard of key, and almost of tune.

Failing to induce them to be quiet, the attendants bundled them back to their cells. There, however, the demonstration was renewed. One of the women took off her boot and speedily broke the window, of which the glass is thick enough to stand most ordinary assaults. As she did so she screamed her battle-cry, "Votes for women." Once started, the outbreak became epidemic, and spread from cell to cell, as the occupants along the corridor became, in their turn, aware of what was going on. Hardly a window or a cell in which a Suffragist was imprisoned escaped, and in several instances even the substantial furniture was broken. Through the apertures handkerchiefs were waved to sympathisers, who it is said, had taken apartments overlooking the gaol, and again the strains of what the performers imagined was the "Marseillaise" were heard.

For nearly two hours the disturbance continued, and was distinctly audible to passers-by, while people in adjoining houses were much interested in the handkerchiefs fluttering from the windows. It was said that the demonstrators would be dealt with "in the usual way", which, it was explained, would mean the ordinary prison diet for those in the second division, and a withdrawal of all privileges of seeing visitors and receiving and sending letters.

Yesterday forty-two women were drafted from Holloway to Lewes to make room for the anticipated increase of inmates as the result of yesterday's trouble.

Cecil Parkinson

"The Prime Minister takes the view that this is a private matter."

6 October 1983
Parkinson admits love affair
"No question of resignation"
By Ian Glover-James

Cecil Parkinson, who as Tory Party Chairman was the principal organiser of Mrs Thatcher's election victory, last night admitted he had had a relationship with his former secretary, Miss Sara Keays, who is expecting his child in January.

In a statement issued through his solicitors, Farrer and Co, Mr Parkinson, now Trade and Industry Secretary, said he had wished to marry Miss Keays, but was now staying with his wife Ann and his three daughters.

A spokesman at 10 Downing Street said Mrs Thatcher knew of Mr Parkinson's statement, but the question of his resignation "does not and will not arise".

Mr Parkinson's statement read: "To bring to an end rumour concerning Miss Sara Keays and myself, and to prevent further harassment of Miss Keays and her family, I wish, with her consent, to make the following statement.

"I have had a relationship with Miss Keays over a number of years.

"She is expecting a child due to be born in January, of whom I am the father. I am of course making financial provision for both mother and child."

"Mr Parkinson, 52, went on: "During our relationship, I told Miss Keays of my wish to marry her.

"Despite my having given Miss Keays that assurance, my wife, who has been a source of great strength, and I decided to stay together and to keep our family together."

Mr Parkinson concluded: "I regret deeply the distress which I have caused to Miss Keays, to her family and to my own family."

Both he and Miss Keays wanted it to be known that neither they nor their families would be prepared to answer further questions about the statement.

The 10 Downing Street spokesman added: "The Prime Minister takes the view that this is a private matter.

"Mr Parkinson is a member of the Cabinet, doing a good job."

Miss Keays's London solicitor, Mr Jeffrey Wicks, later confirmed the contents of the statement, and said it had been made to "place the facts before the public".

News that Miss Keays was expecting a baby was given in the latest edition of the magazine *Private Eye*, but Mr Wicks said the decision to make the statement was "purely coincidental".

Miss Keays, who is in her 30s, has worked for the Conservative Party for some years and has been a secretary to several MPs. Her family comes from Bath.

The Parkinsons have three daughters, aged 23, 21 and 19.

Mrs Parkinson, 48, is a postgraduate student at Brunel University where she is completing a doctorate in political science. Earlier she took a degree in politics as a mature student at Hatfield Polytechnic.

Mr Parkinson was appointed Secretary for Trade and Industry after the Conservatives' General Election victory in June, after being Tory Chairman since 1981.

The son of a Lancashire railwayman, he joined the Labour Party while a pupil at Lancaster Grammar School and campaigned for Labour in the 1950 General Election.

Just 10 years ago he was in a Tory administration as Parliamentary private secretary to a junior Minister at the Department of Trade and Industry, which he now heads.

He has been Conservative MP for Hertfordshire South since 1974, and also held the seat for the previous four years when it was Enfield West.

He graduated with a BA and an MA from Emmanuel College, Cambridge, and qualified as a chartered accountant.

He and his family moved to a former vicarage near Potter's Bar, Herts, 10 years ago.

7 October 1983

Parkinson to ride out storm

Mrs Thatcher was aware of affair

By James Wightman

The Prime Minister and Mr Parkinson, Trade and Industry Secretary and former Conservative Party Chairman, were determined last night that he should try to survive the disclosure of an affair with his former secretary without having to leave the Government.

Mrs Thatcher made it clear she did not regard it as a matter of dismissal or resignation, despite the publicity over his admission that he had had a relationship with Miss Sara Keays and that she is expecting his child in January.

The Minister, now reconciled with his wife and family, indicated that he wanted to remain in office unless the situation became intolerably embarrassing for the Prime Minister and the Government.

He had said he had wished to marry Miss Keays, his former constituency secretary at the Commons, but was now staying with his wife Ann and their three daughters.

The Prime Minister, who had known of Mr Parkinson's situation for some months, took the view that it was a private matter requiring no action from her.

But some senior colleagues said a question mark had now arisen over the future of Mr Parkinson, 52.

Some Conservatives feared his conduct could be seen as a contradiction on the emphasis which the Prime Minister often puts in her speeches and policies on the virtues of family life.

Anxious soundings are being taken of reaction throughout the Conservative Party as well as among the public generally.

The development, which shocked the vast majority of politicians of all parties, is the latest in a series of political mishaps which have troubled the Government since its General Election victory and which are making some politicians say the Government has become accident-prone.

Mr Parkinson's admission was also seen as casting a cloud over the party conference in Blackpool next week. He is due to address the conference on Thursday at the end of a debate on free enterprise and industry.

It has been expected that the Prime Minister's address on Friday would include a warm tribute to the work Mr Parkinson did as party chairman in heading the General Election campaign.

Mrs Thatcher yesterday sent out the message to the party that she was showing to Mr Parkinson the loyalty which he had given to her as a Minister and party chairman.

Mr Parkinson told Mrs Thatcher about Miss Keays's pregnancy some months ago, although 10 Downing Street and his department would not say exactly when. He offered to resign if she wanted him to. But she said he should stay.

There were official denials yesterday of the suspicion that Mr Parkinson's affair had led to Mrs Thatcher's replacing him as party chairman last month with the surprising choice of Mr John Selwyn Gummer.

It was recalled that Mrs Thatcher and Mr Parkinson decided when she promoted him to the amalgamated Trade and Industry Department after the election that, because of his extra duties, he would not continue as party chairman for long.

Some Conservatives suspected that Mr Parkinson had been moved from the chairmanship to avoid the danger of news of the affair breaking out during the party conference.

The new party chairman is a member of the Synod of the Church of England.

Mr Parkinson told a few other Cabinet Ministers about his affair recently. It had been hoped that details would not leak out.

But after some rumours in political circles recently, *Private Eye*, the magazine which has disclosed the secrets of many politicians over the years, carried an item about Mr Parkinson on Wednesday.

Shortly before midnight the same day Mr Parkinson issued a statement through his solicitors, giving details of his relationship with Miss Keays "over a number of years". Within 30 minutes 10 Downing Street had issued a statement from the Prime Minister, saying she knew of his statement but the question of his resignation "does not and will not arise".

The statement also said: "The Prime Minister takes the view that this is a private matter. Mr Parkinson is a member of the Cabinet, doing a good job."

Colleagues said that Mr Parkinson had seemed unusually worried recently, despite his promotion to a higher Cabinet post and the election victory accolades he received. The strain was evident on his face yesterday.

His problems compound the troubles which have hit the Government since the election, raising the suspicion that it has become "accident-prone".

Poor political performances have been given by key Ministers, including Mr Lawson. Chancellor of the Exchequer; Mr Brittan, Home Secretary; and Mr Fowler, Social Services Secretary.

There have been calls for the dismissal of Mr Prior, Ulster Secretary, over the mass escape of prisoners from the Maze. There has also been criticism from some Tories of the Prime Minister's style of leadership.

Lord Alport, a Tory peer and former Commonwealth Relations Office Minister, said in a letter in *The Times* yesterday that many Conservatives were deeply concerned by Mrs Thatcher's "apparent lack of magnanimity, her vindictiveness, her dearth of sympathy for the under-privileged and. her demands for narrow conformity".

But Mrs Thatcher does not accept that the Government is in anything like a crisis. She also hopes that the controversy over Mr Parkinson will soon fade.

Some senior colleagues believe that, if he does survive the present publicity, Mr Parkinson's recently meteoric career has probably reached its peak. Some friends saw him as a future Conservative leader.

The son of a railwayman, he is very highly regarded as a politician by the Prime Minister who sees him as belonging to the same meritocracy as herself.

But whether more traditional Conservatives will take the same forgiving attitude as the Prime Minister remains to be seen.

There was considerable sympathy yesterday for Mrs Parkinson who was extremely hard-working and supportive of his role as party chairman.

Mrs Thatcher once said, in a tribute to Mrs Parkinson, that she had got "two chairmen for the price of one".

It was a surprise when Mrs Thatcher gave Mr Parkinson the Conservative chairmanship in succession to Lord Thorneycroft two years ago. He had been a junior Trade Minister.

But, with his clean-cut appearance, combative speaking style and administrative; skills he became a great success and played a large part in the June Election victory. He was among the small group of senior Ministers who persuaded the Prime Minister, against her will, to hold an early election.

Mr Parkinson's first Cabinet role was the minor one of Paymaster-General. But Mrs Thatcher, again unexpectedly, gave him further promotion when she made him a member of the Falklands "War Cabinet".

Then, as a reward for helping with the election victory, he was promoted to Trade and Industry Secretary.

His future now in the short term would seem to depend on whether the embarrassment for the Prime Minister increases or diminishes. In his favour may be the judgment by colleagues that the social and moral climate of the country has changed over the past 25 years.

His affair is also not seen as serious as the Profumo affair more than 20 years ago when the War Minister, Mr John Profumo, resigned.

15 October 1983

Tories rocked by Parkinson

Minister faced dismissal in 2.15 a.m. confrontation

By James Wightman

Mr Cecil Parkinson resigned in disgrace from the Cabinet yesterday after his fight to remain Trade and Industry Secretary was undermined overnight when his jilted mistress issued an unexpected statement to "put the record straight" about their affair.

Details of the statement by Miss Sara Keays had been relayed from Downing Street at 2 a.m. to the Prime Minister and Mr Parkinson at their hotel in Blackpool, venue of the Conservative Party Conference.

The statement shattered their belief that, after his speech to the conference the day before, Mr Parkinson could survive, at least in the short term, the controversy over his affair with Miss Keays, who is expecting his child in January.

After a brief, anguished talk with Mrs Thatcher at 2.15 a.m. Mr Parkinson, who is 52, tendered his resignation at a longer meeting in her hotel suite at 8 a.m.

She accepted it "with regret".

But if he had not offered to resign he would have been dismissed.

Unusually the exchange of letters between the departing minister and Mrs Thatcher will not be made public.

After the statement by Miss Keays in which she said Mr Parkinson had withdrawn a promise to marry her, his political position had become untenable.

Miss Keays, formerly Mr Parkinson's constituency secretary at Westminster, had asked *The Times*, the newspaper to which she issued her statement to request 10 Downing Street to pass it on to Mr Parkinson and Mrs Thatcher in Blackpool.

The outcome was the departure from office of Mr Parkinson in the way of three other Conservative Ministers caught out in sexual scandals – Mr John Profumo 20 years ago, and Earl Jellicoe and Lord Lambton, both in 1972.

By yesterday morning the embarrassment caused to the Prime Minister had become too intense for Mr Parkinson to remain. Her judgment in insisting that he should say in office despite the disclosure of his affair had become increasingly under question throughout a troubled week at Blackpool.

As Tories headed for home last night relieved that one of their most traumatic conferences was over it was confirmed that Mr Parkinson told the Prime Minister about his affair on the evening of 9 June, General Election day.

But she told him he could remain in the Government and two days later, she gave him promotion to Secretary of Trade and Industry as a reward for masterminding the election campaign as party chairman.

Some Tories at the morning session of the conference yesterday applauded and cheered when the chairman, Mr Peter Lane told them before proceedings opened that Mr Parkinson had resigned.

By then he was departing from Blackpool with his wife Ann leaving Mrs Thatcher to try to repair the political damage with her address to the concluding session of the conference yesterday afternoon.

Sympathy for the Prime Minister over the ordeal in handling the Parkinson case gave extra enthusiasm to the ovation from 5,000 Tories as she entered the hall and at the end of her 43-minute address.

She was given a standing ovation lasting eight minutes and 20 seconds – longer than normal.

She began her speech by recalling the election victory and quickly went into a short tribute to Mr Parkinson.

Thanking all those who had contributed to the landslide win and said: "And we do not forget today the man who so brilliantly organised the campaign."

She did not mention Mr Parkinson by name.

The tribute drew loud applause before the Prime Minister moved on to the substance of her speech about the Government's achievements and its objectives for its second term.

Her hope last night was that she had sent the Conservatives back to their constituencies with their confidence restored alter a week in which they had witnessed a human tragedy and a political crisis resulting in the departure from office of one of the party's fastest rising stars.

Cabinet colleagues, most of whom had been asleep as Mr Parkinson and the Prime Minister had their first meeting, expressed their shock at his resignation but said it was inevitable in the light of the latest unsavoury and apparently unstoppable publicity.

Some women friends of Mr and Mrs Parkinson wept as the couple, both looking dazed, left the Imperial Hotel to travel home instead of taking their places on the conference platform for the Prime Minister's address.

The turmoil which the affair caused to the party throughout the week was highlighted when he cancelled his plan to open a heliport at Blackpool Airport yesterday morning.

The Prime Ministers husband, Mr Denis Thatcher was pressed into service as a deputy for the Trade and Industry secretary.

Workmen had to remove a wall plaque designed to commemorate Mr Parkinson's visit.

The statement by Miss Keays brought public bitterness into the controversy which Mr Parkinson and Mrs Thatcher had insisted should remain private.

Mr Parkinson said in his only comment before leaving Blackpool: "I gave an undertaking and I kept it. Other people can answer for their own behaviour."

His wife said: "The statement Mr Parkinson made last week was with the full agreement of Miss Keays and both families had agreed to say nothing more. We are standing by that undertaking."

Mr Parkinson contacted his solicitors in London about Miss Keays's statement. He disputed some of the claims she made, although it was not disclosed what he was taking exception to.

In a statement last night Mr Parkinson said: "I remain convinced that it is in no-one's interest that our differences should be discussed publicly.

Mr Parkinson said he would continue as MP for Hertsmere.

Mrs Thatcher asked Mr Paul Channon, a junior trade minister, to take over Mr Parkinson's duties for the time being.

Mr Parkinson was to have left London on Monday for a two-week ministerial visit to the United States. No one will go in his place.

Until the statement from Miss Keays reached Blackpool the Prime Minister and Mr Parkinson had been reasonably confident that he had survived the initial controversy over his affair although a question mark remained about his future in the longer term.

Mrs Thatcher had insisted in a statement issued quickly after Mr Parkinson's statement last week disclosing his affair that the question of his resignation "does not and will not arise."

But by 8 a.m. yesterday they both agreed that the controversy with possible implications for the standing of the Prime Minister and the Government had become uncontainable.

Many Conservatives leaving Blackpool last night felt that Mr Parkinson should have resigned before the conference started to avoid the embarrassment to the Prime Minister.

But there was deep sadness at the fall of a much-respected minister and party leader, along with great sympathy for his wife.

Friends said that they hoped that the Parkinson marriage could survive.

Mr Parkinson, a railwayman's son who married a wealthy builder's daughter, had been promoted spectacularly by Mrs Thatcher over the past two years.

He was a junior trade minister when she unexpectedly made him party chairman in succession to Lord Thorneycroft, giving him Cabinet status in the minor role of Paymaster General.

Later, again surprisingly, she made him a member of the Falklands "War Cabinet". Finally she rewarded him for his General Election work by giving him Cabinet promotion to Trade and Industry Secretary.

Mr Parkinson had hoped for further promotion in the next reshuffle, perhaps to Foreign Secretary or Chancellor of the Exchequer. Some friends regarded him as a potential leader of the party.

Some colleagues hope that his ministerial career will not necessarily be over. As one put it last night:

"Perhaps he could come back in about two years after a period of expiation."

But many Conservatives will never forgive Mr Parkinson for the agony he has caused the party, particularly the Prime Minister over the past week at what should have been a celebration of the General Election victory.

The Prime Minister's aides still refuse to discuss the question asked by many Conservatives throughout the conference: Exactly when did Mr Parkinson disclose details of his affair and how much did he tell Mrs Thatcher.

All that could be established last night was that he had told her sometime before she and he went to Conservative Central Office in the early hours of 10 June when it was clear that the Conservatives had won a landslide victory. Together they waved jubilantly to the crowds below from a second floor window at Conservative Central Office.

The question over Mrs Thatcher's judgment is whether she was right to risk political controversy over Mr Parkinson's affair by giving him Cabinet promotion.

But it was not known whether Mr Parkinson had told Mrs Thatcher that he wanted to divorce his wife and marry Miss Keays.

Colleagues are hoping that any doubts about the wisdom of Mrs Thatcher's conduct will be obscured by admiration for her loyalty to Mr Parkinson.

26 January 2016
Lord Parkinson – obituary
Thatcherite star whose career faltered after
revelations of an affair with his former secretary

Lord Parkinson, who has died aged 84, was arguably the best Party Chairman the Conservative Party had since the 1950s and looked set, after masterminding Margaret Thatcher's landslide election victory in 1983, to go on to greater things; but his progression to high office was fatally compromised later that year by revelations that his former secretary, Sara Keays, was expecting his child.

As Parkinson's colleague John Biffen remarked, no living politician more deserved the epitaph "cut is the branch that might have burned full straight, And burned is Apollo's laurel bough". The Keays affair was devastating to Parkinson politically. He was compelled to resign and, although he resumed his Cabinet career in 1987, it never regained momentum.

The future that could not be remained a tantalising question mark over the course of Thatcherism after 1983, since Parkinson was the only senior Conservative politician who, while remaining staunchly loyal to Mrs Thatcher, was also generally liked by his colleagues and at the same time in touch with the real world. He might have replaced Lord Whitelaw as the Cabinet conciliator; he might have been Chancellor of the Exchequer, a job in which his background in accountancy and closeness to Mrs Thatcher might have helped him to avoid the mistakes of the Lawson years; she had certainly wanted him as her Foreign Secretary. As it was, these possibilities remained "what ifs".

Much was made of Cecil Parkinson's Kennedyesque good looks, his monogrammed shirts and easy charm, though he once said that if he were reincarnated, he would like to be born "short, fat and ugly". It was a jest, of course, but there was a serious point, for he was too easily dismissed as a political lightweight, a dilettante who had got where he was by charm alone.

In fact, Cecil Parkinson not only looked good, he was good – and very effective, particularly on television where his contributions were always much sharper than his opponents expected. As a minister, he impressed even the most cynical journalists with his grasp of his subject, his avoidance of clichés and willingness to listen and argue a point seriously. At the same time he could also be indiscreet, funny and gossipy – and thoroughly good company.

At Central Office, he restored the Party's financial position and beefed up the constituency associations that were to play a central part in the 1983 election victory, winning the devotion of staff demoralised by years of cuts and departmental in-fighting. His openness, sense of humour and knack of giving the person he was talking to his fullest attention won round even the most intransigent – and made him adored by the Tory faithful, especially the women.

If the events that led up to his resignation in October 1983 did not reflect well on Parkinson, he paid a heavier price than many colleagues who had done worse and bore his humiliation with stoicism and restraint.

His affair with Sara Keays began in the early 1970s when he was MP for Enfield East and a rising star in the Tory firmament. By the General Election of 1983, she had become pregnant with their child. On the evening of Election day, he confessed the affair to Mrs Thatcher who, though it gave her pause, did not see it as an insuperable obstacle to his becoming Foreign Secretary.

It is unclear whether he told her the whole truth, however, as when, the following day, she received a letter from Sara Keays's father revealing that his daughter was pregnant with Parkinson's child, she decided that, with such a cloud hanging over him, he could not be Foreign Secretary after all. "I urged him to discuss the personal questions with his family. Meanwhile I decided to make him Secretary of State for Trade and Industry," she recalled.

At first, Parkinson felt he should honour his promises and marry Miss Keays, but subsequently, on holiday with his wife and two elder daughters, he changed his mind. Together they decided that "as a family, come what may, we would stick together, and that I shouldn't get divorced".

At the beginning of October, shortly before the party conference, Parkinson, with Sara Keays's consent, made a statement to the press admitting that he had withdrawn an offer to marry her and confirming that she was to have his child. At first it seemed that he might succeed in weathering the storm; his party conference speech received a standing ovation. On Thursday evening, however, it was discovered that *The Times* intended to carry an interview with Miss Keays in which she would complain about the way she had been treated. "It was clear that this story was not going to die down," Mrs Thatcher recalled, "and though I asked Cecil to hold back from resigning that evening, we all knew he would have to go."

She had been baffled by what *Private Eye* referred to as "Ugandan affairs" in relation to Parkinson's affair with Sarah Keays, saying: "I know it's untrue. He's never been to Africa."

Parkinson's conduct was not blameless and although he supported Flora, his daughter by Sara Keays, financially, on her 18th birthday it was noted that he had never met her. The affair overshadowed the rest of his career and he never managed to escape the label of the man who had tarnished the Conservatives' image as the party of the family. The irony was that if Parkinson had left his wife of 26 years and his three daughters – in traditional Westminster fashion – he would probably have saved his political career. As it was, he was punished for standing by them.

The son of a railway linesman, Edward Cecil Parkinson was born in Lancaster on 1 September 1931 and brought up at Carnforth, Lancashire.

The Parkinson family was firmly in the tradition of northern working class Conservatism – his grandmother, the local midwife, was chairman of the Unionist Women – and his early years bore the authentic touch of Thatcherite self-improvement.

Parkinson won a scholarship to the Royal Lancaster Grammar School, where he worked hard and was a good athlete – a long-distance runner, sprinter and rugby player. He was also a fervent socialist, becoming treasurer of the local Labour League of Youth and campaigning for the Party in the 1950 General Election. At the same time he had thoughts of taking Holy Orders and won a place at Emmanuel College, Cambridge, to read Divinity.

When called up for National Service, Parkinson had thoughts of declaring himself a conscientious objector. Although he hated his time in the RAF, the experience convinced him he did not wish to be a clergyman and, at Cambridge, he switched from Divinity to English. But academic pursuits took second place to sport and having fun. He ran for the university against Oxford and represented the combined Oxford and Cambridge teams against American universities, but got a lower Second in English and a Third in Law.

By this time, he had become disillusioned with the Labour Party, though he had not yet made the full transition to Conservatism. It was his marriage to Ann Jarvis, the daughter of a well-to-do Harpenden builder and ardent Tory, that made the difference both to his career and his political affiliations. The two met shortly after he had left Cambridge when he was working as a management trainee with the Metal Box Company. They married in 1957.

During their engagement, Parkinson decided they should emigrate to Canada, where he had been offered a traineeship in an international accountancy firm. But his father had a heart attack and he postponed his departure to qualify as an accountant in Britain. His father-in-law helped him to gain access to the City firm West Wake Price, where he qualified in 1959. He became a partner in the firm in 1961 and a director of several companies.

Meanwhile he had joined the Conservative Party and in 1968 became chairman of the Hemel Hempstead Conservative Association, with Norman Tebbit as his vice chairman. He fought the marginal Labour seat of Northampton in 1970 against the colourful Reggie Paget who disarmed his opponent at his first public meeting by telling his audience: "You will find that Mr Parkinson and I disagree about very little, but we do disagree about one thing – Mr Parkinson dislikes Mr Wilson, the Prime Minister. I hate him."

Parkinson entered Parliament as MP for Enfield West in November 1970 at a by-election caused by the death of the Chancellor, Iain Macleod. In 1972 he became PPS to Michael Heseltine, then Minister for Aerospace and Shipping, then served as a junior whip in the dying days of the Heath administration.

For the February 1974 election the constituency of Enfield West was abolished and Parkinson was returned for Hertfordshire South (which became Hertsmere after boundary changes in 1983). He remained in the whips' office in opposition. Though grander members of the Tory party viewed with disfavour the combination of new money and smooth talking that he personified, he impressed Mrs Thatcher, who picked him out to be opposition trade spokesman in 1976, and appointed him the "supersalesman" trade minister of her first administration.

By now Parkinson was very comfortably off. In 1969, on a tip from his father-in-law, he and a partner bought an ailing Stockport building firm for a down payment of £7,500. They did so well over the next two years that they bought another construction firm in Strood, Kent. When this was sold in 1979, Parkinson was estimated to be worth £750,000.

Even more important, though, he had won the admiration of the Prime Minister who found him a man after her own heart, "dynamic, full of common sense, a good accountant, an excellent presenter and, no less important, on my wing of the party".

Parkinson put their rapport down to the fact that neither of them came from the Tory Establishment and neither was overawed by those who did. "I always say that when you look back at history there are only two types of people – serfs and ambitious serfs," he explained. "This is what united Margaret and myself; we couldn't possibly be chippy or envious with all the opportunities we'd been given."

At Tebbit's urging, Mrs Thatcher picked Parkinson to become Chairman of the Party in succession to Lord Thorneycroft in 1981, with the cabinet post of Paymaster General. In 1982 he was elevated to the Falklands War cabinet as Chancellor of the Duchy of Lancaster. In his memoirs, Parkinson recalled how, on the morning of the Tories' 1983 election landslide, "Willie Whitelaw felt I should have one of the three top jobs, and added he felt I could do any of them". The words had barely been spoken before the Keays affair transformed his life.

Parkinson once likened his fall from grace to "being in a car crash – you can't move. Just utterly stunned". Yet he never lost his sense of humour. One Sunday morning, at the height of the uproar, he sent the doorstepping press two bottles of whisky to keep them warm. His resilience in adversity revealed a philosophical determination to keep going that surprised many.

In exile on the backbenches, Parkinson put his popularity with the party faithful to work by doing the rounds of the constituencies and it was not long before Mrs Thatcher, always relaxed about the sexual misdemeanours of her colleagues, began dropping hints of a return to office.

Soon after the 1987 election (in which Parkinson was returned by a record majority) he returned to Cabinet as Energy Secretary with the task of privatising the electricity industry. "I returned to remove the word 'disgraced' from 'disgraced former cabinet minister'," he said. "And that's why it was essential for me to go back, not just for my benefit but for the kids." But colleagues noticed that the old sparkle had gone and in 1989 he was shifted sideways to the unglamorous environs of the Department of Transport, where he strove, in the wake of Lockerbie and Kings

Cross, to prevent transport issues from becoming an electoral liability by winning huge amounts of extra investment for roads and rail.

Parkinson remained loyal to Mrs Thatcher to the end, but his years in the wilderness meant that he was not in any position to save her from her enemies. As energy secretary he had been designated "Star Chamber" chairman to arbitrate on ministerial spending bids amid speculation that he might become Chancellor. But the Star Chamber never sat under his chairmanship and there were suggestions that ministers ensured they settled their differences privately rather than confer status on a colleague so close to the Prime Minister.

Parkinson belatedly declared in favour of John Major during the 1990 leadership election, but his heart was no longer in it and he resigned from the Cabinet when the new Prime Minister took office. In 1992 he stood down as an MP to take a life peerage.

He resumed his business career, becoming director of 14 companies. He was behind one of the failed bids to build a channel tunnel, established his own public relations outfit, and was chairman of an internet company, Planet Online, which was sold in 1999 for £75m.

In 1991 he became founder chairman of the Right-wing Conservative Way Forward Group, dedicated to upholding Thatcherite values, and as the Conservatives lurched from crisis to crisis as the decade wore on, he jumped on the bandwagon of disillusioned Thatcherites who criticised John Major's leadership.

After Labour's victory in the 1997 General Election and the subsequent Tory leadership contest, Parkinson made a surprise return to active politics when he was picked by the new Conservative leader William Hague to chair the party once again. But he retired from his role after a year and there was nothing he could do to prevent the Tories going down to a second heavy election defeat in 2001.

Cynthia Payne

"It was like a vicar's tea party with sex thrown in."

17 November 2015
Cynthia Payne – obituary
Brothel keeper dubbed "Madam Cyn" who was jailed after
holding sex parties in Streatham in exchange for "luncheon vouchers"

Cynthia Payne, who has died aged 82, became Britain's best-known brothel keeper when police raided her suburban home in Streatham, south London, in 1978, interrupting a sex party that was in full swing; at her trial, she was ineradicably branded "Madam Cyn" and imprisoned for 18 months for running "the biggest disorderly house" in British history.

A rapt media feasted on stories of middle aged and elderly men queuing up in SW16 to exchange "luncheon vouchers" for food, drink, conversation, striptease shows, and a trip upstairs with the girl of their choice. Businessmen, vicars, MPs, lawyers and even, reportedly, a peer were among those who considered Cynthia Payne the best hostess in London. Jeffrey Bernard in *The Spectator* declared her "the greatest Englishwoman since Boadicea".

On appeal, Cynthia Payne's sentence was reduced to six months and a hefty fine. She was unrepentant, however, and on her release from prison she resumed her parties until the police called again in 1986.

Such attention gave Mrs Payne the chance to entertain the nation with her outspoken views on men and sex and, more seriously, to confront the contradictions and shortcomings of the British laws on prostitution.

Detectives who raided her detached Edwardian home at 32 Ambleside Avenue in December 1978 found 53 men huddled in the hall. Most were queuing on the stairs leading up to the bedrooms, and were clutching vouchers to be redeemed for sex; some appeared to have come straight from the office. Of the 13 women on the premises, some were completely naked.

When the case finally came to court, Cynthia Payne's defence counsel Geoffrey Robertson pointed out that his client merely provided a suitable marketplace where otherwise respectable men were able to find a sexual outlet. "She now realises that the party's over," he added, "and she alone has to pick up the tab."

Judge David West-Russell noted, however, that Mrs Payne had appeared in court on four previous occasions, on similar charges. As well as sending her to jail, he fined her a total of £1,950 and ordered her to pay costs of up to £2,000.

The public was as shocked by the sentence as Cynthia Payne herself, and a national debate ensued. Thirty MPs of all parties – among them Sam Silkin, the previous Labour attorney-general, and Tony Benn – signed a Commons motion deploring her imprisonment. They added that she posed no threat to the community, and advocated the prosecution of her male customers.

Cynthia Payne was born in Bognor Regis on Christmas Eve 1932. (The correct spelling of her name was disputed and may originally have been Paine, but she settled on Payne.) Her father, Hamilton, was away at sea for much of her childhood, running the hairdressing salon on board the *Durban Castle*, a liner on the South Africa run.

Her mother died of throat cancer in 1943 when Cynthia and her sister Melanie were still young; the two girls were brought up by a series of housekeepers hired by their father. Expelled from school for being "a bad influence" (a cousin recalled she never stopped talking about sex), Cynthia was enrolled by her father on a hairdressing course at a technical college in London, but she was asked to leave because of her lack of interest. An apprenticeship with some hairdressing friends of her father in Aldershot proved equally fruitless; they insisted she saw a psychiatrist to cure her compulsive swearing, and after claiming falsely that she was pregnant and threatening to swallow weedkiller, Cynthia was disowned by her father.

Back in Bognor in 1950, aged 17, she took a job at a bus garage where she began an affair with a married man (a period dramatised in the 1987 film *Wish You Were Here*). Her lover followed her when she moved to Brighton to work as a waitress and then to London, where Cynthia Payne fell pregnant. A son, Dominic, was born, followed – as a result of another affair – by a second son who was put up for adoption.

When she was 22, Cynthia Payne met an amusement arcade operator from Margate with whom she lived for five years. After her third illegal abortion (the man scorned contraception), she left him and embarked on the career change that would make her name.

Holding down her day job as a waitress in a London café, she rented four small flats which she sublet to working prostitutes. She hit on this idea as the result of a chance meeting in the café with a prostitute who offered her £3 a week to use her room in the evenings. Cynthia Payne quickly realised the profitable potential of such an arrangement (this sum was twice her weekly wage as a waitress); she became a prostitute's maid at her network of flats, opening the door and answering the phone to clients, and when the girls failed to pay the rent on time, decided to try her hand at "the game" herself.

She spent two years working as a prostitute before opening her own brothel. With savings, an inheritance from her mother and help from a boyfriend, she managed to put a deposit on a small terraced house in Edencourt Road, Streatham.

In 1974, she paid £16,000 for a much bigger house called Cranmore in Ambleside Avenue, not far from Streatham's notorious Bedford Hill red light area. Its unusual features included an instruction signed "Madam Baloney" forbidding sex in the bathroom, and a sign in the kitchen proclaiming "My house is clean enough to be healthy . . . and dirty enough to be happy."

Cynthia Payne bought Cranmore with financial help from her devoted friend and "sex-slave" Squadron Leader Robert "Mitch" Smith, with whom she lived until his death in 1981. He was "a bit of a kink", she once testified in court "who liked to be caned and whipped". The house was furnished in a style of overwhelming suburban ordinariness, with nets at the windows, starched antimacassars and plenty of pretty china.

Sensing that her widowed father (with whom she had been reconciled) was missing the company of women, she let him have the run of her house – and the girls. "I can see now why men like coming here, Cinders," he once commented from the depths of one of her red Dralon sofas. "It's because when you look round, you don't feel you are in a brothel."

Brothel days were Tuesdays and Fridays. In addition, bi-monthly parties would be held, starting at 2 p.m. and continuing until early evening. Clients were encouraged to park round the corner. On arrival, each punter bought a voucher for £25, which entitled him to help himself to a buffet, to view a film, watch a live lesbian show and to have sex with one of several women. After sex, the working girls could redeem the voucher for £8 from Cynthia Payne.

She drummed up business by word of mouth, and by distributing her calling card, signed Cynthia Payne LV (Luncheon Vouchers). She barred men under 40 ("all Jack-the-lads boasting about their prowess"); her regular clients included a night watchman in his sixties who availed himself of a special £5 discount for pensioners, a vicar with a penchant for plump angels, an exhibitionist professor, and a barrister who would arrive as if dressed for court, then change into a full tart's costume of extra high heels, black stockings and make-up.

"We had a high-class clientele," Cynthia Payne recalled many years later, "no rowdy kids, no yobs, all well-dressed men in suits, who knew how to respect a lady.

It was like a vicar's tea party with sex thrown in – a lot of elderly, lonely people drinking sherry."

Cynthia Payne and her girls provided a wide range of personal services, to satisfy the requirements of the most exotic male fantasies. She understood completely when one of her clients revealed his penchant for polishing a woman's shoes while she was still wearing them, and always kept her own high heels and cane by her door to please others. At the same time, as the fastidious and orderly proprietor of a disorderly house, she took a motherly interest in the welfare of her staff: each girl would end the afternoon's work with a snack of poached egg on toast and a hot cup of tea.

Having served two-thirds of her sentence, Cynthia Payne emerged from Holloway in 1980 as a fully fledged media madam, and was driven to a south London hotel in a supporter's Rolls-Royce for a champagne reception.

In 1983, the *News of the World* revealed that "the luncheon voucher queen has put sex back on the menu" by resuming her famous parties. This time, Cynthia Payne claimed she was not charging money but leaving clients to make their own arrangements with the women. But according to one guest, nothing much had changed: it began as "an ordinary cocktail affair with . . . polite chatter about politics and gardening.

"Suddenly, three scantily clad attractive girls came dancing into the room and went round kissing everybody and greeting guests like old friends." Normal service had resumed at Ambleside Avenue.

Her celebrity career prospered. The novelist Paul Bailey wrote her biography *An English Madam* (1982) and Terry Jones directed a film about her life, *Personal Services* (1986), in which she was played by Julie Walters.

Meanwhile, the police were still watching. Although Cynthia Payne insisted she no longer ran a brothel, she did admit to throwing "an occasional swinging party". It was at such a celebration to mark the end of filming *Personal Services* that detectives raided her home for a second time in 1986. In an atmosphere of barely subdued mirth, the resulting court case in January 1987 made more headlines and kept the nation amused for 13 days with lurid tales of sex, slaves, transvestites and undercover policemen in disguise. In the end, Cynthia Payne was cleared on nine charges of controlling prostitutes.

She left the court clutching a Laughing Policeman doll which she had kept as a mascot throughout the trial. This time the champagne corks were popped in a suite at the Waldorf. Later she sent Judge Brian Pryor, QC, a copy of *An English Madam*, with the inscription: "I hope this book will broaden your rather sheltered life."

The Conservative MP Anthony Beaumont-Dark thought the case had made fools of the police. "People are wondering why squads of policemen are launching punitive raids on a bit of harmless fun," he added, "rather than getting on with the real job of hammering rapists, burglars and muggers."

Another maverick Tory, Nicholas Fairbairn MP, thought Mrs Payne should have been mentioned in the Honours List for keeping the nation amused. If the police would concentrate on matters of national importance, he told the *Daily Telegraph*, "they would be spending their time more usefully than prosecuting a jokey English lady who has made us laugh during a cold winter".

Following her second trial, Cynthia Payne determined to change what she considered to be Britain's archaic sex laws. She stood for Parliament as a candidate for the Payne and Pleasure Party in the Kensington by-election in July 1988 and again in Streatham in the 1992 general election. Her stated aim was "to provide light relief, to whip up support and to raise funds".

Later that year, Cynthia Payne completed a three-week season at the Edinburgh Fringe Festival playing to packed houses. She became an accomplished after-dinner speaker, particularly at police conferences. In 2004 she raised £325 from an auction of memorabilia, including a French maid's outfit, a mink coat, and a projector used to show blue films. In 2006 she re-launched her range of sex toys and raunchy outfits on the internet. "These days I am still in demand," she said, "but in a different way. In my thirties I was doing it, in my forties I was organising it and now, unfortunately, I can only talk about it."

Latterly Cynthia Payne lived quietly at Ambleside Avenue with her secretary and adviser Gloria Walker. Although always known as Mrs Payne, she never married.

John Profumo

"I want to make it clear that I had absolutely no desire to destroy a Minister."

11 March 2006
John Profumo – obituary

John Profumo, who died on Thursday night aged 91, was associated in most people's minds with the scandal that bore his name and led him to resign from the Conservative government of Harold Macmillan in 1963; but he also became known, in the last 40 years of his life, as a tireless worker for charity and as a man who bore his humiliations with enormous dignity and personal integrity.

Profumo's story is of a man who made one terrible mistake but sought his own redemption in a way which has no precedent in public life either before or since. No one in public life ever did more to atone for his sins; no one behaved with more silent dignity as his name was repeatedly dragged through the mud; and few ended their lives as loved and revered by those who knew him.

Profumo's transgression came when the Tories had been in power for 11 years. He was then a promising Secretary of State for War, married to the actress Valerie Hobson, star of the film *Kind Hearts and Coronets* and one of Britain's leading actresses of stage and screen in the 1940s and 1950s.

On 5 June 1963 he resigned after admitting that he had lied to Parliament about his relationship with Christine Keeler, a call-girl who had been – separately – seeing the Russian naval attaché and spy, Yevgeny Ivanov. The Macmillan government never recovered from the scandal and, for that and other reasons, lost the General Election the following year.

Filled with remorse, Profumo never sought to justify himself or seek public sympathy. Instead, for the next four decades he devoted himself to Toynbee Hall, a charitable settlement at Spitalfields in the East End of London. He began by washing dishes, helping with the playgroup and collecting rents. Later he served with the charity's council, eventually becoming its chairman and then president – the only other person to have held that office was Clement Attlee.

From his tiny office at Toynbee Hall, Profumo kept up a ceaseless flow of letters to anyone who might be able to speak, give money or do anything to assist the charity in its work of helping the poor and down-and-outs in the East End. Largely through his efforts, Toynbee Hall became a national institution.

In his early days at Toynbee Hall Profumo played an active role in fund-raising for the rebuilding after the war, during which half of the site had been destroyed. He arrived at a time when the charity realised that there was still a proportion of society that was not being served by the welfare state; and over the ensuing years, with Walter Birmingham, he established a new and creative programme of services for the local people. These included youth training schemes and facilities for people of all ages.

When Toynbee Hall's centenary came up in 1984, the then editor of the *Daily Telegraph*, W. F. Deedes, a former government colleague, persuaded Profumo to mark it with an article for the newspaper, the first time he had written under his own name since leaving public life more than two decades earlier.

Profumo's dedication and dignity won him enormous admiration from people in all walks of life. The author Peter Hennessy, a fellow trustee at a charitable foundation associated with Toynbee Hall, described him as "one of the nicest and most exemplary people I have met in public or political life; full of the old, decent Tory virtues". Margaret Thatcher called him "one of our national heroes". "Everybody here worships him", a helper at Toynbee Hall was once quoted as saying. "We think he's a bloody saint."

John Dennis Profumo, always known as Jack, was born on 30 January 1915. His father was a barrister with a thriving practice, but the family money was in insurance. The Profumos were descendants of an Italian aristocrat, Joseph Alexander Profumo, who had settled in England in 1880 and owned the Provident Life Association (which the family sold for £6m in the 1980s). Jack Profumo was the fifth Baron Profumo of the late kingdom of Sardinia.

He was educated at Harrow and at Brasenose College, Oxford. Politically ambitious, he became chairman of the Fulham Conservative Association by the age of 21. In May 1939 he was adopted as Conservative candidate for Kettering, and on the outbreak of war joined the 1st Northamptonshire Yeomanry. In 1940 there was an unexpected by-election at Kettering, and at the age of 25 he became the youngest MP in the House.

In the vote of no confidence in Chamberlain's war leadership after the Norway crisis on 8 May 1940, Profumo was one of the 30 Conservative MPs who joined with Labour in bringing Chamberlain down, thus ensuring Churchill's succession.

Profumo had a distinguished military career, being mentioned in dispatches during the North Africa campaign, and being appointed OBE (military) while serving on Field Marshal Alexander's staff in Italy. He was present at the surrender of the German forces in Italy and was later appointed Brigadier and Chief of Staff to the British Liaison Mission to General MacArthur in Japan. He also landed in Normandy on D-Day with an armoured brigade, and took part in the fierce fighting at Caen and in Operation Goodwood.

As an undergraduate Profumo had shown a flair for amateur theatricals and continued his interest during the war. He wrote and produced a musical for Ensa, Night and Day, with Frances Day in the lead, which was a great hit.

Profumo lost his seat in the 1945 Labour landslide and two years later joined R. A. Butler's staff at Conservative Central Office as the party's broadcasting adviser; he returned to Parliament as MP for Stratford-on-Avon in 1950. Two years later he was appointed a junior minister at the Ministry of Transport and Civil Aviation, and in 1954 he married Valerie Hobson, whom he met when she was playing the lead in The King and I at Drury Lane.

In 1957 he was appointed Parliamentary Under Secretary to the Colonies and subsequently Minister of State for Foreign Affairs. Three years later, in 1960, he became Secretary of State for War. This was shortly before the three services and the War Office became merged in a new Ministry of Defence. Profumo's responsibility was the Army, and his principal preoccupation was helping to recruit and establish a regular volunteer Army after the abolition of conscription.

To bring this to a successful conclusion was an important achievement on Profumo's part. At the time the Army had to deal with trouble spots in many parts of the world – among them the Cameroons, Aden, Yemen and Kuwait – and the ending of National Service was in this context a considerable risk. Only by recruiting sufficient young men of the right calibre could the Army's commitments be met. Profumo was essentially laying the foundations for the modern British Army.

Profumo was widely tipped as a future Foreign Secretary or Chancellor, but in 1961 there began the chain of events that would cost him his political career.

The Profumos had been invited by Lord Astor to spend a weekend on his estate at Cliveden in Buckinghamshire. Astor had let a cottage on the estate to Stephen Ward, a louche society osteopath whose client list included Winston Churchill, Sir Anthony Eden, Hugh Gaitskell and Frank Sinatra, but who also specialised in friendships with women of dubious virtue; one of Ward's guests that weekend was the 19-year-old Christine Keeler.

Profumo first set eyes on Christine Keeler when she stepped naked from Lord Astor's swimming pool, her costume having been snatched off her by Ward. Keeler left Cliveden that weekend with Yevgeny Ivanov, a Soviet attaché and friend of Ward, but Profumo asked Ward for Keeler's telephone number and afterwards began an affair that lasted several months.

MI5 apparently learned of the liaison from a tip-off by Ward, and Profumo subsequently ended the relationship after being warned that Ivanov was believed to be a spy. From then on Profumo sought to distance himself from the Cliveden set.

Over the next two years rumours about the affair began to circulate in Westminster, and on the evening of 20 March 1963 the Labour MP Barbara Castle stood up in the House of Commons and asked directly whether the Secretary of State for War had been involved with Christine Keeler.

In the early hours of the following morning Profumo was summoned from his bed by the Government Chief Whip to a meeting with some of his ministerial colleagues at the House of Commons, at which he denied having had an affair with Keeler. In the House of Commons chamber the following day, with Macmillan sitting beside him, Profumo made a personal statement in which he declared that there had been "no impropriety whatsoever" in his relationship with Keeler.

For three months Profumo denied any impropriety; but his denials were challenged by Stephen Ward (then facing trial for living off immoral earnings), who wrote to Macmillan and the opposition leader, Harold Wilson, giving his version of events; it was also rumoured that Christine Keeler had made a series of taped confessions revealing their affair.

Eventually Profumo decided that he had no option but to come clean. After taking his wife to Venice to confess his infidelity, on 5 June 1963 he resigned from the government and from Parliament. In his letter of resignation to Macmillan he expressed "deep remorse" at the embarrassment he had caused his colleagues and his constituents. A few days later he arrived at the door of Toynbee Hall and asked whether there was anything he could do to help.

The Profumo affair was eagerly seized upon by the Labour Party as evidence of sleaze at the top, and the satirists loved every minute of it. One widely repeated limerick ran: "Oh what have you done?' said Christine. / You've disrupted the Party machine; / To lie in the nude is not very rude, / But to lie in the House is obscene." The affair precipitated a crisis of confidence in Macmillan's leadership and helped to create the climate of opinion that led to the Conservatives' defeat in 1964.

Although he never spoke about it, Profumo's friends believed he seldom experienced a day when he did not feel a sense of shame for what he had done. While he maintained a total silence about the affair, his friends sought to shield him from prurient public interest. When two books on the Profumo affair were published in 1987, Lords Hailsham, Drogheda, Carrington, Goodman and Weinstock, plus Roy Jenkins and James Prior, sent a letter to *The Times* arguing that "it is now appropriate to consign this episode to history".

Almost from the beginning, those closely involved in the events that led up to Profumo's resignation began to feel uncomfortable about the way it had been handled. W. F. Deedes, a colleague of Profumo in the Macmillan Government, recalled being cornered by a group of Tory women at a party event in Profumo's old constituency of Stratford-on-Avon: "Why did you let Jack go?", they demanded to know. "He was popular here. We loved him. We'd have worked to get him back. What a damned sanctimonious lot you are."

As one of those present at the late night meeting at which Profumo had lied to his colleagues, Lord Deedes felt in retrospect that the whole affair had been badly handled: "Was it really sensible to convene a meeting of ministers at 2 a.m. at the House of Commons and summon Jack Profumo to this Star Chamber, instantly to answer 'yes' or 'no' to charges which Labour MPs had been bandying in the House earlier in the night?" he asked in 1994.

Because the news media had been besieging Profumo's house, Profumo had taken a sleeping draught not long before being awakened and reached the Commons in a befuddled state. "I have often wondered whether in these bizarre circumstances I would instantly have owned the truth, the whole truth and nothing but the truth," Deedes mused. "I doubt it."

In 1975 Profumo was appointed CBE on the advice of the Labour Prime Minister Harold Wilson, who had played no small part in exposing Profumo's misconduct. The honour was intended as a tribute to Profumo for his outstanding charity work and to his wife, Valerie Hobson, who had stood by him loyally throughout all his difficulties.

After resigning from office Profumo did not withdraw from an active social life. The Queen Mother was a friend, and the Profumos were regular guests at Clarence House. When the film *Scandal* (about the Keeler affair) came out in 1989, they were due to be guests at Maureen, Marchioness of Dufferin and Ava's dinner for the Queen Mother. They offered not to attend, but the Queen Mother insisted on their presence.

In recent years Profumo was often to be seen at memorial services, such as those for Lord and Lady Callaghan, Sir Angus Ogilvy, Sir Denis Thatcher and Sir Paul Getty. He was a guest at Lady Thatcher's 80th birthday party in Knightsbridge last year.

Jack Profumo remained devoted to his family and was deeply stricken by his wife's death in 1998. He is survived by their son, David.

The Duke of Wellington writes: I first got to know Jack Profumo at Oxford in the 1930s, when I found myself sharing digs with him and another Old Harrovian. As an Old Etonian myself, I suffered a great deal of good-natured teasing, but in that house I spent two very happy years. The house was always full of noise, music, pretty girls and parties. Frances Day, a leading actress of those days, was a frequent visitor.

Shortly afterwards the war came and we went our separate ways. After the war we met up again. By that time Jack was an MP, and I remember well an occasion in 1961 when I was about to go to a military appointment in BAOR. Jack said to me: "I shall be coming to Germany shortly," and added jokingly: "You will have to salute me." Equally jokingly, I said that "nothing in the world would induce me to salute you". But he was right, because not long afterwards, as Secretary of State for War, he did come to BAOR; I did have to salute him, and in fact he stayed with me.

Since those days we happily kept in touch, and last year I went to his 90th birthday and he came to mine in July of last year.

He will be much missed by those who knew him, and especially by those at Toynbee Hall, who benefited from his kindness and devotion to serving others in the years after he left politics.

June 1963
Dr. Ward set MI5 on Mr Profumo
Security watch in West-End mews

Dr. Stephen Ward, the osteopath, said yesterday that he had told the War Office security service (MI5) in 1961 about the relationship of Mr Profumo, 48, and Miss Christine Keeler, 21. Then MI5 followed the then War Minister on occasions when he went to meet the model.

MI 5 were informed because Miss Keeler, then a tenant of Dr. Ward's, also knew Cdr. Yevgeny Ivanov, Soviet assistant naval attaché at the time of her meetings with the minister. Dr. Ward was extremely "disturbed" and "anxious".

One night security men watching Mr Profumo and others watching Cdr. Ivanov met outside Dr. Ward's then home in Wimpole Mews, Marylebone.

At Mr Profumo's home in Chester Terrace, Regent's Park, a member of his staff said he would be away for two or three days. A Buckingham Palace announcement said it was expected that the Queen would receive Mr Profumo on Tuesday when he hands over his seal of office.

Mr Wilson, Leader of the Opposition, said yesterday that if there were any questions of security involving Mr Profumo the Commons had a duty to press for further facts. Otherwise there would be no political action by Labour. A letter from Dr. Ward to Mr Brooke, Home Secretary, is the subject of two Parliamentary questions due for answer on Thursday week.

Anxiety over meetings
Dr. Ward Set MI5 On Mr Profumo
Daily Telegraph Reporter

Dr. Stephen Ward said to me yesterday that he had informed the War Office security service about the relationship between Mr Profumo and Miss Christine Keeler at the time in 1961 that the then Secretary of State for War was meeting the model.

He did so, he said, because Miss Keeler also knew Cdr. Yevgeny Ivanov, then Soviet assistant naval attaché in London, "very well" and he was "extremely disturbed about it".

Cdr. Ivanov was a close friend of the Devonshire Street osteopath and artist. He was also a frequent guest at Dr. Ward's London home and Thames-side country cottage on Viscount Astor's estate at Cliveden. Bucks, before he returned to Moscow early this year after Miss Keeler was involved in a shooting incident.

Dr. Ward, a friend of Miss Keeler, and for many years, of Mr Profumo, also told me that he had informed Mr Brooke, Home Secretary, of his approach to the security service in Mr Profumo's Ministry.

He did so, he said, in the letter he wrote to the Home Secretary last month. This letter its text still officially undisclosed, has been a topic of intense speculation inside and outside Parliament.

It is the subject of two Parliamentary questions, one by Mr Chuter Ede, a former Labour Home Secretary, which are awaiting answers by Mr Brooke on 20 June. Dr. Ward said his main purpose in writing to Mr Brooke was to tell him about his approach to the security service.

It was while visiting Dr. Ward's country cottage that Miss Keeler had her first encounter with Mr Profumo. Mr Profumo and his wife, formerly Valerie Hobson, the actress, were at Cliveden at the time as guests of Lord Astor, and they met Miss Keeler when she went up to Lord Astor's swimming pool uninvited and joined a party which also included Cdr. Ivanov.

Other meetings between the Minister and the model followed in London. Dr. Ward said to me yesterday: "When I became aware that Mr Profumo and Miss Keeler were seeing each other I got in touch with a man in the security service at the War Office.

"He came up to my flat and we had a long talk. I told him about Mr Profumo and Miss Keeler. I told him I was very anxious. I also introduced him to Miss Keeler."

Dr. Ward said he could not disclose the name of the security man but said he had given it to Cdr. A. Townsend, of the Administration and Operations Department of the Metropolitan Police at Scotland Yard. Cdr. Townsend, he said, made no comment on this information.

Dr. Ward was also unable to tell me what action was taken by the War Office security service as a result of his information. But I understand that Mr Profumo was followed by security men when he met Miss Keeler at Dr. Ward's London home, then in Wimpole Mews, Marylebone.

Cdr. Ivanov was being watched by security men at the same time, and I understand that one night security men watching Mr Profumo had an encounter in Wimpole Mews with security men watching Cdr. Ivonov.

I believe, too that it was because the security service had a record of the meetings that Mr Profumo was able to say in his statement in the 22 March that he had met Miss Keeler between July and September 1961, "on about half a dozen occasions at Dr. Ward's flat when I called to see him and his friends."

Dr. Ward told me about his approach to the security service while explaining to me why he had taken the steps that led to Mr Profumo's confession and resignation.

Dr. Ward said: "I want to make it clear that I had absolutely no desire to destroy a Minister. My motive in approaching the security service and in writing to Mr Brooke was not to expose Mr Profumo.

"I wrote to the security service because I was anxious about the relationship and in my recent steps my only object throughout has been to clear my own name.

"The relationship between Mr Profumo and Miss Keeler and the fact that their meetings took place at my flat have made it appear that I encouraged this relationship. The contrary was true. I was most anxious about it.

"Miss Keeler met Mr Profumo in the first place entirely by chance and not by my design. I think it is now clear that he subsequently got in touch with her after that first meeting.

"I was not in a position to stop them seeing each other. Miss Keeler is not my ward or protege. I have had no relationship with her other than as a friend, and I had and have no control over her.

"She had rented a room at my flat in Wimpole Mews and at the relevant time was staying there as a tenant with her parents' knowledge and approval. Her meetings there with Mr Profumo took place while I was down in the country.

"I made statements to the contrary when the fact that Mr Profumo knew Miss Keeler was first disclosed because I wished to conceal their relationship in the interests of Mr Profumo and the Government."

Giving his reasons why he later decided to disclose the facts, Dr. Ward went on: "I had at the time done everything possible to conceal the relationship which has now been admitted and it seemed to me that the act of having done so was now destroying my livelihood and the resultant events were being totally disastrous to me.

The case gave rise to a whole train of rumours and all sorts of people were mentioned with the implication that I had been trying to procure them for Miss Keeler. This culminated in questions in Parliament and police inquiries into what was alleged to be a call girl racket.

"My friends and patients were questioned and life became absolutely intolerable for me. I owe as much to my friends as Mr Profumo does to his and I could not stand it any longer. I felt that the only course was to disclose the true facts.

Dr. Ward's first step was to see the Prime Minister's principal private secretary, Mr T. J. Bligh. This meeting took place about three weeks ago. He then saw Cdr. Townsend at Scotland Yard, and later wrote to Mr Brooke.

One of the matters he mentioned in his letter to Mr Brooke was a letter purporting to be from Mr Profumo to Miss Keeler. This letter, Dr. Ward said, had got into the possession of a Sunday newspaper (The *Sunday Pictorial*) and its existence was known to a number of people.

Dr. Ward went on: "At considerable sacrifice to myself I allowed this newspaper to publish an article about me as part of a bargain to obtain the return of this letter. The payment I received for the interview exactly covered the legal expenses I had incurred in trying to recover the letter.

"The letter was handed to my solicitors. Messrs. Coward, Chance, who handed it to Mr Profumo's solicitors. I informed Mr Brooke about the letter and this transaction."

Dr. Ward then said that he had also told Mr Brooke in his letter about how he approached the security service at the time Mr Profumo was seeing Miss Keeler.

He added: "I emphasised that I had told the security service not as a complaint against Mr Profumo but because I feared the possibility of some misrepresentation, particularly in view of the fact that I had a Russian friend."

21 June 1963
Mr Profumo "guilty of grave contempt"
M.P.s' censure: Labour critics claim Ministers abused procedure
By our own representative

The House of Commons agreed this afternoon that Mr Profumo, former War Minister, was guilty of a grave contempt of the House in denying, in a personal statement, that there was impropriety in his association with Miss Christine Keeler. Having approved a motion to this effect without a division, the House decided to take no further action.

The widely divergent political views of Mr Sydney Silverman on the Opposition bank-benches and Mr Selwyn Lloyd on the Conservative side coalesced in the opinion that Mr Profumo should not be further persecuted or prosecuted. But there were further Labour criticisms of the Government's handling of the affair.

Mr Brown, Deputy Leader of the Opposition, backed by Mr Warbey (Lab., Ashfield), submitted that the Ministers who consulted Mr Profumo about his statement before it was made to the House were guilty of an abuse of the procedure for personal statements.

The consultations, said Mr Brown, made this "anything but a personal statement in the proper sense of the words."

At question time earlier Mr Brooke, Home Secretary, was interrogated at length on differences the treatment of Miss Keeler and her friend Miss Rice-Davies in the matter of attendance at court cases. He said Miss Rice-Davies was regarded as an essential witness. Miss Keeler was not.

Opening the debate Mr Macleod, Leader of the House, moved: That Mr John Profumo, in making a personal statement to this House on 22 March 1963, which contained words which he later admitted not to be true, was guilty of a grave contempt of this House.

Pointing out that there had been clear contempt, he said it was right that some formal way should be found of recording the censure of the House.

Another matter which had been raised by Mr Wigg (Lab., Dudley) was that the words twice repeated m the statement "under protection of Parliamentary privilege", were tendentious in a statement which had, in the usual way, been shown to the Speaker.

In the light of what had since been learned the House would agree that that was so. He did not think this was an appropriate occasion to add further censure or comment. Accordingly he advised the House that "we record our displeasure".

Supporting the motion Mr George Brown, Deputy Leader of the Opposition, said that obviously it was distasteful to have return to some aspects of this subject. But the House had to protect its procedures. It had to avoid future misuse by precedents being too easily and wrongfully established.

"I was very glad Mr Macleod only dealt with the contempt conveyed by the inclusion of words that were untrue by the gentleman referred to, but also took up the reference to Mr Wigg and other Labour Members who raised this subject."

That reference reflected on Members who, until now, had not the chance of having their reputations restored. It also seemed to bring the Chair into an unhappy situation.

He hoped everyone could draw that the moral of how careful they must be in personal statements. "A further point which Mr Macleod did not refer to is fact of this purporting to be personal statement.

"When one listened to what Macleod had to say on Monday, it reads very much like a statement which was written for the then Secretary for War by Ministers, which he was then persuaded to make because Ministers thought it would be convenient and proper, or whatever the words are, for everyone that he should do that.

"That was itself an abuse of procedure of personal statements and made this anything but personal statement in the proper sense of the words."

Mr Grimond, Leader of the Liberals, supporting the motion, remarked: "We are not saying the affront to this House is more important than other aspects of the case."

Mr Silverman (Lab., Nelson Colne) said nobody ever thought that a man making a personal Statement in the House and telling a deliberate lie was doing anything but what the motion described it to be. What was the need for formally asseverating a proposition?

Mr Profumo, in a difficult situation, made something worse than a bad mistake. He had paid for it.

Mr Shinwell (Lab., Easington): "Then why don't you leave him alone?"

Mr Silverman continued: "He has involved himself in the irretrievable ruin of a quite distinguished career. I hope he will not be persecuted or prosecuted further."

Mr Warbey (Lab., Ashfield) claimed there had been an abuse the privilege of the House not so much by Mr Profumo as by the Government. The Prime Minister had made it clear that the making of the statement was an act of the Government.

Five members of the Government drew up the statement in the absence of Mr Profumo. He was called in later to endorse it.

But another member of the Cabinet, the Home Secretary (Mr Brooke), could have been at this meeting. He had been in the House that evening when the remarks which led to the statement were made.

The Leader of the House (Mr Macleod) was "very sensitive on this point". When asked about this on Monday he had "a fit of misrecollection."

Mr Warbey added: "I think the House is entitled to know why the Home Secretary was absent, why he was deliberately absent. I can only draw one conclusion, and that is that the Home Secretary knew too much.

"By that time the Home Secretary already knew that Mr Profumo had been engaged in an improper association and the question of whether or not he lied is a secondary point."

The Speaker, Sir Harry Hylton-Foster, stopped Mr Warbey and asked whether he was making a personal charge of dishonesty against Mr Brooke.

Mr Warbey continued: "What I am saying is that this statement which we are asked to express ourselves upon to-day was not, in reality, a personal statement, it was a Government statement.

"As a Government statement, it is one for which the Government should take responsibility. The Home Secretary by his absence from that meeting at which the statement was drawn up, showed that he was not able to be a party to the statement."

The Speaker again asked him if he was making an accusation of personal dishonesty against the Home Secretary.

Mr Warbey: "I am not making an accusation of personal dishonesty at all."

Later, Mr Warbey admitted having said that the Home Secretary knew too much. "What I meant was that by that time he must have been informed of the inquiries made by the police and special branch into the associations of the people concerned in this case.

"And that is why I say the Home Secretary should have been present at this meeting."

It was quite improper that Mr Brooke and other members of the Government, who were present, should not take the grave responsibility of using the privilege of making a personal statement to hush up rumours and to cover up public scandal.

Mrs Barbara Castle (Lab., Blackburn), one of the three M.P.s who originally mentioned the rumours against Mr Profumo in the House, said the statement drafted by the five Ministers contained an allegation that the three Members had wrongly used their Parliamentary privilege.

"For three months we have lived under something of a cloud. We were attacked for raising this matter on 21 March. We were accused in many quarters of scandal-mongering."

The Leader of the House must recognise now that the three Members had made a proper use of Parliamentary privilege. At that time, everyone wanted the air cleared. This could only have been done by raising the rumours in the House.

Mr Macleod should place on record in the annals of the House the apology due to the three MPs.

In a speech of only a few sentences, Mr Selwyn Lloyd (C., Wirral), the former

Chancellor of the Exchequer, said the House should adopt the approach suggested by Mr Silverman.

Mr Emrys Hughes (Lab., South Ayrshire) said there was no precedent for a case of this kind.

Mr Hughes recalled that in January 1957, Mr John Junor, after having been found guilty of a breach of privilege, was brought to the Bar of the House and severely reprimanded by the Speaker (then Mr W. S. Morrison).

[Mr Junor, Editor of the *Sunday Express*, was brought to the Bar over leading article in the newspaper on petrol rationing. The article alleged that politicians were receiving supplementary allowances.]

Mr Hughes said that Members had been impressed with Mr Junor's dignity as he apologised to the House.

It had been suggested in one quarter of the Press, he continued, that Mr Profumo should be brought to the Bar.

"I hope it is not going to be done. If Mr Profumo was summoned to the Bar of the House he might ask who was prepared to throw the first stone. I don't think there you be a rush to Palace Yard to get stones.

Replying, Mr Macleod said that Mr Warbey's unfair point, "in other circumstances I would use stronger language", had been answered by the Home Secretary himself. In an intervention in Monday's debate, Mr Brooke had refuted these allegations.

Referring to Mr Hughes' remarks, he said: "He is quite right. This has no precedent. I cannot believe that the House would wish to bring Mr Profumo to the bar of this House. I think this motion is the right way of proceeding."

The motion was approved.

Mr Pannell (Lab., Leeds, West) then asked the Speaker to consider whether members making personal statements should be allowed to threaten other people, as was done in the last paragraph of Mr Profumo's statement.

{The paragraph was: "I shall not hesitate to issue writs for libel and slander if scandalous allegations are made or repeated outside this House.}

The Speaker said the point could not be dealt with now, but he would consider what had been said.

Oliver Reed

"Look, I'll put my plonker on the table if you
don't give me a plate of mushy peas."

3 May 1999
Oliver Reed – obituary
Actor who starred in *Women in Love* but put his
real energies into hell-raising off-screen

Oliver Reed, the film actor who has died aged 61, exuded an animal magnetism and a sense of danger rare among British actors; these qualities made him a natural choice when the script required a woman to be either terrorised or seduced.

It was seduction which he practised on Glenda Jackson's Gudrun when he played Gerald in the film of D. H. Lawrence's *Women in Love* (1969). On the other hand, he was just as convincing wrestling naked with Alan Bates in the same film.

But Reed's screen career often seemed like a mere rehearsal for the more important business of hell-raising in real life. He once summarised his career as "shafting the girlies and downing the sherbie". A prodigious drinker, he spent much of his later life being escorted from various pubs and hotels after initiating what he regarded as "tests of strength".

Robert Oliver Reed was born in Wimbledon on 13 February 1938, a great-grandson of the actor-manager Herbert Beerbohm Tree and a nephew of the film director Carol Reed. After being expelled from 14 schools, Reed succeeded in becoming captain of athletics and junior cross-country champion at Ewell Castle.

He then worked for a while as a bouncer for a strip club, and did his National Service in the Army Medical Corps. His hopes of becoming an officer were dashed when it was discovered that he suffered from dyslexia and was both illiterate and innumerate.

On leaving the Army in 1958, Reed earned his crust as a fairground boxer and mortuary attendant. For a while he studiously ignored Reed's suggestions that he should attend Rada (founded by his great-grandfather), and only drifted into acting when he discovered that most of his drinking companions were earning good wages as film extras.

He made his television debut in a children's series, *The Golden Spur*. This led to a number of small film roles, as a layabout in *Beat Girl* (1960), as a factory worker in *The Angry Silence* (1960), as a ballet dancer in *The League of Gentlemen* (1960). Appropriately, he was a bouncer in *The Two Faces of Dr Jekyll* (1960).

In 1962 Reed was given his first leading role in the Hammer horror film, *The Curse of the Werewolf*. He starred as the troubled lycanthrope. The film's special effects included a hair-sprouting scene in a jail, and several shots of Reed tiptoeing on his hind paws from the scene of murder.

Altogether Reed made six films for Hammer. In *The Damned* (1963) he appeared as the leader of a motor-cycle gang; in *Paranoiac* (1963) he was a murderer bent on driving his sister (Janette Scott) crazy.

Meanwhile Michael Winner, who had seen Reed in a television play, cast him as a promenade Casanova in a sleazy drama entitled *The System* (1963). Reed then played a brutal fur-trapper in *The Trap*, with Rita Tushingham. After terrorising Carol Lynley in *The Shuttered Room* (1967), Reed was seen in two Michael Winner comedies, *The Jokers* (1967), with Michael Crawford, and *I'll Never Forget What's-'is-name* (with Orson Welles, who became a close friend).

Reed's breakthrough came in 1968, when, directed by his uncle, he made a convincingly savage Bill Sikes in the film version of the musical *Oliver!*. In terms of soft-spoken menace, Reed's performance nearly equalled that of Robert Newton in the earlier version by David Lean. The film won six Oscars and made Reed an international star. By the late sixties, he was Britain's highest-paid actor.

His next project was Ken Russell's adaptation of *Women In Love* (1970). Reed admitted to being nervous about the wrestling scene, which Russell had originally wanted to film in an ice-cold lake. "Alan and I drank a bottle of vodka each," Reed remembered, "before we staggered on to the set." Reed then achieved the distinction of becoming the first actor to appear fully naked in a mainstream film.

Thereafter, his penchant for dropping his trousers sometimes got him into trouble. On holiday in the Caribbean and wanting to show off a newly acquired tattoo, Reed exposed himself in a hotel bar. Unknown to him, the symbol of a cockerel which he thereby displayed denoted to his audience an involvement in voodoo; he was forced to escape over a balcony.

In his second film for Russell, *The Devils* (1971), Reed played a licentious priest who induces hysterical behaviour in a group of nuns. The film dwelt rather more on the physical effects of satanic possession than on its moral implications. Reed followed this with the part of a bullying Army sergeant in *Triple Echo* (1972), again with Glenda Jackson.

This role was perhaps Reed's last attempt at serious acting. Thereafter he appeared to be less interested in the quality than in the quantity of parts he was offered, partly because he needed to pay the cost of the divorce from his first wife, Kathleen Byrne, and partly because he needed money to continue his roistering.

In one celebrated incident in 1974, Reed invited 36 rugby players to a party at his home. Between Saturday night and Sunday lunchtime, they managed to consume between them 60 gallons of beer, 32 bottles of Scotch, 17 bottles of gin, four crates of wine and a lone bottle of Babycham. The entertainment concluded with Reed leading the players on a nude dawn run through the Surrey countryside.

In 1974, Reed made a convincingly doughty Athos in *The Three Musketeers*. On one occasion during filming in Spain, the police were summoned to Reed's hotel to arrest him for dancing naked in a giant goldfish tank. "Leave me alone," shouted, Reed. "You can't touch me! I'm one of the Four Musketeers."

Later that year he told a reporter, "Destroy me and you destroy the whole British film industry. I can afford to say cock-a-doodle-do because I'm the biggest star this country has got, and don't you forget it, you pig." Profiles that celebrated Reed's hell-raising prowess rarely mentioned his loutish, bullying streak, although on set he was always courteous and word perfect.

In the late seventies, Reed moved to Guernsey as a tax exile, where he lived with his companion Jackie Daryl and their daughter Sarah. He returned occasionally to England to appear on chat shows to promote such films as *Tommy* (1975) and *The Prince and the Pauper* (1977).

Reed's notoriety increased yet further in 1985 when he married Jospehine Burge; she was then 21, but had been his companion since she was a 16-year-old schoolgirl. At his stag party, which lasted two days, Reed claimed to have downed 136 pints of beer. But to the surprise of many, the marriage proved a success, although in 1986 Reed was forced to dig up nine acres of his back garden after forgetting where he had buried his wife's jewellery when drunk.

Later that year, Reed went some way towards redeeming his critical reputation with his performance in *Castaway*, based on Lucy Irving's book about her time on a desert island.

In 1991, Reed appeared on the late-night Channel 4 discussion programme *After Dark* (popularly known as *After Closing Time*). The subject was violence, and Reed was determined not to disappoint.

Drinking wine from a half-pint glass, he freely expressed his views on the subject, periodically falling off his chair before kissing a surprised feminist author and announcing, "Right, I'm off to have a slash."

Channel 4 took the programme off the air after 20 minutes; when it returned, Reed terminated the discussion with the words: "Look, I'll put my plonker on the table if you don't give me a plate of mushy peas."

Oliver Reed is survived by his wife Josephine and two daughters.

Keith Richards and Mick Jagger

"She has been described as a drug-taking nymphomaniac.
Do you expect me to let that girl go into the witness box?"

19 February 1967
Drugs search in Rolling Stone's mansion
By Peter Gladstone Smith

Police have raided the country mansion home of Keith Richards, one of the Rolling Stones pop group, in West Wittering, Sussex, and searched the house and all the people present for drugs.

Mick Jagger, leader of the group, and Miss Marianne Faithfull, the pop singer, were in a party of about twelve guests in the house at the time.

Police took away a quantity of substances they found in the house. These are now being analysed in Scotland Yard's forensic science laboratory.

The raid took place at 8 p.m. last Sunday. Earlier in the day West Sussex police had obtained a warrant under the Dangerous Drugs Act at a special sitting of magistrates to search the house, Redlands, Redlands Lane, West Wittering, and all the people there.

It was led by Chief Insp. Gordon Dineley, of Chichester division. He was accompanied by about 20 uniformed and C.I.D. plain-clothes officers, and three policewomen.

Chief Insp. Dineley knocked on the door of the thatched mansion, which is surrounded by a five-acre lawn and a moat, and showed the magistrates' warrant. He explained that police had come to search and was received with the utmost civility.

Keith Richards had invited friends to his home for a weekend house party.

Their cars were on the drive outside. These included a mini car with smoked windows, used by the Rolling Stones to slip away when besieged by their fans, a minibus and a family saloon.

Earlier in the weekend they had formed exuberant beach parties and taken snapshots of each other near the mouth of Chichester Harbour. As they drove past the gardener-caretaker Keith Richards gave him the "thumbs-up" sign to show that all was well.

Mr Richards bought the multi-roomed house a year ago. Throughout last summer builders made alterations to suit his taste.

It was here that the Rolling Stones took their instruments and worked out their best-selling record, *Paint it Black* which has been described as a funereal lament of Indian-style music.

Sometimes teenage fans cross the moat to invade the garden. More often than not they are disappointed, because Mr Richards spends only a few days a month there.

Yesterday a spokesman of West Sussex police issued this statement: "On Sunday evening 12 February police officers, from West Sussex entered premises in the Chichester area under the authority of a warrant issued under the Dangerous Drugs Act.

"As a result several persons were interviewed and certain articles were brought away from the house."

11 May 1967
Two "Stones" for trial on drug charges
Jagger avoids crowd
By a *Daily Telegraph* reporter

Mick Jagger and Keith Richards, of the Rolling Stones pop group, were smuggled out of the back door of Chichester court by police yesterday to avoid several hundred people in front of the building.

The crowd, many of them schoolchildren, had waited several hours in warm sunshine. But Jagger and Richards, both 23, stepped into a chauffeur-driven black car parked at the back of the court.

They had appeared before Chichester magistrates on offences under the Dangerous Drugs Act, 1965. Accused with them was Robert Hugh Fraser, 29, an art gallery director, of Mount Street, Mayfair.

All pleaded not guilty and elected to be tried at the West Sussex Quarter Sessions. The case is expected to be heard on 22 June, and the magistrates granted them £100 bail.

Mr Anthony McCowan, prosecuting, said Jagger told police that tablets found in his jacket had been prescribed by a doctor for him "to stay awake and work".

Jagger was summoned in his full name, Michael Philip Jagger, of New Oxford Street. He was accused of being in unauthorised possession of four tablets containing amphetamine sulphate and methylamphethaphate hydrochloride.

Richards was charged with allowing his house, Redlands, at West Wittering, Sussex, to be used on February 12 for smoking cannabis resin.

Fraser was charged with being in unauthorised possession of a dangerous drug, heroin. He was also accused of unauthorised possession of eight capsules containing methylamphetamine hydrochloride.

Mr Anthony McCowan, prosecuting, said that at 7.55 p.m. on Sunday, February 12, officers led by Chief Insp. Gordon Dinely, of West Sussex police, went to Redlands. A warrant had been issued under the Dangerous Drugs Act, 1965.

The inspector knocked on the front door. There was a lapse of time of about two or three minutes, and he was about to effect entry when Richards opened the door.

The police went into the drawing room, where there appeared to be a party at which there were eight men and one woman. The officers interviewed all people present, and searched them and their belongings.

Dealing with the charge against Jagger, Mr McCowan said that a detective constable found in a bedroom a green jacket. In the pocket was a plastic phial containing four tablets.

Jagger admitted the jacket was his and when asked if the tablets belonged to him replied: "Yes, my doctor prescribed them."

Asked what the tablets were for, Jagger replied: "To stay awake and work." The tablets were later examined at the Scotland Yard science laboratory and found to contain amphetamine sulphate and methylamphetamine hydrochloride, substances restricted under the schedule of the Drugs (Prevention of Misuse) Act, 1964.

The phial containing the tablets had Italian writing on it. Evidence would be given by a Mr Priest, a pharmaceutical chemist, that the label "Stenamina" appeared to be of Italian origin.

The phial contained the name: Lepetit of Milan.

On the case against Fraser, Mr McCowan said an officer named Harris found a dark coloured jacket behind the drawing room door. He took eight green capsules from a pocket. Fraser agreed to be searched.

A small box and a number of small white tablets were found in Fraser's trouser pocket. He said he was a diabetic and the tablets were prescribed by his doctor.

Asked if he had a card, Fraser said it might be upstairs. He and the officer went to a room upstairs in which Fraser was staying, and searched for the card but could not find it.

A detective sergeant said to Fraser: "These look like heroin tablets to me." Fraser replied: "No, they are definitely not." Police sent two white tablets to the forensic science laboratory.

The jacket and eight green capsules found in the pocket were then shown to Fraser, and an officer asked him what the tablets were. Fraser said: "I have trouble with my stomach. I got them on prescription."

He gave the names of three London doctors, but was unable to give their addresses. The white tablets were found to contain heroin hydrochloride, and the capsules methylamphetamine hydrochloride.

On the case against Richards, Mr McCowan said that a police sergeant took from a drawing room table a briar pipe bowl which was found to bear traces of cannabis resin.

When the police arrived at the house they noticed a very strong, sweet and unusual smell. They found sticks of incense and a tin which appeared to contain incense.

There was no sign that any incense had actually been burnt. The prosecution would say that the burning of incense could be used to mask the smoking of cannabis resin.

Continuing the case against Richards, Mr McCowan said a woman detective constable found a deposit on a table in the drawing room. This was found to contain cannabis resin.

Another officer went to a bedroom and took possession of three cigarette ends. These were also found to contain cannabis resin.

Det. Sgt. Stanley Cudmore said that as far as he knew Jagger and Richards were men of perfectly good character. Throughout the time he was at the house they behaved "in a thoroughly adult manner".

28 June 1967
Mick Jagger guilty on drugs charge
No defence, says judge
By Guy Rais

Mick Jagger, of the Rolling Stones was found guilty at Chichester Quarter Sessions yesterday on a drug charge. He is to be sentenced today.

Sentence will also be pronounced on Robert Fraser, 29, West End art gallery director who earlier pleaded guilty to possessing 24 tablets of heroin. The case against Keith Richards, Rolling Stones' guitarist, will be heard today. He was granted bail.

Richard, 23, is accused of permitting His home at West Wittering, Sussex, to be used for the purpose of smoking Indian hemp. The three were charged after a police raid on the house.

The prosecution contended that the four tablets of the drug in Jagger's possession could not be obtained in Britain and could be bought in Italy only on prescription.

Only a handful of teenagers attended the court hearing but about 60 school-boys and schoolgirls thronged round a two-tone Dormobile which took Jagger and Fraser to Lewes Gaol, 37 miles away. Earlier fans tried to pull clothing off Keith Richards.

When the case against Jagger ended, Mr Michael Havers, Q.C., defending, inti-mated there would be an appeal on a point of law.

Judge Block, who tried the case agreed, adding: "I wish you luck."

Jagger, 23, wore a pale green double-breasted jacket with white buttons, olive green trousers a floral shirt and green and black striped tie. He sat in the dock beside Richards, who pleads not guilty,

Richards, with hair down the back of his neck like Jagger, wore a navy blue frock coat, black military-style trousers, a lace collar and maroon and black shoes.

Jagger pleaded not guilty to possessing the four tablets which contained amphet-amine sulphate and methyl amphetamine hydrochloride.

Det. Sgt. John Challen said when he went upstairs to a bedroom he searched a green jacket which Jagger later admitted belonged to him. In the left hand pocket he found a small phial containing the four tablets.

When, questioned, Jagger said they had been prescribed by his doctor and asked what for, he replied: "To stay awake at work."

Mr Lewis Priest, an administrative associate of the Pharmaceutical Society, said that the drug was not available in England and a licence would be needed to import it from Italy.

Dr. Raymond Dixon Firth, of Wilton Crescent, Westminster, said, that Jagger, a private patient, first saw him in July 1965 for a check up.

Asked about the tablets he said they could be called "benzedrine". People who travelled long distances frequently took them and they could be used by people who had had a bad day, were up all night and had another hard day ahead of them.

He recalled a conversation he had with Jagger some months before February 14. Jagger had told him he had had a particularly trying period abroad and that a friend had given him some tablets to help him get through it.

"I asked him what they were and he said he did not know but they were a kind of Italian pep pill. The actual name was not mentioned and I assumed it must have been of the amphetamine type.

"He asked me if they were all right to use. And I said yes, in certain circumstances where he was perhaps short of sleep and faced with a busy day. I said he should not have them regularly."

Mr Michael Havers, Q.C.: "Having been told that he could use them, was he, in your opinion as a medical man, properly in possession of them?" – "Yes."

Answering Mr Malcolm Morris, Q.C., for the prosecution, Dr. Firth said that when Jagger told him about the tablets, he assumed they were something harmless.

Mr Havers submitted that the verbal approval by Dr. Firth to Jagger of the tablets constituted in law a prescription.

But Judge Block, after hearing legal argument, said he had no hesitation in saying the doctor's evidence did not in law amount to the issue of a prescription.

Mr Havers, after an adjournment, said in view of the judge's ruling he would not address the jury. He did not call Jagger.

Summing up, Judge Block said he had ruled as a matter of law that Jagger was not in possession of a prescription for the tablets by virtue of a prescription issued by a qualified medical practitioner.

"It therefore follows that the defence open to Jagger is not available and I have to direct you there is no defence to this charge."

After the jury found Jagger guilty Det. Sgt. Cudmore said that Jagger had "done well educationally". He had seven O-levels and two A-levels.

During the course of the investigation at the house Jagger behaved in an adult manner and co-operated fully.

Earlier, Fraser had pleaded guilty to having 24 heroin tablets in his possession on the night of the raid.

It was said that they were found after he was searched and that he had told the police officer that he was a diabetic and that the tablets had been prescribed by his doctor. He could not produce a diabetic card.

When the tablets were analysed they proved in each case to be 1/12th grain of heroin.

Mr William Denny, for Fraser, said it was not uncommon in these days for people possessing "hard drugs" such as heroin to be workshy, spineless individuals who wandered about and were delinquent.

He was anxious that the court should not accept this in the case of Fraser. He had led an industrious life and was the son of a distinguished financier and went to a famous school. He served with the Army in Kenya during the Mau Mau troubles.

He found he had a taste and flair for modern art and five years ago established his gallery in the West End.

Success came from hard work and because of that he was very prone to temptation put before him about 12 months ago by someone who had worked at the gallery and who had offered him some heroin tablets as a stimulant.

After a comparatively short time he found, to use the modern jargon, that he was "hooked". He had received treatment and had lied to the police because he was so dependent on the drug that he could not bear the thought of all the tablets being taken away from him.

A doctor on behalf of Fraser said that, as far as it was possible to say, he was now cured of his addiction.

29 June 1967
Court told of "nude girl in rug"
Rolling Stones' party
By Guy Rais

The identity of a girl guest wearing only a fur skin rug "which from time to time she let fall" was not disclosed at the trial of Keith Richards, the Rolling Stones lead guitarist, at West Sussex Quarter Sessions at Chichester yesterday.

After the prosecution had concluded its case against Richards, who pleaded not guilty to permitting his house at West Wittering, Sussex, to be used for the smoking of Indian hemp, Mr Michael Havers, Q.C., defending, attacked the prosecution for its references to the naked girl.

He told the jury of 11 men and one woman that it had been brought into the evidence to make them think her behaviour was due to smoking Indian hemp.

Mr Havers asked: "Is that fair? She has not been charged and so is not able to make a defence. She is a girl who remains technically anonymous and one hopes will remain so.

"She has been described as a drug-taking nymphomaniac. Do you expect me to let that girl go into the witness box? I am not going to allow her. I am not going to tear that blanket of anonymity aside and let the world laugh or scorn as they will.

"This is a girl whose name has not yet been dragged into the mud. If I cannot call her to this court I propose to call no one who was at that house."

Mr Havers added: "The prosecution argued for this evidence to be admitted. Having got it admitted, that girl's name was blackened in a way that could affect her career for ever."

Richards, 23, will go into the witness box today when the trial is resumed. He came into court wearing a black four-button Regency-style suit trimmed with black braid and a white high-necked shirt patterned with black stitching.

When the trial started two more of his guests, Mick Jagger, 23, lead singer of the Rolling Stones, and Robert Fraser, 29, were waiting below the court to be sentenced for other drug offences on which they were convicted on Tuesday.

They arrived from Lewes Prison, where they had spent the night, handcuffed together in a prison van.

Mr Malcolm Morris, Q.C., prosecuting, told the jury: "The behaviour of at least one of the guests was such that you may conclude she was under the influence of having smoked cannabis resin [Indian hemp]."

Mr Morris described events on the night of February 12, when a large number of policemen went to Richards' house, Redlands, in West Wittering, with a search warrant. As they went in they noticed an unusual strong sweet smell.

This, said Mr Morris, was cannabis resin and there was evidence that incense was being burned. "You may well guess that if Indian hemp is being smoked, incense may be burned in the hope of masking its distinctive smell."

When police went into the drawing room there were loud strains of "pop" music from the radio.

In the room, including Keith Richards, were eight young men and one young woman. She was sitting on the sofa between two guests facing the fireplace.

Between the sofa and the fireplace was a stone table on which there was a tin containing incense and briar pipe bowl which, when analysed, was found to contain traces of cannabis resin.

On the table ash was also found to contain traces of cannabis resin. In one of the bedrooms upstairs a detective found a pudding basin containing three cigarette ends and ash which were also found to contain cannabis resin when they were analysed.

Mr Morris referred to a man in the drawing room who was now not in Britain, and he would refer to as Mr "X". In his right hand breast pocket a tin containing two pieces of brown substance were analysed and found to contain 66 grains of cannabis resin.

A search of another pocket revealed an envelope containing herbal or untreated cannabis and a substantial brown ball which turned out to contain 150 grains of cannabis resin.

An experienced officer of Scotland Yard's drug squad would tell them about the effect cannabis resin produced after being smoked and its tendency to dispel inhibitions.

Mr Morris then referred to "the young lady on the sofa. All she was wearing was a light-coloured fur-skin rug which from time to time she let fall disclosing her nude body.

"How people behave in their own house is usually no concern of anybody else. The key significance of that young lady's behaviour is that when the police arrived in force she remained undeterred and apparently enjoying the situation.

"Although the young woman was taken upstairs to a bedroom where her clothes were, she came downstairs again still wearing only the same rug, in the presence of guests and policemen.

Det. Insp. John Lynch, of the drug squad, said that after smoking cannabis resin for half an hour "smokers have a smile on their face. In general they are extremely quiet and tend to smile. It is a smile of happiness."

Cannabis removed a lot of inhibitions in most people. There was a particular smell when cannabis was smoked which was difficult to describe.

It was something similar to the burning of hay. The commonest method of taking cannabis in this country was by smoking.

Mr Havers, in cross-examination, suggested that the inspector had got the bulk of what he had said about cannabis from a Home Office circular.

Insp. Lynch agreed that "one of the striking things" about cannabis was that it exploded the myth that it was an aphrodisiac. If anything, it diminished the sexual appetite.

Det. Sgt. Stanley Cudmore, who was on the raid, described the woman guest. He said that when he first saw her on the sofa the light coloured skin rug was draped around her shoulders. "From time to time one could see she was wearing nothing underneath."

During further cross-examination, Mr Havers produced the rug. It was held up by his junior and was about 8ft long by about 5ft wide, orange on one side and fur-backed.

Asked where information had come from which led to the raid, Sgt. Cudmore said he was not prepared to answer the question. After further discussion Sgt. Cudmore agreed it had come from "a well-known national newspaper".

Sgt. Cudmore was asked about the identity of "Mr X". He said he was a Canadian and agreed that a warrant had been issued for his arrest a day or so after the raid, but he had left the country.

After being shown a piece of paper, Sgt. Cudmore said the man was David Henry Sneiderman, alias Britton.

A woman detective constable, Rosemary Slade, told how she saw a young woman in the nude sitting on a settee in the drawing room.

Woman Det. Con. Evelyn Fuller said that the young woman appeared to be in a merry mood. She followed her upstairs and she went into a large bedroom where a man was on the telephone.

As she entered the bedroom the woman let the rug drop and had nothing on. When she went downstairs again still with the rug around her there were a number of policemen in the drawing room.

Asked about the young woman's behaviour she replied: "She seemed completely unconcerned as to what was going on around her."

In his opening address to the jury, Mr Havers said that Sneiderman had gone to the party that day. He was unknown to Richards and unknown to the Rolling Stones. "This man came from across the sea loaded to the gunnels with capsules and he was the only man on whom was found any capsules. He is now out of England. In the words of the judge, he has done a bunk."

Mr Havers said that a week before the raid there had appeared an article about Mick Jagger in the *News of the World* which was a "disgusting libel".

He suggested that Richard had been followed and watched and this had culminated in a newspaper tip which led to the raid. "Can you think of any better way to kill off the ensuing libel action?" he asked the jury.

The hearing was adjourned until today.

30 June 1967
Gaol sentences on Jagger and Richards
Hair cut decision for prison governors
By Guy Rais

Two members of the Rolling Stones "pop" group were gaoled on drug charges at West Sussex Quarter Sessions, Chichester, yesterday. Mick Jagger, 23, leader of the group was sentenced to three months and Keith Richards, 23, guitarist, to one year.

There were cries of "Oh" and "No" from teenagers in the crowded public gallery as the jury found Richards guilty of allowing his house in West Wittering, Sussex, to be used for the smoking of Indian hemp. Robert Fraser, 29, art gallery director, was gaoled for six months for possessing heroin.

Jagger, who was found in possession of four tablets of an Italian-made drug, almost broke down and put his head in his hands as he was sentenced. He stumbled out of the dock almost in tears.

Hundreds of teenagers and schoolchildren waited at the back entrance of the court building to catch a glimpse of the two Rolling Stones before they were driven to prisons in London. But they left handcuffed from the front entrance of the building.

A short while after they were sentenced Marianne Faithfull, in dark glasses and black trouser suit drove to court in Richard's blue Bentley and spent 15 minutes with her friend, Jagger.

She was crying when she came out and got into the Bentley, to drive back to Richard's house at West Wittering. Later she returned to London.

There is no official prison regulation that hair lengths of prisoners should conform to a set length, but it will be at the discretion of prison governors whether or not their hair should be cut.

They can order this to be done if they consider it if unhygienic or untidy.

The Rolling Stones group will not break up as a result of the two members going to prison. A spokesman said that the three other members would remain together and wait for Richards and Jagger to return. They have no further bookings.

It was understood last right that Richards was in Wormwood Scrubs and Jagger in Brixton. Both have long hair covering the back of their necks, and around the side of their foreheads.

Teenagers who had been waiting outside the court said they were "staggered" at what they described as "savage sentences". In his summing up Judge Block referred to "an unfortunate remark" by a Junior Minister of the Crown who referred to this case in detail between the committal and now.

"From what I read of the report it suggested it was impossible that Richards should have a fair trial because of the publicity."

Judge Block added: "That gentleman obviously did not know the qualities of a Sussex jury, such as you are here now."

The junior Minister referred to by the judge was Mr Dick Taverne, Q.C., Parliamentary Secretary, Home Office.

Addressing the Justices' Clerks' Society on 18 May, he said: "One cannot anticipate what the outcome of these proceedings will be.

"But whatever happens elsewhere, can one really say there will be no prejudice in the minds of the public against these defendants, even if they are acquitted?"

Mr Taverne said last night: "The judge is talking nonsense. I stick by what I said, I was talking generally about the need for having some committal proceedings heard in private.

"I was not concerned with legal prejudice, and what I said has nothing to do with the Rolling Stones' case."

Each of the Individual ITV companies will decide for itself whether to engage the Rolling Stones. A spokesman for ATV said: "The last time they appeared was at the Palladium Show when there was a dispute between them and the producer. After this we decided that they would not be invited to the Palladium Show again."

A BBC spokesman said: "We have no plans for using the Rolling Stones in programmes."

Mary Richardson

"Yes, I am a Suffragette. I broke the picture. You can get another picture, but you can't get a life, as they are killing Mrs Pankhurst."

The Canadian-born suffragette Mary Richardson was an enthusiastic proponent of the WSPU's commitment to radical action. Later, like several others in the movement, she would join Oswald Mosley's British Union of Fascists (who, by comparison to the established parties had a remarkably enlightened attitude to women). "I was first attracted to the Blackshirts," she said, "because I saw in them the courage, the action, the loyalty, the gift of service and the ability to serve, which I had known in the suffragette movement."

The "Act" referred to in the text, was the Prisoners (Temporary Discharge for Ill Health) Act 1913, better known as the "Cat and Mouse Act". After its introduction, Suffragettes embarking on a hunger strike in prison would be released as soon as they became ill – thus allowing the government to claim that any harm caused by the starvation was the striker's own fault. If the Suffragette re-offended upon recovery, they could be brought back behind bars.

11 March 1914
Woman's outrage at the
National Gallery
"Rokeby Venus" attacked

The campaign of the militant Suffragettes against property, both public and private, culminated yesterday morning in probably the most wicked act of vandalism ever committed in this or any country.

Mary Richardson, a notorious Suffragette, who is under sentence for burning the Countess of Carlisle's house at Hampton-on-Thames, and has been let out of prison on license under the recent Act, was the perpetrator of the outrage. She chose as the object of her insensate onslaught one of the most precious art treasures of the nation the famous painting by Velazquez known as "Venus and Cupid" and "Venus with the Mirror", or, as it is more popularly called, the "Rokeby Venus", of which a photograph appears on Page Fourteen.

This beautiful work of art, which was purchased eight years ago for £45,000 by subscription, owing largely to the interest of King Edward VII, has been damaged, if not beyond repair, at least to a very serious extent, as the result of six or seven heavy blows with a meat chopper.

Mr Hawes Turner, Keeper and Secretary of the National Gallery, has given it as his opinion that the selling value of the picture has been depreciated to the extent of from £10,000 to £15,000, though the work of restoration would probably not cost more than £100. However skilfully the restoration is carried out, the picture can never be quite the same as it was.

Naturally, news of the attack on the precious canvas caused a deep sensation, and several of the trustees of the National Gallery made calls to see the nature of the injury which had been wrought. Among them was Earl Curzon of Kedleston, who told a representative of the *Daily Telegraph* that the "Venus" was "a sad sight".

The most persistent inquiries could elicit no information from the authorities of the National Gallery as to what had occurred beyond the admission that the "Rokeby Venus" had been injured, and that a woman had been arrested. Fairly full details of the outrage were forthcoming, however, when Richardson was brought before the magistrate at Bow-street Police Court, and from these and statements obtained from independent sources it is possible to give the public – the owners of the picture, who have been wronged by this wanton act – a complete story of this latest Suffragette outrage, and the extent of the harm done to the "Venus".

It appears that for some time Scotland Yard has been in possession of information that an attempt was contemplated on some of the pictures in the National Gallery, and accordingly plain clothes detectives were posted throughout the building, especial watch being kept on the "Rokeby Venus", which was placed on an easel towards the eastern end of the Spanish Gallery. In spite of these precautions the deed of destruction was committed under the very eyes, so to speak, of the police. At the time there was a uniformed attendant in the gallery, a policeman just outside the door, and detective in plain clothes in the next gallery some twelve or thirteen yards away.

The attendant who was on duty in the particular room – Room 17 – in which the picture was exhibited stated yesterday that he was only "eight or nine yards" from the woman and that he "went for her" as quickly as he could get along "on the slippery floor" after he heard the smashing of glass. While he was moving over "the slippery floor" he saw her aim additional blows at the picture in rapid succession. The presumption is that if the floor had been less slippery or the attendant more practised in moving over it, or better shod for the purpose – as, for instance, with rubber shoes – some of the damage might have been prevented.

On Tuesdays the National Gallery is open free of charge, and Mary Richardson entered as an ordinary visitor, unrecognised and unsuspected. She made her way to the Spanish Gallery, in which there were only two or three persons examining the various art treasures. It was a little after eleven o'clock when she took her stand before the "Venus", drew a brand new meat chopper from beneath her coat, and viciously attacked Velazquez's painting. The only warning that Atkinson, the attendant in the room, had that anything was wrong was the sound of smashing glass.

At first he looked up at the skylight, thinking that the noise came thence. Seeing nothing unusual overhead, he glanced around, and, to use his own words, "saw a person hammering away at the picture with a chopper".

Before he and a policeman, moving cautiously over the slippery floor, could reach the woman the mischief was done. The Rokeby "Venus" had been terribly slashed, and when the officials came to make an inspection they were aghast at the mischief that had been worked.

At the first blow the chopper had crashed through the protecting glass and had then cut right through the canvas, making a long gash down the nude form of the "Venus" in vertical direction, almost dividing the picture in two. There were five other clean cuts of varying length, all upon the figure, and also what is described as a scraping "bruise". This last was probably inflicted by the blunt end of the chopper, the final swinging blow, it is thought, having been misjudged as Richardson saw the attendant and policeman approaching her.

The suggestion is that the "bruise" may prove more serious than the outs, as some of the paint may have gone. If such be the case the work of restoration is likely to be rendered more difficult.

No effort was made by Richardson to resist arrest, and she went quite quietly when the policeman took her by the arm. She did not say a word until she had walked some distance from the ruined painting, but then she turned round, and, looking at her handiwork, observed,

"Yes, I am a Suffragette. I broke the picture. You can get another picture, but you can't get a life, as they are killing Mrs Pankhurst."

The instrument used was of the sort which may be found in almost any kitchen. It is straight and a little over a foot long, the blade being about nine inches in length, by two inches deep. Immediately after the outrage all visitors to the National Gallery were asked to leave, and the doors were shut.

Richardson, whose age is given as 31, is described as a journalist of the Women's Social and Political Union, Lincoln's Inn House, Kingsway. She is a slight, pale-faced woman, with somewhat sharp features. Yesterday she was wearing a tight-fitting grey coat and skirt, with a blue blouse, and hat and muffler of the same colour. When put into the dock at Bow-street, before Mr Hopkins, she appeared but little concerned. She wished to put no questions to the three witnesses called. At the conclusion of the evidence she was allowed to make a statement, and, speaking in quiet, level tones, informed Mr Hopkins that that was the tenth time she had been before a magistrate in one year, and described the situation as ridiculous. "Mr McKenna," she went on, "has not rearrested me under the Cat and Mouse Act. He cannot make me serve my sentences. He can only again repeat the farce of releasing me, or else kill me. Either way mine is the victory."

Mr Hopkins made no comment on the prisoner's remarks, simply saying that she would be committed for trial at the next Sessions, and that she would not be bailed by that Court.

In the afternoon a meeting of the trustees of the National Gallery was held, the Marquis of Lansdowne, Earl Curzon of Kedleston, and Lord Ribblesdale being among those who attended. It is understood that the damage to the "Rokeby Venus" was discussed, but no official statement was issued.

At the headquarters of the Women's Social and Political Union it is presumed that the outrage was committed as a protest against the arrest of Mrs Pankhurst at Glasgow on Monday night. Yesterday forenoon a letter arrived at the offices in Kingsway, addressed simply to the Women's Social and Political Union, and written on the union's notepaper. It was a statement signed "Mary Richardson", and the text of the document was given to a *Daily Telegraph* representative yesterday:

> I have tried to destroy the picture of the most beautiful woman in mythological history as a protest against the Government for destroying Mrs Pankhurst, who is the most beautiful character in modern history. Justice is an element of beauty as much as colour and outline on canvas. Mrs Pankhurst seeks to secure justice to womanhood, and for this she is being slowly murdered by a Government of Iscariot politicians.

If there is an outcry against my deed let everyone remember that such an outcry is an hypocrisy so long as they allow the destruction of Mrs Pankhurst and other beautiful living women, and that until the public ceases to countenance human destruction the stones cast against me for the destruction of this picture are each au evidence against them of artistic as well as moral and political humbug and hypocrisy.

(Signed) Mary Richardson.

The following is the record of Mary Richardson's prison experiences:

Arrested on 11 March 1913, for breaking a window, and sentenced to one month's imprisonment.

Sentenced 8 July to two months' hard labour for assaulting the police at Bow and Bromley.

Released 12 July.

Rearrested 18 July.

Released 23 July.

Rearrested 28 July at London Pavilion, and remanded. Rearrested same day for breaking windows outside Holloway Prison, and sentenced to two months' hard labour.

Released 3 August.

Rearrested 9 August at Colonial Office for breaking windows. Remanded without bail.

Released 12 August

Rearrested 4 October for burning the Countess of Carlisle's house at Hampton-on-Thames. Remanded without bail. Forcibly fed. Before her release was brought up on the old charge of breaking Colonial Office windows, and sentenced to four months' imprisonment.

Released (suffering from appendicitis, having been forcibly fed since 4 October) on 24 October.

Four years ago the "Rokeby Venus" came unscathed from the ordeal of examination by an expert committee convened to settle the question whether certain markings on the canvas proved that the painter was Del Mazo instead of Velazquez, to whom the noble picture had always been ascribed. Yesterday a female miscreant left her own markings on the work with an axe, and as long as the doors of houses of detention are open to let out such irresponsible persons the National Gallery must presumably be closed to the lovers of the beautiful. The thief who stole the "Mona Lisa" from the Louvre gabbled about Napoleon's crimes against Italy. The woman with the axe proclaims that, in destroying "the picture of the most beautiful woman in mythological history", she is calling attention to the destruction by the State of what she regards as "the most beautiful character in modern history". Thus does the sparrow attack the canary.

It was on 14 March 1906, that the indefatigable association of friends of Art – the National Art Collections Fund – handed over to the trustees of the National Gallery the superb "Rokeby Venus" as a gift to the nation. Through the laudable efforts of this society a few private donors had been induced to provide the purchase-money, amounting to £45,000, required by the holders of the picture, Messrs. Agnew.

It was one of the works of art brought from Spain in 1808 by the great dealer Buchanan, from whom Mr J. Morritt, of Rokeby Hall, in Teesdale, Yorkshire, acquired it on the strong recommendation of that judge of the beautiful in feminine grace. Sir Thomas Lawrence. According to Carl Justi, in his book, "Velazquez and his Times," the price paid was £500. Painted in the middle of the seventeenth century, the canvas passed from the family of the Counts-Dukes Olivarez to the Duke d'Alba. Godoy, the Spanish statesman, released it to Buchanan. It formed one of the loans to the greatest art exhibition ever held in this country – the Manchester Art Treasures Exhibition of 1857 – and ravished all eyes when it reappeared at Burlington House in 1890. In 1905 Messrs. Agnew bought it from Mr H. E. Morritt, the descendant of the original purchaser, for £30,500, under order of the Court of Chancery.

The National Art Collections Fund then came forward, and by magnanimous effort saved the picture for the nation – and the axe. In this successful endeavour these friends of Art received not a little assistance from his late Majesty King Edward VII. His hearty approval of their labours not only greatly encouraged the committee, but admittedly removed many difficulties.

Everybody knows the famous picture either in the original or from the numerous reproductions of it. In rendering tribute to the glorious beauty of the nude in art Velazquez answered tile challenge of Titian. The canvas measures 48½in by 69½in. Under the directions of Messrs. Agnew it was judiciously cleaned, and the marvellous sparkle and freshness thereby revealed caused many to wonder that the picture could have been painted over 250 years ago.

A "live American" expressed his views yesterday. They were decidedly practical. "Close the National Gallery if you like," he said, "but if the picture belonged to me I should hire the biggest hall I could get in this city of yours and exhibit the picture – just as she is – at one dollar per head. I reckon I should raise a few towards damages and expenses in the first week."

Jacqui Smith

"Quite obviously a claim should never have been made for these films."

30 March 2009
Smith shamed as expenses
sleaze row engulfs Labour
By Rosa Prince

Jacqui Smith, the Home Secretary, faced serious questions over her political future last night following the humiliating admission that she claimed taxpayer-funded allowances for the cost of watching pornographic films at her family home.

In a significant blow to her authority, Miss Smith was forced to apologise for submitting a £10 bill for two adult movies watched by her husband, Richard Timney, while she was away in London.

Mr Timney, who works as her parliamentary assistant, also made a public apology for the "embarrassment" he had caused his wife and promised to pay back the money.

Last night, Miss Smith was fighting to salvage her credibility and her future political career, but the episode also threatened to further undermine Gordon Brown's Government which has been blighted by a series of expenses controversies in recent weeks.

In further examples yesterday, a backbench Labour MP was disclosed to have claimed £300,000 in Parliamentary expenses by registering a seaside caravan as his main home, while a Labour MP couple have built up a £250,000 nest egg courtesy of the second-home allowance. The series of allegations provoked comparisons with the scandals that dogged the dying days of Sir John Major's administration.

Today, an opinion poll for the *Daily Telegraph* indicated that the public's faith in MPs had been significantly eroded by the expenses scandals. A significant majority of those questioned said that they were convinced that hundreds of MPs were abusing the system.

It was Miss Smith's position, however, that was now under most scrutiny. Yesterday, her marriage was also said by friends to be in jeopardy, such is her anger at her husband for having submitted the claim.

Miss Smith is already under investigation by the parliamentary watchdog for claiming the share in the house she rents from her sister is her "main residence". The arrangement allows her to put the cost of running the family home in her constituency of Redditch, Worcestershire, on the public purse, on top of her £141,866-a-year salary.

Ironically, the Home Secretary's arrangements were the reason that her husband's paying for two pornographic films came to public attention. As her Parliamentary assistant, her husband regularly compiles the claims put in by Miss Smith under the Commons' additional costs allowance. He was said to have "accidentally" submitted the television bill which included adult films along with a receipt for their internet connection.

According to the expense claim, the couple was also reimbursed for two other films and items totalling thousands of pounds including televisions, washing machines and even an 88p plug. Under the rules, Miss Smith is required to confirm that all expenses refer to costs accrued in the course of her work as an MP. She apologised for the claim on her television bill, and promised to repay the taxpayer.

Yesterday, Mr Timney appeared on the steps of the family home to express his regret. "I am really sorry for any embarrassment I have caused Jacqui. I can fully understand why people might be angry and offended by this. Quite obviously a claim should never have been made for these films, and as you know that money is being paid back."

Last November, Miss Smith criticised men who paid for sexual entertainment as she announced plans for tougher restrictions on lapdancing clubs.

The films were viewed at 11.18 p.m. on 1 April and 11.19 p.m. on 6 April, while Miss Smith was staying in London. On the evenings in question, Television X, one of nine adult channels available under the terms of their Virgin Media cable television contract, was screening features called *Raw Meat 3* and *By Special Request*.

Miss Smith is said to be "furious" at her husband's behaviour. The couple has two young sons and the relationship was already thought to be under strain due to the amount of time Miss Smith spent in London.

Gordon Brown is understood to have been surprised by the revelations but supportive. A No 10 spokesman said: "She is doing a great job as Home Secretary and will not let this issue detract from her determination to ensure we protect the public and make our neighbourhoods safer."

But the Home Secretary's authority appeared severely undermined, with fellow MPs openly questioning whether she would be able to remain in her job.

Angus Robertson, the Scottish National Party's leader at Westminster, said: "These are serious allegations and only add to the impression that Labour is becoming engulfed in expenses sleaze. The ongoing allegations of expenses irregularities left the Home Secretary's credibility in tatters and present real questions over her future as a senior minister."

David Davis, the former shadow home secretary, added that Miss Smith's poor performance as Home Secretary had already raised doubts about her survival. He said: "I just do think on this circumstance the sympathy for her will be even less than it otherwise would have been because she is not that good at her job."

Even if she survives the immediate furore, angry voters in Redditch suggested that she would be unlikely to be returned at the next election.

The YouGov poll for the *Daily Telegraph* showed that the public was fast losing patience with MPs. Nearly half of those questioned said that the £24,000 second-home allowance was "wrong in principle and should be scrapped altogether".

Even Miss Smith's Cabinet colleagues admitted that the latest revelations meant that reform was now unavoidable.

Sir Alistair Graham, the former Standards Commissioner, said the scandal revived memories of the last Conservative administration, adding: "It was so damaging and lead to the downfall of the John Major government."

3 June 2009
The straight-talking MP whose reputation ended up in tatters
By Andrew Pierce

After Jacqui Smith became Home Secretary at the age of 44, the second youngest since Winston Churchill, her stock was so high some predicted she would be Labour's first woman prime minister.

Gordon Brown, in his first reshuffle as Prime Minister, took a bold gamble with Miss Smith, whom he elevated from Chief Whip over more experienced colleagues to one of the great offices of state.

The Prime Minister believed that Miss Smith, a former business studies teacher in a Redditch school, connected with ordinary Middle England voters.

Within months it became clear the Prime Minister had made a mistake.

Miss Smith, beset by gaffes and errors, was hopelessly out of her depth in one of the most demanding jobs in politics.

Those same people close to Mr Brown, who talked her up in the heady days of summer 2007 after the long-awaited exit of Tony Blair, swiftly revised their opinions.

Miss Smith has been the subject of a series of briefings from the Downing Street machine ever since.

But it is the revelations over her expenses which has cost Miss Smith her reputation as a straight-talking, no frills politician.

First there was incredulity at Westminster that the Home Secretary had designated her sister's second bedroom in Peckham as her principal home while saying the imposing five-bedroom house in her constituency – where her husband Richard and two sons live – was her second home.

It meant that the minister in charge of law and order could, under the rules, claim £116,000 to furnish her family home in the most prosperous neighbourhood of her Worcestershire constituency.

However, Miss Smith was dealt a terminal blow when a full breakdown of her expenses was published which showed that not only had she claimed for an 88p bathroom plug and £550 kitchen sink but also for two pornographic films, watched by her husband, who is her paid parliamentary adviser.

It meant that Miss Smith, who made history as the first woman home secretary, also had the dubious honour of becoming the first Cabinet minister to submit a claim on Parliamentary expenses for blue movies.

In truth, Miss Smith wanted to quit after the toe-curling spectacle of her husband appearing, mercifully briefly, outside the family home – albeit the second one, according to her Parliamentary expenses – to apologise.

But she was dissuaded by some of her political friends such as Hazel Blears, who may also now be in the Cabinet departure lounge. One of the Prime Minister's advisers also convinced her that it would not be "very corporate" to quit. In effect, she was told it was for the "Chief Executive" to decide when she should go.

Miss Smith has now clearly decided to pre-empt the Chief Executive, or Prime Minister as he is known to the rest of the country, ahead of his forthcoming reshuffle.

Briefly, Miss Smith fought back against the tide of criticism that engulfed her, not least in her constituency which neighbours Bromsgrove, whose Tory MP Julie Kirkbride is standing down at the next election after an unprecedented revolt by her constituents over her expenses.

In a television interview, the Home Secretary said: "The charge that is made of me is that I have tried to maximise the money that I have claimed. Well, I haven't."

Well, to a point. An examination of the figures showed that she claimed the full amount available under the second-home allowance in 2004–05 and 2006–07 – £20,902 and £22,110 respectively.

In 2005–06, she claimed £21,596 – just £58 less than the maximum allowed.

Yet, in the beginning, it looked like the Prime Minister's gamble would pay off.

Two car bombs were discovered in London on her first full day in office.

The next day, suicide bombers drove a car loaded with propane gas into the doors of the main terminal in Glasgow international airport.

When she reported to the Commons, Miss Smith exuded authority even if some of the media attention was more about her cleavage than her statesmanlike performance.

She had delivered her statement in a trouser suit, whose relatively low neck line was exaggerated by the camera angle.

All the cameras in the House of Commons are located above head height, so every shot of a politician in the House is taken from above.

Yet talk of Miss Smith as prime minister grew after another impressive display, this time before the Parliamentary Labour Party, when she appealed for support for the 42-day detention period for terrorism suspects.

Miss Smith secured an unlikely victory for a grateful Prime Minister. The gratitude was not to last.

The doubts began to grow after errors such as the rapidly abandoned plan to take convicted knife criminals to hospitals to see for themselves the result of their actions.

There were demonstrations by police officers, whom she angered by agreeing to a real terms cut in their pay.

Last January, Miss Smith said she would not feel safe walking the streets of London at night.

Asked if she would feel safe walking alone through Hackney after midnight, Miss Smith replied: "Well, no, but I don't think I'd ever have done. I would never have done that at any point in my life." It was only Miss Smith who appeared to back the embattled Sir Ian Blair, the Metropolitan Police Commissioner.

Boris Johnson, the inexperienced new London mayor, gained his first scalp when Sir Ian went.

Her position was further undermined when Keir Starmer, the Director of Public Prosecutions, directly contradicted the Home Secretary who claimed that a series of leaks from a Home Office whistle blower, which had led to the arrest of the Tory MP Damian Green, had threatened national security.

Mr Starmer humiliated Miss Smith when he said some of the leaked material was "in the national interest".

One of the most damaging episodes came with the admission that one in five of the foreigners cleared to work in security jobs could be illegal immigrants.

It was particularly embarrassing as 12 of the foreigners were working for a company hired by the Metropolitan Police, including one guarding a repair yard where the Prime Minister's car was taken.

Leaked memos disclosed that Miss Smith had been alerted to the security risk but had accepted the advice of civil servants to keep it secret.

Early this year, when the expenses controversy erupted, Miss Smith was dead in the political water. In desperation, her advisers blamed her husband for the expenses fiasco as she was "too busy" with urgent matters of state.

It was the same officials who briefed the media that her husband had been banished to the sofa with a serious "ear-bashing".

Even in the last dark days of John Major's government no civil servants briefed the media about Cabinet ministers' bedroom arrangements.

Mr Brown's decision to bring back Peter Mandelson from the political wilderness may yet be a master stroke. It could stay the hand of his Blairite enemies if the European and county council elections are as bad as some fear.

However, Miss Smith is no Mandelson and was over-promoted by a new Prime Minister desperate to have a female-friendly front bench.

With a majority of 2,716, Miss Smith may even lose her parliamentary seat which she won in the 1997 Blair landslide.

Miss Smith, who studied at Oxford, will have more time to indulge her favourite pastimes such as supporting Aston Villa and caravanning.

Her modest tastes were credited with her decision to eschew the grace and favour property she was entitled to when she became Home Secretary.

Miss Smith lapped up the praise which reinforced her homely image. If she had taken the glamorous perk of the job she might have been able to remain in the Cabinet.

John Stonehouse

"I am not a criminal in the accepted sense of the word."

John Stonehouse had a brilliant and unconventional mind, but, unable to reconcile the competing impulses of principle, ambition and greed that jostled within him, his life was ultimately defined by scandal and shame, rather than the great wealth and influence he had so strongly desired. It took six months and several failed asylum bids to bring him home from Australia. Somewhat surprisingly he continued to serve as an MP on his return, at least until 1976 when, after a 68-day trial in which he defended himself, he was sentenced to seven years for fraud, theft, forgery, conspiracy to defraud, causing a false police investigation and wasting police time.

Stonehouse suffered three heart attacks while behind bars, but remained sanguine: "The opportunity to sleep nine hours a night and really relax has been extremely good for me. I ask you to disabuse yourself of any idea that prison is harmful." A further twist in his story came in 1980 when a Czech defector alleged that Stonehouse had in fact been a communist spy since 1962 – but a lack of evidence dissuaded Mrs Thatcher from prosecuting him. He died in 1988 at the age of 62.

26 November 1974
Stonehouse mystery deepens
as police check documents
By Henry Miller in Miami Beach

Police and FBI agents in Miami were yesterday no nearer to finding the missing Labour MP and former Cabinet Minister, Mr John Stonehouse, 49, who disappeared after saying he was going for a swim in the ocean from the luxury beach-front hotel Fontainbleau on Wednesday last week.

Police said yesterday that two beach guards, Dick Kholer and Fransicso Gordillo had assured them that Mr Stonehouse had not entered the water during the afternoon.

There was a growing belief that Mr Stonehouse did not enter the water – if he entered it at all – close to the beach on which he was last seen.

On the other hand, a woman employee has told the police that Mr Stonehouse left his clothes with her in her kiosk and told her he was going for a swim.

Since a drowning victim from Miami beach would normally have surfaced in less than two days investigators said there could well be some other reason for Mr Stonehouse's disappearance.

Possessions left behind by Mr Stonehouse at the hotel and now in the care of the police, include an attaché case containing business documents and other papers, several cheques for between £700 and £800 and about £300 in cash. The police are hoping the papers will provide them with further clues.

The police have been told that Mr Stonehouse was aware of an article in the 15 November issue of *Private Eye*, the satirical weekly, which criticised the former Postmaster-General for his banking and business practices, but Mr James Charlton, the business associate and travelling companion of Mr Stonehouse said Mr Stonehouse was not depressed about his business affairs.

Mr Philip Gaye, an aide to Mr Stonehouse, said yesterday that Mr Stonehouse was being sued for £10,000 by London Capital securities, the private merchant bank with which he was connected, but that this was not worrying him.

Lieutenant Jack Webb of the Missing Persons Bureau in Miami Beach told me that he had asked for the assistance of the FBI and that they in turn had asked Scotland Yard for help in building a profile of the missing man.

The family of Mr John Stonehouse, former Labour Minister, who vanished at Miami Beach last week, is convinced that he is dead.

Miss Jane Stonehouse, 25, said yesterday that suggestions that her father had deliberately disappeared were "totally ridiculous".

14 December 1974
Stonehouse check on body in concrete
By Henry Miller in New York

Police in Florida were trying to establish yesterday if a body encased in concrete could have been that of Mr John Stonehouse, the Labour MP and former Minister who disappeared in Miami last month.

The broken concrete casing was found in nearby Fort Lauderdale, but the body had been removed. There were, however, traces of blood and hair which are being checked by forensic scientists against details of Mr Stonehouse gathered by police in Miami Beach.

Detectives said the body was put in the concrete a few days after Mr Stonehouse vanished and they knew from the imprint that the victim was about the same stature. Experts were also examining fingerprints and blood found in a car they have impounded. The car belongs to a man who leases a warehouse in Lauderdale Lakes where, they say, the body was first put in the concrete. The concrete was broken up and about three-quarters of it was dumped near a beach about 30 miles away.

Police chief Albert Kline said yesterday: "We are working hard to prove that the body is not that of Mr Stonehouse. But, of course, there is the possibility that it could be him."

He said the imprints left in the concrete included those of a foot, a leg and the upper torso. There was no imprint of a head.

Police learned about the body when someone reported that a bad smell was coming from a corner of the warehouse. But before they could make a proper investigation the new concrete that had encased the body was broken up and carted away.

For several days they had had the man who leases the warehouse under close surveillance since they suspected him of having been involved in various financial swindles and frauds.

But so far they had not enough evidence to make an arrest in connection with the body – chiefly because they had not located it.

The car the police have impounded formerly belonged to a Mr David Shaver, a long-time associate of the man they regard as their prime suspect. And they say that Mr Shaver himself has disappeared.

Police chief Kline said: "Although Mr Shaver cannot be located; we do not believe it could have been his body because he is of a different build."

It was five days after Mr Stonehouse's disappearance that police were first called to the warehouse about the "pungent smell". They went back the next day and found that the new concrete had been broken up and taken away.

Sergeant Jim Bock, who is in charge of the investigation, said: "There was enough of an impression left in the broken concrete to show that it had encased a body."

Disposal of bodies in concrete has been a method frequently associated with the Mafia.

There had been suggestions that Mr Stonehouse may have been the victim of a Mafia-style killing, but the police in Miami Beach still insist that they have no evidence that this was the case. Mr Stonehouse was in Miami for talks with some bankers about the possibility of expanding his business interests.

One puzzling feature of the affair is that both Mr Stonehouse and the man who is under suspicion in Lauderdale Lakes were both interested in aircraft companies. Sergeant Bock stated: "It is one of the coincidences that we must look into."

Detectives were last night anxiously awaiting Mr Stonehouse's blood type to complete tests in the laboratories.

16 December 1974
Hunt for MP's body continues
By Henry Miller in New York

Florida detectives investigating the disappearance of Mr John Stonehouse, 49, the Labour MP and former minister, said yesterday they were intrigued to learn about the heavy insurance policies taken out on his life by his wife, Barbara.

Mrs Stonehouse is reported to have taken out insurance coverage totalling £120,000 two months before her husband vanished.

The detectives pointed out that this aspect of the case was primarily a matter for British investigators and had not greatly affected the course of inquiries. But it could become a matter for them if any attempted fraud such as a "premeditated disappearance" became established.

Lt Jack Webb, who heads the investigation in Miami beach, where Mr Stonehouse disappeared on 20 November, said "It is, of course, useful information to add to our background dossier and could prove highly significant in due course."

"But we are continuing to treat Mr Stonehouse as a missing person and leaving all possibilities open on what really happened to him."

Lt Webb has now received from London a set of Mr Stonehouse's dental charts and a full set of dental impressions in case a body eventually turns up

Meanwhile, inquiries into the "disappearing body in concrete" in Lauderdale Lakes, Florida, continued last night and efforts were still being made to determine whether there was any link between this mystery and that surrounding Mr Stonehouse's disappearance.

The investigators there still know little more than the fact that a body was encased in concrete in a warehouse five days after Mr Stonehouse vanished. They know also that the concrete was hastily broken up when it became known that they were looking into the matter and that the body was disposed of somewhere else.

Imprints of a foot, a leg and upper torso were left in the concrete.

The police still do not have enough hard evidence to make any formal accusations against the man who was leasing the warehouse where the body was briefly stored.

Our diplomatic staff writes: Miami police have asked Scotland Yard for details of Mr Stonehouse's blood group, for use in checking bloodstains found on the concrete coffin at Lauderdale Lakes.

Mr Pierotti, British Consul in Miami, was in daily touch with the Florida police, a spokesman said.

24 December 1974
Stonehouse found, say police

Police in Melbourne said early today they have detained a man they believe to be Mr John Stonehouse, the missing MP.

The announcement was made by Chief Supt. Mick Patterson, assistant commissioner for crime. He gave no further details about the man or of the circumstances in which he was found.

It is expected that a further statement will be made later today.

Lost MP "did not defect"
By Gerard Kemp

Mrs Barbara Stonehouse, wife of the missing Labour MP, angrily denied reports last night that her husband had turned up behind the Iron Curtain.

"It's absolutely impossible for him to be there," she said at her home in Andover, Hants. "I'll reiterate what the Prime Minister said in the House of Commons: my husband was properly screened. He was as clean as a whistle."

Mrs Stonehouse has always maintained that her husband, Mr John Stonehouse. MP for Walsall North, drowned while swimming off Miami, Florida, on 21 November.

"Unless someone can come up with a photograph of him walking about somewhere then I will continue to believe that he has been drowned.

"He was supposed to have been in Cuba the other day and just before that to have been seen dancing in a Florida nightclub. I don't know where all these stories come from. The police have told me to expect this sort of thing as long as he is still missing."

In Miami. Florida, police and agents of the FBI have for several days been investigating the possibility that Mr Stonehouse might somehow have reached a European Communist country via Cuba.

Investigators in Miami said yesterday that they were treating the possibility seriously although they had no hard evidence to support such a theory.

Lt Jack Webb, who heads the investigation into the Stonehouse disappearance, said: "We still have not ruled out any possibility because no body was ever found."

He said that when it was suggested that Mr Stonehouse could have gone to Cuba this was immediately checked out.

One suggestion was that the MP may have flown from Havana to Moscow and then from there to East Berlin. The FBI, he said, had been making inquiries in this connection.

It would have been feasible for Mr Stonehouse to have swum out to sea some distance from the Miami beach where he was last seen and to have been picked up by a boat and taken to Cuba.

27 December 1974
Freedom plea by Stonehouse
Minister hints at early release

Mr John Stonehouse, the Labour M P and ex-Minister who disappeared last month, appealed yesterday to be allowed to remain in Australia where he was detained on Christmas Eve under an immigration law. And according to one report he could be free within 48 hours.

He made his appeal in the Melbourne court when it was alleged that he had entered the country on a false passport. A magistrate ordered that he should remain in custody for seven days while Mr Clyde Cameron, Australia's Immigration Minister, decides his fate.

Mr Cameron was quoted in the newspaper the *Australian* as saying that if Mr Stonehouse proved that he was an MP "we would not hold him". As an MP he did not need a permit to enter Australia.

At the court hearing, Mr Stonehouse – who vanished from a Miami hotel and was at first thought to have been drowned – told the magistrate: "I am not a criminal in the accepted sense of the word. It is only my wish to do what hundreds of thousands, or millions, have done before me – to come to Australia to establish a new life here as a person in a free community."

In a statement read to the court, Mr Stonehouse was alleged to have said: "I was subject to a great deal of business and political pressure and subject to blackmail by certain individuals. I felt I had to escape from this."

According to the police, Mr Stonehouse explained how he had helped establish a Bangladesh bank, became its unpaid chairman and had to put all his personal resources into it as shares in Britain fell and smaller banks collapsed.

"Certain individuals took advantage of my position in the political world to put me under extreme pressure," Mr Stonehouse was said to have added. "I felt it would be much better for my colleagues if I disappeared from the scene so that they would be spared embarrassment."

Insp John Sullivan told the court that Mr Stonehouse said he obtained a false passport in the name of a dead man – Joseph Arthur Markham – after inquiring at London hospitals about people of his own age who had died.

The inspector said Mr Stonehouse added that he flew from Miami to Hawaii and then to Australia. Later, the alleged statement said, he flew to Singapore and then to Denmark "to test out the reaction to my disappearance" before returning to Australia.

A few hours after the court hearing Mr Stonehouse was re-united with his wife who had flown from Britain. They embraced in the grounds of an immigration detention centre on the outskirts of Melbourne.

Another MP's name used for passport
False name was used
By T. A. Sandrock

The name of another MP, now dead, was used to authenticate the application and photographs for the passport with which Mr Stonehouse entered Australia illegally. The name is being kept secret pending further investigations. The affair could lead to a major inquiry about the ease with which false passports can be obtained.

Scotland Yard received a request for information about "a suspect Englishman" from Australian police on or about 14 December.

Until then, the Yard was convinced that the missing MP was not dead and had not drowned while swimming off the Miami beach. He was treated solely as a missing person.

The C13 department which deals with special crimes and maintains liaison with the American Embassy and the Canadian High Commission made background inquiries at the request of Miami police.

Various reports concerning large insurances taken out by Mr Stonehouse and by his wife were recorded and investigated to some degree.

Then the Yard was told that the Englishman about whom the Australians had suspicions was spending money freely, but that his pattern of behaviour was not satisfactory. He was being kept under surveillance and could be somebody wanted by the English authorities.

Among names suggested was that of the Earl of Lucan, wanted for the murder of his children's nanny and the attempted murder of his wife.

The details sent to England included a description of the man and the fact that he had entered the country with a passport giving the name Joseph Edward Markham. C13 quickly established that Joseph Markham had died in the summer and had no living relatives.

The description sent by the Australians was similar to that of the missing MP, and the Yard sent back to Australia details of Mr Stonehouse, with photographs.

Meanwhile, Mr Wilson disclosed in the Commons that Mr Stonehouse had been investigated by security officials in 1969. The investigation had followed an allegation made to the CIA by a defecting Czechoslovakian intelligence officer that Mr Stonehouse was one of three MPs working in London for a Czech spy ring.

The MP was neither a Communist spy nor a CIA agent, said Mr Wilson. He had not been under surveillance when he disappeared.

Two days after Mr Wilson's statement, the Australian police were sent details of Mr Stonehouse, including a reference taken from RAF files to an 8-inch scar on the inside of his right knee. He was traced and detained.

When he was taken to a police station he was shown a copy of the death certificate of Joseph Markham. This established beyond doubt that the passport was false.

Scotland Yard was informed immediately and further inquiries established that the passport for Markham had been obtained in July. It was also learned that Mr Stonehouse had been making inquiries at London hospitals about people who had died. He had been particularly interested in those who had no relatives and who were of similar age and description to himself.

Mr Markham was 49. The photographs of Mr Stonehouse submitted with the application were authenticated as a "true likeness" of the applicant, Joseph Edward Markham, by the MP who is now dead.

Police are trying to establish whether the MP concerned was "bluffed" into signing the applications and photographs without realising that they were being taken out in a false name.

The obtaining of the passport in July indicates that Mr Stonehouse had at least planned his disappearance well in advance. Police here are anxious to discuss his claim that he was blackmailed.

It is understood that one of the reasons the Australian police were suspicious of the "wealthy Englishman" was that a computer check on passport details of visitors revealed some factor which did not satisfactorily fit the details concerned. This led to a watch being kept on "Mr Markham".

The Australians have always been sympathetic to people entering the country illegally on what is a technical offence of using a false passport.

Mr Stonehouse may be allowed to stay in the country. But if he is returned, there will have to be a number of inquiries, not least into the passport offences. Even in Britain, it is unlikely that there would be any arrest over the passport offence. This could be dealt with by summons.

Also 27 December 1974
Pressure drove Stonehouse to flee
Labour MP who vanished claimed he had
been blackmailed, court told
By Ian Ward in Melbourne

Mr John Stonehouse, the Labour MP detained in Melbourne after being missing for 34 days, vanished because he was subjected to "extreme pressure" according to a statement he is alleged to have made to Australian police.

He said he had helped to establish a Bangladesh bank, and had become its unpaid chairman. He had had to put all his personal resources into it in the past year, as shares in England plummeted and smaller banks collapsed, a Melbourne court heard yesterday.

"Certain individuals took advantage of my position in the political world to put me under extreme pressure," Mr Stonehouse was alleged to have said.

"I felt it would be much better for my colleagues if I disappeared from the scene so that they would be spared embarrassment."

Mr Stonehouse, who was arrested on suspicion of entering Australia illegally, was ordered to be detained in custody for a week.

He listened impassively as his alleged statement was read out by Insp. John Sullivan. Then, speaking firmly and appearing to be in full command of himself, he made an unsworn statement to the presiding magistrate, Mr John McCardle.

In it, he said: "I am grateful for the way the Victorian authorities and Commonwealth police have dealt with me since I came into their orbit. I have co-operated with them fully since I came into their contact.

"I have nothing to hide from the Australian authorities because I have made my position clear. My only wish is to escape the incredible tensions and pressures I have suffered during the last two years in the United Kingdom.

"I wanted to establish a new identity and start a new life as so many other people have done before me in Australia. It is not my wish to be of any embarrassment to the authorities in Australia.

"I hope the people of Australia will appreciate that a man in my position in public life in Britain can at times come under intense pressure as has been in my case.

"A whole web of circumstances developed and it seemed to me my best course was to remove myself from the situation that existed in Britain and establish a new identity."

Mr Stonehouse claimed that be had been a victim of "blackmail".

Mr Stonehouse who used two false names in Australia, then renewed his request to be allowed to remain there. He had received more understanding and sympathy in two days in Australia than in two years in the United Kingdom, he said.

Mr Stonehouse's case was put by his counsel, Mr James Patterson, who was also the lawyer of Ronald Biggs, the escaped Great Train Robber. It was no offence to change one's name, either in Australia or under British common law, he said.

The magistrate, Mr McCardle, agreed. But there were reasonable grounds to suggest that Mr Stonehouse might be an illegal immigrant.

He would therefore make a seven-day detention order so that the Minister for Immigration, Mr Clyde Cameron, could consider whether a deportation order should be made.

Outside the court, Mr Stonehouse, neatly dressed in light sports coat and dark trousers, said: "I certainly have no qualms about accepting the decision of the presiding stipendiary magistrate.

"I'm glad that there is now an opportunity for my application to be considered as a migrant to Australia. For that reason I am very happy to accept the hospitality of the Commonwealth hostels."

His hostel quarters were "not entirely up to Hilton standards but they are getting that way," he said before being ushered away.

Mr Patterson said Mr Stonehouse had decided to change his name when he was in England. This was put into effect after he disappeared in Miami.

He had then gone to Australia under a new name. This represented no offence whatsoever. The fact that he used a second assumed name was irrelevant.

Insp. Sullivan told the court that Mr Stonehouse maintained he had completed passport formalities at the immigration office and left England on a BOAC flight.

He had first arrived in Australia on 27 November with a passport giving his name as Joseph Arthur Markham. However, he had left the following day flying via Singapore to Denmark.

Mr Stonehouse told him he had returned to Europe at that time in order to gauge public reaction there to his disappearance. He had returned to Australia on December 10.

Mr Patterson asked: "Is there any suggestion that Mr Stonehouse will be charged with a criminal offence?"

Insp. Sullivan: "As of this minute, I have no knowledge whatever."

Ordeal of the lonely wanderer
By our staff correspondent in Melbourne

The life of a wanderer was a lonely, depressing ordeal for Mr Stonehouse, normally so suave and brilliant as politician and businessman.

He may have chosen Melbourne as his hideaway because it is one of the larger, more affluent Australian cities, perhaps offering greater opportunity for him to build a new business empire.

After a brief stay in a motel in the bay-side suburb of St Kilda, he moved to a newly built apartment building nestling behind a noisy overpass at the lower end of Melbourne's Flinders Street, jammed between the city's railway and dock areas.

It was anything but the fashionable section of town. But the building was modern and fresh and the surroundings probably suggested the sort of camouflage he felt he needed. He took a small 35-dollar-a-week flatlet consisting of "bed-sitting room, an alcove kitchenette and a bathroom".

By this time, Mr Stonehouse had dispensed with the identity of John Arthur Markham. He booked into the apartment as Donald Clive Mildoon and it was as the quiet, withdrawn Mr Mildoon that he made his first tentative efforts to return to society.

At first, he limited his contacts to watching colour television in the communal lounge. Sometimes he told fellow residents that it was as good as in London, perhaps even better.

The part owner of the building, Mr Rod Wilcocks, took Mr Mildoon for a "very distinguished guest" from the start. "He was almost aristocratic," said Mr Wilcocks. He could tell this from the man's good bearing, his speech, grooming and clothes and luggage of good quality. But Mr Mildoon had "looked more like 55 than 49".

Later, there was the new building's inaugural cocktail party. All the guests received official invitations, including the quiet Mr Mildoon.

Neatly dressed, as always, and now apparently gaining confidence he accepted. According to Mr Max Wechsler, a fellow guest who lives on the third floor, he mingled among the partygoers with great style, sipping from a glass.

Mr Wechsler and Mr Mildoon found they had a common interest: music. Mr Wechsler invited him to try the organ newly installed in the restaurant downstairs. Mr Mildoon just smiled.

During the daytime Mr Mildoon would walk into town. Sometimes he was spotted strolling back to the apartment building in his shirt sleeves in the late afternoon.

He was always alone. He always seemed worried. He always read newspapers.

Then the neighbours read that Mr Mildoon was Mr Stonehouse. As Mr Wechsler said: "I'm not that surprised. I always regarded him as rather strange. He didn't work or seem to be concerned with getting a job."

Police were surprised at Mr Stonehouse's willing co-operation and described him as "extremely relieved it was all over". He was reported to be in very good mental and physical health, and apparently happy to have someone to talk to.

The first authenticated statement of why he disappeared came from Mr Stonehouse himself in a message to the Prime Minister.

In a telegram sent to Mr Wilson at Downing Street on Christmas Eve, Mr Stonehouse said: "Please convey to the Prime Minister my regrets that I have created this problem. And to all others concerned.

"My wish was to release myself from the incredible pressures being put on me, particularly in my business activities and various attempts at blackmail.

"I considered, clearly wrongly that the best action I could take was to create a new identity and attempt to live a new life away from these pressures.

"I suppose this can be summed up as a brainstorm, or a mental breakdown. I can only apologise to you and all the others who have been troubled by this business."

Mr Stonehouse, also thanked Mr Wilson for a Commons statement which cleared him of spying for Czechoslovakia and working for the CIA.

Mark Thatcher

"Thank God my father is not alive to see this.
I will never be able to do business again. Who will deal with me?"

26 August 2004
Thatcher's son held over Africa coup plot
By David Blair in Cape Town

Sir Mark Thatcher was arrested at his South African mansion yesterday on suspicion of helping to pay for a coup attempt in the oil-rich state of Equatorial Guinea.

Lady Thatcher's son is expected to face two charges of violating South Africa's Foreign Military Assistance Act, which is intended to stamp out mercenary activity.

Sir Mark, 51, whose business career has been dogged by controversy, vehemently denied any involvement in the operation.

He said through his spokesman, Lord Bell: "I am innocent of all charges. I have been and am co-operating fully with the authorities to resolve the matter.

"I have no involvement in an alleged coup in Equatorial Guinea and I reject all suggestions to the contrary."

Sir Mark, who inherited his father Denis's baronetcy, was in his pyjamas when members of the elite Scorpions police unit raided his walled house in the Cape Town suburb of Constantia on the slopes of Table Mountain at 7 a.m. Then he was robbed while being held in a cell prior to his appearance before a magistrate.

He was allowed bail of £165,000 and formal charges against him are expected to be laid on 25 November. Until then he must stay at the home he shares with his American wife, Diane, a millionaire.

His twin, Carol Thatcher, told BBC News 24 that she was shocked by the allegations but that she had "lived through scandals before".

Speaking at Heathrow as she returned from Switzerland, she said she had not spoken to Sir Mark and did not know the details of the charges. "My real concern is for my mother because she is in America and I haven't spoken to her and I don't know her reaction and I care about her," she said.

Sir Mark, who moved to Cape Town in the late 1990s, is suspected of involvement in a tangled mercenary plot to oust President Teodoro Nguema Obiang of Equatorial Guinea. The tiny West African dictatorship says it thwarted the plans.

Seventy men, including Simon Mann, an Old Etonian and former SAS officer, were arrested in Zimbabwe in March, allegedly on their way to Equatorial Guinea. Fifteen other men, all South Africans or Armenians, were rounded up soon afterwards in the Guinean capital, Malabo.

The authorities claim that all were mercenaries intent on ousting Mr Obiang and replacing him with an exiled opposition leader in return for a share of the country's oil wealth.

Mr Mann, who lived a few streets from Sir Mark in Constantia, and his group of detainees are awaiting judgment from a Zimbabwean court on firearms offences. All but one of the men arrested in Equatorial Guinea went on trial on Monday; the other has died under torture.

The evidence of one of them, Nick du Toit, a soldier in South African's special forces during the apartheid era, appears to have ensnared Sir Mark. Du Toit told the court in Malabo that Sir Mark had agreed to pay for one of the helicopters to have been used in the coup.

The sum allegedly involved was £153,000, said Torie Pretorius, of South Africa's criminal investigations unit.

Sipho Ngwema, a spokesman for the Scorpions unit, said: "Thatcher is accused of giving assistance to the coup plotters. We are looking for evidence that he was the financial backer."

Police spent seven hours inside the Thatcher home. Mr Ngwema said the officers searched for telephone records, bank statements, invoices and also swept the hard drive of his computer.

Shortly after 2 p.m. Sir Mark was taken away in a convoy of three black police cars, each displaying the crossed claws of the Scorpion's logo and the slogan "Justice in Action". The police carried a cardboard box apparently filled with documents seized at the house.

The convoy drove three miles to the nearest magistrates' court, a gloomy edifice in the suburb of Wynberg. While Sir Mark was waiting in the holding cells for the hearing to begin, his mobile phone was stolen by a fellow prisoner.

In the dock he rocked nervously from foot to foot as Awie Kotze, the magistrate, granted him bail.

"Mr Thatcher, you are released on certain conditions," Mr Kotze said. "See that you comply with those conditions. If you fail to comply with them, then you know what the consequences will be."

Sir Mark did not speak during the 10-minute hearing and he was not asked to enter a plea.

Mr Pretorius, appearing for the state, said that he would face two charges under the Foreign Military Assistance Act. South Africa passed the law in 1996 to end its unofficial status as the headquarters and recruiting base for the continent's mercenaries.

Sir Mark must report to Wynberg police station every day between 8 a.m. and 4 p.m. He must surrender his passport and stay inside the Cape Town peninsula.

The farthest he is allowed to travel without written police permission is the nearby wine town of Stellenbosch.

After the hearing, he returned to his home escorted by one police car, the crags of Table Mountain towering above the thatched house in Dawn Lane. It sits behind imposing, wrought iron security gates and its roof is visible above a whitewashed perimeter wall 10ft high. Many security cameras, all painted white, and three burly guards with shaven heads protect the property.

Amid a throng of police officers and lawyers in the driveway, he greeted his wife with a kiss.

Then he turned towards the escorting officers and said: "OK, well, I'll talk to you if I need to go anywhere."

26 August 2004
Richest member of a famous family and its most accident-prone
No stranger to unhappy headlines, Mark Thatcher is now caught up in allegations of a different order
By Ben Fenton and Christopher Munnion

When Mark Thatcher's mother entered Downing Street in May 1979, she quoted Francis of Assisi to the effect that she wanted to drive out discord, error, doubt and despair.

While there may be debate as to how far she succeeded, few would dispute that these unwanted qualities have attached themselves squarely to the public image of her only son.

Few children of British politicians have so often found themselves the subject of unhappy headlines and on the wrong end of lawsuits.

Born in 1953, while his father, Denis, was watching a Test, Sir Mark Thatcher – he now holds the baronetcy created in 1990 for his father – is the richest member of his family but also the most accident-prone.

His wealth, assessed at up to £60m, a figure he described as wildly wide of the mark, is no mean achievement for a man who left Harrow in 1971 with three O-levels and an assortment of unpleasant nicknames.

He joined Touche Ross only to fail his accountancy exams three times and leave. Unimpressive careers in motor racing, jewellery sales and unspecified "business ventures" in the Far East did little for his reputation but laid the roots of a network of international contacts.

Assiduous students of British politics were aware by 1979 that the still boyish Thatcher was heir to neither his mother's political and intellectual gifts nor his father's jovial charm but he did not really come to public attention until he got lost in the Sahara in 1982.

Sir Mark has since admitted that he was completely unprepared for the Paris-Dakar rally but blamed fellow members of his team for reporting his stranded position wrongly to race organisers. He spent four days in the desert, causing his mother a bout of barely concealed despair that almost shattered her image as the Iron Lady.

The ridicule heaped on him from Fleet Street contributed to his decision to go to Texas in 1984, where family friends established him on a lucrative contract as a representative of British car firms.

But that year he also had his first brush with controversy over business dealings with the Arab world when a Sunday newspaper alleged that he had earned a commission for a £300m deal won by the construction company Cementation after Lady Thatcher recommended it to the Sultan of Oman.

In Dallas, he met Diane Burgdorf, a glamorous blonde whose wealthy father described her as "just an ordinary millionairess", and married her at the Savoy Chapel in London on Valentine's Day 1987. He had already been dogged by further allegations of exploiting his mother's position to earn a commission of £12m as an intermediary for the £20bn Al Yamamah arms deal with Saudi Arabia.

He denied receiving the commission and nothing was proved but he became almost persona non grata among his mother's aides. Asked by Mark how he might help the Conservatives win the 1987 election, Sir Bernard Ingham, her fiercely protective press secretary, is said to have gruffly advised him to "leave the country".

Although he had a wide circle of acquaintances, there were plenty of people to attest to his brusqueness in company and his disdainful treatment of those he considered his social inferiors.

Walter Annenberg, the billionaire American publisher and friend of the Queen, recalled inviting Sir Mark to dinner only to be told that his claret glasses were the wrong shape.

By contrast, there are few – even his twin Carol – who have been eager to defend his character in public. Sir Mark did succeed in staying out of the British press after Lady Thatcher was ousted by her own Cabinet in 1990, but within a few years he was embroiled in an alleged racketeering case in Texas, which was settled out of court, and then in a criminal prosecution, later dropped, over alleged evasion of US taxes.

In 1995, he persuaded his wife and their two children to move to South Africa, where they bought a huge and well-protected house in Constantia, on the southern slopes of Table Mountain overlooking Cape Town.

The house, Number 10 Dawn Avenue, is thatched, providing a fistful of material for local humourists. It is also guarded by large men armed with shotguns. To buy it, the couple sold their house in The Boltons, Kensington, bought for £2m in 1992, but have kept a very large house in the wealthy Highland Park area of Dallas.

Each year Diane returns with their children Michael, 15, and Amanda, 11, to Texas for at least two months, although in 2002 she seems to have left Cape Town for more than a year.

The couple have denied that their marriage is in trouble, although friends say that it is Diane's Christian faith and devotion to Lady Thatcher that has kept things together.

Soon after their arrival, Sir Mark was considered a good catch for the most fashionable Constantia dinner parties. Now his allure seems to have dimmed.

A local industrialist said: "He would keep banging on about his contacts through-out the world and the millions to be made in the Middle East, but when it came to a serious discussion about world affairs, international business or politics he did not seem to have much to offer."

A hostess said: "He reminds me of those rather amiable, entertaining twits that P. G. Wodehouse used to write about."

In 1998 Sir Mark was at the centre of a scandal after he lent huge sums of money at exorbitant interest rates to more than 900 police officers and civil servants in Cape Town. He admitted lending the cash but insisted that he had done nothing wrong.

He is also thought to have profited from contracts to supply aviation fuel in vari-ous African countries.

But it was this summer, when President Nguema of Equatorial Guinea named him as a financial backer of the alleged coup attempt and press reports linked him with its supposed leader, Simon Mann, that the discord, error, doubt and despair began to gather once more over Sir Mark Thatcher's head.

27 August 2004
Thatcher "was ready to flee South Africa"
By David Blair in Cape Town

Suitcases packed for a hasty departure were stacked in the hallway of Sir Mark Thatcher's South African home when he was arrested.

Police said yesterday they believed that the arrival of officers at the Cape Town mansion narrowly prevented him from leaving the country.

Officers discovered that there were plans to sell the house, which was bought 15 years ago during the apartheid era.

Over the past week, Sir Mark has sold four cars. His American wife, Diane, and their children, Michael, 15, and Amanda, 11, were booked on a flight leaving for the US on Monday.

"We didn't want him to leave the country without questioning him," said Makhosini Nkosi, spokesman for the National Prosecuting Authority. "From the state of the house, with suitcases packed, we thought he might be planning to relocate."

Sir Mark was arrested on suspicion of involvement in an attempted coup in oil-rich Equatorial Guinea in west Africa.

When police from the elite Scorpions unit raided the house in the suburb of Constantia on Wednesday morning they already suspected that Sir Mark intended to leave. But they did not know that his plans were so advanced. The sale of the cars and the proposed disposal of the house came to light only during seven hours of questioning.

Mr Nkosi said: "It was confirmed to us that he was planning to relocate and the house was on the market. We would have had some trouble getting him back from the US if he had departed."

Sir Mark, 51, Lady Thatcher's son, has surrendered his passport and is confined to his home until he deposits £65,000 in bail money.

The ownership of the whitewashed house set in two acres of garden was still unclear last night.

Estate agent records show that it was bought on 23 January 1989 – when South Africa was a pariah state under the apartheid regime of President P. W. Botha. Nelson Mandela had not been released from prison and the banned African National Congress was leading a violent campaign to render the country ungovernable. Severe unrest in the black townships had depressed Cape Town's property prices.

Records show that the equivalent of £98,149 was paid for the five-bedroom house with a swimming pool on the slopes of Table Mountain. The property, with title deed T2178/1989, is not registered in Sir Mark's name but under a company called Kosovo Investments Pty Ltd. He moved into the home about 10 years after it was purchased.

Estate agents in Constantia say that the current value of the house on Dawn Lane is about £1.3m.

Three estate agents, including Pam Golding, the largest in South Africa, said that the home had not yet been placed on the market. A uniformed guard carrying a handgun was on duty in the driveway yesterday and all the curtains were drawn. The only sign of activity came when Diane Thatcher drove away.

Sir Mark denies that he had any involvement with alleged plans for a coup and says he is co-operating fully with the police.

The South African authorities suspect that he was linked to the alleged purchase of a helicopter for £153,000. If Sir Mark is formally charged and the case comes to trial, the key issue is likely to be whether he knew of the purpose for which this alleged sum would be used.

Sir Mark is a friend of Simon Mann, an Old Etonian and former SAS officer who is awaiting sentencing in Zimbabwe after being tried in connection with the same plot. Eighty-four suspected mercenaries are in detention in Zimbabwe or Equatorial Guinea.

Another key issue will be the identities of the coup's financiers. James Kershaw, a computer expert who reportedly worked with Mann, has gone missing from his home in the capital, Pretoria. Unconfirmed reports suggest that he has a list carrying the names of all those who contributed to the alleged plot.

Lord Archer, the disgraced Conservative peer, denied through his lawyers that he was one of the financiers and considers the matter "closed". Legal documents say that a payment of £74,000 was made to Mann's company by a "J. H. Archer".

24 September 2004
Guinea "coup plot" police list 43 questions for Thatcher
By David Blair in Johannesburg

Sir Mark Thatcher has been ordered to tell a South African court whether his nickname is "Scratcher" and if he knows a Briton called "Mr Jeffrey Archers".

The questions are in a list of 43 for Sir Mark, submitted in garbled English by the officials in Equatorial Guinea investigating an alleged attempt to overthrow its government.

Sir Mark, who is accused of helping to fund the supposed coup plot, has been ordered to answer the questions before a court in Cape Town on 26 November. The former prime minister's son is challenging the summons and a hearing will take place next month.

Jose Olo Obono, the attorney-general of Equatorial Guinea, submitted two lists of questions to the South African authorities on 3 September.

In a copy obtained by the *Daily Telegraph*, the first is: "Do you know Simon Francis Maan? If yes, tell us the place, date, month and year you met him for the first time."

This presumably refers to Simon Mann, the old Etonian and former SAS officer jailed in Zimbabwe for trying to buy weapons, allegedly for use in the coup plot. He once lived near Sir Mark in the Cape Town suburb of Constantia.

Number 21 asks Sir Mark: "Do you know the following persons," and lists a "Mr (Jeffrey) Archers". The authorities presumably mean Lord Archer, who has denied any suggestion that he agreed to help fund the coup plot.

Question 26 falsely states that Sir Mark "was arrested once in the Kingdom of Saudi Arabia for the crime of trafficking in arms". It adds: "Can you tell us what kind of arms?"

Question 16 asks: "The name 'Scratcher' appears in a letter sent by Mr Mann from prison in Harare. Is this a name by which you are known or have been known in the past?"

Sir Mark, 51, denies any offence relating to the alleged coup. He said compelling him to answer the questions would "violate my right to silence, my right to a fair trial and my right to pre-trial protection".

It would "enable the prosecuting authorities to have a comprehensive insight into my defence", he added.

"I am confident that in any criminal trial to which I am subject in South Africa I shall be acquitted, as I am indeed innocent of any offences relating to the alleged coup."

Fifteen men, all South African or Armenian, are on trial in the Guinean capital, Malabo, charged with trying to overthrow Teodoro Obiang Nguema, the dictator of the oil-rich West African state. The case has been suspended until Sir Mark answers the questions.

25 November 2004
Thatcher must answer Guinea coup questions
By Christopher Munnion in Cape Town

A South African court ruled yesterday that Sir Mark Thatcher must answer questions sent by Equatorial Guinea about his alleged role in funding a foiled coup attempt in the West African nation.

The ruling came the day before Sir Mark, the 51-year-old son of Lady Thatcher, is to go on trial charged with violating South Africa's anti-mercenary laws.

Equatorial Guinea wants to question a number of Britons, including Sir Mark, about allegations that they financed a plot earlier this year to overthrow President Teodoro Obiang Nguema, who has ruled Africa's third largest oil producer for the past 25 years.

The Cape High Court rejected an attempt by Sir Mark's legal team to overthrow a subpoena by South Africa's justice minister ordering him to answer questions posed by Equatorial Guinea's prosecutors.

Sir Mark will now have to answer questions about his alleged financing of the mercenary plot before a magistrate in Wynberg, a Cape Town suburb close to his home in Constantia, unless his lawyers are able to appeal against the decision in South Africa's constitutional court.

Sir Mark denies any involvement in the plot, which was foiled in March when a chartered aircraft carrying mercenaries landed in Zimbabwe's capital, Harare, to pick up arms before flying to Malobo in Equatorial Guinea to overthrow the government.

Simon Mann, a former Special Air Service officer and a neighbour of Sir Mark, was jailed for seven years in Zimbabwe for allegedly organising the plot.

Another 19 alleged mercenaries arrested in Equatorial Guinea are due to be sentenced in Malobo, the capital, this week.

Sir Mark's name has been mentioned in both the Equatorial Guinea and Zimbabwe trials, although he has repeatedly said that his interest was only in raising the funds to provide a helicopter for an air ambulance service for West Africa.

He was arrested at his Cape Town home in April and charged with breaching anti-mercenary laws.

He was released on bail of £167,000, which was said to have been paid by Lady Thatcher.

Sir Mark said that he had been "destroyed" by the charges against him.

He told *Vanity Fair* magazine that they had left him feeling "like a corpse that's going down the Colorado River and there is nothing I can do about it".

He added: "Thank God my father is not alive to see this. I will never be able to do business again. Who will deal with me?"

13 January 2005
All the intrigue of a fantasy blockbuster, written by amateurs
Bizarre tale lacks only a court-room climax for its star, Mark Thatcher
By David Blair in Johannesburg

When Sir Mark Thatcher's lawyers saved their beleaguered client from a possible jail sentence yesterday, they might have reflected that the bizarre tale of the west African coup plot was the stuff of Hollywood fantasy.

Yet the story was true, stretching from the obscure domain of a brutal African dictator to the mansions of Cape Town and the festering jails of Zimbabwe.

The appearance on the cast list of the millionaire son of a former British prime minister was in keeping with the tale's surreal exoticism.

When a Boeing 727 arrived at Harare airport in Zimbabwe last March, the security forces were ready and waiting. They arrested its 67 occupants – all former soldiers in South Africa's apartheid-era armed forces – and rounded up three men who were waiting for the aircraft to arrive.

Among them was Simon Mann, an Old Etonian and former SAS officer who lived a few streets away from Sir Mark in Cape Town's elite suburb of Constantia.

Zimbabwe announced that the men had been on their way to the oil-rich west African state of Equatorial Guinea, where they would have overthrown its dictator, President Teodoro Nguema Obiang.

At first, few took this claim seriously. But it emerged that Mann had tried to buy assault rifles and rocket-propelled grenade launchers from Zimbabwe's state-owned arms company.

Within 24 hours, Equatorial Guinea rounded up 14 men and announced that they were the coup's advance party. Then Ronnie Kasrils, the South African intelligence minister, disclosed that his agents knew all about the plot. The Boeing 727 had departed from an airport near Pretoria and South Africa had tipped off Zimbabwe.

By the end of March, the details of the failed coup had emerged. The mercenaries, recruited largely from black soldiers who fought for the apartheid regime, would topple Mr Obiang. In his place, they would install Severo Moto, Equatorial Guinea's exiled opposition leader.

Mr Obiang's excesses were so egregious that no one would miss him. But he did dispose of immense oil reserves. Once control of these had passed to Mr Moto, the mercenaries, especially their leader, Mann, would be handsomely rewarded. That was the plot that the intelligence services of three African countries had smashed.

The amateurishness of Mann and his fellow mercenaries was astonishing. So lax was their security that everyone in South Africa appeared to know of their plan.

When Zimbabwean officials searched the Boeing 727 in Harare, they found maps and incriminating documents outlining the plotters' target. The 70 captured foot-soldiers in this bungled enterprise escaped with a 12-month jail sentence. But Mann pleaded guilty to trying to buy weapons in Zimbabwe and was sentenced to seven years in prison.

In pleading letters from his prison cell, he referred to one friend as "Scratcher". South Africa's security forces thought they knew who "Scratcher" was and suspected that Sir Mark was involved.

The cast list began to widen even further. A list of those who had allegedly contributed funds pointed to a glittering array of investors. Lord Archer denied he was the "J. H. Archer" on the list.

South African police said later they were also interested in talking to anyone suspected of having prior knowledge of the plot. In London, the Foreign Office denied it had any foreknowledge. Jack Straw, the Foreign Secretary, later admitted that it did.

The South Africans' first lead came from Equatorial Guinea, where one of the hapless 14 accused of trying to overthrow Mr Obiang was Nick du Toit, a former officer in South Africa's special forces. He testified that Sir Mark had paid £153,000 towards a helicopter that would have been used in the plot.

Officers from South Africa's elite Scorpions unit raided Sir Mark's Cape Town home at 7 a.m. on 25 August last year and questioned him for several hours. He was then charged with breaching Section Two of the Regulation of Foreign Military Assistance Act.

This law made funding any mercenary activity a criminal offence. Sir Mark was released on the most restrictive bail conditions and retired to his home on the slopes of Table Mountain.

He relied on his mother, Lady Thatcher, to pay his bail of £165,000. His American wife, Diane, 45, and their two children promptly left for Texas.

Yet Sir Mark could count himself lucky. On trial in Equatorial Guinea, du Toit claimed to have been severely tortured. He faced the death penalty if convicted or, at best, long years in one of Africa's harshest jails.

In November, the presiding judge declined to have him executed and imposed a 34-year jail sentence instead.

The thought of being extradited to Equatorial Guinea and suffering the same fate was concentrating the minds of others involved in the plot in South Africa. Crause Steyl, a former South African soldier who owns a helicopter company, agreed a plea bargain.

He confessed his involvement and escaped imprisonment in return for agreeing to testify against Sir Mark. This gave the South African investigators their key breakthrough.

But last month, prosecutors and Sir Mark's lawyers began secret talks. Yesterday's deal was hammered out and the story ended without the high drama of a full trial. Only in that respect did it differ from the plot of a Hollywood blockbuster.

14 January 2005
Thatcher pleads guilty to aiding mercenaries
By David Blair in Cape Town

Sir Mark Thatcher, visibly tense and nervous, stood in the dock of a South African court yesterday and admitted paying £150,000 for a helicopter that he "suspected" might be used by mercenaries in a coup.

The legal ordeal of the former prime minister's son ended with him admitting an offence under anti-mercenary laws and accepting a fine of £265,000. The court also imposed a suspended prison sentence of four years.

Hours later, Thatcher left Cape Town, his home for almost 10 years, on board a British Airways flight to London. His American wife, Diane, 45, and their children, Michael, 15, and Amanda, 11, have already settled in Texas, where he is expected to join them.

Thatcher, 51, appeared in the high court in Cape Town after his lawyers and prosecuting authorities agreed a plea bargain. He toyed with worry beads in the dock as an agreed statement was placed before Mr Justice Abe Molala.

In this, Thatcher admitted five separate contacts with Simon Mann, an Old Etonian and former SAS officer who is serving a newly reduced four-year jail sentence in Zimbabwe. Mann is accused of plotting to overthrow the government of Equatorial Guinea in return for a share of the West African country's oil wealth.

Thatcher admitted making two payments last January, totalling £150,000, to charter an Alouette III helicopter. This transaction was made at Mann's request and the helicopter would have been for his use.

Thatcher made these payments after being told that the helicopter would be used in mining operations in West Africa. But he admitted doubting "Mann's true intentions" and suspecting that "Mann might be planning to become involved in mercenary activity".

Thatcher paid the money, despite his "misgivings", and hired the helicopter "whether it was to be used for such a purpose or not". This was, he admitted, a breach of the Regulation of Foreign Military Assistance Act which bans any assistance to mercenaries.

During a court hearing that lasted less than 10 minutes, Thatcher gave clipped answers to a series of rapid-fire questions from the judge.

"Do you understand the charge sheet against you?" asked Mr Justice Molala. "Yes," replied Thatcher.

"Do you admit all the allegations on the charge sheet?" asked the judge. "Yes," replied Thatcher. When Mr Justice Molala imposed the fine, specifying that it must be paid within seven days on pain of five years' imprisonment, Thatcher's composure slipped and he visibly winced.

Anton Ackermann, the prosecuting advocate, hailed a "fair and just settlement" and said the outcome of the case was a "bargain" for the state.

Afterwards, Thatcher appeared on the steps of the court and said his only desire was to be with his family again. Bail restrictions, which were lifted yesterday, had forced him to surrender his passport.

"There is no price too high for me to be reunited with my family," said Thatcher.

Directly opposite the court, a mocking banner flew from a third-storey window. It read: "Save me Mummy."

Also January 14, 2005
Taking flight, with his estate left unsold and his reputation in tatters
By David Blair and Robin Gedye

After almost 10 years living in South Africa's most affluent corner, Sir Mark Thatcher emigrated yesterday and sought a new life with his family in America.

By his own admission, the prolonged legal wrangling over his role in a failed coup in Equatorial Guinea had wrecked his standing as a businessman. The former prime minister's son saw no option but to leave his Cape Town home.

Six months ago, his two children moved to Texas and his American wife, Diane, joined them there last September.

Minutes after pleading guilty to breaching South Africa's anti-mercenary laws, Thatcher stood on the steps of the Cape Town high court and said his only aim was to be "reunited with my family". "He looks forward to joining his family in the United States," read a statement issued through his lawyers.

George van Niekerk, a family spokesman, did not deny that Thatcher was leaving permanently.

Later, Thatcher arrived at Cape Town airport shortly before the scheduled departure of a British Airways flight to London.

But building a new life in America may not be straightforward. The evidence in his court case will be carefully scrutinised before a final decision is made on his right to live there, US government sources said.

"The case of any person seeking to enter the United States is judged individually on its own merits. Among many factors of interest is a record of crime or arrest," a spokesman for the US embassy in London said.

While making clear that a criminal record "would not necessarily preclude" Thatcher entering America, he emphasised that the whole area of immigration law was extremely complicated and there were no hard and fast rules that were not open to interpretation.

Thatcher's years in South Africa have ended in pain, acrimony and a ruined reputation. "Who will want to deal with me after this?" he asked in an interview with *Vanity Fair* last year. "Thank God my father is not alive to see this."

He added that the accusations about his role in the planned coup made him feel like a "corpse floating down the Colorado river and there is nothing I can do about it". Thatcher had been the focus of deep hostility from many South Africans since his arrival in Cape Town in 1995. They always resented his wealth. Murky accusations about a coup in West Africa stirred deep resentment of colonial-era meddling by rich whites.

The Youth League of the ruling African National Congress denounced Thatcher's agreed plea bargain, calling it an "abomination and a miscarriage of justice", adding that plotting against "legitimate governments is not only a crime against the people, but one which should be classified as unpardonable".

The hostility did not come only from black South Africans. Thatcher was blackballed from the Royal Cape Golf Club in 1996.

No one was willing to come to his defence yesterday as friends kept their counsel. "On principle, I'm not prepared to say a word," said Rupert Wragg a businessman often seen dining with him in Cape Town restaurants. Vaughan Johnson, a wealthy figure in the wine industry and frequent visitor to Thatcher's home, was equally reticent. "I'm sorry to be rude, but I'm not going to help," he said.

Thatcher's hurried departure from South Africa came before he concluded the sale of his home in the suburb of Constantia. After four months on the market, the house is still available for an asking price of £2.2m.

Described as an "ambassadorial estate", the home Thatcher has abandoned has two acres of gardens. But estate agents say Thatcher's reputation is not hindering the sale. Instead, the property is overpriced and he needs to accept £500,000 less.

Even so, he would still reap a handsome profit. Records show the house was bought for £98,149.

Jeremy Thorpe

"It's no worse than killing a sick dog."

5 December 2014
Jeremy Thorpe – obituary
Charismatic leader of the Liberal Party who fell from grace
in one of the most spectacular political scandals of the 20th century

Jeremy Thorpe, the former leader of the Liberal Party who has died aged 85, suffered a fall unparalleled in British political history when a long-drawn-out chain of scandal dragged him into the dock at the Old Bailey, charged with conspiracy and incitement to murder.

For once the cliché "trial of the century" did not seem misplaced. Thorpe had been a sparkling and successful politician who had come tantalisingly close to realising the Liberals' dream of holding the balance of power. In 1974, indeed, he was invited by the prime minister, Edward Heath – whom he had once described as "a plum pudding around whom no one knew how to light the brandy" – to lead his party into coalition with the Conservatives; he himself was offered the post of foreign secretary.

It was understandable, therefore, that five years later, at Thorpe's trial, even prosecuting counsel should have spoken of a "tragedy of truly Greek and Shakespearean proportions". Tragedy, however, is a large word, implying the destruction, if not necessarily of virtue, at least of some outstanding merit. Only in the context of a man's entire life can its just application be decided.

John Jeremy Thorpe was born on 29 April 1929 into a highly political family. He would claim descent from Sir Robert de Thorpe, who was Chief Justice of the Court of Common Pleas in 1356 and Chancellor in 1371.

More to the point, both of Thorpe's parents were staunch Conservatives. His father John Thorpe, born in Cork, was a KC and, for a few years after the First World War, MP for Rusholme in Manchester. His mother was the daughter of Sir John Norton–Griffiths, 1st Bt., another Conservative MP and one who gloried in the epithet "Empire Jack" – even if he owed his baronetcy to Lloyd George.

Jeremy Thorpe, however, thought of himself as "three-quarters Celt"; and in keeping with this bias, it was from his mother's friend Lady Megan Lloyd George that, rather to Mrs Thorpe's disapproval, he imbibed a romantic attachment to Liberalism.

The boy had two sisters, both older; he was brought up as the cynosure of his parents' eyes. "It never occurred to him," his mother remarked of his early days in Kensington, "that anybody might not be glad to see him."

Young Jeremy adored his father, but it was his mother who exerted the most powerful influence. A formidable woman, who affected an eyeglass, Ursula Thorpe nursed the highest ambitions for her son. "That monocle!" Thorpe recalled in later life. "We were all frightened of her. I have overcome the domination, and I am damn well not going to be dominated again."

Thorpe was only six when tubercular glands were diagnosed in his stomach. For seven months he had to lie on his back in a spinal carriage; he suffered back pains for the rest of his life.

The Second World War caused a hiatus in what promised to be a conventional English education. In 1940 Thorpe and the younger of his sisters were sent to stay with an aunt in America, where he attended the Rectory School in Connecticut, by contemporary English standards a decidedly easy-going establishment.

Thorpe loved it. His histrionic gifts – and in particular his talent for mimicry – began to flourish. He played Miranda in *The Tempest*, became an accomplished violinist, and showed precocious assurance as a public speaker.

In 1943 he returned to England to go to Eton, where the more rigorous discipline proved less agreeable. He was also greatly upset by the death of his father, after a stroke, in 1944. This misfortune left the family in dire financial straits, so that an uncle had to stump up the funds to keep the boy at Eton. It also, inevitably, increased the sway of Mrs Thorpe.

After Eton, Thorpe joined the Rifle Brigade for his National Service, only to be invalided out of the Army after six weeks as "psychologically unsuitable". It has been alleged that he became a bed-wetter to prove the point.

At Trinity College, Oxford, by contrast, the military reject flourished outrageously. His flamboyant dress – frock coats, stove-pipe trousers, brocade waistcoats, buckled shoes, and even spats – received all the attention they demanded; his penchant for Chinese vases suggested aesthetic sensibility; his witty persiflage kept the mockers at a distance.

Theoretically, Thorpe was reading Law; in reality he was laying the foundations of his political career. But though he became in turn president of the Liberal Club, the Law Society and the Union, he attracted criticism from contemporaries for the ruthlessness he showed in the pursuit of these offices.

Thorpe scraped a Third in his Finals. Afterwards, in 1954, he was called to the Bar by the Inner Temple, and built up a modest practice on the Western Circuit. He also, later in the 1950s, worked for commercial television, appearing regularly on current affairs programmes such as *This Week*, and sending back reports from Africa and the Middle East.

But politics was always his master passion. In 1952, with the help of Dingle Foot, whom he had befriended when at Oxford, he was adopted as Liberal candidate at North Devon which, though it had been a Liberal seat in the early 1930s, had a 12,000 Tory majority in the 1951 General Election.

Thorpe, at his very best on the stump, had no rival as a vote-gatherer. He could put any argument with skill and panache; his astonishing memory for faces persuaded voters that they were intimate friends; his brilliant gifts as a mimic kept the audience in stitches; his resourceful mind afforded quips and stunts for every occasion.

At the same time he built up a formidable organisation in the constituency, and drove it with unflagging energy. In the 1955 general election the Tory majority was slashed to 5,226, and four years later he captured the seat by 362 votes. Thorpe would hold North Devon for 20 years, narrowly at first, but in February 1974 with a thumping 11,082 majority. Yet he was never tempted to appeal to wavering Tory voters by trimming his Liberal views on issues such as South Africa or capital punishment.

In the House of Commons he made an immediate impression. A sketch-writer remarked of his maiden speech that "it seemed as though Mr Thorpe had been addressing the House for the past 10 years, and got rather tired of the exercise". But the young MP knew how to draw blood, as with his jibe after Harold Macmillan sacked several of his Cabinet in 1962: "Greater love hath no man than this, that he lay down his friends for his own life."

Thorpe appeared somewhat to the Left of the party, a mouthpiece for impeccable Liberal sentiments, especially on African affairs. He received the distinction of being banned from Franco's Spain.

In 1966 he advocated that Britain should cut off the oil supplies to Ian Smith's Rhodesian regime by bombing that country's railway system. The Liberal conference enthusiastically applauded the idea, but Harold Wilson inflicted permanent damage by coining the phrase "Bomber Thorpe".

Meanwhile, though, the young MP had been working energetically to fill the organisational void left by Jo Grimond's leadership. Thorpe's charm made him especially effective as a fund-raiser, and in 1965 he captured the party treasuryship.

When Grimond retired in 1967, the 12 Liberal MPs elected Thorpe in his place. The new leader immediately gave a foretaste of his style by holding a rally in the Albert Hall, at which he promised "a great crusade that will set Britain alight for the vision of a Liberal society" – a performance relayed by closed circuit television to three other city centres.

Nevertheless, in his first years at the helm the showman for once misjudged his act. "He felt he had to move away from the image of the sharp and witty debater to being grave," David Steel remembered. "It was disastrous."

Yet Thorpe did not altogether abandon frivolity. Colleagues found, to their frustration and fury, that important policy discussions had to wait upon the leader's gossipy anecdotes about the prime minister or royalty. Nor did Thorpe's continuing addiction to outmoded dress and eccentric headgear – notably the brown bowler hat he wore when electioneering – do anything to allay the growing suspicion that he was all style and precious little substance.

His critics acknowledged that he loved the *game* of politics – indeed he took a fiendish delight in its Machiavellian plots and manoeuvres – but they wondered if he knew why he was playing it.

Thorpe's Liberalism was essentially romantic and emotional. He reacted strongly against bone-headed Establishment snobbery, arrogant management or racial injustice, but showed scant interest in formulating any coherent political philosophy.

On the other hand there was no doubting Thorpe's quick mind or his keen antennae. He was to the fore in predicting the 1967 devaluation crisis and in identifying the mounting crisis in Ulster; he also showed himself a consistent supporter of Britain's entry into the Common Market.

Thorpe did not suffer fools gladly. Erring subordinates were treated to the sharp rebuke or the snappish aside; and in the face of any challenge to his authority the mask of the jester quickly gave way to a fixed, distant and icy stare. He was at his most formidable under pressure, as the Young Liberals discovered when they attempted to mount a coup in 1968.

The unsatisfactory opening years of his leadership culminated in the 1970 general election. Thorpe campaigned with his accustomed zeal, sweeping about the country in helicopters and cutting an impressive figure on television, but the results were disastrous.

The Liberals polled only 2.1 million votes and retained only six seats. And then, less than a fortnight after the election, Thorpe's wife Caroline was killed in a car crash.

For a while Thorpe appeared to lose interest in politics. But in 1972 and 1973 the widespread dissatisfaction with the Heath government found expression in a remarkable series of Liberal successes in municipal and by-elections.

Thorpe's style was undoubtedly a factor in attracting discontented Tory voters. But his animadversions against the "bloody-mindedness" of British life were undermined, at the end of 1973, by his involvement in a shoddy financial disaster.

Thorpe had become a director of Gerald Caplan's London & County Securities to boost his meagre parliamentary salary; in his delight at the sudden flush of income, however, he failed to heed numerous and reiterated warnings about the company's viability.

In 1972 the Liberals, and Thorpe himself, put on a notable display of piety over Reginald Maudling's involvement with the Poulson affair. It was therefore more than a shade embarrassing when it transpired that the leader was involved in a company that was charging 280 per cent on second mortgages, and when, at the end of 1973, the collapse of London & County revealed a tangled skein of financial misdemeanour.

British voters, far from being concerned, were apparently impressed by Liberal promises to tackle the national crisis with increased public spending and state control of incomes. At the February 1974 general election Thorpe, though largely confined in his marginal North Devon constituency, reached his political apotheosis. The Liberals nearly trebled their vote to six million; the only fly in the ointment was that this total translated itself into but 14 seats.

Rumour had it that Thorpe was responsive to Heath's offer of a coalition, with the promise of a Speaker's conference to consider electoral reform. His colleagues, however, have gone on record that the decision to reject these terms was "unanimous".

The ensuing months exposed the flaws in the Liberal revival. The party activists were radicals; many of its new-found supporters were dissatisfied Tories. Moreover, the exquisite Thorpe seemed far removed from the community politics advocated by Trevor Jones ("Jones the Vote") and his chums.

In the October 1974 general election, the Liberal leader left his North Devon constituency to its own devices and once more whisked about the country in helicopters and hovercraft. All to no avail: the Liberal vote fell by 700,000.

Thorpe was severely disillusioned. But the most remarkable thing about his political career was not that he ultimately failed to storm the heights, but that he managed to retain the sangfroid to lead the Liberals when, all the while, a large part of his energies was concentrated on repressing a significant element of his personality.

That Thorpe, in his youth, had homosexual tendencies was admitted at his trial. Nor was it in dispute – though he always emphatically denied any physical relationship – that in 1961 he had befriended a young man named Norman Josiffe, who later changed his name to Norman Scott.

Though Mr Justice Cantley's conduct of the trial was widely criticised, no one argued about his description of Norman Scott. "He is a fraud. He is a sponger. He is a whiner. He is a parasite." Scott claimed to have had an affair with Thorpe between 1961 and 1964, and there can be no question whatever that, as their meetings dwindled and finally ceased, he conceived a grievance that nothing but the ruin of Thorpe could assuage. (It should be remembered that homosexual acts between consenting adults were not legalised until 1967.) In pursuit of his vendetta Scott seized every possible occasion, public and private, to advertise his sexual connection with Thorpe. As early as December 1962 he blurted out the story to the Chelsea police, and gave them two letters he had received from the MP, one of which contained the phrase – "Bunnies can (and will) go to France" – that would become notorious when, 14 years later, it finally reached the public domain.

During that time Scott bore the menace of a time–bomb ticking away in the shadows of Thorpe's career. The fuse was unpredictable, but intermittent splutters constantly portended some vast explosion.

Thus in 1965 Scott took it upon himself to write to Thorpe's mother setting out the details of his homosexual relations with her son. This missive prompted Thorpe to make the cardinal error of confiding in Peter Bessell, a fellow Liberal MP.

One of the most striking features of the affair was that Thorpe, for all his public glamour, seemed to have no upright friend to whom he was prepared to turn for counsel. Bessell was a Methodist lay preacher; he was also, as he himself would all too willingly confirm under cross-examination, amoral, hypocritical and untruthful.

Bessell tried to contain the danger to Thorpe by going to see Scott, by purloining compromising letters, and subsequently by paying Scott small weekly sums which Thorpe refunded. He also sought, and appeared to receive, assurances from the home secretary, Sir Frank Soskice, that the police were not interested in pursuing Scott's allegations.

But Thorpe's anxiety could not be assuaged as long as the possibility remained that Scott would one day succeed in finding a newspaper to print his story. And after the Liberal leader had married Caroline Allpass in 1968, he had even more to lose – though the best man, David Holmes, wrote that Caroline Thorpe "knew about Scott" before they were married.

In May 1969 Scott himself married; and his son was born that November. The marriage soon broke up, but not before the experience of connubial penury in a Dorset cottage had lent a hysterical edge to Scott's importuning of Bessell. Worse, there was the threat – never, in fact, realised – that Scott would use the divorce proceedings as an opportunity to blurt out his accusations about Thorpe under the protection of court privilege.

Another crisis developed in 1971. Scott, now living in North Wales, became the lover of a widow, Mrs Gwen Parry-Jones, who, treated to the usual accounts of Thorpe's iniquities, duly reported them to another Liberal MP, Emlyn Hooson. A Liberal Party inquiry into the affair ensued.

Thorpe fought like a tiger, denying the allegations point blank and enlisting the help of the home secretary, Reginald Maudling, to confirm a somewhat misleading summary of police dealings with Scott. It was Thorpe's word against that of his tormentor, and the Liberals chose to believe their leader.

Next year, 1972, Mrs Parry-Jones died, and at the inquest on her death Scott at last had the opportunity to tell his story in court. But no editor cared to print his wild ravings; nor did a South African journalist, Gordon Winter, find any takers when he gathered material from Scott.

It might have seemed that Scott had done his worst, and been repelled. In 1973 Thorpe announced his engagement to Marion, Countess of Harewood, previously married to the Queen's cousin.

About the same time Scott moved to Thorpe's North Devon constituency, where he proceeded to inflict the history of his relations with the local MP upon bemused rustics in pubs. He also told his tale to the Tory candidate, who decided not to touch it.

Just before the first general election of 1974, David Holmes succeeded in purchasing some letters from Scott for £2,500. Nevertheless, Scott the persecutor now appeared in the role of victim.

In February 1975 he was beaten up by two men in Barnstaple market. And in October, when an AA patrolman discovered him weeping beside the corpse of his great dane, Rinka, he claimed that only a jammed pistol had prevented the assailant from shooting him as well as the dog.

In January 1976 Scott, charged with defrauding the DHSS, declared under the privilege of court that he was being "hounded by people" because of his affair with Jeremy Thorpe. This time, at last, the press did take notice. Thereafter rumour blew so loud that by March Thorpe felt compelled to defend himself in the *Sunday Times*, specifically denying both that he had hired a gunman to kill Scott, and that he had had any knowledge of Holmes's purchase of the letters in 1974.

Despite support from the prime minister, Harold Wilson, who appeared to believe that the accusations had been fabricated by the South African secret service, Thorpe was unable to hold the line. After the "Bunnies" letter was published in the *Sunday Times* in May 1976, he resigned the Liberal leadership.

There could scarcely have been any criminal charges against him, however, if Bessell, who had long been exiled in California, had not decided to turn Queen's evidence. He believed, with good reason, that Thorpe would not hesitate to throw him to the wolves in order to save his own skin.

Bessell alleged that in 1968 and 1969 Thorpe had incited Holmes and himself to murder Scott, helpfully suggesting that the body might be chucked down a Cornish mine shaft, or cemented into a motorway bridge. "It's no worse than killing a sick dog," Thorpe is supposed to have remarked, before recommending research into slow-acting poisons.

The second charge associated Thorpe with Holmes and two others on a charge of conspiracy to murder in the years 1974 and 1975; this also depended partly on Bessell's evidence, though in this case the diversion of Liberal funds through Holmes's hands to the hitman, Andrew Newton, was also germane.

Thorpe behaved with marked courage in the face of the cataclysm, observing with his accustomed brio that a man who had the prime minister, Lord Goodman and MI5 on his side could hardly lose.

Even after his committal to trial at the Old Bailey Thorpe insisted on contesting North Devon at the 1979 election, where his opponents included Auberon Waugh, standing for the Dog Lovers' Party. Though Thorpe lost the seat (he remarked laconically to a television interviewer that Scott's allegations had "hardly helped" his campaign), his vote fell by less than 5,000 compared with October 1974.

At the Old Bailey the charges failed after the defence, with the help of Mr Justice Cantley, had annihilated Bessell's character. Thorpe opted not to give evidence in his own defence, thus avoiding cross-examination.

Even so, his reputation was badly damaged by the exhibition of the financial sleight of hand which he had shown in directing funds given to the Liberal Party by the millionaire "Union Jack" Hayward towards David Holmes. He was also revealed as a blustering bully in his attempt to dissuade his friend Nadir Dinshaw, the Pakistani financier, from telling the truth.

Dinshaw, acting on Thorpe's command, had innocently passed on money to Holmes. Before the trial Thorpe told him that if he reported the fact, "It will be curtains for me, and you will be asked to move on."

In short, the trial bore out the impression created by Thorpe's political career, that he was essentially a fixer and an operator. Far from being a tragic hero – a noble nature ruined by a single mole of nature – he appeared, whether innocent or guilty, amply provisioned with common human flaws, cast by his gifts and ambition into most uncommon relief.

Yet this man, who spent so many years trying to avoid imputations of homosexuality, won devoted loyalty from both his wives. "I saw an emotional cripple take up his bed and walk," someone remarked of his first marriage.

For a while after the trial Thorpe seemed to nurse the dream of rebuilding his career. In 1981 he applied unsuccessfully for the job of race relations adviser to the BBC, and the next year he was actually appointed director of Amnesty, only to resign the post after complaints from within the organisation.

Thorpe remained chairman of the political committee of the United Nations Association until 1985, but in the world of the *haut monde* that he loved to adorn there would be no redemption. By the middle of the 1980s, moreover, he was afflicted with Parkinson's disease.

The North Devon Liberals, however, remained faithful to the last, electing him as their president in 1987.

Jeremy Thorpe's second wife died in March of this year; he is survived by his son, Rupert, from his first marriage.

7 March 1976
Yard likely to widen Scott letters inquiry
By Peter Gladstone Smith

Scotland Yard is expected to be called into a broadened police inquiry into the payment of £2,500 for letters and documents to Mr Norman Scott, 36, the male model at the centre of the storm over Mr Thorpe's leadership of the Liberal party.

Mr David Holmes, merchant banker and personal friend of Mr Thorpe, has revealed that he bought the letters which contained details of payments to Scott by Mr Peter Bessell, former Liberal M.P. for Bodmin.

Det. Chief Supt. Proven Sharpe, head of Devon and Cornwall C.I.D., has interviewed Mr Thorpe, Dr. Ronald Gleadle who was intermediary for the payment, and all persons named in connection with the documents.

He will make his final report to Sir Norman Skelhorn, Director of Public Prosecutions, this week. This is expected to lead to inquiries outside the West Country.

A detective of the Yard's C1 pool of chief superintendents is expected to go to California to interview Mr Bessell.

Mr Holmes, 48, who was best man at Mr Thorpe's wedding in June 1968, to his first wife Caroline, who was killed in a car accident two years later, has stated that he made the payment entirely on his own initiative. In particular it was "without the knowledge of Mr Jeremy Thorpe".

He destroyed the letters and documents, but did not know that the Liberal party and the Press already had photocopies of them. If he had known he would not have bought them.

The police inquiry has been concerned with the source of the £2,500 handed over by Dr. Gleadle in two Lloyds Bank accounts at a time when he was treating Scott for depression at a clinic in South Molton, Devon.

At his cottage in Combe Martin, near Barnstaple, yesterday, Mr Scott said: "I don't know the man David Holmes and it came as a complete surprise to me. At the time I think Dr. Gleadle said it was somebody from Manchester.

"I was not *compos mentis* that one and a half years Gleadle had been treating me – I was half asleep, under very heavy dosage."

The Rev. Fred Pennington, Vicar of South Molton, who tried to help Mr Scott in 1973 when he suffered depression, said he had been questioned by Det. Chief Supt. Sharpe.

"I know the line the police are taking," he said. "So much seems to be linked up with the case of Norman's shot dog. There must be some connection."

Mr Scott is a witness at a trial in Exeter Crown Court on 16 March when Andrew Gino Newton, 29, airline pilot of Abinger Road, Chiswick, is accused of possessing a firearm with intent to endanger life.

At his Manchester home yesterday Mr Holmes, said: "I have done nothing illegal, just rather foolish."

He wished he had kept his money and left Scott with the letters. "I bought them and burned them the same evening where I was staying in north Devon," he said.

Yesterday the *Daily Mirror* said that less than 24 hours before he issued the statement Mr Holmes denied that he was the man who paid the money, that he was a good friend of Mr Thorpe and that he had been questioned by the police. He was reported as saying: "I know nothing about this payment. I had nothing to do with it whatsoever."

15 March 1976
I stick to my story, says Scott
By Geoffrey Lakeman

Mr Thorpe's weekend denial of allegations against him prompted the man at the centre of the affair, self-styled author Mr Norman Scott, to say he was seeking legal advice.

At his whitewashed cottage at Coombe Martin, Devon, the 36-year-old former male model said:

"I think the way Mr Thorpe issued his statement was incredible. I am sticking to my story. There were things in the statement that were libellous. I shall be consulting my lawyer tomorrow."

Mr Scott added: "I think Mr Thorpe is just clutching and clinging at straws. It may appear to be vindictive, which I do not want to be, but I must say he is thinking of no one but himself. But then anything I say seems to be taken as the words of a raving lunatic."

In a detailed statement supplied to the *Sunday Times*, the Liberal leader "in the most categorical and unqualified terms" maintained that all allegations made by Mr Scott were totally false. Liberal colleagues also regarded them as "pure moonshine".

With a copy of Mr Thorpe's statement in front of him, Mr Scott yesterday answered the denial of six specific allegations.

On the first and main claim that there had been a sexual relationship between the two, Mr Scott said: "I still maintain, and always will, that the relationship existed. No one will get me to change that story."

Mr Thorpe had next denied stealing Mr Scott's national insurance card. Mr Scott said: "I never accused Thorpe of stealing my insurance card. I have always said I gave it to him because he said he would keep up the payments." The third point in Mr Thorpe's denial referred to an allegation that the Liberal party and others had tried to keep Mr Scott quiet.

On this Mr Scott commented: "Nobody has ever paid me to kept quiet. Peter Bessell gave me money because he was trying to get my insurance card and he said he was worried about my welfare"

Mr Scott would not comment in details on the fourth point made by Mr Thorpe.

The Liberal leader's statement also referred to the identity of a gunman and his occupation which Mr Thorpe said had been alleged to be his helicopter pilot.

Mr Scott said: "The man told me he was a private investigator and was being paid to protect me, so I trusted him. I do not know what this mention of being a pilot is about."

Answering Mr Thorpe's point that he was not involved in the exchange of documents for the sum of £2,500 Mr Scott said:

"Mr Thorpe must have been aware of what was going on because of correspondence between myself and Mr Bessell. I had a letter from Bessell saying he had spoken to Mr Thorpe putting him in the picture regarding my position."

Mr Thorpe, who earlier at the weekend had been at his country cottage in his Barnstaple constituency, was not at home yesterday. A neighbour said he had left North Devon.

17 March 1976
I lived with Jeremy Thorpe, says Scott
By Geoffrey Lakeman

Norman Scott – the man at the centre of the allegations against Mr Jeremy Thorpe – yesterday told a court of "when he first went to live with" the Liberal leader.

"I know it sounds, perhaps, unwholesome. His words as far as I can remember were 'I do not want you to have to worry any longer about money'," Mr Scott told a jury at Exeter.

"In other words I was supposed to live with him and be cared for by him for the rest of my life. Obviously this did not happen."

Before the court was Andrew Gino Newton, 29, unemployed pilot, of Abinger Road, Chiswick, who faces five charges following the shooting of Mr Scott's Great Dane, Rinka.

Mr Scott also alleged that Newton told him that Marion Thorpe, Mr Thorpe's wife, was paying to protect him (Scott) but Newton claims he was being blackmailed by Mr Scott.

Newton pleaded not guilty to possessing a German automatic Mauser pistol and ammunition with intent to endanger life, and possessing the gun with intent to commit an indictable offence.

He admitted three other offences – possessing the firearm without the necessary certificate; having the weapon unlawfully in a public place, and destroying property, namely a dog, belonging to Norman Scott.

Mr Lewis Hauser, Q.C., opening the prosecution's case, said that details of the dog incident were, for the most part, not disputed by either Newton or Mr Scott. But their stories differed completely in the versions of the matters surrounding the shooting.

Newton claimed that Mr Scott had been blackmailing him over a letter and a nude photograph which Newton had sent to a sex contact magazine called *Switch* advertising for "a lady of leisure".

Mr Scott, who had somehow got hold of the photograph and letter had turned up at Newton's Blackpool home and then subsequently blackmailed him for £4 a month, threatening to reveal details of his connections with the magazine.

Newton had travelled to Barnstaple last October to try to get the photograph and letter back and had acquired the gun and shot the dog in an attempt to frighten Mr Scott into giving up the "evidence".

Mr Scott, of Coombe Martin, North Devon – a former male model who describes himself as a writer – was shaking and twice broke down while giving evidence to the packed court.

He said he remembered seeing Newton in his local pub at the end of last summer and some weeks later was approached by the man in Barnstaple's Pannier Market.

Newton, who had called himself Peter Kean, had said it was vital that he spoke to him. "I was rather afraid to talk to anyone because I had already been warned that I was in danger."

This was because of a book he had written about his relationships with various prominent people. Scott went on: "He kept on saying I was in grave danger and that there was a lady who wished to see me and would I please go with him to Knowleston.

"The only lady I could think of . . . " – at this stage Scott broke off and said he did not know if he was allowed to say but was told he could answer the question.

"The only lady I could possibly think it could be would be Marion Thorpe. He (Newton) said 'Yes'."

Scott went on to describe how he told Newton he was willing to meet the lady but Newton had said that he could not be seen with Scott. "He said he was being paid to protect me by this person."

Mr Scott then described the night of October 24 and how he, Newton and the dog got into a car at Combe Martin and drove to the isolated spot on Exmoor. Newton was driving erratically so he offered to take over the wheel.

Newton parked the car on the off-side of the road and got out and the dog started to follow him. Newton then said "this is it" and shot the dog.

Mr Scott, perspiring heavily, described how he pleaded for the dog's life and added: "He tried to shoot me and then the gun didn't work."

He said Newton twisted his arm behind his back and held the gun to the side of his head. Moments later, Newton threatened him again.

Mr Scott demonstrated to the hushed court how he alleged Newton held out his arms pointing the gun at him. "He put up his hand like that and fired, but there was no bang," said Mr Scott.

Newton then screamed: "I'll get you" and drove off. Mr Scott said he tried the kiss of life on the dog before waving down a passing car.

Cross-examined by Mr Patrick Back, Q.C., defending, Mr Scott said Newton's warning had not been the first that his life was in danger. He alleged he had been beaten up a number of times. He had been put in hospital once and thought Jeremy Thorpe's men were responsible.

Mr Back also questioned Mr Scott closely about Dr. Ronald Geadle, who had treated him in 1973 for nervous anxiety, but who has since moved to Welwyn Garden City.

Mr Scott, who had been living alone in a remote spot, had been destitute and was living on raw swedes. He was taking drugs but suspected that the dosages were rather heavy.

Asked if he thought he was being poisoned Mr Scott replied: "That is a bit strong, but I did feel the doctor was perhaps not acting in my best interests."

Mr Scott said Dr. Geadle knew about the book he had written and the various documents. One day he arrived at his cottage and said that he must have the documents, saying: "The sky is the limit."

Mr Scott told him to do what he thought was best and he took the documents away.

Mr Back: "You were showing these documents to people because you knew they were damaging to the Liberal Party?"

Mr Scott: "Absolutely not. I had been hounded, as I said in the other court, for 15 years because of my relationship. I was showing people these documents to prove it existed."

Mr Back pointed out that he had accepted a payment of £2,500 from the doctor but Scott had said he had not known who had paid the money until a few weeks ago when it was revealed in the newspapers.

Mr Back then asked him why he had kept photocopies. "I simply wanted photocopies for my own safety."

Mr Back pointed out that the photocopies were used by Mr Scott and South African journalist Gordon Winter to write a book, which they knew would be damaging to the Liberals.

"It was also a saving for my son and my life, although perhaps that seems irrelevant to you," replied Mr Scott.

Mr Back: Are you really suggesting that a book alleging your various homosexual relationships could be beneficial to your son? – My son would know the truth and why the past 15 years have happened.

The truth of the matter is that by your cunning you have wrought a blackmail. – No, I did not.

Mr Back asked if anyone had suggested to him that he was an incorrigible liar?

"Yes. Mr Thorpe on Sunday," reported the witness to laughter around the courtroom. Then Mr Scott added: "I think Mr Thorpe has problems. I think it would be better if I didn't say anything more."

Mr Scott agreed with Mr Back that he had received £5 a week for nearly two years from Mr Peter Bessell the former Liberal MP for Bodmin.

Mr Back said: "I also know Mr Bessell is reported to have said that was silence money because you happen to know he was having an affair with a young woman."

Mr Scott: "Mr Bessell has said several things to try and get out of this whole situation. But the reason was my insurance cards were not up to date.

"Mr Thorpe had them 1959–60 when I first went to live with him.

"I know it sounds perhaps unwholesome. His words as far as I can remember were: 'I do not want you to have to worry any longer about money.'

"In other words I was supposed to live with him and be cared for by him for the rest of my life. Obviously this did not happen."

Mr Scott said that Bessell had arrived in Dublin when he was there totally out of the blue. "A man I had never known who I subsequently found out was a Liberal Party member. He told me he had an extradition order from Sir Frank Soskice to take me back to England."

Mr Scott said he had written to Mrs Thorpe (the mother) to say he had lost a suitcase containing clothes in Switzerland.

"I had asked Jeremy on several occasions if he would please get it back because the case was full of letters from him to me and I was worried for him because until 1968 I think it was a blackmailable offence."

Asked what offence he was referring to, the witness replied: "Homosexuality."

"I was worried for and that is why I was writing to him and why I wrote to Mrs Thorpe and why Peter Bessell arrived in Dublin.

"That is when he said: 'Norman, until such times as your insurance cards can be sorted out I will pay you a retainer of £5 a week.'"

At one stage Mr Back asked Mr Scott: "Do you find that you sometimes tell yourself a wonderful story, a piece of fiction, and like it so much that with the passing of time you come to believe it?"

Mr Scott: "No. When I first lived with Mr Thorpe, I had to become a totally different character because of my life style with him and having to eat in the Reform Club and do these various parties and ghastly things which I could not stand.

"I had to become another character – in other words, I had to lie for him.

"But now I am able to tell the truth, and for the last year-and-a-half I am able to tell the truth because I am living my own life and not living it for Mr Thorpe any longer."

The hearing was adjourned until today.

19 March 1976
Thorpe praised for meeting smears fair and square
"This man Scott . . . an exhibitionist prepared to go on and on . . ."

Mr Jeremy Thorpe was praised in court yesterday for not yielding to the "persistent intimidation" of Norman Scott, who alleges he had a homosexual relationship with the Liberal leader.

Scott's persistence had the effect "of intimidating certain members of the Liberal Party but not, to his eternal credit, Mr Thorpe who has met it fair and square every time", said Mr Patrick Back, at Exeter Crown Court

"There have been those who, out of a misguided desire to protect the interests of the party or its leadership, have yielded to the demands of Scott," he added.

Mr Back is defending Andrew Gino Newton, 29 an unemployed pilot, of Abinger

Road, Chiswick, who faces five charges following the shooting of Scott's Great Dane Rinka on Exmoor.

Newton has pleaded not guilty to possessing a gun with intent to endanger life and possessing the gun with intent to commit an indictable offence.

He has admitted three other offences – possessing a Mauser automatic pistol and ammunition without the necessary firearms certificate; having the weapon unlawfully in a public place; and destroying a dog belonging to Scott.

In his evidence Newton claimed he shot the dog because Scott was blackmailing him at the rate of £4 a month over a nude photograph which he had sent to a sex contact magazine.

Scott alleged that Newton was being paid by Marion Thorpe, wife of Mr Thorpe, and that Newton had tried to shoot him after killing the dog.

Mr Back said the real issue was whether Newton, in his possession of the gun, intended to endanger human life.

Scott had said Newton had told him his life was in danger and invited him to meet a lady – a lady, by inference, who had something to do with the danger that encircled Scott's life.

The suggestion was that Newton was a hired assassin or strong-arm man and that he came from this lady, or her husband, or that he was employed to "stop Scott's mouth".

"It is a matter of extreme pain for me and for all of us to mention names and I think

I can do this without mentioning any names now.

"We all of us here have tried not to name names. Insofar as names have been mentioned in this court, they have been mentioned by that man Scott.

"Let us consider a little bit more about Mr Norman Scott. I doubt whether, if you sat on hundred more juries, you will ever see or hear a witness quite like that man.

"What can one say about this man? Plainly he is unbalanced, plainly he has been in the hands of a doctor and had treatment for something called neurasthenia. He is a man with an obsession."

Scott was "astonishingly persistent." He was something akin to what was known as a vexatious litigant in legal circles – a person who was prepared to go on and on with his litigation, with his imagined grievances.

"Perhaps one can pause and to be charitable. With people of this kind, there is always a danger they are deluding themselves and maybe this is a man who convinces himself of a situation relative to himself and builds on it."

Mr Back said it was possible for a man to imagine a grievance, insert it into his life history, dwell on it and eventually come to believe it. "I suggest to you, although he refuted it when I suggested it to him, that this was not an altogether bad analysis on my part."

Scott was a self-confessed homosexual. "Again, let us be charitable. A man cannot help very often if he is born a homosexual." Some homosexuals were "afflicted with a terrifying propensity for malice".

Then Mr Back asked the jury: "Did at cross your minds that the man was an actor? Were you really taken in?

"Do you remember how he started with a soft, effeminate voice and a sort of false humility, because it was a false humility, having regard to how he behaved subsequently.

"To begin with, it was a little Uriah Heep. And then at the crucial moment came tears."

It must have been a distressing experience for Scott when his dog was shot. "But be careful about those tears. Ask yourself whether they were real or whether they were crocodile tears."

Because it was not long before they had gone and then you had the charade of fear, the shaking of the hands and the stuttering of the tongue. Do you think that was real?

"Then, eventually there came moments of provocation, prompted by me, and all the stuttering and all the tears and the soft humility disappeared and underneath there was a razor-sharp like quality – sharp, intelligent, witty at times.

"Quite robust and quite able to look after himself, articulate, quick and gaining in invention.

"It was all performance,, wasn't it? And all the time he had his eye on the gallery and was wooing them. Did it cross through your mind that he was an exhibitionist?

"Maybe he was enjoying every moment, every moment of what perhaps he was regarding has his own finest hour. Somebody who, according to his own evidence, has been longing to say all of these things, these damaging things."

Mr Back said Scott had accepted £2,500 for copies of letters – yet before handing them over he had had photocopies made. "The only reason why anybody would pay him £2,500 for these documents would be to destroy them and remove all trace of them," he said.

"Yet he quietly pocketed the £2,500 and kept copies of the letters as well. There is a grave suspicion, isn't there, that this is a man who lives by blackmail."

The cases of the photo-copied £2,500 letters, and the payments from Mr Peter Bessell [Scott alleged he was paid £5 a week from Mr Bessell, former Liberal MP for Bodmin] lent probability to Newton's claim that he was being blackmailed, said Mr Back.

He suggested that Scott was not the bullying sort of blackmailer, but worked cunningly, discovering someone's weak points and using innuendo to claim payment. It might be thought payments of £4 a month were too small to be blackmail demands. He suggested that small payments were less likely to frighten victims into telling the police and so were more likely to be paid.

"If you go for a number of blackmail situations giving you a small return, then you may be making quite a reasonable living. "It must be very easy to blackmail people who are either so puerile as my client seems to be in this matter, or so sexually perverse or twisted as to apply to these contact magazines."

The case, he went on, had surrounding features which made the suggestion that Scott was a blackmailer more likely.

One was "Mr Scott's propensities for blackmail, as I say it is – or if that is too strong, Mr Scott's ability to accept sums of money for what appear to be his silence about certain matters".

Newton had a lot to lose if his employers were shown the nude photo. He was expecting to be promoted to captain. "He had got something very precious to lose.

"The only possible way of understanding this case is to accept the account of Scott as a petty blackmailer blackmailing Newton. It is the only comprehensible account that you have had.

"The Crown account just does not bear investigation because it is an account of Newton arriving as a sort of hired assassin employed by people who would never dream, in a thousand years, of employing an assassin or a gunman.

The Crown case was destroyed "by the very words of the police officer that extensive inquiries show there is no connection whatsoever between Mr Newton, and anybody in the Liberal Party who has been mentioned since this man Scott chose to start this wretched national scandal."

Mr Back said Newton had been irritated by the blackmail, not frightened by it.

"He was, I suppose, to some extent irritated with himself that he had allowed himself to fall for it and he then decided to take action and whatever he did seemed to go wrong."

Mr Lewis Hauser, Q.C., prosecuting, said the real reason for the shooting of Scott's dog may never be known. And he told the jury: "We are concerned with what happened on the night of 24 October and that is the vital matter in this case.

"The prosecution suggests that Mr Newton's blackmail story is quite untrue. If you come to that conclusion you may, of course, ask yourselves the question 'what was he doing down there and what was he up to.'

"It may be there is no answer that can be provided to you from the material available in the court. Maybe we shall never know the answer to the question.

"In the end you may ask yourself what difference does it make because what you are trying to deride is what happened on that night."

Earlier Mrs Henrietta Faulkner, 21, a long-haired blonde, in evidence supported Newton's claim that Scott came to see him in Blackpool, subsequent to blackmailing him over the nude photo.

Mrs Faulkner of Red Bank Read, Bispham, Blackpool, who is separated from her husband, said that on a Saturday morning towards the end of the summer season in 1974 the bell went and Andrew went to answer the door.

"Within a few minutes the door was pushed open upstairs where I was and a man walked in in front of Andrew." She remembered this in particular because bits of a model battleship Newton had been building were knocked on the floor by the door opening and she had to pick them up.

Questioned by Mr Back she said: "I got the feeling I was not wanted in the room and within a few minutes I went out and left the flat."

Asked whether she had formed an impression or noticed any particular characteristic about the visitor she replied: "I thought he was queer."

When she returned to the flat the stranger had gone "I asked Andrew if he (Scott) was queer. I also asked Andrew in a joking way if he was queer."

Mr Justice Lawson remarked to laughter: "Well you had reasons for knowing otherwise."

The trial was adjourned until today when Mr Justice Lawton is expected to sum up and send the jury out.

20 March 1976
Two years for man who shot Scott's dog
By Geoffrey Lakeman

Andrew Gino Newton, 29, who admitted shooting a dog belonging to male model Norman Scott, was jailed for two years at Exeter Crown Court yesterday. And after the verdict, Scott, who was close to tears, said: "I really don't know why he did it – that is what is so terrifying. It is so very, very strange.

"I don't think it is over – only this bit of it is over. I think there is a lot more to come out." He said it would always remain a mystery "what was behind this whole thing".

Scott, 36, who has alleged that he had a homosexual relationship with Mr Jeremy Thorpe, pace nervously outside the court while Newton was being sentenced, and said: "I am sorry for him in a way. But it won't bring my dog back."

The jury, who had been told by Mr Justice Lawson not to be influenced by "party political consideration," were out for three hours before returning verdict of guilty to possessing a gun with intent to endanger life.

The judge then said Newton had taken the law into his own hands for some reason which only he knew.

Mr Patrick Back, Q.C., defending, said: "How it came about that this defendant eventually threatened this man on Porlock Hill nobody can say with certainty.

"It is a very difficult case upon which to mitigate because in order to mitigate one must have some certainty about the background of it.

"In an obvious reference to the lengthy evidence which included further allegations by Scott of a relationship with Mr Thorpe, he went on: "We have ventilated the background with a view to ascertaining motives, but that ventilation, I submit, has left us no wiser than when we embarked on the task."

Mr Back said it would be tendentious of him to reiterate what he had said about the possible motive. "One can only guess at the jury's reasoning. No doubt they are in the dark as are all of us about how all this came about."

Newton was a young man who had led an impeccable life but was rather immature and had been involved in "puerile and a rather undesirable hobby of having recourse to sexual contact magazines".

"Whatever the problem was that led to the eventual encounter between him and Scott on Porlock Hill, certainly it was a situation that was too big for him."

Mr Back said Newton had made the decisions of an immature young man – brash, stupid, and ill-conceived. "The consequences of the verdict are his own undoing and will last him all the days of his life. In short, he has ruined himself."

Newton's version of events, which led up to the shooting of Scott's Great Dane "Rinka" on 24 October on a lonely Exmoor road, were that Scott had approached him after obtaining a nude photograph of him via a sex contact magazine and subsequently demanding money. Newton was afraid that if he did not pay up blackmail money, his promotion and career prospects as a pilot would be jeopardised.

He eventually travelled to Barnstable, Devon, with a gun with the idea of frightening Scott and the result was the incident with the dog.

Scott maintained Newton was a stranger who claimed he had been paid to protect him.

Scott, self-styled writer and self-confessed homosexual, broke down several times in the witness box

More than 20 reporters, some of them representing South African papers, sat through the trial and "house full" signs went up every day outside the public gallery entrance.

Because of the alleged involvement of the Liberal leader and the publicity given to Scott's allegation. Mr Lewis Hauser, Q.C. prosecuting, emphasised to the jurors "There is only one man on trial here, the man in the dock."

Mr Thorpe's name cropped up many times, particularly during Scott's evidence.

But a police witness told the jury that an extensive and thorough inquiry had revealed no link between Newton and members of the Liberal party or other persons mentioned by Scott.

After the trial ended Scott pointed out that he had not alleged that either Mr or Mrs Thorpe had been paying Newton.

"What I said in evidence was that it was Newton who told me that he was being paid to protect me. After the judge said I was allowed to mention the name I told the court that he had said it was Marion Thorpe. I have never alleged this."

Recalling an address to the jury by the defence on Thursday when Mr Back said Scott: "Plainly he is unbalanced," Scott said: "That was a terrible character assassination – it was really quite shattering.

"Mr Back also said I was merciless, but I don't think I have been merciless at all."

Newton, of Abinger Road, Chiswick was sentenced to two years on the main charge which he had denied, together with an alternative charge of possessing the gun with intent to commit an indictable offence.

The judge also sentenced him to six months imprisonment on each of three other charges, which he had admitted, all to run concurrently with the two year sentence.

These were destroying Scott's dog, possessing a Mauser automatic pistol in a public place and not having the necessary firearm certificate for the weapon and ammunition.

The judge told Newton: "This was a cunningly contrived and planned incident on your part. Had it not been for the chance of the pistol jamming, and your being unable to stop it from being jammed, the consequences of this incident might have been very, very grave indeed."

In his summing up the judge had told the jury there was no law which allowed people to shoot blackmailers. "There are processes of law available to take care of blackmail situations and if people take the law into their own hands you can see what the result can be – chaos."

He pointed out that the defence had spent 27½ minutes discussing Scott's wickedness in a closing speech. "You may have formed the view that Scott is a highly nervous man, a man with obsessions, a man who from time to time has quite obviously been in great fear – but you have got to form a view as to how you think his evidence on essential matters is vital."

John Vassall

"I remember someone at the party taking photographs."

14 September 1962

Admiralty man in secrets case

Special branch search in Dolphin Square

By John Owen

William John Christopher Vassall, 37, a clerical officer at the Admiralty, was accused under the Official Secrets Act at Bow Street yesterday. Vassall, who earns £800 a year, is the son of the Rev. W. Vassall, 70, assistant priest at St. James's Church, Piccadilly.

He was charged that between August 18 and September 11, 1962 at the Admiralty, Whitehall, and elsewhere for a purpose prejudicial to the safety or interests of the State, he did record secret official information which is calculated to be, or might be, or is intended to be directly or indirectly useful to an enemy contrary to the Official Secrets Act.

He was remanded in custody for a week. He was told he would be further remanded next Thursday for another week.

Det. Chief Insp. Ferguson Smith, of Scotland Yard's Special Branch, said it might take longer than a fortnight before the case could be heard.

Any person guilty of a felony under the Official Secrets Act is liable to imprisonment for a term not exceeding 14 years.

Vassall, of 807, Hood House, Dolphin Square, Westminster, has latterly been employed at the Admiralty in the department carrying out administration of Naval affairs. He was previously in the office of the Civil Lord, Mr Orr-Ewing, the Admiralty's spokesman in the Commons.

In 1959, Vassall was sent to Moscow to act as clerk to the British Naval Attaché at our Embassy. He served a normal period for a clerical officer on a foreign posting.

Friends yesterday described him as "a quietly spoken man, rather reserved in his manner, who was always beautifully dressed". Strict secrecy measures were in force during preliminary investigation of the case.

Vassall was arrested by Special Branch men in accordance with normal routine. Where a Service security department approves of legal action being taken against an employee, the Special Branch is always called on to make the formal arrest.

During the day, the case was discussed at a high level inside the Admiralty. The head of its security department, Col. John L. A. Macafee, was called in by Admiral of the Fleet Sir Caspar John, the First Sea Lord, for consultation.

At Bow Street, the Rev. W. Vassall was granted permission by the Chief Magistrate, Sir Robert Blundell, to see his son before he left for Brixton. The father, who is a widower, returned last night to his home at Hope Farm, Higham, near Rochester. He lives there with his other son, Roland.

Vassall has lived in his eighth-floor flat at Dolphin Square for over two years. Special Branch officers were yesterday making a thorough search of the flat, which consists of a living room, a bedroom, kitchen and bathroom.

When he went to Dolphin Square as a prospective tenant he gave three references. One of these was from a bank. The others were from the Civil Service and from a friend.

One of his neighbours said: "He appeared to be living alone. I saw him in the lift occasionally, but we never spoke. This block of flats is ideal for anyone who wants to keep himself to himself.

Special Branch officers were also making inquiries in other parts of the block.

The proceedings at Bow Street lasted three minutes. After Chief Insp. Ferguson Smith asked for a week's remand in custody, Sir Robert Blundell asked Vassall whether he was asking for bail or was content to remain in custody.

Vassall started to say: "Whichever you . . . "

Sir Robert: It is for you to say. I am asked to remand you for a week in custody. That will give you time to consult a solicitor if you wish.

Vassall: Yes. I would like to see a solicitor.

Sir Robert: Listen again. I am asked to remand you in custody. Are you asking for bail?

Vassall: In custody, then.

Sir Robert: Very well, you will be remanded in custody.

Vassall was told that if he wished to apply for legal aid he would be told how to do so.

10 October 1962
Counsel tells of drink, vice and threats in Moscow
Admiralty clerk for trial on spying charges
By a *Daily Telegraph* reporter

Meetings in London between an Admiralty clerk and Russian agents were described at Bow Street yesterday when William John Christopher Vassall, 38, was sent for trial at the Old Bailey accused of spying. Police were said to have found 140 photographs at his flat in Hood House, Dolphin Square, relating to secret Admiralty documents.

A statement said to have been made by Vassall told how he was introduced to Russians while he was working in the British Embassy, Moscow. It described a night when he was "plied with very strong brandy" and was involved in "several compromising sexual actions" with three friends of a Pole.

"I remember someone at the party taking photographs," the statement went on. Later, he was shown photographs of himself in compromising situations. A Russian called Gregory and another agent called Nikolai met him on his return to Britain and he handed over photographs of secret documents.

The charges read:

1. Between August 18 and September 11, at the Admiralty. Whitehall, and elsewhere for a purpose prejudicial to the safety or interests of the State, he recorded secret official information which was calculated to be, or might be, or intended to be, directly, or indirectly, useful to an enemy; and

2. In August 1962, for a purpose prejudicial to the safety or interests of the State, he communicated to another person secret official information calculated to be, or which might be, or was intended, to be, directly, or indirectly useful to an enemy.

Mr Mervyn Griffith Jones, prosecuting, said that Vassall recorded and communicated information to the prejudice of the State while employed by the Admiralty in London and Moscow.

"On leaving school he joined the Civil Service and was posted to the Admiralty in 1941." Mr Griffith-Jones went on: "Later in the war he joined the R.A.F. and trained, not perhaps without significance, as a photographer. He returned to the Admiralty in 1947 and served in London for the next seven years.

"In March 1954, he was posted to Moscow in the naval attaché's office. There he remained until July 1956. It was towards the end of that period, it appears from what he says, that the disclosures of information started.

"In July 1956, he returned to the Admiralty in London. He remained there until 12 September last when he was arrested."

Vassall was told it was believed he had been committing offences under the Official Secrets Act and there was a warrant for a search of his flat. He answered: "I suppose it is because I have been working abroad."

On his way to a police station Vassall said: "I think I know what you are after." After being cautioned, he said he had two cameras – an Exacta and a Minox – and that there was a film in the Exacta. He added: "I think you will find what you are looking for in it."

When two keys were found on him he said: "That one opens a drawer in the chest in the bedroom in which you will find the cameras. You will find standing in the standing the corner near the wardrobe a small cornerpiece which has a concealed aperture at its base.

"I know you will find them so I may as well tell you the whole story. On the piece of furniture as you enter the room is an oblong box in which there is a small tool like a knife blade. If you insert this at the base of the shelf in the cornerpiece it will release a spring catch.

"You can lift out the shelf and underneath you will find films of secret information which I recently copied from Admiralty files."

Mr Griffith-Jones said that at Vassall's flat there were five used films with 140 exposures. "They contained between them photographs of pages from 17 official Admiralty documents dated between July 1962. and September 3 last," he continued. "All are secret documents, the exposure of which would gravely damage the State's security."

Diagrams were found on Vassall concerning the setting of cameras. In his diary reference was made to the wattage of electric lamps that might be required for taking photographs.

Mr Griffith-Jones read from a statement it was claimed Vassall had made. It said: "When I was in the Moscow Embassy my work took me to the administrative section where an official who was employed locally was helpful. He was known as Mokoski and was a Pole.

"He invited me to dinner at restaurants. Other people were introduced to me.

"One evening the Pole introduced me to three of his friends whom I had not met before. One suggested I should have dinner at a restaurant near the Bolshoi Theatre. I was taken to the first door which at first I thought was a dining room, but in fact was a private room.

"We had drinks, a large dinner and I was plied with very strong brandy. After half an hour I remember everybody taking off their jackets. Somebody assisted me to take off mine.

"I remember the lighting being very strong. More of my clothes were removed. There was a divan in the corner. I remember two or three getting on the bed with me in a state of undress.

"Then, several compromising sexual actions took place. I remember someone of the party taking photographs."

Later, the Pole introduced him to a military officer, who invited him to a flat in central Moscow. The officer went out.

"Shortly afterwards, two officials in plain clothes confronted me and asked who I was," the statement proceeded. "They asked where I worked and if I had a diplomatic passport.

"Suddenly, one of them produced photographs of me in various compromising acts and asked if this was me. I said it was.

"They said I had committed serious offences and could be kept in Russia for these offences. I remained calm and said as far as I knew I hadn't committed an offence against anybody. They continued questioning me about who I was and showed me the remaining photographs.

"They said if I mentioned the matter to anybody at the Embassy I would not be allowed to leave Russia and they would make an international incident of it."

Finally, they took him home. Next day the Pole arrived. He told the Pole what had happened with the two officials. He accepted the Pole's advice to meet the officials that night.

He met the two men outside a railway station and they took to a private suite at the Sovietskaya Hotel. They again showed him photographs and said they wanted to meet him again.

Suddenly, one of them got angry, tore up the photographs and threw them into his face. Finally, they said they would not let him go unless he promised to meet them again.

Because he did not want to be the cause of an international incident, he met them on subsequent occasions. In the summer of 1955 he began telling them of his work.

"I tried to stall them off with innocuous items, but they said that unless I told them more important matters they would have me hauled off to the headquarters of the M.V.D. [secret police]. I had no alternative."

He handed them documents, some of which would have been secret. He decided to visit Italy and was told he would be under surveillance all the time and unless he returned to Russia they would deal with him.

After he returned to Moscow he continued to meet the men. In June 1956, he was introduced to a third man called Gregory. The Russians knew he was returning to Britain in June and he was told Gregory would meet him there.

Gregory met him in Finchley Road, London, and asked him where he was working and what sort of work he did. At other meetings he took secret documents.

"I handed them to Gregory," the statement went on. "He went around a corner and I presume he handed them to someone in a car. We would then walk around for an hour or two. He would leave me and then return with the documents."

Some time in 1957 he was instructed to photograph the documents instead of giving them to Gregory. He was given the money to buy an Exacta camera.

He used to photograph documents at home in the evening and return them next day He did not develop the films but gave them to Gregory.

Shortly before the Portland spy case he met a man named Nikolai. Gregory did not turn up for the meeting. Nikolai said: "I recognise your face from photographs." Nikolai asked the wav to Belsize Park Tube station. That was a message which Gregory had arranged.

After the Portland spy case Nikolai told him he should not do anything or meet them again until he received a car catalogue. The catalogue arrived last September.

He met Nikolai, who told him no activities were to take place until he (Nikolai) received instructions from his Moscow superiors. The instructions would not arrive until Moscow was certain he was not under suspicion.

Vassall, the statement continued, said he was told to practise with a Minox, photographing newspapers at home. But he was informed the photographs were of no use.

He went to a telephone kiosk near a public house and picked up a parcel which Nikolai had left. The parcel contained an Exacta camera. He had sold the other Exacta.

Last January Nikolai told him to go ahead. The last time he took documents home was on September 3.

Gregory had given him a left-luggage ticket. He used this to get a bookcase with a secret compartment to be used for hiding films and documents.

Gregory described two ways of getting in touch with a Russian agent. One was by ringing a circle in pink chalk on the trunk of a plane tree outside Plane Tree House, Duchess of Bedford's Walk, Kensington. The other was by telephoning Kensington 8955 and asking for Miss Mary. He tried this once to test it.

Among meeting places were Worcester Park, Southfields, Mount Pleasant, Wembley and Edgware.

Mr Griffith-Jones said: "We come to what, perhaps, is the second part of his statement, where it appears that certainly all this was not a result of being blackmailed."

Vassall, telling of receiving money from the Russians, had said: "The first time I received any was before Christmas, 1955, as a gift. I was handed 2,000 roubles – about £50.

"About every fourth meeting the Russians in Moscow used to give me 2,000 roubles. I used the money for food and holidays.

"After I returned to Britain. Gregory or Nikolai used to give me money in sums ranging from £50 to £200. But not on every occasion we met. The sums ranged from £500 to £700 a year."

The money was handed to him in cash, usually in £5 notes. He spent it mostly on clothes, entertaining, holidays and personal effects. He had invested £300 in Premium Bonds.

Vassall had put forward what might be described as his mitigation: "When this terrible catastrophe happened, which happened to me unknowingly, I had to make some decision whether to report these events to the Embassy.

"I also had to have all the terrible responsibility of causing untold harm between our country, Russia and our allies.

"It was explained to me by the Russians that I was only helping them to protect their country and in no way was it to follow aggressive intentions on their part. In no way was it my intention to do anything against this country."

Vassall had recalled that when he joined the Civil Service he signed the Official Secrets Act and said: "I now wish to express my sincere regrets for what I have done."

The statement went on: "I feel the general atmosphere of the Embassy was an unhappy one. Senior staff were occupied with their duties and junior staff left to fend for themselves. If we were cared for as one family I do not think some of us would have got into this trouble."

Chief Insp. Ferguson Smith, of the Special Branch, said in evidence he handed two cameras and some films to a certain witness.

Mr Griffith-Jones said he wished this witness to be called and added: "I would ask that his name be not given. I shall call him Mr A."

When a short, bespectacled man entered the court Chief Insp. Smith said he had handed to him the cameras and films found in Vassall's flat. The man then left the court.

Mr Griffith-Jones: Is it in your knowledge that the telephone number, Kensington 8955, was used by the Soviet Intelligence from June 1959, until September 1960?

Chief Insp. Smith: Yes.

Mr A. called as the next witness, wrote his name and address on a piece of paper. He said he was a security service officer and a photographic expert.

He gave evidence of examining two cameras and developing and enlarging several films. There was a total of 140 exposures.

"I have examined a piece of paper which contains a diagram of the side of a Minox camera with the controls and certain figures which appeared to be time and distance settings for close photography," he added.

On a page from a diary he found three sets of figures which appeared to indicate camera settings in relation to various wattage electric lamps. These settings would be suitable for taking photographic copies of documents.

Col. John Leeper Macaffe, Royal Marines, Director of Naval Security at the Admiralty, said that photographic enlargements of 140 exposures shown to him by Chief Insp. Smith had been compared with the original documents of which they appeared to be photographs.

Mr Griffith-Jones: Would disclosure to a potential enemy be a grave danger to the State?

Col. Macafee: Yes.

Would all of them have been available to Vassall in the course of his work? – Yes.

Did he, or anybody in his position, have authority to remove them from the Admiralty? – No

Col. Macafee added that Vassall's gross salary was £908 a year. His net salary was £700.

Sir Robert Blundell, the Chief Metropolitan Magistrate, then read the charges to Vassall and asked if he understood. Vassall replied: "Yes, sir" – his only remark during the hearing.

Mr Derek Muskett, defending, said Vassall did not wish to say anything at present, or to give evidence, or to call witnesses there.

23 October 1962
18 years' gaol for "traitorous tool of Russians"
Defence plea: "No master spy":
Pure selfish greed, says Lord Parker
By a *Daily Telegraph* reporter

Willlam John Vassall, 38, the Admiralty clerk who said he was blackmailed into spying for Russia, was sent to prison for a total of 18 years at the Old Bailey yesterday. He was described by the prosecution as "a traitorous tool of the Russians".

On a charge that one day in 1955, for purposes prejudicial to the safety or interest of the State, he communicated to another person information which might have been directly or indirectly useful to an enemy, Vassall was sentenced by Lord Parker, Lord Chief Justice, to six years.

He was sentenced 12 years concurrently each on three other charges under the Official Secrets Act, to run consecutively with the six-year sentence. These were that:

Between 1 August 1956, and 31 May 1957, for purposes prejudicial to the safety or interests of the State, he communicated to another person information which might have been directly or indirectly useful to an enemy.

On 17 August last committed a similar offence: and between 17 August and 12 September 1962, for purposes prejudicial to the safety or interest of the State, collected information which might have been directly or indirectly useful to an enemy.

Lord Parker said to Vassall, who had pleaded guilty to the four charges: "You have stated in your confession to the police that throughout you had no intention of harming this country. I am unable to accept that.

"A man of your education, experience and intelligence knew full well that this information and these documents would be of assistance to an enemy. I am satisfied that what you did, you did largely for money."

He accepted that when Vassall first started his spying activities in England it was under pressure, but when he returned to England he could have made a clean breast of the matter, and left his Government work where he would not have access to any secret information.

Also, from 1955, Vassall had accepted money for his work to the extent of doubling his £688 a year salary. "I take the view that one of the compelling reasons for what you did was pure selfish greed."

Although the information Vassall passed was of a haphazard character, it was often of a highly secret nature and capable of doing great harm to the country. "You have got to be punished, to an extent that will also be a deterrent to others."

Sir John Hobson, Q.C., the Attorney-General, for the Crown, said that in a six years period Vassall had passed to Russian agents secret information of the "highest importance" which he had obtained during duties as a clerical officer at the Admiralty.

He had been well rewarded for it by people who used him as a tool. "He has sold some part of the safety and security of the people of this country for cash."

A diary kept by Vassall, found by the Special Branch, showed that about October 1955, he was leading a social life in Moscow that would have been the envy of any London bachelor. He had attended about 150 social functions at Embassies.

"He was already entrapped by his lust and thereafter cash kept him crooked," said the Attorney-General.

Lord Parker: What worries me is how comes it that a man whose real salary is something under £700 gets access to top secret documents?

The Attorney-General: He was a clerical officer, and he only got access because he was a personal assistant and worked in the same room as the person who was the actual head of the section. Everybody requires clerical assistance in the Civil Service.

The Attorney-General concluded: "Throughout the whole period of six years he had neither the moral fibre nor the patriotism to alter the conduct he had embarked upon, but thereafter remained the traitorous tool of the Russians and continued to serve them."

Chief Insp. Ferguson Smith, Special Branch, said Vassall had no previous convictions.

Mr Jeremy Hutchinson, Q.C., defending, said to Lord Parker that he could not hope to tap his springs of sympathy when a man had pleaded guilty to such offences. Vassall was a very ordinary and unremarkable man, an untough man and one who could be described as "unadult".

"He has a weakness and that is that within him he is a latent homosexual, which brings in its train, inner turmoil and suffering. There nothing in him of the master spy."

Vassall went to Moscow with the romantic idea of getting to know Russians well. But his ideas fell flat when he reached the British Embassy where protocol was of paramount importance and junior attaches had to remain junior attaches.

Inevitably, he met the Pole Michailsky, a warm-hearted man who was in control of the tickets for the concert and the ballet and who "had the same unfortunate sexual proclivity as the defendant."

After assessing the harm that Vassall's activities might have done, Mr Hutchinson went on: "So long as powerful nations train men to suborn and seduce, equipped with modern, scientific, psychological methods, then so long there will be victims such as John Vassall.

"Just so long as this canker of espionage continues to rot the goodwill between men, there will be trials such as this.

"If these trials disclose something of the pressures to which ordinary men are not put, then it will serve a greater purpose than anything in your Lordship's sentence, to show society's condemnation of the weakness of one of its members."

He referred Lord Parker to a statement by Sir Alexander Paterson, the late Prisons Commissioner and reformer, that it needed a superman to survive a sentence of over 20 years with his soul remaining intact.

"This is no superman," said Mr Hutchinson, "and I ask you to impose a just penalty to prove once again that here, humanity goes hand in hand with justice."

24 January 1963
Vassall's flat like a woman's, says reporter
Bottles of perfume: Cuddly teddy bear: Corset catalogues
By a *Daily Telegraph* reporter

The bedroom and bathroom of John Vassall's Dolphin Square hat were full of perfume bottles, a reporter told the Vassall Tribunal yesterday. There was a cuddly cheetah and a cuddly teddy bear. "It could have been a woman's flat," he added.

The reporter, Mr Norman Frederick Lucas, of the *Sunday Pictorial*, added that he also found photographs of Mr Thomas Galbraith, former Civil Lord of the Admiralty at the flat. These were of official visits and might have been put by Mr Galbraith in his "out" tray, then taken by Vassall.

He noticed at the flat catalogues for women's corsets and cut-out pictures from French newspapers of "stocky, hirsute Rugby players".

Mr Norman Frederick Lucas, crime reporter with the *Sunday Pictorial*, said that after Vassall was arrested he was authorised by his editor to negotiate for the right to publish his life story. An agreement was reached and he went to Vassall's Dolphin Square Hat accompanied by the managing clerk to Vassall's firm of solicitors.

"The bedroom and the bathroom were full of perfume bottles to an extent which one would expect to find in a lady's accommodation," Mr Lucas went on. "The whole flat, in fact, was not to my way of thinking a bachelor's flat: it could have been a woman's flat."

Asked about the quality of the furniture, Mr Lucas said: "The quality was extremely good. The glassware, particularly, was good.

"The bedroom, too, was extremely well furnished and in the wardrobes the suits all came from a well-known, fashionable West End store. I would have made guess they cost about £35 to £40 each. The bed linen was of good quality."

With the permission of the managing clerk, he took away a number of documents. He also took all pictures he found.

Mr Lawson: Among these documents were there some letters and, I think, one postcard, which appeared to be addressed to Vassall by Mr Galbraith?

Mr Lucas: Yes.

Continuing, Mr Lucas said: "I left behind catalogues addressed to Vassall from a women's corset firm and some cut-out pictures from French newspapers of stocky, hirsute Rugby players, I had no interest in these so I left them.

"I believe there were two or three catalogues addressed to Vassall with the initials before his name, but no 'Mr or Mrs'."

The documents he removed from the flat had been inspected by the Treasury Solicitor. He found between 80 and 100.

He identified two boxes containing photographs as having been taken from the flat. When he was shown a bundle of 12 photographs, he said he found them in a drawer of Vassall's bureau.

Mr Lawson: Are they group photographs?

Mr Lucas: They are.

With what are they concerned? – I would say, without knowing exactly, that they are all concerned with official visits made by a man I now know to be Mr Galbraith.

Mr Lucas was asked to look at one photograph. He said: "That is a studio photograph of a man I now know to be Mr Galbraith."

Mr Lawson: It is right to say there is no dedication or inscription in writing on any of them? – No.

Were the instalments of the Vassall story published in the *Sunday Pictorial* submitted for security clearance? – Yes.

Mr Lawson referred Mr Lucas to a part of his article which said that a list of Civil Servants with records of homosexual offences had been drawn up, that Vassall had no record, but he had many contacts among well-known homosexuals.

Asked what information he had on the matter. Mr Lucas replied: "Many letters which I collected from Vassall's flat were written in abnormally affectionate terms by a number of men.

"I had visited one of these men and I came to the conclusion, purely on the basis of experience in having met homosexuals before, that the man to whom I was talking was, in fact, a homosexual.

"I also know from Vassall's own story that he visited a club in the West End which I knew to be a haunt of homosexuals."

In these letters from Vassall's "boy friends" there was a reference to "a very well-known broadcasting figure, who died recently." There was a reference to his death in one letter from one of Vassall's boy friends.

Lord Radcliffe said he did not want the names of the correspondents to be given for obvious reasons. He thought Mr Lucas should give him the names in private.

Mr Lucas said the letters could be handed to Lord Radcliffe.

Mr Lawson asked: Did you discover that at one time Vassall had had a friendship with a young woman?

Mr Lucas replied: "Yes. We discovered several postcards and Christmas cards and one or two letters from young women. We tried to obtain interviews with several."

According to Vassall's story he and one girl had hoped to marry, but this was impossible because of his mode of life. The girl was employed by the Admiralty Intelligence Department and, therefore, unwilling to talk.

He wrote an article in the *Sunday Pictorial* under the heading, "Woman witness in spy probe," which stated: "A young woman who holds a key position in the Admiralty is to be a vital witness in the John Vassall spy case."

Mr Lawson: Do you know her name?

Mr Lucas: Yes.

Are you prepared to write it down? – I am.

As he did so, Lord Radcliffe commented: "I think she has already been examined."

Mr John Donaldson, Q.C., who appeared with the Attorney-General, asked: You made some inquiries on Vassall's homosexual activities. Did they lead you to any conclusion that anybody in an official position knew of these activities?

Mr Lucas: None at all.

You produced 11 photographs, which included what you called a studio photograph of Mr Galbraith. It is right that that photograph was taken by a Press agency and may have been merely a proof print, or complimentary, submitted by the agency? – That would be possible.

Referring to "photographs of various types" found at the flat, Mr Donaldson asked: You are not saying any of them are photographs which might be described as erotic?

Mr Lucas: No.

Mr Lucas agreed that of the remaining 11 photographs, 10 were prints from newspaper offices or from a commercial photographer with their names stamped on the back and of a type which might have been presented as complimentary copies to a Minister.

Mr Donaldson: They may well have been acquired by Vassall from, so to speak, Mr Galbraith's waste-paper basket – That must be the conclusion, yes.

Answering a question on Vassall's toilet accessories, Mr Lucas said: "The perfumes, bath salts and soap were there for anybody to see. I washed my hands and the smell lasted for two days.

"There were roughly nine or 10 bottles of perfumes, colognes and talcs. I think Elizabeth Arden was one of the manufacturers.

"It looked more a woman's flat than a man's flat. I am allowing that he did have a housekeeper who would have kept the place tidy, but nevertheless with the display of perfumes one felt only the fairy queen was missing."

There was a cuddly cheetah and a cuddly teddy bear "which one would not expect to find in a man's flat".

The *Veronica* Mutineers

"Two of the crew were bad learners – and therefore they were killed."

Perhaps determined to undermine their country's reputation for efficiency and order, Germans Gustav Rau, Otto Monsson and Henry Flohr, along with a Dutchman, William Schmidt, incited a mutiny onboard their ship, the MV *Veronica*. With a crew of twelve, the *Veronica* was supposed to be sailing from the Gulf of Mexico to Montevideo, a voyage of several months. However the mutineers objected to the strict discipline enforced by Captain Alexander Shaw and his two chief mates. The tensions provoked proved irreconcilable and at the beginning of December 1902 the chief mate and two crew members who had remained loyal were battered to death. Captain Shaw survived until the following day, when he was shot dead by Rau, the mutiny's leader. Shortly afterwards his second mate was unceremoniously tossed into the ocean. It was decided by the survivors, some of who had remained neutral thus far that they would burn the ship and set off in a lifeboat. They were more arguments and more deaths. By the time they landed in Brazil, the only non-mutineer left alive was the cook, Moses Thomas.

Once safely aboard the steamer back to Britain, Thomas wasted little time in confiding the story to the ship's captain, and the four mutineers were arrested on their arrival in Liverpool. Rau continued to claim he was innocent, even as the noose was looped around his neck. His last words were: "I am not guilty of the murder of those men."

13 May 1903
Tragedy of the sea.

The trial of the three sailors, Otto Ernst Theodor Mousson, Gustav Bau, alias August Mailahn, and Willem Smith, alias Dirk Herlaar, for certain alleged murders on board the British ship *Veronica*, in December last, came before Mr Justice Lawrence, at Liverpool Assizes yesterday. The accused were charged on four counts with the murders of Julius Parson, Patrick Doran, Alexander Shaw, Gustav Johansen, Alec Bravo, and two others, named McLeod and Abrahamson, and with setting fire to the ship on the high seas. The court was crowded. Accused, who pleaded not guilty, were defended by counsel.

With the help of a model of the *Veronica*, Mr Tobin, K.C., detailed the circumstances of the tragedy. The *Veronica* sailed from Ship Island, Gulf of Mexico, in the middle of October last, for Monte Video, with a crew of twelve hands. On 20 December the vessel was deliberately burnt on the high seas and abandoned, but before she was burnt no fewer than seven of the men on board met their deaths by violence, and of the remaining five the three in the dock stood charged with the murder of the captain, and the other two would presently appear as witnesses. The issue, said counsel, was whether the prisoners were guilty of the murder of the captain; but it would be necessary to consider how the others came by their death. Ill-feeling arose between the prisoners – by nationality two were Germans and the other a Dutchman – and their officers, and this feeling rose to such a pitch that they resolved to get rid of their officers and also of such of the crew as were not Germans. A young lad named Flohr, a German, was overawed into joining them, and was the first told to "remove" Doran, known as Paddy. He shrank from the task, which was carried out by Rau, alleged to be the ringleader, who also stunned the first mate when he came to seek Paddy. The first mate was thrown overboard. Johansen, the man at the wheel, was next attacked, and the captain, coming out of his cabin, was twice shot by Rau, and the wounded commander and the second mate were imprisoned for some days without food and water. But at last it was decided that they should die. So one day Rau arranged the men upon the poop and stood there with a revolver. Smith and Monson were also armed with revolvers, and Flohr with a belaying pin. The second mate came up the steps, and seeing the men armed ran aft along the starboard side. He was shot by Smith, and jumped overboard into the water. The three men then shot him as he was struggling in the sea. Then came the captain's turn. He was ordered out of the cabin, but did not come. Alec, the coolie, was sent by Rau down into the cabin with an axe to bring him out. He came almost a dying man, with his hands before his face, and Rau placed a pistol at his head and shot him dead. The survivors (counsel continued) put their heads together and determined to set fire to the *Veronica*, in order to destroy all trace of the crime, and leave the vessel in a lifeboat. They determined to tell the Consul at whatever port they landed that the *Veronica* was accidentally burnt at sea, that the crew put out in two lifeboats, and that the second lifeboat was lost. That story Rau ordered the whole seven should learn, and they had to repeat it day by day. Two of the crew were bad learners – Alec, the coolie, and Johansen, the Swede – and therefore they were killed. Five men only were then left, and they chartered the large lifeboat, and ultimately lauded on the island of Cajuera, off the coast of Brazil. They were carried from there by the Liverpool steamer *Brunswick* to Lisbon, where the cook made a statement to the Consul which started these proceedings.

Among the witnesses called were Antoine Bellande, a Mississippi pilot, and the lad Flohr, who stated that the ship was not too well provisioned. The trial was adjourned till to-day.

15 May 1903
The *Veronica* murders
Prisoners condemned

The trial of the three foreign sailors, Rau, Mousson, and Smith, members of the crew of the *Veronica*, was continued at the Liverpool Assizes yesterday. The opening of the court was delayed by the indisposition of the juryman who was taken ill on the previous day. At length Mr Justice Lawrence took his seat, and said the best course to take in the circumstances was to get another juryman, and read the evidence to him. This was agreed to by counsel for the prisoners. Another juryman was added, and the jury were again sworn. The reading of the evidence took up the whole of the forenoon, and then Rau and Smith gave evidence on their own behalf denying the charges; Rau's statement tended to incriminate the negro cook. The judge summed up at great length, and the jury at nine o'clock, after a very brief retirement, returned a verdict of guilty against all three prisoners, but recommending Mousson to mercy on the ground of his youth and good character. Sentence of death was passed.

It will be remembered that the British ship *Veronica* sailed from Ship Island, Gulf of Mexico, in October for Monte Video, with a crew of twelve hands. On 20 December the vessel was deliberately burnt on the high seas and abandoned, but before this no fewer than seven of the men on board met their deaths by violence. The first mate was shot and thrown overboard when he came to look for a man who had been already killed, and then Johansen, the man at the wheel, was despatched. Subsequently, the captain and second mate were shot at and injured, and after several days' imprisonment without food or water, were killed. Seven men remained, and they determined to set fire to the *Veronica*, and leave the vessel in a lifeboat. They decided to explain that the ship had been accidentally burnt at sea, that the crew put off in two lifeboats, and that the second was lost. Rau ordered his companions to learn this story, and they had to repeat it day by day. Two of the crew were not proficient, and they were killed. The five men remaining entered the large lifeboat, and ultimately landed on the island of Cajueira, off the coast of Brazil. They were carried from there by the Liverpool steamer Brunswick to Lisbon, where the cook made a statement to the British Consul which has led to the three ringleaders being sentenced to death.

Oscar Wilde

"Sentiments which must arise in the breast of every man
who has any spark of decent feeling in him."

The best, and possibly the worst, thing that ever happened to Oscar Wilde was meeting Lord Alfred Douglas. Bosie, as he was known to his family and friends, was handsome, dissipated and reckless; Wilde fell for him instantly. It seemed sometimes as if he lived only to indulge his spoilt lover's every whim. "It was like feasting with panthers," Wilde would later write, somewhat ruefully, "the danger was half the excitement."

Their indiscretion enraged Bosie's father, the Marquess of Queensbury, whose relationship with his son had long been poisonous. They were confronted a number of times by the creator of the modern rules of boxing: "It was when, in my library at Tite Street, waving his small hands in the air in epileptic fury, your father . . . stood uttering every foul word his foul mind could think of, and screaming the loathsome threats he afterwards with such cunning carried out." Wilde realised he had become enmeshed in a family quarrel, one that promised only two outcomes, both equally hideous: either continue to suffer Queensbury's increasingly lurid insults, or confront him and risk public shame.

When the Marquess left a card at Wilde's club bearing the legend "For Oscar Wilde, posing somdomite [sic]", the playwright launched a libel action against Bosie's father. Queensbury was arrested for criminal libel and in response he and his lawyers set out to prove that his allegations were true. Private detectives were charged with proving that Wilde was a vice-soaked older man intent on corrupting the morals of the young and vulnerable. The trial, which had opened to scenes of something close to hysteria, was brought to a close when the lawyer acting for Queensbury asserted that he had tracked down a number of male prostitutes who could testify to having had sex with Wilde. In short order Wilde found himself bankrupt – he was liable to pay for the costs of the expenses Queensbury had incurred in his defence – and arrested for gross indecency. He lost the second case too and was sentenced to two years' hard labour. Wilde's time in jail crushed his health and his spirits, and the last three years of his life were spent in a lonely and penurious exile in France. His early death might be seen as something of a relief.

27 May 1895
The prosecution of Oscar Wilde

Oscar Fingal O'Flahertie Wills Wilde, 40, author, again surrendered to his bail to answer certain grave charges under the Criminal Law Amendment Act. This was the sixth day of the trial.

The Solicitor-General (Sir F. Lockwood, Q.C.), Mr C. F. Gill, and Mr H. Avory prosecuted on behalf of the Public Prosecutor: and Sir E. Clarke, Q.C., Mr Charles Mathews, and Mr Travers Humphrey defended.

The court was again crowded, the Marquis of Queensberry being present.

The Solicitor-General having concluded his speech on the whole case.

His lordship summed up, pointing out that in a charge like this the jury had no business to act upon such tainted and horrible testimony unless it was corroborated by evidence which led to no reasonable doubt that although it was circumstantial yet it was coherent. In view of the remarkable and horrible character of the circumstances surrounding the case, it was necessary that a cold, calm, and absolutely fair administration of justice should be observed. He regretted that the charges of conspiracy were ever introduced if they were to be abandoned, and, knowing now the nature of the circumstances, that the cases had been taken in the order they were, though he was bound to confers that, from the way the trial had been conducted, the defendant had hot in any way suffered. Alluding to the fact that the defendant had entered the witness-box for the third time, he said that in cases of this kind it was inevitable that the defendant should give evidence if he expected to obtain a verdict of acquittal. When the Criminal Law Amendment Act was passed he confessed that he had doubts as to whether that part which related to the cross examination of the accused would not spoil the whole tone and tenor of the administration of the criminal law; but after ten years' experience of it he was convinced that a number of innocent persons had escaped conviction who might now have been languishing in gaol, and that a still larger number of guilty persons had been convicted who would otherwise probably have escaped what was their just fate. It had, therefore, in every way been, a wise and beneficial change in their criminal system. Having next pointed out that because he could not give a colourless summing-up, which was no use to anybody, the jury must not allow any opinions of his to do more than assist them in the exercise of their perfectly independent judgment, his lordship proceeded to consider the evidence. On learning of the letters between the accused and Lord Alfred Douglas, the Marquis of Queensberry came to the conclusion, as most fathers would have done, that the writer of those letters was not a proper companion for his son, but he seemed to have adopted a method of bringing the matter to a head which he should have thought no gentleman would have done. The plea of justification entered in the Queensberry case threw, of course, a terrible responsibility upon Wilde, who was entitled to the full benefit of the observation that it was impossible for him to remember where and with whom he was two years ago. As to the letter from the accused to Lord A. Douglas, it was entirely for the jury to say what it implied. There were people who were extravagant in the expressions of natural affection, and he regretted that the Solicitor-General should have made so much of particular expressions, instead of treating the letter as a whole. As to the engagement by Wilde of private rooms, he should shrink from drawing any adverse conclusions from that, because it might have been perfectly innocently done, and he could not help saying that it was a pity to rely upon such a thing, which was entirely consistent with the conduct of a respectable and honourable man. With regard to the occurrences at Tite-street, he thought it right to point out that there must have been evidence of corroboration which the prosecution might have produced; and as to the destruction by Wilde of the letters which he obtained from Wood, and which he said were of no importance, he could not but regard it as an act of madness. To believe anything said by Wood would be absurd, as he belonged to the vilest class of criminals, and the strength of this matter depended upon the character of the original introduction of Wood to Wilde as illustrated and fortified by the story with regard to the letters.

The Foreman of the Jury said they wanted to know, in view of the intimate relations between Lord A. Douglas and the defendant, whether a warrant against Lord A. Douglas was ever issued.

Mr Justice Wills: I should think not. We have not heard of it.

The Foreman: Or ever contemplated?

Mr Justice Wills: That I cannot say; nor can we discuss it. The issue of such a warrant would not depend upon the intimacy of the parties, but whether there was evidence of some act. Letters pointing to certain relations would not be sufficient. Lord A. Douglas was not called, and you can give what weight you like to that.

The Foreman: If we are to deduct any guilt from these letters, it would apply equally to Lord A. Douglas.

Mr Justice Wills concurred in that view; but, after all, that bad really nothing to do with the present trial, which was the guilt of the accused. Alluding to the masseur's case, if it stood alone he would not hang a dog upon it, but the other occurrences at the Savoy Hotel was a much more serious matter.

The jury retired to consider their verdict at half-past three o'clock. After being absent two hours they returned, and asked the judge to read the notes he hid made with reference to the evidence of Thomas Price, the waiter at St. James's-place, where Wilde had rooms.

The Foreman: There is no evidence as to Charles Parker having slept there.

His Lordship: No.

The jury then again retired, and after a few minutes' absence again returned into court with a verdict of guilty on all the counts.

Alfred Taylor, who had previously been found guilty, was then directed to be placed in the dock.

Sir E. Clarke, Q.C., applied for postponement of sentence until next sessions, pending the argument on the demurrer which had been entered.

Mr Grain joined in the application on behalf of Taylor.

The Solicitor-General opposed. The demurrer could not be argued until the record was completed, and that could not be until sentence was passed.

Mr Justice Wills said that inasmuch as passing sentence would not prejudice the issue to be argued, and inasmuch as it was desirable on every ground that sentence should follow immediately on conviction, he should not accede to the application. Addressing the prisoners, his lordship said: It has never been my lot to have tried a case of this kind before which has been so bad. One has to put stern constraint upon oneself to prevent oneself from describing in language I ought not to use the sentiments which must arise in the breast of every man who has any spark of decent feeling in him, and who has heard the details of these two terrible trials. That the jury have arrived at a correct verdict I cannot persuade myself to entertain a shadow of doubt, and I hope that at all events those who sometimes imagine that a judge is half-hearted in the cause of decency and morality because he takes care that no prejudice shall enter into a case may see that that is consistent at least with a stern sense of indignation at the horrible crimes which have been brought home to both of you. It is no use for me to address you. People who can do these things must be deaf to every sense of decency which can influence conduct. That you, Taylor, kept an immoral house it is impossible to doubt; and that you, Wilde, have been the centre of extensive corruption of young men of the most hideous kind it is equally impossible to doubt. I cannot under such circumstances, do anything except pass the severest sentence which the law allows, and, in my judgment it is totally inadequate to such a case as this. The sentence on each of you is that you be imprisoned and kept to hard labour for two years.

Prisoner Wilde: Can I say anything, my lord?

Mr Justice Wills raised his hand deprecatingly, and the prisoners were then conducted from the dock, amidst some cries of "Shame" and hisses from the public gallery.

The Marquis of Queensberry and Lord Douglas of Hawick were present in court when sentence was passed. The prisoners were subsequently conveyed in the prison van to Pentonville Gaol.

The Press Association News Agency states: On removal both men were suffering from nervousness and betrayed their mental anxiety. When handed over to the Governor of Pentonville the prisoners were taken separately into the reception ward. Each had to give details of his identity and religion and submit to a medical examination, after which they passed through the hands of the prison bath-room attendants and barber, and then exchanged their own clothes for those provided by the prison authorities, subsequently being handed over to the care of the chaplain. Yesterday they attended the prison chapel with the other occupants of the gaol, and with the exception of exercise time they were confined to their cells, where they will in future be kept unless their health becomes such as to entitle them to infirmary treatment, in which event the prison doctor will decide the nature of the labour they must perform. By the terms of their sentence they will be isolated from their friends, except upon four occasions a year, and even this privilege may be forfeited by indifferent conduct.

Also 27 May 1895

No sterner rebuke could well have been inflicted on some of the artistic tendencies of the time than the condemnation on Saturday of Oscar Wilde at the Central Criminal Court. We have not the slightest intention of reviewing once more all the sordid incidents of a case which has done enough, and more than enough, to shock the conscience and outrage the moral instincts of the community. The man has now suffered the penalties of his career, and may well be allowed to pass from that platform of publicity which he loved into that limbo of disrepute and forgetfulness which is his due. The grave of contemptuous oblivion may rest on his foolish ostentation, his empty paradoxes, his insufferable posturing, his incurable vanity. Nevertheless, when we remember that he enjoyed a certain popularity among some sections of society, and, above all, when we reflect that what was smiled at as insolent braggadocio was the cover for, or at all events ended in, flagrant immorality, it is well, perhaps, that the lesson of his life should not be passed over without some insistence on the terrible warning of his fate. Young men at the Universities, clever sixth form boys at public schools, silly women who lend an ear to any chatter which is petulant and vivacious, novelists who have sought to imitate the style of paradox and unreality, poets who have lisped the language of nerveless and effeminate libertinage – these are the persons who should ponder with themselves the doctrines and the career of the man who has now to undergo the righteous sentence of the law. We speak sometimes of a school of Decadents and Æsthetes in England, although it may well be doubted whether at any time is prominent members could not have been counted on the fingers of one hand; but, quite apart from any fixed organisation or body such as may or may not exist in Paris, there has lately shown itself in London a contemporary bias of thought, an affected manner of expression and style, and a few loudly vaunted ideas which have had a limited but evil influence on all the better tendencies of art and literature. Of these the prisoner of Saturday constituted himself a representative. He set an example, so far as in him lay, to the weaker and the younger brethren; and, just because he possessed considerable intellectual powers and unbounded assurance, his fugitive success served to dazzle and bewilder those who had neither experience nor knowledge of the principles which he travestied, or of that true temple of art of which he was so unworthy an acolyte. Let us hope that his removal will serve to clear the poisoned air, and make it cleaner and purer for all healthy and unvitiated lungs.

"Art for art's sake", that is the original catch-word of half the folly which is talked in our midst. A falser or more foolish sentiment could not be imagined: it is demonstrably an error both on historical and psychological grounds. At the banning of recorded annals art was clearly imitation, at the apogee of its glory it is the necessary expression of the inner moods of the personality, and in neither case can be divorced from the common life of us all. If it cannot be divorced from life, it must be subject to the same judgments, it must be related to the same ends as all our human existence; in other words it, too, must be justified by its bearing on our civilisation, and therefore cannot be exempted from ordinary moral standards. But because art is held to be an independent thing, with its own laws, its own rights, and its own sanctions, we advance to that fatal separation between it and morality which has done so much to degrade and vilify its best work and its choicest aims. Art is, of course, not the same thing as morality – for if so, a religious tract would be its characteristic product – nor yet should it be its business to be directly didactic and educational; but from life and nature, in the true sense of those words, it cannot he disjoined without lowering the one and travestying the other, Observe, however, how the mournful chain of deductions is drawn, ring by ring and link by link, from this misconceived and parodied first principle. Because Kant and Lessing and Schiller talked sometimes as if "l'art poor l'art" were the right axiom or postulate of aesthetics – a doctrine, by the way, which was repudiated by Fichte and Hegel, to say nothing of our own English Ruskin – the modern disciple proceeds to urge that art, being non-moral, has no ethical bearing whatever, and therefore may deal frankly with the immoral. Hence has come upon us the detestable invasion of the foul and the squalid and the ugly, in what is called Realism; hence, too, in other writers, the marked preference for the unnatural, the sensual, the erotic – the suggestion of unhealthy passion, the poison of a sentimental dalliance with vice. We shall never get rid of the products unless we understand the cause; we shall never wash our hands clean of these stains unless we recognise how the waters of art have been fouled at their very source. Art, as existing solely in and for itself, art as separated from life, art as independent of moral stand-ards, art as a cloistered thing apart dwelling in a godless temple, which we can only enter by divesting ourselves of all that has hitherto guided and civilised and elevated us, all that up till now kept us clothed and in our right minds – these are the primal errors which have to be detected and disavowed and spurned, before our literary and artistic sanity can return. And if such a reaction towards simpler ideas be galled Philistinism, then, for Heaven's sake, let us all be Philistines, for fear of national con-tamination and decay.

It is the young men and maidens, the students whose zeal outruns their sobriety, the writers who yearn to show themselves unconventional and daring, who may be especially urged to review the principles on which they work and think. To be cultured is not necessarily to be in perpetual revolt; to be of "the elect" does not imperatively require one to be naked and unashamed. A man can think deeply and yet live cleanly; a woman can be free and happy and yet recognise the obligations of law. It would be absurd to insist on such elementary truths if so much pernicious nonsense from the mouths of self-elected prophets had not found its way into our current literature and our common speech. We are told that Art is the supreme object of activity, which it is not and cannot be so long as the progress of human civ-ilisation depends on knowledge rather than emotion,; we are informed that life and nature imitate Art – the modern painters, for instance, having taught the Thames to wreathe itself in mists and fogs – which would be mere midsummer madness if it were not also indicative of a deep-seated perversion of the artistic instincts. Above all, we are bidden in our æsthetic judgment to worship the form alone without any regard for the content – an attitude which is just possible in sculpture and painting, and, perhaps, some kinds of poetry, but which is wholly out of question in reference to literature as a whole. Will it be said that we take this modern "movement" too seriously, and apply to the fashion of the hour a criticism which misunderstands its essential emptiness and frivolity? In the first place, opinions and principles like those we have been examining have from time to time manifested themselves down the course of history, generally in over-ripe civilisations waving on the brink of decay. In the next place, they are found side by side with great intellectual brilliance, and to the youthful and inexperienced judgement they are clothed in glamour which hides the hollowness within. In our Universities there are certain sections of the undergraduate world, and sometimes even of the young tutorial world, which are captivated by the apish genius of paradox, and seem to believe that Art is eccentricity. It is to these and such as these that the story of Saturday ought to be the handwrit-ing on the wall. Rejoice – the wise moralist would say – O young man, in thy youth; know all the wisest things that have been thought in past ages; do all the best things that can be done on the river, on the running-path, and in the cricket-field. But remember that it is far better to overtax the brain by reading, and to strain the mus-cles of the heart by excessive athletics, than to worship false ideals of art and life, and seek to shift the inalterable standards of right and wrong.